Praise for *Legends of the Dragonrealm*

"Richard Knaak's fiction has the magic touch of making obviously fantastic characters and places come alive, seem real, and matter to the reader. That's the essential magic of all storytelling, and Richard does it deftly, making his stories always engaging and worth picking up and reading. And then re-reading.
　　　　—Ed Greenwood, creator of the *Forgotten Realms*®

"Full of energy.... Great world building [and] memorable characters... It's easy to see why Richard has enjoyed so much success!"
　　　　—*New York Times* Bestselling author R.A. Salvatore

"Richard's novels are well-written, adventure-filled, action-packed!"
　　　　—*New York Times* bestselling author Margaret Weis

"Endlessly inventive. Knaak's ideas just keep on coming!"

　　　　—Glen Cook, author of *Chronicles of the Black Company*

Also by Richard A. Knaak

The Dragonrealm

Legends of the Dragonrealm, Vol. I
(featuring the novels Firedrake, Ice Dragon, & Wolfhelm)

Legends of the Dragonrealm, Vol. II
(featuring the novels Shadow Steed, The Shrouded Realm, & Children of
the Drake, plus the novella "Skins")

Legends of the Dragonrealm, Vol. III
(featuring the novels The Crystal Dragon & The Dragon Crown, plus the
novellas "Past Dance", "Storm Lord", & "The Still Lands")

Shade

The Turning War:
Vol. I - Dragon Masters
Vol. II – The Gryphon Mage
*Vol. III – The Horned Blade

The World of Warcraft

Day of the Dragon
Night of the Dragon
Stormrage
Wolfheart

The War of the Ancients:
Vol. I – The Well of Eternity
Vol. II – The Demon Soul
Vol. III – The Sundering

Dawn of the Aspects

Diablo

Legacy of Blood
Kingdom of Shadow
Moon of the Spider

The Sin War:
Vol. I – Birthright
Vol. II – Scales of the Serpent
Vol. III – The Veiled Prophet

Dragonlance

The Legend of Huma
Kaz the Minotaur
Land of the Minotaurs
Reavers of the Blood Sea
The Citadel

The Minotaur Wars:
Vol. I – Night of Blood
Vol. II – Tides of Blood
Vol. III – Empire of Blood

The Ogre Titans:
Vol. I – The Black Talon
Vol. II – The Fire Rose
Vol. III – The Gargoyle King

The Age of Conan

Vol. I – The God in the Moon
Vol. II – The Eye of Charon
Vol. III – The Silent Enemy

The Knight in Shadow

Vol. I – Dragon Mound
*Vol. II – Wake of the Wyrm
*Vol. III – The Twilight Throne

Individual Titles

The Janus Mask
Frostwing
King of the Grey
Dutchman
Shattered Light: Ruby Flames
Beastmaster: Myth

* - Forthcoming

Legends
of the
Dragonrealm

Volume IV

Richard A. Knaak

Porta Nigra Press

Dragon Tome copyright © 1992 by Richard A. Knaak
The Horse King copyright © 1997 by Richard A. Knaak
Dragon Master copyright © 2002 by Richard A. Knaak
A Wolf in the Fold copyright © 2003 by Richard A. Knaak
A Game of Ghosts copyright © 2012 by Richard A. Knaak

Dragon Tome & *The Horse King* originally published individually by Warner Books, Inc.

Published by Porta Nigra Press
First Printing: March, 2013

ISBN-13: 978-0-9889079-5-9
Cover Art by Ciruelo
Cover Design by Anna Katharina Spanier

TABLE OF CONTENTS

INTRODUCTION

With great pleasure I welcome you to this fourth collection of the Dragonrealm saga. We have at last gathered all of the novels originally published by Warner Books, not to mention the online novellas. In this edition are stories spanning centuries in this world, including tales revealing great secrets about some of the most important characters.

In *Dragon Tome*, we not only meet the first Bedlam to arrive on the shores of the continent, but also discover the truth about the Libraries of Penacles and their creator. Toss in the Lords of the Dead, Shade, and the Purple Dragon and you have a story concerning a pivotal point in the Dragonrealm.

The Horse King is no less significant in that it also deals with the origins of one of the series' most popular and unique characters, Darkhorse. And while Lanith, ruler of the kingdom of Zuu and the villain for whom the novel is named, is ambitious and powerful, his sinister ally is certainly the guiding force behind the story's events . . . not to mention the force responsible for Darkhorse's very existence. Here we also find conflict in the Bedlam family itself, leading to disaster.

With *Dragon Master*, some of the first hints of the complexities of the Turning War are revealed in the discovery that one of those who followed Nathan Bedlam against the Dragon Kings still lives . . . and unfortunately blames anyone with the name Bedlam even while seeking to create a second war between drakes and mankind.

The dark past also rears its ugly head in *A Wolf in the Fold* when the Gryphon's son is kidnapped by Wolf Raiders led by an old enemy. Worse, to rescue his child, the Lord of Penacles must not only venture into the underworld of the Quel, but also leave his pregnant queen alone just as a second assassination plot stirs to life.

And if you thought you knew everything about Cabe Bedlam himself, *A Game of Ghosts* reveals not only just how much remains to be told, but also how those secrets may yet claim his life. What lies awaiting the master wizard within the ruins of Mito Pica will make even vengeful survivors from that lost city and murderous drakes seem slight threat in comparison.

We have also added some teasers from other various novels in the back, including a short scene from the upcoming Dragonrealm trilogy, *The Turning War*. I hope you enjoy not only these glimpses, but also the fact that there are still tales from the Dragonrealm ahead. Even before the trilogy ends, I hope to begin moving forward in the current timeline with some twists and turns that I think will continue to reveal new dimensions to this world.

I thank you again to all of you who have followed and supported this series!

Best

Richard A. Knaak

DRAGON TOME

Chapter One

He always knew when it was the most opportune time for an excursion outside. It was all in the book, so to speak. He knew his adversaries' habits better than they themselves did, just as he had known the habits of their predecessors. He had been at this game far longer than either of the two groups now seeking his legacy and he would be at it when they were only whispers in the winds of time.

They ever underestimated him because of his form, he knew. To them, he was a misshapen little gnome, one of the solitary folk who lived for knowledge and gathered what they could of that rare resource. He was incredibly small and wrinkled with age. His arms had the length that his legs had been cheated of and so he seemed to almost shamble rather than walk or run. There was not one single follicle of hair on his head, which often resulted in him looking like a polished egg when the sun shone down. His nose was long and crooked and his eyes were wide and filled with the wisdom of ages. His clothing was simple, consisting of a cloth robe and hood that made him look like a pile of rumpled laundry than a living creature. He wore simple shoes and a belt from which hung several pouches, but nothing more. There was no need for anything more.

If he looked like a gnome, there was good reason for that; it was he who had given birth to that race when he had taken elfin maidens for mates far in the past. Though those days were past, his offspring continued to spread his mark. It was a sign of his once-great power, one still to be reckoned with even now.

He was no more than a few minutes from his sanctum, but the storm had at last cleared. With the clouds dissipating so fast, it was possible that the dawn would yet reveal a bright, golden sun and a deep blue sky. Dawn was the only thing he really cared about anymore; that and his daily game with those who would seek to steal what was his and his alone.

At the bottom of the hill he paused. From this point on, the land would shield him no longer. Before him stood only wild grass, not nearly high enough to hide even his tiny form. That there was any grass at all was a sign of his own might, for one of his opponents had burned the entire region clean in an attempt to drive the gnome from his sanctum. Left to the weakness of nature, the region would have remained barren. He had no desire to make his home in the middle of a scorched desert, however, and so had sought out the proper spell. That his success only proved to his adversaries the vast extent of his legacy was a moot point. They had seen enough wonders to know that

1

stealing the contents of his citadel would make the victor master over the entire continent.

As for the gnome, he did not cue. At this stage in his vast life span, the pursuit of ever more knowledge was all that was important.

To the naked eye, the field looked empty, save for a peculiar structure some distance from where the gnome stood. The structure, a sort of wide, featureless pentagon three stories high, sat in the midst of the wild grass like a benign tyrant surveying its kingdom. If it seemed that there were no windows nor even a door through which to pass, that was because such was the case. If anyone other than he attempted to seek entrance, then that unfortunate visitor would find himself fruitlessly wandering the perimeter of the citadel. Only *he* knew how to enter, which was why *he* held the trump card in the game of wits. His would-be successors dared not kill him out of hand lest they lose the one key.

That did not mean that they did not try other methods, most of which included pain . . . but not death.

It appeared that the field was peaceful, that his adversaries had abandoned their efforts for the night. This might be true of one, for the time being, but not of the other. Always there was at least one.

Shouldering the brace of rabbits that had been his night's work, he began to trudge through, what was to him, the knee-high sea of dancing greenery. From within, tendrils of invisible power, already highly sensitized to the possible plots of the usurpers, stretched ever farther out. If any spell or physical threat came within a hundred yards of him, he would know. Anything beyond that range would not even "dent" the magical shield that surrounded his person and it was likely that anything nearer would do little more. Still, one could grow too complacent. There were always new and more deadly attacks.

Knowing that always added a little spice to his life. It gave his desire for research that extra little flavor, since his very existence might hang in the balance.

When he had nearly cut the distance between himself and his home in half, the squat sorcerer paused. Nothing had as yet disturbed his network of defensive spells, but a sense of foreboding . . . call it *intuition* . . . told him that someone or something lay waiting in the near vicinity.

Which one? he wondered. *Who's been silent of late?*

The first spearheads of sunlight rose over the horizon. The aged spellcaster admired the sight for a moment, then resumed his trek. He was still slightly curious about the sensation he felt, but since it did not hint of danger, the gnome was not overly concerned.

Perhaps an enterprising elf? Once or twice, that race had made overtures to him, seeking his friendship, but no longer interested in dallying with the female of the species, he had ignored them. Compared to the other watchers, the elves were inconsequential.

Now his sanctum, his home and place of research, was little more than a hundred feet away and still he had not been attacked. The wizened sorcerer grew bemused, wondering if his handiwork would go wasted this time. He had not even really needed the rabbits, able as he was to summon them to him, but the walk and the challenge always stirred his blood. It was almost disappointing.

There *was* that sensation still . . .

Standing at last before the gray structure, he raised his hand to open the way— and felt every protective spell activate as something hurtled straight down from high in the sky above him.

It was strong, *far* stronger than he had expected. It shrugged off his initial defenses as he might shrug off a leaf that had fallen on his shoulder. Whatever it was

2

must have been high up indeed to have avoided detection sooner and it evidently moved with a speed that would have left even a dragon dumbfounded. The sorcerer dropped his brace of rabbits and focused his attention upward at the startling new threat. Whichever of his present adversaries was responsible for this assault had outdone themselves.

A huge, bat-winged shape formed in the dim light of pre- morning. It shrieked, much the way the night flyer it so resembled did, and reached out with long, taloned fingers for him. Like a bat, those fingers were part of the webbed wings themselves. It had long ears and a body that was essentially humanoid, but that was all the detail he could make out under the circumstances.

Ugly as sin, no doubt, the sorcerer thought even as he moved to defend himself from it.

With a speed remarkable for one of his build, the gnome reached into one of his pouches and removed a small stick. Holding it up above his head, he gave the tip a flick of his thumb. The tip of the stick burst into a brilliant white light, brighter a hundred times more than the sun at its zenith. He was prepared for searing illumination and so his eyes had closed just before his thumb had struck.

The night flyer was not so fortunate.

It squealed, wavered, and finally whirled out of control. Though he suspected it could guide itself by sound as well as by sight, he knew that the light had disoriented it too much for the moment. Its masters might have created it so that it would be used to the light of day, but few things could stare into the gleaming white flare in his hand and not lose their sight permanently. What made the trick more enjoyable to the sorcerer was that the source of the light was a product of nature and not a costly bit of spellcasting. Making the stick had cost him only a few minutes' work.

By no means had he stood still while all this happened. Even as the creature, seven feet in height at least if he were any judge, clawed at its eyes, the gnome was already opening up a path for himself in the side of the pentagon. A swift series of gestures with his left hand resulted in a circular hole that formed directly before him. He stepped through, dragging the retrieved rabbits along with him, but paused before sealing the entrance up again.

The beast was already fluttering off into the retreating night, its mission a quick and embarrassing failure. From experience, the gnome knew the mental and physical agony the monstrosity was going through. He felt no sympathy, save for the wasted effort on the part of the beast's creators. Seeing now its sickly white coloring, odd for a creature of the night, he had a good suspicion which of his opponents had been responsible.

"Hmmph! The Lords of the Dead. Of course it would be one of theirs!" Necromancers who had appointed themselves gods. Fools in one way, but still quite challenging and able. They had, with their own vast storehouse of power, created quite a formidable weapon, but one that evidently lacked the cunning needed for its task. Yet, he could hardly believe it had been so short and simple. It was almost anticlimactic after all his expectations.

"Almost farcical, if you ask me," he muttered, though those involved would have hardly questioned him on the subject. "Waste of good material! Never use a good weapon with a bad plan!"

Watching the massive shape disappear into the clouds, the gnome's brow suddenly wrinkled. It might not be an ill- conceived attempt after all. They should have known by now that such a weak attack would be destined for failure. This might have been an exploratory assault, a preamble to the true attack.

He smiled in anticipation of what their next move might be and when it might take place. Whatever they plotted, he would be ready for it, of course, but the thought that they might have come up with some novel approach stirred his hunger for research. He would have to research the possibilities this incident presented, even if it turned out that any such possibilities were nothing more than the products of his inventive imagination.

The hole had just begun to seal itself when he again felt the presence of that patient watcher. Freezing the doorway spell, the bent sorcerer peered outside again. He saw nothing, not that he had expected it to be that simple, but in his mind's eye, where the power flowed, there came an image of a tall figure, human perhaps, wrapped in a shroudlike cloak.

That was all. As if his sensing this had broken a fragile bubble, both the image and the feeling of being watched vanished.

Frowning, the gnome allowed the wall to finish sealing itself up. He had protected his precious legacy from foes human and otherwise for endless millennia and he saw no reason that he could not protect it from one more. Be his rivals birdmen or cloaked sorcerers, they were nothing next to him.

Another image flashed through his mind, but this one was merely a memory of his most persistent and patient adversary yet. He chuckled at some of the clever but futile tricks that one had pulled. "Yesss, and that goes for you, too, *lord dragon*!" the aged spellcaster muttered. "The book's mine and that's all there is to it!"

The squat figure resettled the rabbits on his shoulder and trundled down the hall, thoughts of dragons, bats, and such now giving way to memories of the sensual aroma of roast hare. He so enjoyed the peaceful life. This was not at all like his former home, the place that he had abandoned so very, very, very long ago.

No, this domain was nothing like Nimth.

Chapter Two

"There!"

It was Captain Yalso himself who planted the flag. With the aid of his great bulk, he shoved almost two feet of the wooden pole into the soft earth at the inward edge of the beach. As two sailors unfurled the banner—which was actually a ship's identification banner borrowed for just this occasion—a cheer went up from both those who made up the shore party and those watching from the three-masted vessel anchored in the natural harbor. After months of treacherous sailing, the *Heron's Wing* had reached its destination.

The myth was now a fact. There *was* a fabled Dragonrealm! *Or at least a continent in the same general location,* Wellen Bedlam thought, staring in sour humor at the tiny flag, one that had not even been his idea.

The guiding force as well as the master of this expedition, he should have been the one most excited by this turn of events. His dream had been fulfilled. From the first time his parents had told the children the tales of Lord Drazeree and the Dragon Men to the final days of his own researches in the ruins of the ancient city, he had believed that the Dragonrealm had existed as more than just a storyland. Somewhere there had to have been a basis for such tales.

His entire reputation as a master scholar had been at risk these past few years, but that had hardly been a concern to him. Even when the Master Guardians, who ruled the nebulous region called the Dreamlands from mysterious Sirvak Dragoth, had warned him

4

of the dangers of delving too deeply into the past . . . a shaded threat? . . . he had pressed on. After his researchers had finally, *conclusively,* pointed to the west, beyond the terrible seas, Wellen had somehow gathered the support to finance this expedition. When it had appeared that the effort was about to flounder just as the *Heron's Wing* was about to set sail, he had even taken his own meager finances and spent every last coin to make certain that the ship would leave.

Brushing sand from his brown, cloth shirt, he pulled his long, green cape about him and turned from the merrymakers. Yes, he had made his dream come true, but now Wellen wondered at what cost that might be. In the safe seclusion of his chambers back home, he had only imagined the dangers. The reality of those dangers, however, was more than he truly wanted to face. It bothered him that he of all people might most jeopardize the expedition.

I'm afraid! The thought had burned its way into his soul. *I'm afraid. I've spent my entire life with the deadliest threat to my existence the possibility that I might fail to graduate!*

Sand flew up as he walked aimlessly across the beach. Even with knee-high boots, some of the granules still managed to get inside, making his feet itch. Wellen wished all of his sufferings could be so tiny. How would it look back home if the expedition leader was the first man to crack? How would it look if Prentiss Asaalk had to take over?

Thinking of the northerner, whom other interests had chosen as Bedlam's undesired second, Wellen now recalled his own *physical* deficiencies. It was bad enough that he was afraid, but he had to compete against a man who looked like some demigod hero out of an ancient myth. Where Wellen was short, barely topping the midway point between five feet and six, Asaalk was nearly a foot taller. The shorter man was by no means unathletic, but his broad frame more resembled a flat gate when compared to Prentiss Asaalk's herculean dimensions.

Facially, there was no comparison. Wellen's own features could be called unremarkable at best. Slightly rounded face, simple nose, unassuming mouth . . . only his hazel eyes, which somehow always snared the attention of those he spoke to, rose above the ordinary. Penetrating eyes, however, added up to little compared to the aristocratic features of his second. Not only did Asaalk have the bearing of a leader, but he had the arrogant beauty that all those story heroes had seemed to have, save for the legendary Drazeree.

Despite his constant listing of his faults, however, the short man still found himself very much in charge. For some reason, people were more willing to listen and follow him. It confused Wellen and it almost certainly annoyed the ambitious Asaalk. That added yet another fear to those of the scholar. When would come the point when he led his people into disaster and, should they survive, Prentiss Asaalk finally and irrevocably took his place as leader?

The day was young. The wind fruitlessly tried to tousle his brown hair, which had been cut short in order to save him the trouble of having to take care of it any more than he had to. He pushed a few loose hairs aside, trying not to think of the damnable silver streak that his fingers touched, and paused to stare at the woodlands beyond the beach. They seemed quiet and unassuming, but was anything so in this strange land? A part of him argued that he worried needlessly, but the rest of his mind knew that such worry was the only thing that kept him from growing too dreamy, a dangerous tendency of his youth. Though not quite three decades old, Wellen liked to think that his reckless days had ended with the broken leg and arm he had received because he had been daydreaming instead of making certain that the library ladder was stable.

"So just what're you doing here?"

He nearly jumped, so startled was he to hear the question that he had just been asking himself spoken out loud. Then, realizing it was not he himself who had spoken,

Wellen knew that the question had a different, far more mundane basis behind it. He exhaled in relief and turned to face Captain Yalso.

The mariner was ancient, but no one could say just *how* ancient he was. *As old as the seas,* one crewman had said, but if Yalso was that old, he was holding up well for one of his age. Though the hair on his head was shockingly white and his beard stretched down to his chest, the captain was by no means a frail old man. His girth alone proved that, if not also the way he was able to manhandle his crew during the roughest storms and get them working in order to save the *Heron's Wing* and all those on board. He had done that more than once on the long journey. Like most men, it seemed, Yalso also stood several inches taller than Wellen. Again, it always surprised him when men such as the sea captain deferred to him in matters.

"You're driftin' off, you are," Yalso told him in tones designed not to carry beyond the two of them. If there was a man on the ship that could be called Wellen's friend, it was Yalso. Until the scholar had come along, he had been looking at nothing but a long overdue retirement. Wellen had given him one last great adventure . . . the *greatest* one, in fact. No one had ever sailed this far west. No one that had come back to tell of it, that is. The young scholar had had an insistent, knowing way about him, however, and that had been enough for the seaman. He had never lost faith in Wellen.

"I'm sorry," Bedlam muttered. "I keep wondering what we'll find out there." He gestured inland.

"Oh, trees, grass, animals, birds . . . " Yalso winked. "I think maybe a few lost cities, damsels in distress, and gold aplenty. . ."

They both smiled at that image. While there were always those aboard who expected the expedition to find such things, the two were more practical. As far as the captain was concerned, sailing here had been a reward all its own. He had proved once more that he was the best captain there was and that the *Heron's Wing* was the finest lady ever to set sail. Wellen, on the other hand, cared mostly for the history.

His spirits had risen a little, but Wellen could not shake off certain fears. Not after the first attempt to land.

Here be dragons was a warning essential to the tale of this distant land. Dragons they had not seen . . . at least not enough so that they could be identified as such . . . but there were strange dangers aplenty here, of that Wellen was certain.

"You're thinkin' of that blasted city again, aren't you, Master Bedlam? Don't. This here's safe harbor, not like that haunted, monster-laden cove."

Haunted, Wellen could not recall, but the ruined city to the northeast, the wind-swept region that was their first sighting of the legendary Dragonrealm and *was* to have been their initial landing point, was indeed 'monster-laden' as the ancient mariner had just commented.

Their first sight of land had brought a cheer and when the city had first been spotted it was thought that here might be people open to trade. Only when they had sailed closer had the crew and passengers of the three-master noted that the port city was in ruins and had been so for centuries. Part of it had apparently even sunk into the sea. Still, it had been a marvel to see, what with its almost inhuman architecture and beauty, and so they had talked of exploring it, possibly even finding riches long abandoned.

Then, the lookout had seen the sleek, scaled backside in the water.

Sea-blue, that was why no one had noticed them at first. Possibly they had been swimming too deep, also. All that the daring explorers still knew was that suddenly there were several murky shapes in the waters around them that promised leviathans. Captain Yalso was of the opinion that they had come across a breeding ground or something. Prentiss Asaalk had wanted to hunt one. He was, fortunately, in the minority.

The shapes had remained no more than that, ever diving out of sight when the explorers moved closer, but that did not mean that the ship was left alone. When the first tremor rocked the *Heron's Wing*, they knew that several had swum underneath. Oddly, very little damage occurred to the ship, but possibly because Captain Yalso instinctively understood what it was they wanted. Each strike was focused at the bow of the ship, halting the three-master's progress and soon forcing the vessel back.

"They want us out of here!" he had informed Wellen. "They're givin' us a chance to leave in one piece!"

Sure enough, when the *Heron's Wing* had finally turned about and headed away, the fearsome shapes had receded. The explorers had kept sailing and had not looked back until the city and its denizens of the deep were no more than a spot on the horizon.

"Drifting again." The comment scattered the shorter man's memories. The scholar stared down at the sand beneath his feet, reorienting himself to the present.

Wellen started walking up a small rise, wanting to stand among the foot-high blades of wild grass. "Sorry, captain. I don't mean to do it. It just happens."

"Nothing wrong to dream; that's what got you, got all of us, here. You just have to know where the dreaming ends and the reality begins . . . otherwise ya put your foot in something terrrrible!"

He was never certain whether Captain Yalso affected a salty accent at times or whether the man just switched back and forth without realizing it. Yalso was far more cultured than the short man had expected, but that might have just been the personal prejudice borne of having been highly educated. "I'll try to remember that."

"Good!" The heavy-set sailor joined him, his boots sinking a bit in the soft earth. "If anything happens to you and I have to listen to the blue man's royal orders for very long, then there's gonna be a mutiny!"

The "blue man" was Prentiss Asaalk. For reasons only the Dreamlands might know, Asaalk's folk were blue-skinned. It was not a dye of any sort; they were born a dusky blue from head to toe, including their hair. The only people so colored, they felt it marked them as special, which explained to a great extent Asaalk's arrogant manner. He was a product of his culture.

Still, even for a blue man he could be demanding.

"Come on back to camp, Master Bedlam! If you want a search party ready for tomorrow, we've got plenty to get done before then! I've sent out a few men to scout the nearby area, but I'm goin' to need your presence of mind to keep them enthused and the blue man from takin' over!"

Knowing what an opportunist Asaalk was, Wellen readily agreed. He also knew that keeping himself busy was the best way to maintain a steady rein on his fears and self-doubts. It was one reason he enjoyed his research so much; for a time he could depart from the world and his deficiencies.

Sure enough, when they arrived back among the others the blue man was already attempting to seize control. His expression was bland, much like a king's might be when commanding his subjects.

"There and there," he was saying in a clipped, slightly accented voice. Though most folk spoke the common tongue in the same manner, the northerners put a certain twist in their inflections, making them sound to Wellen as if the ceremonial daggers they wore on their kilt belts were digging into their abdomens. No one, of course, ever joked about Asaalk's voice, in keeping with his heroic image, he was a deadly swordsman and wrestler. "Create a perimeter here, yes?"

Despite their mild dislike for the blue man, the sailors' minds were so ingrained with the concept of obeying the voice of authority that they were grudgingly following the northerner's commands.

"Thank you kindly, Master Asaalk!" Yalso roared, his beard fluttering as he spoke. "I can take such a meager task off your worthy shoulders!" The captain gave Wellen a conspiratorial glance. "Master Bedlam! Certainly you have something more pressing that would not be so beneath the able control of your second!"

It was likely that Prentiss Asaalk knew very well what the seaman was doing, but the northerner was nothing if not capable of masking his true feelings whenever need be. Instead, he smiled and broke from his self-appointed duties in order to join the two. Yalso, having no intention of submitting himself to the one-man oratories Asaalk thought conversations were supposed to be when he was a part, bowed to the young scholar and made his excuses. He made certain to avoid glancing at the blue man as he departed to organize the camp . . . providing Prentiss Asaalk had left him anything to do.

"Master Bedlam!" Asaalk greeted him with such fervor and pleasure that the expedition leader expected the larger man to envelop him in a bear hug. Asaalk did not, however, choosing instead to cross his arms and stand in cobalt splendor before Wellen like a storybook champion who has just bested his archrival. "Glorious day, yes?"

"The weather seems to be holding---"

"Weather? Not weather!" The blue man smiled broadly, as if appreciating Wellen's comment as a joke between good friends. "The weather is good, yes, but I speak, of course, of our being *here!*" With a finger, he indicated the ground beneath his feet. Asaalk's tendency to emphasize points always reminded Wellen of an actor onstage. He wondered if professional acting was yet another talent of the northerner's. Probably. There were few things that Asaalk did not seem to have some ability in. In fact, Wellen could think of *nothing* so far that was beyond the skills of his second.

Maybe I should let him take over! Then, I might find his limitations! What would happen, however, if Prentiss Asaalk proved to have none, though?

A hand twice as large as his own fell upon his shoulder. He was jostled again and again as the blue man patted him. "This is your day, Master Bedlam! Those who scoffed will hide their faces in shame when we return with our vessel laden with riches, yes?"

Riches? This was to be a voyage of discovery, not plundering! He wanted to shout that in the northerner's perfect countenance, but did not. It would have only made Wellen look ridiculous and Asaalk would not have paid any real attention to his words, anyway. Asaalk was not the only one who sought riches. Most of those aboard, even Captain Yalso, dreamed of returning home with a king's ransom. It was not that they had no interest in the knowledge that might be gained; they were merely of the opinion that one could have knowledge *and* wealth. Asaalk's people had only invested in the expedition because they were certain that the *Heron's Wing* would return with *something* of value . . . providing, of course, that it returned at all. Neither the ship nor Wellen dared return otherwise.

"The city in the north," his mighty second was saying, entirely ignoring the frustration that was evident in the shorter man's eyes. "We could reach it by land, yes? The creatures in the sea would then be no threat! Think what might be there!"

Wellen did and shuddered. "There might be things other than those monsters, things that move about on land. Besides, as ancient as the city looked—what was still above water, I mean—it's probably been picked clean already. Probably hundreds or thousands of years even."

"There is always something . . . and did you not want to find your knowledge? Surely, this must be a good place to seek it, yes? A city as mighty as this might have once known the great Lord Drazeree!"

It was doubtful that things could work out so neatly for him, but the scholar could not deny that a place as massive as the ruined city *might* contain countless answers and endless surprises. There was one other problem, however, that Prentiss Asaalk was evidently oblivious to, but that Wellen could hardly forget.

"It may take too long a journey to reach that land, Prentiss, and we'd spend more than half the time wandering through a mist so thick we wouldn't be able to see a thing around us! Have you forgotten *that?*"

"Pfah!" The tall northerner waved off his concern. "A little fog, yes! I have not forgotten it! I would worry about dragons and demons, but *fog?* Hah! Of what danger can the gray mists of that land be?"

What danger? He had no answer for the massive figure, only a sense of dread that had remained with him all the time they had been within sight of the mist-enshrouded land far south of the ruined city. Certainly, the fog had done nothing to warrant his distrust, but he found it unsettling the way the weather of this realm was so distinctive from one region to the next. The region occupied by the partially sunken city had been sunny and warm. Only two days later, they had entered a storm that had not let up until they came across the mists. Neither the storm nor the fog had shown any sign of relenting. With his scholar's eye for detail, Wellen had noted that the rain had only broken off when the gray cloak became dominant over the distant landscape.

Almost as if someone had *divided* the land between two or more elemental lords.

It was a preposterous notion even to Wellen and so he had not spoken of it to anyone, the captain included.

He held back a sigh and finally said, "We'll see. I'll let everyone know tonight after evening meal. Right now, my only concern is making certain our encampment here is safe and secure."

"You have no need of fear, then! I have placed pickets at the edge of this portion of the beach and I have also men scouting beyond. . . all the way to the first hills. I have our supplies safely ensconced near that sandbar." He pointed at the aforementioned landmark, which was located to Wellen's right. "And I have placed four men by the longboats as a safety precaution. Satisfactory, yes?"

"Are you expecting a war?" It was a rhetorical question, one Wellen had not even meant to ask out loud, but Asaalk's preparations—how he had managed to get everything so organized in so little time astounded the scholar—seemed more apt for someone fully expecting an armed assault.

The blue man flashed him a smile. "I, too, do not take this land as harmless. I, like you, Master Bedlam, know that caution is a very good thing, yes?"

"Yes . . . " He wished his second would stop abusing that last word. It always sounded as if Asaalk were answering his own questions.

"So! There are many things to discuss, but also many things still to do! Tomorrow will begin the glorious trek! I leave you to make your decision, Master Bedlam; I know there is much to consider, yes? You have but to send for me if my assistance in the matter is needed!" Prentiss Asaalk executed an abrupt, ninety-degree bow. "I am your servant."

As the majestic northerner departed, Wellen tried to decide which side of Asaalk he disliked more, the arrogant lord or the patronizing comrade. He finally gave up, knowing in his heart that he would have preferred dealing with neither of them. Whatever side the blue man showed, one could be certain that there was more hidden beneath the facade. Someday, the true Prentiss Asaalk would reveal himself. Wellen hoped he would not have to suffer the misfortune of being around when that occurred.

Yalso would not doubt be upset at the northerner's return to duty, but there was truly nothing Wellen could do about that. For all his faults, no one could deny Asaalk's efficiency. There had been too many instances where his abilities had enabled Wellen to pull the expedition through some crisis. That was what made the man most infuriating. He was as invaluable as he was insufferable.

The blue man's associates had chosen well.

Between the captain and Asaalk, there was actually little for Wellen to do but think.

Most of the men had captured a glance of him upon his return with Yalso, and that was all they needed; his mere presence reassured them and renewed their enthusiasm.

Sighing, he stalked his way back to the edge of the beach. The woodlands and the fields beckoned to him. Daring Yalso's wrath, he stepped out into the high grass and wandered slowly toward the nearest tree. His mind was far beyond his physical location, however. Far beyond even the hills in the distance. Somewhere out there, the scholar knew, were mysteries and legends to unravel. Asaalk had a point about the ruined seaport; even stripped by scavengers it would contain many secrets. Who had built it? What were they like? Was the city the last legacy of civilization in the Dragonrealm? None of the stories Wellen recalled had made mention of such a place, but that was not to say it had not existed then. If what he had seen so far held true, then the Dragonrealm was a mighty continent. It might take several expeditions just to map its coastlines. That was something that could wait until later, perhaps after he had achieved his other, more private dream . . . starting a colony. A colony would give him a permanent base for his studies.

His left foot sank a bit in the soft earth, causing him to stumble slightly. Cursing both his daydreaming and his constant worries, he regained his balance. It was while he was wiping the bottom of his boot off on the root of a small tree that he caught a glimpse of something.

He blinked, but it was still there, a black shape moving about within a copse of trees far off in the distance. Wellen had no idea what it was, but his imagination introduced him to several tantalizing possibilities. He took a tentative step toward it, then another.

"Master Bedlam!" Yalso's voice seemed to echo through out the land, not to mention the young scholar's head. "If I might have a word with you?"

The captain's voice must have carried, indeed, for Wellen, about to turn to the man, saw the figure bound out of the copse. It was a stag.

Nothing more.

His disappointment was overshadowed only by the dread of facing the captain of the *Heron's Wing.* He had been warned once by the sailor about wandering off on his own. Despite his being in command of the expedition as a whole, Wellen also had to follow orders, especially where his own safety was concerned. Yalso was a man who had sailed to many exotic places and dealt with countless excursions into the unknown. Until this voyage, Bedlam's closest brush with the unknown had been his examinations.

Steeling himself for another respectful lecture, the scholar made his way back across the soft, grassy earth. Yalso was shaking his head and smiling, but Wellen still felt like a schoolboy caught missing classes. Not wanting the captain to gain the same impression, if he had not already, Wellen met the man's gaze and held it as he walked.

The elder mariner crossed his arms and tried to look like a scolding father. His success was somewhat debatable, since both he and Wellen could not keep from smiling at the scene they presented. "I know there's a siren song that pulls a man at times, Master Bedlam, but I'll not have you wanderin' off on your own, even if ya *are* in charge. *No man is* safe here alone; not until we have a better idea what's out there."

"I was feeling a bit useless."

"The blue devil's got a tendency for making folk feel so. If he wasn't so damned anxious to be top man, he'd make a fine officer on my vessel."

Wellen paused at the edge of the beach and finished wiping off his boot. "I doubt that he'd be satisfied with that."

"You're right on that!" Uncrossing his arms, Yalso heaved his bulk nearer to the scholar. In a quiet voice, he asked, "What was it you saw out there? Someone watchin' us from the woods?"

"No, just a deer."

Yalso chuckled. "Maybe it was some mystical white stag watchin' over the forest!"

"It was a male deer, it was brown, and it scampered off the moment it heard your bellowing."

"They just don't make woodland spirits too strong these days, do they?"

Rising, Wellen shook his head. "Careful, captain. I might find I prefer Asaalk's company to yours if you keep that up."

"That would be *your* nightmare, not mine."

Bedlam took one last lingering glance at the woods and hills beyond the beach. Tomorrow, he would lead the expedition out into that unknown land. The thought drove away much of the good humor that Yalso had brought with him.

"You'll see plenty of that come the morn."

He nodded, then joined the captain on the beach. "I still haven't figured out where exactly we're going."

"Not the city?"

"You, too?"

"Is that where the northerner wants to go?" The sailor scratched his furry chin. "Much as I hate to be agreein' with him, I'd say it's our best bet. We can't stay too long and that would likely be the quickest way to prove our claim here."

"Not to mention possibly making us rich, too."

"I've never been ashamed about the thought." Yalso's eyes gleamed. "You wouldn't deny us that, would ya?"

Wellen raised his arms, dropping them almost immediately after. "I surrender! The city it is, then."

"Now you're talkin'!"

What choice did I have? Wellen wondered. Hopefully, he could keep the men from tearing things apart before he had an opportunity to look the area over. They owed *him* that much, at least.

"Let's get back to camp now," Yalso suggested. He straightened as much as it was possible for him to do and added, "And *this* time you're gonna stay there or I'll clap half a dozen men to your backside who'll see to it that you do!"

The young scholar knew better than to argue. Turning his back on the land of his childhood dreams, at least for this day, he headed back to camp.

This time, Captain Yalso stayed at his backside.

Had he not been interrupted during both brief visits, it is very possible that Wellen would have noticed the print in the soft soil. He had, in fact, stepped in the very same region, but the other print was so large that the mark left by the scholar's boot covered not even a tenth of the area. It is possible that even if he *had* looked down, Wellen might not have noticed it, for the wild grass that had been stamped down into the earth upon the other's arrival had long ago, as plants will do, risen to once more follow the sun. Thus, more than half of the other print was obscured.

Whether or not he would have noticed it was not so important as the fact that Wellen Bedlam would have recognized what creature had made the print even though he had never actually seen one. He would have also likely realized how close the camp might be to one of the monsters.

The print was that of a reptilian beast far larger than any man. A dragon.

A *huge* dragon.

Though she sat alone in the midst of the dark wood, she had no fear of the night. The fire was slow and barely illuminated even the surrounding area. Xabene did not care; the fire only existed because she liked to watch the flames dance their brief lives away. She liked the dance because it played at both life and death, as she did.

A flutter of wings warned her of the Necri's coming.

Xabene looked up as the monstrosity descended. In the dim light, she was a study of contrasts, a thing of beauty wrapped in the darkness of death. Her visage could best be described as perfect. Cat eyes that glowed when something drew her interest. Long lashes nearly hid those eyes when they narrowed before the kill. Her skin was unblemished, but as white as ivory. The spellcaster's nose was small and perfectly aligned, while her mouth was full and bloodred. A slight crease in her chin was the only feature that might have marred her countenance, but no man had every truly noticed it, not when confronted with all else she had to offer.

Ebony hair cascaded down to her brow in front and past her shoulders elsewhere, framing her pale features. A single streak of silver coursed down the left side of her head. It was difficult to see where her hair ended and her gown began, for it too was as black as pitch. Xabene had *a* form that matched her features and the gown emphasized that fact. Thin and cut low both in the front and back, it hardly seemed appropriate for one who spent much of her time in the wilds. Yet, no stain had ever marred it and the sorceress never appeared uncomfortable, no matter what the weather.

Many a man had fallen victim to Xabene's beauty, but that beauty served only herself and those she called master.

As for the Necri, it probably found her as repulsive as she found it. Its clawed feet touching earth, the Necri trotted toward her, looking much like a runner bent forward during a grueling race. The winged abomination did not stop until it was within a few feet of the fire. It then folded its wings about it and stood waiting, white, soulless eyes staring at the tiny human before it.

Xabene knew the danger of the Necri, knew the speed with which it moved and the sharpness of its claws. As if to remind her it had yet more weapons, the massive creature gave her a smile, revealing row upon row of dagger teeth. Though its general form was manlike, everything else was a twisted parody of the animal from which its kind had been spawned, the bat. Had it been able to stand completely straight, the Necri would have been more than seven feet tall; even bent it was almost six. Like Xabene, its flesh was pale, but the pale of something long dead.

A shift in the wind reminded her of something else. The Necri smelled. The odor of carrion and decay clung to it like a shroud. The dark enchantress was fairly used to the smell, having been forced to confront it whenever her masters had summoned her, but coming from this horror it took on an added strength. Given an opportunity, the Necri would be more than happy to add her to its dinner table. It was one of the functions for which it had been created. Human agents might command them for a time, but a Necri's ultimate loyalty was to the Lords of the Dead.

After all, they had *created* the monstrous race.

The snub nose and long ears of the creature twitched as it impatiently waited for her to speak.

Xabene did not rise, although that would have brought her almost eye level with her companion. Instead, she held out one hand so that the Necri could see the small, copper figurine resting on her palm. It represented two figures in struggle. Birdmen. The sorceress had never asked where it had come from. . . one *never* asked the masters such silly questions ... but she assumed it was an artifact left behind by the Seekers, the avians who had ruled this land before the coming of the Dragon Kings. They had always been fond of using medallions and talismans for their spells. The race still existed, but their power was a mere shadow of their former greatness. Still, Xabene had to admire them if they had been capable of such work as this.

"Do you know what this is?"

The Necri leaned forward, avoiding the light of the fire as much as it could, and studied the copper piece for a moment. It squeaked what the sorceress knew was a positive response. She hid her smile. It always amused her that a monstrosity as deadly as the Necri spoke in a high-pitched squeak.

"Observe." With her free hand, she stroked the side of the figurine.

A blue, spherical light formed above the copper talisman. It turned and pulsated, growing in intensity with the passing of time. The Necri lowered another lid over its eyes to dim the illumination.

The ball of light was now as large as the beast's head. At that point, it ceased growing and a form within began to take shape. Both figures watched with interest as a familiar adversary solidified in the midst of the ball.

The Necri hissed.

"The master of the citadel," Xabene whispered.

Before their eyes, they saw the gnome at work. He was busy scratching away with a feather pen, jotting his notes down. In the background, there were vague images of other things, but only the gnome and his desk were sufficiently in focus to be of any interest.

"Your predecessor achieved this success."

It's eyes focused on her again. The Necri knew what had happened to its predecessor. Damaged permanently in mind as well as body, it had no longer been of use to its creators. They had disposed of it as they saw fit. The winged servant understood that action, but what it did not care for, Xabene knew, was the blindness and madness it had suffered due to the sorceress. It was she who had devised the suicidal plan and had commanded the other Neal to obey, in the name of their mutual lords.

"We have his image trapped. We have the ability to observe him now. The first step to victory and achieving possession of his precious book."

The talons of the creature's hands played against its chest. The squeak it emitted was full of disbelief and contempt.

Xabene was prepared for defiance. No Necri believed that human agents were worthy of their support, but they obeyed because the masters commanded them to do so. A plot hatched by a human, therefore, was sheer madness.

"My work has been approved by the lords themselves. If you care to request an audience with them . . . " She smiled at the Necri's sudden discomfort, revealing her own perfect but somehow predatory teeth. "This image is proof that all is proceeding well."

Disbelief was still evident, but the pale abomination remained quiet. If her plan failed, not that she could foresee *that* happening, the punishment would fall upon *her* head alone, providing that the Necri could prove it had performed its part to the letter. She knew that the winged servant understood that as well.

The image of the gnome vanished as Xabene cupped her free hand over the artifact and withdrew the object from the sight of her ghoulish partner. "We have been given another task, too."

It cocked its head and waited.

"There are strangers in the realm, men from beyond the sea."

For the first time, the Necri's expression caught her by surprise. Puzzlement. Complete puzzlement. The creature could not comprehend the idea of men from beyond the vast body of water. Xabene herself found the thought unsettling. The Dragonrealm

13

was the only world that she had ever known, but the lords had said that these men were from a land beyond and so she knew that it was true.

What was also true was that they were traveling in a direction that would take them much too close to the citadel of the damnable gnome. The Lords of the Dead wanted no other competitors. The Dragon King of this region was trouble enough, thought he would, of course, fail in the end.

The Necri squeaked harshly and flexed his talons in expectation.

She shook her head. "No, we are to watch and wait for a time. The Dragon King will surely note their passage, as will the keeper of the citadel."

Baring its teeth, the batlike monstrosity protested this decision. In the dark of night, it would be easy to pick off several men. Despite its sickly white coloring, it was somehow able to conceal itself from the eyes of all but the most wary.

"The decision was not mine."

Squeaking once more, the Necri grew subdued. It would not go against the wishes of its masters.

"We watch for now," Xabene continued, toying with the copper artifact. "Perhaps later, there will be time for your games."

That mollified the winged horror, at least for the moment. The enchantress wondered just how long it would be able to resist the temptation to slay at least one of the intruders. Long enough, she supposed, for it knew the fate that would await it if the lords discovered its disobedience in this matter.

She pointed to the southeast. "They camp on or near a beach directly south of the hills. Pass within sight of the gnome's citadel and you will have no trouble finding their vessel."

The Necri nodded its understanding. It would find them. Nothing escaped its kind for very long.

Xabene remained silent as the creature spread its expansive wings and turned from her. As it rose into the night sky, a ghostly death on wings, the sorceress pocketed the Seeker artifact and studied the dying flames. She had not informed the Necri of their masters' desire to speak with the leader of the outsiders. They had not required her to and so she had made the decision to leave the horrific beast in the dark.

The Lords of the Dead were very curious about the newcomers. Had the dark enchantress been more daring in her thoughts, she might have almost suspected them of being just a bit frightened as well. Such a thought had never occurred to Xabene, however, for to imagine fright among her masters would have seemed very much like heresy.

In truth, the reason she had not informed the Necri of their lords' desire was because *she* wanted to be the one who brought them the expedition's leader. It would give her an opportunity to ask a few harmless questions of her own.

She smiled. If the newcomers' leader was a man, and she supposed that was the most likely case, then before long he would tell her *everything* she and her lords desired to know.

The dawn had come earlier than they had expected. Under the guidance of Captain Yalso and Prentiss Asaalk, the expedition readied itself. Most of the necessities had been brought ashore the previous evening, including the dozen horses and wagons. Yalso had had the latter reassembled as soon as all the pieces were accounted for. Once more, Wellen felt as useful as the sand on the beach. He knew that was not the case, for it had been his efforts that had brought about the expedition and it was to be his decision when it came to the direction the expedition's future was to take. Certainly, they would investigate the ruined port city first, but there were other priorities. If there was thriving civilization somewhere on this side of the continent, it was up to the party to discover it.

Wellen knew they might find the locals warlike, but the men he had hired, including those of Yalso's crew who were to accompany them, were, for the most part, capable in such situations. He was grateful that the captain had chosen to leave things in the hands of his first mate and had joined the explorers. If there was anyone who knew how to handle a desperate situation, *besides* Prentiss Asaalk, it was the sturdy Yalso.

Around mid-morning, they got underway. Only the scouts and those commanding the expedition had steeds; there simply had not been enough money or room for all those that they would have required. Even enterprising merchants were willing to risk only so much on such a daring venture, and to have carried all that Wellen had needed would have required one, possibly *two* more ships as massive as the *Heron's Wing.* As it was, Wellen, the blue man, and the captain had three of the animals. The scouts had three more. The remaining horses, all draft animals, pulled the wagons along. For the time, their loads would be light, but the expedition hoped to fill those empty wagons with valuables before time considerations made them return to those waiting at the beach encampment.

The first few hours passed as uneventfully as the night. After several miles of walking, most of the men had lost interest in the surrounding landscape which was, even Wellen had to admit, not very different from some of the regions back home.

Wellen called a halt about midway through the afternoon. Asaalk was all for continuing on for a few more hours, but the scholar reminded him that not only was *he* riding and the men were not, but also that most of them had not yet fully gotten their land legs back.

"They've only had a day to recover," he reminded the blue man. "Whatever ground we cover after they've had a short time to rest will be a bonus as far as I'm concerned."

"You plan to travel on until nightfall?" Captain Yalso asked, dismounting.

"I do." Wellen followed suit. After a moment, a reluctant Asaalk joined them on foot. "That should mean about another four, maybe four and a half hours. I'd hoped to reach the hills—"

"Humph! Not today!"

The hills were an annoyance to Bedlam. He had estimated them closer and thought they might reach the base of the nearest by the time the sun set, but that was no longer likely.

"Whatever we can add to what we've already traveled, then." He had no intention of putting the column through a grueling death march.

"There is rain in our future."

The northerner's words made both men look skyward. In the distant northwest, Wellen observed a line of clouds. He shook his head. "Cloud cover, maybe, but those don't look like rain clouds. . . not yet. It'll cool things down a little, at least."

It seemed likely that the white mass would not reach them until some time during the night. If it appeared threatening by then, they could always make arrangements, but Wellen doubted that would be necessary.

The scouts returned just as the column began moving again. Riding beside the scholar, the lead scout, a young, narrow man with a crooked nose and no hair whatsoever, reported their finds.

"All clear up to the hills, Master Bedlam. Not a soul around."

Wellen caught a note of uncertainty in the man's voice and asked, "Does that bother you for some particular reason?"

The scouts looked at one another before the leader finally answered. "Just seems too pretty and too damned organized. My ma had a big garden and I keep feelin' like I'm ridin' in the middle of it now."

"Garden? What does that mean?" Prentiss Asaalk urged his mount closer and stared down the lead scout.

"I mean the hills, what we could see of them, are awfully nice and organized!" His face screwed up as he thought about it. "They're all pretty much identical, too!"

Glancing forward at the distant hills, Wellen had to admit there was something to what the man was saying. The hills *were* nearly identical. They varied in size, true, but not in shape. There was also a definite trend; the hills grew taller the more to the north one looked.

"Preposterous, yes?" Asaalk asked, looking at the scholar. "I suppose . . ."

"Is that *all* you men have to report?" Captain Yalso asked, sounding both relieved and disgusted. No one wanted to be told that there was danger, but at the same time everyone wanted to know if there was something of interest ahead. The thought of finding nothing but endless woods and fields appealed to no one. While that meant plenty of good land for colonizing, it also meant no riches.

"You told us not to go too far ahead, sir."

That was true. Since the column would be turning north in another day or two, no one had seen much sense in sending the scouts too far west. Wellen was already regretting that decision. Who knew what lay farther inland? Had he not had the others to consider, he would have ridden deeper into the Dragonrealm. Unfortunately, the scholar knew that he would be lucky if they managed to map most of the eastern coastline before they were forced to return home. It might be years before he had another chance, though.

He came to a decision. "Would you men be willing to scout farther west?"

There were nods from all three. The leader asked, "How far should we ride?"

"As far as you can and still be back by the time we've turned north. That'll give you . . . three days."

"Three days?" Yalso's half-buried mouth curved upward on the ends. "Change your mind?"

"No, I just want to make certain that we bypass that mist-enshrouded region completely." That, at least, was true. More so, now that he was thinking about it. The sense of foreboding was so great that he almost thought he felt it. . . but that was *ridiculous.* Wellen wore the mark of a spellcaster, the streak of silver in his hair, but he had never so much as manifested the least of skills.

The lying shock of hair was a sore point with him, but he knew better than to brood about it, especially now. Thrusting it from his mind, he told the scouts, "That's all I can give you. Ride at your own pace and be careful. We can't afford to turn around once we get started north."

More enthusiastic than they had been upon returning, the scouts saluted Wellen and rode back the way they had come.

"On horse they should make some distance, yes?" Asaalk looked as if he wanted to join them. In that, he was one with the young Bedlam. "Perhaps they will find something for us, something we may turn to if the city is a loss."

An encouraging thought, but Wellen did not want to get his hopes up. At least they knew the ancient city existed. There might not be another such place on the entire continent. There might be nothing.

Wellen hoped that was not the case, if only because it would mean his dream would become only that, a fool's imaginary wonder.

The rest of the day's excursion passed quietly. Several of Yalso's men had been constantly at work jotting down landmarks that would later be compared for a final map of the region. Now and then, the captain retreated to speak to these men, leaving an uneasy Wellen to ride in silence beside the massive blue man. Fortunately, Asaalk seemed lost in his own thoughts, for he made only one comment when they were alone and that was to point out a rather large bird in the distance. From what little they could make out, the two estimated it to be almost as large as a man. That made the northerner check his bow and Wellen reconsider the tales of the Dragonrealm.

When the sun finally began to sink over the hills and Yalso suggested they stop for the night, he was more than willing to acquiesce. They chose a lightly wooded location that would give them some protection. Any locale would have actually suited Wellen, even a rocky hillside. Exhaustion mingled with anticipation had taken a worse toll on him than he had thought possible.

"You look all done in," the sea captain commented after they had handed their mounts over to one of Yalso's men. Around them, weary souls were preparing meals and bedding. Wellen nodded to a few and tried to look encouraging. He had no idea whether he was succeeding or not.

"The trouble of being a scholar, I suppose. My life has been too sedentary and my body just can't take all of this."

Yalso's expression indicated he did not really believe the shorter man's excuse, but the captain liked Wellen too much to pry, at least for now. "Get some food and then go to sleep as soon as ya can. I'll handle sentries and the like, providin', that is, that the blue devil's not already done *that* again."

The blue man had not joined the two of them, but rather had darted off in the opposite direction as soon as he had dismounted. Wellen did not really care what Asaalk was doing now; the blue man's ambitions had no outlet here in the wilds. Perhaps when they reached the ancient city, he might be able to turn the lure of riches to his advantage, but not at the moment. Wellen had the column moving as quickly and efficiently as possible and he knew that his caution concerning the land to the north was one that most of his men shared.

Food was welcome at this late point in the day, as was the tent that he found waiting for him when he went to retrieve his things. Both Yalso and Asaalk insisted that the expedition's leader warranted a private tent. To everyone else, it seemed a plain and simple thing, but Wellen always felt embarrassed when he was treated so. He had led a quiet, unrigorous life and so he always carried the fear that no one would respect him if he did not work as they worked and lived as they lived.

Still, the tent *did* give him somewhere private that he could use for his research. His food half-forgotten beside him, the scholar began rummaging through his notes and theories concerning the Dragonrealm. It was always best to check and double-check what he had written earlier. So engrossed did Bedlam become in his work that he did not look up until he realized that someone had called his name.

It was Captain Yalso. "Knew I'd be findin' you pourin' over those things! What do you find new in them each night? You were readin' them each night on the ship and here you are again!"

Wellen gathered up his papers. "There's always something new. A different perspective, a clearer thought; it could be anything."

"So you say. Well you may be in charge, but I'm orderin' you to bed les' of course you want to fall off your horse tomorrow!"

Sleep suddenly sounded *so* good. Wellen eyed his dinner, part of which was still untouched. "I'll just finish eating."

"Do it without readin'," suggested the aged mariner. "Just so you know, too, the blue devil's out huntin' with a couple of men. Said there's plenty of game out there."

"Long as he doesn't mistake anyone for a deer." Yalso grew somber. "He'd better not."

Reading the captain's expression, Wellen shook his head. He doubted that Prentiss Asaalk would bend to anything as crude as murder. A man of pride, the northerner would be more interested in letting his skills prove him the rightful leader of the

DRAGON TOME

expedition. Yalso, however, was a man who had lived a far more violent life. Between pirates and such, he had developed a very harsh opinion of life.

The captain, seeing that Wellen would not hear his warnings, switched to a more mundane subject. "The clouds've moved in a lot faster. They may not be rain makers, but I doubt we'll be seem' much sun tomorrow."

After the heat today, that seemed more of a godsend to Wellen. "Means we might get a few extra miles. We'll have to keep an eye out. No telling if the weather here changes abruptly. Wouldn't do to be unprepared for a downpour."

"I'll be keepin' that in mind. That's *all* I had to tell ya. Get yourself some rest. You'll need it." The bulky seaman started to depart, then paused and added, "If you're *not* asleep in an hour, I'll be havin' the sentries tie ya down!"

Wellen laughed as the captain retired, because he knew very well that Yalso meant what he had said. Organizing his research into a neat pile, he thrust it back into a weathered pouch and then set about finishing his evening meal. There would be days enough to go over it a hundred times and Captain Yalso was correct when he said that Wellen needed rest. Now free of the hypnotic pull of his work, the short scholar felt the renewed weight of exhaustion attempting to overwhelm him.

He wondered whether he would be able to finish his food before sleep finally triumphed.

Wellen gasped and sat up. He had no way of knowing just how much time had passed since he had retired, but he was certain the night was well underway. Outside, he could hear nothing but the sounds of night: insects, birds, and other small, nocturnal creatures. The scholar frowned. None of those sounds had disturbed him; rather, he had the sensation that there was something *else* out there, something beyond his experience.

He gathered his clothes and dressed quietly but quickly. It was still quite possible that Wellen had heard one of the sentries wandering by, but he doubted that. He could not say why he felt doubtful any more than he could explain why these sensations were occurring.

The clouds covered most of the sky, which made the night that much darker. Wellen stepped out of his tent and surveyed the area, trying to identify the few things he could make out from where he stood. He heard a man cough in his sleep and saw the vague shapes of several sleepers. Nothing unusual.

A few tentative steps left him standing in the dark, perplexed and annoyed at what was happening within his head. It if was real, then what was it? If it was all imaginary, then was he suffering from paranoia? Asaalk, if no one else, would welcome that. The young scholar knew that he could not remain leader of the expedition if he started dreaming up imaginary dangers left and right . . . and *above.*

It was *above.* As if he had actually heard or seen it, Wellen knew that whatever it was lurked directly above him. In the overhanging branches of the nearest tree.

He looked up and perhaps it was the vehemence with which he moved that settled the matter, for a large, dark form suddenly stirred to life. Wellen instinctively let out a yell, bringing the entire camp into frenzied life. The creature in the tree, despite having the advantage, did not fling itself down upon him nor did it flutter off into the night. Instead, it moved about the branches, as if lost or confused.

A hissing noise made the short man stumble away. He saw a long, skinny shape bury itself in the upper portion of the tree's trunk and realized that someone had let loose an arrow. He had no time to wonder who could have moved with such speed and accuracy, however, because the watcher in the branches had finally had enough and was pushing its way out of the tangle.

"What is it? What's happenin'?" Yalso roared from an unknown location to Wellen's right.

18

Another hiss. The winged figure, just launching itself into the sky, squawked in agony as the shaft bit into it. Wellen watched it tumble toward the ground, wings desperately trying to control its crazed descent. A moment later, it struck the ground with an all-too-solid *thump.*

"Master Bedlam!" Captain Yalso, shirtless, rushed to his side. In his hand he held a torch. "Are you well?"

He could not answer the other man, his eyes snared by the sight before him. In the flickering light, the injured creature became a tale come to life. The humanoid torso, the avian visage, despite its small size—standing, it probably came up to Wellen's chest—it was as a few of the fragmented stories had described.

A Seeker. One of the bird folk in the legends of Lord Drazeree.

Other men were gathering, but Yalso waved them back. The Seeker, whether male or female was hard to say, tugged at the shaft, which had caught it in the thigh. It completely ignored the humans.

An adolescent, Wellen decided. *Small wonder it grew confused instead of departing immediately.*

"I struck it, yes?"

Prentiss Asaalk broke through the gathering men, his longbow ready. Suddenly, Bedlam wanted to take the man and shake him. The northerner would never understand why, though.

He would have to act quickly. "Everyone remain where you are! Leave this to me!"

Slowly, Wellen walked toward the bleeding avian, his hands out and open for the creature to see. It failed to notice his nearing presence at first, still caught up in its futile attempt to remove the arrow. When it finally did notice him, its reaction was to reach out and try to claw at his legs. Fortunately for Wellen, its desire was greater than its reach. Its swift defense, however, proved too much for it and it slumped to the ground. The scholar continued to move cautiously, noting that the eyes still watched him.

"Don't go any closer," Yalso warned him.

"It's all right."

"We should finish it off, yes? Much easier to study when it cannot snap a finger off." Asaalk's comment made Wellen's gaze shift for a brief time to the Seeker's beak. There was no doubt in his mind that the avian could not only bite off his fingers, but possibly his entire hand. Still, he did not stop.

When he was well within claw range and still the young Seeker had not attacked him again, Wellen dared to kneel down by the injured leg. The eyes of the avian stayed on him at all times, but it now seemed to understand that he, at least, meant it no harm. He touched the shaft carefully, noting how deep it had sunk into the leg. The pain had to be almost unbearable.

"This will hurt. I'm sorry, but I can't help that. There's no other way." Wellen doubted that it could understand him, but he hoped that his soothing tones would relay his intentions.

Though he had lived most of his life in the throes of research, Wellen Bedlam was not unfamiliar with such wounds. Part of his training had included aiding the injured. With raiders such as the Sons of the Wolf forever harassing settlements, it behooved a traveling scholar to have such knowledge.

His hands steady, something that surprised him quite a bit, Wellen carefully worked the shaft outward. The Seeker's breathing grew ragged as the adolescent flyer struggled with the sharp increase in pain. Smiling encouragement and hoping that the bird understood his expression, Wellen continued. The head of the arrow was giving him great difficulty, causing him to wonder just what it looked like. Trust the blue man to utilize a tip with jagged barbs or something equally nasty.

He nearly fell backward when the arrow came loose. The Seeker gasped and shivered, but still did not pass out. He had to admire its stamina. Had it been himself, Wellen was certain he would have blacked out long before. He glanced at the arrowhead. Sure enough, it was lined with hooked ridges. Any animal suffering the misfortune of being struck by one of Asaalk's toys would tear open its wound further when it tried to pull the arrow out with its teeth or claws. In all probability, the head itself would end up remaining lodged in the wound until the victim perished from blood loss or disease.

Thinking of the wound, he turned his gaze back to the leg. Blood continued to streak down the sides. The wound was a good two inches across and probably extended down to the bone. He would have to bind it lest it grow worse, but first he had to inspect it a little closer. There might be other damage.

As his fingers touched the edge of the gaping wound, a wondrous thing happened. Wellen removed his hand as if a snake had been about to bite it, but only because he had hardly been expecting this latest shock.

The wound was closing. It was *healing* itself.

Sorcery! I should have recalled! The Seekers, so the stories went, had ruled the Dragonrealm before the coming of Lord Drazeree. They had a magic of their own.

"What's happenin' there?" Yalso finally dared ask, having grown frustrated with being unable to contribute anything to the situation. "What's it doin' now?"

"Healing itself." *Odd,* Wellen thought. *I thought it would have entailed more than this.*

The Seeker stirred, and rose so quickly to a sitting position that several of the onlookers thought it was about to attack their leader. Asaalk's bow was at the ready, but Wellen held up a shielding hand.

"No!" He made a calming gesture to the Seeker, too. Fear might make it do exactly what everyone had thought it was about to do.

What the avian did do was gingerly touch the closed wound. A taloned finger gently ran the course of the injury, almost as if the Seeker could not quite believe what had happened. Wellen was perplexed; perhaps the young creature had never had to make use of its powers in such a way, but surely it had seen others of its kind heal themselves?

His confusion swelled when the Seeker removed its hand from its leg, reached out slowly, and touched the scholar's arm.

A sensation of gratitude . . . that was the only way Wellen could describe it . . . washed over him. He swayed under its intensity.

Mutterings from the men warned him of their misconceptions. He shook his head and quickly assured them of his safety. "I'm fine! It was only trying to thank me!"

"What do we do with it?" someone asked. "Put it over a fire and cook it?"

Normally, Wellen might have joined in the laughter, but not in this case. He slowly rose and turned to face the others. "We let it go."

"Let it *go?*" It came as no surprise to the scholar that the loudest dissenting voice belonged to Prentiss Asaalk. "So it may bring its flock back to murder us in the night, yes? We should kill it and preserve its hide!"

There were more than a few agreeing nods. Wellen quelled his rising anger. "This is a *child,* gentlemen. You can see that for yourselves. Is there anyone who would like to kill this child? Is there anyone brave enough?"

A cold silence draped itself over the expedition. As he had hoped, putting the killing in such terms had made it an unthinkable act in the eyes of the others. There might have been one or two men who would have performed the horrific deed had they been alone, but no one now dared even speak of it, lest they be marked by their compatriots. Though Wellen had tried to choose men with few familial ties for the expedition, he knew that some *did* have children.

"You heard Master Bedlam!" growled Yalso. He somehow towered over the men. "And a right good decision it is! I'll want no child's death . . . whatever that child *be* . . . on my hands!"

The blue man looked a bit frustrated, but he had lowered his bow and was already replacing the unused arrow into the quiver that had been slung rather haphazardly across his back.

The Seeker rose, careful to remain behind Bedlam at all times. Wellen encouraged it with *a* smile, indicating that it could fly off into the sky as soon as it desired. The Seeker spread its wings, but instead, walked up to the short man and placed one clawed hand on his arm again. Once more, there was a sensation of immense gratitude such as only a youngster could convey. Wellen shook his head, trying to indicate that he had done nothing for the adolescent.

Cocking its head to one side, the Seeker released his arm. Expansive wings stretched, flapped, and lifted the avian into the air. There was a collected exhalation from the party. While their homelands were not without wonders, especially for those who lived near the wilds claimed by hidden Sirvak Dragoth, the Seeker was a new creature and one that few besides Wellen recognized from childhood stories.

It hovered over the scholar a moment longer, then turned and soared with remarkable speed into the concealing night.

A *youngling,* he thought, watching the sky even though he knew he would see nothing more. *The entire camp turned about because of a curious youngster!*

Yalso, as ever, was the rational force among them. He waved the men away, saying, "That's all! It's over! I want everyone back to sleep . . . 'cept you sentries! You I want to keep awake! Lettin' sprats go right past you! If I find another one in here, you can be certain. . ."

The captain's voice trailed off as he followed the men. Asaalk remained just long enough to retrieve his arrows. He picked up the one that had been removed from the avian's thigh by Wellen, ignoring the blood, but the other arrow snapped in two when he tried to free it from the trunk.

"A pity! They are costly."

Bedlam said nothing. He stared at the blue man until Asaalk, seemingly oblivious to Wellen's disgust, bid the scholar good night and retired.

Alone at last, the tired scholar gave the heavens one final scan, then retreated into his tent.

Inside, his other emotions gave way to the wonder of it all. A *Seeker! I saw one!* He could not get the thought out of his mind. The fables and legends bore more truth than he had thought likely. If the Seekers existed, what *else* might? Wellen seriously doubted that he would get any more sleep tonight, so awed was he by the experience. He settled down and stared at the ceiling of his tent, recalling every marvelous detail of the avian. Time would have to be devoted to a piece on the creature before the memories grew indistinct. That meant now. Wellen decided to allow himself a few minutes to regroup his thoughts before he began to write down his notes on this discovery.

Three minutes later, he was sound asleep.

In a tree beyond the camp, its eyes focused on the habitat of he was leader of these new folk, the winged figure watched. No one would notice it here. Learning from experience, however, it had also cloaked itself in warding spells, just to make certain.

The leader of the humans was the one to watch. Already, he had marked himself different from the rest. Soft as he appeared, the others respected his decisions. That meant

21

there was more to him than appearances suggested.

Reluctant as it was to share the information, the watcher knew what would happen if it did not. Closing its eyes, the Necri linked with its unwanted partner. The human called Xabene would be very interested in this particular man, of that the Necri was certain.

It almost pitied him.

Chapter Four

Reddish eyes the length of a man opened, taking in the darkness of the cavern. Reptilian eyes, monstrous eyes, filled with vast knowledge.

There was something amiss in his kingdom, something more than just the annoying intrusions by the insignificant creatures calling themselves the Lords of the Dead.

In the darkness of the cavern, the shadowy form of the Dragon King rose, nearly filling the entire chamber. There was something amiss.

His claws scratched at the rocky floor as he contemplated this affront to his reign. Who *now* dared threaten what was his and what should rightfully be his? Did someone else seek the tome? What was the source of the strange presence? Who was the fool?

His talons gouged great crevices in the rock as he thought of the punishment he would mete out. In the darkness, no one could see his dragon's smile, toothy and full of hunger.

There was something amiss in his kingdom, *oh, yes* . . . but not for very long.

Despite the events of the night, the column was underway soon after dawn. A different mood prevailed. Most now recalled the tales from their youth and were beginning to wonder just what other shocks the Dragonrealm had for them.

Wellen, especially, wondered. As he rode beside Captain Yalso, he could not shake the uneasy feeling that had been with him since the discovery of the Seeker. The young scholar had assumed that the sensation would dwindle away once the avian was gone, but such had not been the case. Waking that morning, he had felt the same, possibly even worse.

Why?

The clouds that had moved in during the night had failed to vanish with the morning. Rain was still not likely; the clouds were not the right type. There were even several patches of clear sky, windows in a wall of mist. Wellen found himself constantly leading the expedition from shadow to light and back to shadow again. Under other circumstances, Wellen might have found it amusing. Not today, not with the sense of foreboding.

"Somethin' wrong?" Yalso asked. "You look all out."

He decided to be honest with the mariner. "I can't help shaking the feeling that something's going to happen. I had the same notion when I woke up and discovered the Seeker!"

Yalso glanced at the telltale mark of silver decorating his companion's head. "But I thought you didn't have any sort of magic, despite that—"

"I *don't!*" Wellen snapped.

Both men stared at one another. Embarrassed, Wellen looked around. The men in the front of the column stared straight ahead. Twisting, he faced Prentiss Asaalk. The blue man met his gaze with an indifferent one, but Wellen was certain it was a mask.

Asaalk was likely smiling inside at the shameful display. Bedlam had always prided himself on his ability to hold his temper. For most men, such an act would have been nothing, but for him . . .

A shadow broke across one of the patches of sunlight and vanished.

His anger at himself temporarily put aside, Wellen studied the clouds. The bit of open sky was there, but nothing that could have created the shadow was evident.

"Somethin'?"

The young leader shook his head. "Nothing. Just my imagination running off."

Neither one brought up the subject of sorcery and Wellen's lack thereof. The column moved in relative silence for the next couple hours. Comments were restricted to the notation of landmarks and where the best point to turn north would be. Bedlam finally chose the edge of the hills. The scouts had not yet returned, and he could no longer wait. Somewhere there had to be a break that would allow him a view of the lands beyond.

The column was just entering another patch of sunlit countryside, but Wellen's mind was hardly on something so insignificant. The nearer to the hills they came, the more the lead scouts comment concerning the gardenlike quality of the land came back to haunt him. Was there a break? Did the hills just continue unbroken, as they appeared to do so far?

Had someone arranged them so? Again, it seemed a silly notion, but . . .

For the second time, a huge shadow blotted out the sunlight.

He was not the only one to notice it. Yalso muttered an epithet and even Prentiss Asaalk seemed disturbed. The shadow, however, disappeared from sight before any of the three could look up. Wellen looked at the two for suggestions. The northerner shrugged, weather not being of much import to him unless it was about to storm. The captain thought about it, then suggested, "Clouds."

That was the obvious answer, but it did not settle well with the scholar. He was the first to admit that weather was *not* his forte, but *swift* clouds?

The massive sailor could see that neither man understood him. He tried to explain, "I know most landleggers don't pay *that* much attention to weather, 'cept maybe farmers, but a man on the sea has got to, 'cause if he don't he might find his ship torn apart on the rocks and him takin' the biggest drink of his life . . . and the last, of course."

"And how does that concern us?" the blue man asked.

"There're currents in the air just as there're currents in the ocean. Sometimes, ya got one current going one way and another, lower, goin' a different way."

"And you're saying that it's the same above?" Wellen wondered for the first time what knowledge he had ignored by paying so little attention to the sky.

"Might be, is what I'm sayin'. I've seen clouds high up go different directions than the ones below them, faster or slower, too."

"Clouds . . . " It was apparent that the blue man was ready to forget this subject. "We have no reason to fear clouds, yes? Not these."

"Maybe."

None of this talk had satisfied Wellen, however. He looked again to the heavens, trying make out something in the patches of clear sky. "I don't think it was a cloud, not a normal one, captain. It moved too fast."

"Then what?"

The scholar had no answer, none, at least, that he could verify. Whatever it was seemed to be gone now.

Or *was* it? The sense of foreboding was so strong that it threatened to drown out all thought. He put a hand to his forehead and closed his eyes for a moment, trying to ease the pounding. Neither Yalso nor Asaalk said anything.

I have no powers! I have no skill! This is all in my mind! Wellen tried deep breaths.

DRAGON TOME

For a brief instant, he felt an inhuman presence in his head. "Gods!" His head snapped up and though he stared forward, what he saw was beyond mortal vision.

An overwhelming sense of mastery. A hunger that can never be sated. A contempt for lesser things . . . for the tiny warm-bloods below.

"Master Bedlam!" Yalso was shouting. "Listen to me!" He grabbed the captain's thick forearm. "It's up there! It's up there watching us!"

"What does he speak of?" Asaalk yelled.

"I *don't—Mother of the Sea!"*

Shouting erupted from the ranks even as Wellen joined Yalso and the blue man in gazing up at the source of the growing panic. It had wings that spanned the length of the column with ease. Talons that, even at this distance, must be capable of easily picking up a man and a horse. It had a tail at least as long as its body. When it roared, they could see the vast array of long, sharp teeth in its maw. It was green for the most part, but another color mingled with that green in a manner so subtle that one almost accepted it being there without realizing what it was. Purple or something near it.

Here be dragons, so the stories said.

No one, not even Wellen Bedlam himself, had actually believed that the horrific leviathans of their childhood tales existed. But what flew above them, looking very much like a vulture circling its meal, was no massive, stupid beast like the dragons of home.

As they stared, still unbelieving, it began to dive. Wellen's shout surprised even him. "Scatter!"

What *else* was there to do? They were not armed to fight such a monstrosity, even if a spellcaster or two had deigned to join the foolhardy quest. The sorcerers of their homelands were too busy fighting each other or simply did not care. Now, that lack might mean the death of every man.

"There's nowhere to run to!" Yalso screamed. "That thing'll tear trees from the earth if we run to the woods! It'll probably scorch the entire field!"

"What else is there to do?"

There was no time for talk after that. The dragon was much too close.

With Yalso and Asaalk behind him, Wellen urged his mount to the hills. The hills offered the best protection and he wished that there was some way to transport his men there. The entire column was facing destruction and *he* was to blame!

A massive shadow raced across the land. The roar of the dragon deafened everyone. The frantic scholar thought that the beast almost *laughed,* but that was impossible, wasn't it? The question became moot as a strong wind caused by the dragon's passing buffeted the riders.

"We must stand and do something!" the blue man shouted. He had a peculiar look in his eyes, but Wellen had no time to decipher it. He was only concerned with saving himself and those who had followed him into this chaos.

"You're welcome to try!" Yalso replied, his eyes glued to the receding backside of the dragon. Its first pass had resulted in little damage and no bloodshed whatsoever. No one thought that the party would be that fortunate on its next pass.

Prentiss Asaalk seemed to be considering his weapons. Wellen shook his head. "You've nothing that could slay that beast! Hiding is the best hope we have!"

The dragon turned in a great arc and began its second dive.

Despite the oncoming danger, the scholar hesitated. His eyes scanned the scene beyond, where men either ran in full panic or buried themselves in whatever bit of cover the landscape provided. Both attempts were futile, save that *some* men might survive with such numbers as they had. From above, the dragon could see them all.

"We can't *do* anything for them!" Captain Yalso cried, taking his arm. The anguish in the sailor's voice surprised Wellen. For all his gruffness, Yalso cared for his crew as if they were his sons. He cared for the rest of the expedition almost as much, since they were under *his* care as well as Bedlam's.

The dragon, persistent as all large drakes were, came toward the earth again, but this time it did not simply pass over and return to the clouds. From its maw, a fine smoke flowed forth, settling on the earth as the drake raced over. Men caught in the midst of it rose and began to run.

The strongest of them ran perhaps five, maybe six steps before clutching their throats and falling face down into the grass, which was itself turning brown and withering.

"No!" Wellen almost whispered the protest, so taken aback was he by the deaths. What sort of weapon was that the dragon had, a poison smoke? "No!"

He urged his anxious steed back toward the dying, his thoughts entirely on their lives and not his own.

"Come back!" Yalso raced after him. "You can't be of any help, Bedlam! You'll only get yourself killed, too!"

The shadow enveloped them then and grew at an alarming rate. The dragon had already turned back.

It did not strike this time, but the wind its streaking form caused was enough to send men falling to the ground. Wellen barely held his place in the saddle and even his steed stumbled in the midst of the blast. He still did not know what he intended to do, only that *something* had to be done.

"It comes again!" Prentiss Asaalk materialized next to him, the blue man's horse already panting from the combination of fear and its rider's great mass.

Even though he knew the leviathan was deadly, the scholar could still not help but admire its grace and beauty. The dragons of home were indeed dull-witted cattle compared to this monster. The vast, batlike wings spread so far that a dozen horsemen on each would have been able to stand their mounts ready and still have no fear that they and their animals would be cramped for space. The scales of the beast shone whenever the sunlight hit it. Truly a wonder to behold . . . but not when it was trying to kill them all.

It was no longer possible to keep track of the men. They were scattered everywhere. Wellen wished he had the dragon's point of view. At least then, he could see where everyone---

A *sudden image of landscape seen as though from a mountain peak, yet it kept changing. Tiny, silly figures scurrying about in blind panic, knowing that he was above them, their death. All merely prey to be toyed with except for one who rode, whose mind seemed to reach out . . .*

Gasping, Bedlam found himself atop his mount once more. Had he *dreamed* that? Had his wish come true, albeit only for a moment, and granted him the ability to see as the drake did? How could such a thing happen?

You are the one . . .

The voice was in his mind and though no more was said after that, the cloying, inhuman sensation of it remained with him despite the scholar's best efforts to clear his head. He reined his horse to a frantic halt, surprising both Asaalk and Yalso, who rode several lengths past him before they could bring their own frightened animals around. As they rode back to him, the danger to both grew frighteningly clear to Wellen.

He rose in the saddle. "Go back! Ride away! Keep away from me!"

The northerner hesitated, slowing his steed a bit, but Captain Yalso continued on, his weathered visage deep-set in determination not to abandon his friend.

Wellen turned his horse and desperately urged it into motion. The sweating horse needed no encouragement; it broke into a gallop that left the other two riders quickly behind.

25

"Master Bedlam! Wellen!" Yalso would not be so easily deterred. Wellen, looking back, saw the seaman racing after him, a reluctant Asaalk close behind. He knew that the two men were unwittingly rushing to join him in death.

What the massive beast's limits were, Wellen had no way of knowing. His only hope was to ride and try to block its thoughts. Somehow he and the monster had briefly formed a bond, one that had worked in both directions. He did not think the dragon could read his mind that easily, however; its thought message had seemed forced, as if it had struggled to break in. The frenzied scholar knew that he might be badly mistaken, that the dragon might even now be laughing silently at his suppositions, but there was little he could do about that.

Once more, it was the sudden plunge into deep shadow that warned him of the leviathan's nearness. The black shroud crept up rapidly from behind him. Oddly, his fears were not for himself, but for those who followed.

Someone screamed, *"Jump!"*

Wellen reacted instinctively and dove off his horse.

The animal cried out in horror and pain, but the rolling Bedlam saw only the dust and earth that rose and beat him mercilessly. He heard the thundering of hooves and a voice that sounded like that of the blue man, but little more. As he turned face down again, his nose was pushed against the ground. Wellen grunted as it bent to one side and blood splattered his countenance. The world took on an ethereal quality, fading into and out of existence. As he finally slowed to a stop, it was all he could do to keep from passing out. The stunned explorer refused to give in to his injuries; there was no promise that unconsciousness would save him from the dragon's claws. Wellen, despite his upbringing, was one who preferred to die, if he had to, fighting the loathsome process to the bitter end.

He tasted blood on his lips as he turned over and tried to right himself. A broken nose and torn lips were miniscule wounds. He was thankful that nothing else seemed broken. Had the ground been rocky, it might have been worse.

The dragon was high in the sky, something large squirming in its claws. Wellen's mount. Beast and prey vanished into the clouds.

Captain Yalso rode to him, reining to a stop just in front of the bleeding scholar. "How bad are you?"

"Bruises, nothing more." That was a lie. There was dizziness, too, but he did not want to tell the mariner that. "Leave me; I'll go on foot."

"Don't be bigger fool than you've been! Climb aboard!" Yalso stretched out a hand.

Wellen eyed the captain's mount. It suffered from the combination of the weight of the sailor and the frantic pace it had already been put through. Adding a second body would only kill the animal in short order at this rate. At the very least, it would quickly grow useless for both of them.

The dragon was still above the cloud cover, no doubt finishing off his snack. There could only be seconds before the leviathan returned. "Captain Yalso, if we ride together, we're both lost! If we keep separate, one or both of us could survive!"

"Listen—"

Bedlam would not be silenced. "Go now! You can make it to safety! He wants *me!* Our minds, our thoughts, touched! He will not rest until he has taken me!"

It was obvious that the captain did not understand anything that Wellen was saying, but the grim determination in the scholar's eyes could not be denied. Yalso sighed and gave his companion a weary smile. "At least take the horse!"

"You need it more than me!" Strong the mariner might be, but running was not something his monumental girth allowed him to excel at. "Go!"

Yalso blinked, then nodded and rode back in the direction the column had originally traveled from.

Dirty, disheveled, and wracked with pain, Wellen chose a path going opposite that of the captain. By leading the dragon away, he hoped to give the survivors, including Yalso, a chance to make it to safety. Perhaps the drake would even lose interest in them once it had dealt with the one who had invaded its mind.

He was still not certain how he had done that. The silver streak in his hair had always lied; never had Wellen revealed so much as the most modest of sorcerous skills. Why now?

Any theory he might have formed was lost, for the dragon broke through the clouds and dove like an avenging demon toward the spot in which the scholar stood. Wellen broke into a desperate run, knowing he could not outpace a soaring beast such as this. He only hoped his sacrifice would not be in vain. If even a few of the men survived, it would be worth it.

The shadow blanketed the field around him. Wellen stumbled and fell. There was no time left. He had hoped to get farther, to draw the dragon's notice for a bit longer, but such was not to be. He rolled onto his back and watched the descending form grow. What madness made him desire to face his scourge he could not say. Some insane hope, perhaps, that a miracle would yet save him.

Only a short moment from his victim, the dragon suddenly veered off.

The confused and unbelieving human rolled over to watch the monstrosity fly around. The dragon's pattern was erratic, as if he did not know where he was going. Wellen touched the silver in his hair without realizing it. A tentative smile played at his lips as he marveled at his astonishing escape.

Rising once more to a great height, the green and purple leviathan scoured the earth. Reptilian eyes scanned the very region where Wellen Bedlam lay, but still the beast did not return for him.

"Wellen!"

The horrified voice made him whirl about. He stared in knowing fear as the captain, thinking that the dragon must have injured but not taken the scholar, rode back.

"No!" His shout went unheeded. He was as invisible and silent to Yalso as he was to the drake.

The rider, unfortunately, was not invisible to the menacing form above. Frustrated at losing his prey, the leviathan turned in the air and dove. Captain Yalso realized his mistake at the last moment and tried to leap from his mount as the dragon neared. The winged monstrosity was not to be fooled this time, however. It watched the man and not the beast and when the seaman jumped, unleashed another deadly cloud.

Already knowing it was too late for his companion, Wellen blindly ran west in order to escape the onrushing cloud. Behind him he heard the startled cry of the horse and a mortal cough that could only have issued from a human throat. Wellen did not look back.

The dragon remained low after the attack, evidently searching for its escaped victim. The shadow fell over Wellen and the wind nearly wrenched him from the ground, but still he ran free. Better to just keep running and hope that somehow he might live through this nightmare.

How long he ran, Bedlam could not say. Always it seemed as if the dragon was just behind him. The hills loomed closer and closer. Wellen briefly wondered what had happened to the scouts. Had the dragon caught them sooner? Had something *else* taken them? Such questions only made him run harder, despite the growing pain in his body and the shortness of his breath. It might very well be, he thought, that he would escape the scaly predator only to die of exhaustion.

Something came charging toward him.

A horse. Saddled. One of their own. Wellen had lost his own mount and Yalso's had perished with its rider. That meant that this was Prentiss Asaalk's animal, but then where was the northerner?

He realized he had no time to worry about the blue man. The horse was a gift of circumstances; Wellen could hardly not make use of it. Calling to the animal in as quiet and smooth a voice as he could manage, the battered scholar tried to encourage it over to him. At first the horse was skittish . . . and with good reason, of course. . . but then it slowly trotted his way. When the animal was within arm's length, Bedlam reached out, stroked its muzzle, and carefully sought out the reins. There was no blood to be seen. Other than being frightened and exhausted, the steed was healthy. Again, he wondered what had become of the blue man. While Wellen had hardly cared for Prentiss Asaalk, he did not hate him enough to see him dead or injured.

A quick glance skyward revealed the dragon still searching fruitlessly for the tiny figure who had vanished before his very eyes. Wellen thanked whatever gods had chosen to protect him and mounted. He did not dare ride east, not with the poisonous mists still enshrouding most of the region, and his inability to return to the ships left him with few other options. Riding north or south would leave him too open for his own tastes. Wellen had no idea how long he would remain invisible to the drake and whether or not this protection extended to other dangers. The horse had not been blinded; other creatures might also be able to see him.

That left the west and the hills, the destination he had been fleeing toward already.

Turning the nervous steed about, Wellen rode. Now able to relax a bit physically, if not mentally, the scholar found himself fighting the exhaustion that his earlier panic had kept at bay. He shook his head and tried to clear his thoughts, never assuming for a moment that he was free of danger. The drake might come in his direction and bury this part of the field under a cloud of death. It might finally pierce the mysterious barrier—one which Wellen could not believe *he* was responsible for—and once more be able to see the human morsel who had escaped it.

Sweat dripped down from his forehead, stinging his eyes. Wellen wiped his arm across. As he lowered his arm, he noticed a stain of red across his sleeve. The bleeding scholar knew it was a good thing that he could not see his countenance; between his broken nose and the wounds he had garnered during his fall, he probably looked more dead than alive. That he felt no pain from his wounds worried him, and for the first time he tried to take stock of his injuries. It was impossible to do so now, however, for between the horse's bouncing gait and his own exhaustion, the injured man could not keep track of what he was doing.

The first of the hills was nearly within reach when a second, louder roar shook the rider.

Wellen fought for control of the horse, then twisted, with effort, to an angle where he could study the cloudy sky over the plains.

Something moved about the clouds that *dwarfed* the leviathan that had destroyed the expedition.

Something *purple?*

He wiped his eyes clean again and stared. Whatever it was chose not to reveal itself again, but it was still there. He knew that, if only because the drake was rising swiftly to meet the newcomer. Yet, the monster's movements were not those of a beast about to attack, but rather those of a lesser creature answering the summons of a greater.

There and then, Bedlam knew he did *not* desire to remain where he was any longer.

With a last effort, he guided the stumbling horse into the hill region. The way was rough going at first. It almost seemed as if the same being who had shaped the hills with such uniformity had placed them so no path ever went straight, or remained level, for that matter. The path twisted and wound with such frequency that when Wellen and his horse finally reached a smooth, clear point, he paused and studied it. The thought of a subtle trap wormed its way through his clouding mind, but he soon rejected it. For what reason he did so remained unclear to him; the scholar could only recall that it seemed to make sense.

Wellen looked back on occasion, but after the first few minutes, the hills permanently blocked his view of the plains and the eastern sky. He could not hear either the dragon or the newcomer, which he assumed, with much trepidation, had to be yet *another* of the species. But that did not mean that they had departed.

The longer he rode, the more difficult it became for Wellen Bedlam to remain conscious. The leap and its aftermath had taken much more out of him than he had first supposed. Once in a while, Wellen found himself stirring from periods that he could only describe as blankness. He had been neither conscious or asleep, merely *not there*. When he tentatively checked both his broken nose and the forehead wound, he found both still bleeding profusely.

"I hope you can go on without my help," he muttered to the horse. The sound of his own voice, as dry and cracked as it was, kept him somewhat coherent. He began talking to himself more and more, not caring how mad he might sound. Besides, who was out here to listen to him besides the scholar himself?

"I had this dream once." Wellen forced himself to turn his head so that he could study the landscape around him. More and more trees were dotting the path. He vaguely wondered if that meant he was coming to the western edge of the hills. "I had a dream that I would become a great warlock, a sorcerer without corn—compare."

He coughed. The noise echoed throughout the area.

"Kept waiting for those magnificent powers to manifest them—themselves. They never did." Wellen glanced at his mount, as if waiting for it to respond. He started to think about what sort of life the animal had enjoyed before being picked for this expedition. "Bet you wished you were back in the stable. Nice and boring, but safe." A ragged laugh. "I had a life like that. . . and to think *I* wanted out of it."

The hills kept rising before him, shattering any idea that an end might be in sight. Wellen scratched his nose despite both the blood his hand came away with and the fact that since the nose was numb it had not itched in the first place. "Should I . . . should I stay here or go . . . go beyond the edge?"

Something fluttered about the trees, something fairly large. Wellen doubted that a dragon could hide itself so well, then thought of the young Seeker. Could one of the legendary avians be watching him? He leaned in the direction of the noise, and an owl darted out of the trees and off into the sky.

Wellen wanted to laugh, but there was not enough strength left for that. He satisfied himself with a brief smile, then once more concentrated on the myriad path running through the hills.

There had been no sign of the dragon or dragons for some time now, but not once did the scholar think to turn around. He was committed. This far into the hills, he was determined to at least complete the crossing. Beyond the sloping, turning land there was something so valuable that it needed dragons to guard it. Bedlam was certain that such had been the drake's purpose in being here, to guard what lay beyond the hills.

The horse shied.

Wellen twisted in the saddle, gazing up in full expectation of sighting a diving form.

He saw nothing. The sky that was visible here was clear, save for a few high clouds. Now, there was nowhere the dragon could have hidden. Frustrated and worn, he turned to shout at the skittish animal. . . and saw the grisly remains poking out from behind some high bushes.

They were recognizable as a horse and a man, but little more. From the shreds of clothing that still lingered on the bloody torso of the unfortunate rider, Wellen knew it was one of the expedition scouts. Some force had torn the man quite literally apart, much the way one might tear apart an orange.

Weakened as he was already, the scholar did not have the stamina to resist the sickening sight. Half falling from the saddle, he went to his knees and vomited. Little more than spittle and blood issued forth, but the act itself was nearly enough to make him completely collapse. Wellen succeeded in maintaining consciousness, but that was all. For more than ten minutes, the hapless rider kneeled where he was, trying to pull himself together.

No dragon had killed the man. If such had been the case, not a shred of clothing would have been found. This deed had been performed by a smaller but savage creature, something perhaps the size of a . . . of a *Seeker?* Wellen could not see the avians killing so, however. The legends and his encounter with the adolescent Seeker were enough to convince him that the bird folk, however dangerous they might be, were capable of more *civilized* methods of death. More likely, an animal of some sort had gotten the unsuspecting scout while he had been engaged in studying the landscape.

So where were the *other* scouts, and why had they left his body unburied?

He was afraid he knew the answer already. Dragging himself to his feet, Wellen took hold of his mount's reins and, forcing himself to endure the sight of the ravaged remains, continued down the path. Each step tore at his already fragile system, wracking him further. Nevertheless, Wellen continued until he found what he was looking for.

All in all, the other two had not gotten very far from their comrade before whatever horror had murdered the first had caught up to them. One of the figures, the man Bedlam recalled as the spokesman of the trio, was actually in recognizable shape. Perhaps the beast had tired by that point. What did matter was that Wellen was now absolutely alone in the Dragonrealm. The scouts were dead, Yalso had perished, and the scholar had found no trace of Prentiss Asaalk, save the blue man's mount. Any survivors from the column were undoubtedly on their way to the waiting ships. There had to be a few, despite the thoroughness of the dragon. He had no doubt that the acting commander would order both vessels underway once he heard what had happened to the grand expedition. With such tales to tell, it was doubtful that anyone would risk returning to this continent for years to come.

He would be *alone* in the Dragonrealm.

His dream had become a nightmare.

Wellen desperately wanted to do something about the remains of the three men, but he barely had the strength to stand, much less dig a grave or build a pyre. In fact, as shameful as it might seem, Wellen did not even want to remain in the same area any longer. In his present state, he could barely stomach the rising stench.

Disgusted with himself, the expedition leader tried to remount his horse. The animal was understandably nervous and Wellen's first two attempts failed miserably. Wincing at the pain coursing through his body, Wellen took a tighter hold on the reins and whispered to the beast. The voice calmed the horse to a point where the young Bedlam finally felt it was safe to try again. Carefully, he started to swing himself upward.

In the undergrowth near one of the bodies, a heavy form moved toward them. The horse shied. Wellen, caught midway, could only hold on. He did not even have the breath to talk to the shifting steed.

The creature in the undergrowth hissed and crawled out from cover. The scholar, turned to face it by the movements of his panicking mount, marked it immediately as a carrion creature, one of the lesser drakes that always seemed to have a nose for finding the dead. Unless there were more than a dozen, such beasts rarely attacked the living. They were possibly the biggest cowards amongst their kind.

The horse, already at its wits' end from everything else, saw only teeth and claws. It rose onto its hind legs and kicked wildly. Try as best as he could, Wellen could not maintain his grip. He fell to the earth, striking his head on the flattened path.

The drake hissed again, but held its ground, unwilling to give up the morsels it had found. Wellen had a blurred glimpse of hooves and then was bowled to one side as the horse, unwilling to contest with the newcomer, caught him a glancing blow. It galloped off even as its former rider rolled to a stop.

Wellen tried to rise, but much like the steed, he too was at his limit. Even when he heard a louder hiss and saw the second drake appear, the strength would not come to him. The drakes were cowards, yes, but not when it came to the helpless. Wellen had as much chance of fending them off as he did of casting a spell. The bitter irony that here his lack of true power would finally prove his undoing, made him curse the heavens for ever having created the silver mark as the symbol of sorcery.

"Such, such language," came a voice.

The drakes froze, then scattered as if one of their more violent cousins had come for them. Wellen tried to turn over and see his rescuer, but that was now beyond him.

"Where . . . who . . . ?"

Darkness coalesced in front of him, taking on the vague shape of a cloak and hood. In the deep shadows cast by the hood, he barely made out the general visage of a man. That was all he could tell about his rescuer. The massive robe all but buried its wearer within.

"You should be more careful, Dru," the cloak said. Wellen tried to speak, but then even breathing became difficult and he passed out.

Chapter Five

Xabene stood by the long-dead campfire, her silence condemning the Necri in front of her as no words could. The Necri refused to be cowed by this mortal creature. It had performed its part as commanded.

At last, the enchantress turned on the monster. "You were caught up in your *entertainment*, weren't you? You were too busy with your *playthings* to keep an eye on the leader of the newcomers!"

The pale, batlike servant hissed. Through its own peculiar method of communication, it had let known all that had happened, but Xabene still did not believe it.

She shook her head. Time and time again she had warned her masters that the Necri had only limited uses. They were too savage, too single-minded. While it had vented its eagerness upon the outsiders' scouts, the dragons had struck at the column itself, slaying most and scattering the few survivors. The winged monstrosity claimed it had followed the short one who was leader, but somehow the two had become separated in the hills. The dark sorceress was certain that *she* would not have lost track of a man, but then men were her forte.

What bothered her most was the sensation she had felt at roughly the time the

Necri indicated it had lost sight, both normal and magical, of the human. It was a feeling she had only associated with two other forces, the gnome and the Lords of the Dead . . . yet she was certain it was neither.

"We have to find him again! You"—*she* stared into the white, dead eyes of her inhuman partner—"have to find him, or the failure will be on *your* head!"

The Necri bared its long, glistening teeth, but it did not argue. Their masters were not ones to debate the reasons for failure, they would merely execute punishment. Still, both knew that it was just as likely that they could find fault with Xabene. After all, it had been her duty to back up the Necri in its mission.

Yet, she too, only came up blank when she sought to tear away the darkness that had enveloped the outsider leader.

At least we have your face, she thought. The Necri had been able to relay that much to her. A short man, true, but not unsightly. A learned man from what the Necri's sensitive ears had picked up during its visitation to the men's camp.

Also a man who wore the mark of the warlock, the sorcerer, yet did not display any power whatsoever.

You will be so much more entertaining then most, she thought to the mind image of the one called Wellen Bedlam. She hoped that her masters would leave something of him when they were done; it was rare that she encountered a man who wanted more than conquest, riches, or even women. Here was one that wanted knowledge, too.

Certainly he would make a better companion than that! Xabene decided sourly, giving her monstrous counterpart a glare that would have chilled most mortal creatures. The Necri only twitched its long ears and waited for her to return her attention to it. She buried all personal thoughts of the missing outsider in that secret part of her mind that no one, not even the Lords of the Dead, could touch.

"He has to be somewhere," she told the Necri.

Its nose wrinkled as if it had smelled something unpleasant, though what a carrion beast such as this could find unpleasant was a good question. Xabene knew what the response truly meant; the Necri was not one for the nuances of human speech and thought. Its kind had no use nor could even comprehend the use of obvious statements such as the last.

"We have no choice but to search until we find him."

This time, it shook its head. Searching the hills would take it days, perhaps weeks, even with the use of its sorcerous powers.

"Would you rather we go to the masters and tell them of our—"

The Necri had begun to vehemently shake its head, but then something beyond Xabene made its soulless orbs widen in outright fear.

The sorceress whirled about, thinking that perhaps the Dragon Kings had seen past her spells of concealment.

An odd, greenish hole had opened up behind her, one that stood in open air. It was nearly a third again her height and twice as wide as the Necri. Though nothing was visible within, she could already detect the sweet scent of decay emanating from the hole.

Now beside her, the Necri hissed. It was not a challenging call, but rather a meek, fearful response to something they both recognized.

The Lords of the Dead *already* knew of their failure, and they had come to their own decision concerning the twosome.

From within the hole, a second Necri emerged.

"Awake, are you?"

Wellen opened a pair of protesting eyes and tried to focus on his surroundings. For a time, there was little more than a vague light. Then, things slowly began to take form.

To say he was in a cavern was to understate matters. This simple cavern was tall enough to house a castle in its midst. Much of it did not seem natural, as if some ancient had carved out most of it, then left a good deal abandoned. He wondered whether it was the same being that had possibly shaped the landscape.

"No, the cavern is not the work of any Dragon King."

The scholar rose quickly to a sitting position, then waited for the wracking pain to punish him for his transgression. When nothing happened, he looked down at himself. Not only were the blood, scars, and dirt gone from his hands, but his garments looked new. Wellen put a hand to his nose and delighted in the sensation of skin touching skin. There was no blood when he pulled the fingers away. A quick inspection of his forehead wound revealed that it, too, neither bled nor pained him.

He finally recalled the voice and also remembered the murky figure that had rescued him from the minor drakes.

It . . . *he* . . . was seated on a stone throne overlooking much of the cavern. Only the voice lent any clue to the identity of the figure and that only of the gender. The hood and robe obscured so perfectly that Wellen Bedlam would have almost assumed he was staring at a pile of clothing rather than a man.

"I took you for another," the cloak said. "I sometimes forget that so much time has passed. He's likely dead by now, don't you think?"

"Who?" the confused Bedlam asked. He thought of Yalso, but the figure surely did not mean the sea captain.

"Dru . . . but then, you didn't know him. Still, I see him in you."

"Who are you? I mean . . . I thank you for what you've done, but I don't know where I am or why you—"

The robe waved him to silence, revealing by the act the fact that the figure did indeed have a hand. A gloved one. Like the robe, it was dark gray. Everything about the figure seemed to be gray.

"I've watched you for the past day. You're here because I thought you someone else . . . then it was too late. I decided to continue rescuing you, after all."

Wellen began to wonder whether his host was completely rational.

"No, sometimes I lapse and forget where and when I am." The hood leaned forward, revealing just a bit of proud chin and stern mouth. "The forgetting of *when* is by far the worst, I warn you."

"Are you reading my thoughts?"

"Something like that. It is so much easier when you are conscious, though. Besides, you've hardly kept them hidden, now have you?"

Though he had never manifested power, Wellen did know of mental shields from his studies. He raised one instantly.

"Now is that any way to build *trust?*" The hooded warlock rose, but made no threatening gestures. "Well, I've always believed in the sanctity of one's privacy, so I have no qualms if you desire to protect yourself." The hood tilted to one side. "Besides, I'm certain we'll come to an understanding before long."

"Who *are* you?"

The warlock turned from him, seemingly caught up in other matters now. He moved to a table where a collection of artifacts and drawings were scattered and began to collect the latter. The table, as far as Wellen was concerned, had not been there a moment ago.

The cloaked figure finally managed to respond to the scholar's question. "I am the shadow of the past, a ghost of your past . . . and even mine. Whatever name I had, it hardly matters now. Those who knew it are dead. Dust. My people live on in you and those above, but the memory of greatness has been forgotten." The warlock shrugged, his back still to Wellen. "You may call me Shade; it's appropriate as anything and I

33

have become attached to it over the past few centuries."

"Past few—" Bedlam cut off the remainder of his stunned reply. He knew that spellcasters could extend their lives, but that was generally limited to three or four hundred years. Though the one called Shade had not indicated otherwise, Wellen suspected that he was speaking of much more than four hundred years. There was a presence about the warlock so alien, so ancient, that the expedition leader would have been willing to judge the sorcerer in terms of *millennia* rather than centuries.

He realized that his fantastic host had turned to him once more. In the left hand was a plate upon which fruit had been piled. Wellen was aware that the plate had been nowhere in sight, just as the table had been earlier.

"It would be best if you ate. I have tended to your wounds and replaced your clothing. You will need to be at your best when the time comes."

The temptation to ask the warlock exactly what it was the scholar had to be ready for was great, but Wellen decided to wait until after he had eaten. The food would give him strength he might need in case his host proved to be too unstable. The shorter man did not know how he might defeat a master warlock, but he was prepared to try, if necessary.

"I thank you. I could use food."

The plate floated from Shade's hand and landed in Wellen's lap. "When your constitution is a bit stronger, then perhaps you can try something other than the fruit. For now, it will serve to revive your strength."

Wellen tore into the food, finding his hunger suddenly growing into a monster as huge as the dragon that had slaughtered his men. Thinking of the drake made him pause. The warlock also paused, as if he, too, knew what his guest was thinking. Bedlam wondered just how strong the mental shields he had put up really were. Was Shade reading his mind again?

"Something disturbs you?"

"I was thinking about the dragon and the attack."

"Oh." The cloth-enshrouded spellcaster shrugged again, apparently deciding that the deaths of so many good men were of little consequence to him. "You find that such things happen here."

"Is that *all* you can say?" At last roused to anger, Wellen Bedlam rose, spilling the plate of partially eaten fruit all over the smooth cavern floor. "They died needlessly!"

Quietly, patiently, the warlock said, "I have seen more deaths in my life than there are fish in the seas. Only my own now concerns me . . . even after so many failures."

The scholar stood where he was, shaking in frustration. He could think of nothing to say to his host that would likely break through the apathy that had built up over a lifetime at least tenfold, possibly a hundredfold or a thousand fold longer than his own.

Bitterness growing, Wellen reached down and retrieved the fruit. There would come a time, he reflected, when the warlock would regret those words. When death finally came for the man, the angry scholar hoped Shade would recall what he had said now and how he had reacted. Wellen's men at least had their leader to mourn them; no one would ever wish to mourn for someone such as Shade.

For a time, he ate in silence. The dark spellcaster seemed satisfied to simply stare his way. He tried not to stare back, but more and more the shadows that hid the warlock's visage bothered him. What did Shade truly look like? What effects would living so long have on mortal flesh?

Wellen knew he would get no answers if he chose to question Shade about his past. It might be that the warlock barely remembered his own history.

As he completed his meal, something else began to nag at the scholar, something concerning the cavern. Wellen looked up and scanned the area, ignoring Shade's suddenly stiffening posture. What was it about this place . . .?

For the first time, he realized that he could see *nothing* of the cavern, save the walls, the throne, and the table. .. and the last only because the warlock had walked over to it. Every time Bedlam sought to focus on an object, he found his eyes turning away and seeking some view of less significance. With concentration, he was able to make out a series of tables, but what lay upon them, the curious explorer could not say.

"So you pierce the mists," his gray, nebulous host commented. "So there is a bit of Dru within you after all."

At the mention of the last, Wellen lost concentration. The cavern once more became a place of the almost-seen, the shadowlands. He hardly cared. Twice, perhaps more, Shade had made mention of the name "Dru."

"Do you speak of Lord Drazeree?"

"Drazeree? Lord?" Shade chuckled. It was a dry sound, as if the warlock had only just rediscovered it now. "I speak of things long dead, my friend. I speak of myself and others."

A *typical Shade answer,* Wellen was realizing. There was no point in pursuing the matter. His speculations would have to remain just that. Still, if this warlock *was* what he claimed, a contemporary of the legendary lord, would that not make him over . .
.

The confused scholar shook his head. *No one* could live so long.

Shade surprised him then by reaching up and pulling back his hood.

Perhaps, he amended, *one* could *live so long!*

From a distance, the warlock would have resembled an elder scholar, a man nearing the end of his term, but not yet ready to give up the fight. There was strength there, incredible strength. In any other being, that would have been all Wellen noticed . . . if not for the fact that Shade's skin looked so dry, he wondered whether it would turn to powder at his touch.

It was the skin of a man who *should* have been dead, but *was not.*

Tearing his gaze from the stretched, parchment skin, he met the eyes of the sorcerer. Too late, Wellen Bedlam wished he had not abandoned his previous view. The eyes of Shade were *crystalline.* Not eyes created from crystal, but actual ones like Wellen's own that merely exhibited perfectly the attributes of gems.

If the eyes were the mirror of the soul, then the warlock no longer suffered the existence of the latter. Outside, he might still live; inside, he had died long, long ago.

Why the words that came then should choose this moment to be blurted out was a question the explorer would wonder later, but Wellen suddenly found himself asking, "What do you plan to do with me?"

Questions like that had been the death knell of many a character in the plays the scholar had enjoyed back home. Under present circumstances, it would have hardly been surprising to find real life similar.

Again, the dry chuckle. Shade smiled, but it was forced, as if it, too, had only now been rediscovered and its true use still uncertain to the hermitic spellcaster. "I plan to help you. . . if you choose to help *me.* "

He was acting much more lucid, but Wellen was hardly encouraged by that. What would a warlock of his host's obvious abilities need with a mortal who could only dream of casting spells? "I can think of no way that I would be of use to you," Wellen admitted, knowing he might very well be throwing away his life but unable to lie under present circumstances. "I ask again; what do you plan to do with me?"

Shade walked slowly about the cavern, and as he walked, the chamber grew more distinct. Tables and alchemical equipment filled the chamber. Crystalline artifacts flowed with power. Diagrams and patterns that Bedlam had never come across before were hewed into the very stone. The scholar within Wellen desperately wanted to inspect each and every artifact and experiment. He wondered why the warlock would be willing to reveal so much. Either he was extending his trust to his guest or he had no fear that anything Wellen did would be a danger to him. "When I saw you . . . and I came to realize how lost my mind was then . . . I thought you another, a man of great courage and strength." The hooded warlock paused and stared at one of the blank cavern walls. He whispered something, a name, Wellen believed, then seemed to recall himself. "A man of ingenuity and determination. A man who could help me with a situation that prevents me from achieving my goal."

"And that is?" Daring the nebulous figure's wrath, the scholar purposely phrased his question so that it might be referring to either the problem or the goal.

The crystalline eyes narrowed and focused on Wellen as the warlock turned to him. Wellen had never thought to stare Death in the face before, but surely here was the closest earthly equivalent.

"You know as well as I. Your reason for journeying here was too transparent. I know the true reason was carefully *buried* within the folds of your mind." The crystalline eyes seemed to burn. "I know that you've come for the *book.*"

"What book?"

Shade frowned, causing Wellen to fear that the warlock thought he was being patronized. "You know its appearance. A massive tome with a stylized dragon on the cover. It is possibly green, though it may be another color. It is kept there by a gnome who is the only one who knows the way in and out."

The scholar hesitated, but finally asked the next logical question. "In and out of *what?"*

A sigh. "Beyond the western edge of the hills lies another field like the one in which you were . . ." Shade shrugged and let the last part hang. "In this field is a single structure, a five-walled place with neither doors nor windows."

The curious explorer wanted to ask what purpose was served by such a place, but he suspected that the gray warlock would not care for yet another interruption at this juncture.

"The tome lies within. The gnome has guarded it jealously for . . ." Glittering eyes blinked and Shade seemed to lose track of his present surroundings for a time. At last he shook himself and finished, " . . . for as long as I can recall."

"I know nothing about any book, gnome, or bizarre structure sitting out in the middle of nowhere," Wellen responded in flat tones. He took a step toward his host. "I came here only because I had grown up on legends of such a land. I—"

"Ridiculous." For the warlock, there seemed to be no answer but his own that would satisfy. He cut off yet another attempt by Wellen to explain, then slowly returned to the throne that he had been seated in when the scholar had first awakened. Shade pulled the hood back over his head, all but obscuring the upper half of his visage, and sat down again. His breathing was quick and short.

"We have . . . things to discuss . . . you and I. The book, your . . . being here, and *what* you are."

"What I *am?"*

The shadowy spellcaster settled back, seeming to sink into the very rock. "What the lands have made you . . . what sort of power . . . and, more important, what sort of monstrosity . . . hides within you . . . that I do not see."

The tone was cool, almost indifferent, but Wellen read a well-nurtured fear behind it, one the spectral sorcerer had carried for very, very long. It concerned not just his mortality, though that was a part of it, but something more, something at least equally important. He hoped he would not remain with the warlock long enough to find out. Shade was as dangerous to Wellen as the dragon, and the fear within the ancient figure might one day prove too much.

A mad man with great power was a man to be feared.

He dared to respond, not wanting Shade to think that his silence was an acknowledgment of the accuracy of the warlock's dark statement. "I'm no monster. I'm as human as anybody."

At that, the master warlock *did* laugh, but laugh so that Wellen feared for his existence. Only madness, never humor, tinged the laughter of his host. Bedlam had thought the chuckle dry and unnerving; the laugh made him wish to find a place to bury himself.

From the dark within his hood, the eyes of Shade *gleamed.* Though the cloaked figure had not moved in the slightest, it was as if he loomed directly over Wellen, so forceful was his presence. *"Nobody* is human, anymore!" he informed his anxious guest, the authority in his voice almost making his words believable. "Nobody on this forsaken world is human anymore, save for *me!* The lands have changed you *all,* no matter how you might appear!"

As if punctuating his insane words, a roar echoed throughout the cavern. The scholar looked about, trying to find the source and cursing himself for being impotent against the chaos around him.

The roar was followed by another and then another. Wellen readily identified their source, the knowledge turning him as pale as ivory. He had heard dragons roar before.

"Pay them no mind," Shade commented in disdain, acting as if he had completely forgotten his outburst. "They often grow lively this time of day. Merely the clan males reaffirming their status with one another."

"Dragons?" Wellen stared wide-eyed at his host. "There *are* dragons here?" What sort of fool lived among dragons, especially ones like the horror that had killed his men.

"They never come this deep into the caverns. They fear the older magics." This satisfied the warlock, but not the scholar.

"You *live* beneath dragons?" Visions of the monstrosity in the air made the explorer shake. What if they chose now to start descending into this chamber?

"I live beneath the foremost of the dragon clans," Shade corrected him. Straightening just a bit, the warlock used his hands to indicate the entire cavern. "Welcome to the interior of Kivan Grath, emperor of the vast and treacherous Tyber Mountains!" The eyes glittered again, then faded into the darkness that was so much a part of Shade. "A most appropriate place, I think, for the dwellings of the Dragon Emperor. . . don't you *agree?"*

Wellen neither agreed nor disagreed with the warlock. He could only stand, stare, and once more curse the silver streak in his hair that should have promised so much but instead only *mocked* his continual helplessness.

Chapter Six

Amidst the clutter, the gnome worked feverishly. Tables and shelves filled the tiny room that he had set aside for his research and upon each table and shelf were notes, discarded experiments, and miscellaneous artifacts that he had either created or located over the years. Once every hundred years or so, he cleared everything away in order to make room for more.

At the moment, the gnarled spellcaster was completing his notes. The feather pen, animated by his abilities, danced about the sheet of paper, scribbling down its master's every notion as he thought it. When that sheet was filled, the pen would lift and the paper would fly off to join those which had preceded it. The pile was already several dozen sheets high. A new piece landed below the quill, which dropped down and hurriedly resumed its momentous task. Even as swift as it was, the pen had to work hard to keep pace with the gnome's thoughts.

Time, be it measured in hours or days, meant nothing to him when he worked. He had long diverged from his original course, that being the possible explanation for the weak assault by the potentially deadly night creature controlled by the Lords of the Dead. When he had thought about that particular situation at all .. . and that had been rare. . . the gnome had decided that the attack was a ploy and that his adversaries had hooked a more subtle spell to his person. Locating it had been child's play. In the end, the short mage had chosen to leave it attached; while they watched him, he watched them. Besides, they now only saw what he permitted them to see.

The gnome had been at this game much too long to be taken in by a trick such as this. Once again, he marveled at his own brilliance.

"End," he abruptly informed the pen. It straightened, shifted to one side of the sheet it had been writing on, and laid down. He stretched out a hand toward the pile of papers, which leaped to him. With his free hand, he indicated an uncluttered spot on the table.

A book materialized on that spot. It was green, or perhaps red, or perhaps any of a number of colors, depending on how one looked at it. On the front was a stylized dragon.

Placing the sheets to the right of the tome, the wizened figure took hold of the book and carefully turned the cover over.

The front page was blank. Taking the first sheet of notes in one hand and the quill in the other, the gnome began to write. This part he always did by hand, for this would be the final version of his research, and because of that he liked to savor each and every word.

So used to this task, he finished the first page in only a little more than a minute. He pulled the pen back and allowed the page to turn itself.

A tug in his mind warned him that someone had activated the watcher spell planted during the attack. The gnome carelessly released a spell of his own, one which would give the faraway observers something to interest them. This time it would be him in the midst of some suitably brilliant experiment. Of course, if they tried to follow his work, their own experiment would *somehow* go awry. He doubted they would watch for that long, however. They were only concerned with books.

Finished with the second page, he began work on the third. The thrill of his own brilliant discoveries urged him on and on with his writing. That suited him just fine.

After all, he had an entire book to fill.

They stood atop the peak of one of the Tyber Mountains, Shade observing the land below and beyond and Wellen observing that he was going to freeze to death if he did not stumble to it first. The two of them were here, apparently, because the master warlock simply liked the view.

A day had passed since Wellen had first woken in the cavern. The spellcaster had taken him to this place once before, shortly after his talk of how all those around him were monsters in disguise. He had still not yet explained that insane statement, nor had he "decided" about Wellen himself, who was supposed to be just as monstrous as the rest of humanity. The scholar chose not to bring up the subject, fearing it would only be detrimental to his own chances. There was so much he already dared not bring up. Shade was nothing if not mercurial; he brought up and dropped subjects as rapidly as he breathed.

"Here is your kingdom, Father," the shadowy figure whispered.

Wellen had already learned to pretend to ignore these various comments that his host muttered. Shade lived half in another world and time. He talked of and to a vast panorama of folk, many of them apparently related to him. The scholar had already counted five certain brothers and two more likely candidates. None of the names were familiar to him save *Dru,* which he believed *must* be the basis for Lord Drazeree, and another that sounded like *Sharissa,* the legendary lord's daughter.

If it were not all simply a case of madness, then the cloth- enshrouded figure beside him was many, many millennia old.

Shade turned from his musings and observed his hapless companion. "You should clothe yourself better."

"I *told* you that I have *no* power of my own!" Wellen had long gone beyond the point of civility where this question was concerned. Try as he might, he could not convince the other *that* the silver streak was only a mistake, not a sign of greatness.

"Very well, if you insist." Without so much as a negligible wave of a hand, Shade clothed Wellen in a furred cloak with hood. "Thank you," Bedlam replied, his voice on edge. The warlock missed his sarcasm. "Not at all."

"Are we through here?"

"A moment more."

Knowing protest was futile, Wellen tried to occupy his thoughts. He had been awash with relief when he had been told they would be leaving the caverns, not to mention the drakes who lived above, but that relief had died quickly when the scholar had learned where the two of them were headed. Worse yet, Wellen, who had never experienced teleportation, nearly lost his meal upon arrival. It was not the trip itself, which had been so swift that he had missed it by blinking, but rather the abruptness. To find himself going from the depths of a cavern to the precarious heights of a mountain peak had nearly been too much. He was disgusted with his weaknesses.

Despite having dropped the subject, it was obvious Shade still believed that he was here to obtain the mysterious dragon tome. All of Wellen's protests had gone unheeded. He knew that he could have opened his mind to the warlock, but to Bedlam his mind was the only private place he had left, and the sanctity of that was not something he was ready to give up. Besides, the warlock would have likely claimed his thoughts all false, the product of a clever spellcaster like himself.

So far, he did not know why his companion wanted the tome, but Wellen was beginning to suspect it had to do with the pale warlock's incredible age, since that seemed the one topic Shade continued to recall. What part the book played was still a question whose answer or, quite possibly, *answers,* evaded the scholar.

"Do you hear them?"

Wellen could hear nothing but the wind howling.

"They'll not see us, of course, not unless I will it. My power is forever beyond them now that they've changed. I reestablished the link to Nimth, only this time no one noticed it because I was so much more careful." Shade had mentioned the place called Nimth before, but always talked of it as if it existed *elsewhere.* Several scholars and spellcasters had begun to debate about worlds beyond this one and the emptiness termed the Void. The latter was a realm of nothingness which those who used certain types of teleportation passed through before arriving at their destinations.

While much of what Shade said had little bearing on what Wellen knew or understood, there were always a few tidbits that made the younger man pay fairly close attention. One was the status of the legendary Dragonrealm. Wellen had been horrified to discover that the old saying was more than true. Not only were there dragons here, but many of them were intelligent, such as the one that had devastated the column and the many who lived in the upper caverns of Kivan Grath. Worse yet . . . they ruled the *entire* continent!

"We have spent enough time here," the gray warlock suddenly announced.

Wellen let out a gasp. The two of them were now standing on a small hill overlooking a town of some sort. The shaking scholar was surprised to see people in the distance, apparently unconcerned about the fact that they lived in a land ruled by monsters.

"Mito Pica."

He glanced at the warlock. "What?"

"Mito Pica." Shade indicated the village. "It will be a grand and glorious city in another century or two. Much traffic flows through it."

"How can they hope to build anything with the dragons loose?" Despite his question, Wellen Bedlam could already see that the village *was* thriving. There was new construction going on in the western portion of the village.

"The Baron of Mito Pica obeys the edicts of the ruling Dragon King. His people perform the tasks that come down from the ruling drakes. In return, they are left in peace."

"They . . . they *deal* with those beasts?" Throwing off the warm cloak given to him by Shade, Wellen took a few steps forward in order to better view the village. *Sycophants!* An entire community of them! Dealing with murderous monsters that—

A restraining hand caught his shoulder. Wellen discovered two things. The first was that, in his anger, he had started down toward Mito Pica. The second was that the warlock was not only a being of great magical power, but also great *physical* strength.

"It would not do to go wandering down there. Not for our needs. As to your question, they deal with the dragons because doing so allows them to live and flourish. The Dragon King's folk have become dependent on many services performed by the . . . the *humans.*" Shade seemed reluctant to actually use the word *human* to describe his fellows, but apparently had come upon no other word that satisfied him.

"What could they want that humans have?" *Besides the flesh on their bones,* Wellen added bitterly.

Shade shook his hooded head and looked down at the scholar as a disappointed schoolmaster might at student who has not lived up to his potential. "The drakes are not mere beasts. They are thinking creatures. Despite their savage nature . . . " Here the warlock paused, seeming to drift off. "Yessss . . . their nature has always been rather savage."

Wellen was already thinking of his brief contact with the mind of the attacking dragon, an act he still had no satisfactory explanation for. In retrospect, he could recall the complex workings of that mind.

"The humans tend their food herds," Shade continued, not, evidently, noticing his own lapse. "They act as trade emissaries between the various clans because two drakes of opposing groups tend to become combative after a time. Humans are beneath them, but the Dragon Kings know their skills at trade. There are many other ways that the human race has proven itself worthy of survival. The population has *grown* continuously because of that." The warlock shook his voluminous cloak, as if trying to rid himself of something not to his taste. "Not bad, considering how few survived the original chaos."

Forcing himself not to ask about the last statement, which he knew that Shade would not explain anyway, Wellen decided to deal with his own immediate future. "And we have some reason for coming here now?"

"We do, but our route will be quicker and more subtle." Wellen barely had time to prepare himself before they teleported again.

This time, he found himself in, of all places, a smithy. The smithy, actually a barn, was filled with all sorts of metal creations, including a few that he could not identify. To Wellen's right, an open doorway taunted him with false promises of escape. Ahead, a heavy, muscular man, nearly bald, was hard at work on something that his back hid from the sight of the scholar.

"Master Beam."

The smith seemed not at all startled by the voice. With great deliberation, he put aside what he was working on and turned to face the twosome.

"Master Gerrod. Good to see you, sir."

Wellen made note of the educated tones of the smith, but his interest focused more on the name Shade had given himself. He debated whether or not Gerrod might be the warlock's true title, then decided that the cloth-enshrouded spellcaster would hardly have utilized it. Shade had probably chosen the name at random, not because it had any meaning.

Beam seemed not to notice the scholar, which was fine with Wellen.

The warlock's visage was shadowed by his hood, but his voice hinted at his anxiousness when he asked, "And have you completed my task?"

In response to the question, Master Beam seemed to shrink. He now appeared only slightly overwhelming. His tone was bitter. "I have not. In the year since last, I have made many breakthroughs, but none worthy of your project." Beam spread his hands, "If you should choose to go to another, I would understand."

"You are the most suited for the task, Master Beam, as your father and grandfather were before you. Each of you has presented me with discoveries which, while not of use for that which I have described, have proved worthy in other ways." The almost soothing voice of the warlock surprised Wellen, who had not expected to find so much humanity still remaining in the shrouded figure.

"Here." A pouch materialized in one of the smith's empty hands. The smith gripped it, causing the pouch's contents to jingle. "Until next year, Master Beam."

"I have *not* earned it—"

For a brief breath, the crystalline eyes burst through the darkness caused by the overshadowing hood and glowed with an inner fire that, even after millennia, had evidently not been extinguished. "When you or your descendents *have* completed my commission, smith, it will be worth *all* the money your family has been paid . . . and more!"

Beam went down on one knee and thanked the warlock. Shade gripped Wellen's shoulder. "Come."

As simple as that, they stood on a rocky hillside. Wellen started to look around, then gasped and covered his eyes when the glittering brilliance almost blinded him.

"The peninsula . . . can be quite bright when the sun is sinking," Shade informed him. The warlock pressed something into the scholar's hand. "Put this on. It goes. .. over your eyes."

Wellen cautiously looked down at the object. It was a pair of transparent lenses attached to some sort of frame. A notch in the center seemed to indicate it should rest on his nose. After a few tries, he got the artifact to fit, if not comfortably.

He looked up. . . and was dazzled.

Even with the protective lenses on, the landscape still sparkled. He had seen crystalline deposits before and so he knew *what* was causing the magnificent glitter, but the sheer immensity of *this* place . . .

"It's . . . it's . . . "

Beside him, Shade nodded. "It is. That is why he and they have chosen this place."

Wellen was suddenly wary again. "He'? 'They'?"

The cloth-enshrouded figure pulled his voluminous cloak tighter. "The first you have no need to be concerned about. He never interferes. He has no interest. As for the latter . . . they are here now."

And the earth at Bedlam's feet erupted.

They burrowed free of the rocky soil, two monstrosities that overwhelmed both men in size. Their clawed hands were good for both digging and grasping. They had dusky brown shells that covered most of their bodies, and their heads were long and ended in a peculiar, tapering mouth. Even with the lenses on, he could see that they, like their land, glittered.

One of the creatures hooted. It was a long, baleful sound that made Wellen's heart flutter. At the same time, however, the scholar in him was fascinated by these incredible creatures. Interest and reason, the latter reminding him that he had no chance of escape anyway, kept him riveted where he was.

"He is with me," the warlock informed the beast who had sounded.

The second horror also hooted, albeit at a higher pitch. Though the sounds meant nothing to Wellen, other than that both creatures appeared disturbed, the ancient spellcaster evidently understood them perfectly.

"Not yet. You have not completed your end of the bargain. Have you found it? Is there one?"

The two armored figures eyed one another, seeming to confer. . . and then one dared to reach out and try to snare Wellen.

Its speed was so unbelievable for so bulky a beast that the scholar, on his own, would have moved much too slowly. Even as the huge, taloned hand closed on his shirt, however, he found himself standing several feet behind Shade, who now was positioned directly between his mortal companion and the earth dwellers.

Shade reached out and touched the would-be attacker with only the tip of his gloved index finger.

It squealed and began folding into itself. The other one, sensing that they had overstepped their bounds, backed away and sounded a similar squeal. The warlock paid the second no mind, but watched the first. Wellen, daring to step closer, could not help but watch also.

Like the armadillo it so closely resembled, the monster folded itself into its shell. Yet, the change did not stop there. Rolled tight into a ball, the hapless monstrosity squealed what was obviously a frantic plea to forgive its transgression. Shade simply folded his arms. As the other watched, the rolled-up form stiffened, grew more indistinct. Wellen noted that the monster looked more and more almost like a . . . like a *rock.*

That was what it was. The image was no longer indistinct. Where once the mighty beast had been was now a large, quite real, boulder.

A short, dry chuckle escaped the warlock. "Not much of a change in personality when you think of it."

The survivor fell to its knees.

"Get up," the spectral figure commanded. Wellen saw a different Shade now. The warlock had multiple personalities, likely developed from his eternity of near isolation.

The armored monster obeyed.

"You have to watch the Quel," Shade informed his companion offhandedly. "They have vile tempers." To the sole remaining Quel, he said, "Your companion will return to normal in two days, long enough for him to contemplate the foolishness of his actions. *We* have a bargain. Just because you have been unable to fulfill it so far is no reason to demand things from me! If you no longer wish to deal with me, you can always deal with *him!"*

The plaintive hoot the kneeling Quel emitted left no question as to the beast's opinion on the last suggestion. Whoever it was that Shade spoke of, the Quel feared almost as much and hated more.

"I thought not. I shall return next year then, as agreed. Perhaps your successors will be more fortunate."

The finality in Shade's tone was signal enough to the lone Quel that its presence was no longer required. It cast one disturbed glance at its ensorcelled companion, then dug its claw into the hard earth below.

With a speed and skill that would have been the envy of many animals, the creature burrowed into the ground. In only a few breaths it had vanished below the surface. In only a few more, there was barely even a sign that it had ever been there. Only a small mound of unsettled dirt. The Quel evidently filled in its tunnel behind it as it burrowed. Wellen wondered about its lung capacity.

"Nothing," Shade whispered to himself, "but the pieces will slowly gather." He did not bother to clarify for his companion. "Perhaps in another century the preparations for this spell will be ready . . . "

Wellen, carefully silent, shivered then, but not because of anything the warlock had said or done. The shivering came on its own and, while it existed for only a brief time, its reappearance made him stiffen, for the sensation was akin to those he had felt just prior to his experiences with both the Seeker and the dragon. He shifted his position as he tried to calm down.

The warlock, sensing something was amiss, whirled around. "I had almost forgotten." He began to revert to the dark, dreaming persona that Wellen had met first. "It is time to talk again . . .

"Time to speak of lives and how they change . . . or perhaps how they *are changed* literally," Shade added, now sitting once more upon the throne in the cavern.

Spitting out a very unscholarly epithet, Wellen tried to orient himself *again*. He only barely heard the shadowy figure's words. The constant shifting from one location to another was wreaking mental havoc on him. He did not know if he simply hated the teleporting or the fact that he always found himself so helpless. Dragons and spellcasters; what chance did he have? Despite the 'drake clans above, Wellen hoped that he and Shade would remain in *this* location for awhile; at least until he ceased feeling like a leaf caught in a whirlwind.

As if purposely choosing a moment when Wellen was most open to attack, the sensation of impending danger struck him again. This time, it lasted longer than a few seconds. Like the last occurrence, however, it eventually did pass, again leaving no reason for its existence. Was it merely because he was a captive of the warlock? Was it possible that he was just *imagining* the sensation?

That will make two *madmen,* the bitter warrior silently cursed.

Shade, half lost in his thoughts, barely even noticed his "guest." He looked skyward, staring through the cavern ceiling to some place beyond, both in time and space. "Do you know, monster, what it is like . . . to live so long . . . but to live in constant fear for. . . your very self?"

The scholar thought he had a fair idea of the latter portion of the question, but it would hardly have been to his benefit to mention who was presently the cause of that fear.

"Dru Zeree . . . " The dreaming warlock gestured. A vague apparition began to take form before him. "He always seemed to see so much, yet he could not see what was happening."

The apparition swelled and coalesced, gradually taking on a more distinct appearance. It was a man, one who swayed back and forth like a leaf in the wind. Wellen squinted, noting the height, the beard, and the streak of silver. Was this Dru Zeree? Was this truly what the legendary Lord Drazeree had looked like, or was it a stylized phantasm, an image borne of ancient but colored memories?

"Master Zeree . . . " Shade whispered. He met the gaze of the misty figure.

"What did you finally become?"

Wellen could have told him, but he knew that Shade would never believe the legends. The warlock would refuse to believe that his companion of old had lived a long, fruitful life and that there were those, like the scholar himself, who had some claim that they might be his descendents. Shade would hardly care anyway; to him Dru Zeree had become a monster like all the rest.

Bedlam wondered if Shade had ever looked in the mirror to see what *he* had become.

Another form began to materialize on the warlock's other side. Shade barely paid any attention to it at first, caught up as he was in some one-sided conversation with the ghostly Dru Zeree, but when he did, he fairly buried himself in the depths of his cavernous cloak. His voice was barely a whisper, but Wellen, watching the new specter take shape, already knew who now haunted the spellcaster.

"Sharissa . . ." The warlock whispered.

The depths of his insanity were ever surprising the explorer. It was clear from Shade's reaction that even though he was responsible for conjuring up these apparitions of the far past, he did not entirely control them, at least, not on a conscious level. He had, in fact, succeeded only too well in haunting himself.

What price immortality?

She was tall, albeit not so much as the other conjured ghost, and slim. A magnificent robe of white covered her very female form and silver-blue hair cascaded down her back. She was beautiful, so *very* beautiful, this possible distant relation of Wellen's, that the scholar knew she must not be real. He was seeing her, and Dru Zeree, as the hooded spellcaster *wanted* to recall them, not as they had been. Still, there had to be some truth to their appearances. They were too distinct to be entirely fashioned from Shade's madness.

Rising, the warlock joined the shades of his past. As he moved and talked, they floated about him, taking in his words and responding in silent mouthings that the ancient spellcaster evidently heard.

"I did care for you, Sharissa," he told the female image, "though I knew you would never be mine."

Her smile brought sunshine. She said something that made Shade laugh, much to Wellen's astonishment. The laugh was young in direct contradiction to his deathly countenance and his previous, darker moods. "Yes, I think I knew that. I just did not want to admit it."

Fascinated, Wellen stepped closer. Now might have been the perfect time to seek escape, but he found he could not pull himself away from the fantastic tableau before him. That this scene confirmed the madness of his captor was not so important as what it revealed about the history of Wellen's kind.

Though it was not likely pretending to him, Shade took the insubstantial hand of the Sharissa image and pretended to pull her nearer. "I hated most of all to think of you changed. I thought you would be a physical horror, like my brethren . . . like my father. Now I see, though, that you of all of them could not suffer such a fate." The image put a hand to his cheek. He moved as if truly being caressed. "I see that you could only have become *a goddess!*"

Is this what near-immortality does to one? Wellen found himself saddened despite his own predicament. *Is there a point where your existence becomes only a never-ending look back at your failures, your losses?*

The Sharissa image wavered around the edges. The explorer glanced at the unmoving figure of Dru Zeree. It, like the other, was just beginning to grow indistinct. Shade was slowly returning to the present, Wellen assumed. Soon, he would recall his 'guest' and the questioning would begin again.

Then he looked closely at the warlock and discovered that he also had grown vague around the edges.

Wellen blinked and tried once more. If anything, Shade had become even more murky. *What becomes of him?*

Somewhat belatedly, the sensation of possible danger returned.

On the dais, Shade was still caught up in his conversation with the two phantasms. Wellen found he could no longer hear the warlock. In fact, he could not hear *anything.* The scholar turned uncertainly and scanned the cavern chamber, his fears almost immediately justified.

It was not just the warlock who was fading, but rather the *entire* cavern.

Or was it Wellen himself?

"Shade!" he called frantically, hoping to stir the dreaming spellcaster. To his growing horror, the shout emerged as no more than a whisper, one that even he found barely audible. Wellen started forward, but despite movement, he drew no closer to the dais.

The domain of Shade dwindled without pause. Bedlam finally stopped running. The effort was futile and he was only expending his own energy. Yet, he could not just give up. There was no telling what had become of him. It was even possible that the dream-struck sorcerer himself has been responsible for the scholar's predicament, though Wellen was of the opinion that the source was from somewhere beyond.

A tiny gleam before him caught his attention. With nothing but emptiness now surrounding him, he focused on the gleam with the fervor of a starving man eyeing a crumb of bread. The gleam seemed to slowly grow in intensity, but Wellen doubted his senses at first. It seemed too much to hope that he would so quickly leave this oblivion. Not with the way his luck had turned so far.

I am destined to be some sort of human ball, forever being tossed or carried from one place to another! Despite that thought, however, he did not regret coming to the Dragonrealm. He had already seen and learned so much. His despair lay in the fact that no one else would ever hear of his discoveries. All he had come across would again sink into the mire of legend, especially if no one else in the expedition returned. Had the others turned around and sailed home? Did the dragon continue east and destroy the rest of his expedition? How many *had* died?

Wellen tensed as the gleam defined itself. Suddenly, he found himself staring at a medallion of gold. It drew his eyes as Shade's crystalline orbs had. He tried to turn away, not trusting, but this time his will was not strong enough. The medallion pulsated. . . at least, he thought it did. . . and pulled him closer and closer. Resistance was useless.

Shapes representing many things formed around the artifact. A scene grew around him. Wellen felt like a character in a painting who watches as the artist draws in the world around him. He saw trees and hills, but what he saw most of were a number of figures who surrounded him. Almost immediately, it was evident that they were not human. One of them was holding the medallion at chest level.

He made out wings on the still-vague images and knew then who had taken him from the very sanctum of Shade. The Seekers.

Beneath his boots, he felt the solidity of earth. The wind caressed his countenance. The sounds of birds and other forest life assailed his ears. A rich forest landscape surrounded him.

As, he reminded himself, so did the avians.

The one with the medallion lowered it and stalked toward him. Like the bird it so resembled, it cocked its head to one side as it observed him. Wellen could not help but fix his own gaze on the sharp, predatory beak. It was quite clear that here was a creature who made meat part of its diet.

The Seeker leader, if that was what it was, came within arm's length of him and stopped. Wellen swallowed but tried to give no other sign of his uncertainty. He had no idea why he was here, but the feeling of impending danger was still with him, not that he needed to be told how precarious his position had become.

Gazing behind the human, the avian nodded.

Strong, taloned hands took hold of his arm. The talons dug into his flesh, but not enough to hurt.

Raising a hand to Wellen's face, the apparent leader displayed its own long, sharp talons. The captured scholar needed no one to tell him what those claws could do to his unprotected body.

It came as a surprise, then, when the leader stepped back, the threat of the talons receding with it. Bedlam doubted he was safe yet, at least not if his peculiar new sense was correct.

The tall avian turned back to the circle of winged figures. As if reacting to a silent command, the circle broke open. Through the opening stepped another Seeker, this one smaller than the others. A female?

It joined the first and turned to study Wellen. One clawed hand went to its leg as if it were trying to indicate something. The human's eyes widened as realization struck.

Before Wellen stood the young Seeker he had protected from the expedition. He breathed a sigh of relief, deciding that it had convinced the others to save the one who had aided it earlier. The Seekers were a strange, alien race, but gratitude, it appeared, was a concept they shared with humanity.

The smile was just spreading across his visage when the talons of the young avian shot toward him.

Chapter Seven

They were displeased with her. Her masters were displeased with her. Xabene shuddered. The Lords of the Dead had *never* found fault with her skills before. She had seen others fall victim to their displeasure, but the thought that she now balanced on a precipice . . .

For the first time, she began to regret her pact with them. They had always given her what she had felt the world owed her and in return she had given them absolute loyalty. The enchantress had never had cause to wonder what would happen to her if she could not fulfill her end of the bargain. Now that thought was ever in her mind, reminding her that those dismissed by the demonic lords did not merely ride off into the distance.

It was a combination of things that had brought about the fall from favor. One had been the suspicion that her watchdog spell, the one she had sacrificed a Necri for, had failed. Her masters were of the opinion that the gnome had tricked them again, that he knew he was being watched. The other thing that had endangered her was the loss of the man called Wellen Bedlam, the one who evidently had led the ill-fated expedition. He had survived the dragon, but somewhere in the hills, both she and her monstrous companion had lost him . . . and to that mysterious personage whom the lords refused to discuss . . . but clearly worried about.

To her right, the Necri she had been paired with hissed in consternation. A sick joke, the beautiful sorceress decided. A sick joke that she and the beast were allies in spirit, too. They were bound by their mutual failure and now they had only one chance.

A dozen other Necri stood scattered around them. Here to aid the two, supposedly.

46

Yet these monsters did not treat either her or their counterpart as superiors. Rather, they seemed more like executioners awaiting the signal to swing the ax and put an end to their predecessors.

"Be silent!" she warned them. Let them think that they were the cause of her lack of concentration.

She would have preferred to work her spells at night, when she was more comfortable, but the masters had deemed time of the essence. Her only bit of satisfaction lay in the knowledge that the band of Necri found the sunlight far more distressing than she did. Had her own existence not been at risk, Xabene would have stretched the working of the spells for as long as possible, just to watch the pale horrors squirm.

In her smooth, deceiving hands, she held a tattered notebook. It was her special prize, the one thing that had redeemed her so far in the eyes of the lords. She had suspected that some object of the expedition's leader might remain in the field. The dragon that had attacked the column had not been particular about clearing away the carnage. A search by the Necri and herself had brought this item, evidently something that had fallen out of one of the saddlebags on Bedlam's unfortunate mount.

The notebook was well used. His trace was strong. Given a little time, she would be able to locate him.

Given a little room, too! The Necri were starting to cluster together, trying to draw comfort from one another in the revealing light of day. Unfortunately, that meant that they were crowding her.

"Away from me, you decaying misfits!"

They gave her a little breathing room. She sighed. Now there were no more excuses. This time, Xabene knew that she had to succeed.

Sliding the notebook so that it rested on the palm of one hand, she stroked the top of the foreigner's journal as a child might stroke a beloved puppy. Love had nothing to do with this, however. Rather, the constant, active contact stirred the trace, made her connection with it stronger. The stronger the contact, the better her chances of reaching out and finding the notebook's owner.

What is your own world like, Wellen Bedlam? she wondered as she concentrated on the spell. *What wonders exist over there?* From what she had glanced at in his journal, he was an intelligent if somewhat isolated man. A knowledgeable scholar, but one lacking in practical experience. Still, someone closer to her own ways than most of those she had encountered during her service to the lords. For them, Xabene had generally had one of two purposes, both designed to put them into the debt of her masters.

A pity that we may not have time to talk, Master Bedlam.

There came a tugging in her mind. She forgot all else as she opened herself to the link. An image slowly formed before the raven-haired enchantress, an image of a forest and . . . and . . . the view was being blocked by whatever or whoever was with the man. There were several figures, however. Xabene tried to delve into the mind of her target, but found a very impressive wall blocking her probe. The spellcaster pondered her dilemma for a moment, then used her link to pick up peripheral information about the region.

She recognized the place, which in turn answered the other question. Xabene smiled, an entrancing yet chilling sight that, this time, did not involve humor in any way. She knew who was with the man, even though she did not know how he had come to be in their talons rather than the grip of the cloaked warlock. *You are very popular, my scholar. I look forward to meeting you face-to-face . . . should the Seekers leave anything left of yours by the time they're through with you.*

There was no time to lose. It might already be too late to save him from the avians, but she had to try, if only for her own sake. Xabene broke the link and leaped to her feet, the notebook crushed in one slim hand.

DRAGON TOME

"I've found him!" The Necri stirred, at last able to do something. Her own demonic companion hissed a sigh of relief and almost looked thankful, although the savage visage of the batlike creature was hardly designed for such expressions. "We must hurry! Even now the bird folk might be finishing with him!"

Xabene revealed to them the image she had conjured and where it was located. The Necri, to their damnable credit, wasted no time. In rapid progression, the horrific bat creatures took to the sky, a line of unreal terrors that scattered the few birds nearby and brought silence to the forest with their sudden activity. The sunlight did not deter them, for they knew that the responsibility was now as much on their bone-white shoulders as it was on Xabene's.

The enchantress watched them vanish into the distance. Alone, for even her Necri companion had joined in the flight, she contemplated her own plans.

The Seekers would meet her masters' servants with all the power they had. Chaos would reign. If the outsider was not already dead, there was a good chance that he might die in the madness of combat. For some reason, a dead man was of no use to the Lords of the Dead. They had made it clear that they wanted him alive if at all possible. That in itself interested Xabene, who began to wonder at this sudden limit to their power. Why had she not noticed it sooner?

For now, that did not matter. Wellen Bedlam, explorer and scholar, did. Which meant that Xabene herself would have to join the battle . . . and enter the very thick of it. She hoped that the man was worth the trouble.

If not, she would make certain he knew that before she was through with him.

Wellen gasped as the talons came at him. He prayed that at least the attack would finish him quickly, else he would suffer horribly. It seemed that fate had stopped toying with him at last. He almost looked forward to death, if only because it might mean an end to his being tossed and chased about the Dragonrealm like a cat's prey.

The talons, when they touched his flesh, were astonishingly gentle. He barely even felt them.

Was this a test?

A vision assailed his mind. Wellen was so stunned, he tried to back away. The avians holding his arms tightened their grips, preventing any escape. Unable to resist, the scholar gave in and allowed the vision to take root.

He saw a world in which everything was slightly distorted. Odd men came forth and, with a start, he realized that he was the foremost of them. The others were various men from the column, including a menacing, much more avian-appearing version of Prentiss Asaalk. The group was surrounding something and the blue man looked ready to pounce on whatever it was.

It was the young Seeker, the explorer realized. He was seeing the event as the feathered creature had. It . . . were there different sexes among the race? . . . was trying to explain something.

He felt a touch in his mind, a feeling of acknowledgement. The concepts being revealed to him almost made Wellen gasp. Communication through images in the mind was not unknown, but not with such efficiency, such skill. Yet here was a race that did it on a daily basis!

Gradually, the entire scenario unfolded. Most important was the last part, where Wellen Bedlam had refused to allow the hatchling to die and then had healed the deadly wound.

Healed it? He tried to think in the negative, to deny that he could have ever performed such a feat. Magic was not for him. He pictured himself casting a spell and failing, hoping the meaning got across. It did, but the bird creature sent back another image, one of him casting a series of spells, each progressively more successful. The

Seeker was of the opinion that the ability was there. In its mind, Wellen had already proved that.

It was useless to argue. Moreover, the tantalizing thought that he *might* yet become a sorcerer of some skill appealed to him. There were so many things he could have done if magic had been there to aid him. So many things . . .

An urgent touch by the young avian informed him that there was more. Wellen opened up his mind to the link. This time, he saw the hatchling returning to the flock. It was well received, for there were few young in this aerie, a magnificent old castle that the Seekers had taken over and made their own after the unknown builders had abandoned it. The birth rate among their kind had been at a low since some ancient disaster. It had happened long ago, but the Seekers were *still* trying to recover. What it was Wellen was not told. He sensed fear in the mind of the adolescent being before him and knew from contact that this fear touched the adults as well.

The Seekers had noted his deed, but little more. It was not until the devastation of the column that they tried to aid the one who had proven his worth to an otherwise proud race. Wellen had the suspicion that the Seekers looked down on the other races, but his act had raised him almost to their level. He did not feel insulted by that; humans could do worse.

Shade had reached him first, much to the consternation of the Seekers. The warlock and the birds were old acquaintances. It said something about Wellen that they had attempted a rescue. Shade was both respected and feared; to the Seekers he was almost a demon. His madness was his only weakness, at least so far as they knew, and they had dared exploit it this once. *They* had instigated the visions from the past, drawing them from the warlock's drifting mind in a rare moment of strength. Still, the spell summoning Bedlam had barely succeeded. There had even been a point where the Seekers had almost lost their target to the Void.

The scholar shivered, happy that he had not known that then. He had wondered why the bird folk had foregone their advantage and not attacked their adversary. But now Wellen knew that they barely had had enough strength to free him. Entrancing Shade for a brief time and actually doing him harm were two different things. Many avians in the past had learned the folly of assaulting the warlock. If left alone, he generally left them alone. If disturbed . . . the images that flashed across Wellen's mind stunned him. Never had he heard of a spellcaster with power of such magnitude. Even the mysterious Dragon Kings feared him, if what the images indicated were true.

And all that power in the hands of a madman! What would Shade do when he discovered his "guest" missing? The young Seeker reassured him that they could protect him from the threat, but he was doubtful.

At last, contact was broken. Wellen looked at his inhuman companions with new respect and hope. He still had no idea where they hoped to hide him, but he was willing to go along with their plan. What choice did he actually have? Whether they lied or not, he was definitely helpless before them. Yet, where once he had revealed magical skill, could he not again?

If given time . . .

"What happens now?"

Though contact had been broken, he was certain they understood him. The young one pointed skyward. Wellen looked up, but saw only clouds and blue. He turned his gaze earthward again, focusing on the hatchling. "I don't—"

The two Seekers who held his arms rose into the air, taking their prize with them.

It took a moment, but Wellen regained his composure. He was certain he was safe in the claws of the avians, not only because the sensation of danger had vanished but also because the Seekers had had too much opportunity to prove themselves his enemies. He was helpless, something that seemed to be the pattern of his life since coming to the Dragonrealm. Admittedly, Wellen was not so certain that Shade had meant him harm, but with as unpredictable a force as the shadowy warlock, he preferred not to find out.

Fears and doubts fell behind him as he and his two guardians rose above the trees. Flight was something new to the explorer and he marveled at the experience. The sights below could certainly not compare to his excursions with Shade, but Wellen much preferred this method to standing and shivering on the top of a chilling, inhospitable mountain peak.

Other Seekers joined the trio. He saw no sign of the young one. Likely they had not wanted to take any risks with it. It? Though contact with the adolescent had not lasted that long, he had come away with the vague notion that the young one had been female. It was hard to say and he had noticed that, to his eyes, the adults all looked more or less alike. Wellen scanned the small flock fluttering around him. They were probably males, if only because what little he had learned about their history made that seem more likely. With births so few, a race would be mad to waste its females on a task such as this. Wellen had no misconceptions concerning his own worth; he was probably fortunate that the young Seeker had been female. It explained even more why the avians had finally chosen to rescue him.

They flew for what was probably two or three hours, with periodic stops to allow different pairs to take control of the wingless human. The avians were strong, but carrying so much dead weight—not a term Wellen liked to use for himself but true nevertheless—would tire anyone after a short while. As time progressed, the sun slowly moved on a downward arc on the scholar's right side, which meant that the party was heading more or less straight south. He hoped they would reach their destination before nightfall. While not a child afraid of the dark, Wellen did not care for the thought of flying blind or coming to a rest in some mysterious wood. It was a foolish fear, since the avians obviously knew what they were doing, but Wellen had already gone through enough for anyone. He only wanted a safe and secure place in which to rest and hide from the world for a time.

His head began to pound. Wellen grimaced, thinking that a headache was mild in comparison to what he had already suffered.

As if taking umbrage with that thought, the pounding grew incessant. Had it not been for its intensity, which was becoming staggering, Bedlam almost would have thought that it was—a *warning*.

He quickly glanced around, almost dislodging himself from the grips of his guardians. One of the Seekers squawked at him, no doubt reminding him that humans did not fly and so he should stop squirming. Wellen shook his head and tried to indicate that something might be wrong. The avian blinked and turned its attention back to the flight.

Around him, the other Seekers flew with an equal lack of concern. By rights, that should have been enough to satisfy him, for they certainly had to know their homeland better than he, but the warning would not cease. He looked below, thinking that there might be a threat from that direction. The incredible height from which he peered down gave him an excellent view of the region for miles around, but the most dangerous thing he noted was a small pack of minor drakes at work on a kill. They were of the wingless variety and fairly slow-witted from the looks of them, hardly a threat.

So what was there, other than being dropped, that would endanger him? Wellen tried to look up, but the angle at which he was being held allowed him to scan only those areas ahead of the flock. Twisting around only threatened to loosen his companions' grips, something he did not want to cause. Yet, where else was there to look?

At last, unable to resist the constant nagging in his mind, he carefully tried to turn enough to see. The Seekers holding him squawked, but he merely shook his head. His attempt was not entirely successful, as it would have required the ability to twist his neck in a complete circle, but he was able to shift enough so that he could see some of the clouds just behind and above them.

The explorer stared narrow-eyed at the clouds. It had been clouds which had hidden the dragon that had murdered his companions.

He could not take the risk. Twisting back, he regained the attention of one of the avians and shouted, "The clouds! I think there's something in the clouds!"

The Seeker merely looked at him, one eye cocked as usual. He repeated the warning, wondering if it understood his words at all. Wellen had no right to assume that all Seekers understood human common language. In fact, it surprised him that people on this continent still spoke the same tongue. Why was that?

Time for questions later! he reprimanded the scholar within. His two guardians matched gazes, possibly speaking in that silent manner of the race, but nothing more happened. If they had mulled over his warning at all, either they had not believed it or they thought it not important enough. Perhaps they had even known in advance but were merely allowing possible watchers to fall into some secret trap. He hoped but did not believe the last was the case.

Minutes later, the flock began to descend. As the earth rushed toward him, the human searched for a possible destination. He saw nothing but more hills and woods. Only another pause, then. Wellen quickly scanned the rest of the landscape and noted some hills far to the southeast. Their regularity made him wonder if they were the same hills where Shade had first rescued him from the scavengers.

Thinking of the warlock made him wonder what the murky figure had thought when he had woken from his musings. Had he even gotten that far? Was Shade still conversing with the images of long-dead companions? For all the danger that the ancient warlock represented, Wellen could not help feeling sorry for him, for all the years of fear and uncertainty he knew the spellcaster had gone through.

His feet touched the ground, erasing such notions. The avians released him once they were certain momentum would not send him tumbling forward. Around him, the other creatures landed. None of his companions were at all concerned, but the broad human was not so certain. While very nebulous, his sudden ability to detect danger had not failed. Each time there had been a threat, however remote it might have been.

Able to stretch his legs, Wellen went through a methodical listing of possibilities. Why would he not see a danger, yet feel its presence? First, because it was not there. Second, because it was far away . . . which did not seem that likely to him. Third . . . he paced, both to think and work his muscles more . . . third . . .

Because it doesn't *want* to be seen? Shade's cavern had been masked by a spell, but Wellen *had* seen through it, much to the warlock's surprise. That meant that he had more than average potential. Would it be possible to do the same here?

Not exactly certain what he should be doing but willing to experiment, Wellen Bedlam tried to open up his mind completely. He had not been concentrating when he had broken Shade's spell, so he suspected that such a route would not work here. As with many things, trying too hard often led to failure. Perhaps if he allowed his premonition to guide him, he might find something.

To his surprise, he found himself turning his gaze to the east and high up in the sky. There was no conscious effort; Wellen simply moved. Still, he saw nothing, despite scanning the sky carefully, and doubt began to resurface.

Then vague outlines began to take shape in the sky above them. He could not tell what they were, but he could see that they were closing the distance between themselves and the flock in swift fashion.

Grabbing hold of the nearest avian, he pointed at the oncoming shapes. "We're about to be attacked!"

A number of the Seekers looked in the direction the explorer pointed, but none of them reacted as if they had seen what he did. The one that Wellen had grabbed hold of gave him a glance whose meaning was the same in either human or avian terms. Wellen refused to give up, however. He took the Seeker's claw and pressed it against his own forehead. With as much will as he could muster, the human envisioned what he had discovered.

Almost instantly, the avian pulled back his hand, eyes wide. At first, Wellen was not certain he had succeeded, but then the Seekers as a whole turned toward the sky. A change came over the flock. Their feathers bristled and they readied their talons for combat.

Wellen saw that the shapes were nearly upon them.

The bird folk began to take to the air, save for one that remained by him. As they rose, a transformation took place among the winged figures descending. Their cloaking spell uncovered, they evidently saw no more use for it. Just before the two groups met, the last shreds of sorcery burned away, revealing in its place . . . horror.

"Gods!" Bedlam had expected birdlike creatures, thinking that the wings meant the attackers must be like his avian allies. These were not, however. The monstrosities that the Seekers now faced resembled another flier, the bat. Yet, no bat ever resembled these. The attackers were as tall, if not taller, than Wellen and almost as manlike as the bird folk. Where the avians wore the mantle of civilization, however, the bat creatures were without a doubt savage killers.

He did not doubt that it was he they were after. Coincidence could only be stretched so far.

Why? Why does everyone want me? Whatever the reason, Wellen knew it was a mistake. He knew nothing and had nothing anyone would desire. For some insane reason, though, fate had chosen Wellen Bedlam to be its jester.

The two sides were evenly matched in terms of numbers, but the Seekers were badly lacking otherwise. They had power, true, but so did the bats. Spells were unleashed and spells were cancelled out. A few did some damage, but most caused a flash or a crackling sound and nothing more. The bats were also not mere animals; they moved with too much skill and daring and reacted too efficiently when attacked to be thought of as such. It was physical strength that would decide victory and that, unfortunately, belonged to the deathly pale horrors.

Even as he realized that, Wellen saw a Seeker plummet to the earth, its chest a gaping, blood-covered hole. Another was torn apart by two monsters who then threw the remains about. Intelligent, yes, but bloodlust clouded their senses a bit. One of the two died suddenly when a Seeker came from nowhere and slashed the back of its throat completely open. The other reacted, however, and raced to meet its companion's killer.

The Seeker beside Wellen put a claw on his shoulder. The human nodded, knowing without looking what the avian wanted. Assured, his feathered guardian leaped into the air to do its part in a battle it must have known was lost already. Wellen could not have blamed it; he would have done the same had he some way of assisting. His sorcerous abilities were limited to say the very least. The explorer had a knife, but his sword had been taken from him. Wellen pulled the blade free nonetheless, knowing he would need it whether his next decision proved to be running or fighting.

Either way, he expected to be dead or a prisoner before the sun had set.

"Run! This way!" a voice, female, called.

The voice came from his right. Wellen searched that region, but saw no one.

"Run, I said!" A figure, as female as the voice, materialized next to one of the trees. The woman wore a long cloak that blended in with the colors of the forest, which was the reason he had not noticed her at first. She waved for him to come to her. "Hurry! It's your only chance!"

It twisted Wellen's stomach to abandon the Seekers, who were giving their lives for him because he had saved one of their most precious ones, but they fought in great part to keep him from the bats and this looked like the only way their desire might still be fulfilled.

Still holding the blade ready, the harried scholar ran toward her. All the while he wondered. *What now? Who else wants me?*

"A little farther!"

He tore through the foliage and came up next to her. For one brief breath, Wellen froze and stared at the exotic, pale countenance. Then, she broke the spell by tossing a cloak like her own at him.

"Put this on over your other clothing!"

With all their power, he doubted that the cloaks, however much they resembled the forest, would fool the bats for very long. While he was donning the bulky garment, though, Wellen noticed that its pattern *shifted.*

"It adjusts to whatever your surroundings resemble. Precisely adjusts."

True camouflage. It was still doubtful that the trick would work for more than a few minutes, but any time it bought might give Wellen time to think of something else . . . that was what he *hoped.*

When he was finished, she gave him a very brief inspection. "That'll do! Follow me!"

The two moved swiftly through the woods. Wellen marveled at how the branches and the grass never seemed to touch his guide. She moved like the wind, something he wished was possible for him, for every bit of foliage grabbed at his garments or sought out his face.

The sounds of battle had died down. Wellen heard a heart- stopping shriek of anger that no Seeker would have been capable of unleashing and suspected that the bat creatures had discovered him missing. It would not be long now. The only positive note, and it was indeed a slim one, was that of the dozen or so monsters, at least a few had likely died or been badly wounded by the unfortunate bird folk. With their numbers diminished, they would not be able to cover the region as thoroughly as they might have before.

It gave him slim hope.

His guide, who moved like an elf but did not resemble one, slowed and reached out a hand. Wellen grasped it, feeling a tingle run through him that had nothing to do with warnings of danger. He had time to think of how smooth and cool that hand was before she commanded, "Close your eyes and hold tight!"

Close my eyes? "Why?"

Her smile was a bit crooked, but the perfection of her lips made him ignore that. "To live."

He could hardly argue with that. Wellen shut his eyes and prayed it would not be his last mistake.

There was a ripple, as if he had struck and passed through the surface of a lake. Wellen heard the distant shriek of a bat creature, but it broke off abruptly. He collided with his rescuer, who had stopped running almost at the same moment as the shriek had ceased.

"You can open your eyes again."

Once more, he was stunned by her beauty. The hair was at least as black as night, if not more so, and it worked to perfectly accent her ivory skin. His gaze met her own. Wellen thought of the cat people in the mountains east of his homeland.

With eyes such as hers he would have almost suspected her of being a crossbreed.

"You may relax now. We'll be safe here for a time." Seeing that he was sweating from all the clothing, she added, "You can take that off, too. It was just a precaution. I didn't know how fast they might be after us."

"Who are you? What were those things? How did you know where I was?"

"Such an inquisitive man." Her change in demeanor was disconcerting. She talked as if they had not been pursued by ungodly fiends but rather had been out for a stroll after a picnic. "I like that. You don't demand like so many I've known. Polite even under the circumstances."

"Then perhaps you would be so kind as to answer some of my questions," he returned, undoing the cloak. Wellen hated to part with it, especially without examining it, but the heat was getting to him.

Slender fingers worked as she began to remove her own cloak. "My name is Xabene."

"Xabene." Her name was all he could think of to say, for the woman dropped her cloak at that point.

"And yours?"

"Wellen. Bedlam."

"An interesting name." She reached toward him with two smooth, pale arms. "May *I?*" When he blinked, the raven-haired woman added, "May I take the cloak?"

The scholar pulled himself together. Handing her the fascinating garment, he asked again, "What were those things that attacked the Seekers?"

She began folding his cloak. "Those were the Neat You wouldn't like them."

"I didn't." Bedlam noticed that the garment in her hands kept decreasing in size as she continued to fold it. The bundle was now only half as big as when Xabene had started. "What did they want of me?"

"Probably the same thing that the birds wanted." The bundle now fit into the palm of her hand, yet she still folded. "Do you know what *they* wanted from you?"

He watched as the cloak became a tiny square of cloth. When Xabene seemed satisfied, and the bundle was hardly bigger than a large coin, she deposited it into a pouch at her waist.

"*Do* you know?" she asked again.

"They were rescuing me. I saved the life of one of their young."

Her visible impression of him rose. He felt unreasonably pleased at that. "It's not many a human that the birds respect at all."

"It seems to be the only good piece of luck that I've had since coming here." *Other than now,* he added in silence. Xabene's mere presence disconcerted him.

"And where did you come from?"

"Overseas." An unanswered question of his own nagged at him again. "Why did you rescue me? How could you even know I'd be there?"

She did not seem inclined to take it any further at that point. Bending over, Xabene retrieved her own cloak. She bundled it up rather than folded it. "There's a time for questions later. I've been remiss." Her smile bewitched. "I know of a place where we can be alone . . . and talk in peace."

The idea of actually being able to relax and exchange information appealed so much to the brown-haired man that he was almost able to forget the bloodshed he was responsible for. Perhaps Xabene would be able to shed light on the situation, including the secret of the mysterious dragon tome that Shade had wanted and thought that Wellen had come to steal.

Admittedly, he did not mind the thought of remaining with Xabene for a time.

The lithe, commanding woman was crumpling the second cloak together. Like the first, it seemed to shrink as she packed the cloth tighter. Since she had not bothered to fold it, the garment ended up resembling a small pile of loose material shoved together. When it was no larger than the other, she put it away.

"You are a sorceress."

"Sorceress, witch, enchantress . . . the titles all mean the same thing now, but, yes, I am." Her eyes half-closed and she gave him a look that reminded him of a child who thinks it has disappointed a parent. "Does that bother you so much?"

"Not at all. You might be able to help me." Perhaps she would be able to instruct him in the development of his own abilities. For the first time in quite some while, he felt truly encouraged.

Xabene almost came to him. "I'm so glad. So many people do not understand. Now come. We have just a short distance to cover, but the sun is about to set." The enchantress reached out and took his hand again. "You don't want to be out here at night. There's no telling what sort of dark things might be roaming about."

He allowed her to lead him along, but they only had gone a few paces when he pulled her to a halt.

"What is it?"

Wellen pointed to the east. The trees had kept much of the landscape in that direction hidden, and now was the first time he had been able to get some bearing on his location. To his surprise, the sight before him was very, very familiar. "Those hills. Are there others like them?"

"None." There was something in her tone that hinted he should not waste any more time, but Wellen wanted to be certain. "I think . . . they look like the ones where I was rescued by. . . where I was rescued." He decided not to mention Shade, not wanting to worry Xabene further.

"If you think that those hills look familiar, they probably do. The first Dragon King of this region is supposed to have raised them up that way. That was when their power seemed limitless. The present ones can't do that as far as I know, although you shouldn't underestimate them."

"I won't." More questions to ask. Who were the Dragon Kings? He was just about to return his attention to the trek at hand when he noticed a tiny structure vaguely east of the two of them but not quite as far as the hills. It seemed to be sitting in the middle of nowhere. Nothing else existed around it, save empty field and a few wooded regions. Why would someone build such a place here? "What is that building?"

For the first time, she looked at him with suspicion. "That's the citadel of the gnome. It's where he works and where he keeps his secrets. No one get in or out of that gray place but him."

Wellen was not deterred. "I think . . . I think I have to go see him."

"No." Her voice was flat. "You don't want to see the gnome."

"Why, is he dangerous?"

She shrugged. "There's a vast, ruined city on the eastern edge of the Dragonrealm. Part of it extends into the sea now."

The city guarded by the sea serpents. "I remember it. We passed it on our way to the southern shores."

"A good thing. The Dragon King who took it over is very possessive." Her smile held no warmth. "It'd been in ruins for over a thousand years before that."

"What had that got to do with the gnome?"

Xabene laughed. "Who do you think made it that way?"

He gave her a doubtful look. "Not *him?*"

"Of course. Now tell me; is *that* dangerous enough for you?"

DRAGON TOME

Chapter Eight

"I have waited so very long for the book," the Dragon King Purple rumbled. He lay just outside of the caverns where the clans made their home. The setting sun reflected off his scales, causing him to glitter. Purple might have seemed a strange color for a dragon, but he felt it quite regal . . . and no one laughed at a purple dragon, anyway. No one who lived for very long after, that is.

"My sire waited. So too did his predecessor. They waited, but they never succeeded." The great drake's fore claws gouged ravines in the rocky, unrelenting soil. The region just around the clan caves had been baked hard by generations of fire-breathing beasts, yet it was no match for the Dragon King's might.

The tiny human figure before the leviathan did not look up. That was one of the first rules the Dragon King taught those within his presence; you knelt and looked down, showed the proper respect until given permission to stand. Ashy remains attested to those who did not obey with sufficient swiftness.

"I will *not* allow this task to fall to *my* successor! I *will* have the gnome's secrets!"

Those few drakes in attendance tried to make themselves as small as the human. When the dragon lord grew angry, it did not matter whether the one who suffered the consequences was human, drake, or otherwise.

Purple eyed his human. "I spared your life because I desired information. You were fortunate, for the one who decimated your kind was too eager for his own good. He disobeyed. He will not do so again."

The other dragons hissed and the human shivered. A reptilian smile, so very toothy, spread across the Dragon King's horrendous visage. There was no question as to his authority in his kingdom.

He brought his massive head lower to the earth, the better to further terrify his man-toy. The tiny creatures were so predictable, it was pathetic.

"You claim that you did not come here for the book, which I do not believe. I suspect now, though, that you are not the one who led. There is another and he is the one I seek. You are hardly clever enough to hope to gain entrance to the gnome's infernal lair!"

"No, my great and imperial lord!" came the muffled response.

"So." Purple pulled back, his countenance masked in an expression of nonchalance . . . or as close as was capable for one of his kind. "Who, then? All of your companions are dead. Your vessels are scattered. Can you give me a reason why I should prolong your existence?"

"The one who commands still lives!"

"Indeed?"

"I saw him escape into the hills! He rode a horse he had stolen!"

"The hills . . ." The leviathan was having difficulty hiding his interest. These outsiders, as weak as they were, would not have dared come from so great a distance if they had not had a plan they felt sufficient to outwit the cursed gnome. The Dragon King Purple was certain of that, for it was the way he would have thought, and of course his cunning was paramount. "He is one of your learned ones?"

"He is very learned! It was by his decision that we have come to this damn—this land!"

There was hatred in those tones. The Dragon King found that amusing. It was something that might be played upon later. "And what is this human's name?"

56

His puppet dared to look up, knowing that his life relied on this next moment. As he stared at the insignificant creature, the drake lord marveled at its coloring. *Perhaps I shall give him to Irillian. He is, after all, more to their liking, being blue.*

Prentiss Asaalk, looking much more worn and beaten, responded, "His name is Wellen Bedlam!"

Xabene's choice for a hiding place was not what Wellen had expected. When she had first revealed it to him in the first minutes of night, he had stared at the giant, misshapen form, not certain that what he saw was what she wanted him to see.

"The tree?"

"It's more than just a tree," she had assured him. In the darkness, the enchantress had been almost invisible despite her pale skin.

In truth, it *had* proved to be more than just a tree. Much, much more.

It was almost another *world.*

She had led him to a crack in the side of the trunk. It had been a tall, narrow thing, hardly big enough for him to even slip his fingers into. On the other hand, Xabene's slender fingers had fit perfectly. While Wellen had watched, mystified, she had run her fingers up and down the crack. The enchantress had performed the strange deed twice, then had stood back.

With a groan, the crack had *widened.* It had continued to widen until it was somehow spread far enough apart to admit the two humans.

"Come with me," she had whispered, her hand seizing his to assure that he would not be left behind . . . or possibly choose to turn and run from her.

If the outside of the tree had stunned him, the inside had *overwhelmed* him. From without, the trunk had looked massive enough, if it had been hollowed out, to contain five or six people . . . provided, of course, that they had stood still and barely breathed. From within, however, the tree had revealed a chamber almost as great as the vast, ageless cavern Shade called his domain.

Even now, hours later, Wellen could still not believe it.

He sat cross-legged on a fur, one of many covering this part of the floor. Xabene lounged nearby, uncomfortably close. She smiled as she noticed him once more surveying the unbelievable room. It had been, other than his tales of his life back home, one of the most prevalent subjects they had spoken about.

There were shelves along nearly all the walls and tables upon which books and various artifacts had been neatly organized. A rack of jars attested to the enchantress's interest in alchemy. Specimens of many small but exotic creatures floated in other jars nearby. A desk with writing supplies resting atop it stood in one corner. There were even two subchambers, one filled with various items the raven-haired spellcaster had collected over the years and the other sealed off. Wellen, unable to find a good reason to pry about the closed chamber, tried to ignore it from then on.

"Is it that disconcerting here?" she asked from where she lay.

Wellen tried not to pay too much attention to the way her gown, which somehow had never so much as snagged against a branch or bush *once* during the trip outside, molded itself to what little of her body it covered. He had no doubt that she was aware of her physical attributes, but he was not trusting enough to think that she merely found him attractive. Nothing could be accepted at face value, even so perfect a face, in the Dragonrealm.

Her question was safe enough. "It is disconcerting, yes, but at the same time I feel so at home. The books, the experiments, the collections . . . I might almost be back in my own study."

It might have been wishful thinking on his part, but he thought she was pleased. Certainly her next words sounded sincere. "I'd hoped you would find my secret place to your liking. There is much similarity between us, I think."

"I still don't understand how this chamber came to be, though. The skill with which the spell was cast is astounding."

She nodded, shifting closer as she replied, "It is, as I said, very ancient. Before the Dragon Kings, the birds, the Quel, or even those that came before them. We are not exactly in the same world once we enter the tree. You might call it a pocket world, one created long ago by someone and then abandoned. I found it purely by chance."

Wellen mulled that over. This place reminded him of Sirvak Dragoth. He wondered if there might be a connection, but since Xabene had never been across the sea, he could hardly have asked her to make a comparison.

She reached forward and handed him a mug that must have been conjured by sorcery, for he could not recall her holding it the moment prior. Wellen readily took the proffered mug, as he had had food and drink previous to this, and sipped it approvingly. After so many meals aboard the ship, he still found fresh food a grand novelty. The brief life of the expeditionary force had not been a long enough time for him to accustom himself anew to normal meals.

Throughout most of their time here, Xabene had offered little information about herself. She admitted to having seen Wellen earlier during the Seeker's flight. It had been her intention to rescue him from the bird folk, whom most humans did not trust. That circumstances had caused that rescue to come off a little differently was just the workings of fate.

He did not, of course, completely believe the story, just as he did not believe some of the other things she told him about. Most of her explanations twisted or turned whenever they grew too close to what he suspected was the truth. The puzzling thing was that he had felt no premonition of danger since entering this place. It pleased him that he could feel safe in the presence of the enchantress, as safe as any man would *be* from her, that it, but it perplexed him that all her deceit did not present some sort of threat. Almost everything else in the Dragonrealm had.

Since she had not mentioned Shade, Wellen chose to continue to keep his time with the warlock secret. There was no single particular reason; at some point he had just decided *it* would be better if he kept silent.

His mind was just beginning to drift when the mug nearly slipped from his hand. After the day's events, Wellen was worn almost to nothing. Even the rest Shade had allowed him had not been sufficient, for the scholar had found himself shifting and waking constantly, each time feeling the eyes of the hooded warlock upon him.

"Let me take that," Xabene offered, retrieving the mug from a drowsy Bedlam. "You look exhausted."

"I feel exhausted." Had it been just a little too sudden? The thought that his food or drink might have been drugged had occurred early on, but the lack of warning had made him complacent. Now, the novice warlock was wondering if his own small skills had betrayed him. Not possible . . . or could it be that he could be drugged as long as no harm was meant to him?

Wellen grimaced. His thoughts were all muddled.

With gentle pressure, the pale enchantress pushed him down onto the furs. Her action had just the opposite effect from what it should have; the weary explorer stirred at her closeness. For a moment, their eyes locked. Xabene stared as if seeing something new, then, with lips parted, whispered, "You have demanding eyes, Wellen Bedlam. What is it they demand now?"

"Sleep," he blurted, half-mumbling the word. Her catlike eyes widened, almost tempting him to a knowing smile. If she had expected his defenses to be down, she did not yet know him well enough.

He drifted off after that, his last memory that of the frustrated sorceress folding her arms across her exquisite form and glaring at him.

She never looked more beautiful.

He had a dream, the only one he could remember, that is, and it included Xabene, the monstrous batlike creatures, and a figure who reminded Wellen of nothing less than Death itself. There were words and tones filled with anger and supplication. That was all there was to the dream, save that a vague sense of danger touched him. As the dream, or rather nightmare, faded, however, so too did the warning.

Puzzled but relieved, Wellen Bedlam sank deeper into slumber.

When he finally woke, it was as if the last few moments of the night before, especially his rejection of Xabene's advances, had never happened. As fresh, somehow, as the morning itself, she gently prodded him to consciousness. Wellen, on the other hand, felt as if he had slept among the very animals from which the furs on the floor had been skinned.

"I have some clothes for you." The smile was back and possibly even warmer than the day before. Having witnessed many a play during his years of study, Wellen came to the conclusion that the enchantress was as good an actress as any he had seen. "There is also a place where you may renew yourself."

The latter proved to be the mysterious subchamber the brown-haired scholar had wondered about during his initial hours in the tree. His first glimpse of it was as stupefying as his first glimpse of the tree itself.

The Dragonrealm is truly a place of wonders, a magical paradise . . . when it is not trying to kill you!

It was, as Xabene explained it, a pocket world within a pocket world. What it truly was, was a tiny woodland scene with, of all things, a stream running in a complete circle around the rest of the view. There was no end or beginning to the stream; it just went around and around.

"The water is always fresh," she assured him.

It was cold, but marvelously so. Wellen spent half his time enjoying the luxury and the other half trying to investigate the astonishing creation. The trees and grass were very real. A light source he could not locate played at being the sun.

With some reluctance he finally abandoned the place, knowing that it was time to move on. For the first time, the scholar was relatively able to decide his own fate. He had come up with the only choice that seemed reasonable to him. Wellen hoped that Xabene would join him, but if she did not, he would move on without her. . . even if it meant confrontation. The enchantress might not like the thought of losing him before she succeeded in gaining whatever it was she wanted. The explorer was under no delusion that her interest in him was strictly personal.

The clothing he now wore was an exact replica of that he had arrived with, save that it was both clean and untorn. The boots were still his own, however, being a very serviceable pair that Xabene must have decided did not need to be replaced. As for the sorceress, she was clad much the way he had seen her the day before. There were subtle differences in the style of her gown, but it still served the same purpose he now knew all her clothing seemed to have been designed for; addling the senses of men. It was certainly not practical for the outdoors, although the enchantress had not seemed at all put out by the weather.

It came to him then that despite her words of warning concerning the gnome, she also had an interest in the enigmatic book. She had been too quick to warn him about staying away and her attitude had revealed her belief that he was there for the same purpose she was. That was the connection that Wellen had somehow not been able to make yesterday—the reason for which she had *actually* rescued him.

One question remained; did she herself have masters or was she, like Shade, a single force?

He blinked. Vague memories of voices and the smell of sulfur. A flapping of wings. Had that happened during the night? The memories slipped free and escaped as Wellen was forced to focus his attention on Xabene. She was seated on the furs, *a* small table filled with meats and other items before her. He noticed that none of the food had been touched and that the majority of it was placed near the side where he would have to sit.

"Are you hungry?"

He was, but was too restless to sit down. Wellen took a piece of fruit, confident that it was safe, and bit into it. After he had swallowed the first bite, the explorer said, "I need your help."

Xabene's eyes narrowed in interest. "In what way?"

"I want to speak to this gnome."

She looked at him as if he had asked her to marry a Seeker. "The gnome? After what I told you?"

"You told me only that he destroyed a city long, long ago. I think there must be more to it than that. I also think that if the gnome were so powerful and so evil, he would have conquered the Dragonrealm long ago. For that matter, how do you know it's the same gnome? Could he have really lived so long?"

"Throughout time as far back as legends go there's always been a gnome there. From what I've seen and heard, he has looked the same for generations. Could he really be that old?" Xabene shook her head. "I've heard of stranger things!"

"He appears to be my only hope of ever extricating myself from this chaotic farce."

"There is the matter of the Dragon King of this land. It was one of his that tore apart your expedition and slaughtered your friends!"

He winced at her casual way of speaking about the massacre. "He cannot be too great a threat or else you would not keep returning to this place." Wellen indicated the tree chamber. "Although it could also be that other things draw you to this region. You've a great interest in books, I've seen."

Xabene crossed her arms and met his gaze. Her words were not accusatory, only confirming. "You already know that I've an interest in the gnome's book. You've known for quite awhile. If you'd asked, I wouldn't have denied it."

"But you would not have mentioned it otherwise." He smiled. "Am I your prisoner? It seems to be a habit with me."

"I could have conjured up some chains at any time. Have I?"

"No." The scholar did not add that her not having done so did not preclude his captivity. He hesitated, pretending as if the thought was only just occurring to him, and then suggested, "It might be the case that my needs coincide with your needs."

Her interest was instantly piqued. She moved closer, using every step to her advantage. Wellen worked hard to prevent the facade he wore from cracking. Xabene played her role well. From many another woman, Xabene's manner would have seemed overdone, too obvious. Not so from the enchantress. It *was* her. She was so natural that Wellen almost shivered. What could she do to a man who *did* succumb to her charms?

Not all the answers that flashed through his mind were pleasant.

"Are you speaking of the book?" she asked. "Or other things?"

"The book." His reply was a bit too quick and, unlike the night before, not at all to his advantage. Both of them knew it.

"Then you are saying that if I help you gain an opportunity to confront the gnome. .. and there's no guarantee that he'll even bother to acknowledge you standing outside his citadel . . . you'll help me obtain the book?"

60

"If that is possible; I cannot promise that the chance will arise."

From her tone, the sorceress seemed to think otherwise, likely because she still assumed that Wellen secretly *did* want the dragon tome. He did not attempt to dissuade her. If it helped him escape this madness, all the better.

I was willing to risk death to reach this land, but I'm not willing to risk it for something! care nothing about! Given the opportunity, he would have been more than willing to take the gnome's damnable opus, throw it as far as he could, and then sit back and watch the others fight over it.

Xabene looked him over and visibly contemplated his offer. He had no doubt about the outcome, however.

"All right. I agree." She turned away with a whirl, as ever, perfectly orchestrated, and added, "But we'll have to move in swift fashion. This place does not allow spells to extend beyond it; we'll have to transfer from outside."

"No."

"No what?"

He waited until she was looking at him again. "No more teleportation. Not after what I have been through."

"Traveling any other way will take too long. The more time we linger in the vicinity of the pentagon, the more chance that one of the Dragon King's sentinels will see us! If not his minions, then those of someone else interested in the gnome's secrets!"

Deep down, he knew that Xabene had the right of it, that taking their time would only increase their risk. Wellen was adamant, however. He had been pulled along like a toy once too often. Magic was not yet his element and it might never be. His premonitions of danger aside, he felt lost in its presence. Wellen wanted some semblance of control over the situation and sorcery, especially teleportation, left him feeling defenseless and befuddled.

The enchantress saw that it was useless to argue. If she wanted to maintain his trust, she could only give in.

"As you like it, then." Even when she merely shrugged, the ivory-skinned witch exuded her charms. "I could summon up a pair of mounts, but it could mean waiting for quite some time. They might be very near, but they also might be very far."

"Would it take longer than walking?"

She sniffed, not caring for that suggestion at all. Wellen knew his hostess thought him mad and it might be that she was correct. He was not so certain about his sanity, either.

"I will not walk to the gnome's citadel. That is asking too much, Wellen Bedlam."

The night before, she had been calling him strictly by his first name; now, she had become more formal. It was the one inconsistency. If she sought to draw him in, why distance him so? Calling him by his full name reminded both of them that they were relative strangers.

Wellen knew not to press. "Very well, we'll ride."

Her smile returned. All was well, indeed. On the surface. "It will not take so long, I think. This will not be the first time I've summoned these particular mounts. They *should* be fairly near."

She had yet to call them horses. *Were* they?

"I'll have to summon them from outside, of course." It was one of the things Xabene had explained to him after their arrival here. Spells worked within or without the tree's tiny world, but only if the sorcerer was in the same region. A spell cast in the tree would not make it to the Dragonrealm. At the same time, someone utilizing magic in the Dragonrealm could not send their spell into the tree. It made for a wonderful sense of security as far as Wellen was concerned.

"I'll join you," he replied. While keeping the enchantress in sight was a pleasant task in one way, Wellen was aware that his future might depend on being wary when it came to Xabene. She might decide at some point that he had overextended his usefulness... and *then* what would happen?

"Of course."

Where gaining entrance to the tree had required physical effort from the enchantress, leaving proved to be not so cumbersome. As the two walked to the hidden doorway, it slowly split open. Bedlam noted that it opened only enough to allow one person through at a time. He wondered whether this was the way it worked or if Xabene had caused it to part only so far.

It was early morning, just after sunrise. Even before he stepped back out into the Dragonrealm, Wellen knew that. It surprised him, for he had come to assume that his slumber had lasted far longer. So much the better. While night might have its uses, he preferred movement during the day. Too many things stalked this land after dark. At least in the daylight he would have a chance to see what was coming for him. Wellen had never been good at stealth.

"This will only take a moment." She turned from him and faced north. He took a step away from the shielding tree and breathed in the sweet morning air.

The inside of Wellen's head fairly screamed.

"Xabene!"

Too late did he realize what the world within the vast tree had done to him. His own powers had become muted in there because the danger was outside and he was inside. Now the warnings ripped through his mind, as if stored up and waiting for the first chance to tell him the truth.

There came a rustling noise in the woods beyond. Something large moved with great speed toward the duo. It trampled through the underbrush. Wellen glanced at the enchantress and saw that she was still caught up in the summoning. He turned his gaze from her to his hands, as if staring at them would somehow unleash the power he supposedly contained. Bedlam felt no different, however, and almost immediately gave up the attempt as hopeless. As the unseen threat neared, the desperate scholar quickly searched the surrounding ground and located a broken tree limb. His head ached with the urgency of the situation. Wellen wanted to laugh at how sad his defenses would be. Anything that caused such dire warnings to ring in his head had to be monstrous. The stick would probably annoy rather than harm it or them.

"Xabene!" he hissed, trying one last time to awaken her. "What?"

Her sudden, calm voice threw his guard completely off. He was about to turn to her when two massive shapes crushed through the foliage and raced toward the enchantress and him.

Wellen raised the branch then dropped it when he saw what had joined them. He knew his face was red.

Two horses. A black and a spotted one. The mounts that the sorceress had been summoning. They were the danger? It hardly seemed possible.

The animals trotted to within a few yards of the duo but refused to come nearer when Xabene called to them. She noticed the branch in Wellen's hand. "You won't need that. Throw it far away so that they see you don't mean them any harm."

"I—" The sensation would not leave, yet how could these horses be a threat? Wellen reluctantly threw the stick far to his right, then revealed his open palms to the animals. He felt foolish, but the enchantress nodded her approval.

"Do not underestimate them, Wellen Bedlam. These are very intelligent creatures."

He knew of legends revolving around a demon horse whom Lord Drazeree, or rather *Dru Zeree*, had befriended, but neither of these could be the demon.

So why was his head still pounding? "Xabene . there's something wrong here."

"Nonsense." Her tone might have been a bit sharp; Wellen could not be certain. He had not explained his peculiar ability to sense possible danger, mostly because he still did not understand it himself. It had also been his one reliable weapon . . . until now, perhaps. "The Dragon King is nowhere near and I sense nothing else."

Were her abilities superior to his? The novice warlock was willing to believe that. Xabene was a sorceress of no little ability. To think that his skills could in any way be more finely tuned than hers was presumptuous to say the least.

The spotted horse trotted up and tried to smell him. Wellen backed away before the nose touched him, not knowing why he did but glad regardless. Both animals disturbed him despite their innocent appearances.

"I think your horse has been chosen for you," Xabene commented wryly. "If you have no objections, then mount up so that we may be gone from here."

He looked the horse over. "There are no reins. No saddle, either."

"And there will be none. These animals will not accept them. You may trust that they will not lose us, though. I have ridden both of them countless times."

Still not assured but unable to argue, since it had been *his* choice to enact this plan, Wellen reached over the spotted one's backside in order to get a good enough grip to help himself up.

His fingers barely grazed the animal's skin. Wellen withdrew them as if the horse had tried to bite him.

Xabene, already atop her mount, looked down at the confused figure. "What is it now?"

"There's . . . " How could he describe what had happened when he hardly knew what had happened himself? When his fingers had touched the flesh of the spotted horse, they had not felt the warmth of life, but a coldness that he could only associate with the *long dead*.

Brief images of the dream flashed through his mind. Xabene. The figure she had been speaking to. A figure that brought up thoughts of ancient tombs and corpses long putrefying.

"Are you having second thoughts?" the enchantress asked coyly, her interruption banishing the dream images to his subconscious again.

"No." Gritting his teeth, Wellen searched his clothes, then recalled that these were not his originals. Knowing that he looked more like a plaintive child than a grown, educated researcher, the scholar asked, "Do you have a pair of gloves?"

"Look in the belt pouch just under your left arm."

"I looked there already."

"I know."

Removing the gloves from the pouch a moment later, he reflected upon how spellcasters seemed to have an annoying habit of playing games with those unable to reciprocate in like fashion. While having had little personal experience with sorcerers, a *planned* maneuver on his part, Wellen had heard more than one tale. Whether a master mage or a permanent novice, sorcerers were all the same. They enjoyed toying with their *lessers*.

It in no way helped to constantly recall that he was, by the loosest of definitions, a spellcaster himself.

The gloves on, he tentatively mounted the horse. It was an extremely calm creature, but that failed to sooth his distrust. The sensation of danger, or perhaps it was just possible threat, continued to plague him.

"Are you ready?"

He was not, but it was too late to back down. With a mask of bravado in place, he simply responded, "Lead on."

Xabene gently touched one side of her mount's neck and whispered in an ear. The animal started off on a slow trot, which, despite her interesting, almost lounging manner of sitting, did not dislodge the alluring black-clad woman. She and her horse were almost one, an effect amplified by the way her clothing melded with the color of the steed.

Wellen's own beast followed. He was certain that its first movements would send him sliding off, but the horse's body countered his every shift. After a few moments, Wellen grew a little more comfortable about his chances of staying on. He still did not trust the horse, however. Even with the gloves and pants, the sickly feel of the horse's cold flesh belied its outward appearance. If not for Xabene's words and his own inability to put his finger on exactly what was amiss, he would have leaped to the ground and followed the sorceress on foot instead.

It would be no more mad than this journey I've chosen to take.

He settled in and tried not to think about the animal beneath. It was not as it he had nothing else to consider. There was still the matter of his upcoming confrontation with the gnome, providing the latter even deigned to meet him. What would he do if the end result of his quest turned out to be either sunstroke or finding himself a tidbit for one of the Dragon King's minions?

For that matter, what would he do if the gnome *did* appear? Now there, the explorer thought, was a *truly* disturbing aspect!

From where they huddled in the treetops, trying their best to avoid the unforgivable light, the seven remaining Necri, including the one who had originally accompanied Xabene, watched as the enchantress and the other mortal rode off. The one Necri in particular noted the man's discomfort with the beasts the Lords of the Dead had secretly provided. The batlike horror could not blame the human for his distaste; the two mounts had been dead far too long. Their meat was tasteless and dry. Only the glamour cast upon them made the horses seem so lifelike.

The Necri who had served alongside Xabene pondered the sorceress's plot. On the surface, it seemed reasonable, but her other plans had failed in the end. On her head and its would lay the most blame. The others . . . the masters might choose to include them in the punishment . . . but more likely was the possibility that they would be made to watch the slow, painful elimination of the two who had failed greatest, despite more than one chance to redeem themselves.

It would be the female's fault, then, if *it* perished so ignobly. No battle. No blood. Not the way a Necri desired to ends it existence.

It had already noted the hesitation with which the enchantress had acted now and then where the man was concerned. The winged horror still recalled the betrayal, when she had taken him while the Necri had been fighting the feathered ones. *That* had not been part of the plan. Xabene had not spoken of that, even with it.

The Necri glanced back at its anxiously awaiting fellows, than turned its blank eyes back to the receding figures. It hissed in frustration, ever mindful that its existence now depended upon a human female.

The toothy maw opened and closed. The claws that had torn stronger foes to bloody gobbets flexed. If she failed, then before it perished it would do its best to see that the sorceress died first. Slowly, too.

After all, a good death was one that could be savored for a time. Even if that time would be short-lived.

While the Necri watched Wellen and the enchantress, another watched them both from a short distance behind. Even though no tree or hill provided adequate cover, the batlike horror neither noticed him or the telltale stench of his odd sorcery.

This will do just *fine*, Shade decided. *They head to the citadel. I could not have planned it better myself!*

Chapter Nine

The Lords of the Dead gathered in a world where light was but a dim memory. They were eleven and always had been ever since they had discovered the path to godhood. There were vague outlines to each, hints of what they once had been, but anyone who sought to ferret out details of their features would find that little remained but the memories. They were not much more than emaciated figures, some worse than others but all of them reminiscent of the long dead.

Such was the price of their rule. They only knew that they had carved for themselves an empire of sorts, one that stretched beyond the boundaries of this plane into the world of the Dragonrealm. They were the final judges. When those in the Dragonrealm died, it was only to become vassals for them. Someday, their subjects would also include the living and then their empire would be complete.

So they had always liked to believe.

Their kingdom was decay. Things long dead slowly rotted or were eaten by scavengers, yet never entirely disappeared. Lakes and rivers of dark, moldering green were the only color in the landscape, save for clouds of sulfur that rose above volcanic vents. Ungodly creatures scuttled about, seeking food and trying to escape being food.

The sky was a black cloud that rolled and turned, ever threatening a storm. No moon or stars existed here. The only light came from the vents and it was just barely enough to let the scavengers sight their next meals.

In the citadel, the Lords of the Dead took their places. A huge pentagram marked the floor of the room. Ten of the shrouded forms moved toward points and corners of the pattern, while the eleventh waited for them to take their places. As nominal leader, his place would be at the center, where the array of power would be the strongest.

To his eyes, they had not changed at all over the millennia. None of the Lords of the Dead saw themselves or their compatriots as other than the armored, dragonhelmed sorcerers of long ago. It was a measure of their power, not to mention their madness, that they had never seen their kingdom as it truly was. To them, they had rebuilt the magnificent world of their kind. In truth, there *was* a close resemblance between this place and that ancient world, for their birthplace, forever barred to them, had also become a twisted reflection of its inhabitants. It was why they had come here in the first place, to escape the destruction their people had caused.

When the others had moved into position, the leader joined them. He stepped into the very center of the pentagram, then turned around in one complete circle so as to acknowledge the presence of each and every one.

"The pattern is complete," he intoned. His voice was nearly emotionless, though he did not realize it. "The power flows. Who will be first to speak?"

A shorter specter shifted just enough to warrant the attention of the others. His voice was almost identical in timbre to the leader. "The servant Xabene rides with the outsider."

"Where did they find horses?"

"The animals were ours, ensorcelled to seem living."

The spokesman nodded slowly. "Then, they are on their way to the gnome's accursed sanctum."

"Yes." The shorter figure lowered his shadowed head, a sign that he was finished speaking.

Another, this one akin in size and shape to the master speaker, moved forward one step. "The Necri are upset. Many were lost in battling the Sheeka. They slaughtered the bird folk, but they felt that the servant Xabene had wasted them, not informing them of her own plan until afterward."

The leader turned, setting in motion a wave of sulfur that wafted throughout the featureless, dank room. Moss on the walls withered, but the other lords did not notice. They had long passed beyond the normal senses of men. "Her actions have been questionable of late."

"The outsider's doing?"

"Perhaps." The ruling lord waited for his counterpart to withdraw, but the other was not yet finished.

"There is . . . one more thing."

Hesitation. The coven leader arched a brow he no longer had at the sudden show of uncertainty. "That is?"

"He has taken an interest in the outsider and the gnome. It may be that he too desires the book."

No one had to ask who it was the one spoke of. He had been the bane in their existence for longer than they cared to recall, ever since they had sought to steal the power that he had brought with him from the birth world. Unfortunately, his link made him stronger than they and he had refused to see the inevitable and die. Century after century he had kept himself alive by one means or another.

Now he was after the gnome's secrets. That meant that he was growing desperate, but it also meant that their own plans were in jeopardy, for it anyone understood them, it was he who now called himself *Shade.*

Shade. The name was a mockery. The Lords of the Dead preferred the use of his true name, when they could recall it, for it served to remind them that he was, after all, no more than their errant relation.

"There is no choice," the ruling speaker intoned. "We cannot allow the dragon tome to belong to anyone but ourselves. Even if it means confronting . . . our cousin." He found that this time he could not recall the name. There were many things he especially had forgotten over time. With effort, the name would come, but like so many other such moments, it made more sense to utilize that effort for their plots than for recalling little-needed things like the past.

One whose memory in regard to Shade was a bit stronger than the others, supplied the name that the others could not recall. "Gerrod. His name is Gerrod, Ephraim."

Ephraim, who realized with a start that he had forgotten his *own name* as well, moved from the center, breaking the pattern. The others saw determination etched into his features, but only because they shared the same delusion when it came to one another. "Then we will know what to call him when we summon him later . . . from the lists of the dead."

The gnome's citadel did not loom over them, but regardless, its presence unnerved them both. It was not as big as Wellen had thought, but the fact that it stood here was impressive enough. From what he had learned, the citadel was as solid a landmark as the mountains Shade had dragged him to . . . was it only a day or two earlier?

"Do what you must and hurry," Xabene demanded, her eyes darting this way and that. He knew she expected to see a dragon or some other threat come swooping down from the sky or springing up from the earth. In truth, the scholar was somewhat surprised at his change of luck. The determination to reach this place had dwindled the nearer they had come. It was almost as if geas had been put on him, one that had now served its purpose.

His head throbbed with undefined warnings of danger, but Wellen was beginning to understand a little about how the ability worked. There were things with the potential to threaten him and things which *were* a danger to his existence. The horses, a mystery yet unsolved, were one of the former. Shade he considered one of the latter.

Xabene was an enigma. Bedlam knew she should have been one or the other, yet she was still one of the few things that apparently did *not* mean him harm. That was contradictory to everything he knew or thought he knew about her.

He dismounted and walked toward the blank, ominous structure. After a moment's hesitation, the enchantress followed suit. Wellen had expected that. Xabene wanted to get in more then he did. In fact, had it been up to him, he would have turned around now and ridden back as if a thousand hungry dragons were nipping at his heels.

Too late now. He glanced at the wall that rose before him. Not a leviathan, but still more than three times, probably more than four times, his height. Careful to avoid touching it, the curious explorer leaned close enough to inspect the substance from which the edifice had been built. It looked like stone, possibly marble, but there were differences. He started to walk along the side, trying to find a place where blocks had been joined together, but more and more it seemed that the gnome's citadel had either been carved from some single massive rock or that it had been formed and baked into shape, like a clay pot. Neither theory was very plausible. There had to be another explanation. Lost in curiosity, he continued along the wall.

"Where are you going?"

Wellen glanced back. "I have to look it over. How do you think he breathes in there? There's no opening that *I* can see. Are there vents or windows on the top?"

"No." She folded her arms in aggravation. "Is this necessary? I though you had some plan to make the gnome listen to you."

"Plan?" Wellen turned the corner. After a moment, he heard the soft steps of Xabene behind him. "Until this morning, I hadn't even thought about coming here. I was going to ask you to help me get back to the coast so I could see if the *Heron's Wing* was still anchored there." He began to walk faster. "It was not until this morning that I felt I had to come here. I don't even know what I expected from him."

"Do you mean I—" Xabene snapped, her words cut off so abruptly that the scholar turned to see if something was the matter.

"What was that you were saying?"

"Nothing."

Nothing? Wellen pondered the possibility that Xabene had been responsible for his overnight change of mind. Could the vague recollections he had assumed were dreams actually be some true scene? If so, why did he not sense any danger from Xabene?

Wellen continued around the ancient structure until he had come back to his starting point. The enchantress followed him all the way, her expression sour and possibly a bit fearful.

Of what?

"Did you find anything?" she asked.

He shook his head. "Only that I have wasted my time. Have you ever touched it?"

Hesitation, then, "Yes."

"Nothing happened?"

"See for yourself."

Taking a deep breath, Wellen reached forward. His fingers grazed the surface. When no bolt of lightening smote him, he planted his palm flat against the wall.

"Extraordinary, wasn't it?" Xabene asked, the sarcasm in her tone sharp and biting.

The disappointed explorer removed his hand. The wall felt like any wall, save a little smoother. He had no idea what he had been hoping for, just that he had been . . . hoping.

"And so it ends," the enchantress chided. Wellen met her gaze. Xabene looked away and began to walk to the horses. For some reason, Wellen saw that she was more upset with herself rather than with him. Another puzzle.

The logical thing would have been to follow his companion, remount, and ride off. In a few years, he might be able to forget his debacle, providing he lived that long. Yet, now that Wellen found himself here, he knew he could not just walk away. There had to be something else he could do.

Facing the wall, the scholar quietly spoke. It might be that he talked only for his own benefit, but at least he could say he had tried. Perhaps the proper words could do what force had not.

"I do not know if you can hear me in there, but my name is Wellen Bedlam. I've come from across the seas to explore this continent." He shrugged. "I have no designs on your secrets. My only reason for coming here was to see if you could help me return to my land. Right now I want nothing more than to begin my studies anew."

A breeze tossed his hair about. The gray, flat face of the edifice remained as indifferent as it had before. No magical portal opened in the side. No voice boomed in the heavens. For all he knew, the gnome might not even be inside.

Xabene, mounted and ready to retreat from this disaster, leaned forward and called, "What was that you were saying?"

He was about to turn and tell her when a tingle ran through him. It was not a premonition of danger, but rather some effect from outside his body. Wellen stared at the blank wall for a few seconds, then reached out and touched it.

With a yelp, he pulled his hand back. His fingertips felt as they had been *burned.* A belated throbbing warned him that he should not touch the wall.

"What did you do?" the stunned sorceress cried.

Explanations had to wait. The tingle increased. Though he sensed no danger to himself, Wellen stepped back just in case. The entire pentagon shimmered.

"No! Don't!" Xabene tried to urge her mount forward, but it was strangely still, almost like a frozen corpse. She cursed the animal, then called to Wellen. "Get away! You might be killed!"

He could not. The shimmering structure nearly had him hypnotized. A panoramic display of colors surrounded the gnome's citadel, a display that grew brighter with each passing breath.

"Wellen!"

Bedlam put a hand over his eyes to shield them from the brilliance.

With what sounded like a hiss, the entire building *vanished.* "Lords of the Dead!" Xabene swore.

Slowly, Wellen took a step toward where the edifice had stood. His hope that it had merely been an illusion and that the gray structure still stood there, invisible, was quickly shattered. For all practical purposes, the gnome's sanctum might never have been built. Grass as high as his waist fluttered in the light breeze. There were no indentations, no fragments. The citadel was simply gone.

The enchantress leaped from her mount and ran over to him. She took him by the arms and spun him around to face her, displaying at the same time incredible strength for one of her size. "What did you *do?* What spell did you cast?"

68

Spell? He realized that she had taken his words, unintelligible to her, as some sort of complex spell. He knew that sorcerers sometimes found need for vocal guides, what the ignorant called "magic words," but surely she did not think that *he* was capable of such sorcery?

Or was he? The novice warlock gazed thoughtfully at his hands. *Had* he somehow unleashed a spell of such potency that it had taken the entire building, gnome, book, and all?

"This was not his fault."

The two turned at the sound of the voice, Wellen's heart sinking, for he knew all too well to whom it belonged. Xabene, on the other hand, ignorant of who faced them now, took a step toward the newcomer and held up a fist that crackled with power. The disappearance had wracked her far more than it had Bedlam. He, after all, had only wanted escape; *she* wanted the tome . . . and not, Wellen suspected now, for herself.

"Who are you?" the enchantress demanded. "This is your doing, then?"

"You may call me Shade," the hooded warlock advised her quietly. As usual, his deathly visage was half-obscured by shadow. "And I am no more responsible for this than Master Bedlam here."

Wellen could not meet her gaze. "You know him? You lied all the time? The book *was* what you wanted?"

"No! Shade assumed I did, just as you have! He's the one who wants it."

Xabene looked from her companion to the elderly but potent figure before her. "The dragon tome is mine!"

To their surprise, Shade simply walked toward them. Wellen quickly stepped aside. The enraged enchantress, confused by the peculiar action, finally stepped away just before Shade would have walked into her. The shadowy warlock continued on a few more feet until he was at the edge of where the citadel had been. He went down on one knee and studied the grass with avid interest.

"A masterful piece of work. Worthy of him."

Despite circumstances, Wellen was interested. "Worthy of who?"

"The gnome, of course."

A movement by Xabene drew the explorer's attention. In horror, he watched as she stretched out her hand and pointed at the shrouded backside of Shade.

"Xa—" was as far as he managed before her spell was unleashed.

With perfect timing, Shade raising a single gloved finger. Xabene's attack faded with only a spark to mark its brief existence.

"There will be no more of that," the kneeling figure commented in an absent manner, still studying the ground. "For Master Bedlam's sake, I will forgive it this once."

The disheveled sorceress began to shake. She looked at Wellen with sudden pleading in her eyes. He frowned, not understanding her growing fear, and joined her. To his further consternation, Xabene fell against him and started crying

"What is it? What's wrong?" he whispered. There was no reason to include Shade in this, whatever it might be.

"She has failed her masters," the hooded warlock interjected. He rose, his back still to them as he surveyed the field. "They will, of course, see that she pays appropriately for that failure. This is, after all, a very important task and they do not generally take failure well. Still, do not take all of her anguish to heart. She's hardly given up."

Xabene's shivering had grown worse as Shade had talked. Her tears had lessened, though. She looked up at Wellen, gave him a shadow of her seductress's smile, and then focused on the cold figure of the ancient warlock.

"Who are you that you know so much? Who are you that thinks you can best the gods?"

Grimacing, Wellen quickly whispered, "Take care! He's mad!"

"They are no more gods than I am." Shade faced them. "Their power—" began the scholar.

"Has its limits. You may trust me on that." He cocked his head to one side, almost resembling a Seeker. "They and I are related, as a matter of fact, though neither side is willing to admit it at times. We also have a tendency to forget, it being so long."

His explanation was hardly what she had expected. "How could you—"

"Cousins, actually. Perhaps half brothers in some cases. Father . . . he had a tendency to . . . share."

Wellen, mind busy in what was so far a futile attempt to find a way to extricate the two of them from Shade's hands, recognized the telltale signs of the aged warlock's insanity seizing control again. Shade was beginning to drift back in time.

"Xabene." He tried to keep his voice as low as possible, hoping that she would be able to understand him and that Shade, in his present state, would not pay attention regardless of his exceptional hearing. "Forget what I said earlier. Teleport us away from here now!"

He was gratified to see her nod slightly. She, too, realized that this situation was beyond her abilities, especially if all the master warlock had said were true.

Xabene tensed in his arms and then—

Nothing. Nothing, save that Shade was walking up to them and Wellen discovered that he . . . and Xabene . . . could not move so much as a finger.

"I think we should go elsewhere to discuss this further," the warlock suggested offhandedly. This close, even the shadows could not hide the fact of his parchment skin. He looked ready to crackle. "There will be others along shortly and they will raise a fuss."

The Dragon King! The reptilian monarch of this land would surely know of the catastrophe before very long, unless, of course, he knew already. The choice was not one that he would have preferred to face, but Wellen decided that departing with Shade certainly had to be better than awaiting the scaly presence of the angry drake lord.

"I'm not going anywhere with you!" Xabene swore.

"Then you may remain here, if that is your desire." He stretched out a hand toward Wellen. "Come, Master Bedlam."

"I won't" —Wellen discovered himself now standing *next* to Shade—"leave her!" he sputtered, mentally cursing teleportation and its misuses.

"Wellen!" The enchantress, also released from the movement spell, rushed to his side. Whatever her goals, she evidently did not want to separate herself from him. He wondered how much of it had to do with fear for herself because of her failure and how much had to do with the chance that she still might be able to redeem herself in the eyes of her masters if she remained with Wellen and Shade. Possibly she was evenly split; the short scholar *still* had no delusions about her attraction to him. What did he have to offer?

"We all go together then." The corners of the warlock's mouth crooked upward at the sight of the twosome holding one another for reassurance. Shade seemed most coherent when he had an audience or something that particularly piqued his interest. If not for his indifferent attitude toward the lives and deaths of others, Wellen might almost have been able to like him. As it was, the best he could do was again pity the aged spellcaster.

The shrouded figure began to curl within himself. It was something he had always done prior to teleporting himself, but this was the first time that Wellen had actually paid attention to it. He wondered if that was the way he had looked when the hooded warlock had teleported him.

A force tugged at the duo, Shade's spell pulling them in. Bedlam and the enchantress held one another tight, if only because neither of them cared for the idea of entrusting themselves to their spectral companion. Wellen thought the spell was drawn out much more than it had been in the past and wondered what Shade might be doing differently. He glanced back up at the warlock.

Shade, twisted sideways in a manner that turned the anxious scholar's stomach, froze . . . and *untwisted* with a scream.

The cloth-enshrouded figure crumpled to the ground, his spell dissipating even before his face struck the grassy earth. At the same time, Wellen felt a heavy weight he had not noticed earlier lift from his mind. A cold shiver passed through him as he realized what it might be. He looked down at the motionless form.

"What happened to him?" Xabene separated herself from Wellen and took a tentative step toward Shade. She leaned forward and studied the warlock.

"I think . . ." It was insane, but he could see no other explanation. "I think! might have fought him off."

"You?" The enchantress rose and inspected him, trying to see something that neither she nor Wellen had noticed before. "You think you stopped him?"

Her disbelief was reasonable. He shrugged. "When he started to collapse, I felt different, as if something had been accomplished or . . ." The confused man spread his hands in surrender. "I cannot explain exactly how I felt. It just makes sense somehow. I knew that I wanted his spell to fail. The thought of teleporting again . . ."

"Perhaps you have something there. Now that I think of it, I thought I sensed a difference in you, but my first notion was that it was just an effect of his sorcery." She dared to prod the still form with her foot. "His power . . . so different, yet still like theirs . . ."

Her masters. Shade had spoken about them, called them *kin* of all things. The idea that Xabene followed such masters repulsed him. What had she spouted after the disappearance of the citadel? *Lords of the Dead?* His eyes flashed to the two horses, still standing quietly exactly where the duo had left them. Wellen's hands curled as he thought of the flesh he had touched. Now he understood.

A horrible thought sprouted from that memory. Could Xabene be like the horses?

He stared at her pale skin, such a contrast to her raven-black hair and the dark gown she wore. Impossible. There was too much vibrancy in her, even if most of it worked to trick men into doing her bidding. She could never be one of the walking dead.

She caught him staring at her and, despite the situation, smiled. It was not a smile that beguiled, but rather one that he thought was tinged with open pleasure at his interest in her. Again, though, Wellen could not forget that the enchantress had already proven herself competent at playacting.

"There's nothing more to be gained here." Xabene glared at the innocent-looking field. "I can't sense it anywhere. Are you certain that it wasn't you?"

"No, but he was." He wondered what they would do with the warlock. Leave him? Abandoning an unconscious Shade to the whims of the Dragonrealm did not appeal to the explorer. There was also the thought that the ancient warlock, should he escape harm, would immediately set off after them.

"Him. Should we find some peace for a time, I would like to hear about the circumstances of your acquaintance. You seemed to have forgotten to tell me earlier."

He met her reprimand with one of his own. "As you seem to have forgotten your masters."

Xabene bit her lip. "No, I could never forget them. They, on the other hand, might be more than willing to forget about me."

"For failing?"

"I never have before. I never thought I *could.* It was so perfect!"

His head was throbbing harder. Turning his gaze to the sky, he scanned the region.

At last, Wellen discovered a tiny dot on the northern horizon, one that was rapidly growing larger.

"Xabene, whatever our differences, they can wait. I think we have to *leave—fast.*"

"You sense something?" From her tone, she had not. Wellen was vaguely interested to note how his sorcerous abilities, however limited, occasionally proved themselves superior to those of much more powerful spellcasters. He tucked the fact away for later contemplation. Their lives were what mattered now.

"I sense *and* see something. Look north."

She obeyed. "I don't . . . no . . . I do see it."

"Dragon?"

"I wish it were only that simple. Try *dragons!*"

Squinting proved Xabene was correct. There were three of them. They flew in a formation, much the way birds did, with the flock leader in the front.

"Wellen," Since Shade's intrusion, she had gone back to speaking to him in more familiar terms. Whether that was good or bad was something only time would reveal. "Whatever has come between us, I agree that we are together in this at least. You were the one able to overcome our friend here; can you also summon up a portal or teleport us away from here before it is too late?"

"What about you?" The thought of trying to perform a conscious spell, something he had really yet to do, unsettled him. "Shade is no barrier now. Your powers—"

"Are not sufficient. I tried at the moment he collapsed, hoping to take us away before he recovered. Instead, I found my abilities reduced to almost nothing." She glared at the prone figure in bitterness. "Much the way they were *before* I *made* my pact."

It was up to him, then. "All right. Any suggestions?"

"It differs with everyone, but this might help. Think of us elsewhere. Pick a place you know and trust. A stable place."

Pick a place he knew? He was a stranger in this land. When had he had time to become familiar with *any* part of this realm? Wellen looked around in frustration, trying to stir an idea to the surface.

He caught sight of the hills to the east. Their unreal uniformity was something he could never forget.

"I have it. The hills."

"Then think of us there. Wish that we were there. That is all I can tell you. The rest happens within your mind."

The would-be warlock tried. He pictured the symmetrical hills and tried to recall various parts of the range. Choosing one, Wellen formed an image of himself and Xabene standing there, safe and sound.

Nothing happened. After several precious seconds, he shook his head. "What now?"

Her eyes on the rapidly approaching leviathans, Xabene suggested, "The horses . . ."

Both their mounts were gone. Neither Wellen nor the sorceress could recall when the beasts had vanished. Xabene was particularly upset. "They've abandoned me! I failed them and this is my reward!"

Running would have been futile. Wellen doubted that even the horses would have been fast enough to escape the soaring drakes. Were they just to stand there, then? What else was there?

It came to him. "Can you cast illusion?"

She understood. "I might be able to do that. We have to huddle together, though. The less space I have to cover, the better."

Wellen nodded and walked over to Shade.

"What do you think you're doing?" Xabene demanded.

"He doesn't deserve to lie here helpless. He could have killed you rather than muted your spells. Besides, we might need Shade to help us later. If you cannot accept that, think how much more carefully they'll search this area if they find him."

His pointed was not arguable. With some distaste, she joined the explorer and took hold of the unconscious warlock. "It will be better if we kneel or sit."

"We do not have much time remaining."

"I know." She closed her eyes. A breath or two later, she opened them again. A triumphant smile played on her full lips. "I've done it!"

Wellen, who still saw the three of them sitting . . . in *Shade's* case, lying . . . in the middle of the field, frowned, not having noticed anything. "I don't see any change!"

"We are not the ones who should, but you can feel it, can't you?"

"Feel?" Concentrating, he did finally notice it. A tingling, much like what he had felt just before the citadel had vanished, but almost unnoticeable. In fact, Bedlam had to concentrate hard just to continue sensing it.

"Now," Xabene said, moving closer to him, "we have to hope it fools *them!"*

Even as she whispered, the dragons, reptilian visages twisted in fury, swooped down toward the field.

Chapter Ten

One fear that Wellen had tried to stop thinking about was that even if the dragons did not notice them, one of them might decide to *land* upon the very bit of ground that the hapless humans had chosen for their spell. That, fortunately, proved not to be the case. The nearest drake was more than twice its length from the still figures.

If there *was* a problem, it lay in that the trio was within the triangle formed by the three behemoths. None of the drakes wanted to be too close to where the building had stood, just in case it came back, Wellen supposed.

They were giants. Wellen's scholarly curiosity came into play even while part of him prayed for a quick and painless end if he and the others were caught. The drakes had jaws capable of easily swallowing a horse and rider and sharp, daggerlike teeth stained by the bloody meat diet their kind preferred. Their claws looked strong and deadly enough to tear apart mountainsides, which made it more amazing that the citadel had looked unmarred by battle. At least two of them were larger than the leviathan that had slaughtered the column. The third could not have been much smaller. All three were of the same coloring, a dark green mixed with hints of purple. On the dragons, it was actually a beautiful color, especially when the sunlight caused their scales to glitter a bit.

He forgot all about colors and scales when the smallest of the three *spoke.* "It issss asss feared! There issss no trace!"

Wellen almost smiled, so fascinated by the sights and sounds. This was the first time he had actually heard one of the monsters talk like a man. The dragon that had killed Yalso had laughed, if the scholar recalled correctly, but had never really talked much, if at all.

Thought of the friendly sea captain and all those others that had perished turned the would-be smile to a scowl.

"But it wassss here!" roared another. An old scar ran across its torso, one that indicated a wound almost mortal, for it looked as if it had run long and deep. That the dragon had lived to see it heal spoke of the fate of the one who had caused the wound.

A sudden, low groan by Wellen's side made him tense.

"Wassss there ssssomething I heard?" asked the short one, raising its head to listen.

"I heard nothing," muttered the third.

Shade was beginning to stir. Wellen matched frantic glances with Xabene.

"It wassss ssssomething!" insisted the smaller one. His stature in no way detracted from his leadership. The other dragons clearly respected his power.

The three menacing beasts twisted their heads around and began to scan the field. The eyes of the scarred one glanced over to where the trio hid, but did not stop.

The waking sorcerer shifted.

"Ssssomething?" roared the smaller one, its burning eyes focusing on a point just a few paces to Wellen's right.

"Nothing." The one with the scar clearly wanted to be gone from this place. "There issss *nothing* here."

Xabene's hand came down and covered Shade's mouth just as the warlock was about to mutter something. His eyes flashed open, gleaming crystalline orbs that almost made the enchantress, who had never seen them unshadowed, cry out. She was able to smother it at the last moment.

This time, they were fortunate. The drakes had not noted anything.

"He will not be pleassssed!"

"What elsssse can we do? There issss nothing! Perhaps the gnome hassss destroyed hissss infernal sssself!"

"Would that ssssuch were true," agreed the leader.

The dragon with the great scar abruptly raised its head. "I ssssmell manlingssss!"

A shift in the wind. Neither Wellen nor Xabene had counted on that. The scholar silently cursed his stupidity. A boy on his first hunt would have known to prepare for such a situation.

The other behemoths sniffed.

"I smell nothing!" argued the third.

"It issss the gnome'ssss doing!" hissed the leader. "A ploy to confuse ussss while he furtherssss hissss plotssss!"

They were taking much too long. Although Shade was awake enough to be aware of the danger, Wellen doubted that the warlock would remain complacent for more than a few minutes, shorter, if his madness flared.

If they would only finish their search and depart! he thought, eyeing the smaller dragon, whose decision was the one upon which their lives hinged. If only that creature would satisfy itself and give up! There was nothing for them to see. Wellen knew that all too well.

He felt a tug.

Wellen blinked, and found himself facing two dragons. "What ailssss you?" one of them, the *scarred* one, hissed anxiously.

The explorer, stunned, eyed first the one who had spoken, then the other, who looked as frantic as Wellen felt. As for the third, the leader, he was . . . he was . . .

He was *Wellen.*

I've leaped into its mind! Unlike the first time, when he had touched the thoughts of the dragon in the sky, Bedlam had complete control. There were no thoughts of puny humans and how well they might taste. He was himself. How long that would last and what happened afterward were two very good questions, but Wellen had been given an opportunity that he dared not miss.

"There is no more to be seen here!" Belatedly, he recalled how the dragons had a tendency to hiss. "If the gnome issss gone, it issss our lord who issss besssst suited to find him!"

It proved easy to convince them. In what might have been a flash of insight from his host's mind, Wellen realized that all three leviathans feared the might of the gnarled gnome. That said much for the tiny sorcerer's power, that *three* such as these would fear to face his sorcery together.

With a swiftness that almost caught him napping, the other two drakes lifted into the air. The wind created by their vast wings stormed over the field. Wellen wondered how the others were taking it, then realized that he was still trapped inside the dragon's body. Unless he wanted to live his life out as one of the beasts, Bedlam had to find a way back or—

No sooner was the desire made known than Wellen found himself clutching onto Xabene and even Shade as the three behemoths rose higher and higher into the heavens. The wind threw grass and dust all about, nearly choking the humans. Even Shade seemed disinclined to do more than cover himself, easier for the warlock with his expansive cloak, and wait for things to settle.

Gradually, the situation did. The wind became no more than a light breeze again and the dust and grass returned to the earth from which they had been torn. As for the dragons, they were already far to the north of the field by the time Wellen and Xabene looked up.

It was also at this time that they noticed that the third member of their party was no longer huddled beside them.

"You have my gratitude," Shade said, standing over them. He might have been talking about some minor gift they had given him, so disinterested did he sound. The warlock peered around at the open field. "So the drakes are at a loss, too."

Xabene was silent, perhaps measuring her chances against Shade, but Wellen was not going to wait for the ancient sorcerer to make their decisions for them. He had shown the master warlock that he could be entrusted with his life; now he intended to show the hooded titan that he could be respected and listened to, also.

Strengthening his resolve, he stood before Shade. "You just thanked me. I don't think you realize just how much you owe to us."

The near smile returned to the undead countenance, but no words escaped the lips to condemn Wellen for his impertinence. Shade was amused at the very least.

Wellen pushed on. "You lay unconscious, my doing, I admit—"

"Yours?" He had the warlock's interest now. The smile was not so deprecating anymore.

"Mine." The novice spellcaster waved it aside as something that could be discussed later, when he had finally had an opportunity to try to puzzle it all out for himself. "What matters is that we could have easily left you there, helpless, for the drakes to discover! The Dragon King would have found you most interesting considering what had happened here!"

"Indeed." Shade's gaze drifted to Xabene, who had come to stand behind and to one side of the angry scholar. Her left hand rested on Wellen's shoulder. "You have forever forsaken your masters now, female. I am the one being they can never forgive you for saving. Had the dragons seized me, they might have even forgiven you for losing the gnome and the book."

Xabene did not say anything, for which Wellen was appreciative, but the crushing strength with which she grasped his shoulder was a sure indication that the weary enchantress had not considered that.

The warlock returned his attention to the short figure before him. Standing face to half-face, Wellen knew that even if he had been of a more normal stature, he still would have not quite stood at eye level with the cloth-enshrouded titan. Shade was several inches above average and had such a commanding presence that he seemed even taller.

"You are correct in part it seems, Master Bedlam. I owe you, but not for simply saving my existence." Shade reached up and pulled back the hood. His glittering eyes flashed into and out of existence as he blinked in the sunlight. Xabene inhaled sharply, still not used to the sight. Wellen, too, found the eyes arresting. Who *was* Shade that he looked so? There was the name, Gerrod, but that hardly explained anything about the man. He was not even certain the name was a true one. That he had known legends also said something about him, but hardly enough.

Who was the man?

The warlock brushed hair back from his eyes. "I owe you for something just as essential to me. For the past few years it has become increasingly difficult to retain my mind. I've seen *so* much time go by, but so slowly! It has a withering effect, I can tell you."

And through nearly all of it you've been alone. The scholar was amazed that Shade had retained as much of his sanity as he had.

"You are an anchor, Master Bedlam, an anchor that has enabled me to plant my feet firmly on the ground again. Part of it was due to the simple fact that I pursued you, thus giving myself active purpose. That was minor, however. In truth, what drew me back more than anything else was seeing myself . . . in *you.*"

"This is all very pretty," Xabene interrupted. Her hand continued to squeeze Wellen's shoulder. She was nervous about remaining here and he could not blame her for being that way. "But there must be a better time and place to discuss this than in this field."

"Indeed there is." Shade pulled the hood forward without thinking. Wellen felt as if some gate had been shut. For only the space of a few breaths, he had captured a glimpse of the man behind the shadows. Now, the master warlock, the mask, stood before him. "And I shall take us *all* there, since no one else seems able."

Shade started to curl within himself, then paused. He glanced at Wellen, an appraising look spread across the portion of his visage that the explorer could see. "You have far greater potential than I imagined, Master Bedlam."

"What do you mean?"

"I find I still cannot teleport no matter which variation of the spell I try. You seem to have anchored me *too* well to the earth."

With neither Wellen nor Xabene able to cast such a spell themselves, Shade was their only hope. "Do I need to remove whatever I did?"

"That would be kind."

He tried to think of the spell being removed. Vaguely, Wellen saw a spectrum of colors that seemed to beckon to him, but when he tried to reach out with his thoughts, the spectrum vanished.

Shade shook his head. "It appears that we are destined to walk."

"We could summon something," the novice warlock suggested, trying to make up for his mistake. As a scholar and researcher with some success over the past few years, he had forgotten what it felt like to be a first-year student. The Dragonrealm had brought all those humiliating memories back a thousand fold.

"Risky, Master Bedlam. At this point, we're liable to summon back our scaly friends. No, walking is our best bet. The only thing that remains now is a destination." Shade frowned in thought. "My own sanctum, I regret to say, is both much too far away and too dangerous to reach from here. We would have to cross the clan caverns of Purple, who would be delighted to see all of us. A shame, Mito Pica is beyond that and west of Mito Pica is the Dagora Forest. We could find aid there."

Xabene was aghast at the idea. "Dagora Forest! The Green Dragon rules there!"

"Yes, I know. His line has always proved a benevolent one where humanity is concerned."

"I will not willingly place myself in the claws of *any* Dragon King!"

The warlock laughed, a raspy sound. "You have a spirit much in common with one I knew in my youthful days! Then *where,* my lady, do you desire to go? We have already spent much too much time jabbering with one another! Purple himself may return here before long, and he and your former masters were hardly the only ones interested in the gnome's treasures!"

"There's the tree." Wellen stared down Xabene, who flashed dagger eyes at him for betraying her secret place to the fearsome warlock. "We really don't have a choice, Xabene."

"Not anymore," she snarled. Despite her anger, the enchantress did not argue. "We could probably make it there just after nightfall."

"A tree?" It was clear that Shade desired to ask questions, but the spellcaster held back, likely because he and Wellen both knew that Xabene would not readily volunteer answers.

Although it was Xabene who led the trio, she being the only one who knew exactly where the tree was, it was Wellen who found himself in command. Neither of his companions trusted one another very far, but both had faith in the outsider. Wellen had proved himself time and again. Trust was evidently a rare and precious commodity in the Dragonrealm.

The walk was not so strenuous at first. Xabene had the worst of it; though she still moved with astonishing grace, she was no longer immune to the landscape. Things scratched her legs now and snagged on her clothing. As the journey progressed, she became more tight-lipped. Wellen began to understand just how much of her power had been granted to her by the mysterious Lords of the Dead. Without their favor, Xabene had little more ability than he did.

For all that the enchantress had lost, Wellen found her even more desirable that ever. He knew why; she had lost none of her beauty, but now she seemed *human.* Little things affected her. Xabene no longer passed through the world. She was now a part of it.

They contemplated running, but a near fall by Wellen quickly squashed that suggestion. The nigh uniform look of the grassy plains hid the fact that there were treacherous gullies and holes. It was amazing that the horses had not thrown them at some point, but then the creatures had been more than they had seemed. The Lords of the Dead had probably calculated for worse dangers than uneven ground.

Shade ever remained behind them, keeping pace but never catching up. *He* might have been out for a stroll. He had no trouble with footing and neither the grass nor the insect life sought his attention. Wellen, who could not make his abilities work for him in regard to the infestation problem, envied the warlock. What made it worse was that the sun, quite triumphant in its efforts to heat up the world, had also failed to touch Shade.

It hardly seemed fair.

There was still no sign of activity. Each moment, Wellen expected hordes of dragons or flocks of batlike creatures to come swooping down. The latter especially bothered him. It was not just that the three of them would be hard pressed to defend themselves in the open field. What bothered the scholar more was a realization that the woman beside him had once been a servant of the same masters who controlled the winged terrors. He had not forgotten the slaughtered scouts or the massacred Seekers. There was no doubt now that Xabene must have known, too, possibly even plotted the second attack.

What other horrors was she responsible for?

"We have trouble," the enchantress warned. Wellen was almost grateful, for now the answer to his question could be safely put off for a time.

Riders were approaching. At least a dozen. They were small figures in the distance, but they obviously were heading toward the trio. A banner fluttered above the newcomers, but it was impossible to make out in the wind caused by their passage.

Wellen's first impulse was to run. He had only the knife and a few untrustworthy magical abilities. Run where though? The closest shelter was a clump of trees a hundred or so yards to the south and it was hardly sufficient to hide or protect them from the determined horsemen. There was nowhere, in fact, where the trio could escape before the riders caught up to them. The newcomers were familiar with the land, that was evident in the easy manner in which they navigated the plains without falling prey to the many hidden gullies.

"We have to make a stand here," he informed his companions. "Unless we split up. It might be that one of us could get away."

"Not likely," Xabene countered. "Not with at least four riders apiece to chase us down." Her hands opened and closed, the frustration of no longer having the power to deal trouble to her enemies tearing at her. "Repeating the illusion would not do any good, either. They've seen us and I do not doubt that at least one of them has some sorcerous ability. They will be ready for most any trick that I can still muster."

"We will do nothing."

They looked at Shade, who calmly walked up to them, then continued past until he had the lead. "We will do nothing at all."

"He's betrayed us!" the pale woman snarled. Xabene looked ready to take the master warlock on no matter how great the imbalance of ability between the two.

"Be silent and observe." The tall, hooded figure took up a stance of authority, his voluminous cloak fluttering loosely in a wind that seemed stronger around him than it did anywhere else.

Wellen knew they had no choice. Shade had volunteered his services and the other two could only hope that he knew what he was doing. The scholar had not seen any lapses in sanity so far since the ancient warlock had woken; that, he hoped, was a good sign.

The riders were close enough now that Wellen could see they were soldiers. Most were clad in a cloth-and-chain combination of armor. The patrol leader, a large, black man with graying hair, wore a more elaborate chain-and-plate outfit. A purple cape danced behind him. Wellen did not have to ask which human solders would be allowed such free access in this region. Only those who served the lord of the land. A glimpse of the full banner verified all too well that assumption, for he saw a winged, masterful drake posed in triumph. The leviathan was clearly purple.

He began to fear that he had overestimated Shade's sanity. The warlock was asking them to wait to be captured by men serving the Purple Dragon.

Xabene had come to a similar conclusion. Pulling Wellen back a step, she whispered, "He's mad! Why else wait to be captured by servants of a deadly enemy? Look! He has no intention of fighting! With his power, I could have killed them all!"

"Which makes it fortunate, does it not, that I am the only one with the ability to do so," the shadowy spellcaster called back. Both of them had forgotten Shade's uncanny hearing. "Rest easy, though. You have my word that I know what I am doing."

The promise had little effect on either Wellen or Xabene. The explorer doubted that Shade was even concerned about their misgivings. He had given his word and that was that. They would have to trust him.

"We've little choice in the matter," Wellen reminded her. "If he wanted to betray us, he could have done so much earlier. Why give us to the patrol when he could have easily turned us over to the Dragon King's own kind?"

"Why indeed?" Shade asked, his back turned to them. He calmly watched as the riders spread out in a manner meant to cut off escape. Bedlam tried his best to look as unconcerned, but the surly visages that began to surround them would have made it nigh impossible for the bravest of men to not reveal at least a little uncertainty.

The patrol leader urged his bay charger toward Shade, not stopping until the mount's flaring nostrils were almost in the warlock's shadowy visage. Shade gave the rider and animal the same expression of indifference that he had given to Wellen and Xabene earlier.

"Master Shade." The black man nodded in respect. He had a short, well-groomed beard and an aristocratic countenance. In comparison to the four other dark-skinned men in his party, he was night itself.

I am surrounded by shadows, Wellen could not help thinking. Compared to Shade, Xabene, and now this man, he looked positively colorful in his simple green and brown clothing. Everyone else was black, white, and *Shades—the* pun could not be resisted—of gray.

The late Prentiss Asaalk would have stood out like a flower in the desert.

"Benton Lore. Commander." Shade added the rank after a disappointed expression began creeping over Lore's face.

"I'd not been expecting to see you again, sirrah. Three years it has been since last we were in this position. I gather it is you who are the cause of our routine being disturbed."

"Not this time."

"No?" Lore gazed at Wellen and the enchantress. Not surprisingly, he spent more of the time studying Xabene. "You will, of course, explain all of this to me . . . and my lord."

The meticulous politeness was becoming too much for the explorer. Why was the warlock on such terms with a servant, a traitorous *human* servant, of the Purple Dragon?

The patrol leader studied his chief captive again. "You seem. . . more fit."

"It is the company I've been keeping."

Lore misunderstood, his eyes briefly flashing to Xabene, who scowled back. "And such splendid company!"

"Careful," Shade teased. "She has killed men for less than making that assumption."

"Well can I believe that." Lore leaned forward in the saddle. "May I ask how you escaped the notice of the three drakes? I must admit I was surprised to discover you here after they departed."

"In time, we all meet again."

It was refreshing to the scholar to see someone other than himself perplexed by the warlock's inscrutability. "If you . . . say so." The soldier straightened again. "I will not bother to try to decipher that response. Oh, by the way, you are my prisoners, sirrah."

"Of course. You have my bond."

The commander was satisfied with that. "And your friends? Their bonds?"

Shade shrugged. "Of Master Bedlam, I can promise you a word of honor. Of the female . . . I can promise you that she'll remain with him. No more than that, though."

Benton Lore snapped his fingers. One of the men began unlooping rope from the back of his saddle. "Then she will have to be properly bound."

"What?" Xabene's eyes first grew round as the moons, then as narrow as a dagger on its side, not to mention as sharp as the selfsame weapon. She was all set to summon up what little skill was left to her and teach the soldier a lasting lesson.

Wellen seized the rising hand and forced it down. He matched gazes with Commander Lore and, to his hidden pleasure, forced the other man to look away, if only for a second. "I'll be responsible for her. There's no need for the rope."

The massive officer chuckled. "You may change your mind before long, Master . .

. Bedlam, was it not, sirrah? Very well, I accept your bond for her, also."

At a nod from Lore, the man who had been unwinding rope returned it to the saddle. The patrol leader then pointed at Shade and Wellen. Several riders broke from the ring, two converging on the scholar. Each one grabbed him by an arm and lifted. Wellen found himself deposited on the back end of one of the large mounts. He saw that the same had happened to the warlock.

Benton Lore, in an amazing show of strength, pulled Xabene up and almost threw her over the front of his saddle. At the last second, he allowed her to slip into a sitting position. The enchantress had death written on her face, but Lore only laughed. "You would tempt many a man, Milady Xabene, tempt or terrorize them!"

As her hand came up, the dark man caught her wrist. The smile took on a slightly taunting atmosphere. "Temper, temper, milady! You would ruin your fine nails on my tough hide! Lest you think your spells would do you better, let Master Shade yonder tell you otherwise!"

"You would be wise to listen to him, child," the hooded warlock chastised. "Commander Lore has a bit of talent of his own."

"He has no streak of silver in his hair!" she argued, not wanting to give the soldier any more advantage over the trio than he already had.

"I am, milady, a bit of a confusing situation for my friend Shade here . . . for my master, too. Rather than explain, I ask that both you and Master Bedlam inspect my graying hair.

Both of them stared uncertainly at Lore's head. At first, Wellen saw only the coming of the elder years. Then, he noticed what was almost a twinkle. Trying not to slip from the horse, he leaned forward for a better view.

Lore turned his head to the side. Wellen again saw the twinkle and this time knew what it meant. "There's silver in your hair," he blurted, "but it's scattered about like little *bits!*"

"I prefer to think of it as 'peppered,' but, yes, that is more or less correct, Master Bedlam."

"Showing that even the 'gods' are not perfect." Shade seemed to find much satisfaction in that, the explorer noticed, almost as if he had known those very gods he spoke of . . . known and cared little for.

"So"—Lore made certain that Xabene was secure—"if there is no other reason to delay, it is time to leave this place."

One of the other soldiers, apparently the commander's second, ordered the riders into a more military formation and then faced them northwest. When the patrol was ready, Benton Lore gave the signal to advance.

A short distance into their journey, Wellen began to have suspicions about Commander Benton Lore and his men. It was not just because of his inexplicable relationship with the aged warlock, although that was a good part of it, but also the officer's choice of routes out of the gnome's former domain. Once clear of the field, the party made no attempt to turn due north, the direction that the dragons had indicated was where their infernal monarch awaited. Bedlam was certain that the Dragon King would have desired to question the three humans as soon as possible. Any delay was likely to cost those responsible, yet Lore was heading farther and farther away.

Why?

Although on the surface it was a ridiculous gamble, the scholar leaned close to the guard he was riding with and asked, "Where are we going?"

The man did not respond, but his eyes narrowed as if Wellen's question had hit too close to the truth. *Only I have no idea what that truth is!*

Xabene was more or less hidden by Lore's expansive backside, but Wellen could see Shade, who rode a little ahead on his right. His visage remained hidden by the wide hood of his cloak regardless of the gusty wind caused by the patrol's quick pace. Nonetheless, the warlock's body radiated a sense of satisfaction with the present situation.

What lay northwest of their location? Xabene had given him vague lessons in the geography of the Dragonrealm, but most of those lessons had melted away. The veteran scholar tried to recall the maps he had been shown. Unfortunately, only a few names came to mind, most off in the wrong directions. Lochivar was the mist-enshrouded land to the east; far, far north of it was Irillian By The Sea, the city that the gnome had supposedly ravaged centuries earlier. Mito Pica, the thriving village that Shade had dragged him to was more or less north, although it might be west enough to be their destination. He doubted that, however.

His head, strangely enough, disturbed him very little. If the signs were to be believed, he was in less danger now than he had been when the trio had been walking. Wellen wanted to accept that, but found it impossible to do so. There were so *many* things he found impossible to accept. The list, he thought, must surely stretch longer than his arm.

At least we aren't teleporting, Wellen thought, trying to boost his morale. It was not the greatest of comforts, but it was one of the few he had at the moment.

Then a massive hole in the very air opened wide, right before the racing charger of Benton Lore.

In the comfort of his sanctum, the gnome laughed as he observed the havoc and consternation his spell had caused among those who would have his secrets. Dragons in a panic and humans racing hither and thither. Would-be gods afraid to step upon the very world they desired to rule.

"*Children!* All of them . . . nothing but children! They cannot even see what lies under their noses!"

He leaned back and once more observed. The best, the wizened sorcerer knew, was yet to come.

Chapter Eleven

"It seemsssss that you will forever be a thorn in my sssside, warlock!"

The Dragon King was a horribly magnificent being, so large that he was forced to lie nearly flat on the cavern floor in order to speak to the small band of humans brought before him. His eyes were fiery red and, in the glow of the torches his servants had placed about the chamber, his scaly form glittered like the stars on a clear night. Each paw could have enveloped a horse.

He was everything the other dragons were and more. He radiated majesty and power. When he moved, it was with a grace that a creature of his form and bulk should have been denied.

Only . . . the Dragon King before Wellen and his companions was not purple in any way, but rather *emerald green.*

"I have never attempted to disturb you, Your Majesty," Shade returned with politeness. "Our paths have only crossed in times of necessity."

"Necessssity on your part, *not* mine!" Nevertheless, the Dragon King smiled. Xabene unconsciously pressed her side against the scholar's and he, in turn swallowed hard at the toothy sight. "Sssstill, you may be of ssssome usssse to me thissss—this time!"

"I live to serve." The master warlock bowed.

"Or be sssserved."

Wellen chose the moment to observe Benton Lore. The soldier had removed his cloak and donned a new one upon arrival here. Green dominated the garment. The banner standing tall over the patrol also had changed; it now bore the stylized image of a proud, almost *thoughtful* dragon.

They were in the domain of the Green Dragon. That was the Dagora Forest. Northwest of the field, but much farther than a day's swift ride. This was the drake lord that Shade had called sympathetic to humans.

The portal had been the work of Benton Lore. The disguises he and his men had worn would have only served to momentarily fool a true servant of the Dragon King Purple, and so the patrol had planned to be in and out of the region once they found out what they wanted to know. Unfortunately or fortunately, depending on how one looked at it, Lore had sensed Shade and the others. He had judged rightly that the shadowy warlock and his companions would garner his master much more information than the patrol could have obtained in such limited time. More important, it meant getting out with their skins intact, always desirable for any sane spy.

The cavern of the Green Dragon was much like the one Shade lived in, save that it seemed more alive. The warlock's citadel had reflected its master; it resembled more a ghost of the past, a memory. There had been nothing there that sparkled with life. It was a gray place for a gray figure. Not so this cavern. While that might have been in part to the bustling activity and someone's attempt to decorate the carved-out chamber with amenities a human noble would have appreciated— sculptures and the like—it had more to do with the smells. Benton Lore had explained that the dragons here had a slightly different system and so methane, not sulfur, tainted the air.

"I must admit," the warlock was saying, "that I had not expected to sense Commander Lore nearby just when we needed his services."

The dragon acknowledged Lore with what was an almost affectionate nod. "The commander is a very valued servant. He looked at the situation, saw what needed to be done, and performed his duty in exemplary fashion."

They were all quick to note the change in their host's voice. The Dragon King was being very precise in his speech, as if the sibilance that was common among the dragons embarrassed him.

"Quite a coincidence that he should be riding under the banner of your brother at the time."

"Quite." The short, succinct response informed them that the drake lord wanted no more said on that subject. Spying on the domain of a fellow Dragon King probably had worse potential repercussions than if one human monarch had spied upon another. The lords of the Dragonrealm were not afraid to use their might, whatever the consequences.

"I don't like this at all!" the enchantress whispered. "They're all too polite!"

Green chuckled. Had he heard Xabene?"

"As I said, it may be that you can serve me, warlock. Lore has told me what he knows already. Now, you tell me what happened to the gnome. Tell me what you did."

As politely as it was requested, no one doubted that the Dragon King was to be obeyed or else. Wellen only hoped Shade's mind continued to function in the present. It would not do for him to start drifting just when it appeared their lives might be in danger.

The warlock was far from mad at the moment, however, Bedlam discovered just how in control the shadowy figure was when Shade stepped aside and, with a vague smile at the scholar, informed the drake, "You will find Master Bedlam a much more reliable fountain of information than myself."

Wellen blinked, refusing to believe what he knew he had just heard.

"The *outsssssider . . .*" The Dragon King Green's interest made Wellen feel like a rabbit held up before a hungry wolf. He steeled himself. Now that Shade had pushed him before the leviathan, there was no choice but to hope that he would impress the dragon enough to earn his continued existence.

"I am Wellen Bedlam, Your Majesty." He bowed, trying to think of the emerald behemoth as just another noble.

"From across the sea! Fascinating!"

"Yes, my lord." Did the Dragon King sound almost childlike in his enthusiasm?

"You must tell me all about it when things are calmer! I have gathered artifacts and legends that connect your lands and ours, but until your coming, it was only my dream, nothing more!"

This is a dragon? Wellen was both befuddled and bemused. He felt more at ease. However great and ferocious a leviathan this drake lord was, he had interests so very much akin to the scholar's that it almost might have been enjoyable to forget all else and just compare findings.

Benton Lore, perhaps used to this type of behavior, cleared his throat. Green blinked, looked the black man's way, then nodded. "Perhaps later." A puff of smoke escaped the flaring nostrils. "Tell me now, Master Wellen Bedlam, of the gnome, his citadel, and your part in this."

Wellen did, omitting nothing. It might have been an elaborate ploy, but he was tempted to trust the Dragon King more than he had most other beings he had met since the massacre. That the great beast shared his interests in the far past had much to do with it, but Wellen tried not to think that such a reason alone had swayed him. It was also that he sensed almost no danger at all from the emerald monarch. Considering the premonitions he had felt, prior to this during various other encounters, a dragon who was little or no threat was something quite easily noticed.

As he spoke, Wellen grew more and more relaxed. He felt again in charge of himself. True, his future was still in the talons of the Dragon King, but the interest with which everyone listened to what he had to say was near enough to make him feel it was so. By the time he was through, Wellen was feeling more like his old self than he had since he had made the terrible mistake of boarding the *Heron's Wing* back home.

The Dragonrealm is my home now, such as it is, he reminded himself. *I have to make it a place I can live or else I'm lost!* There was no doubt in his mind that the remainder of the expedition had either lifted anchor and headed east or had been decimated by one threat or another, most likely by the clans of the Dragon King Purple.

When the scholar was finished, Green addressed Shade again. "And you?"

"I find his account as accurate as any I could give. There is nothing I can add, save that I believe this was the gnome's masterful work. Master Bedlam merely fell prey to his somewhat peculiar sense of humor. The gnome has simply come up with a new way to confound us all."

"It would sssseem strange if he did not. My predecessor was of the belief that the gnome finds this all some sssssort of game. I am inclined to believe that. He acts too precisely, introduces us to his tricks at too perfect a moment, to be doing this haphazardly."

"He was the greatest of his kind," Shade remarked somewhat distantly. For a breath or two, Wellen feared that the warlock's mind was slipping away. The ancient warlock visibly pulled himself together and retreated in the security of his enveloping cloak.

"I must consider all you have told me," the Dragon King declared. "I must also consider what to do about your predicament, Master Shade. It issss humorous that you have been laid low by so untrained a warlock, though."

"It is only my ability to teleport anything to anywhere. My talents for all else are still exceptional."

"I will do what I can for you. I think there is something in one of the tomes I have gathered. This will require much more than simple blink-of-an-eye sorcery." The reptilian monarch raised his head and summoned Commander Lore. "Thesssse three will be my guestssss . . . guests! You will guide Master Shade and the dam to appropriate quarters. Master Bedlam, however, issss to remain with me."

"Wellen!" Xabene refused to budge from his side, seeing in him her only ally. Both of them knew that Lore and the others were fully aware of who *her* masters had been.

"I assure you, Mistress Xabene, you are in no danger whatsoever." Benton Lore smiled at her discomfort. "We will treat you as you deserve."

Now it was Wellen who did not trust the commander. He stood ready to fight the soldier, if necessary, even though Lore outweighed him by a good sixty pounds or so, and all of it well-honed muscle.

"Rest easy, Master Wellen Bedlam." The Dragon King tried to look pleasant, not something he had been born to achieve. Instead, the leviathan looked hungry. "Your female will be treated as an honored guest." He eyed the enchantress. "Sssso long assss she recallssss who issss ssssovereign of thissss realm!"

Bowing to the inevitable, the sultry enchantress took a moment to urgently whisper in Wellen's ear. "See me when you can!"

Taking her arm, Benton Lore led Xabene away. Shade followed behind them. Most of the officer's men formed a very secure "honor guard" around the visitors. The hint was not lost. Xabene went meekly.

When they were alone, save for a few solitary human guards who could only be there for show's sake, the massive head tilted down toward Wellen. "Tell me about your life, human."

More relaxed then before, Bedlam gave him a brief discourse, skipping quickly through his young years, save when his interest in the legends had first arisen, and then concentrating on his time spent in research and studying. He told of his dream, of the actual voyage, the storms, and the pleasure of the expedition when it had at last sighted land. With bitterness, he told of the ill-fated column and its fate.

That part of the tale made the Dragon King hiss in anger. Although Wellen had never met the Green Dragon's counterpart, he felt certain that they were as far apart as could be. What were the others like?

He finished with the attack by the ghoulish, batlike terrors. The drake lord's eyes widened as he spoke of the monsters and the ferocity with which they had slaughtered the avians. It was clear even before he was very far into the tale that the leviathan knew of the creatures.

"The infernal onessss who think themselves godssss sent thosssse monstrossssities after you! The creaturessss are not natural beings! The Necri are like golems of flesh! They only exist because of the foul necromancy of the Lords of the Dead!" The Dragon King hesitated, then, in a calmer voice added, "You know that your female followed their path of decay. I could smell their tainted touch upon her."

"I know she did. She does not any longer."

"That is ssssomething time will tell."

"Meaning?" Was there something Wellen did not know about Xabene that the drake lord did?

"Meaning many things or nothing at all. Hmmph! I sound like Shade now! I will not detain you much longer, human. You are in need of sustenance and rest. Besides, there are things I must do myself."

"I haven't minded."

The head cocked to one side. "I am not what you expected, am I?"

Wellen had no trouble with the truth. "You are what I hoped for, Your Majesty. What I expected . . . I perhaps discovered all too much of."

"Well said! I find, as the dark one has probably told you, that I have an affinity for your short-lived kind. More so than any of my brethren."

"Are they all so . . . so different from each other, your . . . brothers?"

That brought a laugh. "They are . . . and we are not actual brothers, if that is what confuses you. We call one another brethren because we are equals, just as the ancient covenant of the first of our forebears declared. Equal, save that the *Emperor* has final say on all things." At the sight of the confusion spreading over the scholar's visage, the Dragon King shook his head. "Never mind our ways for now, human. Just know that most will tolerate your kind, you being so adaptable to our needs, but only a few actually care. I have worked so that my successor . . . the eldest of my own get . . . will likewise care."

"If I may ask, why?"

The dragon grew serious. "Because one before me foresaw a time when it might be humans who control the destiny of the realm . . . and I would have our races live together rather than watch my kind fade away as sssso many racesss did before ussss. So I will impress upon my get and so he who follows me will impress upon his."

Benton Lore rejoined them. Instead of armor, he wore an elegant, forest-green tunic that ended in a kilt much like that once worn by Prentiss Asaalk. A short sword hung at his side and a cape similar to the one he had worn earlier covered his shoulders and back. "Your Majesty needed me? I thought I felt your summons."

"I did, my loyal sssservant. It is time that Master Wellen Bedlam wassss returned to hissss companions." The drake lord's sibilance seemed to grow more pronounced every time he became distracted or emotional, Wellen thought. If not for that, it would have actually been possible for the scholar to forget that he talked to a gigantic, winged beast.

"We will talk again, human. The matter of the gnome and Brother Purple is a priority and we can certainly not forget about the most irritating Lords of the Dead! They have surely not played their last hand!"

There was no gesture of dismissal, but Commander Lore suddenly bowed, indicating with his hand that Wellen should follow suit. When the weary explorer had, Lore turned to him and said, "If you will come with me, sirrah, there are fine quarters awaiting." His voice dropping to a whisper and his face breaking into a smile, the dark-skinned warrior added, "You will also find *a* volatile but glorious visitor waiting there, too. She has refused to leave until she has seen you again."

Certain that Xabene's concern was more for herself than for him, Wellen did not respond to the latter statements. Instead, he turned back to the Dragon King, who watched them with veiled amusement, and said, "Your Majesty, I look forward to our next discussion."

"As do I," the reptilian monarch rumbled.

With Lore leading, the two humans departed the cavern of the Green Dragon.

Xabene fairly flung herself on him when he entered his new quarters. Benton Lore stayed only long enough to give flustered Wellen a look of barely concealed mirth, then departed.

As soon as he was gone, the enchantress released her hold. She looked at the scholar with a calculating expression. "What did you talk about with the monster?"

"We talked of many things," Bedlam replied, a bit disgusted with her behavior. "I told him about myself. We discussed this land a bit."

"All nicely civil, I suppose."

His anger stirred. "As a matter of fact, it *was*. More civil than this conversation, in fact."

She looked chastised, but he knew better by now. "I *was* worried about you, you know."

"Because I might be all that stands between you and the Green Dragon," he retorted. Wellen studied the room. It had been purposely carved out of the wall, as much of the cavern system had. He wondered whether the drakes or an earlier race was responsible. The chamber was actually rather roomy, almost as much so as the one in Xabene's tree. Emerald and blue drapery covering most of the walls nearly gave the place the illusion of being other than a cave. Cavern plant life, mostly mosses or fungi of a sort, added to the decor. Someone with an eye had sculpted them into astonishing shapes and patterns, further enhancing the wonderland appearance of Wellen's quarters.

Almost mundane by comparison were the desk and bed, despite the fact that an artisan had obviously carved the wooden parts. Wine of some sort sat waiting on a table next to the bed. A rich, bright green carpet, which turned out to be *grass* when the intrigued scholar inspected it closer, covered all but the entranceway of the chamber.

Xabene had remained silent and brooding after his comment. When she saw that he had run out of things to inspect, however, she reinitiated the conversation.

"We're no safer here than we were in the field, you know."

"I am; you might not be."

"Wellen." The seductress was back. "I would never harm you."

"I know." He said it with such conviction that she stepped back to stare at him.

"You *do* know!" she blurted. "I can see it in your face! But . . ."

How could he know when she herself did not? Wellen knew too little about his ability to answer that question. He also knew too much about Xabene. She was not the sort of person who liked being predictable to others.

Best, he thought, to turn to another, albeit sensitive, subject than this one. "What do you think the Lords of the Dead will do?"

She was wary. "Do you think I know?"

"No, but you're far more familiar with them than I am. I hoped you might be able to guess."

His response was acceptable to her. "I don't know! If what that walking corpse of yours says is true, they will not tolerate his presence! Lords! He looked more like one of their servants than I ever did! How old do you think he *is?"*

"As old as they are and don't try to turn from the question I asked, Xabene. Please."

The enchantress was genuinely worried. Whenever the subject of her former masters arose, Wellen caught a glimpse of the hidden Xabene. *How the offer of power must have appealed to her! She must have been so afraid before that!* Someday, he would ask her about her early past.

Someday? That was assuming that they were still together and, more important, had survived this chaos.

"I think . . . I think they will strike after we leave here. They must know where we *are;* that would require the least of their power. Maybe they'll wait until we've left the safety of the Dagora Forest."

"But they *will* strike?"

The look on her otherwise beautiful face told him all he needed to know, but the sorceress added, "Oh, they will. When they do, we'll be lucky if any of us survive!" Her hands shook. She clasped them together. "I won't talk of them any more. Talking draws their attention." The wine attracted her. "If you can withstand my presence a little longer, Wellen, I think I need some of that."

Xabene sat down on the bed and waited in silence while he poured wine for both of them. He handed a goblet to her, and sat down beside. The sorceress sipped the clear, golden elixir.

When he saw that she had calmed somewhat, Wellen dared ask, "How did you come to be one of their servants?"

She looked at first as if he had taken his knife and cut her throat. Then, the look faded into an expression of resignation. "You want some tragic tale, don't you, Wellen Bedlam? You want to hear how I turned to them in desperation? How they were my last chance? Not at all! I was a minor witch, someone destined to life in a small village where I would do little things for little people but be shunned otherwise! I turned to the Lords of the Dead because I saw that my life would be a wasted nothing, that I'd grow old, live uselessly, and die to be buried and forgotten! Forgotten like so many before me and so many after me."

"Xabene—"

"They gave me power to do what I wanted! I could go anywhere and look down upon those who would have looked down on me! I *was* power!" She turned away from him, swallowed a large portion of wine, and finished, "So much for your idealistic imagination! Not what *you* thought, was it?"

Rising, the bitter enchantress tossed the goblet to the floor. The remainder of her wine slowly sank into the grassy surface.

"If you'll excuse me, Wellen Bedlam, I think it's time I rested. I'd like to leave in the morn if you can persuade our host to let me. There doesn't seem to be much need for me here . . . and I think I'd only attract more trouble, isn't that so?"

He could not respond, still overwhelmed as he was by her initial outburst. Xabene seemed ready to take the slightest thing as a provocation. His question perhaps had pushed too much at something she no longer cared to recall, but he had done it with their safety in mind. It was his own attempt in trying to understand the ivory-skinned enchantress.

Xabene stared at him for several seconds, waiting for *what* he could not say. Then, frustrated, the proud goddess stalked out of the chamber.

The exhausted scholar fell back on the bed, all too aware that he had missed something that he should not have. Under better circumstances, it would likely have been very obvious. Now, though, his mind churned so much that Wellen found it a wonder that he had been able to keep as much straight as he had.

He fell asleep still trying to make sense of it all.

In her own chamber, nearly identical to Wellen's, Xabene fell onto her bed and tried to bury her turmoil in one of the pillows. What she felt was unfamiliar to her and, because of that, frightening. The enchantress also hated losing control, a thing that had not happened since before her pact with the Lords of the Dead.

Some of what she had shown the outsider Wellen Bedlam had been playacting. It was so much a part of her nature now that she found she could not avoid using that ability, even when events might have warranted otherwise. He, especially, encouraged her playacting, although he did not know that. There was something about him that made her afraid to reveal too much of herself, yet desire to.

He would be gone after this was over, one way or another. They might die, but, if they were fortunate enough to escape with their lives, he would find his way back to his home. Why would he desire to remain in a land that had tried to kill him almost before he had even set foot upon its shores?

The thought that he would leave tore at her. The enchantress grimaced, recognizing the unfamiliar feeling. *Not me! It could never happen to me! I'm stronger. It would serve me no purpose to care for him! It would make no sense!*

Part of her mind argued that those she had seen under that selfsame spell never cared about whether it made sense. They just succumbed.

"Not with *him*," she muttered. *Certainly not so swiftly, either!*

Xabene closed her eyes and began to drift away from the true world, never actually falling asleep but sinking into a state where she sensed things around her but only from a great distance. It was a pleasant sensation, for her fears and anxieties became tiny, insignificant creatures of no concern to her. Once more she was the powerful enchantress. Men fell prey to her form while her spells wreaked havoc with their plots.

All except one man.

He can be yours . . . if that is your desire . . .

Her dreams took on a different twist. A horribly familiar darkness slowly crept through her mind.

You are deserving of a second chance . . .

Xabene's nose twitched as she relived the memory of a chamber filled with the smell of sulfur and decay. She saw the multitude of scavengers crawl over and through things that had been rotting since, it seemed, time itself began. A pool lay before her, one covered with a thick layer of fetid slime. The pool bubbled, as if something lurked beneath it.

Let your power be yours again . . . all that is asked is this one . . .

A distorted, monstrous image of Shade loomed over her dream self. He laughed at her insignificance, his crystalline eyes gleaming. She would not be sorry when Wellen and she parted company from the mad warlock.

Your power . . . and the man . . . yours . . . for so small a price . . . What was the price? Her brow wrinkled as she struggled to understand. What price?

A doorway formed in her thoughts. Not anything that *she* had ever imagined. The rest of the scene around her, the pool and Shade, faded as the doorway strengthened. There was no actual door, but the sorceress knew somehow that something still barred whatever waited on the other side. Some sort of barrier.

The power to be respected . . . more power than ever before . . . to make yourself feared by those who would otherwise make you fear them . . .

It was tempting . . . and the power would also give her back the self-control that she had been losing.

Open the door . . . that is all that must be done . . .

Open it? How? Her image reached out and touched the darkness in the center. There was nothing before her, yet her hand would not go through.

The barrier exists only in you . . . *but you are also the key . . .* The barrier *and* the key. To power. She wanted that power. Slowly, her image pushed at the invisible barrier. This time, it began to give where her hand was. Xabene knew that she did not have to destroy the entire barrier. All she had to do was make a hole . . . then the Lords of the Dead could act.

So close to attaining her desires. The barrier struggled, but it was already straining to her limits. She had no qualms about betraying Shade. In her eyes, he was deadly, a mad creature that would bring only death to her and Wellen and then depart, laughing at their foolishness in believing in him.

The barrier gave. One finger burst through its membrane. She felt a tug on the other side, as if they were trying to help pull her completely through. Only a little more . . .

Then, pain struck her and she realized just *what* barrier it was that she was fighting.

Herself. A part of her that did not want to give in again to her former lords . . . but why?

Once asked, the answer, since it came from her own mind, was instantly known. To betray Shade was also to betray Wellen . . . both his belief in her and in himself . . . for the Lords of the Dead saw much potential in him.

They also knew that he would never become one of their servants.

"No!" Xabene called out in the scene. She tried to withdraw her hand, but whatever tugged at her held the sorceress and, in fact, pulled her farther in.

She screamed, but whether in the real world or the dreamland, she never knew, for the barrier broke then and the enchantress was overwhelmed by what had been waiting for her all this time.

Waiting in hunger.

Chapter Twelve

"Issss thissss the one?"

Prentiss Asaalk, looking much more fit than he had after his capture and feeling a bit more in control of himself, studied the image the crystal revealed to **him. He stood in** the imperial chamber of the Dragon King Purple, the monarch of the realm stretched out before him in all his horrific splendor. Unlike the "throne room" of the Green Dragon, that of Purple was barely more than the cavern itself. Only those things that the drake lord thought necessary to his pursuit of knowledge, and the power that such knowledge would in turn lead to, were present.

Asaalk was very respectful in both manner and response, despite now being granted the privilege of gazing at the glory of his new master. The blue man had been treated well these past few days, but he knew that his footing was still precarious. Wellen Bedlam was still loose and the drake lord was growing furious, especially after the debacle involving the gnome's cursed citadel.

"That is not him, no." The image was that of a strange old . . . *old?* Asaalk thought he looked a thousand years *dead* . . . clad in a cloak and hood that seemed ready to swallow him.

"Then, I know who it musssst be." The leviathan raised a fore claw. A human clad in a robe of deepest purple touched the crystal. The sheer size of the dragon made it impossible for him to manipulate such tiny objects without endangering them. The artifact was also so sensitive that to use his vast sorcerous power might have resulted in the drake lord destroying its effectiveness.

Prentiss Asaalk had noticed many humans working for the Dragon King. They did all the things that the drake clans found beneath them and also those things that the tinier, more adept hands of men could do better. The blue man had also come to realize that for all the drakes there were in the clans, they were actually few in number. Humans already outnumbered them and would increase that margin before too long. It would be interesting, he thought, to see what the future held.

His future held nothing but oblivion if Bedlam was not discovered soon . . . and then what? Asaalk would have to find a new way to make himself valuable. *So I will, yes!*

"Concentrate on what floatssss before you, human, or elssss I shall feed you to my get as a sssspecial treat!"

The blue man looked up . . . and gasped. His eyes narrowed and his mouth curled in bitterness. He could never forget the face now. "It is him, yes! It is Wellen Bedlam!"

He had come to hate that face for putting him in this situation. Had *he* been in charge of this expedition, this would have never happened.

"Sssssoooo . . ." The leviathan raised his head. As far as the northerner was concerned, there were far too many teeth in the smile of the Purple Dragon. "Brother Green treadssss where he should not!"

The statement made no sense to Asaalk, but he remained silent. If the reptilian monarch deigned to explain his outburst, Asaalk would be more than pleased. If not . . . he would have to live without the knowledge.

The important thing was to *live*.

"Your Bedlam issss in the care of my brother to the northwesssst! The Dagora Foresssst! Green hassss grown too pressssumptuousssss! I shall tear his kingdom assssunder! There will be carnage everywhere! Hissss damssss will become mine; hissss get will feed my own!"

Another Dragon King had Wellen Bedlam and had stolen him . . . somehow. . . from this one. The blue man understood that much. He also understood that his captor was speaking of a war between the clans of two leviathans, with Asaalk caught in the midst! In desperation, he sought ways to prevent the coming war. Asaalk was a survivor. Better to throw himself into a plot of his own making than sit by idly waiting for death to come for him.

A solution came to him. It was not the best, but time did not warrant long and careful planning. While it had risk to him, he preferred it over doing nothing. "My great and honorable lord!"

He was forced to call twice more before the Dragon King noticed him. The head of the behemoth swung down and Asaalk found himself staring into a dripping tunnel from which there was no returning. Sulfur and the smell of blood combated with one another to smother him. He stifled the look of disgust that was attempting to surface, knowing that it would only lessen his chances of convincing his new master of the worth of the plan.

"Ssspeak, manling! Or should I ssssimply disssspense with your annoying pressssence now?"

"My lord, I have a plan which may gain you what you desire without the danger of loss!"

His phrasing, he discovered, did not entirely agree with the leviathan. "Do you think my clanssss *cowardly?*"

"By no means, great lord! That which I meant was . . . was that why risk what you seek? Such a war would likely kill Wellen Bedlam!" A new thought, based upon what he had learned about the society of the drakes, gave him more ammunition. "The Emperor would surely not like seeing your two lands torn apart either! He would grow suspicious and learn of what you have hidden from him!"

Purple's mouth clamped shut. Asaalk had never seen a dragon caught unaware before, but here was such a sight.

"The tome musssst be mine!" the drake lord muttered. "Only I have the right to it!"

"It was found, after all, in your proud domain, yes?"

The handful of human servants in the chamber were all staring at Asaalk. He flashed them an arrogant smile, to show them who had their master's ear now.

"What issss your plan?"

Here it was. Always it seemed that his existence depended upon something. "It is simplicity itself, yes. Master Bedlam and those who control him will leave the other kingdom soon. They must, for they, too, want what is rightfully yours." He spit on the cavern floor to show what he thought of their presumptuousness. "When they leave, they will find one waiting for them. One who will gain their trust and lead Wellen Bedlam into your very claws. That one will be me, yes."

"You? And why should I trusssst you, human? If I let you loosssse, you will ssssimply try to run!"

"How could I run from you? I am merely a mauling. Besides, I have come to see that my desires are best served by serving you, yes." There was truth to that. If he was condemned to live out his life in the Dragonrealm, it made sense to choose a path leading to power. The drakes *were* the lords of the realm and Asaalk had learned enough about the others to know that his chances were probably best with this one. There was just enough similarity between himself and the Dragon King to make that so.

Of course, by that same reasoning, there was less reason for the leviathan to trust him.

"A pretty little sssspeech . . . and a plan which, while ssssimple, might be acceptable! There musssst be a few *minor* alterationsssss, though! I musssst alsssso ensure your obedience!"

Prentiss Asaalk had known that would be the case and steeled himself. Whatever happened, it could not be too severe, else it ruin his chances of tricking Master Bedlam. While the squat little scholar had led a sheltered life, he was by no means a fool, save perhaps in being too naive at critical times.

The Dragon King tilted his head and eyed one of the guards standing just behind the blue man. "Ssssee to it that thissss one issss fitted for a collar! Then . . . return with him to me!

Would it not have risked his new status, the blue man would have exhaled a tremendous sigh of relief. The collar was what he had hoped for. He had seen the sorcerous toy in action. There were other, stricter methods that Purple used to keep his more enterprising servants at bay, but the collar was the simplest. Most humans needed nothing; they were cowed by the drake lord's mere presence. Collars and such were for those too crafty or too important to be left unguarded, people who might actually *defy* their rightful monarch.

The collar, despite the little tricks it contained, was something Prentiss Asaalk knew he could circumvent. The blue man had tricks of his own that no one, not even his late and unlamented companions in the expedition, knew about.

As he was led away, much more respectfully than when he had first been dragged in here days ago, the northerner began to think that life in the Dragonrealm might not be so terrible. . . once he had made a few changes in the way things were done.

The look on Wellen Bedlam's terrified visage would be good enough incentive, too.

"Wake up, lad!"

Wellen was once more on the *Heron's Wing*. He was trying his best to sleep, but Captain Yalso kept shaking him. Part of him knew that was wrong, for Yalso was dead, but the image was insistent. Somewhat distractedly, he noticed that his head was trying to warn him of some danger.

"I said for you to be wakin' up!" A beefy hand slapped him on the right side of his face. His eyes opened wide but, as is often the case with those startled to consciousness, he could focus on nothing. He only knew that the torches that had lit the chamber were still burning, albeit not nearly so brightly.

"That's better!"

The startled scholar blinked, looked up at the source of the voice, and then tried to scramble off the other side of the bed. Unfortunately, a steely grip around his arm kept him from going anywhere.

Captain Yalso's pale visage came within an inch of his own. "Someone might

91

think you're not pleased to be seem' me, Master Bedlam!"

"You . . . you're *dead!*"

The sea captain smiled. "That I am, lad."

The next connection was not difficult to make. "The Lords of the Dead! *They* sent you!"

Still keeping his hold on Wellen, Yalso sat his heavy bulk down on the edge of the bed. "That they did. A queer lot, them lords, but their power can't be argued with. I heard me name and there I was!"

Bedlam noticed that Yalso never breathed, even when he spoke. That should have made it impossible for him to speak at the very least, but the corpse seemed unimpeded by that fact. Yalso also stunk like a fish left rotting on the deck during a hot, sunny day. "It . . . it's good to see you, captain. I mean that, regardless of the circumstances. I wish . . . "

The undead mariner nodded his sad agreement. "I know. We made our choices and that's all there is to it."

"How did you get here?"

"How else? Through your comely lass."

"Xabene? But she—"

"Was made an offer that sounded too good. Can't blame the girl; I was in her shoes not too long ago." Yalso stood up, his hold on Wellen's arm never easing. "Speakin' of which, it's time we got goin'! I've got a bargain to keep and you're part of it, Master Wellen." With one hand, he lifted Wellen up and stood him on his feet. "Good to see you're wearin' your clothes, my boy! Would hate to think I had to drag you naked before their like!"

The befuddled explorer gazed down at his crumpled clothing, which he vaguely recalled having fallen asleep in earlier. Then, realizing the import of the ghoul's words, he asked, "Where are we going?" What's to happen to me?"

Yalso tried to look comforting, but his ghastly appearance had the opposite effect. Wellen, having more time to observe him, noticed that the words he heard were not in sync with the movements of the late captain's mouth.

"No need to be worryin' too much, *friend.* They've promised not to harm ya. They just want to be knowin' what *you* know."

The hapless explorer tried to pry the death grip loose, but touching the sailor's hand was like touching the cold flesh of the horse Xabene had summoned for him. Wellen drew his own hand away and shivered. Yalso's face darkened.

"D'you think *I* like it? They've offered me a new chance at life, Master Bedlam. I just have to bring you to them to answer some questions! Then I bring you back and they give me what the cursed sky serpent stole from me! Is it too much to ask ya, then, to help me out? You're still livin', you are! *You* escaped!"

The bulky corpse began to drag him toward the hall. Wellen forced himself to touch the hand again and struggled to free himself. "Yalso! Listen to me! I've mourned the deaths of all of you and I wish I could bring you back, but you can't trust the Lords of the Dead to keep their promise! They've only resurrected you because they know I feel guilty about what happened!" It was true; he had still not forgiven himself for ever having put together the expedition. "They know I won't fight you as much as I can!"

Small cracks had materialized in the mariner's hands and face while Bedlam had talked. They reminded Wellen of the sort of cracks a badly formed clay pot might develop on hardening. The sight made him nauseous. Yalso did not bleed as living people did. Even as the unnerved scholar watched, a dark, thick substance began to drip from the wounds. What was slowly seeping out of the corpse was blood, he realized, but it had long ago congealed.

The undead captain did not notice what was happening to him. "I can't take that chance, Master Bedlam! I'll not stay dead if I have a choice about it! C'mon, man! You'll be okay! They've promised to give you to your lass! Ya can't call *that* a fate worse than death, now can you?"

"Where *is* Xabene?" Had she really betrayed him? It seemed reasonable to suppose that she had to have been their key to the protected realm of the Green Dragon. Like the tragic figure before him, Xabene had been made an offer that encompassed all she could ever want. Life without power was as horrible to her as being dead was to Captain Yalso.

"She's *fine,*" the corpse replied in what was supposed to be soothing tones. The cracks had spread so much that the mariner was now covered with dripping wounds, none of which he had yet noticed. Yalso's visage was taking on a less-than-pleased expression. "Now, come with me, Master Bedlam, so that what needs to be done *will* be done!"

"I cannot, captain!" Wellen lifted his knees into the stomach of his undead companion.

The sailor shook his head. Bedlam's kick had not even slowed him. "You shouldn'a fought me, Master Bedlam. Now, I'm afraid I'll have to take you more forcible like."

Yalso's eyes turned up, becoming pale white orbs. More and more the scent of death permeated from his body. "I'll have to make you more agreeable. I'm sorry, lad, but it's me *life* I'm talkin' about!"

This is not the captain! Wellen told himself. *Yalso was never this way in life and he'd not be this way in death!* This was a shadow of the man, manipulated by the soulless necromancers Shade claimed were his kin.

The scholar fought the rage that welled within him. What the Lords of the Dead had done to Captain Yalso was unforgivable. "Captain, if I could give you what you desire, I would!"

A brief spark of the old mariner resurfaced. Yalso's horrific visage twisted into a look of genuine sadness at what the two had come to. "I know ya would. I . . . I really can't help meself! They promised me, though!"

"They promised Xabene many things, but I've seen that they like to take back those promises! Think of how they've treated her!" Wellen was gambling that the enchantress had not been so willing to return to the fold as the corpse had said. Perhaps she had been tempted, even almost succumbed to their offerings, but if she had accepted, why send Yalso, then, instead of her? Xabene was not one to leave something she had started to others. *She* would have gone after Wellen, if only to erase her earlier failure.

"I—" Yalso froze, caught between whatever he had been told and what his mind argued might be the truth. Wellen's spirit rallied, although not for his own sake. That Yalso hesitated meant Bedlam had been correct concerning the raven-crested sorceress. Xabene had not betrayed him.

"I have to . . . " Though the captain's loyalties, enforced or otherwise, tied him to where he stood, it was all too likely that the necromancers' power would prevail in the end. Wellen could not hope that the undead mariner would decay away if stalled long enough. The Lords of the Dead surely had that contingency covered.

Power within, if there was ever a time for you to come forth, it's now! He wished with all his might for some spell to save him from the clutches of his rotting captor, but nothing happened. His mind still screamed uselessly of the danger he was in, yet no other bit of sorcery sought to free him of that danger.

For that matter, he wondered why no one was rushing to his aid. With the arguing, it would have made sense for *a* guard or two to come bursting in . . . unless the forces behind Yalso had taken care of that beforehand.

Staring at the entranceway, Wellen abruptly spotted his one chance for salvation. It would mean risking all, however, for if he failed, his plan would only serve to turn his late comrade against him.

"I know it's hard, Captain Yalso," he said in his most understanding voice. "You still have time to consider everything. I could be wrong. Perhaps if we start on our way to wherever it was you were trying to lead me to? By that time, you might be able to think clearer."

Yalso's now blank eyes stared his way. "What are you trying to do, Master Bedlam?"

"Help you."

"Help me . . . all right."

Wellen had banked on this shambling parody being less than the living sailor or else his plan would have failed in that instant.

As the captain turned them both toward the entranceway, Wellen stared at the torches that were still burning on each side.

Yalso only held him by one arm, too.

His captor was silent, either still engaged in mental battle with himself or simply deciding that speech was an unnecessary drain on his false life. Wellen walked almost beside him, trying to keep up his show of support until the end. "It's always possible that there's another way, captain. Shade is a masterful warlock, perhaps he—"

"He'll be dead, lad, like I've been."

Wellen almost gave himself away at the announcement. Just how great an attack was this? Did the Lords of the Dead seek to take on *all* of their adversaries while they slumbered under the mantle of false security? Was even the Green Dragon in danger? If so, it only made %lien's need to free himself that much greater.

The torch on his side was almost in his grasp. Another two steps. Then, it was only one. Still Yalso did not notice. Would he react as Bedlam assumed?

The final step. The burning torch was within reach. Wellen lunged for it.

"You shouldn'a had, Master Bedlam!" a sad Yalso announced. He pulled hard on Wellen's arm, nearly yanking his prisoner off the floor. His strength was enough that the explorer could not help but fall toward him.

Which was what Wellen had wanted. Prepared, he added his own strength to the zombie's. The two crashed into one another and, despite Yalso's dead weight, both living and unliving were sent stumbling into the torch on the captain's side.

The horse that Xabene, or rather the Lords of the Dead, had provided had been a cold, lifeless thing like the unfortunate Yalso. It had felt like a dry, long-dead corpse, although at the time the realization had not sunk in. Wellen had wondered just how dry both the mount and the unliving captain were.

The answer was . . . *very*.

Yalso's back and far side burst into flames like kindling.

"Put it out!" roared the sailor. His visage, already crumbling, was half ablaze. He released his charge without thinking, trying desperately to beat out the flames. Bedlam did not pause, backing quickly to the other torch and taking it from its stand. With it, he confronted the macabre figure.

There were tears in his eyes. If he had thought there was actually a way to resurrect his friend . . . "I'm sorry, Yalso, I am."

"You will *come* to us!" a chorus of voices decreed. What was left of the sailor's face no longer resembled him. Yalso was gone; the Lords of the Dead had taken complete command. One of the corpse's hands was completely burned away. The other, flames wrapped around it like a glove, reached for the waiting human.

Wellen thrust the torch at the horror's midsection. The flames rushed up the length of the torso, turning the entire top half of the ghoul into an inferno. The furnishings and curtains behind it were also ablaze. Bedlam, sweating from the head and half blinded by the light, backed out of the chamber. The thing that had once been Captain Yalso tried to follow, but the flames had spread to its legs and, being so much dry timber, they easily crumpled under the combination of sapping flame and the creature's still-bulky form.

He watched the corpse burn for a few breaths, his face tear-streaked and his mind recalling Yalso as he had known him in life. Wellen had no doubt that a part of the captain had been there, but at the same time, it had been the necromancers who had guided the strings.

No one should make a mockery of life like they do!

There was no time to mourn Yalso and, he reminded himself, he had done so before. It was the living who were important now. Falling back to the cavern corridor, Wellen started to throw the torch away, then remembered that Shade and Xabene might face attacks similar to the one on him. The torch might prove handy. The enchantress, he suspected, was in less danger. If he understood correctly, the Lords of the Dead needed her to maintain penetration of the Dragon King's lair. He was under no misconceptions about his chances of trying to free her on his own. He had only escaped because the necromancers were probably concentrating their power on their most dangerous adversary. Shade.

It was Shade who represented Wellen's best, possibly only, hope of freeing Xabene, yet, he found he could not bear the thought of rushing to the warlock first. He *had* to see if he could help her.

The tunnel was dead silent. tie heard neither drakes nor battle sounds. Either all were killed or they were unaware of what was going on. Likely the latter, for the disarrayed explorer doubted that the death lords could defeat the hooded warlock *and* destroy the combined drake clans.

Benton Lore had placed all three outsiders within only a few minutes from one another, yet Wellen saw nothing. Had Shade been caught unaware or in the throes of his madness? Wellen started down the tunnel, still trying to convince himself to rush to the warlock first. What if they had acted against Shade as they had against him? It was the one area where Bedlam held the advantage. The Seekers had struck at the shadowy spellcaster, successfully releasing his memories and using them as distractions. Could the Lords of the Dead have utilized the same trick, only more effectively?

Riming a corner, he stumbled to a halt.

There were two human guards standing in the tunnel, facing one another. Human guards for human guest, Bedlam decided. They looked neither ensorcelled nor dead. Both of them looked his way and one brandished a short sword.

"Identify yourself!"

"Master Wellen Bedlam! What are—"

"One of the outsiders brought in by the commander," the other sentry, an older man, explained to his compatriot. To Wellen, he said, "You should not be wandering the system, Master Bedlam. Those unfamiliar can get lost very easy. It's sometimes hard to explain to the drake's young that they shouldn't have eaten a guest of His Majesty."

"Haven't you *heard* anything?"

"No, should we have?" The sentries looked skeptical. Wellen knew he looked like a wild man.

"I was just attacked by a man who I last saw dead at the claws of a dragon!"

"Then, he couldna been much trouble, could he?" the younger one asked, chuckling.

"Your master—"

"Save your breath on these blind ones," came a voice that was doom incarnate. Wellen was reminded of the tones a judge used when sentencing someone to death . . .

95

or perhaps it was the voice of the executioner himself.

It was all and neither.

It was Shade.

He stood in the midst of the tunnel, directly behind the two guards, who whirled and readied their weapons. Shade raised a finger and the two soldiers fell against the sides of the corridor. They were conscious, but they could not move. Not even speak.

"Shade! Were you—" He stopped as he caught sight of the warlock's tattered garments. Even the cloak and hood had been torn. The ancient spellcaster still wore the hood over his head, but it failed now to hide the burning rage in those jarring, crystalline eyes. Shade teetered on the brink of an insane rage and it was possible that he had even begun plummeting over that brink.

"They have gone too far this time," the warlock muttered. He did not seem entirely focused on Wellen. "They chose the one they thought I could not deny in the end, the one most likely to bring me down."

Memories of the two phantasms floating around mad Shade's head returned. Sharissa and Dru Zeree. Had it been one of them? The woman? Had they used her?

"They, of course, had never defied him until then. *They* would never have believed that I could have defied him so." Shade turned to the elder guard. The man, unable to move anything but his eyes, could only stare back in fright. "You. Tell your commander . . . tell your liege . . . that the necromancers have invaded his domain. *Now!"*

Suddenly free, the sentry ran. Wellen fell flat against the wall as the man sped past, obviously under a geas or some similar magical compulsion.

Shade recalled the other sentry. "There may be risk. You had better go with him."

Compelled, the wisecracking soldier hurried off to join his compatriot.

"I will not sacrifice any more lives to them," the hooded sorcerer commented coldly. To Wellen, he said, "I come to save you, but I find you coming to save us."

"I was . . . " Wellen could not get his tongue to work for him. Listening to the sorcerer speak, he had been reminded of Captain Yalso.

A bit more rationality, but perhaps even more chilling anger, returned to the warlock. "Yes, my cousins no doubt sent someone they thought you might hesitate to resist. Like myself, however, you found that you could." At the shorter man's unasked question, Shade added, "What they sent me wore the shape and form of my dear, unlamented father, but it was not his spirit. I know. That was their fatal mistake. They could re-create the form, but they could *not* imitate the spirit of the Patriarch of the Tezerenee. It would be unmistakable to me." To Wellen's surprise, Shade actually shivered. "I cannot say what I would have done if it *had* been him . . ."

"Shade . . . "

"They will pay for this debacle . . ."

"Shade!" Bedlam stepped directly in front of his companion and forced the warlock to look at him. The expression he received almost made him regret his action, but it was too late. Besides . . . "Shade, Xabene needs us! She's the way they were able to pierce the Dragon King's defenses! She's their key!"

A grim smile stretched his dry skin to its utmost. "And ours. Come."

Without preamble, the two of them materialized in the enchantress's chamber. Wellen barely noticed this time, his concern for the pale sorceress far outweighing his dislike for teleportation.

She lay on the bed, almost serene.

"Xabene?" He started to go to her, but the shadowy warlock stayed him with an arm.

"They would hardly leave her like this without another trap."

"Are you certain?"

"We are kin. We were Vraad. Worse, we were all Tezerenee."

The names meant nothing to him, but if Shade understood the necromancers, Wellen would bow to his judgment.

"What could it be?"

Given a task, the master warlock once more gained a stronger foothold in reality. He took a tentative step toward the motionless figure. "Something surrounding her, deadly to the touch, would be the obvious way."

Wellen's head, which had been screaming danger since his awakening, somehow succeeded in becoming even more adamant. The danger seemed much closer than a spell surrounding Xabene, almost as if a great *physical* threat was lurking . . . *above?*

Hanging from the cavern ceiling, motionless until Wellen's glance upward, were the Necri.

"Shade!" was all the harried scholar had time to shout before the winged horrors were upon them. Four dove at Shade, while only two found Wellen of interest. He held up the dying torch, a pitiful thing by now, and wielded it like a sword in the desperate hope that it would have sufficient flame to ward off the oncoming pair that had chosen him for their meal.

His torch became a sunburst, swelling upward in size yet never so much as singeing his fingers. It caught the first batlike monstrosity by surprise, turning the creature into a living fireball that squeaked once and dropped to the chamber floor. Wellen jumped back, but did not lose track of the second horror, which had now grown much more cautious.

An explosion shook the furnishings and forced Wellen to fight for balance. He was pelted by a rainstorm of stench-ridden gobbets of white flesh and a sickly sweet liquid he did not care to identify, although he had his suspicions. The Necri above was also showered by the ungodly rain, but where the human shook in disgust, the demonic creature was aquiver with rising fury. It hissed.

Wellen's protective flame winked out of existence.

The Necri dove, claws bared and maw wide open.

He fell to the floor and rolled aside. Claws raked his backside, causing him to scream. Fortunately for the scholar, the winged terror had either overestimated the width of the chamber or its own ability to maneuver in closed spaces. As it turned to finish its prey, it caught one winged arm against the rock wall. The sudden loss of the one wing forced the Necri into a short-lived spiral that ended with the monster colliding fully with the wall.

Panting and wincing from the jagged cuts, Wellen leaped up and charged the Necri's backside. He raised the dead torch above his head, then brought it down as hard as he could. Not once did he consider the creature's skull, suspecting that it was solid as it looked. Instead, Bedlam utilized his momentum and weight as much as possible and focused the head of the torch onto the less protected neck.

The monster's neck did not crack; Wellen had never thought it would. The blow did, however, send the Necri to the ground, shrieking in agony. Wellen struck again and again. The batlike creature twisted in frustration and confusion, succeeding at last in throwing the scholar from its backside. Still, even free of the human, the Necri could not rise at first.

An inhuman roar filled with agony overwhelmed Bedlam from behind, but he had no time to see what had caused it. The torch was beyond him now. That left only his knife. Wellen wished he had asked the Green Dragon for a new sword, but doubted that the drake lord would have given him one so readily. After all, what reason had there possibly been for Wellen needing a sword while in the safe claws of Dagora's monarch?

What, indeed. Only ghouls and savage horrors from beyond!

Wishing there were another way, for his own sake, Wellen pulled out the knife and attacked the slowly rising Necri.

The demonic servant of the Lords of the Dead turned to face him . . . a moment too late. The blade, intended for the neck, caught the beast in the snout. Wellen was startled but relieved to discover that the Necri did not have impossibly thick skin near that region. The knife sank all the way to the hilt. A thick, brackish fluid covered both the hilt and the scholar's hand. It stung terribly, making Wellen release the blade without thinking.

The Necri was squealing, trying to grasp the slick hilt and remove it. It took a halfhearted swipe at its human target, but the knife insisted on attention. The batlike terror clawed futilely at the moist blade, only doing more damage to its snout. Wellen fell back against the edge of the bed and looked around in desperation for something to finish the beast. Even wounded as it was, the Necri would soon enough come for him . . . and now it partly blocked the only way out.

Benton Lore, wielding a falchion, chose to materialize in that selfsame entranceway, followed closely behind by at least two or three guards bearing similar short swords. He looked in horror at the necromancers' servant, then immediately brought the wide blade down on the neck of the wounded monster. The falchion sank deep into the Necri, splattering more of the foul liquid over the area.

The Necri shivered once . . . and collapsed.

The commander quickly wiped the blade off on one of the cloths decorating the nearby walls. Disgusted, he looked at the battered and worn outsider and demanded, "What is happening here?"

Wellen did not answer him, but turned instead to Shade, who he feared might already be a victim of the other Necri.

He was not. The shadowy warlock glanced his way as he dropped the tattered remnants of a Necri arm to the ground. Shade appeared tired, but the fury had not left him. The course of the battle had knocked his hood back and Wellen heard Benton Lore and the other soldiers mutter at the sight before them. If anything, Shade seemed almost as much a demon as the savage beasts he and the scholar had fought.

"You took your time getting here, Lore." In contrast to his appearance, the ancient sorcerer's voice was almost nonchalant, as if Benton Lore had been a few minutes late to a noble's party.

"Not our fault. We were barely more than two or three minutes . . . and that because a barrier of some sort blocked our way in this hall until moments ago."

Two or three minutes? Wellen blinked. Had it only been that long?

"Two or three minutes in battle with these can seem like an eternity. Fortunately, they prefer tooth and claw to their magic, else they might have utilized the latter to better advantage. Typical of the lack of thought that their creators suffer from."

"Xabene!" Mention of the Lords of the Dead brought the disheveled explorer to his senses. He rushed to the still enchantress's side and reached for her.

"Stay!" Shade was suddenly there on her other side, his gloved hands gripping Wellen's wrists with such strength that the mortal grunted in pain. The warlock pushed him back. "The link must stay intact. I need it."

"I cannot let her stay like that! Not even for you!"

Shade's smile was mocking. "Would it make a difference, Master Bedlam, if I told you that breaking the link would not return her?"

"What does that mean? Who is responsible for this transgression?" asked Lore, coming up to the foot of the bed. He glanced down at the unmoving Xabene. "What has happened to her?"

"Always this need for infernal explanations," Shade mocked. "She is the link that the Lords of the Dead used to invade your liege's kingdom. Her body and mind are here, but her spirit, her ka, now resides in *their* domain."

"She's *dead?"* Wellen paled.

"I did not say that. I said that her spirit resides in their kingdom, though I cannot say how long before she does die. I sincerely doubt her former masters will have any use for her once they realize they have failed."

"I should think they would know by now," Benton Lore commented, pointing at the still sizzling remains of one of the Necri the hooded warlock had destroyed.

The smile crept onto Shade's face. "I have seen to it that they do not . . . for a time. Time enough, if there are no more interruptions, for me to do what I must."

Wellen looked the warlock in the eye, not an easy thing to do even now. "You have to save her!"

"If that is possible; my hands will be filled . . . with my cousins. Now if someone joined me . . . " He stared pointedly back at the scholar.

Wellen nodded without hesitation.

"We shall come, too." Lore snapped his fingers. The guards quickly lined up in two columns.

Shade winked at the scholar, such a disconcerting sight that Wellen almost thought he had imagined it. "I think not, Commander Lore."

He seized the explorer's hands again.

The world twisted in and out . . . and so did Wellen.

It was so dark that his first thought was that someone had doused all the torches in Xabene's chamber. Then the terrible stench of sulfur and rotting flesh informed him that he was elsewhere.

A blazing light formed in the air only a yard to his right. In its glow, he saw a wretched landscape. The few things that resembled plant life were twisted and black. The scholar was reminded of terrain after a horrible battle in which the only true victors were the carrion crows and their ilk. Things, frightened by the intense light, scurried into holes. A few did not move fast enough and were swallowed up by less frightened, much larger monstrosities that failed to resolve into any distinct shapes when Bedlam tried to see them better.

"I once knew a place like this," came Shade's voice. Somehow, he had not seen the warlock. Wellen finally made out, the shrouded form standing an arm's length from the floating light. "In some ways, I have never left it."

The tone was all too familiar to the younger man. It was the same one that the ancient spellcaster generally used as he was slipping into madness. Wellen rushed to prevent that. "Where are we?"

His spectral companion, seeming almost as much a part of this nightmare world as the things that had hidden from the illumination, quietly responded, "We are in the reflection of another place, a world that long ago died yet still is . . . and only they would think to re-create such despair." A cloak-covered arm rose and a gloved finger pointed ahead. Wellen followed with his eyes and saw something, some *structure in* the distance. "And there is where they wait."

The warlock began walking, the ball of light ever floating ahead. Wellen kept pace, knowing that to lose Shade and the light was to lose more than his life, for here were things that fed on souls as well.

Here were the Lords of the Dead.

DRAGON TOME

Chapter Thirteen

In the field abandoned by the gnome, there occurred a strange thing. It happened when no one seemed to be looking that way, curious since, until that point, countless prying eyes had studied the land in a futile attempt to understand what the citadel's master had done.

The pentagon rematerialized . . . but not quite in the same place.

Then it disappeared again.

Wellen and Shade stood at the front gate of the twisted castle that served as the meeting place of the Lords of the Dead. The magical ball of light that the master warlock had summoned was their only illumination, but it served to give the anxious scholar some idea of how the bizarre structure looked.

What it looked like a hodgepodge collection of many places all fixed together by insane craftsmen. Towers jutted at impossible angles and the style of architecture in one region sparred with an entirely different style next to it. The only thing they all had in common was a presence of despair and decay . . . and madness, too, Wellen corrected himself.

"Shall we go inside?" the hooded figure asked rhetorically.

And just like that, they *were*.

Shade looked up into the darkness. "Come out, my cousins, and let us speak of family!"

Save the scattering of tiny, hideous forms at the silence- shattering call, there was no response.

As willing as Bedlam was to save Xabene, he wondered what his companion thought he could do against the ageless necromancers. His own abilities were too unpredictable, too reluctant. They had saved him from one of the Necri, but seemingly abandoned him to the other. The only skill he trusted was his ability to sense oncoming danger and that was of no use to him now, for the screaming in his head only told him what his normal senses had from the beginning. This was not a place for a living mortal.

"We shall have to go to them," Shade informed him. "I would recommend staying near my side for now."

Where else would I dare go? the explorer wanted to ask. Too many larger things moved about at the edge of the sorcerous illumination, as if biding their time. Wellen tried not to contemplate what would happen if the light spell failed.

Shade began leading him through a moss-covered hall. The stench was, if anything, worse within the walls than without. Now and then, a large mass lying sprawled on the floor required them to step carefully. The entire place seemed orchestrated to emphasize what it was the Lords of the Dead were. The scholar whispered so to his dread ally, not so much out of fear of discovery, but because the silence was so absolute that any noise was an intrusion that struck to the soul.

His words did not surprise the shadowy form beside him. A dry, sardonic chuckle escaped the mass of cloth. "There has ever been in my family a sense of the theatrical. Still, I doubt this world we see is the one that they perceive. It has been said that the one most susceptible to an illusion is often the one who has cast it, for he of all people *must* believe in its worth."

Rolling the last past over in his mind, Wellen dared ask, "Who said that?"

"I did."

Somehow, Wellen found that the answer did not surprise him.

The hall abruptly ended at a flight of stairs leading up . . . and *up*. Even when Shade expanded the ball of light, they could see no end.

"I see they are expecting us." Shade raised a gloved hand. In the extended brilliance, Bedlam noted that his clothing and that of his companion had been repaired. It was a bit consoling, he admitted to himself, that Shade was powerful enough to deign to reclothe them while still concentrating on the danger at hand. Wellen knew he himself would have been hard pressed to conjure even a good glove, if even that much was possible for him.

"Enough of these childlike games." The warlock's hand folded into a fist as he called out, "By the dragon banner, *I* demand a confrontation!"

"The banner is torn," mocked a whispering voice.

"The staff is broken," said another.

"And the clan is dead," uttered a third.

The staircase was gone. For that matter, their entire surroundings had changed, though Wellen would have sworn it was the room that had come to *them*, not the other way around. They stood in a chamber where an immense pentagram had been etched into the floor. A dark circle marked each point and corner of the pentagram, eleven circles all told when the one in the center, one fairly close to the duo, was counted, too.

"We are all that remains of the glory," said yet a new voice from almost behind them.

Bedlam whirled, but Shade seemed not at all put out by the sudden intrusion. He stood his ground and Wellen, trusting his judgment in this case, relaxed, but only a bit. They were, after all, in the sanctum of the Lords of the Dead.

A shape began to coalesce in the region where the last voice had originated. Basically manlike, but in the way a cloud can look like a person. Temporary. Always shifting, as if the memory was hard to recall. Wellen had an impression of a fully armored figured wearing a cape. The more he stared, the more the impression became clearer. The necromancer, for it *surely* had to be one of them, wore a helm with some sort of intricate design. Much of his countenance was covered, which the scholar thought was probably a good thing.

"What do you see?" Shade whispered.

Wellen hastily described it.

"You perceive memories. To me, there is a walking cadaver, a thing less alive than the false father I confronted in my chambers. It wears the armor that you mention, but it is rusting and ill-fitting on so emaciated a torso. *All* of them look so. Yet, even I see only memories."

"All of them?" He looked around and discovered that there were ten other murky figures around them, each one standing near a darkened circle. When they had appeared he could not say. "Are they . . . dead?"

"For all that they should be, they are not."

"We are immortal, cousin," said the one nearest to them. "No more than I."

"We have become the gods we once were and *more."*

"Gods?" Shade laughed. "We were never gods. Just spoiled children with godlike powers, children who did not know how to use those powers." The warlock pretended to look around. "And I see you have learned nothing in that regard."

"Our kingdom is a paradise." As the leader spoke, the others moved to the center of their respective circles. "We have re-created the Nimth of old."

"True . . . you have re-created the twisted, sick child we left behind."

The air crackled with barely suppressed power. Despite their air of indifference, Wellen could see that the Lords of the Dead were very much disturbed by both the intruders and the words of their cousin. He wondered why Shade did nothing. Surely his companion saw what was happening around him?

"We have mastered life and death."

The hooded warlock purposely turned away from the speaker and addressed Bedlam. "They think that because they can steal a piece of a dying person's ka, that they have captured the entire thing. They think that a scavenger stealing a morsel is the same as a hunter catching his prey. Have you ever seen such naivety?"

"*You* demanded confrontation and we have given it to you!" The necromancers grew larger. The nauseating stench they raised made Wellen's eyes water.

"The female is your responsibility, Master Bedlam," Shade remarked quietly. "Follow her trail. You cannot miss it from here."

"His words are ensorcelled," one of the other necromancers commented. "He hides something from us."

"To little avail," intoned the leader. He took his place in the center and faced the warlock. "To little avail, cousin."

Shade wrapped himself tightly in his cloak and turned around to stare at the thing that claimed kinship. "Nothing I do is to little avail, Ephraim."

The ball of light circling above the duo's heads became a nova.

It was as if the necromancers' world itself screeched in agony. A howl rose among the Lords of the Dead as the blinding illumination revealed to all what they truly were. Wellen swallowed hard. Neither the image he had seen nor the view Shade had described left him ready for the dark mages' true forms. Wellen found it hard to believe that these things could be alive in any sense.

A hand caught his shoulder and a voice, Shade's voice whispered, "Now is the time, scholar. Find her and take her from here. Go!"

Propelled in part by the warlock's hand, he ran blindly toward the only exit he could see.

The light died. Not faded away. Died. Wellen felt it, just as he felt the summoning of great strength by the Lords of the Dead. The running explorer stumbled, then discovered that despite the absence of illumination, he could still see the arched exit. Wellen increased his pace, regretting for the thousandth time that he had not been able to secure some sort of weapon, such as the falchion that Lore had carried. His knife was gone now, too. Now he only had his sorcerous skills to trust, not a great consolation in this dismal place.

It occurred to him that he was running without thought, that Xabene could be on the opposite side of the necromancers' citadel. For some reason, though, the novice mage was almost certain he was on the right trail, almost as if the two of them were linked to one another.

A hiss warned him of approaching danger. Wellen came to an abrupt halt and flattened himself against the nearest wall. He tried not to think of the things he had seen crawling around on other walls in the castle, reminding himself that they could be nothing compared to what moved ahead of him.

Whatever source, be it Shade's doing or some stirring of his own power, allowed him to see in the darkness, he was hard pressed to make out what shambled slowly toward his location. Wellen was reminded of a beehive with tentacles, but that was all the detail he could make out. He thought that something, some sort of slime, dripped from it, but that was based purely on the sounds the horror made as it moved slowly along.

Wellen was certain that it was coming for him, until it suddenly turned and went *through* one of the walls without so much as a second's hesitation. An illusion? With great care, the curious explorer stepped over to where the monstrosity had disappeared. Just before the wall, he stepped into something moist, certain evidence that what he had seen had not been the product of overtaxed imagination. The scholar within could not help taking a moment to study the phenomenon.

Tentacles burst from the wall, *seizing* him by the arms and throat.

Crying out, Bedlam tried to pull back. The thing proved stronger, however, and he found himself slowly but surely edging toward the wall. Wellen wondered what would happen when he and the stone met, then decided that it was a question better left forever unanswered. Frantically, the would-be warlock tried to summon up some sort of spell.

Nothing happened. He cursed his premonitions; the ability was so overwhelmed by the necromancers' kingdom that the warnings had become one constant headache, with no definition between near and not-so-near danger. Such was the trouble of becoming too accustomed to sorcery; one could forget it had limits.

In desperation, Wellen gave up attempting sorcery and tried the only thing he could think of. Bracing himself, he kicked the stone from where the tentacles projected.

If anything, the tentacles pulled with more fervor.

"Let me help you," came a quiet but, somehow, commanding voice. A single, delicate hand, female, reached out and touched one of the tentacles.

The appendage unwound and snapped back into the wall with such haste that it took part of Wellen's sleeve with it. Again the graceful hand, attached to a slim arm clad in white gossamer, reached out and touched a tentacle.

Whatever was happening, the beast had decided it had happened once too often. Wellen fell back as the tentacles were frantically withdrawn. He coughed as air rushed into his lungs. There was no doubt in his mind that he had scars around his throat and wrists. Still trying to draw breath and also watching to make certain that the wall stalker did not attempt to renew its attack, he said, "My . . . my thanks!"

"I would always help one of my children."

He raised his head and twisted around to see who had saved him.

She was taller than him and nearly as tall as Shade. Her well-formed figure was outlined in white, making her appear to be some snow goddess, and her hair, long and flowing, was silver-blue. A streak of very solid silver also ran through her hair.

His next statement died as he studied her more closely. The hall behind her was visible *through* her.

She smiled, almost a bit sadly, and somehow the smile made up for the fact that she was one of the undead. This was not Yalso. This was not one of the necromancers' toys. Here was one who could not, *would* not, hurt him.

"Tell him I always cared about what happened to him," she whispered. Then, in slightly lighter tones she added, "There are still a few facets of crystal in *your* eyes."

"Wait!" He knew without knowing how, that she was leaving. "What—"

The white wraith pointed backward at the hall behind her. "She lies that way. You won't be impeded anymore. I can see to that before I go."

She was growing less distinct, looking more and more like a bit of smoke in the wind than a woman.

He hesitated, then asked, "Did I . . . did I summon you?"

"I will never belong to the children of the drake," was her dwindling response.

Wellen shook then, feeling as if he had both found and lost something. He rose, thinking that the spirit had looked familiar, almost like . . . like the phantasm that had haunted Shade? Lady Sharissa?

Did she call me one of her children? The scholar found that hard to believe. If true, the bloodline had grown diluted over time. Many families, including his own, had laid claim to being descended either from the Lord Drazeree's . . . Dru Zeree's . . . daughter or from the children his elven bride had borne him. He had liked to think there was some truth, had even subconsciously used it as *a* reason for his obsession, but to actually *be* . . .

As astonished as he was, Wellen recalled what his true task was and rose. If he was a descendent of the legendary lord, it behooved him to prove himself more than he had so far.

DRAGON TOME

Wellen followed the path both his mind and the wraith's words told him was the true one. He was relieved to discover that she had not lied about one thing; nothing larger than a hand-sized, dead-white spider crossed his path and it had retreated quickly. All the time, the castle was silent. What had happened to Shade and the Lords of the Dead was an enigma. Wellen had expected the castle to rock from the intensity of their battle. He had anticipated explosions, thunder, and the screams of massive monsters brought into the fray by both sides. The silence, however, reminded him too much of the invasion of the Green Dragon's domain. The scholar was unfamiliar with sorcerous duels, but he assumed that they involved *some* noise.

Turning a corner, he found a wooden door. There was no question in his mind that this was his destination. This was where Xabene, or a part of her, was kept. He had no idea what he would find behind the door. A wraith, like the one in the hall? Conjectures were useless; it was easy enough to find out.

As Bedlam reached for the handle, the citadel *shook.*

A roar like *a* thousand storms raging all around nearly deafened him. Wellen put his hands to his ears and fell to one knee as the floor began to ripple beneath his feet. Pieces of stone dropped from the ceiling as shock wave after shock wave rocked the castle. It was as if all the effects of battle had been saved up for this one movement. Perhaps Shade had confined the battle somehow so that Wellen could find Xabene without too much trouble. If so, it boded ill that the hooded warlock's intentions had failed.

The stone floor tilted, nearly sending the hapless rescuer crashing into the opposite wall. He tried to grab the handle again, but it stayed just out of reach. Wellen managed to stand in one place, but then his boots started to *sink* into the stone floor. Not wanting to sink through to whatever lay below, or worse, find himself *trapped* in the very stone itself, the determined explorer struggled his way back to the more solid walls and pulled himself up by what little fingerhold he could find. The floor still had some solidity, too. With effort, he found himself making progress toward Xabene's chamber again.

A flurry of tentacles in his face made him throw himself to one side. A wall stalker sprouted full-grown next to his chest, but it had no interest in him. Wellen watched as the monster frantically wiggled its multitude of appendages in a useless attempt to stay attached to the wall. With what must have been a despairing hiss, the creature lost total control and plummeted to the floor.

It did not fall through as he expected. Instead, the wall stalker struggled as a drowning man might. One or two tentacles of the beehive creature shot in his direction, but not far enough. The thing rolled about in the liquid floor. It seemed to be trying to *swim* its way to the opposing wall. Unfortunately, the wall stalker was not built for that. All it succeeded in doing was miring itself further.

As abruptly as it had liquefied, the stone floor reverted to normal . . . much to the distress of the necromancers' pet.

Wellen swore as he turned away from the stomach-wrenching sight. As simple as it had been for the wall stalker to shift through stone, there was evidently some conscious effort needed. Caught unaware as it struggled, the monstrosity was *crushed* in the sudden reversion. A shower of entrails and fluids narrowly missed Bedlam. A wave of sulfur made his nose burn and his eyes water, but fortunately, it was only a momentary thing.

Testing the stone, Wellen dared put his full weight on the floor again. Tremors still shook the castle. Although there were no windows here, he did not doubt that if there had been he would have seen a panoramic display of colored explosions lighting the generally dismal landscape. Light seemed a key element in dealing with the Lords of the Dead. They and most of their abominations had an aversion to it. Only a few servants, mostly humans like Xabene and reluctant creatures like the Necri, the latter of whom probably *preferred* the night, were likely to be of any use during the daytime.

He touched the door. To his surprise, it swung open easily. Almost too easily, he thought, but then it was doubtful that the necromancers had contemplated someone actually invading their citadel. Either that or once they had made use of Xabene, she had become unimportant to them.

"Xabene?" His voice echoed.

He stepped into the chamber, not understanding. Xabene *had* to be here. It felt correct. Shade had said he would be able to follow the trail; the wraith of Lady Sharissa had pointed the way. This *was* the place.

It's not her true body I'm looking for, Wellen reminded himself. *It's her spirit.*

Follow the trail . . . he had followed it to the room, but could it be followed farther?

Slowly, he wound his way into the middle of the room. There did seem to be more to the path. It was as if he was at his destination but not.

As he circled the center, still tracking the trail, the scholar saw a form shimmer into and out of existence.

A woman on a platform.

He continued to circle the center, finding somehow that the trail overlapped itself again and again but did not come to a definite conclusion. *What sort of mad sorcery is at work here?*

Wellen glimpsed the image again. It *was* Xabene. She seemed a little more solid now, although the image itself lasted little longer than it had the first glimpse. The enchantress was stretched out much the way she had been in the Dragonrealm, yet now she was more ephemeral, more like a dream.

This is not her true body. Would he be able to touch her, much less wake her? Wellen tried calling out to her again, hoping that his voice would do what his hands might not. "Xabene! Awaken!"

She remained as she was, but the image of her grew more constant, albeit still ghostly. Bedlam circled like a vulture, both marveling and despairing at the way the path seemed destined to go on forever. Still, each revolution appeared to bring him closer to his goal. Closer, but never actually there.

"Xabene!" The chamber quivered as another tremor shook the castle. A piece of ceiling stone crashed to the floor just to the right of the scholar. Neither the sudden crash nor the tremor so much as caused the sleeping enchantress to shift.

She must wake! he thought, *before the entire citadel comes crashing down on us!* Or just him, he corrected. It might be that Xabene was beyond the physical danger. "Xabene!"

Her eyes opened wide and stared skyward. He was overjoyed until he realized that nothing else was happening. Xabene merely lay on the platform, arms crossed, and watched the ceiling. She made no move to acknowledge him nor did she appear to notice the destruction going on around her.

"Xabene, I won't leave without you!"

The enchantress turned her eyes toward him. Though her mouth did not move, he had the impression that she spoke his name.

Madness or not, he seized the straw. Wellen held out his hand. "I have come to take you back with me."

She stretched out a hand toward his. It was not insubstantial, as he had assumed it would be, but very light. Slowly, her ghostlike form rose from the eerie platform and joined him. Xabene said nothing else, but the enchantress did *smile.*

Now what? Shade had not told him what to do after this. Wellen had assumed that he would recognize the way back when the time came, but nothing struck a chord.

DRAGON TOME

Shade! What do I do?

In the chamber of the pentagram, the twelve still stood. The eleven Lords of the Dead and Shade. None of them had moved so much as a foot or even a finger in all the time, yet the signs of their savage battle were everywhere. The ceiling was gone, opening the chamber to the pitch-black sky that was occasionally lit by fire. Portions of the castle lay strewn about both the room and the landscape. Things glowed or melted or died, depending on the spell that had been cast.

Near the center, whirlwinds failing to dislodge his hood, stood Shade. He stared ahead at the one called Ephraim, but his mind, like theirs, was all over the landscape.

One part of his mind heard Wellen's anxious thoughts. Slowly smiling, an act which instantly pushed the Lords of the Dead to renewed efforts, the warlock responded.

Xabene's spirit, her *ka* as Shade had called it, turned toward one of the far walls with such abruptness that Wellen expected to see a horde of tentacled stalkers come crawling through. That was not the case. Instead, his unworldly companion began trying to pull him toward the wall. Uncertain but not knowing anything better to try, he allowed her to lead him, careful never to lose his hold. The enchantress's hand was so light it was almost possible to forget one was holding it. That could prove dangerous. If he and the ka were separated, Xabene might never wake.

He might never return.

She continued ahead, even when it was evident that the wall was not going to move for her. Bedlam started to warn her, then closed his mouth as first her fingers and then her arm disappeared through the stone. Within seconds, the enchantress had vanished, save for the hand the scholar still held.

"Xabene!" *She* might be able to walk through walls, but Wellen could hardly be expected to follow—

His own hand sank into the stone without even the slightest tingle.

Gritting his teeth and closing his eyes, the novice warlock allowed himself to be led through. He did not open his eyes until he was certain that enough time had passed.

Wellen almost regretted reopening his eyes. They had left the castle interior and the spirit was now pulling him along with even greater force, almost as if she were nearing an important destination.

It would not have been so bad if the two of them had not been more than twenty feet above the ground.

He knew that Xabene did not have to fear falling, but he wondered what held *him* up. Certainly not his own skills. Could it be that Shade was aiding him again?

They flew swiftly over the landscape. Wellen dared to look back. For the past few moments, the citadel had been deathly quiet, but he doubted that the battle was over. If Shade had won, he would have joined them. If the warlock had fallen victim to the Lords of the Dead, the two mere mortals would hardly have been allowed to escape.

Something began to take form ahead of them. It resembled Shade's ball of light, but much, much larger. Xabene's spirit focused on it.

Behind them, there was a slow, building growl of thunder. It did not end after *a* few seconds, but continued to grow in intensity. Wellen did not have to be told that the final showdown was coming. When his wraithlike companion picked up her pace, he did not argue.

They were nearly upon the fiery sphere. It was wide enough to admit a score of riders traveling side-by-side and taller than the gnome's citadel. The heat made Wellen sweat, but he would have been willing to face the burning might of the sun, if only to escape this place.

He *assumed* this was escape.

With a final effort, Xabene dragged the two of them into the inferno.

"—back here, warlock!"

Wellen Bedlam looked up at the startled countenance of Benton Lore, who actually dropped his sword as he stared at the battered and torn figure lying in a heap on the rug next to Xabene's bed. The officer retrieved his weapon and, still stunned, stared into Wellen's face.

"Master Bedlam!"

The worn scholar tried to say something, but only a low croak escaped his now parched lips. He felt as if all fluid had been drained from his body.

"Get him water!"

One of Lore's men brought a mug. Wellen accepted the water and gulped it down. A sense of reality finally returned to him. "We're back!"

"You barely left! First the two of you vanish, then a second later, *you* return! What *happened* to you?"

He was not certain he had heard the officer's words correctly. "Only a few seconds?"

"No more."

"I do not—" The stench of the dead Necri attacked his sense of smell. What was left of the monsters had not been removed, something that Lore would have definitely had done at first opportunity. Memories tame tumbling back to him. With an effort he would not have thought left in him, Bedlam whirled around and pulled himself up. "Xabene!"

His heart sank. The pale enchantress lay as she had before. "What did you expect?" Commander Lore asked in open curiosity.

Wellen wanted to tell him about all that had occurred and how *hours*, not seconds, had passed, but he could not take his eyes from the still figure. For all she had to answer for, he did not want to lose her. When he had been younger, the scholar had smiled in mild amusement at stories of people who were drawn together almost from the first they had met, despite their differences. Now, Wellen was not smiling, for with him it was true.

He put a hand on her arm.

Xabene stirred.

The soldiers tensed, as if expecting some new trap, but Lore signaled them to relax. "What have you done, Master Bedlam?"

"Nothing!"

She opened her eyes wide, quickly scanning the chamber as if unable to believe where she was. Then the enchantress focused on Wellen. To his surprise, Xabene turned away.

"I'm sorry . . . it was so tempting at first."

"What was?"

Xabene turned back. Her expression was hard, cynical, but her eyes were moist. "What do you think? They offered me all that power back . . . and more . . . "

"And did you accept their offer?" Benton Lore asked. His manner was easy but his falchion was ready. Wellen glared at him, but the soldier did not lower the blade.

"I almost did . . . but then I realized what that would mean."

"Yet, you still let them through!"

"I had no *choice* by then! They were too strong!" She tried to rise, but it became apparent almost immediately that her strength was far from replenished. "Too strong!"

"Commander Lore, I will vouch for her!" Wellen understood the officer's concern, but Lore seemed too determined to have *someone* to punish for the embarrassing intrusion. "She was hardly an honored guest! You also might recall what Shade said . . . not too long ago . . . about how she would have died before very long if the part of her the Lords of the Dead had stolen had not returned."

Lore was by no means convinced, but he quieted nonetheless. "And where is Master Shade? Will he be returning shortly, too?"

"He isn't here?" Xabene looked around, as if expecting the shadowy warlock to materialize in some corner. "But he *was* the one who showed me the way back!"

"He stayed behind." The rolling thunder echoed in Bedlam's mind. "He was still fighting the necromancers. Shade must have wanted us out of the way."

"But I thought that she was the only path open to you," Benton Lore commented, forgetting his distrust of Xabene for a time. "If she is awake and well now, then that path is closed to him."

Taking the enchantress by the arms, Wellen asked, "Can you open the path again? Can you?"

"No!" She looked away, not wanting to see his disappointment. "They've severed the link! I'm cut off from them forever! I'll never be . . . " Xabene's voice faced away as she contemplated her future.

The thunder seemed to roll even louder in his head. He closed his eyes and tried to will it away. "Then, Shade's trapped in their domain."

Chapter Fourteen

The rest of the night passed without any sign of Shade's return. Wellen was surprised at the depth of emotion he felt for the peculiar, often tragic, warlock. Shade had saved him more than once and the last time for no reason at all. His only comfort lay in the fact that the Lords of the Dead had been conspicuously absent, too. They had not attempted a second invasion. Wellen could only hope that if the warlock had perished, he had at least taken the necromancers with him.

Xabene was still asleep on his arm when Benton Lore quietly returned to their chamber. The enchantress, in a complete reversal of the sort of personality she had exhibited upon their first encounter, had pleaded with the weary scholar to remain with her. He could hardly blame her. Had he suffered as she had, it was likely he would have made the same request.

"Good morning," the black man quietly said with just a touch of mirth in his eyes. "Sleep well?"

The scholar shook his head. He had dozed, but nothing more. Each sound had made him think that either Shade or the Lords of the Dead had finally made a reappearance.

Hearing Lore, the enchantress stirred. When she realized where she was lying, she quickly sat up. "What is it?"

"Morning, nothing more."

"Morning . . . " Xabene grew wistful. "I used to love the nights . . . "

"His Majesty would like to see you," Lore announced. Wellen looked down at his ruined clothing. "Do we have some time or are we required there now?"

"You have time to make yourself presentable, of course. Her presence is not required."

Before Xabene could say anything, the scholar replied, "I think he will want both of us there."

"As you wish." The commander snapped his fingers. Two human servants brought in food and fresh clothing. Benton Lore seemed more than just a loyal soldier serving a Dragon King. He was more of a major-domo, ever making certain that the kingdom, *his* kingdom, ran as smoothly as possible. Lore was probably almost as much the ruler as the Green Dragon. "A guard will be posted outside. When you are ready, you will be brought before His Majesty. Until then."

The officer departed, leaving Wellen and Xabene in the care of the servants, who, it seemed, were there to see that the duo did not dawdle. The two chose to eat first, hunger having quickly stirred once they were awake.

"What do you do now?" Xabene asked between bites of a juicy fruit called a srevo.

"What *we* do depends on the Dragon King." Whether she was distancing herself for his sake or her own, Wellen had no intention of parting just yet.

A passing smile, only a shadow of the once-seductive one. "And what do you think he'll want of *us?"*

Wellen knew the answer to that one without thinking about it. "It will have something to do with the gnome, I'm certain. What else is there?"

She grimaced. "You're probably right."

They ate in silence after that.

At first, it seemed he was wrong.

"I have utilized all options open to me," the dragon *informed* them almost immediately upon their arrival. "And I find no trace of either the Lords of the Dead or Shade. None of the gateways that they use are open and my power is insufficient to break through the lock spells they have set. Insufficient, that is, for the time being."

The Dragon King's almost clinical manner reminded Wellen of one of his instructors in school. An image of the drake lord teaching a bored class formed in his mind. He quickly stiffed it and waited for the reptilian monarch to continue.

It almost seemed as if the Green Dragon was hesitant to add to what he had already said. "Your warlock friend still lackssss hisss . . . *his* ability to teleport, that is, if your spell still holds true."

Consternation filled the novice sorcerer. He had completely forgotten about the accidental 'curse' he had laid upon the hooded warlock. Shade had brought them to the domain of the Lords of the Dead and then had shown them the way out, but in neither case had he needed to rely on a spell of teleportation, although what spell Shade *had* used to send them to the necromancers' foul kingdom was beyond him. Wellen was almost certain that the warlock *had* materialized in the hall during the initial chaos, but if the Green Dragon had not had an opportunity to free Shade of Bedlam's blunder, then the scholar was mistaken. In the rush of things, it had probably just seemed as if the warlock had teleported.

"Then, he has no chance." In a sense, Wellen realized that *he* had condemned the ancient spellcaster to his fate. "That is where you might be wrong."

"You know something?"

"I fear you will not like it, human."

He knew then what the Dragon King was suggesting. "You want me to go and seek out the gnome."

"Insanity!" Xabene, who had kept quiet since their arrival, mostly because the reptilian monarch had stared her down almost immediately, dared step toward the massive figure lying before them. Benton Lore and several guards readied their weapons. While Wellen could not fault their loyalty, he did find it hard to think that *they* could possibly protect the Dragon King better than he himself could. What were swords and spears compared to *one* paw?

"I merely offered the choice, female," snarled Green. The enchantress, staring up at his open jaws, stepped back behind the dubious protection of Wellen's body. "I feel that Master Bedlam would have wanted to know regardless."

"Thank you, yes." The idea of returning to the field and seeking out the hermitic gnome, a creature who had baffled and foiled would-be conquerors for as long as anyone could remember, appeared ludicrous on the surface. It also appeared ludicrous below the surface.

And yet . . .

"Shade might be dead," Xabene reminded him, seeing the calculating look on his visage. "Could he possibly hold on for so long?"

He remembered the rolling thunder again. If the shadowy warlock was dead, however, why were the Lords of the Dead not moving? Surely they still wanted Wellen. There was also Xabene. He doubted that they would leave her be.

It was no use mulling it over and over. The explorer knew what his decision was already. He had to know. He had to *try.* "How can I do what no one else has in all these centuries? How can I gain entrance to the gnome's citadel?"

The burning eyes of his host lowered. "That, I fear, I do not know. I cannot even ssssay how you might find the curssssed place!"

"Then why bring it up?" Xabene asked, her voice and stance mocking.

"Because I *am* in debt to the gray one!" The Dragon King would say no more about that. "And if I knew of a way to send mysssself to hissss . . . his aid, I would."

"Wellen, listen to me!" The raven-tressed woman turned to him so that they faced each other. She moved close, too close for his peace of mind, and said, "It would be madness to put yourself in the claws of Purple. While he is a lover of knowledge, like this one, he lacks any care for humanity. As long as you are useful to him, you stay alive! Become useless and you perish!"

"She is correct in what she says."

He knew that, but it made no difference. Somehow, he had to find a way. Wellen silently pondered his own abilities, physical and otherwise, and tried to find something that would aid him. There was not much. He was a researcher, a would-be explorer, a man of books who lived for knowledge but did not always use it to his benefit. Wellen admitted to himself that he knew facts, not the world. It was not an entirely shameful thing. Even now, the thought of merely conversing with the gnome, learning a few of the things the master of the citadel had learned, exchanging knowledge . . .

Exchanging knowledge?

Would it work?

The others, even the Dragon King, had waited in silence, seeing that this was an inner struggle on which everything here hinged. Wellen smiled at Xabene, thanking her for what he was certain was true concern, then turned so that he faced Lore and his monarch, too.

"I think I have a plan."

"Indeed?" The lord of the Dagora Forest lowered his tremendous head. Benton Lore looked skeptical, but that was the way prime ministers and major-domos were supposed to look as far as Wellen was concerned.

"What can you tell me about the gnome?"

Green acceded to his second. "Lore?"

The pepper-haired soldier thought. "There is not much, my lord. No one knows much about him. If he has a name, it has never reached the ears of a talespinner. Legend says that it is the same gnome, that he is immortal, but I find that hard to believe."

"What about Shade?" Xabene could not help asking slyly. "Shade is Shade. He is an entirely different matter."

"Of *course."*

The commander went on. "Now and then it's claimed he is seen in human settlements. I have even heard he appears in the aeries of the Seekers or, more doubtful, the underworld dwellings of the imaginary Quel."

"They are not imaginary," Wellen commented, recalling the massive, armored monsters.

"No?" The Dragon King was interested in pursuing the subject, but held back while Lore continued.

"No one knows what he does when he appears. He is seen and then not seen."

Wellen scratched his chin. "What sort of people have seen him?"

"My spies, but I assume they are not who you mean. Learned folk for the most part. People whose word I can trust in this matter. There have been others, some trustworthy, some not, but the majority are as I said."

"I think he must love knowledge," the scholar commented. He knew that his idea might be foolhardy, but no more than some of those ideas attempted already. How many more ridiculous plots had been hatched over the millennia as desperation grew among those seeking the dragon tome and its owner?

"What do you propose?" Lore asked, his doubts in whatever Wellen had planned quite evident.

"Something simple and straightforward, but it still required knowing *where* the citadel is."

"I think . . . there may be a way," Xabene interjected. She did not want to speak, but if Wellen intended to seek out the gnome again, everyone knew that she would go with him. Therefore, it behooved her to increase their chances of success as much as possible.

"And what might that be, female?" asked the Dragon King. He was as doubtful of her suggestions as Benton Lore had been of whatever plan Bedlam had come up with.

The enchantress grew thoughtful. "I'd rather not say until I've had a chance to try it. There is a problem, though."

"Of course."

"Not one beyond the skill of the enterprising Commander Lore, however," she added, smiling knowingly at the officer. "I need you to gather grass from the region where the structure rested. Grass and cloth for weaving."

"Grass?" Lore was incredulous.

"You shall have whatever you desire, female," the reptilian patriarch interrupted. His nostrils flared, sending tiny clouds of smoke flying. "But I shall expect some results. Your skills are not what they used to be."

Xabene was more confident now, despite the polite reminder of her present status. "If you can get me what I need today, than two days from now should be sufficient to find out if I'm correct, Your Majesty. What I hope to do doesn't require much sorcery. Just concentration, cunning, and some talent for *weaving."* She looked at her hands in disgust. "Something I thought I'd never have to do again."

"And you, Wellen Bedlam," the Dragon King said. "Is there anything beyond the usual preparations that you will need for this undertaking?"

He could think of only one thing. "Luck."

Green chuckled. The sound echoed. "That, I am afraid, is a treasure likely beyond even the gnome."

Perhaps because of the task Xabene had set before him, Benton Lore had been determined to retrieve the grass himself. He presented her with his catch only two hours after the audience with the Green Dragon. The major-domo's eyes dared the enchantress to tell him that he had failed in any way. Xabene, however, indicated she was quite satisfied with the bundle of wild grass. She took it and other materials she had requested to her chamber, where some of the other human servants had set up a device to aid her in her weaving. With it, the enchantress promised that even with her rusting skills would be able to finish the project by nightfall. Wellen was almost certain that she actually looked forward to the work, if only to keep her mind off of her former masters.

The explorer's own plans were so simple that he had much time on his hands. Part of that time he spent with the Dragon King, who more and more became simply a fellow scholar and not an emerald-scaled leviathan who could have swallowed him whole. The drake lord told him more about the Dragonrealm and how the Dragon Kings ruled it.

There were thirteen kings and twenty-five or so dukes. The truth as to their origins was lost to the drakes; as far as most were concerned, the past really did not matter. It was where the Green Dragon differed from most of his brethren. "The past matters very greatly. We are but the most recent monarchs of this land. I do not think, human, that I am remissss in believing that our predecessorssss also thought that they would rule forever."

It was a sobering thought even to the human. He thought of his own race and the ever-growing menace of the Sons of the Wolf back home. Most thought the raiders were a temporary menace, but Wellen sometimes wondered.

As she had promised, Xabene did finish the weaving portion of her plan. The enchantress forbid anyone to touch or even look at her work, but not because she was embarrassed about its quality. With her meager magic, the sorceress-turned-weaver had instigated the next step, which would take all night to complete itself and was so sensitive to outside influence that even Bedlam, with his limited abilities, might disturb it.

The night passed so uneventfully that Wellen, unable to believe it, found he still could not sleep. Again, the sounds around him made him think of either Shade or the Lords of the Dead. Sleep finally did come, but then his dreams were haunted by cloth-enshrouded specters and rotting ghouls that slowly stalked him.

Morning, as horribly quick as it came, was a blessing by comparison.

Xabene remained ensconced in her chambers. What she was doing was still a mystery, since she had forbidden even Wellen to enter, but the smell of melting wax wafted from the entranceway. Feeling rather useless, again, he decided to see if he could convince the Dragon King to teach him how to bring his abilities to the surface and use them with some consistency. The idea had originally come to him because of the constant nagging in his head. His premonitions could not cope with dragons nearby, even if those creatures were either indifferent or, in the case of the monarch himself, fairly friendly. It was especially irritating this morning.

The dragon, however, had been reluctant so far to instruct him. As with many things, he had not said why. Wellen, who had seen few other drakes during his stay here, had an idea why. Making use of humans was one thing. While Bedlam knew that Benton Lore was very important to the leviathan and even respected by the Green Dragon's clans, part of that respect was due to the knowledge that he was fiercely loyal to his lord. He had been born and raised in one of the human settlements and considered it *as* much his land as his lord's.

The scholar, on the other hand, was an outsider. Not merely someone from a neighboring kingdom, but from a land beyond the control of any Dragon King. He was an enigma and, as Wellen had discovered, the drakes disliked, perhaps even *feared,* enigmas.

A guard met him in the tunnel just a few yards from his destination. "Your presence is requested by His Majesty."

"I was just going to him."

The guard insisted on leading him back the short distance. Protocol was protocol even in the kingdoms of the Dragon Kings.

Raising his head, the emerald behemoth acknowledged the human's arrival. "Master Bedlam. So good of you to come so quickly."

"I was on my way to see you when your guardsman found me."

"Then you heard."

"Heard?" Wellen's hopes rose. "Shade's returned?"

"Alas, no. This concerns an intruder captured in the eastern edge of my forest. A most unique human."

"And how does that concern me?"

The dragon's mouth curled into a toothy smile. "He claims to know you."

"Know me?" Wellen tried to recall who had been left in charge of the *Heron's Wing*. With all that had happened, however, he could not even summon up a distinct face, much less a name. "Who?"

'Riming his head, the dragon commanded, "You may bring the creature in."

Two guards stepped from a side corridor into the cavern chamber. Between them was one of the last people that the explorer had ever thought to see again.

"Asaalk!"

"Master Bedlam, would you so kindly please tell these two that I am friend, not foe?" The blue man partially turned so that Wellen could see the ropes that bound his arms back.

"You do know thissss . . . this creature?" The drake lord was visibly amused by the northerner's blue skin.

"I do, Your Majesty. He is likely the only other survivor of the column, unless, of course, some made it back to those waiting for us." The hopeful explorer looked to Asaalk for confirmation.

"Alas, I do not know," Prentiss Asaalk replied with great sadness. "Until yesterday, I was a prisoner of the beast who rules the land to the east, yes!"

"The Purple Dragon?"

"The Lord Purple, yes. I was not laughing, either, despite his peculiar appearance. He is not a forgiving master."

"He is not," agreed the Green Dragon, interjecting at this point. "It issss a wonder you succeeded to escape!"

Prentiss Asaalk bowed. "Master Bedlam will tell you that I can be enterprising when I need to be, yes?"

Wellen nodded. Deep down, he was sorry that it had not been Yalso who had survived, although he knew that could not have ever been the case, having witnessed the captain's death himself. He was ashamed that he was less thrilled by Asaalk's survival than he would have been if the mariner had walked through the door. The blue man had probably gone through at least as much hell as he had.

The huge dragon nodded to the guards. From their faces, they were not that pleased to release the blue man, but when their master commanded they obeyed.

"My great thanks, Your August Majesty!" Asaalk rubbed his arms where rope marked had formed.

"In gratitude, you will tell us all, in detail, of your captivity and your escape."

"Only too gladly!" With gusto, Prentiss Asaalk talked about being thrown from his horse and stumbling his way north. Twice he had thought that the dragon was coming for him, but both times it veered away. The northerner, weaponless, had nevertheless continued on bravely to the north. There were incidents, but his skills of survival had always come through for him in the end.

Until he had been spotted by servants of the Purple Dragon. His strength depleted, the northerner had been easily captured. Asaalk was taken before the drake lord himself and only quick thinking had saved his life. He had immediately discerned that here was a beast who admired knowledge and gathered it to him as if it were gold.

"And what did you have to offer him?" the Green Dragon interrupted.

"I told him of my homeland and of the place I came from. I . . . embellished a bit for him, yes, in order to keep his interest." The blue man glanced at Bedlam. "You, I think, would have done the same."

Wellen nodded.

Asaalk skimmed through his captivity, something the scholar could not blame him for doing. It could not have been a pleasant time. Escape had come by accident. He had been fitted with a magical collar to keep him under control, but after a couple of days, he had discovered that the control was weakening. His probing fingers came across a crack that had formed when they had sealed the device around his neck.

"By the end of the third day, it threatened me no more. I wasted no time, yes. When my chance came, I *walked* out of their lives like a cat." The rest of his tale the blue man summed up in a few sentences. He had headed west, knowing from information he had gathered that here he might find sanctuary. "And what do I find, but a face so familiar to me! This is fate, yes?"

The northerner's exaggerated speech pattern made Wellen wince. He was certain by now that Asaalk's shifting from one manner of speech to another was calculated. Now and then, the blue man might slip, but for the most part, he seemed to purposely change. Why he continued to do so was something the scholar doubted he wanted to know about. Perhaps now that he was safe again, the blue man's ambitions were returning. Did Asaalk think he could toy with the Dragon King?

It hardly mattered for now, Bedlam reminded himself. What Prentiss Asaalk chose to do was up to him. Wellen had his own path to follow.

The northerner apparently did not think so. He strode up to the shorter man, clasped him on the shoulders, and bellowed, "It is good to see you again, yes! I thought you dead! Now, the two of us can leave this place together and return home!"

"Home?" Once, he had planned to try and start a colony here, one that would not have to deal with the machinations occurring across the sea. That idea had died a lamented death with the unfortunates in the column. "How can we return? The *Heron's Wing is. . ."*

"Is still anchored off the shore where we left it. It has not been so long since we departed, has it?"

It had not been, but Wellen had assumed that the rest of the expedition had either departed in haste or been taken by the minions of Purple. "It's still there?"

"Before my escape,"—here Asaalk gave him a theatrical impression of craftiness—"I gained access to a device that could study most every region of the cursed purple one's kingdom, including the shore."

"Ssssuch a device is known to me," Green interrupted. "All of us control such artifacts. There are other methods available assss well."

Home! It almost seemed too good to be true! "Could we see the ship from here?"

"That issss doubtful. While we may call one another *brethren,* each of ussss . . . each of us guards our domain very carefully. Not that we do not have our spies, of course. Finding out about this vessel is another concern, however. Purple is particularly jealous at the moment, what with his prize stolen, and so he has stepped up his defenses. Perhaps after a time I will be able to overcome his spells. It would take many days of work."

"We can't afford to wait," Wellen reminded him. "Shade can't afford to wait. As soon as Xabene completes her work, we have to move." Even now, it was probably too late. Yet, he still could not believe that Shade was dead.

Asaalk listened with great attentiveness. "Please. What is it you speak of? Who is this Xabene?"

"I'm Xabene." The enchantress was standing by the entrance to the Green Dragon's imperial chamber. How long she had stood there, Wellen did not know. Somehow, she had found yet another form-enhancing outfit, again black, but this time it was a little more practical. Still a gown, yet it was sturdier, more able to combat the elements and plant life.

She was no less desirable and she likely knew it.

The lengthy northerner eyed her with open appreciation. He shook his head and said to Wellen, "Here I struggle and you have found this one! All adventures should be so treacherous!"

"Oh, it was . . . for both of us." The enchantress gave him a winning smile, which made Bedlam scowl. She then smiled at Wellen and joined him, giving clear indication to Prentiss Asaalk where her interests lay.

"Human relations are always sssso amusing," the reptilian monarch baldly stated, "but there are other, more pressing, concerns. How goes your task, female?"

The enchantress did not take kindly to the drake lord's general refusal to acknowledge that she had a name. "It goes well, dragon. I have to return in an hour and begin the next stage." She had been up for hours already, but fatigue was not evident. Sorcery gave Xabene life where nothing else could. "After the next stage, we just have to let it sit until it is ready."

"And when will that be?"

"Tomorrow sometime." She held her head high. "As I promised. It should function perfectly for our purposes. I could, of course, do more if I had the time."

"What is it we speak of?" Asaalk wanted to know. Wellen saw no harm in telling him. "A way of tracking down an elusive building."

"You jest."

"Did the Dragon King Purple never speak of the gnome?" The northerner nodded. "There was talk of such a creature and his sanctum, yes. For a time, I was questioned, but I knew nothing. What does this have to do with a building that . . . *hides?*"

"It vanished. I was standing almost as close to it as I am to you."

"Aaaah! This explains much, yes! Small wonder they did not expend so much effort on me! I know of the value that the Dragon King put on the place. If it is gone, he would be very furious."

The Green Dragon chuckled at that. "He issss, indeed, human! He would rather his get all be slaughtered than lose the gnome."

"It is a book he wants, I think."

Green's more vicious counterpart had evidently told Asaalk more than Wellen had first imagined. "That's right. A book."

"And you also want this book?"

The scholar was saved from trying to explain by Xabene, who cryptically said, "Among other things, if possible."

Prentiss Asaalk seemed to measure Wellen. "And you plan to go to this place then? You plan to risk the evil of the land's monarch?"

"I do."

"I have not found you only to lose you again!" The blue man put a companionable hand on the explorer's shoulder. Wellen tried not to wince at the strength Asaalk used when he squeezed. "Then *I* must go with you!"

"That won't be necessary," Xabene blurted.

"But it will! I must see to it that Master Bedlam here survives to return home and claim his glory!"

DRAGON TOME

The enchantress grew rigid and glanced at Wellen. She did not appear to like it when the blue man spoke of him departing. The thought had been discussed on and off, but no one had truly believed he would be leaving. Until Asaalk's return, it had been assumed that there was no longer a vessel waiting for him. Without a good ship, the explorer was trapped here. Now, however, it appeared he had a definite means of escape. Whether he made use of it was up to Wellen.

Prentiss Asaalk was not going to back down. Bedlam knew the man well enough to realize that. It might be that the northerner *would come* in handy. They could hardly go marching in with Benton Lore and his soldiers and expect the gnome to listen. More important, they could hardly expect the dragon Purple to ignore a small army. A diversion had been planned by the lord of the Dagora Forest, but this would only work if it was more noticeable than the truth. Three or four people riding swiftly and shielded by some spell of the Green Dragon would have a better chance of avoiding detection. If one of those people, Prentiss Asaalk, knew something about the workings of Purple's kingdom, it might increase their chances. While the Green Dragon was the best source of information, they could hardly bring him along.

"All right," Wellen told him, trying not to sigh in resignation. He turned to Xabene, but she was finding ways to avoid his eyes. The time was coming for the two of them to ask and answer some questions for one another.

It may be that the Dragon King saw some of this, though it was more likely he had his own questions and answers to discuss. "Human," he said to Asaalk. "These guards will take you to a place where you may feed and rest. I have things that I must discuss with Master Bedlam. You will be summoned when your presence is required."

The northerner bowed and obediently followed his guards out. Wellen knew that Asaalk did not like being dismissed like that, but protesting to a dragon was utter foolishness.

When it was certain that the northerner was far enough away that he could not possibly hear them converse, the Dragon King asked, "You trust this peculiar-skinned human, Master Bedlam?"

"I do." He was basing his assumption on pure conjecture; with his head throbbing as it was, Asaalk could have been ready to murder him and he would not have known. Still, the two of them shared a bond. They were outsiders in a mad world.

Green tilted his head to one side and called out, "You may enter now, Benton Lore."

The black man stepped in from one of the outer corridors. "Yes, Your Majesty."

"You are certain, Wellen Bedlam, that you might trust this man?"

"I am . . . I *think* so, anyway." What were they driving at? What was wrong with Prentiss Asaalk? From Xabene's perplexed expression, he gathered she did not understand, either. Disliking the man in general was one thing, but sinister mysteries was another.

"Lore, tell him what you ssssensed."

The pepper-haired warlock looked at the curious duo and calmly reported, "Nothing."

Wellen shrugged. "So what then is the problem? If you sensed nothing amiss, then why should—"

"That was not what I said," Lore interrupted. "I said I sensed *nothing.* Your companion is magically blank to me."

"Asssss he isss to *me,"* added the leviathan.

"I do not understand."

The reptilian monarch smiled grimly, his toothy smile, as ever, making Wellen uneasy. "What Lore seeks to say, is that as far as the blue-skinned one is concerned, we do not feel his presence on a magical level."

"He does not exist," completed Lore. "Bodily, yes, but the man you call Prentiss Asaalk is not altogether *human.*"

Chapter Fifteen

Wellen spent several hours with Prentiss Asaalk, but unlike the Green Dragon and Benton Lore, not once did he sense anything amiss. Asaalk seemed a bit more flamboyant than he recalled, but not enough that the scholar could interpret the difference as anything significant. Still, Wellen was willing to think about what his host had said. The Dragon King was of the opinion that Asaalk might be a spy of sorts for the Purple Dragon. It might not be the blue man at all, but rather something or someone made to resemble him. Bedlam was therefore careful about what he discussed with the possible double and regretted that the subjects of Xabene's work and the gnome had come up.

In order to keep everything seemingly normal, Asaalk had been given one of the chambers near those of Wellen and the enchantress. The guards, however, were tripled in strength. No one informed Asaalk that there had ever been a change in numbers.

Day had passed into the night, although that was not a simple thing to realize in the perpetually lit caverns. Wellen first knew it from the exhaustion that threatened to overtake him. A short conversation with Lore had verified the lateness of the hour. Asaalk had already retired and his chamber was carefully watched. No one wanted a repeat of the attack by the Lords of the Dead. The Green Dragon was very certain that this was a ploy set up by his counterpart to the southeast and not the necromancers. The style was identifiable, the leviathan had informed him, even if the plot was not one of Purple's most cunning. Its flaws had been spotted almost instantly by the master of the Dagora Forest.

The Green Dragon intended to turn that ploy against its originator.

"He thinks we do not suspect that this creature is possibly not the real human. The frustration of losing the gnome has made him act in too much hasssste!" The reptilian monarch had greatly enjoyed his counterpart's gross error.

Wellen was not so confident. He could not help wondering if there was more to the situation than they knew. Had the other Dragon King grown *that* careless?

The scholar paused when he reached Xabene's chamber. A thick curtain covered the entranceway, but he could tell it was dark within. Wellen had wanted to talk to her, but waking the enchantress would not start the conversation off in the correct mood. This had to be done just right.

He continued on to his own chamber, nodded to a couple human guards . . . did the rest of Green's clan have *nothing* to do with humans? . . . and brushed aside the curtain as he entered.

Xabene lay casually across his bed, waiting for him. She smiled slyly at his dumbfounded expression. "I had to talk to you, Wellen Bedlam."

Her formal use of his name did not bode well. He strode to the bed and stood before her, arms crossed. With languid movements, the well-formed sorceress rose and faced him.

"Still untrusting?"

"I trust you." He stepped back when she came too near. Xabene laughed lightly at his reaction.

"I can see that you do. Don't worry, I won't come any closer than this . . . unless you decide to let me."

"What do you want?"

She folded her own arms and turned away. Wellen could not help but follow every detail of her movement. The ebony-haired enchantress had resumed her role of seductress. Bedlam was not certain whether he welcomed the return or not.

"I've wanted many things in my life. Most of them were beyond me before I sold myself to the Lords of the Dead for power. When I was finally able to gather those things, I discovered that they were not what I had expected. There were always other things, though, so I was not unhappy so long as I had those goals, those treasures, to pursue."

Xabene turned around again. Wellen broke the momentary silence to ask, "What does that have to do with me? Am I supposed to be like those treasures? You no longer have to toy with me for the necromancers; does that mean it's time to turn elsewhere?"

In response, she took hold of Wellen and kissed him hard. Like a candle's flame abruptly doused, the world around the scholar winked out of existence. His world was now the woman in his arms. Shade, the gnome, the Lords of the Dead, the Dragon Kings . . . they seemed such distant things that he was almost tempted to believe he had dreamed them.

When they finally separated, Xabene once more had a calculating look in her eye, but this time Bedlam had a better idea of what it concerned. "I still don't believe in love at first sight," she said. "But I do believe that two people can find that they are meant for one another. I was bothered by that thought when I first noticed how I reacted to you. You struck something within me that should have been as dead as . . . " Xabene forced the unspoken thought away. "Let's just say that I knew I was yours even when I fought not to be."

"I'm not certain I understand some of that."

"It doesn't matter, but something else does. You know what I was like, Wellen; you know what I've done. Can you accept me as I am now?"

He blinked. "I thought I had."

"Kissing me doesn't necessarily answer that. I've done far more with men before and neither side thought of love."

"Are you the same Xabene as then?"

"Only in form."

"You almost sound like Shade," the scholar commented. "My answer still holds. If what I've seen these past few days is the true you . . . and not some playacting like both you and Asaalk seem to enjoy . . . then I have no intention of giving you up."

"What about your vessel?"

Wellen had forgotten about that. "If it exists, which is doubtful, it has room for one more." He grimaced. "It has room for *many* more now. More likely, the Dragonrealm is now *my* home."

She took hold of him again. "Do you still intend your madness with the gnome?"

"I do. I owe Shade that much."

Xabene sighed. "I suppose I do too." The enchantress kissed him briefly, then began to lead him toward the bed. "If we are destined to walk arm-in-arm into the maw of Purple, then, let us do it as one, not two."

"Xabene . . . "

A finger to his lips silenced him. "No argument, please." She smiled and though her smile was seductive, it was not calculating, this time. "After all, tomorrow may be too late."

He could not argue that no matter how much he might have wanted to. Tomorrow was all too likely to end in disaster . . . and one or both of them would probably be dead.

The blame, much like the choice, would be his.

All too soon it was the next day. With much enthusiasm, Xabene revealed her handiwork to Wellen and the others. There was no way of avoiding the inclusion of Prentiss Asaalk, or whatever or whoever the blue figure might actually be, from the gathering. If Asaalk was other than he appeared, to exclude him was to warn the one who had sent him that the plot had been uncovered. The Green Dragon did not care for events to occur that way.

At Lore's order, two servants had brought a large, oak table into the cavern chamber so that the enchantress could better display her handiwork. The results, needless to say, were curious enough to bring even the Dragon King to silence.

"Thissss issss a tapestry of ssssorts," the leviathan finally stated.

"It is," she responded. "Given more time, I could have made it much more elaborate, but that would've probably taken years."

"Time we do not have," Wellen agreed. If this worked, they would likely be leaving soon after. The Dragon King wanted everything perfectly coordinated. It was possible that the citadel would move again, too. The nearer they were when they did their final check of its location, the less chance they had of riding fruitlessly back and forth across the plains.

"How does it work?" Asaalk asked rather eagerly.

The tapestry was fairly simple. Three feet in length and two across, it barely fit what Wellen would have thought the size requirements of a tapestry. He recalled the huge, intricate cloths hanging in the great houses and the university corridors. This . . . this seemed more something to wrap a small baby in.

Its pattern was also simple, although time, again, had played a hand in that. The explorer recognized a crude representation of the region where the gnome's five-sided citadel had stood until recently. The material used to weave that section was different from the rest. He suspected it was the grass Xabene had requested. That she had been able to make use of it in her weaving indicated that some of her sorcery still remained.

The hills and grasslands were easy to identify, but one mark puzzled him. A five-pointed star. He assumed it must represent the citadel, but it stood far away from the field, almost as if it were part of some other illustration not yet complete.

Wellen repeated Asaalk's question.

"The best way to explain it is to show you," Xabene replied. She turned the tapestry toward her, then pulled a small crystal from a pouch on her waist. Nothing their eyes, she held up the piece. "I used this in an attempt to spy on the gnome while he worked. I also used this and. .." Her eyes lit up and she rummaged through the pouch. Xabene retrieved a tattered notebook and thrust it toward Wellen. ". . . and *this* to search for you."

He looked at the ragged object. It was his notebook. The scholar felt a momentary rush of affection, as if a favored pet had been returned to him. The journal was all he really had left from his once-peaceful life.

"It occurred to me," the enchantress continued, "that I could use the crystal in another way." So saying, Xabene lowered the crystal onto the waxy star. She held it in place for several seconds, closing her eyes during that period and whispering something to herself. When she opened them again, there was an intense eagerness.

"What did you do?" Prentiss Asaalk asked. Everyone, including the Dragon King, had turned their attention to the sorceress during her brief display.

She glanced down at the tapestry, smiled widely, and indicated that they, too, should study her creation.

The star was no longer situated under the crystal. It now marked a spot in the northwestern region outlined on the tapestry.

Xabene leaned back and put her hands on her hips, pride at her accomplishment radiating from her. *"There* is where the gnome is!"

"So simple!" Wellen marveled. He touched the star lightly, almost afraid he would nudge it away. Examination proved, however, that it was as much a part of the illustration as the plains were.

"Not so simple. I had to chip the crystal to make this work. There are fragments incorporated in the wax. Only because of them does the tapestry work."

One observer, however, was not so impressed with the results and what they indicated. "That cannot be! From all that my ssssourcessss have informed me, there hassss been no ssssign of the citadel! It doessss not ssssit there! Not sssso closssse!"

"It must!" The enchantress looked ready to fight to protect her success. She had proven that her abilities were worth something even without the added power that the Lords of the Dead had given to her. One Dragon King was not going to make that success a failure. "I planned it all out carefully! If the star is there, then that's where the building is!"

"Then where issss it, female? Floating high in the ssssky? I think one of my cousins would have sssseen it there!"

Wellen's eyes narrowed as he considered the suggestion. The sky, obviously, was not a proper choice, but what if the gnome had traveled in the opposite direction? He recalled how the Quel had burst from the ground. They *lived* down there; why not the gnome?

The short scholar leaned over the area where the star was located. "He's taken it below and shielded it."

"What?" Prentiss Asaalk stepped back as if struck. Not the reaction Wellen would have expected from the true northerner, but it was possible that Asaalk, out of his depth now, was truly surprised.

"What do you ssssspeak . . . speak of, Master Bedlam? The cursed gnome has taken it *under* the surface?"

"Why not? Is it beyond him?"

"Hardly! Yet . . . " The Green Dragon could come up with no argument against Bedlam's suggestion. Xabene was visibly grateful for his quick thinking.

Pressing on, Wellen added, "We have to move as quickly as possible. You were the one who first said that. He could send it elsewhere at any time. An entire army might waste weeks hunting him, even if he's only limited to the plains . . . which we do *not* know is a certainty."

The Dragon King shifted. His claws scraped at the rocky surface of the cavern floor. "Below . . . and *moving*. Hissss skillssss never cease to amaze me!"

"A question, Master Bedlam," the blue man said. "How will you speak with the gnome even if you do find where he is located? He will be far underground, yes? It will make for difficult hearing."

"I doubt if the gnome pays any less attention to the outside world now that he has moved under the earth. Despite his hermitic existence, he's proved to be very interested in what is going on around him. That's one of the reasons I hope to contact him this time."

"And assss you indicated, human, time issss a great factor." The drake lord considered matters. He seemed to come to a decision he found both daring and dismaying. The emerald leviathan studied the scholar for several breaths, then finally asked, "Are you and yours prepared to leave within the hour?"

The Dragon King very much wanted to finish this, but Wellen thought that Green might be pushing ahead too swiftly. Wellen would have preferred to leave after nightfall, thinking that quick enough, but as he had realized before, one did not argue with a drake.

Bedlam exchanged looks with Xabene. She nodded, seeing the inevitable.

"We can be ready," he said with confidence.

"Good! Lore."

The black man appeared from nowhere. How long had he been lurking nearby? "Your Majesty?"

"Have the animals been readied?"

"I ordered men to make them ready more than an hour ago . . . in anticipation."

"Sssssplendid."

"We are to ride?" questioned Asaalk. "Not teleport?"

"Not until late in the journey. Teleportation works best when one is familiar with the region." Commander Lore's bored look was a mask; Wellen knew he did not care to stay in the northerner's presence any longer than necessary. "There has been no reason to remember that area until now; it was like any other part of the region. With the exception of a few masters, such as Shade, most spellcasters are better off using line of sight for such unfamiliar places."

"We would need to see where we are going, yes?"

"Exactly." No longer needing to look at the blue man, Benton Lore awaited further commands.

The truth was that there would be no teleporting at all. Neither Wellen nor Xabene was capable of casting the spell, but that was not the reason why. After all, Lore, who was to follow behind in order to keep their backs covered from possible treachery, did have the capability. The Green Dragon, however, had pointed out that excessive spellcasting would only attract the attention of his fellow monarch. A small group of riders had a better chance, especially if Purple was intentionally looking for the telltale signs of teleportation.

Asaalk was the reason they hinted at utilizing teleportation at all. Whether he was not truly the blue man or was willingly serving the other drake lord, the figure beside them was not to be trusted as far as the Green Dragon was concerned. False information fed to him might make its way to Purple. That would give them two distractions. At the very least, it would certainly keep the blue man at a disadvantage.

Their efforts might be for nothing; the Purple Dragon by no means could see everything that went on in his domain. Wellen and the others could feasibly reach their destination, succeed or not at contacting the gnome, and return without any incidence of danger.

No one was willing to believe it would be so easy.

Wellen wanted to leave Prentiss Asaalk behind, but the master of Dagora Forest would not have that. Drakes were apparently fond of overdone subterfuge and the Green Dragon reveled in it. The scholar was certain only disaster would come of it in the end.

The drake lord shifted, bringing everyone's attention back to the situation at hand. "The time for talk is over, then. Lore, see what activity occurs in my brother's domain. Master Bedlam, you will ready yourself and see to it that your companions are ready." Hesitation, then, "Would that I could be there when he finally realizes he has been tricked and that *we* have gained access to what he, the Lords of the Dead, and all their predecessors failed to capture!"

Feeling uncomfortable with the Dragon King's overconfidence, Bedlam reminded him, "The plan is hardly foolproof; the gnome may laugh at me from within his citadel! I am only relying on the thought that in certain cases, he and I are of like mind."

"I have faith in you, human. Besides, as has been brought up more than once, nothing else has succeeded. Why not try *your* plan? At the most it can only fail!"

He was not certain whether the Dragon Lord was serious or not, but he could hardly ask. Wellen took one last look at the tapestry, exhaled sharply, and said, "Let's hope that *is* all that happens."

121

No one had to remind him of what failure by itself actually meant. Wellen and the others might still return to the forest, from there to continue on with their lives as best as possible. For Shade, however, it meant death sooner or later at the rotting hands of the Lords of the Dead.

That was, of course, assuming he was not dead already.

Prentiss Asaalk confronted him a short time later in the corridor by the former's chamber. Servants had taken what few things Wellen was going to carry and brought them ahead so they could be packed. The explorer had intended on trying to talk to the Green Dragon for the few minutes that still remained. There were details about the diversions he was uncertain about and wanted clarified.

"Wellen Bedlam, you and I must speak."

The scholar's throat tightened. "About what?"

"Please! Inside the room." Asaalk's voice was low and just a little uncertain.

After the necromancers' invasion, it was doubtful that anything could occur that Lore's soldiers would not respond to in a matter of seconds. Nonetheless, Wellen was somewhat leery about being alone with the blue man. "Perhaps we could talk later, when—"

"No! It must be now!" The massive northerner seemed to fill up the corridor. "Please, Master Bedlam!"

The intensity with which Asaalk spoke, moved, even *breathed*, made Wellen acquiesce. Nodding, he allowed the blue man to lead the way into the chamber. Asaalk had never struck him as a man who did things for no reason and if he needed to speak so urgently with Wellen, then it might do the scholar some good to listen. Perhaps some questions the Green Dragon had brought up would be answered. Still, the scholar did not consider himself a complete fool. As he followed the northerner in, Wellen put one hand on the hilt of the sword that he had convinced the Dragon King to let him wear.

Asaalk studied the chamber, possibly seeking magical eyes that might report his words to the drake lord even as he spoke them. Satisfied, the blue man finally talked.

"Master Bedlam, I must warn you about myself."

"Warn me?"

The blue man's eyes darted back and forth. "I spoke of escaping the collar put on me by the Dragon Purple, yes?"

"Yes."

"I did not escape that collar, my friend."

"But the marks . . . " At one point when they had last spoken alone, Prentiss Asaalk had shown him the marks left by the metal collar. They were purplish, scaly scratches. Wellen had been certain at the time that removing the collar must have been painful if it had caused these.

"Aaah . . . " Asaalk gave him a grim smile and fingered one of the scars. "These do not show where the collar was, but where the collar *is!* Like the building whose master has buried it, the cursed thing lies *beneath* the surface, yes! Beneath the skin!"

Without thinking, Wellen started to reach forward to touch the other's neck. Asaalk jerked away. "No! Only I may touch it! Anyone else's touch is agony! One of my captors put a hand to the back of my neck, yes, and I almost doubled over!"

"How is it you are able to tell me? That hardly seems like a thing that the Purple Dragon would neglect to prevent. He does not mark me as a simple tyrant."

"And he is not, no. I have some small magic of my own and I have my own indomitable will." He swelled with pride. "I am never totally beaten! I always strike back!" Prentiss Asaalk twitched then, moving like someone just whipped. The blue man deflated a bit. "The collar always fights to regain even that bit of ground from me. I fear that sooner or later it will triumph, yes. Yet, no one can remove the collar, save the Purple Dragon and he will do that only if I obey his commands—

"And what are those?"

"To bring you to him, of course."

"Me? In particular?" Wellen recalled standing before the pentagon and watching it vanish. Had the other Dragon King been observing and decided, like so many others had, that the would-be warlock was responsible? Wellen was beginning to wonder himself. Was he absolutely certain that the tingle he had felt had not originated from him? Absurd, yes, but still not entirely improbable. After all, he had not meant to bespell Shade, yet he had.

"You." The blue man seemed to bemoan this fact. "He has come to believe you must be here to steal the dragon tome from him . . . he is certain that it is his by right, yes."

"I only want to be left alone, to live in peace."

Asaalk shrugged. "But we cannot and now we must think of what to do."

"The Green Dragon might be able to do something."

"He cannot. I believe my accursed master, yes, when he says that he has planned for that, but"—suddenly, the crafty northerner's eyes narrowed—"could the gnome, do you think?"

Even from what little he knew about the short, squat figure, Bedlam thought it quite possible. "If he can do everything that's been hinted to me, then I think it's very possible that he can help you."

"That is good. If he cannot, I must face the wrath of the Dragon King. I assure you that he is not a forgiving creature, no."

Asaalk twitched again. Wordlessly, he stepped away from Wellen and turned his back to the scholar. The blue man's entire backside shook from effort. Bedlam purposely found other things to study, thinking that the struggling northerner deserved to preserve his pride. As much as he disliked many things about Prentiss Asaalk, he admired the blue man's spirit. Wellen was not so certain he could have been as strong under the circumstances.

At last, the blue man turned around. His countenance in no way betrayed his struggle with the pain Wellen had watched him go through. "You must let me come with you. I must speak to this little man."

The Green Dragon would forbid him doing that and Benton Lore would be with the trio to assure that the scholar obeyed. Still, if there was anything he could do to aid the blue man, Wellen knew he had to try. "I'll see."

"I can ask no more."

They heard the sounds of armored men marching through the tunnel. As the two of them turned to face the entranceway, a guard stuck his head inside. He pulled it back almost immediately. There was some muttering, then Commander Lore stepped in.

"Everything is prepared. We do not know what Purple himself is doing, but our eyes watch his lackey's every move. He seems to be waiting, nothing more."

"Which means your lord wants us to leave now."

"Unless there is still urgent need to complete other matters, Master Bedlam. It is for your own sake, I must point out. His Majesty does not desire to endanger you any more than necessary. He cares."

"How noble," Asaalk sneered. Wellen gave him a severe frown, warning him not to provoke the major-domo.

Lore's eyes flared, but his visage remained polite and cool, as it always was around the blue man. "Yes, very much so. The same could certainly not be said for most of his kind, especially the tyrant whose land you reenter."

The blue man said nothing.

Wellen stepped between them, pretending interest only in the coming quest. "Have you provided Xabene with a map case for the tapestry? We need to keep it clean and out of sight."

"I have." The dark-skinned officer nodded, his eyes acknowledging his understanding of why the scholar had interrupted. "Even now, she waits by the mounts."

"Good. Then we had best be on our way."

"As you desire." Lore stepped aside and, with a sweep of his arm, indicated that the two outsiders should depart first. Asaalk stalked out of the chamber immediately, with Wellen following close behind. *A good thing we won't be here any longer than necessary!* he thought. *Each time these two meet, they come closer to blows!*

Whether or not they succeeded, he was determined to help the blue man free himself of the Dragon King's deadly ring. Then, Asaalk would be encouraged to go somewhere, *anywhere,* that he might like. Wellen intended to spend some time discussing the history of the realm with the Green Dragon, but he could hardly do that if Asaalk remained with him. Xabene also had a say in the matter, a very essential say, and her dislike of the blue man's ways was more than obvious.

It occurred to Wellen that he was assuming they would all be returning. That was still in doubt even with the information that Prentiss Asaalk had provided him.

Their footfalls echoed throughout the corridor, a feature of the caverns that he had grown so accustomed to that he barely noticed anymore. That was why when Benton Lore stepped up beside him that the shorter man was surprised when the officer commented, "The echoes have always fascinated me."

"Oh?"

"Actually, the acoustics of this entire system of caverns must be experienced over a long period of time to fully understand their complexity. One hears so much." The commander's expression was entirely innocent.

That settled the question of whether the Dragon King knew what the two foreigners had discussed. Wellen did not reply, but he took it as a mark of the monarch's trust that he had even been given a hint.

Prentiss Asaalk, several steps ahead, scratched his throat at the sore marks.

When they reached the animals, Xabene was there. Her eyes, first slits when she spied Asaalk, lit up when Wellen entered the chamber. He returned her smile, but his attention was momentarily fixed on his surroundings. They stood in what was an organized and very well-kept stable. Row upon row of stalls attested to the great capacity of the place. Most of the stalls were empty, but a few held tall, ready animals. The party's mounts were already saddled and waiting.

"Tell me, commander," Wellen said, noting the walls and ceiling of the chamber. "Was this entire system carved out or did any of it exist before the coming of the drakes?"

"Much of it was as you see it, sirrah. Even this place. But there have been many ruling races in this land, as my lord made mention, and some of those used this place before. We have had to make few additions."

"A ready-made kingdom," Xabene commented. "I hope the next rulers appreciate it as much as your masters do."

"Your mounts await you," Benton Lore reminded them, the enchantress's comment diplomatically ignored. It was impossible to believe he did not think about who those rulers would be. The Green Dragon had already hinted that the human race was becoming more and more an influential force in the realm. The major-domo himself was part of that force, having almost gained a kingdom of his own from the looks of things. The human habitations of this cavern system had to nearly equal in size those of the drake clans unless the entire cave system was even more extensive than it seemed. With men like Benton Lore to lead the way, humanity was indeed gaining a stronger foothold, especially in this region.

Not all the Dragon Kings were likely to appreciate that as much as the Green Dragon did.

Lore watched in silence as they mounted their horses. Because of Prentiss Asaalk, he did not mention that he would be following, but Wellen knew that they would barely be beyond the cave entrance before the commander himself mounted. He felt a little better knowing that Lore would be behind them; in some ways, the efficiency of the man reminded him of the late, lamented Yalso. Recollections of the captain, both before and *after* his death, renewed Wellen's decision to go ahead with this lunacy. Unlike Yalso, Shade might not yet be beyond his ability to save.

"You will be led to the entrance," the officer informed them solemnly. "From there, you will be on your own. You have the maps I gathered for you and you have the tapestry. That should be all you need. Follow the timetable we agreed on and there should be no trouble. Lord Purple will be too busy with other matters to watch out for you."

"Let us hope so." Asaalk's whisper was loud enough for all of them to hear.

"May the Dragon of the Depths watch over you," the black man concluded.

Two soldiers on horseback joined them. One of them, a dark-skinned man he recognized from the initial patrol, saluted and said, "Master Bedlam, if you and yours will follow me."

They did as he requested, Wellen and Xabene riding alongside one another and the blue man a length behind them. After the trio came the other soldier. Lore was taking no chances.

From the torch-lit stable they entered a darkened tunnel. The soldiers were undaunted by this change, but Wellen disliked it. There was no complaint from Asaalk, however, and Xabene, more used to the night than the day, likely was at peace. Wellen wished he could adjust his eyes to the way they had been during his sojourn into the realm of the dead.

A tiny light blossomed in the distance, the entrance to the outside. Bedlam wanted to ride hard toward it in order to escape the darkness, but he was aware how that might appear to the others. They would reach the light before long, anyway.

Then their troubles would truly begin.

Chapter Sixteen

The gnome smiled as he watched his adversaries play their games. The flurry of activity beyond his domain had given birth to a new, typically remarkable idea and he looked forward to implementing it when the time came.

The time was very near. Only a short *distance* from him, in fact.

When the time chosen for the diversion came, they acted as planned. They rode with speed and determination, their course rechecked just prior to the appointed hour. The citadel was still in the northwestern region, so close to where they had waited that it seemed almost a shame they had waited at all. Yet, wait they had, for no one, with the possible exception of Prentiss Asaalk, wanted to go charging in until their chances were best.

Somewhere behind them, Benton Lore was supposedly keeping pace. There had

125

been no sign of the man, but the soldier was an expert at scouting . . . as he seemed to be expert at almost everything else.

Wellen's head, of course, pounded with dire warnings all the while. He needed no overly sensitive albeit consistent ability to tell him that he faced possible danger. He had known that from the first time the Dragon King had suggested this.

To the scholar's left, Prentiss Asaalk stared sullenly ahead. He had not forgiven them for their lack of trust, at least, that was what Wellen had decided. It was possible that would change if they were successful and the gnome showed them not only how to free Shade, but also how to rid the blue man of the magical collar just underneath his skin. The thought of the collar being there made Bedlam cringe every time he considered it; a fine but horrible piece of sorcery. He was amazed that anyone could live with such a thing attached, but the Dragonrealm probably held worse than that.

"It has to be just a short distance ahead!" shouted Xabene. "If we go too much farther, we'll be too much to the east!"

So far, there had been no sign of activity on the Purple Dragon's part. Wellen was both wary and relieved by that. True, the Green Dragon's deception was already at work, but from what he had heard of the master of this land, Bedlam could not help considering that this drake lord might not be so easily fooled.

Could it be he *wanted them* to locate the citadel for him? If so, how did the Dragon King think he was going to seize the prize? If the gnome deigned to speak to them, then they would surely be under some protection, as, of course, would be the tome everyone wanted so badly. If they failed, then Purple would be back where he started.

Benton Lore probably held the key. It would not have been surprising to learn that the lord of the Dagora Forest had held back a few plans even from Wellen. Not a betrayal, as Xabene or Asaalk might see it, but rather caution, for if the party did not know what else had been plotted, then it was doubtful anyone watching them would.

Raising a hand and slowing her mount, the enchantress cried out, "This is it! We're here!"

"Are you certain?" The blue man reined his horse to a stop. He peered around. "It all looks the same. I sense nothing, either."

"Let me look." She unrolled the tapestry. Wellen saw now another reason it was so small. Anything larger would have been cumbersome and nearly impossible to study while on horseback. Xabene glanced up several times, studied the landscape, then finally nodded. "If I'm correct, we're only about fifty feet from it."

"Which way?" Like Asaalk, Wellen could not see or sense anything that told him where the citadel might be buried. If they had not had the tapestry . . .

She rolled the magical item back up and placed it in the case Lore had given them. The enchantress then pointed to a spot to the southeast. "There. It lies somewhere just in front of us."

They dismounted. Bedlam experienced *a* sense of *déjà vu,* save that this time he was hoping that the gnome's stronghold would reappear.

"You know," the sorceress said quietly, looking somewhat ashamed, "the first time you came here, when the place vanished, it wasn't entirely by your choice."

"I wondered."

"I was told to put the desire into your mind and enforce it. Given a choice, I would have preferred not to, but they were adamant. You can see how well it worked."

"Are you suggesting that I might have been influenced again?"

"By the drake who plays at being your friend?" Xabene shrugged. "I'd say I wouldn't be surprised, Wellen, although I do think he likes you. That might save your life in the end if it happens to be true."

"Or not. I've already considered the things you mentioned now, though, and I think

I still would have come here. I owe Shade that, even if it's only to bring his body back."

She smiled sadly at him. "An idealist!"

"Worse. A dreamer." He did not try to explain the difference.

"Are we there yet?" asked the blue man, who had been trying all the while to find something, anything, that would lend credence to the tapestry's revelation.

Xabene took a few more steps, then stopped. "This should be good."

"Am I facing it?" Despite the danger of their situation, Wellen also feared the gnome's opinion of him if he happened to be facing the wrong direction. The wizened spellcaster's opinion was paramount, else he had not a chance of convincing the creature to hear him out.

"You should be. I'm sorry, but the tapestry was put together in quick fashion. As I said, if I'd had more time, I could have made it more elaborate."

"This will do."

"You are merely going to *talk?*" an incredulous Prentiss Asaalk spouted. "This is your masssster plan? This is to succeed where all other plans have failed?"

Wellen looked at him, trying not to think about how his own face must be turning red at the northerner's accusatory tone. "You knew that was what I planned."

"Yes, but I expected that . . . " The blue man trailed off. From his outburst, the scholar understood what Asaalk had left unsaid. Considering the distrust surrounding him, Asaalk had expected not to be told everything. That expectation had already been justified.

"Get on with it!" Xabene urged. "The longer we wait here the worse our chances."

Bedlam nodded. He reached down and removed the sword and scabbard he had been given in what he hoped was an obvious enough attempt to show the gnome he came in peace. Xabene stepped near, took the articles from him, and retreated again. Taking a deep breath, he organized his thoughts. "Master of the citadel, I know you by no name save 'gnome' but I hope you will hear me out this time. A plain and simple offer is what I bring. An exchange. I need your aid, your knowledge, to save a life and free another. I want nothing else from you. Your precious tome, what the Dragon King Purple and so many others have sought over the centuries, is none of my concern."

To one side, the enchantress wore a bitter mask. She had likely spent much of her service to the Lords of the Dead in pursuit of the very object he was telling the gnome he wanted no part of.

"In exchange, I can offer you only one thing. I come from a land beyond the seas east of here. My former home is one of only many, but I have spent my life, short as it is compared to your own, studying all those realms. You seem one forever searching for knowledge; I am the same. If you can aid me in my quest, a simple one for a spellcaster of your proven skill, then whatever I know I offer to share with you, scholar to scholar."

There was nothing more he could think of to say that would not make him sound like he was babbling. Wellen folded his arms and glanced Xabene's way again. She nodded her satisfaction. Prentiss Asaalk, a bit farther back, had eyes only for the patch of grassy ground before the shorter man. Wellen might have been invisible for all the interest the blue man had in him.

The scholar returned his own gaze to the still, innocuous- looking piece of field and waited.

Several minutes later, he was still waiting.

"We've failed," Xabene said at last, breaking the uneasy silence. "We'd better leave."

"Not yet."

"He won't respond, Wellen! We're all next to nothing to the gnome, even the Dragon Kings!" She stepped closer, intending to take his arm.

A powerful wind erupted in the grasslands Wellen watched. The startled sorceress stepped back.

The patch of grass shimmered, grew indistinct.

Asaalk muttered something that was lost in the roar of the unnatural wind.

The scant outline of a tall structure briefly formed before Wellen. He blinked, finally marking it down as wishful thinking when it did not rematerialize.

"Wellen, come away!"

"No! He musssst not!" shouted the blue man. The ferocity in his voice so snared Bedlam that he started to turn toward the northerner.

A vaguely recalled tingle coursed through his body. He stumbled back, but not too far. His head barely throbbed and that meant that he was not in any true danger from what was happening . . . at least, not at the moment.

With a crackle of thunder, the five-sided citadel of the gnome once more stood before him.

There was a difference this time.

A hole just large enough to admit the scholar marred the otherwise smooth, featureless side of the sanctum.

"We can enter!" Prentiss Asaalk raced toward the hole, which Wellen realized *was* an entrance, and tried to go through.

The wall sealed up just as he was about to put his hand into the opening.

The tall warrior pulled back his arm with a snarl. He pounded a fist against the blank wall and shouted, "This is the last trick! Open! Open or I shall tear this place down around you!"

"I doubt *that* threat means much to him," a more practical Xabene interjected. She had quickly grasped the situation. "Wellen, I think it's only meant for you."

"What?" Watching the fruitless pounding by Asaalk had made him think of something, but the notion faded like dew in the sunlight the moment the enchantress spoke. *Perhaps later,* he decided. "What did you say?"

"I think . . . " She put a hand against the wall. Her success was no better than that of the northerner. "I think you might be the only one allowed to go inside."

"It must be *all* of us!" Asaalk argued.

"We do not have a say in the matter. Only the gnome, and he's chosen Wellen alone."

"Me . . . but I cannot leave you two out here!"

"I don't like it either, but you can't pass this up! It's you alone or no one."

She was probably right, but he did not like the thought of the two of them alone. Not merely because of the danger around them, but the certainty that the longer Xabene and Asaalk were alone together, the more likely they would come to blows about something.

Xabene confronted the taller man. "You. Move."

Seething, Prentiss Asaalk nonetheless obeyed. His eyes, more narrow than Wellen recalled them, darted back and forth between the scholar and the treacherous wall.

The hole sprouted into existence, this time more directly aligned with where an anxious Wellen stood.

"See what I mean?"

He nodded. "I do, but it's all of us or none of us. I cannot leave you behind." He faced the inviting hole. "All of us . . . that's not too much to ask for! I will vouch for them!"

There was no reason for the eternal to do anything but laugh at his daring. Nonetheless, he was determined that his companions join him. Even if Prentiss Asaalk

128

was a spy for the Purple Dragon, certainly the gnome knew that already. With trepidation, Bedlam approached the gaping hole. It seemed to widen the nearer he came, as if seeking to accommodate him as well as possible. The way the stone, if that was what it was, shifted and flowed made him think of a gigantic maw opening to accept a meal. He wondered if the citadel was somehow alive, then tried quickly to drop the horrific thought as he ran out of distance between the structure and his body and discovered that his next step would take him inside.

One foot through. The hole remained still. It had not attempted to relieve him of his leg as part of him had secretly feared. Wellen leaned forward, planted his boot on the smooth, marble floor, and peered inside.

A blank corridor, impossibly long. He could not make out what was at the other end, although he assumed it was a doorway. The scholar recalled circling the pentagon and was certain that it had not been this lengthy. A trick of the eye? The citadel's master *was* a spellcaster of seemingly limitless ability. It could be real. Almost as an afterthought, he noticed a corridor on each side of him as well. For some reason, however, he did not give them the consideration that he gave the one in front.

He turned back to the others. "Inside. Quick."

The ancient mage might choose to crush his body in the very wall, but Wellen was willing to risk it. That the gnome had expressed interest in him at all meant that the mage might hesitate. The other two were of no consequence to the master of the citadel and he hoped they were hardly reason enough to send a certain presumptuous scholar to his gory death.

Asaalk removed his own weapons but held back, allowing Xabene to be the first. The enchantress, unarmed, walked up to the portal, but then hesitated at the threshold. Her fear was no mystery; she wondered if the hole would close as soon as she dared put a hand or foot through. This close to the goal her masters had set for her, the ivory-skinned sorceress was frozen.

Prentiss Asaalk solved the problem by *pushing* her through.

There was a collective gasp from Bedlam, the stumbling enchantress, and even an anxious Asaalk.

Nothing happened. Xabene continued across and then spun around, her eyes aflame and her hands twitching as if she sought to utilize what little strength remained to see that the blue man regretted his maneuver.

"Xabene!" the scholar hissed. "Remember where you are! For all our sakes!"

She did, and the knowledge drained her of the desire if not the anger. The seething woman relaxed as best she could and muttered, "I won't forget that, blue man!"

"I had faith," the northerner replied in cool tones. He dismissed her as if she had ceased to exist. Asaalk stepped calmly through the hole, gazed down the corridor, then turned to wait for Wellen.

The apprehensive explorer, moving with a speed enhanced by a well-honed sense of mistrust, finished crossing the unnerving portal, then stood transfixed in the corridor by the sheer thought of being inside what so many had fought fruitlessly to enter. Here was the domain of the enigmatic, immortal gnome.

"Wellen!"

Xabene's warning shout shook him from his stupor. He whirled about and watched in dismay as the circular portal shriveled. Smaller and smaller it grew, a gaping wound magically healing itself before their very eyes. Wellen reached toward it, then pulled his hand back when he realized that all he might succeed in doing was trapping his arm in the side of the citadel.

With a slight hiss, the hole ceased to be.

After some careful consideration, Wellen ran his fingertips across the region where the entrance had been. There was not even the slightest trace of its existence. For all practical purposes, it might never have been.

"What issss this?" Asaalk snarled. "Where is the gnome? Why is he not here?"

Turning, Wellen stared at the endless corridor. "I suspect that we're to go to him."

"Down the corridor?"

"Do you see anywhere else to go?" he asked. Sure enough, when Xabene and the blue man looked around, they too, saw that the corridor was the only path open to them. Wellen wondered if the same thought was going through their minds that had gone through his . . . had there not been other corridors running along each side? Now, there were only blank walls. The notion that they were being herded was not an attractive thought.

"Let us be done with this!" Prentiss Asaalk began stalking down the corridor, his lengthy strides taking him several yards from his comrades before either could even react. Wellen hurried after the northerner, not wanting Asaalk to run off too far on his own, for both his sake and theirs. Especially theirs. Xabene kept pace with him.

"Perhaps we should let him keep a distance ahead of us," she whispered. "Maybe there's a trap or two and he'll spring them."

"We stay together, *regardless* of you two."

"A pity."

The blue man, despite their best efforts, continued to lead the way. Wellen soon settled for merely keeping pace a few feet behind the warrior. He was not too concerned with Prentiss Asaalk's attempt to seize control of the situation. Let Asaalk lead the way; it was still Wellen who the mysterious gnome wished to see. The blue man could be no more than a minor irritant to someone as omnipotent as the lord of this magical place.

Several minutes passed without incident, but everyone sensed that something was awry. Still walking, Wellen glanced over his shoulder to observe the path they had already trodden, then faced forward again. While he was still mulling over his discovery, he heard a muttered curse from the figure before him.

"What ails our friend now?" Xabene asked quietly. "He's likely discovered the same thing I did."

"What's that?"

"That we are no closer to the end of the hall than we were just after we *started.*"

She blinked, scanned the entire corridor, and finally frowned. "I'd wondered . . . it didn't seem right, but . . ."

"I know. It's hard to sense it; part of the spell, I imagine." *Is he laughing at us?* Wellen asked himself. *Have we been admitted only to amuse him?*

Asaalk paused. When the others had caught up to him, he turned and snarled, "The faster I go, the less distance I seem to cover. What do you suggest we do, Master Bedlam?"

There was only one thing to do, but he dreaded telling it to the frustrated blue man. "We keep walking."

"That is all?"

"We could turn back."

"Never!"

The northerner's outburst was much too intense. Wellen regretted having him with them now, but it was too late. Perhaps Prentiss Asaalk merely fretted over the collar, which was reasonable enough, but his interest was more of a coveting nature. He wanted the dragon tome as much as the Lords of the Dead or the Purple Dragon did.

"Then we continue on." Wellen, taking Xabene's arm, stepped around the seething blue man and resumed his trek. As she passed, the enchantress could not help displaying to Asaalk a brief, mocking smile.

They walked for a time more and then it became obvious that while their progress was slow, it was definitely progress. Wellen squinted and thought he made out doors both at the end of the corridor and on the side walls farther ahead. He asked Xabene if she saw them.

"I do. What do you think lies behind them?"

"That's not the question that runs through my mind," he returned, eyeing the distant portals. Considering where the trio was, such doorways were tempting, indeed. "I was wondering whether we're allowed to open them or not."

The doors had also captured the blue man's curiosity. Prentiss Asaalk broke past his two companions and increased his pace further.

"Asaalk!"

The hulking figure ignored them. Now the distance melted away with a swiftness. In only a few minutes, the rows of doorways became apparent; Wellen estimated that there had to be over a hundred on each wall. They were simple in design and blended with the white walls. A handle was the only thing that decorated each, a plain, metal handle that like so much else, seemed austere in design for something conjured by one with the power to do almost anything he desired.

The more evident it became that they were nearing the doors, the faster Asaalk traveled. He moved as if the Dragon King himself was on his heels. The last few steps he fairly leaped. When at last he reached the doorways, the blue man did not hesitate. Asaalk seized the handle of the closest one and pulled.

It would not open.

He pulled harder. Despite his strength, the door did not even so much as shake. Cursing, the blue man released the handle and tried pulling the one next to it. That portal, too, rebuked his efforts.

"Asaalk! Wait!"

Ignoring them, the enraged northerner turned to the opposite wall and took hold of the handle of the nearest door there. It, like the others, refused him entrance. He put his foot against the wall beside the portal and tried to use his weight.

Still nothing.

"Asaalk, it's obvious these paths are not meant for us." Wellen tried to pull the ever more furious figure from his obsession, but the blue man pushed him away with a snarl. To his surprise, the smaller man barely saved himself from flying into one of the other doors. Instead, he roiled to a stop just inches away. Asaalk's strength was so incredible that Wellen was surprised his companion had not torn the entire door from its hinges.

"Stop that!" Xabene called, stepping toward Asaalk. She, like Wellen, was ignored.

"One of thessse must open!" He turned toward the final portal at the end of the corridor. "Sssso be it!"

Before they could stop him, Prentiss Asaalk was running toward the far doors.

"He's gone mad!" the enchantress cried, helping Bedlam to his feet.

"Mad or ensorcelled! The collar, remember?"

"Then this was all—" She had no time to finish. Prentiss Asaalk had nearly reached his goal, and showed no sign of slowing down.

The hard, massive form of the blue man struck the twin doors where they met.

With a shriek of metal resounding through the hall, Asaalk's body continued through as the barrier before him gave way.

Wellen and Xabene rushed after the blue man. The scholar feared that all hope of peaceful contact with the gnome was lost. The citadel's master surely would not long tolerate this vandalism, this plundering.

"There!" roared Asaalk from within. The chamber was fairly well lit. With his large form blocking most of their view, however, they could not entirely make out what was in the room beyond, save that Wellen thought he saw some sort of pedestal upon which something lay.

There was an inhuman quality about the northerner now. His breathing grew heavy and fast and his stance was a bit awkward. He seemed even larger for a moment or two.

"At lasssst!" he hissed. "My *dragon tome!"*

"Did he say . . ." Xabene hesitated at the battered doorway. " . . . the dragon tome?"

Bedlam only partly heard her. He was still staring at Asaalk. A horrible, unthinkable notion was creeping into his mind, one he tried to reject but could not.

He started to move, realizing that whatever the truth, one thing was certain. "We have to keep him from taking that book!"

It was already too late. Heedless of whatever else might wait in the chamber, the blue man rushed toward his prize. As much as Wellen both hoped and dreaded it, nothing stayed the crazed figure. The scholar had some hope that he and the enchantress might still have a chance when Asaalk suddenly slowed just before the pedestal. The northerner, though, wasted only a few seconds as he seemed to study the area before him for traps. Evidently finding none, he reached for the massive book.

Wellen did not need any magical warning sense to tell him to stay back. He grabbed hold of Xabene's arm and pulled her to the floor.

Prentiss Asaalk lifted the dragon tome from its resting place. He laughed.

Then vanished.

With a heavy thud, the ancient tome fell to the marble floor. It bounced twice, then settled a few yards in front of the two gaping onlookers.

"Predictable in the end," commented a voice behind them. Wellen had a sense of great age and authority . . . and not a little pride. "Obsession will always do that, even to a creature like a Dragon King."

Very slowly, the two humans, still lying on the floor, turned around.

The figure towered over them, but only because they were not standing. *He cannot be any taller than my chest!* Bedlam decided. *And that if he can straighten up.* The latter seemed doubtful; the figure before them had been permanently bent by both centuries of study hunched over desks and by the centuries themselves, for though he might be immortal, this being was old.

The gnome, clad in a brown robe that nearly touched the floor, smiled at them. It was a smile reminiscent of a dragon, but without the warmth. "Rise, please."

The duo obeyed immediately. The master of the citadel glanced over Xabene, found nothing of interest, then studied Wellen. He stared longest at the scholar's eyes.

"A few flakes of crystal, I see. A throwback, no doubt. Most interesting."

His words raised questions, but nothing that Wellen would have dared ask now.

A staff was in the gnome's left hand. It had not been there the previous moment. With it, the aged figure prodded at the two humans. "Step aside."

Again, they obeyed without hesitation. The gnome moved with amazing grace to the fallen book. It lay flat with its pages fanning upward.

"Wellen," Xabene whispered. "Do you sense anything?"

He thought about it. He had not sensed danger in the corridor and he had not sensed danger in the chamber, despite the trap offered by what had to be a false book.

His ability had vanished. From the moment Bedlam had entered this place, it had ceased to be. *How* had he missed its sudden absence?

The answer was the squat creature before him.

She understood his silence. "It's the same with my own power. I've lost it all now," the enchantress muttered. "I think it was the moment Asaalk touched the book."

Blocking out his ability to sense danger was one thing, but the citadel's lord must have known he would give his plot away if he stole the last of Xabene's power. Unlike Wellen, she was not one to fail to notice the absence of something so important to her.

"That it was him at all was the most fascinating part of all this," the smiling gnome explained to his baffled audience. He flipped through the pages of the tome and chuckled at something he saw within. "I have always wondered just how he planned to get in even if he succeeded in capturing me."

"What is it . . . " The scholar took a deep breath. "What is it you're saying?"

"You know very well," the gnome admonished him. "You know that he was not your companion of old."

Xabene's eyes rounded. "Not the blue man?"

"I would say that your blue friend . . . what was his name, my young friend?"

"Prentiss Asaalk," Wellen responded. "Is the true man dead, then?"

"Probably so. If this is the kind of spell I think it is, then he died the moment our scaly friend put on this form. That he mastered even a human one is astonishing, but that he wore the shape and form of one you knew, too, is impossible."

"Who is he talking about, Wellen? You and he both seem to understand what you're saying, but I—" The enchantress broke off. "He just said *scaly* . . . "

"Indeed I did, young woman." The staff turned to so much smoke as the gnome made use of both hands to hold the huge tome open. He held it much the way it had lain on the floor, both covers down and the pages all displayed like a peacock's feathers. "Allow me to show you what he looks like. .. without the spell of seeming that made him be your friend."

The spellcaster tore a page from the false tome and tossed it into the air before them. The single sheet fluttered about for several seconds, at last coming to earth roughly in the trio's midst. It did not settle, however, but rather continued to turn and turn, a top spun by an invisible hand.

The page stood on one end. Transfixed by this continuing feat of sorcery, Wellen and Xabene watched as the paper expanded, swiftly rising to a height equal to the scholar's own and then rising even higher. Bedlam estimated it ceased growing when it was a little over eight feet tall.

It was still turning, but now that its growth had ended, it began spinning faster and faster, raising a breeze that forced the two humans to turn away until they could shield their eyes.

Beyond them, beyond the whirling page, the gnome chuckled.

As Wellen, his hand above his eyes, squinted, much of the sheet started to darken. The darker the paper grew, the slower the turning became. He made out a manlike form, but one taller and more massive than even Prentiss Asaalk.

The hairless spellcaster nodded. With a stop so jarring it made Wellen and Xabene jump, the page froze before them. There, in all its inhuman glory, stood what had truly traveled with the two humans to the citadel.

A demonic warrior clad in enshrouding scale armor. The monstrous countenance was all but hidden within a helm, but they could make out the fiery eyes and part of the flat, horrific face within nonetheless. Atop the helm was an elaborate dragon's head crest, a crest so lifelike that one expected the head to open wide its maw and snap up the onlooker. No weapon hung from the warrior's waist, but it was doubtful that any was needed. The gauntleted hands and the savage mouth looked readily able to tear apart a foe gobbet by bloody gobbet.

From head to toe, the fiendish knight was colored a very distinctive shade of purple.

"Allow me to introduce, albeit in a form much removed from his original, His

133

Infernal Majesty, the lord of this land . . . the *Purple Dragon.*"

The illustration on the page was so very lifelike that Wellen could see the evil, the power, and at the moment, the incessant frustration of the trapped drake lord.

It *was* the Dragon King.

Not an illustration. Not an image of the captured creature as he stood waiting in some hidden dungeon. The *true* dragon. Held prisoner on the very sheet of paper—a prison of only two dimensions—that stood before them.

The gnome shuffled toward them. It was all the humans could do to keep from stumbling back. There could be no doubting the short, squat mage's skills now, not that the scholar ever had.

"And since it seems time for introductions," the gnarled figure continued, closing the book with a finality that was all too noticeable, "you may call me *Serkadion Manee.*"

Chapter Seventeen

Benton Lore had not believed that the outsider Bedlam would succeed with his insane, sophomoric plan, but his lord had thought differently. Now he saw that the Green Dragon must have made a careful study of both the outsider and the gnome, for who could have predicted Bedlam's success otherwise?

From his hiding place in a copse of trees not too distant from the featureless pentagon, he watched. There was little else to do until they exited the cursed place.

If they did leave, he wanted to speak with the scholar in private. Whatever secrets or even passing knowledge that Bedlam picked up would be useful to the major-domo's true cause. He could have cared less about the fate of the mad warlock Shade, whose chief concern, in Lore's eyes, was always his own existence. The gnome had the potential to give all humans their freedom from the Dragon Kings, make them master of their own fate. Wellen Bedlam represented a possible bridge for Lore to that knowledge and power.

His lord knew of his desire, of that the officer was aware. The Green Dragon, however, foresaw mankind's ascendancy as a certainty, whereas Lore saw it as something attainable only if he and those like him strained to reach it. Nothing was certain as far as the black man was concerned, especially freedom.

All of that would be a moot point if the trio never departed. Benton Lore and humanity would be back where they had left off. Nowhere.

He settled down to wait, knowing that his own sorcerous abilities would warn him of any approaching threat. The forces of the Dragon King Purple, however, were very absent tonight. That could only mean that they had fallen for the diversions. Asaalk was still a problem, but not one he could not handle. After all, it was not as if the blue man, human or not, were the Dragon King himself.

Another pair of eyes, white, soulless ones, also watched the pentagon. Another watcher, just as eager as the dark man, waited for the trio, especially the scholar, to leave the safety of the citadel.

The gnome spoke his own name with such authority that Wellen supposed that he should have recognized it. He did not. Neither, he saw, did Xabene. Name or not, though, Serkadion Manee was to be respected, if only because of his power.

Something about the name did strike him, however. Wellen could not say what it was, save that it reminded him of another name . . . two, in fact. Shade had used those names, Dru Zeree for the legendary lord Bedlam had known as Drazeree, and Sharissa Zeree, the wraith who had also been the lord's illustrious daughter. In fact, there had been another title with the same distinctive syllable at the end, a mysterious people called the Tezerenee.

Could Serkadion Manee, like Shade, be a representative of the same ancient race?

Xabene was not so concerned with history. Her priorities surrounded the menacing figure of the Dragon King, who literally seemed to be struggling to free himself of the page. "Can he escape?"

Manee glanced back at the prisoner. A brief frown crossed his unsightly visage. "He is stronger than I imagined; I had not thought it possible for him to fight it as much as he has." The rounded shoulders rose and fell in a shrug. "But struggle is all he shall do."

The bizarre, flat image did not seem to agree. The Dragon King only increased his visible efforts.

"How did he obtain such a near-human form?" the unnerved yet fascinated woman asked, ignoring the annoyed look on Serkadion Manee's visage. Wellen hoped he was not the type that used his sorcery to erase from his existence all those who irritated him, however slight the irritation might have been.

"There are ways, but it would have been a struggle. You see that while he has obtained size and the basic form, he would *hardly* have passed for human without the other spell. He has tried to compensate for his ineffectiveness by masking himself in a form that, at least from a distance, might pass." A chuckle. "Although I can say without a doubt I have never seen such a beastly knight. Oh well, the helm hides his worst ugliness."

Despite her anxiousness, Xabene was fascinated by the complex and physically draining spells that the Dragon King must have utilized to achieve as much as he had. Wellen could not blame her for the way she stared at the sight. He knew that she was wondering what she might have achieved with such ability available to her.

"Now, then," started the gnome. He paused when he saw that the two were still eyeing the ensnared drake. "Whether in man form or beast, he *cannot* escape." Manee sighed and added, "I can see that we will not be able to speak in peace so long as he is around. No matter, this was hardly a comfortable place for conversation."

The three of them were suddenly in another chamber. Wellen's stomach rose and fell. He still detested traveling in such a manner, but it was becoming less and less disturbing to his system. Much of his pain was in his mind, anyway. The scholar knew that, but so far had not been able to convince his stomach of the fact.

Their new location was a place so very familiar to the scholar, not because he had seen it before but because he had seen its like. As with Xabene's secret domain, Wellen almost felt at home. Shelves of fascinating and mysterious objects lined the walls. The familiar desk with candles. Paper and quill pen. Notes and sketches laid here and there. It was evident that the room had been reorganized only recently, but things were already forming into random piles. It was a chamber typical of men like Wellen. Researchers and scholars.

"This should be much better." Once again, the gnome smiled and once again his guests were repulsed. "Sit."

He discovered then that Serkadion Manee's study was not so typical after all.

135

DRAGON TOME

The floor beneath the two humans' feet swelled, throwing them off balance. Helpless, Bedlam fell backward. He envisioned the back of his skull striking the hard surface and cracking into a number of pieces. He saw Xabene's head do the same and the vision of her lying dead on the floor stirred him more than his own fate had.

Midway to his doom, something soft caught and nestled him. A gasp from the enchantress informed him that she had met with a similar experience. He looked down at what his body rested in.

A chair had formed from the very substance of the floor. Wellen rubbed a finger over what should have been a harsh surface, only to find it smooth and pliable. He looked at his companion, who was likewise studying the astonishing sight. Even shaped as it was, the floor still retained an appearance of stone.

"I trust that is comfortable." Serkadion Manee, still standing, folded a partially obscured leg under him. Bedlam expected to see him teeter, perhaps even fall, but the ungainly sorcerer somehow maintained perfect balance.

Then, he folded the *other* leg under him and simply floated a few feet in the middle of the air.

Summoning up his courage, Wellen said, "Master Manee, I thank you for allowing us entrance to your domain. I know that you rarely have congress with others—"

"More often than you think." The smile broadened, no pleasant change. "You are hardly the first I've allowed entrance to, my young friends."

That contradicted everything that he had heard, but Wellen tried to take it as a good sign. Certainly, the gnome would not advertise that he dealt often with others, yet how could he keep it a secret?

"That is neither here nor there," Manee continued. His fingers absently stroked the book's cover.

"Please," Xabene asked, a bit more at ease now that she knew the chair was not going to swallow her whole. "Is that the dragon tome or not?"

Another chuckle. "In a sense."

"What does that mean?"

"It means what I said."

Wellen interrupted, already seeing that this was going to turn into a conversation of confusion, which the inhabitants of the Dragonrealm seemed to delight in creating. "You said we were hardly the first to be allowed inside. Why are there not tales of the others? I would think the Dragon Kings or the Lords of the Dead would have discovered them."

"I take measures." It was all the gnome would say on that subject. "I believe that you made me an offer, Master Wellen Bedlam."

The scholar burned within. He realized that he had set aside Shade's existence for a brief moment so that he might satisfy some of his curiosity. "Yes. Knowledge of the land from which I began this journey in exchange for aid for two of my companions . . . although it seems too late for one."

"Perhaps. We shall see. What of the other one then? What fate has befallen him? Explain carefully the details."

Wellen did. That the Lords of the Dead were involved did not shake Serkadion Manee for a moment. When Wellen hesitated after first introducing their threat to the tale, the gnome merely raised one hand from the book in his lap and indicated he should continue. The scholar told of the attack and Shade's determination to track down the necromancers and make them suffer.

When he spoke of Shade's claim of blood ties to the self-styled gods, Bedlam noticed Manee's eyes widen, then narrow. Curious as to what effect his encounter with the wraith would have on the aged sorcerer, he slowed down at that point and gave as descriptive an image of the scene as possible.

136

Serkadion Manee hung on every word. From his expression, he seemed to be thinking that what the mortal before him was relating was impossible yet true. It was very likely that the ancient mage could tell whether Wellen was lying or not, so everything that left the scholar's mouth was the truth. It was not the entire truth, but at least there were no falsehoods. Wellen did not want to give everything away if he could help it.

After the story ended, Serkadion Manee leaned back. Wellen expected him to fall, but the sorcerer shifted as if a chair also held him. He appeared to be speaking more to himself. "So Nimth still reaches forth from her far grave. She should be dead by now, and all her children little more than a few vague memories in the souls . . . or specks of crystal in the eyes. . . of their descendants."

"What is Nimth? I heard it mentioned."

"Nimth, my young mortal companion, was my home. It was the home once of those who call themselves the Lords of the Dead, although I consider them shadows now, not living examples of its former greatness like *myself.*" It had already become obvious that Serkadion Manee held himself in great esteem. He scratched him chin in thought. "This Sharissa, who claims ancestry, fascinates me, but I will leave the visitation for another time. The one called Shade, the one you desire to free, he might also be *Vraad* after all. This is worthy of note."

From the desk, a quill and a sheet of paper leaped into the air and darted to the waiting warlock. Manee did not take the items, but rather had them float to one side of him. The two newcomers watched as the paper stiffened and the pen readied its point just above the top of the sheet.

"Proceed," the gnome commanded the implement.

Writing at a furious pace, the quill filled the sheet with words. Manee's eyes were little more than slits. Although no words escaped his lips, he was evidently directing the pen's efforts.

When the first page was filled, a second flew from the desk and took its place. Xabene actually smiled at Wellen. The dancing quill and the soaring sheets seemed so fanciful, it might have been pulled from a child's dream.

After a third page, the pen froze. The final sheet joined the other two, which were floating serenely above the gnome's head, and then both paper and pen returned to the desk.

Manee was visibly amused by the attitudes of his two guests. Wellen was entirely baffled by the gnome. Was he as benevolent and understanding as he appeared now or was the master mage who had trapped the Purple Dragon more what the true Serkadion Manee was like? Could he trust the gnarled figure or was the gnome only biding his time for some reason?

"Tell me, Scholar Bedlam, did this Shade ever say the word `Vraad'? I should have paid more attention to him, but he seemed only to watch, and the necromancers and the Dragon King were so much more interesting."

One of Wellen's questions was partly answered. The true Serkadion Manee was more like the sorcerer who had tricked the drake lord and countless would-be conquerors through the ages. He enjoyed the challenges, even as certain as he was of the outcome of each. Over the centuries, or rather millennia, they had probably become one of his chief ways of battling boredom. Even the most avid scholar could not study *all* the time.

He wondered just how mad Serkadion Manee was.

Belatedly, Wellen recalled the gnome's question. He pretended to be considering the answer, then finally responded, "He may or may not have. It sounds familiar, but I could be mistaken."

The gnome uncrossed his legs and returned his feet to the ground. His eyes looked to the ceiling as he stared at something that existed only in his memory. "You have no idea what your ancestors were like, my young ones. We wielded power such as even the Lords of the Dead only dream of. Our world, Nimth, was our plaything . . . and play with it we did. We began to twist and turn its laws, make it a parody of both itself and us, its children."

Swinging one hand in an arc, Serkadion Manee summoned forth an image in the air. A landscape, but one that lived and breathed, not simply a flat picture. Clouds floated serenely overhead and a winged creature or two soared into and out of the tiny domain. Leaning closer, Bedlam saw that the landscape was sculpted, not natural, yet to such a masterful degree that one became so caught up in admiring it that one did not notice immediately the handiwork of the unknown artisan. In the distance, one or two high and elaborate buildings, possibly towers or castles, could be made out.

"This was the view from my domain." Manee seemed to age as he spoke. The spellcaster might deny it, but he missed his former world. He stared at the scene a breath or two longer, then wiped it away with a single slash of his hand. "But it exists no more and even as I chose to depart, knowing what was to come of our playing, it was *decaying* already."

He arced his hand again, summoning up the image. There was something different about it, however, something subtle that neither Wellen nor Xabene could define at first. The scholar only knew that he sensed a mood of uneasiness, almost like that of a person who suspects he is dying but does not wish to know the truth for fear he is correct. Clouds lingered too long in the sky. Nothing flew. Those were the only physical differences that Wellen could see, but that hardly proved a thing. If, as Serkadion Manee had said, this Nimth had already been decaying, much of that decay would begin with the unseen things, the breakdown of the natural laws that bound all.

Again, the gnome slashed his hand across the image, literally shattering it into a thousand ephemeral fragments that dissolved before they stuck the hard floor. "I can only imagine what the world this Shade and your kind left must have been like. A sick, twisted thing. The Lords of the Dead, they do not remember their own past very well, but I have often suspected that their domain is a mirror of those times."

Wellen nodded. Shade had made a similar comment.

"I was right in abandoning that place." Manee drew himself together. "But the Vraad still live on, if only in a distant manner, through you."

Xabene leaned close to Wellen. "He sounds more and more like Shade."

The gnome put a gnarled hand to his bald head in obvious discomfort. "None of that now!" he reprimanded to the air. "Struggling will achieve you nothing but more pain, you know!"

The scholar rose. Behind him, the chair instantly sank back into the rocklike floor that had birthed it. "Are you all right?"

"The Dragon King is becoming a bit of a bother, nothing more. Some of them will not accept the inevitable. Some of them cannot accept that Serkadion Manee is ever their superior. I, a *Vraad* of the highest achievement! I was the one who *opened* the path of power to my kind, showed them what they could *do* . . . not that they listened properly! The drake lords are novices. I have in this place the accumulated knowledge of *two* worlds and it is all for my use whenever I need it!"

Despite his words, Manee winced. "I can see that I will have to do something about him, but later." Serkadion Manee looked up at the two outsiders. "My own words remind me of the task at hand; you have promised me knowledge in exchange for a service. I see no reason to delay any further. What little I have garnered from observing you makes me fascinated. I never thought to explore beyond the eastern seas or the Sea of Andramacus to the west." He indicated the citadel as a whole. "How could I leave all that I had obtained over time? It would be better if I could take all of it with me, *then* . . .

Take it with him? Is that what he hopes to do? the explorer wondered, thinking of the sudden change in the citadel's location after all this time. Was the sorcerer trying to make his sanctum capable of transporting itself from one land to another? From one *continent* to another? What Wellen understood about teleportation indicated that Serkadion Manee needed to know much about a region before he could safely materialize there. He was probably capable of a blind teleport, but for something as distant as Bedlam's homeland, such a feat was too risky even for him.

Riskier still if he truly sought to teleport his entire citadel with him.

The idea did not defy Wellen's imagination, but it did defy his belief. He had never heard of a sorcerer with such power and ability.

"What about Shade?"

"His time will come after you have given me what is mine."

"He could be dead by then."

"If he is Vraad, then he is not. If he is not . . . then he perished long before you came to me, my young friend."

"What must I do?" Suddenly faced with the task, the scholar was uneasy. Manee might just as easily strip his mind clean, reduce him to less than a newborn child. That might even be what the gnome intended.

"Nothing much . . . just trust me." Serkadion Manee chuckled as he watched the two.

From his empty hand the robed spellcaster produced a flat, square object made of some gray material of the like Wellen had not seen. It was not the same substance as the citadel walls, but did have similarities in appearance. A piece of finely forged metal was wrapped around one end of the mysterious artifact and on the metal, inscribed in black, were runes of *an* unreadable language. Humans generally spoke one language, the *why* of that never having been settled, but there were records of other types utilized by some of the races that had preceded the Dragon Kings as rulers of this land.

Serkadion Manee held the metal-clad end toward the two waiting figures. He contemplated Xabene for a time.

She stepped back, shaking her head. "This was not *my* bargain, gnome! I made no offer to you to go stealing around in my head!"

"Perhaps you will change your mind before long," he retorted, the sinister smile playing on his lips again. His attention focused on Wellen. "And have you decided to back down from this deal?"

Shade's life aside, Bedlam pondered their fate if he chose to abandon his part of the bargain. Immediate ouster from the gnome's sanctum; that was the least they could expect, that and forever to be haunted by the hooded warlock's ghost. "Do what you have to."

"I always do. Please understand that."

While he was still attempting to mull over the last, something seized him. Xabene called out, but there was nothing that Wellen could do. Something had hold of his legs and his arms, something with tentacles as strong as iron. The enchantress, too, was tangled in tentacles. Wellen tried to make out their source, but he could only see a thick darkness behind her. Trying to glance over his own shoulder, the struggling man saw only shadows. The limbs just seemed to begin somewhere in the darkness.

The gnome was slowly moving toward him, the peculiar artifact held tight in his extended hand. Manee shook his head. "I'm sorry, but I find this necessary. Every time."

The cephalopodic limbs had him wrapped tight. Bedlam could barely move his head from side to side, which was what the wizened spellcaster desired. At an unspoken command, the scholar was pulled down to his knees. Serkadion Manee smiled one last time and touched the metal portion to his captive's forehead.

Wellen's head rocked back as what seemed like a lightning bolt shook him. A second shock, slightly less intense, rattled him just as he recovered from the first. The second was barely gone before a third, a bit less intense than the second, rocked him.

Only one variation jarred the otherwise rhythmic sequence. A brief flash of memory of the dismal domain of the Lords of the Dead interrupted things for only the blink of an eye. The vision of the tortured castle of the necromancers was enough to make him shiver.

The shock waves decreased with each successive one until finally he could sense them no longer. The scholar blinked, then realized that he had shut his eyes tight almost from the moment Serkadion Manee's toy had touched him. As the chamber came into focus, Wellen noticed slight alterations. Not understanding why and how Manee would change things during the few moments he had been out, he turned to where Xabene had been held.

She was not there, but the gnome was.

"That took longer than I expected," the squat figure commented in almost companionable tones. "Not many have dedicated themselves to knowledge as you have. Not in so short a life span, that is."

"What did you do to me?" Wellen's struggle was futile. The tentacles still held him tight. "Where's Xabene?"

"The typical questions. No originality? Here." Manee touched one of the limbs with a finger. The coils began to unwrap; the scholar was free in less than a minute.

"What did you do with her?"

"I sent her elsewhere. Would you have wanted her to wait in discomfort for so long?"

"So long?" He stared down at the stooped figure. "How long was I . . . it was only a few moments, wasn't it?"

Manee shook his head in sympathy. "Day has turned to night, my young scholar friend. There was much in your mind to gather, much more than even I had supposed. We are more alike than I thought. I must say it is refreshing to know that there is someone else."

Flattery was not what Wellen wanted to hear. "What did that thing do to me?"

"It merely read your mind, both the conscious part and the part where all you have learned or perceived is stored. Nothing is ever lost, you know. Even things you learned in passing are retained. My creation finds it all and reproduces it."

Bedlam eyed the magical artifact in the gnome's wrinkled hands. "What will you do with all that?"

"Go through it later. There's always time. It may be years, but there will always be time."

Wellen almost thought he sounded tired.

"Can you take me to Xabene?"

"Of course." Serkadion Manee touched his forehead and winced.

"What's wrong?"

"The Dragon King is becoming most offensive. Had I known he would be so much trouble, I would have left him outside pounding on the walls."

That brought something to mind that Bedlam had briefly contemplated earlier. "Why didn't you kill him? It certainly seems as if you had a chance."

"I've not studied him yet nor have I made a copy of his memories." Mance looked at Wellen as if all this should have been logical. "I waste nothing."

Then, they were standing in another room. Xabene, in the act of pacing, something she had evidently been doing for a long, long time, stiffened. The rage and frustration boiled over when she saw the gnome.

"You! How dare you keep me in here all this time!" She rushed to Wellen and held him tight. "Are you all right? Say something!"

"I'm fine, Xabene. Other than a few jarring moments, I felt nothing. He didn't hurt me."

"Not that he would've cared!" Still holding the scholar, she glanced at Serkadion Manee. "Ask him about that, Wellen! Ask him if he would have cared if you were injured!"

"It would have been regrettable," Manee responded, not waiting for Bedlam to ask. "The loss of knowledge is always regrettable."

"More so than the loss of a life!"

"Life can be replaced; knowledge is often lost for too long, sometimes forever."

There was no doubt that he meant what he said. What similarities there were between the gnome and Wellen did not include this. Life was more important than anything. The death of those who had journeyed to this land, even the unseen, far-off death of Prentiss Asaalk, would remain with him to his own demise.

Serkadion Manee did not seem to see a problem with his way of thinking. "I do what I can to make certain that the process is safe. I will not waste what might again be useful."

Was this an example of their ancestors? Wellen hoped not. The ghost of Sharissa Zeree had not been at all like this. She had cared about life.

"We could discuss this until the end of all," Manee continued. "But I am assuming that you still desire your end of the bargain fulfilled."

Shade! "I do."

"Then we shall commence with it now."

"What should I do?" He expected the gnome to order him to lie down. The Lords of the Dead had put Xabene into some sort of trance. If the necromancers and the wizened spellcaster were of the same people, then it stood to reason that their methods would be similar.

Wellen was proved wrong. Manee looked up at him. "You should do nothing. All I require is your presence as a focus. You may sit, sleep, talk, or try to walk on the ceiling. As long as you stay nearby, I can search."

Opening his hands, Serkadion Manee suddenly held the dragon tome again. For the first time, Wellen had a good view of the stylized image on the cover. It was as had been described to him. A fierce and very elaborate design. The color of the book confused him, however, for he recalled that it had been some color other than gold. That he could not say for certain did not surprise him; events just prior to the mage's use of the memory device were still a bit cloudy. Bedlam hoped nothing had been lost permanently. He preferred his memories to fade away, not to be snatched.

"Here it is." Serkadion Manee ran his fingers down one of the pages. He winced at a momentary pain, then resumed his reading. "Yes. Short but complex. Simple thought would hardly do. No one could maintain all those patterns and still be able to search .. ." The gnome grew more and more interested.

Xabene had shifted to the scholar's side. "Is this wise? He might bring forth one of the lords themselves or, at the very least, a Necri!"

"It's too late now."

Manee was muttering under his breath, his eyes no longer on the page but staring up into another world. For the first time since he had entered the pentagon, Wellen felt the familiar throb of warning. With the Dragon King to control and the spell to complete, Serkadion Manee did not need to waste power on something as insignificant as the novice warlock's poor abilities.

He felt the enchantress shift beside him and knew that her powers, too, had returned. Wellen hoped she would not try anything at this juncture. If Xabene thought now an opportune time to strike back at the gnome, Manee might indeed summon forth something other than Shade. Something they might all live . . . for a short time . . . to regret.

A faint scent of decay and death turned their noses. Xabene, who should have been more adapted to the odor, shivered, possibly thinking that one of her former masters might be the next thing through Serkadion Manee's spell.

Then, the gnome frowned. He twitched once or twice, searching, Wellen decided, but why was there need? Manee had been confident that even the otherworldly realm of the necromancers could not hide from his prying senses.

With a sigh, the tiny figure finally opened his eyes. His gaze darted from one side of the chamber to the other, as if he expected to see the hooded warlock standing with his companions.

"What's happened?" the scholar asked. Was it too late? Was Shade beyond *everyone's* power to save?

"He should be here. In fact, it almost felt as if he had . . . impossible . . . not likely at all . . . could it?"

A moment ago, Wellen would not have been able to picture the gnome caught up in uncertainty. Serkadion Manee knew everything, orchestrated everything to satisfy his goals. Yet, here he was now, at a loss.

"It *has* to be!" the sorcerer finally muttered. "It has to be! Devious! Worthy of a Vraad!"

"What is he babbling about?" Xabene whispered. "I don't—"

Serkadion Manee, his mind returning to the reality of the room, extended a twisted hand toward the duo. "Come! He must be there!"

This time, Wellen was prepared for the teleport.

They were in another corridor, but its contents did not immediately register with the scholar, for his attention was snared by the gnome, who was clutching his head in obvious agony. Bedlam started to reach for him, trying to give aid in some way, but Manee waved him back.

"It is nothing! Nothing!"

"You! You have tricked me!"

Wellen forgot all else at the sudden shout from far down the corridor. He turned, unable to believe that his ears had heard true.

"Wellen! He's here!"

Shade stood in the midst of the long, narrow hall, a demonic fury. Though distance and the hood shadowed his features as usual, there was no doubt as to the intensity of his anger, an anger directed not at Bedlam or the enchantress, but rather at the short, squat figure who had brought them here.

There was no sign of injury, no indication at all that the warlock had suffered in his battle against his cousins. Wellen knew that not all wounds were visible, but Shade seemed to suffer from none, not if his manic activity was a sign.

"Which one is it, Serkadion Manee?" the cloaked figure roared. "Which one is it? I've gone through shelves already and none of them have it!"

Shade picked up a massive, crimson book and threw it at one of the empty shelves. Wellen blinked; he had been so caught up in the discovery of the warlock that he had not even noticed what lined the walls of the corridor.

Books. Row upon row of books stretching far off into the distance. If anything, this hall was longer than the first he had traveled. Perhaps it even went on forever.

All the books were identical in color and form. There were hundreds . . . no . . . *thousands* of volumes in this corridor alone and from the looks of things, there were side hallways in the distance. More shelves with more books? Small wonder that Shade was growing frustrated in his search for . . . for *what?*

Then the maddened spellcaster pulled another volume from one of the walls, allowing the scholar to at last see the cover.

A stylized dragon. Without seeing the other books, he knew that they, too, would have the same design.

"Which one is it?" Shade snarled. "Which one is the true *dragon tome?"*

Serkadion Manee chuckled. From his hands he produced the volume that Wellen and Xabene had watched him utilize only minutes before. The gnome tossed the book toward the enraged figure. It flew with unerring accuracy into the waiting fingers of the other spellcaster. Shade forgot the others and began paging through the tome. After several seconds, however, his anger began to resurface. What he sought was not in the book Manee had given to him.

"This is not it, either!" The book fell to the top of the pile that had accumulated at Shade's feet. "Another useless collection of dribble!"

The gnome's countenance darkened. "Dribble? Yes, you are Vraad! No concern with anything except what you desire! All else is to be swept aside as inconsequential!"

"I want only one thing! I want nothing else this accursed, parasitic world has offered! Where is the true dragon tome?"

He could not see it. Wellen pitied Shade, so caught up in his quest and his madness that he could not see what Serkadion Manee was trying to show him.

It was apparent to the gnome, too. He produced another book, identical in design but this time a forest green in color, and held it up before his shadowy counterpart.

"This is the *true* dragon tome."

"Give it to me!"

Manee ignored his demand. Releasing the book, he sent it floating a few feet before him. At the same time, a new volume materialized. This one was deep blue, but otherwise *a* twin of the others. "This is the true dragon tome."

Shade began to say something, but stopped. He simply stared at the gnome and the floating books.

A rainbow of literature formed before the eyes of all. Wellen had never seen so many variations of color at one time. He counted more than a dozen shades of green and was certain there were more. Book after book materialized and dematerialized, only to be replaced by another.

"These are *all* the true dragon tome." The gnome took amusement at the horrified expression stretching across the warlock's deathly visage. "As is every volume on every shelf in every hall."

"All . . . of them?"

There was something Serkadion Manee had not yet said that Bedlam suspected would finish whatever reserves of anger and hope that Shade had left.

"All of them, yes, my dark and annoying friend." Manee waved a hand and every book that had been torn off the shelves returned to its rightful resting place. The countless volumes that he himself had summoned also vanished, no doubt to their own shelves.

Serkadion Manee smiled widely and finally concluded, "And you have yet to see the *other* libraries."

Chapter Eighteen

143

In Serkadion Manee's intricate trap, the Purple Dragon continued to struggle. Now and then, he found he made a little more progress. Soon, it would be enough to free him. Soon.

The old sorcerer ran a hand over his hairless head. Wellen noticed him wince again. The jabs, or whatever they were, were becoming more frequent. He wondered if Manee understood that he was overtaxing himself.

Shade was still refusing to believe what he had heard. He took a few steps toward the master of the citadel. "You lie! You have to be!" With a sweep of his arm he indicated the other volumes. "These are ploys, an elaborate plot to hide the one, true tome!"

Sounding much like a disappointed parent, Serkadion Manee returned, "You know who I am, Vraad."

"I do! Master Dru Zeree studied your works long and hard! It was because of your writings that he searched and found this accursed land!"

"I wish I had met him. From what else I have gathered, he was rather remarkable. A Vraad who did more than fulfill his childish fantasies was a rare one even in my time . . . and I have lived *much*, much longer than you, stripling!"

"Which is why I know you must have what I seek!" Shade looked triumphant and not a little mad. "You could not be alive otherwise! Not after all this time!"

Manee arched what had once been an eyebrow. "Is that what you want? Is that all? A thousand thousand years of research and that is all you want?"

His almost matter-of-fact tone made all of them curious. If he was talking about immortality, a thing sought after by so many over the millennia, then his manner was puzzling. Wellen doubted that he could be so nonchalant about such an amazing discovery. No mage that he had ever met had discovered a way to tap into the world's life and extend his own for more than three, possibly four hundred years. Even the Dragon Kings were mortal.

Pulling back his hood and fully revealing his horrific state, the warlock almost pleaded. *"Yes, that is what I want! That is all that I want! I will give this world neither my body nor my soul!"*

"Hmmph." Serkadion Manee saw what Shade could not. Wellen was certain that anyone other than the shadowy warlock would have noticed the truth. Shade had long ago given his body and soul to this world, or at least a good portion of each. The rest belonged to the place called Nimth. The warlock was a man caught between two worlds, neither of which he saw as promising him a simple and quiet fate.

Shade looked for help. "Master Bedlam, I am sorry. The spell used on Xabene by my cousins urged me to a sudden and daring plan, a spell hidden in *your* mind. I desired no harm to come to you. This the Green Dragon and I agreed upon."

They had both betrayed him. Only Xabene, who had proven herself to him, still earned his trust. If not for her, Wellen would have wished that he had never thought of searching for the legendary Dragonrealm. It was a place of treachery and greed, nothing more. "How did you escape from the Lords of the Dead?"

"They are shadows of what we once were. Only I still have ties to Nimth, to the power that is both our right and our curse."

"He means he has broken through and linked himself to a world ravaged by my kind," Serkadion Manee argued. "Only a true Vraad would think of allying himself with a force I estimate had been perverted beyond repair."

"As have you."

"I have not."

"I don't believe you." There was, however, a touch of uncertainty in Shade's voice.

"It matters not what you believe." The gnome was disgusted. "I had forgotten what happens when two Vraad meet. Very well, before we come to blows, I shall give you what you desire and then you can leave." He winced. "Do not bother to come back. Our mutual heritage will not open this citadel to you again. Rather, it should have never let you inside."

"All I want is the secret of immorality . . . and the promise that Master Bedlam here will not become a part of your collection." .

Serkadion Manee wore a pained expression. "He will remain here only so long as he chooses to. Now then," the gnarled spellcaster reached into the confines of his robe and removed yet another book. Pitch black, Wellen would have thought it more appropriate for death rather than immortality. Manee held it out. "This is what you were seeking. Read it, use it if you will, and depart. You may thank Master Wellen Bedlam for your safety and the fact that I am even giving you this one chance."

"He has my gratitude. I hope one day he will understand, if only for the sake of one we both know."

Bowing his head, Wellen would not meet the crystalline gaze. Whatever Shade or Gerrod had been to the scholar's ancestor, the warlock had to be a shadow of that man now. He truly lived up to his self-chosen appellation.

The warlock grabbed the proffered book and began thumbing through it. His eagerness made him bat the pages aside with such intensity that it was a wonder he was able to ready any of it. Serkadion Manee watched him for a breath or two, then *tsked* at the cloaked figure's impatience.

"That is not how you will find it. Do what you are doing and you will search through the tome forever. Simply think about what you desire. My book will do the rest."

Shade visibly debated believing the gnome, then decided it was worth a try. He held the dragon tome slightly away from him, unnecessarily, Wellen suspected, but Shade had always seemed to live the dramatic, and stared at it.

The pages flipped by. Nearly two-thirds of the way through the volume, they ceased. Shade slammed a gloved hand on the page, which made his counterpart frown, and pulled the book to him. He began to read avidly, not caring at all the sight his desperation made of him.

All was well at first, but then the warlock's brow furrowed. He reread part of the page, silently mouthing the words as if he could not believe what was written there.

"You cannot be *serious!*" he snarled. "You would not have done this! It would mean giving yourself up to this land and its accursed, covetous mind! It would mean forever being tied to this one place!"

"What you see is truth."

"You have been seen throughout the Dragonrealm!"

"There are ways. Temporary measures that allow me access and the ability to taste outside life."

Now it was Shade who was disgusted. "You are truly Vraad after all even though the rest of you belongs to this domain! I could only dream of such a travesty!"

Serkadion Manee held his head. "I have given you what you wanted. If you choose to decline it, then our business is ended. You may leave us any time you like."

"Leave you?" The warlock *threw* the dragon tome to the floor. One hand went up and pulled the hood back over. Shade was a different person when all but hidden by the voluminous cloak. "Only with them!"

"I knew he could not be trusted!" Xabene whispered. "He let you think he was a prisoner or nearly dead just so that you would help him gain entrance!"

"I don't know . . . "

Serkadion Manee had stepped in front of the duo. "They do not wish to depart with you. Leave now or not at all."

Holding out a hand, Shade tried to appeal to the confused scholar. "Master Bedlam, have him explain what has happened to the others he allowed inside! Ask him why neither the Dragon King nor any of the others who sought, foolishly, I see, the secrets of this monster ever questioned those folk! Ask him what became of them!"

"It is time you left." Serkadion Manee pointed at the other Vraad.

A brilliant emerald green aura bathed Shade. The warlock smiled and the aura winked out of existence as abruptly as it had formed.

"My cousins showed more imagination."

Helpless, Wellen and Xabene stepped back from Manee. The gnome ignored them. "You want imagination?"

Every book from the shelves before, next to, and behind the hooded figure shot forth.

Shade covered his face as the paper hailstorm battered and buried him. Though he must have sought to protect himself with his own skills, several volumes struck him soundly on the head. The warlock went down on one knee. The dragon tomes, what he had desired for so very long, continued to come to join their brethren in the assault.

Unable to stand it any longer, Wellen ceased his retreat and came up behind the gnome. Manee, still holding his head and now breathing with a little difficulty, paid him no mind as he concentrated on defeating his rival.

"A little knowledge is a dangerous thing!" snarled Serkadion Manee. Despite his seeming triumph, however, each passing second saw him more and more exhausted. He clutched his side.

Wellen's head screamed of the danger he was thrusting himself into, but the novice warlock patently ignored both the warning and the fear he felt rising. Perhaps it was still the memory of Shade and his silent talk with the phantasms of the scholar's ancestors or even Wellen's own brief conversation with Sharissa Zeree's specter, but he could not allow Serkadion Manee to continue.

Praying that something, *anything*, would happen, Bedlam touched the gnome's shoulder.

In the chamber where the Dragon King struggled, the magical page that held him prisoner burst into flames.

The Purple Dragon roared.

Wellen had hardly expected Serkadion Manee to scream, but the master of the citadel did so—and very loudly. Manee doubled over, falling to the floor. One hand still clutched his head. "Too much . . ." he muttered. "Too much . . . but it cannot be! Not me!" Then, "He will escape . . . he will . . ."

"What did you do?" the enchantress asked, joining Wellen. The gnome, curled up, seemed to be in shock, although it might have been the effect of sorcery. Slowly, his words became quieter. Serkadion Manee eventually froze in one position. Wellen stared at his hand, uncertain as to whether he was the cause or not. When Xabene moved even closer to him, he was almost afraid to touch her for fear the same fate that had befallen Serkadion Manee would befall her.

"I don't know . . . it *could* have been me . . ." He reached toward the fallen figure, but pulled his hand back at the last moment. Wellen had no desire to kill Manee. That might happen if he touched him again. He still had no control over his abilities.

Understanding his quandary, Xabene knelt and inspected Serkadion Manee for him. Her first touch was tentative, but when the still figure did not respond, she became less cautious. After a brief inspection, the enchantress pushed aside some hair that had fallen forward and said, "He's either in a trance or there's a spell on him."

"Is there anything you can do?"

"I could care less about doing anything for this parasite . . . but the answer is no; I can't. What has him is beyond my meager powers."

"I could try to touch him again," he suggested with some hesitation, his hands clenched, "but it might only harm him. I . . . I do not even dare touch *you.*"

Xabene reached out and took hold of his left hand before he realized what she was about.

"No—" His protest faded when nothing happened. Bedlam glared at the woman.

She smiled. "You seem to work off your emotions. I counted on the fact that you wouldn't want to hurt me. I was right."

As a scholar, he would have argued her logic, especially as it did not take in so any other considerations. On a more personal level, he agreed with her . . . not that he planned on telling the enchantress that.

His eyes drifted beyond her, alighting on the massive pile of bulky tomes. "Shade!"

Nearly dragging Xabene along, he rushed to where the warlock had made his last stand. While Wellen could not forgive the mad spellcaster, as with Serkadion Manee, he wished Shade no injury. Wellen admitted to himself that there was still a trace of compassion for the warlock. In the same position, the scholar wondered how *he* would have held up. Would he have been as insane as Shade? Worse?

They dug their way into the pile. The scholar was amazed at both the sheer number of books and how none of them had been damaged in any way. Serkadion Manee's assault had initially surprised him, for he had not thought the gnome would risk his own work. Now he saw that the gnome had assured the condition of the dragon tomes before sending them at his adversary.

Deeper and deeper they burrowed, Wellen as swiftly as he could and Xabene with much reluctance. As far as she was probably concerned, two great problems had been removed from her life. Wellen was aware that the only reason she helped was because she knew he would not leave without trying.

The literary avalanche gave way in short order to his efforts, but still he could not find Shade. Bedlam began moving around the massive pile, thinking perhaps that he had chosen the wrong location to dig.

Shoving aside yet another dozen tomes, Xabene cursed in the name of her former masters and said, "Wellen, we have to forget him! I think it might be a good idea if we search instead for a way out of this place!"

"Not without Shade! He saved your life, remember!"

"And we've repaid him for that! Just because it turned out to be a ploy on his part . . ." She shivered, recalling something for the first time. "I wonder what he did to them. He *must* have defeated them." Her eyes grew round. "Gods, what power and skill!"

"Thank you . . ." came a hissing voice from where they had left the unconscious gnome. "It wasssss really nothing at all!"

A leviathan in scale armor, the Purple Dragon was a thing of nightmares. He filled the hall, so massive was he even in humanoid form. The dragon's head crest leering down on the twosome made him come nearly to the ceiling; Within the helm, they saw the reptilian eyes burning. Now and then, a forked tongue would dart out of a mouth filled with jagged teeth. The image of a monstrous knight was so real it was almost impossible to believe that the armor was actually just the Dragon King's scaly hide twisted by the spell that allowed him this shape.

With one hand he carried the unmoving form of Serkadion Manee. The other was raised toward the duo.

"You are mine at lasssst, manling! I have *everything* now!" He indicated the two should come to him.

Wellen's body rose, although Wellen himself tried not to obey. Xabene was already moving toward the armored figure. He caught a glimpse of her horrified expression and wondered about his own.

The Purple Dragon made them pause just within arm's length. One swipe of his clawed hand could have torn both their throats out. This near, the scholar noticed that the drake was not as at ease as he had tried to make them believe. There were signs of strain. Wellen could see that Purple was feeling the weight of trying to maintain his control over the situation.

If nothing else, it was the sibilance in his voice that most betrayed the Dragon King. The more excited or weary he became, the more the hissing grew dominant. "At lassst! Now all I need issss the interfering warlock who wassss the final sssstraw!" The drake gave a raspy chuckle. "If not for him, I might sssstill be sssstruggling! Not that the outcome wassss not inevitable regardlessss! I would have sssstill triumphed, jusssst a bit later!"

Wellen and Xabene once more moved without their own consent. Lugging the gnome with him, the Dragon King stepped between them and confronted the sea of knowledge under which Serkadion Manee had attempted to drown Shade.

"Let it be assss it wassss."

The dragon tomes flew back to their various shelves. There did not seem to be any order to what the Purple Dragon did. He did not seem to care about organizing the books, merely putting them where they would be out of the way. For the moment, Shade, the last loose end, was all that concerned him.

When all the books had flown away, however, there was no trace of the hooded warlock. The Dragon King stalked over to where the center of the mountain of tomes had stood and peered down at the floor.

"Bah!" He turned back to Wellen. "Your comrade issss either a victim of thissss damnable little ssssprite or hassss fled in mindlessss fear at my coming! Either way, he will trouble ussss no more!"

That Shade had turned coward was not a notion that Wellen Bedlam believed. That the warlock had fled, however, he found more likely. With Serkadion Manee's spell of rejuvenation not to his liking and the Dragon King now in control, there was no reason for Shade to stay.

Yet, he *had* fought with Manee over Wellen's freedom.

The Purple Dragon's breathing quickened. He put Serkadion Manee down and leaned against one of the corridor walls. For a brief moment, the horrific warrior shimmered.

Wellen found he could move his fingers. It was not a great victory in the scheme of things, but it was a victory nonetheless. It meant that the Dragon King was weaker.

Slowly, the drake regained control of himself. He glared at the two humans, daring either of them to comment on his weakness. Still under his spell, they could not have said anything even if they had been insane enough to want to. Satisfied, the drake contemplated his next move.

"There issss no need for the two of you for now," he informed them. The truth, Bedlam knew, was that like Serkadion Manee, it was becoming harder and harder for Purple to spread his power over so much. If he could find another way of keeping his two human prisoners secure, then it would allow him to redirect his efforts. "I shall sssend you to the royal caverns. Then, when the time permitsssss, I will be better able to disssssect what information you know from your mindssss."

He waved a negligent hand at them, then hissed in anger when they simply stood there. The Dragon King stared at them long and hard. Wellen felt a faint tug, but it soon faded.

"Why do you not vanish? What holdssss you here?" The Purple Dragon picked up the wizened sorcerer at his feet and held him at eye level. "Thissss issss your doing!

It will not ssssave you, though! Your preciousssss tomessss are now mine and they shall stay mine!" A sinewy tongue darted out and in. "You would like me to assssk you for aid, would you not? You think I am foolish enough to risssk your essscape by freeing you from thissss ssspell for *any* length of time? You will neither move nor sssspeak until I can be certain your cooperation issss assured!"

The fearsome knight lowered his motionless captive and then scanned the library hall in both directions. There seemed no end to the corridor no matter which way one looked. Cursing, he turned back to the two helpless humans.

Wellen found himself able to move once more. He looked up expectantly at the Dragon King.

"There issss no need for me to wassssste my strength on you, manling. Neither you nor your mate have shown power of any ssssignificant level. Therefore, you will hardly be able to essscape me should you both be mad enough to try."

The scholar was well aware of their present chances. Later, things might change, but for now they had little choice but to obey. "I understand."

"I am certain you do. Both of you."

Xabene gasped as mastery of her body was once again hers. She quickly nodded her agreement.

"We underssssstand one another. Good." The Dragon King studied the corridor behind where he had originally materialized. He nodded to himself and added, "Ssssince I may not teleport you out of thissss place, we musssst find a portal like the one we entered by. You two will lead the way . . . jusssst in casssse."

Wellen reached for the enchantress, but the drake's free hand came between then. Nothing was said but die message was clear. The Dragon King did not trust their apparent weakness *that* much. He would not allow his captives to conspire against him.

Side-by-side but nearly an arm's length apart, the two began walking. The horrific knight followed only a few paces back, Serkadion Manee's small form not slowing his stride in the least. The sorcerer was carried the way one might carry a light sack, an ignoble position if ever there was one.

Their trek began in silence, the Dragon King possibly taking inventory of his gains. Wellen doubted that his success was going to be as complete as he imagined. Something about the citadel, especially the libraries, seemed to hint at a reluctance to accept this new master. If defeating Serkadion Manee was all that the drake lord had needed to do to triumph, then why was he unwilling to teleport *within* the pentagon even if teleportation out of it was impossible? Surely if everything was now his, then there was no danger.

If that were the case, Purple would not be using them as shields. No, the Dragon King knew that the battle was not yet over. He had captured only the master, not the servant.

After a time, the scholar decided to chance talking to his captor. Anything to break the leaden silence that suppressed them all. "Is Prentiss Asaalk truly dead?"

Almost to his surprise, the reptilian sovereign responded. "The gnome had the right of it. Your azure companion quickly proved himsssself too devioussss to live. I tolerate ambition in thosssse who are usssseful, but only assss long assss they undersssstand their place. I knew he would never undersssstand and sssso I played on hissss very arrogance and ambition." A hissing laugh. "There are collarssss and there are collarssss. Assss if I would be so foolish assss to trusssst him with the tasssk of sssseeking you out and bringing you back to me!"

Asaalk had offered him to the Dragon King. *Would I have done the same in his position?* he asked himself.

"There will be one for you and your female eventually. Collarsss that will only teach you your place, however, unlike some of the otherssss I have usssssed in the passsst. I needed the blue one'ssss appearance and mind but not hissss untrusssstworthy waysss. The collar he ignorantly donned drained him of all memoriesssss. It alwayssss workssss sssso much better when they are not aware of what issss to happen. Alassss, it meant his eventual death, for in draining his memories, it destroyed what was left." A pause. "Pray that you do not annoy me assss he did. I might forget which collar to pressssent you."

The last brought a return to silence. Wellen exchanged glances with Xabene, but that was the extent of their communication. Escape was essential. The reptilian monarch's hint at their future had made that all too clear. Unlike the Green Dragon, this drake lord had no qualms about disposing of his guests on a whim.

Shelf after shelf after shelf of book after book after book. All of them forming the accumulation of the gnome's millennia-old search for knowledge. Did any of them hold a key to their rescue? He would have liked to thumb through a few of the volumes, if only to see what was contained within.

"Sssso much knowledge," the Dragon King commented in what might have been an admiring tone. "Will there be time for all of it?"

For just that brief instant, the scholar and the Dragon King shared a desire.

"There are no titles on the sssspinessss. How does one know what issss contained in what?"

The question had bothered Wellen, too, but unless the drake chose to release Serkadion Manee now, he doubted he would ever find out.

"Manling."

As the Dragon King had not stopped, neither did Bedlam. He turned and waited for his captor to speak again.

"Doessss thissss place sssseem almost *alive* to you?"

He gave it some thought. "It wouldn't surprise me."

"Agreed." Burning eyes darted from one bookshelf to the next. "Sssso many marvelssss . . ." The look of admiration died as the drake lord turned his gaze forward. "But the one I could do without issss thissss cursed, endlesssss hall!"

The words no sooner escaped his lipless mouth then they saw a lone metal door in the distance. The discovery was so abrupt that Wellen eyed the ensorcelled gnome with some suspicion. Did Serkadion Manee still have mastery over his former domain?

The door, when they at last reached it, was a simple iron thing with only a handle. There was no lock, but then the ancient sorcerer had never needed one. Pausing, the party stared at the exit for several seconds. What lay on the other side only Serkadion Manee knew. After some silent debate, the Dragon King looked at the explorer. "You!" he hissed, thrusting a clawed finger at Wellen. "You will open it!"

Bedlam stepped forward, knowing he had no choice. All he could do was pray as his fingers wrapped around the handle and pulled the door open.

Xabene gasped.

"Nothing . . ." murmured the Dragon King. "Almosssst a dissssappointment."

His heart still pounding in his ears, Wellen surveyed what had been hidden behind the door. Only another hallway. No trap. No visible threat.

Save perhaps to one's eyes. Evidently, Serkadion Manee had his whimsical moments, for there seemed no other explanation for the design and pattern of the place.

They entered an immense hall that was a chess master's board run amok. The floor, the walls, and the rounded ceiling were all covered in a black and white pattern resembling one massive game board. There were no doors, save at the far, far end. Neither were there fixtures or decorations. Because of the pattern, it was even hard to tell where the floor ended and the walls began. Wellen would not have been surprised if the party could have walked up one of the walls without even noticing the change.

"What issss thissss new madness? My head poundssss jusssst sssstaring at it!" Purple, squinting, turned to his two mobile prisoners. "The female will go first, I think. A few paces ahead. Then you and I, manling. Side-by-side. If you should stray even a foot beyond my reach, I will act. I do not need to touch you to kill you."

"I understand."

A taloned finger scraped the stubble that was growing on the scholar's neck. "I am sure that you do."

The trio started down the hall at a slow but steady pace. From his position, Wellen studied the profile of the horrific warrior. The Purple Dragon, marching along from square to square, looked like the soul survivor of some massive game in which he played both knight and king. The scholar pictured an entire board of such figures, with Serkadion Manee for some reason still coming to mind as the opposing lord. Xabene was a queen, but one whose side she was he had not figured out. As for his own position, Wellen could only see himself as a pawn in the middle.

But it is the pawn in the middle who starts the opening gambit sometimes . . .

It was a peculiar thought and he could not say what had caused him to summon it. Chess was *a* game he had once played avidly, but not during the past few years. In the end, the expedition had demanded his complete devotion. There had been no time for games.

"Issss there no hall in thissss accursed place that doesss not ssssstretch on and on and on?" the Dragon King complained. The strain was beginning to show on the drake. Not only had he exhausted much power in escaping his prison and capturing Manee, but he was expending even more keeping the gnome secure while also, at least so Wellen assumed, probing for any sorcerous surprises left by the citadel's former master.

It rose through the floor, clad in black mail and plate armor, simply decorated but skillfully crafted. A helm obscured all trace of the fighter's countenance. In his gauntleted hands, the dark knight held a battle-ax nearly two-thirds the size of Wellen himself. As for the mysterious warrior, he topped the Dragon King in both height and build.

"A challenge?" mocked the drake. "No challenge at all!" He raised his free hand.

The newcomer glowed liquid-metal red.

Purple suddenly snarled and withdrew his hand as if something had bitten it. While he rubbed it, the silent guardian took two steps forward, then shifted a square to his right, bringing him parallel to the rounded form of Serkadion Manee.

Another figure, also black, rose behind the original position of the first. This one was smaller, but clad in nearly identical armor. He looked no less threatening for being shorter, although the ebony mace and shield he carried might have had something to do with that. The second guardian took two steps forward, then also waited.

The Dragon King hissed.

Scarlet tendrils of sorcery entwined the two attackers.

The larger one shook them off like so much mist. He took another step forward, then two to his left so that he ended up facing Xabene, who quickly backed away to where Wellen was standing.

After a brief struggle with the drake lord's attack, the second warrior took a single step toward the party.

Behind the black figures, two more, identical to the smaller one, joined the confrontation. Far to the scholar's left, a different gladiator rose. This one was almost as tall as the lead figure, but slimmer and carrying a crimson longbow. A sleek, glittering arrow of gold was already notched.

"We have to go back to the libraries," Xabene whispered. "I don't think the Dragon King will find these so simple to defeat!"

Nodding, Bedlam glanced back in order to locate the doorway . . . and found that it no longer *existed.* "It seems we have no choice in the matter." He faced forward again and squinted. "The other door is still there."

"But we have to go through them first."

Beside them, Purple heard everything. "They are nothing! I have dissssscovered their weaknessss."

He held up his ensorcelled captive for the warriors to see. "I have your massssster here! Ssssurrender or I will kill him now!"

The archer took several steps forward until he was even with the original guardian. The Dragon King spun around and held Serkadion Manee between himself and the bowman, but the latter did nothing.

The shorter warriors all took one step forward.

It struck Wellen then what sort of predicament they faced. This hall was not simply decorated like a chessboard by chance. Rubbing his chin in thought, he happened to glance ceilingward.

"Xabene!" he whispered.

She followed his gaze.

More than half a dozen ebony warriors stood scattered on the upper walls and ceiling. They seemed not at all put out by the fact that in some cases, they stood completely upside down. Most were identical to the ones already confronting the trio, but there was one wearing black raiments and an obscuring hood who resembled some insidious cleric.

All of those clinging to the walls and ceiling were armed and eyeing the intruders below.

Hearing Wellen's voice, the Dragon King turned just enough to see the humans. When he caught them staring up, he glanced that way. "Dragon of the Depthssss!"

The archer released his arrow.

It might have been an exceptional shot, but Bedlam was almost positive that only chance made the bolt miss Serkadion Manee, who still hung unknowing and unprotected from the massive Dragon King's hand. Hampered by his living baggage, Purple could not turn in time to avoid the arrow. He was, however, able to react fast enough with his sorcery to cause it to deflect. A normal arrow would not have concerned the Dragon King, but it was doubtful that Serkadion Manee would have been satisfied with such for this macabre, life-size game.

Yet another dark knight rose through one of the squares, this one out of the wall to their left. Though armored like the others, it had a definite feminine shape and in its hands it carried a jeweled scepter.

"Pawns, knight"—the scholar studied one of the archers, then continued—"rooks, I suppose, then bishops, and now a queen." Wellen glanced hurriedly around the mind-wrenching corridor. "But where's the king?"

"What are you talking about?" the enchantress muttered, her eyes still on the unsettling tableau above them.

"This is some bizarre and deadly chess game!"

If the drake lord heard them this time, he said nothing. His hands were full in more ways than one, for several of the stygian figures were moving toward him, each one following a peculiar movement pattern. Even the ones on the ceiling and walls were shifting closer. So far, only the archer, Serkadion Manee's idea of a rook, had posed any problem, but the attackers were slowly cutting off the party from any hope of escape . . . and there was no telling what powers the queen or the yet-to-be-seen king controlled. There might even be more than one. Who was to say that the gnome's version of chess was the same as the one the scholar was familiar with? With so large a board and so many dimensions, Wellen would have added pieces. He suspected that Manee had done just that.

The Purple Dragon unleashed another spell. Mist enshrouded the chessmen, for a moment bringing all movement to a halt. More was expected if the drake's irritation was anything to judge by. Hissing, the Dragon King muttered under his breath. The mist took on a greenish tinge.

The nearest pawn fell face first onto the floor and faded away.

"Ha!" Encouraged by his success, the Dragon King increased the intensity of the green mist. The knight in front remained still, but the other pieces moved closer, as if the death of one had strengthened the others.

Wellen saw the queen raise her specter. He was caught in a quandary. Warn the Dragon King? Let him be attacked? Either way he and Xabene lost. They needed the drake to save them from these silent sentinels, but they also needed the chessmen to rescue them from the clutches of the dragon.

He was saved that decision by the Dragon King himself, who noticed the queen at the last moment. The jewel in her scepter glowed a warm rose. Purple's eyes narrowed and darkness seemed to come from them. He reached out and swiftly blocked the queen's scepter. A crimson flash was all they could see, then the darkness vanished. The queen slowly lowered her royal weapon and stood there as if nothing had happened.

"Can't we do anything?" the enchantress asked. "I have some power! Perhaps I could pull one of those from the ceiling onto some of the ones coming toward us!"

"Do nothing!" the scholar uttered in sudden inspiration. Perhaps they were not in so great a danger after all!

She looked at Wellen as if he had lost all sense of reality. "If we do nothing, we die."

"If we do nothing," he responded in as low a voice as possible, "then they may ignore us completely. So far, they've only attacked the Purple Dragon!"

"I think I would prefer not to wait until they have killed him. By then we'll be surrounded!"

He nodded. "When I said do nothing, I meant only in terms of attacking them. I think that they may only be interested in the Dragon King"—Wellen pointed at the archer above—"or else we would have been dead already."

The original chess piece, the knight, finally attacked. With a rapid one-step, two-step run, he moved close to the Dragon King. He brought the axe up and around in a vicious arc, his speed so astonishing that the drake lord barely had time to react. Not trusting to his spells at so close a range, the reptilian monarch stumbled backward. It almost proved a fatal mistake, for Serkadion Manee's weight made just enough difference that the drake nearly fell.

Cursing, the Dragon King shot a glance at the frozen figure. With little ceremony, he dumped the still form of Manee on one of the squares a few feet back and to the side. In his now-free taloned hands materialized an incredibly long, curiously curved sword. No human that Wellen had ever met could have wielded so great a giant, but the Dragon King did so with ease.

He moves and acts with confidence, the scholar noted. *How long has he held this spell from the eyes of his brethren? One would almost think he had been born in such a body and not shaped himself through masterful sorcery!*

The ebony knight brought the axe around again, this time in a downward arc. The gleaming head missed its target by less than a foot, but it forced Purple back another square. If he was not careful, Wellen thought, he would be in danger of stepping on———

Serkadion Manee was no longer lying prone on the square where he had been so roughly deposited.

Xabene noticed it at the same time. "The gnome!" she hissed. "He's escaped!"

It hardly seemed possible, but there was no sign of the libraries' creator.

153

Wellen could not even say exactly when he had disappeared.

A golden streak flashed by them, narrowly missing him. Reflex action made him fall to the floor away from the path of the bolt.

"We may die whether they intend to kill us or not!" he managed to gasp.

There was no response from the sorceress. Fearful that she had somehow been struck down by the arrow, despite the fact that he was almost certain it had continued on, Wellen rolled over.

Xabene was gone.

Something heavy and metal crashed to the floor beside him. Not Xabene, as his mind first imagined, but the knight who had crossed weapons with the Dragon King. The helm was cracked and for the first time he caught a glimpse of the warrior within.

The sight almost made him sick. Within the armor, thankfully only barely visible, was the mummified visage of a man. By the explorer's calculation, he had been dead for years. There was hardly anything but dried skin and bone. By comparison, Shade almost looked robust.

Then, to his horror, the head began to *turn* slowly toward him. He scrambled back.

Something that would not be denied pulled him from every direction.

The chessboard corridor and his macabre companion faded. For the first time, Wellen welcomed a teleportation spell, regardless of where it might be sending him.

A darkened chamber formed around him. He breathed a sigh of relief . . . and looked up at the looming specter of a huge, ebony-armored warrior clad in scarlet cape and crown and bearing a long scepter upon which was fixed a rainbow gem whose power even an inept novice like Wellen Bedlam could sense.

He had found the king of Serkadion Manee's chess game at last . . . or perhaps the king had found *him.*

Chapter Nineteen

The black king continued to stare in silence. Wellen remained where he had materialized, uncertain if even the slightest movement was allowed.

After a long, breath-holding wait in which the ebony figure did not stir, the scholar began to wonder if he had misjudged the situation. He looked at the visored head and dared talk to it. "Are you the one who saved me?"

Nothing. Yet, knowing the abominable thing that must lie within, he could not take a lack of response as meaning that he was safe. "I'd like to stand, if you have no objections to that."

He decided to take the silence for agreement. Wellen slowly rose from the floor, his eyes ever locked on the monarch of night. The armor spoke of a being gargantuan in proportions, larger than even the humanoid form of the Dragon King. While such giants were not unknown among humanity, it was possible that the armor enhanced its wearer, made the thing within appear larger than it was.

Either way, if it chose to strike him down, he doubted he would be able to defend himself.

When he stood before it, and it did not react, the shorter scholar took a step toward it. Still nothing. He continued until he was well within arm's reach. The scepter did not rise and crush his skull. The gauntleted hand did not seize him by the throat and squeeze.

He reached up and touched the black king lightly on the chest. The chessman might as well have been a marble column for all he moved.

"Praise be!" Bedlam exhaled. Thinking of the need for a weapon, Wellen tried to take the scepter. It was held so tight, in fact, that it was more likely he would end up crushed under the fallen figure of the king if he continued. Exasperated, Wellen stepped back from the monstrous toy and finally studied his new surroundings.

Choking down a gasp of disgust, Wellen for the first time saw the *other* playing pieces of the gnome's macabre game. A full score at least, all surrounding him, a legion of the dead. There were a few more black pieces and an entire range of white. There were duplicates, too, evidently in case one of the others became too damaged to use again. They were the only things he could see in the chamber, but that was not surprising, since the only illumination was a pale blue ball just above him.

He was alone. No Xabene. No Serkadion Manee. Where they had vanished to he had no idea. Worse, where *he* had vanished to was a complete mystery. Just how vast was the gnome's citadel? The libraries alone were a phenomenon in size, but now he was discovering corridor after corridor and room after room.

There was little choice but to seek a way out of this place and hope he could find Xabene. Then, the two of them would have to find a means of escaping Manee's paradoxical pentagon. What happened between the Dragon King and the gnome was of no interest to him. Wellen merely wanted his freedom.

Choosing a direction unpopulated by the grisly warriors, the explorer started out. The throbbing in his head had begun again, although he could not say exactly when, but here it was fairly useless. There was too much within a near distance that was genuinely a threat to the would-be warlock. His ability informed him of nothing he did not already know about. Had one of the chessmen raised a weapon against him, Bedlam would have been no better warned.

If this was the extent of his powers, then he doubted he would ever be a competent sorcerer. At this point, he doubted he was much more competent at *anything*.

He found, to his relief, that the blue light followed him as he progressed. It would at least be possible to wander about without having to worry about walking into something in the dark. The illumination was still not the best, but it always kept a yard or two of the path around him visible, which had been more than he could have hoped.

Now if only I can find a doorway or a gate out of this chamber! The fear that this was a place accessible only by a teleportation spell had already occurred to him, but Bedlam tried not to think about the possibility. If such was the case, then he was doomed to capture, or even worse, to die here and become one more rotting corpse.

Wellen increased his pace.

After what he estimated to be at least three or four minutes, Wellen began puzzling over the lack of walls. Not once had he noticed one, not even when he had stood in the midst of the chessmen. Looking up, he realized that there was no visible *ceiling* either. Only the floor beneath his feet, the blue globe floating over his head, and the horrific army he had left behind seemed to exist. There was no sound, save his breathing and his footfalls. He might have been in limbo.

Limbo . . .

He came to a dead halt, trying to hear again the voice whispering in his head. Had it been his imagination? A single word, one sounding more like a gust of wind than speech, that was all it had been. Just a trick of his anxious mind?

Mind . . .

Again, a single word! "Is someone there?"

The proverbial silence of the tomb was all that greeted him, but Wellen was certain it had been another who had spoken.

"Where are you?" His voice did not echo. Even sound died here.

Died . . .

This time, Wellen thought he noted a direction. It was difficult to say if he was imagining *that,* too, for the voice still appeared to exist in his head alone. Yet, he felt that turning to his right and walking in that direction for a time was the correct choice. Perhaps the only choice.

"Please," the scholar whispered, running a hand through his hair as he tried to think. Despite a quick and lengthy stride, Wellen still saw nothing. "Who are you? I don't mean any harm."

It could all be another game, either Serkadion Manee's or the Dragon King's, but he doubted it. With each other to have to concentrate upon, neither could waste time on such a game with him.

Having little other choice, he continued walking. Wellen guessed that he might be underneath the rest of the citadel. Perhaps this was a storage area for Serkadion Manee's abandoned experiments or his monstrous toys, if the chess pieces were any indication. Either way, the scholar only cared about escape.

No escape . . .

"No escape? But . . ." He closed his mouth. The voice within was not speaking of his fate, but rather its *own.* For the first time, he sensed the mournful, beseeching tone, the sense of agony and loss.

The cry for release.

More than mere words were being conveyed into his head. Emotions. Vague memories. A warning.

Its fate *could* be his, if he was not careful.

"But where are you?" He had to find out what the source of the voice was. He needed to know if he could free it from whatever torment held it. Wellen had to find out if he could avert his own fate.

Then, the dim blue illumination touched an array of small, glittering objects before him.

They stood upon a pedestal, each in its own little slot. Vials no bigger than his index finger. There were ten vials in all, each sealed tight with wax. What was within he could not say, only that it shifted as he tried to see it, almost as if it did not want to be seen. His scholarly side seized control. Wellen crouched near the pedestal and surveyed the scene from eye level. The slots had been designed to securely hold the containers. No simple jostle of the pedestal would shake them loose. For that matter, the stand itself had been created from the same stonelike substance that formed the pentagon itself. The pedestal literally grew from the floor, which made it doubtful that anything short of a dragon would actually be able to disturb it in the first place.

"But what is it?" he muttered.

There came an almost undeniable urge to reach forward and touch the nearest vial. The urge was desperate, needy, and not of his own doing. It was the same sensation as the voice. Whoever or whatever had chosen to speak through his mind desired him to touch one of the vials. It pleaded through sheer emotion for him to do so. He started to comply, but as he eyed the odd array, the arrangement of the containers registered.

He was staring at a pentagram. The pattern was almost identical to that utilized by the Lords of the Dead. This was not just a display, but part of a complex spell of which the sealed vials were likely of the utmost importance. There was one at each point of the pentagram. The only difference was that instead of an eleventh container, a clear gemstone filled the center. It was not an overly brilliant stone, which was why he had not paid that much attention to it, but he saw now that someone had cut the stone to certain specifications. If things followed as they had with the necromancers, then the centerpiece was a focus of sorts.

What was in the vials, that they were used in this spell? What sort of power had the gnome captured in each? What was he doing with it?

The urge to reach for the nearest vessel struck him again, but he shook it off. Touching the magical construct of a creature like Serkadion Manee could easily prove very, very fatal. He had his life to consider. His and Xabene's. She was still trapped here somewhere, perhaps the captive of the immortal.

Trapped . . . A chill wind enshrouded him. Indignation amidst despair rocked his senses. Pleading struck him again while he fought off the other emotions.

There's more than one! the scholar thought. More than one . . . soul? . . . trapped . . . *trapped?* Wellen dared lean close enough to minutely study the foremost flask.

A soul? No, not a soul. A mind.

Ten of them.

"Lord Drazeree protect me!" he uttered, falling back on the inaccurate version he had grow up with. This was what Shade had hinted at! This was what the twisted gnome did with those he invited in! *He doesn't like to waste anything. He said so himself!*

How did he progress? Did he take their memories, as he had taken Wellen's, and then used their bodies for whatever purpose the gnome needed them for? No, the bodies had to be the last thing, else the minds would have been damaged, possibly destroyed.

The possibilities became too grotesque. Bedlam forced the thoughts to the back of his mind, but they continued to make their presence felt. He concentrated on the vials. Within was something not quite white, not quite liquid, that tried to hide from his sight. Each vial held similar contents.

With a deep breath, Wellen took hold of the closest.

Pleadingsobbingshatterchildrenfatherhelphusband

Wellen gasped and tore his hand away from the vessel.

"Too much!" he shouted at the mind he had touched. "I can't take that all in!" The memories and the message had kept mixing. It was probably as confusing and difficult for the trapped thing within as it was for the scholar.

Shatter, he recalled. *It said 'shatter'.* A plea to destroy the vial? That would *kill* it---

He shook his head. Not kill it. In truth, the ten were already dead; they had just not been allowed to rest. How long since they had been forced into this tortured nonexistence? The minds must burn out eventually, but they went through agony in the meantime. Bedlam had felt that. Not just from the one he had touched, but from all of them.

There were many questions the dark-haired explorer desired answers to, but to delay in what had to be done would only be adding to the cruelty that Serkadion Manee had instigated.

The vials would not come free of the pedestal; Wellen had learned that during his brief physical contact with the vessel. He would need something to smash them with, but his choices were sorely limited. Anything that could have been used as a weapon had been removed. While he did not want the immortal's victims to suffer further, Wellen did not relish using his bare hands.

He looked down, trying to think, and noticed his boots. They were of the sturdy kind, designed for the tremendous trek originally intended. Comfortable, but with sturdy enough soles and a bit of heel that, admittedly, had been added in vanity to give him a little more height than nature had provided.

Stepping back, Wellen measured the pedestal. If he raised his leg high enough . . .

Balancing himself, Wellen kicked with as much force as he could muster.

157

The vial shattered, pieces flying everywhere.

Something like a wisp of smoke shot forth from the remains of the vessel. A trilling sound assailed the explorer's ears as the smoky form whirled about his head once. Wellen caught a glimpse of a face, or at least thought he had, belonging to a woman. That was all he could see. The smoke curled around itself then and, without further fanfare, *dissipated.*

He became awash in a sea of emotion. Pleading and hope from those still trapped. The ease with which he had liberated the first still somewhat surprised Bedlam, but it was possible that Serkadion Manee had never considered an intruder down here. Wellen suspected that the reason he was here in the first place was due to the very beings he was now aiding. The Dragon King's presence likely had something to do with their sudden freedom to act in their own behalf.

Shifting his stance, Wellen brought his boot up again. This time, he aimed so that more than one vial would be in the path of his heel. The sooner this was finished the better.

Three more containers shattered under the impact of his second strike. A harmony arose as three tiny forms intertwined with one another and then, like the first, circled his head once. He saw no ghostly visages this time, but he felt their overwhelming gratitude, their relief at being freed from their torment.

As the three faded, the scholar studied the remaining ones. The anticipation they exuded permeated him, making Wellen all that more desirous to put an end to the travesty. He considered his arm. The vials were actually fairly fragile, perhaps a necessity for the spell. While his hands were unprotected, his arm was covered in cloth. One good sweep of his arm could do what would have required his heel two or three attempts to complete.

He stepped around to the other side of the pedestal, measured, and pulled his arm back.

His head shrieked a dire warning.

Wellen fell to the floor and rolled away from the pedestal, the blue light, as was its manner, shifting to compensate. The scholar came to a crouching position. The pedestal was only a dim outline at the edge of the ball's illumination. He could see no threat to warrant the alarm.

"What . . . have . . . you . . . *done?"* came a voice from somewhere behind the vials.

The despair he felt was not just that emitted by the minds in the vials. His own more than matched theirs.

"Do you know what you've done?" What was most frightening about the voice was its detached quality, almost as if the questioner had gone beyond anger to something far colder and far deadlier.

An inferno lit up the region, momentarily blinding Wellen. When he was able to see again, a tiny part of the scholar's mind noted that beyond himself, the pedestal, and the newcomer, there seemed to be nothing but emptiness.

Emptiness and Serkadion Manee.

"Six left," the wizened gnome commented, looking down at the broken pentagram. "But not at all in a viable configuration. That means that control is gone."

Perhaps it was Wellen's imagination, but he thought he felt an aura of satisfaction emanating from the remaining victims.

"He shall treat you no better than I, my little friends," the gnome snarled. His attention turned to the human. "And you have finally made a place for yourself in the Dragonrealm." Manee indicated the now empty slots.

Wellen knew his only hope was to stall. It was the only thing left to him, a momentary halt to the inevitable. Unless a miracle occurred, nothing would prevent Manee from adding him to his vile collection.

He wondered if Xabene had already been added. Was one of the minds hers?

"I'd like to ask a question if I may?"

Something much like the strange square memory device materialized in the gnome's wrinkled hand. "I have no time for questions or rebellious creations! Each moment allows that infernal lizard to further set back my precious work! The chessmen do not respond now and the corridors are beginning to buckle. . . and you have made the situation intolerable! Without a properly coordinated system to maintain the balance, this entire structure cannot exist! The libraries will fold in on themselves as they try to take up limited space . . . and they will not be concerned with the presence of any of us!"

"Stealing my mind will hardly give you the added control you need."

Serkadion Manee glanced at the vials. "I can create another viable configuration, one that will work until I've gathered enough replacements. The female, for one. Perhaps the drake, too. I've never tried one of his kind." Despite his talk of time limits, the sorcerer became caught up in his own suggestions. "I had to rely on elves and dwarfs and the like. They lasted longer, but were too scarce. When humans appeared, they looked to be perfect, but they only last two or three centuries." He scratched his chin. "What would be perfect is an immortal, but the drakes live centuries. They will do perhaps as a good substitute."

"How do you propose to get the Dragon King to accept such a task?" Wellen asked. If his choices consisted of three hundred years of agony or a quicker death in the collapse of the citadel, he would take the latter. He only hoped the destruction was imminent.

"Once I have this realigned, I will have time to consider that." Manee smiled. "A pity we do not have more time to discuss things. You have potential. Unfortunately for you, it is time for me to make use of some of that."

Wellen's legs abruptly gave way, sending him to a kneeling position on the floor. He felt the other minds mourn their lost hope and his lost life.

"Just one thing," Wellen asked, no longer trying to stall but wanting to know. "Where's Xabene? What have you done with her?"

The gnome's smile soured. "I do not have your companion, but do not worry, my young friend; she will be joining you soon. There is no way out of here without *my* assistance."

"You weren't responsible for the chessmen?"

"Talkative until the end?" Manee stepped around the pedestal. "Yes, I was. . . in the beginning. The drake's presence has muddled things. I lost control and these"—he indicated the *vials*—"*these* dared to exert some independence."

Their hatred for their captor could be felt even now. Serkadion Manee shrugged it off. "Their agony cannot be helped, nor will yours. It is essential that my work continue and that the results are available for possible later study. I need this spell to maintain that system. I could use the memory disks, of course, but they do not last. The memories fade." The gnome's smile broadened again. He appeared to be trying to be kind about the situation, as if Wellen had a choice. "Otherwise I certainly would not do this, believe me."

He held up the gray, square device with the metal side toward the straining human. "You will find this a bit more shocking than the other one."

Whether it was his own latent ability come to the forefront in this desperate moment or some carelessness upon the immortal's part, the novice spellcaster felt a weight lift from his entire body. Movement was his again.

Wellen did the only thing that he could think of under the circumstances. He *threw* himself against the shorter Manee.

The gnome just had time to open his mouth before the two of them met. As they fell, his disk slipped from his hand. Wellen cared not; if Serkadion Manee recovered, the gnome could easily retrieve his dark device. The scholar had to keep his adversary off balance. Only if he succeeded could he even consider the menacing artifact.

Manee struck something solid, jarring both men hard.

The pedestal! Wellen, taking advantage of the fact that the sorcerer had taken the brunt of the collision, lifted the much lighter gnome and threw him over the top of the stand.

There was a crackling noise as the immortal sprawled over the pedestal.

Stumbling back, the explorer watched in relief and awe as the six remaining victims were released. For a breath or two, the smoky creatures cavorted over the stunned figure of their murderer and enslaver. Then, they drifted over to Wellen, enveloped him in a wave of gratitude, and drifted off, fading as they went.

A tremendous groan marked their passage. Wellen felt the floor beneath him shift.

Without the imprisoned minds to coordinate his spell, could Serkadion Manee's libraries be beginning to collapse?

"No!" Rolling off the pedestal, the gnome turned and gazed upward. After a quick study of something that Wellen could not see, Manee glared at the scholar. Wellen found himself again frozen in place. "I hope you enjoyed your moment of magical glory, my young, impetuous friend, because even if you can manage another spell, it will not be as easy to escape from my domain as it was to break free of the holding spell!"

"What are you going to do?" He fully expected the worst. He had possibly caused the destruction of the work of ages. The scholarly side mourned its imminent passing but the practical side reminded him that it had to have been done. Whatever fate awaited him would be better than what the immoral had planned.

In point of fact, however, Serkadion Manee was smiling, albeit this time without any pretense of enjoyment. With grim satisfaction, he replied, "No, things are not quite ready to crumble yet. You have caused, though, an imbalance. Things will begin to shift in an attempt to keep the citadel from collapsing . . . and that will cause yet more chaos. Worse, there is no control over anything." The gnome shook his head in mock pity. "But I am hardly in dire straits. I planned for this eventuality. There is a method, albeit a rather drastic one, by which I can restore control of this place. If I could only remember what it entailed I could . . ."

"You speak of a lack of control? Does that mean you've lost control of the citadel?"

Manee did not answer his question. Staring off into the emptiness, he said, "It has been too long. I can't remember what it was." He reached out to his motionless prisoner. "Come. We have a book to read."

Once more, they suddenly stood in the libraries.

It was not the same corridor, not unless the tomes had changed the color of their bindings. These books were sky blue. Again, Wellen was amazed at the sheer volume of Serkadion Manee's studies.

"This way." Under the gnome's guidance, the scholar followed his captor down the corridor. Manee seemed at ease despite the fact that somewhere the Dragon King was searching for them.

The gnarled sorcerer began running his fingers over the spines of one particular row of books. He muttered something under his breath. Wellen could do nothing but walk and watch.

"Here!" Manee pulled out one of the volumes. He opened it. Like a living creature, the pages began to turn of their own accord. Manee perused them, telling the book to continue when he did not find what he was looking for.

"Ah! Stop!"

The pages flattened out.

A bent finger ran down the length of the left page. Serkadion Manee nodded to himself. "Of course! How silly of me! That's why I created it like that in the first place." He *tsked* and looked up at his captive. "Time takes its toll even on the most brilliant of minds. It has been so long that I forgot and yet what I forgot was so simple in the first place!"

Closing the dragon tome, the gnome sent it floating to its rightful place. He started to speak, then squinted at something behind Wellen. The scholar, of course, expected the worst.

"Odd. The corridor did not end so close. The pentagon must be readjusting itself. I'd hoped the control had not slipped that badly."

Wellen said nothing but his eyes widened as the part of the corridor he was forced to gaze at abruptly ended no more than a few yards behind the gnome. When they had first appeared, it had been as endless as any. Now, a shelf full of books, *silver* copies, adorned the area.

Noting the look, Serkadion Manee turned. "Nimth's blood! This is more fouled than I imagined!" he snarled at his reluctant companion. "It is only appropriate that since you are responsible for this disarray that you be the sole means by which it is tidied up."

Wellen expected to find himself teleported again, but the gnome did nothing but fold his arms. For several seconds, the human pondered what it was that Mance intended. Then, a prickling sensation coursed through his feet. He wanted to look down, but Manee's spell prevented him from looking anywhere but in the direction the squat mage stood.

"What's happening to me?"

"I regret this, I really do, my overcurious friend. It will be a waste. You probably will not last more than, oh, three or four years, being mortal, but I have no better choice at the moment. A pity you are not immortal, like myself. Then, you'd last forever. The spell for that takes too long to prepare, however. You would need the life span of a Vraad for that and I am afraid the blood has been watered down by too long exposure to this world." The gnome became thoughtful again. "Perhaps I can entice the hooded one into returning. He might be useful once you fade. Yes, I'll have to consider that."

The unnerving sensation had spread upward to Wellen's knees now. He gritted his teeth and asked again, "What are you *doing* to me? At least *tell* me!"

"Now that it has progressed so much, I suppose I can. It appears your own power will not save you this time. You are more of a carrier than a mage. I suspect that your children . . . which you will not have, of course . . . would have been exceptional sorcerers." Serkadion Manee reached up and tapped Bedlam on the chest. "As for satisfying your curiosity, it is the least I can do for a fellow scholar. Put quite simply, you are going to become part of my domain. At present, the floor is slowly encroaching upon you. It lives in a sense, have I mentioned that? It has no higher thought, only base instinct, but that might change now. I have never really tested its potential; so much else to do, you know. It is a radical solution and I fear you will not be as efficient as the matrix was, but this will have to do."

Wellen tried to struggle, but the part of him that had not succumbed to the encroaching floor was still frozen. Manee had only allowed him speech. "For god's sake, don't do this!"

"I am the closest thing to a god around here, I imagine, and this *is* for my sake. Bear with it, won't you please? I have other things to look up. There is still your companion to find and a rather annoying pest to clean out." The insidious gnome bowed. "I am afraid that I will not be back before it is too late. Please believe me, Master Wellen Bedlam, when I say that it was both a pleasure and a pain to meet you. Who knows? Perhaps enough of you will remain coherent so that we might have a discourse or two in the future."

With that, Serkadion Manee vanished.

Blinking, the scholar realized he could move again. Unfortunately, that meant being able to move only the top half of his body, for the living stone that was the citadel had already crept up to his waist and was continuing its climb at far too fast a pace.

Xabene! was his first thought, but she was probably almost as powerless as he seemed to be. Shade was the only one who might be able to help him but he had vanished, either a victim of Manee or simply a wiser soul who had departed the moment he could. Still, Wellen wished that one or both of his companions were here. Perhaps there was some spell they knew that would free him or—

Before him stood both the hooded warlock and the pale enchantress.

To say they were as surprised as he was would have been understating matters. Xabene looked as if she expected either the Dragon King or the gnome to snatch her. When she realized who it was she stood next to, the sorceress stepped away. Her gaze drifted to Wellen, but her sudden joy died when she saw the fate that had befallen him.

"Wellen! By the Lords of the Dead!" She took hold of him and tried to pull him free, not understanding the true nature of his predicament.

"Stop! Unless you desire to become a part of him permanently!" Shade separated the two. Xabene raised her hand, but instead of the spell that the warlock likely expected, she *slapped* him instead.

Shade looked at her, mouth a grim, straight line, and then laughed. "I think I like you after all, female, despite the fact that you remind me too much of my dear, unlamented family."

"Like me or hate me; I could care less! Do something about Wellen!"

"I was going to." The warlock turned glittering eyes on the scholar. "You need not have shouted in my head, Master Bedlam; a simple summons would have been sufficient."

"Shout?" The shadowy figure extended a gloved hand, which Wellen immediately took hold of. All at once, he felt able to move his legs again.

"You brought us here, you know. That infernally unpredictable power of yours."

Looking down, the novice spellcaster saw that the stone was receding. It had taken on an almost liquid quality and was so soft he was able to pull one of his legs entirely free. With a hand from both of his companions, he was soon away from the treacherous spot. The trio watched as the floor reformed its flat self, then solidified.

"A Vraad through and through," muttered the ancient warlock. Now free, Wellen took hold of Xabene. "Where were you? What happened to you in that madcap corridor?"

She gave Shade a chilly glare. *"He* did. It was he who rescued me."

"I would have rescued you also," the hooded warlock added, "but you vanished before I could. It was Manee, then, who took you."

"No, Manee didn't." Wellen relayed what had happened to him, not excluding even the tortured minds he had discovered.

When Wellen was done, Shade shook his head. "Worthy of Lady Melenea." When the other two stared at him blankly, the warlock added, "An old acquaintance. Your ancestor, Master Bedlam, was the last to see her before she herself vanished forever. No loss." He grimaced. "All this activity stimulates the memory too much. I was better left dreaming in my cavern, going ever more mad."

"You are welcome to return to your madness," Xabene snapped, "but not until we've escaped this place!"

"Xabene—"

Shade raised a hand to forestall arguing. "Have no fear that I take her words the way she meant them. I am a child of the clan of the Tezerenee, the dragon men." He paused dramatically for reasons Wellen would never understand. At last, twisting his dry features into something resembling pleasure, he finished, "I have been threatened and bullied by far more intimidating forces than her."

"Listen you—"

"This can wait," Wellen said, taking charge, much to his surprise. "What concerns us now is escaping."

"Do you have an idea?" Shade asked. His parchmentlike countenance had slipped back into the shadows of his hood.

"Then," responded the master warlock, reaching into his flowing cloak, "perhaps you might be interested in my idea, after all."

His gloved hand emerged with a dragon tome of a pale white that reminded the scholar of the color of the undead Yalso's decaying flesh.

"What's so special about that particular volume?" the raven- haired enchantress asked. She no longer seemed to have any interest in the gnome's treasures. In fact, the very presence of all the other books had made her even more anxious. Wellen had seen her gazing at them every now and then out of the corner of his eye and her expression had not been one of desire but the opposite.

He found he was glad.

"This," Shade said, "tells us the citadel's weaknesses in detail."

"You're joking! Why would he put together something like that?"

"Because," the dark warlock replied, opening to a particular page and turning it toward them, "he *is*, after all, Serkadion Manee."

In another corridor of the vast libraries, the gnome rematerialized. By now, the unfortunate mortal scholar was a well- integrated part of his citadel, but it would take a little time for the shock to recede. It was much the same *as* the first few minutes after a mind had been introduced to the pentagram. Not until the spell completely took control was it worth trying to get what had once been a living being to obey even the simplest of instructions.

That meant that the citadel was open to further infestation by the Dragon King and there was only one thing that Serkadion Manee knew of that was quick and cunning enough to foil the intruder.

A creak made him glance around, but he saw nothing out of the ordinary. With no guidance, the citadel's vast interior was shifting randomly. This was not the first such noise he had heard and he doubted it would be the last. Things would need time to return to normal.

A gray book leaped into his hand from one of the shelves. The pages turned until he found what he wanted. Manee read and, by reading, cast the spell.

The squat gnome allowed himself a chuckle as he sent the dragon tome back to its resting place. That would teach the would-be conqueror a thing or two. It would almost be worth the risk just to watch the drake open one of the books now.

See how much you learn now! The stooped Vraad chuckled again. The spell had almost been a joke when he had devised it, a change of pace from his more serious work. Now, it would be the final strike in his counterattack.

Jagged streaks of pain shook his body. He felt moisture on his back and neck. The world around him began to blur.

What is happening to me? It almost feels—was his last coherent thought.

He fell to the floor, the blood from the gaping tear in his neck and shoulders spilling over onto the floor.

Looming over the quivering figure of the dying gnome, the Purple Dragon dropped his spell of hiding and wiped his bloodied talons on Serkadion Manee's robe, only briefly pondering what it was that might have amused the former immortal so much.

163

Chapter Twenty

Torches lit by themselves as the trio teleported into the chamber.

"Where are we now?" Wellen asked. He looked forward to a time when he could once more travel purely by conventional means. *Still, I suppose to a spellcaster teleportation is a conventional method.*

"In the lair of the beast," Shade replied, unfurling himself. There was something foul about the way he teleported, something so different that Wellen had so far been unable to pinpoint it. The grotesque manner in which the warlock twisted himself . . . and the two of them, this time . . . before each teleport was not what the scholar wondered about. It was the way Shade's magic always made him want to shy away.

To a lesser extent, the same applied to Serkadion Manee's power, albeit with the gnome it had always seemed more of a residue, as if he no longer drew from the same source that his counterpart did.

What was the land called? Nimth, that was it.

"I could think of many other places to be than Serkadion Manee's private study," Xabene muttered, her eyes darting around the room as if she expected the gnome at any moment. Quite possibly that just might happen, but they had no choice. Shade had indicated that a key to their release lay in the very heart of the immortal's domain.

Wellen was not entirely trustful of the shadowy spellcaster, but Shade had rescued him more than once.

"What are we looking for?" he asked.

The quiet laugh startled him. "A key, of course."

"A key?"

"Serkadion Manee is either often literal-minded or has a touch of dry humor. The key to opening the portal in the wall without his aid is to use a *key*. He apparently created a few precautions in case something happened to his powers. Very kind of him, don't you think?"

Neither Wellen nor the enchantress bothered responding. The trio commenced a rapid search of the crowded chamber, discovering almost immediately that like so much else in the citadel, appearances were deceiving. The more they searched, the more to search there seemed to be. It was as if random things simply materialized from some pocket world, like the one in Xabene's tree. In only moments, they were already wading in stack after stack of abandoned experiments and notes. Wellen could not help returning to his early days as a student, when all of his assignments had seemed so mountainous.

"What do we have here?" Shade finally asked.

The others quickly joined him. It was not a key he had found, however, but a tapestry.

Looking it over, the master warlock could not keep the admiration out of his tone. "Exceptional work! Still so new! It might have been weaved yesterday!"

"It reminds me of the tapestry *I* weaved," whispered Xabene to Wellen.

"I would not be surprised," Shade interjected. "Since in that respect it serves a similar purpose to the one Serkadion Manee influenced you to create."

"*He* did?" A flush of red filled the cheeks of the pale sorceress. She did

164

not like being used, but especially by the crafty gnome.

"It appears so, but this is not a Vraad thing. I think, despite its condition, that it was weaved even before our cursed host came to this world." Shade touched the side of the cloth artifact gingerly. "Yes, no doubt about that. He may have learned the method of its creation and passed it on to you, but this was created by another hand . . . or claw, depending on who ruled here then."

"That's it! I will not be used again!" Xabene raised a hand toward the artifact. Shade, seeking to protect the tapestry, caught hold of her wrist. Wellen saw the look on her face and tried to warn the aged warlock, but it was too late. Not caring what happened, the enraged sorceress unleashed raw power at the struggling Shade.

He shrugged it off as a dog might shrug off rain.

With the release of her anger, Xabene grew sullen. Letting go of her wrist, the hooded figure blinked his crystalline eyes and said, "That tickled. Was that your intention?"

Wellen took hold of her before her anger, now directed at Shade, renewed itself sufficiently. "Forget it! We need him. He needs us."

"He doesn't need us. He could find this thing and leave without dragging us along with him."

The cloth-enshrouded mage shook his head. "I abandoned her. I will not abandon her children."

She looked at him in angry puzzlement. "And what does that mean?"

"Master Bedlam knows." Leaving it at that, Shade returned to admiring the tapestry. "If he did not weave this, then at the very least the gnome has made many changes in its usage. Some of them quite new. I can sense as well as see them. I wonder what purpose this marvel now serves."

Wellen, caught up by Shade's interest, was forced to admit to himself that the tapestry was certainly worthy of the attention being given to it. As with Xabene's creation, it was a representation of a region, but with such stark detail that it was like gazing at a true image. A tiny book marked the location of the Libraries. Scanning further, he easily noted the hills to the east, but then did not recognize something that lay to the southwest. He pointed at it and asked Shade, "What is that? A town? Every building looks to be there."

"Penacles. One of the human habitations that the Purple Dragon allows in his domain. Only a small human town now, but once, long before refugees from Nimth foolishly invaded the Dragonrealm and even before the reigns of the Dragon Kings, the Quel, or a dozen races who preceded them, Penacles was known as a city of knowledge. Its original builders, who may have also created this tapestry, were not human, I think . . . at least not in the end."

"It seems a strange coincidence that Serkadion Manee would pick this location," Wellen commented. His eyes narrowed and he looked at the hooded warlock. "Could he have been here that long?"

"Perhaps, but I suspect it predated even him. Despite his talk of a thousand thousand years, Manee is not that old. Not hardly. Perhaps it just seems so long to him, I do not know." Shade put a hand to his face, as if growing exhausted. "I think he must have stripped the city's ancient bones of whatever he could find, though. I once searched its ruins, even spied upon the human town in the course of my own desires, but I learned all too soon that ancient Penacles was bare of anything that might have aided me. I wondered then where it had gone. That was before I knew of him." He leaned forward. "Interesting. The entire plain, I see, was part of the original city."

"Is this thing of any use to us or are we wasting precious time?"

"It may very well be useful to us, enchantress." Shade reached up and removed it from where it hung. "This is the method by which our host may reenter the citadel directly from no matter where he is. Normal teleportation does not work, as you know. Not even for Serkadion Manee. This would have been good for times when it was vital to materialize within and not outside. I wonder . . ."

Wellen noticed a tiny slot in the wall where the tapestry had been hung. He reached into it and felt something metallic. "I think I've found our key."

"Be careful, Wellen!"

Despite Xabene's warning, he was not worried. So comfortable had Serkadion Manee become in his private quarters that he had evidently felt little reason to overprotect them. Those few who he had allowed in had never had free access to this chamber.

The key, if that was what it was, had a rounded end for holding and a stem, but that was all that resembled a key that Wellen would have recognized. The other end, the part that must touch the wall, was a wicked five-pronged affair that looked as it if were more designed for torture than opening a lock. The scholar wondered how it was supposed to work. Turning it so that the prongs faced him, he noted that with so much else here, the five points made up the corners of a tiny pentagram. He mentioned this to his companions.

"A Vraadish taste, that. Pentagrams and fives." Shade folded the tapestry and thrust in into his deep cloak. He reached for the key, but Wellen chose to hold onto it. The master warlock already had the book and the tapestry. Shade took it in stride. "We have no more need to be here, then. It is time to leave this infernal place. Let the gnome and the lizard decide who its master is."

He was just beginning the spell that would teleport them out when his entire frame coursed with light. Shade, a burning sun, gasped once and fell.

"The decisssssion hassss been made, thank you."

The Purple Dragon stretched forth a taloned hand and flames from the torches encircled the two mortals. Xabene tried a counterspell, but the flames would not be denied. Wellen tried to shift out of the way. He failed. Like a snake, the magical fire followed him, then darted around him again and again, tightening its circle until he could no longer move without burning himself.

"Thisss has been a mossst informative conversation. I appreciate your effortssss on my behalf." The key flew from Bedlam's fingers and into the waiting hand of their captor. The Dragon King gazed at it in fondness. "At last! The cursssed gnome hasss made it impossssible to open the portals without thissss!"

A scratching sound made them look down. Shade was still alive. His gloved hand scraped against the floor, as if even while unconscious he sought to escape.

"Resssilient. I ssssuppose I shall have to take you with me," the drake lord said to the still figure. "You might have some knowledge of worth."

Shade's body rose into the air, making him look like a limp marionette with invisible strings. The Dragon King turned to his other two captives. "This time, I will not trust to chance. My will is your will. Your bodies will move as I command."

Wellen, with Xabene beside him, staggered toward the drake. This time, Purple had assured that his control was complete. The only movements left to the scholar were blinking and breathing. He could not even ask the question that burned on his tongue.

The Dragon King must have noted his expression, however, for he held one of his taloned hands before the human. "For an immortal, the gnome died assss eassssily assss any mere mortal!" Straightening, the drake looked at the key, then back at his prisoners. "Now I truly have everything. All I need issss to ssssecure you ssssafely and then I can return and begin the processss of going through thissss treasure trove." Purple's eyes blazed with anticipation. "Sssso much to do!"

Even if he had been able to speak, Wellen Bedlam would have not contradicted the Dragon King. Let the drake believe that it would now be a simple task to escape. If there was one thing the young scholar had learned, it was that nothing was simple in this place. Serkadion Manee might be dead, if what the Dragon King had said was true, but this *was* his creation.

The Purple Dragon could continue to believe his own words, as far as Bedlam was concerned. Let him think that he could simply walk out of this place. Let him believe that with the gnome no more, he was now unchallenged master of the libraries and their contents.

Wellen knew better. Even without their creator, the libraries were *lethal.*

Had the Dragon King waited for a few more moments after delivering the mortal blow to Serkadion Manee, he would have perhaps seen a strange thing happen to the Vraad sorcerer. With a few vestiges of life still remaining, the body began to *sink* into the false marble floor and, as it sank, it changed, becoming less and less the gnome and more a part of the very floor itself.

Serkadion Manee had designed his libraries so that nothing would be ever be wasted.

Not even him.

In the corridor where they had first entered, the party appeared. Shade was still a silent corpse. He might truly have been dying for all Wellen knew, but there was nothing that could be done about it at the moment. All of their lives were in the scaly claws of the Dragon King and his concern at present had little to do with their well-being.

Holding out the pronged key, Purple returned control of the scholar's body to him. Wellen savored the ability to move, then looked up at his captor.

"How doessss thissss work? There issss no hole."

"Shade knew," Bedlam replied with some satisfaction. "But you made certain he wouldn't be able to help."

For his remark, he received a backhanded blow to the face. It was only a tap, but from the Dragon King it was enough to send the human falling back. When Wellen rose, he felt blood trickling down the left side of his mouth. Now, not only did his head throb, but so did his jaw.

"Again, how doessss thissss work? Another flippant remark and I shall tear your head off! Then, we shall ssssee if your female will be more obliging!"

The threat to Xabene was sufficient. Looking at the blank wall and then back at the key, Wellen shrugged. "I would guess that the first step would be to place it against the wall. From what little the—Shade said, it sounds like the only thing you *can* do." He had almost mentioned the single volume that the hooded warlock still had secreted on his person. That single dragon tome might yet save their lives. "After that, I can only assume that it will either open or you'll have to turn it first."

"Ssssimple. Ssssensible. I agree." The Dragon King stepped past his captives and placed the key against the stonelike wall.

Nothing happened. He tried turning the key, causing it to scrape against the substance. Wellen almost expected the living stone to rebel against the sharp prongs of the key, but that was not so.

This time, there was a reaction.

With great hesitation, the wall began to separate around the region where the prongs of the key had touched it. The drake quickly pulled the device away and hissed in triumph as the crack became a circular opening which in turn grew larger and larger. Once again, the scholar was reminded of a giant maw, only this time he was inside looking out. Not a comfortable thought.

DRAGON TOME

"Much better!" Purple roared. "Much better!"

The opening of the wall was much slower this time than when they had first arrived here. Now, with success at hand, the Dragon King grew impatient. He stood before the expanding portal and tried to use physical means to make it widen faster. That failed. In an attempt to keep his impatience at a minimum, the drake turned away from the exit and faced Wellen.

"Consssssider yoursssself fortunate, manling. You have been witnessss to the end of one era and the beginning of the next. Thissss will be the dawning of a new kingdom. The Dragon Emperor will ssssoon on longer ssssit in the Tyber Mountains. He shall rule from here! From . . . from a new *Penaclessss*, yesss! I shall ressssurrect the ancient city!" It was obvious that the Purple Dragon did not intend to turn over the gnome's vast knowledge to his golden counterpart but rather intended that *he* become new lord of the realm. Even with the knowledge of Serkadion Manee, Wellen wondered whether Purple was taking on more than he was capable of controlling. Certainly, the other monarchs would have something to say.

The portal was now large enough to admit the Dragon King through. Wellen was surprised to see that the sun was setting. Was it the same day? Another? Time here, he was certain, did not pass as it did outside.

Purple started to step through, then recalled something. He turned and went back to the silent form of Shade. With little care, the drake rolled the warlock onto his backside and reached into the voluminous cloak.

Move, Shade! Bedlam expected a trick, expected the spellcaster to leap up and take on the Dragon King, but Shade remained motionless. This was no ploy, which meant that now there truly was no hope.

"Dragon of the Depthssss! How far musssst I reach to find it?" A moment later, the horrific knight smiled. He pulled his hand from the confines of the cloak. In his claws he held the tapestry. "Yesss. Lessst I forget it and it remain losssst in your infernal clothes. Thissss piece issss definitely worth inssssspecting."

Outside, a wind whipped up the nearby grass. Wellen contemplated running for the portal, but he could not leave Xabene nor even Shade.

Rising, the Dragon King looked over the intricate work of the artifact. "I wonder. A few changessss and I may be able to usssse thissss. No more keyssss. I will have the only way in and out."

A flutter of wings caught Wellen's attention.

A huge, white form that seemed all claws and wings darted through the portal and made for the backside of the drake.

The reptilian knight dropped both the key and the tapestry as he went down under the onslaught of a monstrous Necri.

Acting on sheer instinct, Wellen rushed to Xabene's side. She, of the three of them, was the only one still under a spell of paralysis. Shade, after all, was hardly in a condition to crawl, if he was even still alive. Taking hold of the enchantress by the waist, he started to drag her toward the opening.

Despite his lack of height and his scholarly background, he was far from weak. Xabene was also light, which helped. Even before Purple had recovered from his initial surprise and started to fight back, Wellen had her in the mouth of the portal.

What he hoped to gain, he could not say. Wellen was aware that he could not carry her all the way to safety. There was nowhere to hide for miles. No matter who won the battle, the victor would easily be able to chase down the runaways.

Still, he did not give up. Wellen would not have been able to forgive himself. Too many had died. If he could even buy Xabene a little time . . .

The wind cooled him a little bit, which helped, but the soil was too soft. He could not get much traction. The oncoming darkness, which he would have once thought

168

a plus, also worked against him. Both the Necri and Purple would be able to find him, day or night. Wellen, on the other hand, could already tell that he was no longer gifted with night vision. Bumbling around in the dark, with Xabene an unwieldy load, he would not be far from the pentagon when the winner came to reclaim the two of them.

"You look as if you could use my aid, sirrah."

Bedlam swore.

"Such language," Benton Lore said, adding a chuckle.

"Does no one walk or simply ride anymore? Did you have to materialize right behind me?"

"I did nothing of the sort. I crept here."

Feeling somewhat abashed, the scholar apologized.

The black man waved his apology aside. "Never mind that. Let me help you with her."

A single touch of his hand to her forehead and Xabene was released from the Dragon King's spell.

"Lords of the Dead!" she muttered.

"Good," Lore commented almost clinically. "I did not think he would waste anything fancy upon you."

"How are you feeling?" Wellen asked her.

"Good enough to run if we have to."

"There is no need, my lady. I can teleport us all back." The major-domo raised his hand.

Wellen wanted to go. He wanted to travel as far as he could, and then find ways of allowing him to journey farther. By no means did he desire a return to Serkadion Manee's former domain. Yet . . .

"I can't leave him, Xabene."

She seized his arm. "There's a Dragon King and a Necri in there! *My* Necri! If that thing should win or be fought off, it'll come for me! I failed the Lords of the Dead! Shade may have repelled them, but that monstrosity won't care! It only knows that I have betrayed its creators!"

"Go with Commander Lore, then. I have more than one reason for going back! Just trust me!" He tore free of her and hurried back to the gaping hole.

She did not cry out for him, but Bedlam knew she was still behind him, refusing to leave if he did not. Wellen hoped that neither Xabene nor Benton Lore would suffer because of his decision.

The drake and the Necri had taken their battle farther down the corridor. Wellen had expected the batlike creature to fall quickly under the massive power of Purple, but the dragon appeared to be holding back. Either he was weaker than Wellen had thought or he was afraid to unleash his full strength so near his precious books. The drake had, after all, resorted to physical violence when he had finally taken down Serkadion Manee. Neither the gnome nor the dragon had likely been able to utilize their full strength.

Shade was where he had been left. The fear that he had accidentally been included in the deadly duel had proved false. Wellen slipped through the circular entranceway and rushed over to the warlock, ever careful to keep an eye on the combatants. With two such as they, the battle could turn at any moment.

"Shade!" There was no response to his whisper. He was forced to begin dragging the injured figure as he had Xabene. Unfortunately, Shade's much larger and more limp body proved at least twice as laborious to carry as the slighter enchantress. The false marble floor added to the difficulties, for Wellen found that he was in danger of slipping now and then.

Something fell from the cloak. Wellen leaned down and saw that it was the dragon tome that the aged spellcaster had appropriated much earlier. He picked it up and stuffed it into his shirt. There would be time to deal with it later.

Benton Lore called to him from the other side. "Do you need help?"

"Take Xabene and leave!"

"She does not desire to be reasonable, sirrah, and I find that neither do I!"

He sighed. A part of him could not help but he relieved at their reappearance. "Help me, then."

The black man came around and took Shade's feet. "I tried to teleport you out, but it did not work for some reason."

"One of the gnome's tricks . . ." Thinking of tricks, he started to look around. A metal object a few feet to his left caught his eye. "Wait!" Lowering Shade, he reached over and retrieved the pronged key that the drake lord had dropped during the initial assault. Wellen pocketed the key and repositioned himself.

"What is that?"

"Something which could buy us time." Continuing his search as he began to back through the gateway, the scholar finally located the tapestry. It had evidently been carried partway down the hall with the two combatants. Wellen calculated his chances. Once Shade was outside, he might still have time to—

He heard the Necri shriek.

Both Wellen and Benton Lore turned to the agonized cry. Far down the corridor, the Dragon King had finally gained the upper hand. His adversary was pinned under him. The talons of the drake had torn both the demonic creature's wings to shreds and now an odd foam was spreading over the batlike horror. Purple released his hold on his opponent and stepped back to watch as his spell enveloped the dying beast. The Dragon King himself did not look well. He was bleeding from severe wounds. His stance was none too steady.

"We have to hurry, Master Bedlam!"

They had the warlock nearly through when he began to mutter and struggle. Wellen heard Shade speak to someone he referred to as his father, warning him about some scheme. Then, Lore lost his grip and Wellen stumbled. The warlock's words grew garbled, but he did not cease struggling.

The anxious scholar looked up in the direction of the Dragon King.

The reptilian knight had noticed them. With some effort, he started toward the open portal.

"Step through!" Wellen roared. "Pull him out from my side!"

As the soldier hastened to obey, the scholar reached into his pocket and pulled out the key. His idea was desperate, but not completely mad.

"What are you doing?"

"Just pull him through!"

Xabene joined them, much to his annoyance. *We can all die together!* "Go back!"

She ignored him. Leaning, the enchantress helped Lore with the mad warlock. Shade's words were complete nonsense now, but his hampering of their efforts was not.

Wellen could wait no longer. He reached forward with the key, choosing a part of the wall just to the left of the portal. A crash nearly made him drop the key.

"It's all right!" Xabene called. "I reached in with one hand and blocked his spell with one of my own! It was a weak attack!"

"He will summon up something much more troublesome in a moment, I'm certain!" the officer added. He gave a final tug. "Your friend is free, Master Bedlam!"

All too aware that he might be totally mistaken, Wellen turned the key as the drake had done, only in the *opposite* direction.

The mouth of the portal began closing.

The party fell back as sorcerer's tendrils reached forth from within. They were not the target, however. Instead, the tendrils sought to keep the entrance open. The spell on the citadel was far more potent, however, and the portal continued to shrink unabated.

Even as the tendrils failed, Purple stood at the threshold.

"If he gets outside, we're lost!" the enchantress shouted. "He could shift form!" Both she and Lore unleashed their sorcery.

Their spells died at the wall. They could not hope to repel the drake unless he was outside, and if he was, then it would be too late.

Wellen looked at Shade. The injured spellcaster's eyes had opened, but it was apparent he was not seeing the world around him. *If only we had his strength! We might be able to do it!*

Perhaps there was yet time for one more miracle.

Hurrying over to Shade's side, he knelt and took the warlock's head in his arm. Wellen faced his mad companion toward the portal and leaned down to whisper. He was working on an assumption, one based solely upon the master warlock's triumphant return from the dank domain of the Lords of the Dead. "Shade, they've broken their word! Your cousins have broken their word! They're coming!"

Purple had a claw through what remained of the gateway and was crawling through. Despite his wounds, he shrugged off the desperate attacks of Benton Lore and Xabene.

Shade stirred, but still did not act.

Wellen tried the last thing he could think of. "They want her, Shade. They want her descendents. They want Lady Sharissa!"

Crystalline eyes blazed. Shade gritted his teeth. For a moment, a much younger, more arrogant figure lay in the scholar's lap.

"It's coming through the hole, Shade! It's coming for her!"

The Vraad glared in the direction of the Dragon King.

A rain of needlelike thorns shot forth at the drake. Concerned only with his escape, he did not see them. Only when they first pierced his armored hide did the drake realize his danger.

A full score more struck home. Several entered wounds left by the Necri. Roaring his agony, the drake lord tried to pull them free, but for every one he pulled out, more than a dozen found root. In mere seconds, he looked like some sort of grotesque parody of a pincushion.

Still the needles flew.

His breathing a ragged hiss, Purple finally realized that to remain outside was to invite certain death. He began to slide back even as more of Shade's missiles hit. His pace was too slow, however. It was clear that he would not escape the closing portal on his own.

Then, just before the blood-covered knight would have been crushed, Wellen saw a small hand drag him back.

The gateway closed.

He breathed a sigh of relief. "Thank you, Shade. Thank you."

Then the weary Bedlam looked down and realized he was holding nothing but air.

Chapter Twenty-One

171

"We think he has returned to his caverns beneath the realm of the Dragon Emperor," Benton Lore informed them. "With Shade it is almost impossible to tell, but our spies reported sightings of a cloaked and shadowy wraith." He smiled. "I can think of no one else to whom that description would be appropriate."

"Why did he leave?" Xabene asked.

Wellen, the enchantress, and the Green Dragon's majordomo sat astride horses in the middle of a glen just west of the main portion of the Dagora Forest. In the four weeks since escaping Purple and the citadel of Serkadion Manee, the scholar and his bride had made the small settlement of Zuu their temporary home. The two of them had both agreed that they needed to find a quieter, safer place than even that, but not until Wellen was satisfied as to Shade's fate. Even Xabene agreed they owed the ancient mage that much.

"I think the madness has returned," Lore replied, his smile fading a bit. "He is said to seem a bit at a loss, as if his memory is incomplete or, at the very least, muddled. He may not even recall that he was ever inside the citadel. His failure to secure a method of achieving immortality may have also sent him back to the real of fantasy. From what I have discerned, it would not be the first time."

"I'm not so certain I would ever want to be an immortal. The Lords of the Dead dangled that above my head, but the price seems too high now."

"Two or three hundred years is enough for the two of you, then?"

"Enough," Wellen agreed. One of the benefits of sorcery, even for an inept carrier like himself, was an extended life span. Both he and Xabene might live another two centuries, maybe more, and most of it looking little older than they did now.

"No one has yet seen Purple depart the libraries," Lore said, changing the subject. "Perhaps he will be trapped forever."

"Perhaps." The scholar still had the key. Just in case. He was not so certain that the Dragon King would not escape someday, though. Given time, if he survived his wounds, Purple would eventually reason out the tapestry and how it could be used.

He had not spoken to anyone about the hand he had seen, a hand belonging to an obviously short being.

"My lord fears what his brother will unleash if he does escape. All that knowledge in his vile claws."

Here, Wellen relaxed. He smiled at Xabene, who nodded. It was time to show Benton Lore what they had discovered. Reaching into a pouch, he removed the book.

The black man's eyes widened. "A dragon tome! You have one!"

"Here."

Lore caught the book and quickly opened it. After a few pages, he looked mystified. "It is *blank!*"

"Not quite. Think of a subject involving the construction of a magical fortress . . . like Serkadion Manee's pentagon."

The major-domo did. Before his eyes, the pages began to turn. At last, they stopped. The smile reappeared, then almost instantly disappeared again. "What *is* this gibberish? It looks almost like a . . . like a riddle or a poem! I do no understand!"

"Shade stole that particular volume, then lost it. I picked it up, intending on giving it to him if we escaped, but then he vanished first." He looked a bit abashed. "I know I didn't mention its existence, but my curiosity got the better of me. I promise you I would have told the Green Dragon everything."

"I believe you and so will he." Lore inspected the riddle. "What does it mean?"

"The secret is within, one merely has to be willing to spend the time . . . years, even."

"Then . . ." The officer laughed. "If Purple lives it may take him years just to decipher one?"

172

Wellen joined him in laughing. "It gets worse. Unless you really work at it, what you read in the book will not be retained in your memory. You can't even write it down. Somehow, it always disappears."

"The gnome must have done this!"

"I think so. Just before he died, I imagine." *Was* he dead, though? What had Wellen seen?

"So the price of Purple's victory is endless searching for even the minutest bit of information. He may spend his lifetime simply deciphering a simple experiment for telling time!"

Knowing how complete the knowledge contained in the libraries was, Wellen had no doubt that there was such information listed. The Dragon King might have won, but his victory would keep his ambitions curtailed. If anything, the rest of the Dragonrealm had gained much more than it had lost with the change in masters.

Xabene glanced at the sinking sun. "It's time we returned to Zuu. Tomorrow, we head north. I know a settlement up there that the Dragon King Bronze never bothers with. A pleasant place."

"You would both be welcome here. It would be safer. What about the Lords of the Dead?"

"Shade did something to them, that's all we know," Bedlam replied. "We can only tell you that we have this feeling that they will not bother us, neither in this life nor the next."

No one desired to contemplate what could have made the necromancers abandon their plans and their vengeance.

"I think this would be better off in your hands," Lore finally decided. "I only ask that you share whatever you find." The dragon tome was returned to Wellen. "I shall depart, then. Farewell to both of you. Good luck with everything."

"Farewell to you, Commander Lore," the enchantress said, taking a tighter hold of the reins.

Wellen simply nodded. He was savoring being his own master at last, not to mention riding a horse rather than teleporting. His children, on the other hand, would likely be materializing and dematerializing before they were adults. Still, much of the fact that he was now able to live his own life was due to one person. As Benton Lore rode off, Wellen muttered, "May you find your future, Gerrod."

"Shall we go?" Xabene asked him.

They urged their horses to a trot. The sorceress, her lengthy dark hair fluttering, moved her mount alongside Wellen's and asked, "What do you really think is going on in the gnome's place? Couldn't Purple be dead?"

"He might be, but I doubt it. He probably won't recover completely for some time, but I think he survived."

She did not care to think about that. "At least we no longer have to worry about Serkadion Manee. His death is the one good thing we can thank the Dragon King for."

"Mmm . . ." Wellen turned the dragon tome over and stared at the cover. He was tempted to throw the book away and try to forget Serkadion Manee, but curiosity made him put it back where he had originally packed it. It might not hurt to try and decipher the contents. Besides, unlike the Purple Dragon, Wellen only had *one* book to muddle through.

With two hundred years ahead of him and some peace at last, he was certain to make *some* progress.

Hissing, the Dragon King threw the yellow-backed book across the corridor. His rage unspent, he cleared shelf after shelf until finally, exhausted, he slumped against one of the library walls.

"You seem ill-tempered. How may I serve you?"

"You again?" Purple whirled on the tiny, calm figure. "You are *dead!* Dead! Leave me!"

The gnome bowed. "I am here only to serve you, the present master of the libraries. It is all I exist for now, thanks in great part to you."

"Ssssstop sssssaying that, cursssse you!" The Dragon King reached forward and took hold of the gnome by the collar. The bald figure simply stared back blandly. This further antagonized the drake. "I killed you once and I shall do sssso again!"

He brought a taloned hand down on the gnome's head.

The squat figure vanished.

"Perhaps if you tell me what it is you search for," came the voice again, this time from behind him. When the Dragon King turned, he once more found himself facing the libraries' former master.

"I want out of thisssss place! I want the secret of why it hassss turned mad!" He picked up one of the tomes and held it open for the other to see. "Mosssst of all, I want to know what you have done to thessss precious volumessss! What is thissss foolishnessss written here?"

The gnome calmly held forth another book. "I am only an extension of the libraries' purpose; I cannot aid you in that. The one you have there is the wrong volume, however. The one with the information you seek is this one here."

A hand batted the book away. "I *cannot* decipher it!"

"Perhaps if there was someone to help you . . ."

"There issss no one but me!" Purple stepped back and glared at the shelves. "When I am free of thissss place, I will rebuild Penaclessss! I will take humanssss, who are insssssufferably adaptive, and educate them! The bessss will work to aid me in ssssolving these quandaries!"

"That seems a reasonable course."

"But I have to find the way *out* of here first!"

"It is in the book . . ." responded the gnome, bending over to retrieve the volume. "All you have to do is read it."

Hissing in frustration, the Dragon King fell to his knees. "Very well, then. Give it to me."

"This is a simple one, truly," the shadow that resembled Serkadion Manee commented. "At the most, it would take one as clever as you no more than forty, perhaps fifty years to solve it. Possibly as little as a year or two."

In sullen silence, the Purple Dragon took the proffered tome and began reading. His eyes narrowed and his breathing slowed. He knew he would need all his concentration to decipher the cursed poem/riddle. He also knew that he would have to struggle to retain whatever he read.

"The key . . ." the drake lord muttered. "It would have been sssso much eassssier with the key."

"Yes, my lord." There *was* still the tapestry, which the gnome recalled presently lay in an obscure part of one of the hallways, but it was not his place to offer such information. His purpose now consisted entirely of maintaining and protecting the libraries, as he himself had commanded before his demise. That was all he was to do and he would perform that task until the libraries themselves were no more, for he, unlike the minds trapped in the vials that had once monitored his creation, had tied his own immortality to this place.

As he watched the new master of the libraries at work, the gnome could not help but smile.

END

174

THE HORSE KING

Chapter One

He was sorry, but the king had to die.

Miklo Vinimus respected, if not liked, the king of Zuu, but for the sake of peace, Lanith had to die before his ambitions grew to fruition. It was not that the muscular, graying monarch was so terrible a ruler, but he had begun gathering forces that Miklo and a few others understood would eventually overwhelm Lanith himself, then spread unchecked over much of the Dragonrealm.

Back in the quarters of the Order, all the others save for Hysith would be sleeping now. Miklo did not fear that particular would-be mage. Hysith only had a shadow of Miklo's power, just enough to become a member of the king's Magical Order, and most of the time the aged figure could not even recall his own name. He had been drinking heavily tonight and Miklo had left him even stronger drink on his way out. Hysith would definitely be no danger. Lanith only kept him around because human sorcerers were still very scarce. Zuu could now claim a dozen, but most were little better than Hysith.

Miklo had only been a baby when the Dragon Emperor had perished, a death that had opened the way for a new generation of human mages like himself. The last generation had been hunted down by the draconian emperor and his servants after the drakes had nearly lost a war against the Dragon Masters. The human spellcasters forming that legendary group had been out to free their kind from the oppression of the drakes. They had nearly succeeded, failing more because of betrayal in their ranks than because of the Dragon Emperor.

A few spellcasters with resources or, more often, no discernible power had escaped the hunt. Meanwhile, more newcomers with potential appeared every year. However, Miklo would be old and wrinkled before mages became more than legend to most common folk. Only in Zuu and perhaps far-off Penacles did common folk see sorcery on a daily basis.

But not much longer, if I succeed. It'll all crumble without Lanith to urge it on. Clad in robes the color of the night that made his rather trollish features look even less human, the short, swarthy Miklo stalked quietly through the corridors of the palace. The Magical Order had its living quarters in a converted stable next to the palace . . . near enough if Lanith desired the presence of his mages but far away enough for when he did not. The place still smelled of the memory of sweaty mounts, but then, so did the rest of Zuu as far as he was concerned. The murals Miklo passed were illustrations of the natives' great passion. Each one represented some scene of equine majesty, the animals gamboling, racing, or charging into battle. The kingdom was renowned for the horses it bred, horses purchased by eager folk from every corner of the continent. The horse folk earned a good living from raising and running the animals. It should have stayed that way, but Lanith was too ambitious a monarch. With most of the Dragon Kings dead or their power in disarray, he had

175

decided that the time to expand his lands was near at hand and his grand Magical Order was to be one of the weapons he would use to achieve that desire. Even horses seemed now a secondary passion to the king.

Torches lit the corridors through which the self-appointed assassin silently moved, but Miklo left no shadow as he passed. The trick that *she* had taught him worked well, even better than either of them could have hoped. Although he had started learning to use his gifts just shortly before reaching adulthood, he had quickly proven himself a capable and fairly powerful sorcerer. Not at all as powerful, say, as the great Bedlams, but powerful enough. His abbreviated training had been enough to gain him entrance into Lanith's Magical Order and a position of some trust. He was one of the Order's more competent mages and, therefore, one of the more better treated.

Of course, without her quick training, he would never have made it to this point, the assassination of the king. She was the reason he had finally dared to take this great risk, even if she had not actually wanted him to make such an attempt. However, Miklo's home in the independent barony of Adderly lay just to the north of Zuu and was an attractive first target for the horse king's campaign. For that reason alone, Miklo had to stop Lanith.

Adderly consisted of rich farmlands barely defended by a few large towns and one castle, a land that had prospered since the death of the Dragon King who had lived there. Miklo 's parents, his sister and her family, and his younger brother all lived in the heart of the barony, near the castle itself. Although he had not seen them since leaving for Zuu a year before, their possible fates if Zuu went to war were always on his mind. Adderly could not hold out against the horse king. It would be trampled by his armies in one day, two at most.

There would be no aid. Gordag-Ai, the nearest other great kingdom, lay much farther north, too far away to be of assistance. Besides, Gordag-Ai had a marriage treaty with far-off Talak, and Talak a treaty with Zuu from over twenty years ago when both had fought for freedom against the drake lords. Neither of those kingdoms would likely risk their treaties simply for his home. They would probably be preparing their own defenses instead, waiting for the day when the horse king unveiled to all his mad crusade.

Miklo's own people could not believe that their neighbors to the south, neighbors with whom they had traded for generations, would suddenly turn to war. Frustrated at their lack of comprehension, he had finally come to Zuu on his own with only the intention of seeing if his notions were simply delusion. However, his chance meeting with her two days after his arrival had introduced him to revelations so great and terrible that had he not seen proof Miklo would have not believed them himself.

Lanith has opened the way to a future darker than the one the Dragon Kings once intended for our kind, she had informed him that first night. *There's something already alive in the palace that should not be a part of our world. I can feel it.*

He had not seen that thing, but he had seen evidence of its existence, evidence that frightened Miklo yet steeled his resolve to kill the horse king.

A guard stood before the doorway through which Miklo needed to pass, but the bronzed, braided figure neither heard nor saw the mage slowly walking toward him. Miklo allowed himself a brief, satisfied smile. His potential had both stunned and pleased his mistress. Miklo knew very well that his ability to perform sorcery had been the reason she had also chosen him as a lover; she herself was quite accomplished in sorcery, not to mention a few more fascinating fields, and more than once she had spoken of how the marriage of Cabe Bedlam to the legendary Lady of the Amber had produced offspring reputed to be even more powerful sorcerers than their parents. Knowing nothing about the Bedlams save from tales passed on by visitors to his village, Miklo took her word on the abilities of the children, but he was also aware that each time she spoke of them, she did so with envy. She clearly desired a similar union and the results thereof and he was the prime candidate. Once this was over, there would be time . . .

When he was next to the guard, Miklo reached up to the man's chest and tapped it. The guard immediately went rigid. Impressed by his success so far, Miklo paused a moment to admire his work. True love had not been a part of the relationship between the northerner and his mistress, at least not where she had so far been concerned. Miklo was already hopelessly her slave and had been so from the moment he had first stared into that perfect face. Only on one other had he seen such beauty and that beauty belonged to one who would flay him alive if he was captured. Saress was very protective of her royal lover and her power of sorcery was as great as that of Miklo's mistress, possibly even greater.

They will both be in the bed, asleep by now. One simple target. She said that even Saress would have no defense against this attack How his mistress knew so much about the horse king's devil woman Miklo did not know, but everything had so far worked to perfection. The guards he had passed were now ensorcelled, the Magical Order slumbered on without knowledge that their protective spells had been temporarily negated, and King Lanith and Saress had only a few steps left worth of life.

He tried the door, but found it locked. Reaching into his robe, Miklo removed a small vial from an inner pocket. For some reason, locks remained impervious to his skills no matter how much he practiced. Miklo would have stood a better chance of breaking the door down with his shoulder than of opening the door with sorcery.

Miklo poured some of the contents into the lock, then leaped back as the liquid immediately began eating into the metal. A low, sizzling sound accompanied the process, but other than the would-be assassin the only one within earshot was the frozen guard. Miklo Vinimus counted to twelve as he had been instructed, then pushed against the door. It resisted at first, but with a little more effort, he at last opened it. The slight groan of the joints was not enough to worry him. As soon as the door was open wide enough, he slipped through.

"Almost there . . ." he whispered. Miklo gazed around the chamber, somewhat disappointed at the dust-encrusted but otherwise bland decor of what had once been a royal bedroom. Dark shadows clung to the farthest corners of the room. The dust made his nose itch, but Miklo held back his sneeze as he stepped farther inside.

It had once been the chambers of Lanith's brother Prince Blane, but Blane had perished years ago in some old battle against the forces of the long-dead Dragon Emperor. The previous king had ordered the chamber sealed up and guarded after his son's death and Lanith had carried on his father's eccentric desire. Miklo felt a touch of guilt at the thought of utilizing the room of one dead son in order to eliminate another, but for the sake of his homeland and the lives of many, it was best that Lanith walk the Final Path.

With one last glance down the hall, Miklo closed the door. Slowly his eyes adjusted to the darkness. The details of the decor did not interest him save that the center of the chamber had to be clear of any objects. He saw that this was so, something that pleased him immensely, and eased a sudden nervousness that had just a moment before spread over him. Miklo had been anxious from the start, but this near to his goal the ramifications of what he was about to attempt now became overwhelmingly clear. He was about to assassinate the monarch of one of the leading kingdoms of the Dragonrealm. He was about to change the course of the land, save the lives of countless innocents.

Almost Miklo Vinimus turned to flee, but her voice echoed in his head, almost as if she stood in the room with him. *If you're going to do it, do it then, Miklo! There's*

THE HORSE KING

no hope for any of us otherwise.

His brow furrowed as he briefly thought over the last, but the urge to complete his task again took precedence, pushing away the fear and all else. The horse king had to die for the sake of the Dragonrealm.

Moving to the center, Miklo dropped to his knees. Lanith's personal chambers were directly overhead. Surely the fact that providence had supplied Miklo the perfect location from which to cast his spell of death meant that he was destined to succeed.

If all worked as planned, the spell would come up from below the horse king's bed and envelop its occupants before they had a chance to stir. Saress no doubt had set her own defenses, but Miklo's mistress had insisted that what they plotted would work, defenses or not. It was clear that she knew Saress reasonably well.

He coughed once because of the dust, then began to concentrate.

Like many sorcerers, he saw the power as lines of force crisscrossing everything. Even here, it cut across the darkened room, creating a strange glow visible only when he used magical sight. The sight was useful when one had to draw upon substantial levels of power, but otherwise interfered with normal vision. Miklo was still amazed that more competent spell- casters such as the Bedlams could shift into and out of magical sight in the literal blink of an eye. It always took him a few moments to adjust, both when shifting into and out of the phase. Perhaps those like the Bedlams did things differently than he did. If he survived this, he would ask her.

Tendrils of power—thin, misty things that only he could see—floated with purpose toward the ceiling. They paused there, as yet unable to penetrate the man-made barrier, but Miklo was not perturbed. He still had to bind the power a bit more. Her instructions had been explicit. If he wanted to slip past Saress's defenses without disturbing anything—

A sudden shifting of forces made him pause. An oddly foreign presence briefly touched his mind. It vanished before he had a chance to try to identify it, leaving him only with an unsettled feeling. Miklo waited, but when it did not return, he finally shrugged it off as nerves and decided to push on with his effort.

He raised one hand toward the ceiling.

A giggle escaped him—no, he realized, the giggle had come from somewhere in the chamber.

"You've been very amusing, very amusing indeed, little Miklo. I watched and waited with anticipation as you wended your way despite all obstacles to your moment of destiny," piped a voice from the shadows surrounding him. "Very amusing it was, but now I can't let you go on. I've so many plans, so many things to do, and if I let you go through with this, it'll just take that much longer for me to achieve them!"

Gasping, Miklo rose from the floor. The forces he had been gathering he now turned toward the darkest shadows in the chamber, those being the only place he could imagine the source of the voice hiding. Green and red flashes of energy momentarily illuminated dead Prince Blane's room and stirred up so much dust that despite his predicament Miklo Vinimus had to pause to cough and sneeze.

A massive hand seized him by the collar and raised him into the air.

"Don't fret, though, little Miklo. I shall find a place for your name in this great epic I'm creating. A small place, to be sure . . ."

The hand released the hapless, would-be assassin. Instead of the floor, a huge maw of darkness now opened beneath his feet. Miklo Vinimus found himself falling and falling and falling without end in sight.

His scream grew distant.

In the hills overlooking the city, the golden-haired enchantress stirred from her

178

self-induced trance, sweat suddenly enveloping her. She blinked and looked around as if afraid that something terrible now stalked her. Then, her somewhat elfin features twisted into an expression of annoyance, frustration, and not a little guilt at having used a loyal if very naive man whose magical potential was now lost to her.

"Damn . . ." she muttered. If what she had sensed before breaking contact with Miklo was true, there was no hope left for the ugly little northerner. "Damn . . . damn . . . not another one . . ."

Lanith stirred from his slumber, slightly disgruntled at having lost the thread of his dream. He had been breaking in a magnificent stallion, a creature more elemental than animal. He dreamed such dreams often, for in his mind there was only one mount worthy of him.

A giggle from nearby pushed away the last vestiges of the dream from the graying, bearded king's mind. Lanith blinked, allowing his eyes to grow accustomed to the darkness. He saw that the giggle could not have come from Saress, for she still slept deeply. He admired her long, flowing mane and the curves of her body before sitting up and looking around for the true force.

"What is it?" he asked.

A part of the darkness blacker than the rest coalesced into a tiny figure much like a puppet without strings. It had no mouth or nose; in fact, the only discernible features were a pair of ice-blue, narrow eyes that lacked any sort of pupil. The presence of the macabre nighttime visitor did not disturb the horse king. Lanith was too familiar with the thing by now.

Despite the lack of a mouth, the figure had no trouble speaking. "Are you sleeping well, my great king?"

"I was until something woke me." Lanith's craggy features twisted into an expression of annoyance. He liked being woken by no one in the middle of the night.

The thing, now perched on the end of the bed, giggled. "I think that you will find one of your Magical Order missing, King Lanith."

"What's that?" The monarch stiffened, dark piercing eyes fixing on the inhuman orbs of his companion. "What have you done, imp?"

"He was about to send you to join your brother Blane. I thought you might not want to do that, but if I was wrong, then I do apologize."

"An assassin? Where are the guards? What about the defenses? They should have been sufficient—" Lanith started to rise, but the puppetlike figure shook its head. To his surprise, the king obediently sat back down. Beside him, Saress continued to sleep. She had not so much as shifted since the creature's arrival.

"He was naughty, so I've sent him away. You'll have to inform Ponteroy that the amusing little Miklo has decided to forgo the rewards of the Order."

"Miklo Vinimus?" Lanith had nurtured hopes for Vinimus. With a little training from Saress, Vinimus would have been able to replace Ponteroy, something of an egotistical popinjay, as second in the Order. Saress had been hesitant to teach the northerner, however, and now Lanith saw that her judgment had been sound. "You sent him away? Bring him back! There may have been others involved. He'll have to stand for questioning."

"Oh, dear . . ." Even devoid of features, the ebony puppet somehow physically displayed comic dismay. "I'm afraid that he won't be coming back from where I've sent him." The thing giggled. "They never do."

Lanith frowned. "Nevertheless, this does not end here. If a member of my Order attempted an assassination on my life, there will have to be some changes made. Fewer privileges. More proof of respect and loyalty to the one who feeds them and pays them good gold. I will have to draw a tighter rein on them."

"A tighter rein." Another giggle. "You're right, of course, and I shall help you achieve that, but not yet. Let them have their freedoms, their rewards. When their loyalty is demanded, good King Lanith, I'll make certain that they pay their due. Have I failed you thus far?"

"No . . ." Sleepiness once more touched the monarch of Zuu. Vague images of the magnificent black stallion again began to sprint through his thoughts. "No, you've not failed me, although I do not know why you—"

"Because I *like* you, good King Lanith! Because I want to do things for you! You've given a poor, lost soul a home and hearth! That's why soon you'll have the mount a conqueror and emperor deserves . . . because I want to do it for you."

The horse king leaned back, eyelids barely able to stay open. He did not question how swiftly sleep was overtaking him; he never did. A grin tried to spread across his face, but he was already too exhausted to complete it. "The shadow steed? You'll . . . help me . . . capture him?"

"Help you snare him, saddle him, and break him. Oh, especially *break* him . . ." The shadowy puppet rose from his perch and completed a comic bow of obeisance that King Lanith barely noted. "Rest easy now, my lord and master. When all things are in place, *I* will tell you what to do and you will do it, won't you?"

"Tell me . . . to do. . . do it. . . yes. . ." The warrior king drifted off to sleep.

"And no one but you and I will know that I'm helping you, will they?" As he spoke, the thing on the edge of the bed began to grow and as he grew he became more diffuse. Only the eyes remained strong.

"No . . . one . . ." spoke Lanith even though he was now deep into his slumber.

"You will be my puppet, great king. You'll serve me, bring me glorious battles and wonderful chaos for my epic, and in return I'll give you a most disobedient and ungrateful child, an offspring who has long been due a lesson."

"Shadow . . . steed . . ." mumbled the horse king. "Dark . . . horse."

"Yes. . . oh, yes, indeed. . . nothing will give me greater pleasure . . . well, *one* thing, but that can wait . . ."

King Lanith of Zuu did not respond this time, for no response was desired by his visitor.

Ice-blue eyes studied the horse king a moment longer, then the thing giggled once more and faded from the bedchamber.

Chapter Two

Penacles. The City of Knowledge. A place of wonders. It was the location of the magical libraries, a fount of history and information older than the kingdom itself. It was the land ruled by the Gryphon, sorcerer, shapeshifter, and warrior. Here the first victories against the centuries-long reign of the Dragon Kings had been won. Here humans had finally gained the chance to be truly free.

RICHARD A. KNAAK

It was a kingdom that had witnessed many astonishing events and played host to a variety of unusual guests throughout its long history, but for those gathered in the royal court, there was one guest who ever unnerved most of them simply with his presence.

His arrival tended to do even more.

A crackle of thunder. A burst of wind. A flash of light.

Someone screamed. Someone generally screamed, even though it was likely they had witnessed the same entrance a dozen times or more. The shadow steed did not try to hide his amusement as he trotted onto the marble floor. The brightly decorated chamber, newly renovated in the year since the Gryphon's return to the throne, contrasted greatly with his ebony color. The clatter of his hooves echoed throughout, the only sound now other than the gasping of one courtier or another as he passed among them.

He resembled a huge black stallion, although everyone there knew he was much more. How much more, even his dearest companions did not understand. He would have been hard-pressed himself to explain all that he was and was not.

There was nothing else in the Dragonrealm that was at all akin to Darkhorse.

The last humans scurried out of the way. Darkhorse cared little about any of them. Only the three figures ahead were of great importance to the steed. The one seated on the throne, sharp beak clamped tight in an obvious attempt to hold back his laughter, was the Gryphon. He was a humanoid variation on the traditional winged creature, a being as unique and as fascinating in his own way as Darkhorse was. The face was that of a bird of prey, although the feathering at the back gave way to a mane of hair more akin to that of another predator, the lion. A loose robe of crimson and gold covered most of the Gryphon's form, but Darkhorse knew that although the monarch of Penacles seemed perfectly human in body, the knees bent backward and the feet were taloned. The Gryphon also had vestigial wings, although as with the legs and feet, he kept those differences well hidden.

Standing alongside the Gryphon and looking slightly uncomfortable was the sorcerer Cabe Bedlam, Darkhorse's truest friend. Cabe Bedlam was a plain man by the standards of humanity, save for the silver streak in his dark hair that marked him as a spellcaster. However, his plain demeanor hid a sense of fairness and honesty achieved by very few beings that the shadow steed had met over the centuries. It also hid power such as few had ever attained. Cabe Bedlam could have laid waste to much of the realm just as his father Azran had attempted once, but where the elder Bedlam had been a monster, the son was a protector. It was he more than any other force that had helped shape the peace effort between not only the kingdoms, but also the races.

But there is still much work ahead, Darkhorse thought. *And some kingdoms will never accept a peace they have not achieved through war.*

The other figure standing near the throne was the sorcerer's mate, the fiery-tressed Lady Gwendolyn. Like Cabe's, her hair possessed a streak of silver. Unlike her husband, she was by no means plain. Accenting her beauty most were her emerald eyes, eyes that perfectly matched the sleek gown she wore. Those very eyes now fixed on the newcomer, dampening some of Darkhorse's humor. Lady Bedlam somehow had the ability to make him feel embarrassed, an emotion he otherwise rarely experienced.

Darkhorse had expected the two sorcerers to be here, having stopped briefly at their abode before journeying to Penacles. Their daughter, Valea, had informed him that her parents had transported themselves by sorcery to the Gryphon's palace only a few hours before. He was glad that they had done so; it would save him from having to repeat himself.

Just a few yards from the throne, the shadow steed dipped his head. It was as close as he ever came to bowing. "My greetings, Your Majesty! I apologize if my coming has greatly disturbed things!"

The Gryphon briefly flexed one clawed hand. "No. In fact, you are quite welcome this day. We had just begun discussing some matters that you may be able to lend a . . . hoof . . . with at some point. That can wait, though. To what do we owe your visit, my friend?"

There had been a time when *friend* would have been the last word the monarch of Penacles used to describe Dark- horse. There had been a time when the only one who had really trusted the demon steed had been the faceless warlock Shade, himself hardly the trustworthiest of characters. Shade was long dead *now— supposedly—but* over the past two decades, Darkhorse had gained for himself more friends than he had ever had before. Not only the Gryphon, but the Bedlams and their remarkable children. He was also good friends with the queen of Talak and her daughter, although the king of that mountain realm would never be too comfortable with him.

"I have the news you wanted about the drake confederation."

Everyone in attendance quieted. The Gryphon fixed one avian eye on his fearsome guest. "And what news is that?"

"Sssaleese appears to have strengthened his position. Two competitors seem to have . . . disappeared. The drakes have solidified their holdings in the northwestern region of the continent. They presently hold what used to be the northern half of the Iron Dragon's old domain. They've not moved on the hill dwarves to the east, but I suspect that is coming soon."

"Just as we suspected," commented Cabe Bedlam. "Sssaleese intends on becoming a Dragon King even if the others will not acknowledge him so. He probably believes that if his confederation grows large enough, Kyl will have to give him such rank."

"Do you think the young emperor will do that?" The king rubbed the underside of his beak. "He might lose the support of the other Dragon Kings. Storm and Black will certainly not accept Sssaleese as one of them."

Both the Storm Dragon and the Black Dragon were neighbors of sorts to Penacles. The Black Dragon had already tried to seize the kingdom and although his forces had been repulsed, no one believed that the lord of Lochivar was not constantly watching for weakness.

"I can't say. We're due to visit Kyl very soon. I'll try to put the question to him then." The Bedlams shared a unique relationship with the young emperor of the drake race, having raised him after his predecessor's death. That relationship had not always been easy, Kyl not always liking the human way of life.

"I could pay a visit to Sssaleese." Darkhorse stared at the sorcerer, one of the few who could look into his pupilless, icy blue eyes without flinching. "I could suggest new options to him if you like."

"That would not be wise, Darkhorse," Lady Gwen interjected. "Don't underestimate Sssaleese's power. We suspect that he has gotten his hands on some artifact. Certainly his success so far has been astonishing."

"I still say he had some hand in Toma's efforts to subvert Kyl to his cause." Darkhorse snorted. Toma had been a renegade drake, half brother to the new emperor, who had tried to control the throne to which he had not had any right. First he had attempted to manipulate his sire, the former emperor, and then, masquerading as a human teacher, he had sought to twist Kyl's mind. Toma was dead, but some believed that Sssaleese had given him refuge during the many years the renegade had remained hidden.

The Gryphon nodded. "Perhaps." He looked around at those gathered in the court. "My friends, please forgive me, but I must delay all other requests for an audience at this time. I apologize for letting you wait. Tomorrow, those of you who had business set for today will be first. Now, if you'll excuse me."

While those gathered still attempted to digest his words, the lionbird departed from the high-backed throne. He did not look at anyone as he hurried away, but the Bedlams followed him as if given some signal. Darkhorse paused only a moment longer, then proceeded after the mages. The shadow steed heard much whispering behind him, but nothing that sounded angry. The people of Penacles knew that their inhuman monarch, however brusque his manner, worked constantly for the benefit and safety of his subjects. He did not cut an audience short without good reason.

Guards came to attention as the Gryphon passed through the hall. At last they reached an open area in the palace where the sun could shine through onto a small inner garden. Benches circled the garden. To one side, a small pool populated with a few golden fish added to the feel of nature.

"I never know how to end audiences," grumbled the monarch of Penacles. "I never did. Toos was always more at home with the trappings of state, even if he was a crusty old soldier like me." The Gryphon looked to the heavens and raised a fist in frustration, a maimed fist missing two fingers. "You should've remained ruler, Toos, not me."

Toos had been an invaluable comrade and friend to his former commander, and Darkhorse, who had lost his share of friends, sympathized with the Gryphon. He turned his gaze toward the Bedlams, unable to keep from wondering what he would do when they, like all the others he had known, would fade into the past.

"I'm sorry." The Gryphon shook his head as if to clear it. "I think I would rather face the hordes of a Dragon King than sit on the throne, but the people refuse to see that others would be better fit to reign. They won't even let me very far out of their sight for fear I'll go running off to fight in some far-off war again."

"Troia might have something to say about that, too," remarked Lady Gwen. "Especially now that you have a child to raise."

Life and death, thought the shadow steed. *Everything always comes down to life and death.* Darkhorse could die, but he had lived so long that such a concept always seemed distant to him. However, such was not the case for his companions. Besides his old comrade, the Gryphon had also lost someone even dearer to him . . . his son. The lad had died in that same far-off war that the king had just spoken of. Of course, if the Gryphon had not journeyed across the sea to fight the wolf raiders, then he would have never met his mate, the cat-woman Troia, in the first place.

Life and death. It was a never-ending circle, the one villain Darkhorse could not defeat.

Which was why he sought other, more earthly foes. At least he could achieve some sense of satisfaction from overrunning a drake war party or barreling into a flock of arrogant Seekers. "My Lord Gryphon! You mentioned something else you wanted of me! What might that be?"

"It can wait a moment, Darkhorse," interrupted Cabe. "There is something we need to finish discussing with the Gryphon."

"Which is why I decided to bring us here instead of remaining in the court. The fewer ears the better, my friends." The lionbird glanced at his companions. "But my manners are slipping. Please, be seated."

Darkhorse noted the tension mounting in their host. Whatever topic he had missed because of his late arrival greatly disturbed the monarch.

"I've forgotten if you answered me earlier, Cabe. How many does that make?"

"Three. Two might have been coincidence, but the third one makes it all too clear that someone is hard at work here. The last was named Ilster. Fairly promising younger man."

"They've all been younger men," Gwen commented.

"And what do you mean by that, milady?"

She frowned. "Nothing. Just an observation. It might mean something more, but I can't be certain."

Darkhorse had to break in again. "Would it be possible for someone to clarify what is happening? I gather from what I hear that this has something to do with the school for mages?"

"That's right." Cabe's expression was a mixture of worry and puzzlement. "Three of our students have vanished over the past few months. No trace whatsoever."

"Three? They did not just simply give up their attempts and go home?"

"We thought of that, Darkhorse, but no one has seen them. If they left, then they didn't head for their homes."

"Aah! Then that leaves only one place where they could possibly be! They have gone to . . . Zuu!" Darkhorse uttered the name of the southwestern kingdom with the expectation of surprising his companions with his quick thought, but his pleasure faded as he saw that his announcement was far from a shock to them. "You know that, then . . ."

"It's what we *suspect,*" returned the Gryphon. "There is a difference, my ebony friend."

"Well, then, we simply have to go there and find out!" Darkhorse backed up to give himself some room. "Come, Cabe! You and I will ride there now and be back with them before King Lanith can even blink!"

The Gryphon bristled. "With all due respect and for the sake of peace between Penacles and Zuu—at least for the moment—I'd prefer we handle things a little differently. This calls for treading a little more carefully, if you don't mind, Darkhorse."

"Are you suggesting that I cannot be delicate, my Lord Gryphon?" He looked from the monarch to the spellcasters, read their answer in their expressions, then dipped his head. "Well, perhaps you have a point."

"Zuu has been building up its strength for years, Gryphon," remarked Cabe. "Especially where mages are concerned. These disappearances have to be related to that."

"I agree, but we need proof. I have agents at work on it now. I'd prefer to hear what they've discovered before we move against Zuu. I—"

The clatter of metal made the entire group look around. A guard raced down the hall toward them, his face pale.

"Your Majesty, my pardon! Lord and Lady Bedlam! Your son! He's—"

"Aurim!" Gwen was on her feet. "What is it? Has something happened to him?"

The guard paused to catch his breath. "Not . . . not to him, my lady! He was showing . . . you just have to come, my lady!"

Cabe held on to his wife. "His sorcery. He was using sorcery again, Gwen."

"Where is he?" demanded the Gryphon.

"Your practice field, Your Majesty."

"Not far. Everyone with me."

With the Gryphon and the guard in the lead, the band hurried through the palace. Although the royal guard had a vast practice field by their quarters, years ago the king had usurped part of the royal gardens for a walled practice yard specifically designed to test his own unique abilities. Most humans would have found themselves hard-pressed to successfully navigate some of the features the Gryphon had added over time. To him, practice did not just concern swordplay; it also involved gymnastics and problem solving.

Just moments before they would have reached the field, a scream reached them.

"Is there someone with him?" the Gryphon snapped.

"He was with the daughters of Baron Vergoth of Talak." Vergoth was one of King Melicard's chief advisers and often played ambassador to Penacles. He had been good friends with Toos and also got along well with the Gryphon. Vergoth had many children, and Darkhorse vaguely recalled that two of the daughters were only a few years younger than Aurim Bedlam.

"I suspect that he was trying to show off." Cabe shook his head. "Not again."

No one else had an opportunity to comment, for they were suddenly standing outside facing the Gryphon's private field. It was a living nightmare.

The ground rose and fell as if something huge were trying to punch its way to the surface. A series of poles, originally set up for gymnastics, popped up and down at random, rising at times with such force that they surely would have badly injured anyone who happened to be standing too near. Climbing bars set in one wall seemed to believe that they were snakes, to coil around whatever object was within reach.

At various points around the field, weapons darted about of their own accord. One long blade buried deep into one of the poles was attempting to pull itself free.

"Animation," Gwen whispered. "He should know better than to try animation."

In the center of the chaos huddled three frightened figures. The daughters of the visiting baron—pale, tiny women clad in wide gowns—clung to Aurim's side. Aurim Bedlam was a golden-haired youth who might have escaped the pages of an epic tale, so physically did he resemble the handsome, noble heroes of such stories. At the moment, however, the younger Bedlam did not act the part of the epic hero, his face almost as terror-filled as those of his companions.

A pole shot up from the ground. It was close enough to strike one of the females a hard blow on the arm, but at the last moment, the pole bent away. Despite his fear, Aurim had at least put together a protective shield, albeit one that did not allow for much movement.

"They're all right." Lady Bedlam breathed a sigh of relief. Darkhorse knew that she had not only feared for her son, but for anyone near him. Although Aurim's difficulty with sorcery extended back to when he had been a small child, there had been surprisingly few injuries and none of those serious. Still, considering the lad's great potential, Darkhorse and the others still feared that one day the unthinkable would happen.

"He is not without some control of his abilities," the shadow steed offered, trying his best to soothe the Bedlams' worries.

Cabe stepped forward, arms outstretched. Darkhorse felt him summon up power. The sorcerer stood motionless for several seconds, then frowned. "I can't put a halt to it."

"Let me try." The Gryphon's eyes narrowed. Again, Dark- horse felt power build up . . . then nothing.

"It's Aurim," decided Cabe Bedlam. "He might not have complete control of his abilities, but that doesn't make him any less powerful." The sorcerer studied the mad scene. "I'll have to go in and get them out before we can put a stop to his spellwork. He can tell us what he did."

"I'll do it, Cabe. This is my practice field and although it's a little more lively than even I prefer, I stand a better chance of reaching them."

"Neither of you should go running into there." Lady Bedlam anxiously clenched her fists. "If I thought it was safe to just go in, I'd do it myself. You know that. Aurim's abilities are unpredictable. They're safe so far because he cast both the spell that caused this chaos and the protective one now covering them. Our protective spells might not be so effective in there."

Darkhorse tired of listening to them discuss their options. He understood their fear, but could not fathom why the obvious solution had escaped them. "Never fear, my friends! The answer to your dilemma stands before you! I am not as fragile as you! I will not be bothered by a few enchanted blades or some dancing poles! Allow me!"

Before they could say anything, he had entered the pandemonium. The two females had their faces buried in Aurim's rich red mage's robes, but Aurim saw him immediately. The fear turned to relief and the youth opened his mouth to say something.

One of the serpentine bars wrapped itself around the stallion's neck.

The action was so startling that for a moment Darkhorse could not react. The bar should not have been able to touch him; his will alone should have made him a ghost, a phantom, which the enchanted bar should have passed through. The shadow steed concentrated, willing himself even less substantial, but the thing's hold did not slip.

Darkhorse reared, pulling the bar from the wall. It squirmed around his neck, seeming unable to tighten its hold but unwilling to give up. The stallion moved forward again, but found his hooves sinking into the stone surface. He pulled one loose, but the other three sank deeper. Try as he might, Darkhorse could not make himself light enough or insubstantial enough to completely free his legs.

His power is astonishing. Many had said that Aurim had the potential to be a spellcaster several times stronger than his parents combined. His deficiency had lain in his concentration, not his actual skills. Darkhorse had not understood just how powerful his young friend was until now. Aurim *was* much stronger than his parents . . . strong enough that this enchanted practice field could injure, possibly even kill, his would-be rescuer.

Darkhorse was an eternal creature, never aging, but he could be destroyed. He had faced death many times for those he considered worthy. Aurim had been the accidental cause of this sinister chaos, but that was certainly not reason enough to abandon both him and the two females.

He surged forward, pulling his hooves free, then burying them again as he moved closer and closer to the trio.

Only at the last minute did he see Aurim pointing frantically behind him. Ignoring the futile movements of the serpentine bar, Darkhorse twisted his neck at an angle all but impossible for a true equine. A buzzing sound passed over him.

An ax buried itself in a wooden pole to his side. It had been aiming for his head and although Darkhorse was fairly certain that it would not have actually harmed him, he was grateful for the human's warning.

At last reaching the three, Darkhorse found that he, like the animated weapons, was unable to pierce the protective barrier. "Aurim! Disperse your shield, then help them mount up! I will protect all of us!"

Aurim closed his eyes and concentrated. Several seconds passed without any discernible change to the shield and Dark- horse began to fear that the three were trapped within. Then, just as he was about to give up hope, he sensed the shield fade away.

To his credit, the young mage moved the moment the defensive spell faded. He dragged both women forward. Darkhorse adjusted his form, growing longer and shorter. Aurim helped both of his companions to mount, then proceeded to do so himself.

A pole burst from the ground, knocking the mage backward. One of Baron Vergoth's daughters shrieked and it was all the magical stallion could do to keep both from falling off. He heard Lady Bedlam call out, but what she said was lost amidst the pandemonium.

Again one of his passengers began to shriek, but Dark- horse, both impatient and anxious, twisted his head completely around and roared, "Be silent!"

Both clamped their mouths shut and stared wide-eyed at their rescuer. Darkhorse turned his attention back to Aurim, not caring at all if the females were now frightened to death of *him* so long as they stayed put and quiet. Up to now, he had been able to keep his footing, but his luck was certain to fail soon. He had to take hold of Aurim and get them away.

"Darkhorse!" Beside him, seeming to materialize from nowhere, was Cabe. "Take them! I'll get Aurim!"

The ground gave way more and more. A pole shot up just before the shadow steed's muzzle, startling him. He wanted to help Aurim, but arguing would take too long. Darkhorse trusted the master sorcerer to rescue his elder child. If anything went amiss, however, he would come back.

Twisting around, the ebony stallion fought his way back toward the opening where Lady Bedlam and the Gryphon waited. Several others had gathered in the short time since he had entered the enchanted practice field and one of those was Baron Vergoth. The Talakian aristocrat stood poised by the very edge, as if debating whether or not to go charging in after his daughters. Darkhorse knew that he had to escape the field quickly lest the man do such a foolhardy thing. Vergoth already sported two ragged scars on his right cheek; if he entered the practice field while Aurim's spell still held, the baron risked losing his head.

The Gryphon had one hand on Vergoth's shoulder. Gwendolyn Bedlam stood before him, shaking her head and pointing in the general direction of the ebony stallion and his passengers. *No doubt she is assuring him that his daughters are safe with me!* For some reason, though, the baron did not seem convinced.

The going was still slow. Darkhorse silently cursed as he pulled back before what appeared to be a dancing sword. He did not fear for himself—he rarely did—but human life was precious to him, more so because they lived so few years in the first place. Whether his passengers had been aristocrats or beggars would have made no difference to him; Darkhorse would have protected either with equal effort.

At last he reached the end of the field. The humans parted way for him as he leaped the final few feet and landed silently on the marble floor.

Vergoth retrieved his daughters. The two young women clung to him. "My gratitude, Lord Darkhorse."

"I am lord of no realm, Baron! I am and shall always simply be Darkhorse! No gratitude is necessary! Besides, there are still others in danger—"

"Not any longer." The voice was Cabe's. With him, still very pale, was his son. This near to one another, the two humans looked more like brothers than father and son, but mages aged very slowly. Cabe Bedlam might have seemed only in his mid-twenties, but he was nearly twice that.

"Thank you, Darkhorse. I'm . . . I'm sorry." The last comment appeared to be directed at everyone, not simply the shadow steed.

The baron, his expression neutral, ignored Aurim, instead turning to the Gryphon.

"If you will excuse me, Your Majesty, I would like to take my daughters back to their quarters. They are understandably shaken up by this and I am certain that they need to rest."

"By all means, Baron Vergoth. If there's anything you need, please let me know."

"I will." The aristocrat bowed. His children attempted to curtsy, but Vergoth steered them away before they could finish.

"That is going to require some diplomatic work," the Gryphon quietly commented. "I'll have to have some of my best wine sent to his guest quarters . . . along with some of the young women's favorite flowers and treats."

A tremor shook the hall, followed immediately by a loud clatter. Everyone glanced back at the practice field. The flying weapons had dropped to the ground. The poles and bars were motionless. The entire field looked normal once more.

The monarch of Penacles looked relieved. "Thank you, Aurim."

The golden-haired sorcerer looked sheepish. "I didn't do it, Your Majesty. It just . . . stopped."

"Well, I'm sure you tried your best to make it stop."

This only seemed to make Aurim feel worse. Darkhorse knew full well that such statements had flooded the boy's ears for most of his almost twenty years. People were always consoling him over this mistake or that. The eternal could identify with his situation. Despite his great age and power, Darkhorse was often reprimanded for his impetuousness. He did not see things quite in the same way as humans even though he had lived among them for lifetimes. Even now, he did not understand why some of the things he did worried his companions so.

Many of those who had gathered were now drifting away, aware that this situation was one the king would prefer to handle more in private. Darkhorse carefully kept from saying anything, wanting to hear the decision of both the Gryphon and the elder Bedlams before adding his own thoughts. He hoped that they would not be too severe with Aurim. The spellcasters' children were most dear to him.

"What happened?" Gwendolyn Bedlam asked.

Aurim refused to look at anyone. "They wanted to see me perform some sorcery. Just something little. Queen Erini has power, but she doesn't use it unless necessary and there's really no other spellcaster in Talak. I . . . I didn't think I'd have any problem with something so little, but I brought them out here just to make sure there was enough room."

"What did you try to do?" The Gryphon's tone had softened.

"I took a chess piece from your set and—"

"From *my* set? The set that was sitting in the palace library?"

"Yes." Aurim tried to back away, unnerved by the Gryphon's sudden anxiety.

"That set is ancient. Possibly magical in some ways. Very intricately carved. I was a fool to leave it out like that, but I never thought—"

Darkhorse recalled the chess set and although he had suspicions concerning its lost origins, he decided now was not the time to mention them. What was important was that the Gryphon did not realize how his words were cutting deeper and deeper into the young mage. Even Darkhorse, who would ever observe the workings of humanity from far away, could see that the more Aurim's confidence sank, the worse it would be for him in the long run.

Perhaps the king saw this also, for he then added, "But I can hardly condemn someone for something so little when I consider some of the things that I did during my life. What did you do with the chess piece?"

Brightening a little, Aurim explained how he had taken the chess piece and led the two young women outside. From the way he talked, Darkhorse gathered that Aurim was attracted to both, but more to Vergoth's elder daughter. Cabe's son seldom had the opportunity to associate with one attractive female near his age, much less two. He had grown a little reckless, telling them how he had animated things before, including, once, a number of stick men. Of course, Aurim had failed to mention that they, like so many other things he had animated, had gotten out of his control. This time, however, he had been certain that he had the proper concentration.

Everything had gone well at first. The power was his to control. He had fed it into the chess piece as his two admirers had watched in fascination. The figurine, which he had chosen at random, had started to shiver as if about to move.

Then a backlash of energy had thrown Aurim to the ground. That was when the practice field had suddenly come to life.

"I don't understand *what* went wrong! Everything was going just as it should have!" He looked at his parents. "I swear I kept my concentration perfect. It should have either moved just like I wanted or stood still. I don't know why the spell backlashed into the practice field."

"It may have been your choice of items," his mother answered. "If, as you said, Gryphon, the chess set contains some trace of power, then perhaps that's what caused Aurim's spell to go awry."

The lionbird rubbed the bottom of his beak. "You may be right. I'll investigate it. I've always meant to, but I just never got around to it. Perhaps the time's overdue." To Aurim, he added, "In the future, though, I'd like to be asked for permission before you attempt to dazzle attractive young women with your magical skills."

"Yes, Your Majesty."

"Where is the chess piece now?"

"I . . . don't know." Aurim looked around. "I don't see it, but it must be somewhere in the yard. I'll look for it—"

"Never mind. I'll hunt for it myself later. If you did succeed in animating the piece, it could be anywhere." To the elder Bedlams and Darkhorse, the king remarked, "I still need to discuss those other matters with the three of you, but I think it might be good if I first talked to my queen about what else can be done to smooth things over with Baron Vergoth. Troia's become quite friendly with Queen Erini and through her has come to know the baroness. She should be able to give me more insight on what to expect from Vergoth's wife. I know that the baroness has much influence with her husband. In the meantime, I'd like you all to stay as guests. Your usual chambers are available for you and your family, Cabe, if you'd care to use them."

"We'd be honored, Gryphon," returned the sorcerer. "Valea is overseeing the Manor while we're gone and I think she's been looking forward to proving that she can do as well as her mother and me. She's not often had the opportunity to oversee things on her own."

"I'm certain that she'll do an excellent job. She's grown up quite a bit since Kyl's ascension."

Unspoken but understood by all, including the shadow steed, was that there had been some fear that the Bedlams' daughter would have a difficult time shaking off the emotional turmoil caused by the young Dragon Emperor's attempt to seduce her and then his brother Grath's betrayal of her to Toma. However, instead of caving in to the damage to her heart, Valea had turned around and seemed to grow to adulthood overnight. Her power was already at a more advanced stage than her mother—who knew better about these things— had predicted, and her handling of her skills was already superior in some ways to that of her older brother.

Thinking of that, Darkhorse cast a quick glance at the youth. Aurim frowned slightly, but the moment he realized that someone was watching him, the frown disappeared. The younger Bedlam suddenly found the ceiling of the hall diverting.

There is more turmoil in the lad than we have suspected. Should I mention this to Cabe?

While he was trying to decide what the proper human course of action would have been, the Gryphon and the Bed- lams evidently came to the end of their conversation. The king bowed to the spellcasters, something he did for few others, then departed.

Cabe sighed. "Aurim, I—"

"I'm going into the city." The golden-haired figure started to walk off.

"Wait, Aurim!" The elder mage reached out.

His wife took hold of his arm and whispered, "No, Cabe. Let him go. Let him burn away some of his frustration. He's been like this before. You know that he won't do anything foolish."

"I don't like to leave him alone, though, Gwen. I know what it's like to be so uncertain about one's abilities. Maybe if I walk with him—"

"And what if you only succeed in reminding him that your abilities and your handling of them were enhanced by the memories that your grandfather Nathan instilled in you? You had some benefits to your training that few ever had, you'll have to admit."

"I did at that, but I still don't like leaving him alone."

Darkhorse brightened. He had wanted to help his friends, but until now had not known how to go about it. "Have no fear, my dear companions! There's no need for your son to be on his own! I will join him, be his companion during his troubled times, and, coincidentally, keep him from any mischief!"

Both spellcasters immediately opened their mouths, no doubt to express their gratitude to him, but now that the decision had been made, Darkhorse wanted not to waste a single moment. He wanted to join Aurim before he left the palace.

Darkhorse felt a surge of power and recognized it immediately as the work of the younger Bedlam. Aurim had decided to transport himself out of the palace rather than walk or ride. The shadow steed immediately followed suit. When focused by a great desire, such as escaping his parents after a debacle like today's, the golden-haired mage's ability to properly complete his spells increased dramatically. *If he could only focus as well when not so upset . . .*

The hallway of the Gryphon's palace faded away, to be replaced immediately by a busy street in the market district of Penacles. People whirled around as Darkhorse materialized, some screaming and others turning so pale they might have been denizens from the realm of the Lords of the Dead. The crowd around him melted away, leaving only one other figure besides the huge ebony stallion.

Aurim turned around and looked up into the pupilless, icy blue eyes of his friend. "Get away from me before I kill you."

Chapter Three

190

"What's that?" The eternal could scarcely believe what he had heard. "What are you saying, Aurim? You are distraught! You cannot mean such a ridiculous thing!"

"Don't I?" Aurim approached the shadow steed heedless of the spectacle the two of them were creating. "Look at me, Darkhorse! Look what I did! I nearly killed Adelina and Mersi and all I was trying to do was show off for them! I should have known better. I can't control my powers; I'll *never* control my powers! Better I stay at the Manor for the rest of my life before I injure or even kill someone I care about . . . including you!"

"I am a bit more durable than you think, my friend."

"I saw how you had to struggle in the practice field. I *could've* killed you. I know that."

Darkhorse looked around at the still startled crowd. Penacles was an enlightened city, thanks in great part to the efforts of both the Gryphon and the Bedlams, but watching a sorcerer argue with a creature out of legend was too much for most of the folks around them. He tried to think what Cabe would do.

"Aurim, there is an inn nearby run by a man named Gullivan. It is a place where the students from your parents' school often go and one where even I am considered . . . less of a curiosity now. Let us go there and talk this out. You can find some drink and I . . . I can listen."

The human calmed a little. He looked around at the rapt audience, then visibly pulled himself together. "All right, but you better take us there. If I try another spell, I could leave a gaping hole in this part of Penacles."

That was hardly likely, but Darkhorse did not want to become entangled in another argument concerning Aurim's fear of his own powers. That could wait until they were at Gullivan's.

It took the slightest effort to transport the pair of them from the street to the interior of Gullivan's inn. A few faces looked up at them in surprise and one serving woman gasped, but the overall reaction to their astonishing appearance was far more reserved than it had been outside. Months of dealing with the students of the fledgling school of sorcery, not to mention visits from the shadow steed on rare occasions, had steeled most of the regulars. The Gryphon also paid Gullivan a fairly good amount of money to tolerate the antics of the students and their possible effect on other business, although any serious incident was to be reported to either the king or the Bedlams immediately.

Cabe had once informed Darkhorse that Gullivan's inn had actually benefited from its unique clientele in an unexpected way. Many newcomers to the city found the thought of seeing the students or even possibly Cabe Bedlam himself enticing enough to risk any magical mischief the practicing spellcasters might unleash. Even now, a pair of Irillian merchants, their bluish, wide-legged sea garb the newest rage in their kingdom but rather out of place here, watched with open fascination the arrival of the two newcomers. Feeling a bit mischievous, Darkhorse looked at them and winked. They stiffened, then leaned forward and whispered to one another rapidly. The shadow steed studied them, deciding that they were what they seemed and not actually spies for the Blue Dragon. While a treaty existed between Irillian By the Sea and Penacles, it was not unheard of for agents of both kingdoms to circulate around. One never knew what information might be needed if a treaty was later broken and war was declared.

Of the other five or so humans in the room, two were students he had noted several times. They watched with interest until a look from Darkhorse made them return to their own conversation. The remainder consisted of two serving women, one of them Gullivan's niece, and the innkeeper himself. While Gullivan's niece was used to strange sights and only smiled at the new pair, the other woman, obviously new, was already retreating to the back room.

Gullivan, a former soldier, as were many in his present trade, was a muscular man just beginning to thicken at the waist. He was only slightly older than Cabe Bedlam, but, lacking the sorcerer's abilities, looked more like the master mage's father. What little hair remained on his head made him resemble a monk until one noticed the scars on his face and his arms.

"Darkhorse . . . and . . . it's Master Aurim, isn't it?"

"Greetings to you, Gullivan!" The first time the ebony stallion and the ex-soldier had met, they had, by mutual consent, dispensed with the titles they generally used for all others. No Lord Darkhorse or Master Gullivan. Darkhorse liked the man although they did not see one another that often.

"Hello, Master Gullivan." Aurim turned from the innkeeper and, after a study of the interior, located a booth far away from the rest of the people. It was a wide one, but hardly wide enough for Darkhorse in his present form. Nonetheless, the eternal made no attempt to either transform himself or request Aurim to change booths. The youth was still sensitive. The stallion settled with standing next to the table.

The door to the back room opened and a brawny but younger version of Gullivan walked out. "Zaysha said that there was a *horse* in the place, Father! What could she mean—" His eyes alighted on the shadow steed. "Gods!"

"It's all right, Pietr. You haven't been here for any of his visits. This is the legendary *Darkhorse.*"

"Darkhorse, but he's just a . . . no, I guess he isn't, is he?" Pietr shook his head. "I never know what to expect in this place. I'm sorry, M-Master Darkhorse."

"Simply call me Darkhorse, young human, and I have taken no offense."

"My son, Darkhorse. Been away for a few years. The other woman is his wife. She's from a coastal village to the south where the weather's been the most she ever had to worry about."

"I'd better go explain," Pietr added, already retreating into the back.

A brief smile lit Aurim's features. Darkhorse chuckled. Aurim quickly looked down.

"Come now, Aurim! Surely there is no reason to continue feeling so terrible! It was a minor thing. No one was hurt. The baron has kept his daughters under his protective arm for all their lives; a little adventure is good for them."

"A little adventure? Is that what you call what happened? It could've been a disaster . . . it *was* a disaster!"

"Hardly that, but the point is, it is over and all is well, Aurim! You need not worry. You simply need more time!"

Aurim slammed his fist on the table, causing the Irillian merchants to briefly look at them again. Gullivan immediately blocked their view, asking them if they required anything else, then came over to his new customers.

"Did you care for anything, Master Aurim? On the house for you and your family; that's the way I set things. I owe your folks for a lot of business."

"Nothing, thank you."

"If you change your mind . . ." Gullivan retreated without asking Darkhorse if he desired anything. By now he understood that Darkhorse did not eat.

"Now perhaps we can talk a little." The shadow steed paused, however, noticing a peculiar expression on his young companion's face.

"I'm sorry. I don't really want to talk. Why didn't you just leave me alone? All I wanted to do was walk around for a little while until I could bring myself to face my parents or the baron's family. Is that asking too much, Darkhorse?"

"Your parents were concerned about you, Aurim, and as both their friend and yours, I thought I would join you on this walk! Surely I am no great bother! I will walk or stand quietly by as you work matters out in your head. You will hardly even notice that I am nearby!"

"I think the fleeing crowds would keep reminding me," the youth snapped. A moment later his expression became apologetic. "I didn't mean it to sound so severe, Darkhorse, but you know how most folks react to you. They didn't have the fortune to grow up knowing you as I did. You're still the demon steed of yore, the monster only their king and the wondrous wizards Bedlam can control."

"Is that what they think of me?" He laughed. "I would have been disappointed if they thought any other way."

"The point is, I can hardly relax if you're with me. I need time to wander around, think for myself." Aurim's tone grew more imploring. "Darkhorse, I hardly ever get to see anything other than the Manor unless I'm with Mother and Father in Penacles or Talak . . . and I rarely get to see much of either kingdom save the royal grounds. My parents have been through so much, seen so much—"

"And I daresay they would like you to avoid much of what they had to fight through, young one. You and your sister have also had your share of excitement. Let us not forget that Toma lived among you and your family for a long time without anyone realizing that he was not your tutor Benjin Traske. I am not completely versed in the desires of humans and I doubt that I ever will be, but most would find your adventures more than sufficient to last them their lifetime . . . even if it may be a sorcerer's lifetime of three hundred years."

"I've been doing some thinking, though." The young spellcaster paused and glanced briefly at the two students.

Darkhorse followed his gaze and saw that once again they had been studying the two newcomers. Darkhorse supposed that they were in awe of him, not an uncommon event. He decided that some time soon he would visit the school again and give all the students the benefit of his centuries of peerless wisdom. Surely no one had a view of Dragonrealm sorcery to equal his . . . even if his own abilities followed a different path than those of a spellcaster native to this world.

"I think I do need to be on my own for a time," Aurim continued. He leaned nearer. "All the teaching, all the tutoring, can't do for me what being out in the real world can. If I was on my own for a little, I think that maybe I would be better able to focus. I'd be less nervous each time I attempted some spell. I *would.*"

Aurim on his own. Did his parents know of this desire? "And how long have you had this notion? Did you come to this conclusion after the incident in the practice field?"

"Actually, I've been thinking about it for some time on and off. It came back to me while you were talking with Gullivan and his son. I realized that I shouldn't be dwelling in pity, but trying to overcome my difficulties. That's what Father and Mother have always preached and I know that Great-grandfather Nathan believed the same as Father. Even . . . even Grandfather Azran would've agreed with them on that."

"I would prefer to keep Azran Bedlam out of this conversation just as I suspect your parents would. If this notion is at all influenced by your grandfather's foul memory, then it is a notion best dropped!" Even Cabe rarely mentioned his father. Azran would forever be a bloody stain on the Bedlam name.

"No, I just used him as an example." Aurim shuddered. "I would never want to be like my grandfather. You can see what I mean, though, don't you? If I could just spend some time on my own, maybe visit Gordag-Ai in the northwest or Irillian By the Sea, I might gain the confidence and will I need to set myself straight."

Darkhorse's quandary grew. He was certain that neither of the lad's parents would agree to something like what Aurim desired, but he himself was almost willing to agree with his companion. Why was it not possible? Gullivan, he knew, had started as a soldier when he had been at least two or three years younger than Aurim was now. What was so dangerous about visiting either of those two kingdoms? Both were relatively safe. Gordag-Ai had always been a peaceful land and since the treaty Irillian and Penacles had come to trade with and respect one another. Surely Cabe and Gwen would see that, too.

They might agree if they knew that I would secretly be keeping an eye on the lad . .

The door to the inn swung open. Aurim looked up, eyes widening with interest. Darkhorse shifted his gaze to the entrance. A young woman with dark brown hair that flowed down over the back of her bright green cloak looked over the interior as if uncertain that she was in the correct location. Her eyes grew especially round and questioning when they fixed on the black stallion.

"Greetings, my lady!" Gullivan hurried up to the young woman, hands folded together. "Looking for a room or simply a meal? You'll find the finest of both here at Gullivan's!"

"There's . . . do you usually allow your customers to bring their horses into your place of business?"

"Him? My lady, that is not an animal there; that is the legendary Darkhorse, friend and companion to the Bedlam sorcerers and the king of Penacles himself!"

She either did not understand or did not believe him. Dark- horse decided that he had to intervene before the innkeeper lost a customer because of him.

"What he says is true, my lady." The shadow steed paused while the newcomer registered his words. Her expression tightened and her hands trembled, but otherwise she remained calm. Darkhorse was impressed by her reaction; most women of her station—her flowing, colorful clothing indicated that she was the educated daughter of a wealthy merchant from Gordag-Ai—tended to gasp, back away, and possibly even faint in his presence. Others simply fled.

"I've heard. . . you *are* real, then."

"Some would still say unreal, my lady, but yes, here I stand, in the. . . well, *flesh* is perhaps not quite the proper word!" He chuckled, in part hoping it would ease the situation.

"You rescued the princess once." She walked toward him, fascinated.

Erini. Before becoming King Melicard of Talak's queen, she had been Princess Erini of Gordag-Ai. He had rescued her, but she had also rescued him. There was a statue of Darkhorse, or at least a statue of what the sculptor believed he looked like, in the royal gardens of Gordag-Ai, a tribute from her parents. He had never journeyed there to see it, although Erini had always insisted he should. "Queen Erini is a good friend of mine."

Her gaze abruptly shifted to Aurim, who had remained speechless so far. "The silver streak in your hair. You're a sorcerer? I've never seen a powerful one."

"I'm . . . I'm Aurim."

"My name is Jenna."

Darkhorse did not have to be human to understand his companion's slow reactions. Cabe Bedlam had reacted much the same during the first days after meeting his future mate. Aurim was fascinated by the young woman. Jenna had large, expressive brown eyes and a small but sloping nose. Her lips were full and her mouth seemed always to be smiling. She was, the shadow steed suspected, very attractive by the standards of any human male.

Perhaps here is a different and possibly safer adventure to take the

194

lad's mind off of his difficulties. Jenna seemed attracted to Aurim as well. Perhaps if the young sorcerer gained more confidence in his dealings with others outside his family, he would gain more confidence—and therefore more focus— concerning his powers. Even if it did not help Aurim in that respect, what was the harm in a little flirtation? The boy needed to enjoy himself.

"Are you a powerful sorcerer?"

"Aurim is the son of Cabe Bedlam!" Darkhorse proudly announced, certain that such news would impress the woman. He saw immediately that he was correct, but for some reason Aurim did not appear to appreciate his aid. "And a fine sorcerer himself, although he, like his parents, has promised to keep their use of power to a minimum while in the city. Most folks are not used to such skills."

"Darkhorse—" Aurim looked even more frustrated. He rose and bowed for Jenna. "Aurim Bedlam, at your service. It's a pleasure to meet you."

"And you, too." Her smile grew wider and as it did, the sorcerer's countenance turned faintly red. Jenna looked around. "My father's stayed here on occasion while he had business and he said that this was a fascinating place, but I never dreamed he was telling the truth about those he met here." Her attention focused on Aurim again. Darkhorse might not have been there for all the interest she now had in him. He was both amused and pleased. "He told me I should try to find a room here. Father thought that I might like it because . . . because I have a little magical skill myself."

The eternal stirred. Although Darkhorse had not actively tried to sense power within her, he generally noticed such, anyway. It was surprising that he had not sensed her presence before she had even entered. However, now that the merchant's daughter had mentioned it, he could sense a trace of power buried deep within her. It was faint and a little peculiar in signature, but each spellcaster seemed to have a unique link to his or her abilities. What was odd was that she did not have any silver in her hair. Human spellcasters always had silver in their hair.

"You're a sorcerer, too?" Aurim's eyes lit up.

"Not a very good one." Jenna reached up and lifted her hat, revealing a tiny lock of silver hair. "Father likes me to keep it hidden." She replaced the hat, then held out her hand toward Aurim. "This is all I know how to do." Jenna stared at her hand. After a moment, it began to gleam. The illumination was not very strong, however. Jenna stared at it for a second or two longer, then blinked. The gleam vanished.

Curiously, Darkhorse noticed that he did not feel any tug of power as he did with other spellcasters. Jenna's skills, he decided, were so meager as to be nearly nonexistent.

"That's very good," Aurim assured her. "Most people can't even do that."

"But I want to do more. I've tried, but this is all I've been able to manage."

"Sorcery can be pretty difficult at times. I *know*."

The shadow steed watched both of them with growing interest. More and more he was certain that what the younger Bedlam needed most was time with a woman such as this, someone who he could confide in and understand. Humans seemed to need such relationships throughout their lives.

"Aurim." The cross expression with which Cabe's son briefly presented him was sign enough to Darkhorse that his assumptions were correct. "As you are in Gullivan's and in trustworthy company, there are some tasks that your father and the king require of me which I should deal with now. I trust you will return to the palace before nightfall?"

"I will."

"Then I shall bid you both fond farewell! A pleasure to meet you, Jenna! I hope to see you again soon!"

"Oh, I think you will." She smiled at Darkhorse, as if sharing some jest of which only she was fully aware.

Both of the young humans seemed to appreciate his departure. The shadowy stallion glanced at Gullivan. "Good day to you, innkeeper! My gratitude for your tolerance of my presence!"

"Come whenever you please, Darkhorse. Come whenever you please."

Darkhorse could not resist doing one more thing. He turned to the two students, who had ceased their attempts to continue their conversation and were now simply watching him, and added, "I trust your studies are going well! I may test you later!"

They both immediately nodded, evidently too dumbfounded to speak. He had no true intention of testing their skills, but he was certain that for some time to come they would study with more passion than they had ever managed in the past.

Darkhorse laughed, then, with everyone watching, vanished from the inn.

He rematerialized in the palace, this time avoiding a location where he might surprise a crowd. The palace library, not to be confused with the legendary magical Libraries of Penacles for which the City of Knowledge had earned its title, was generally utilized only by the Gryphon, his queen, and the Bedlams. Therefore, it was not at all surprising to discover it empty. The king was likely still trying to make amends to Baron Vergoth. What Cabe and Lady Bedlam might be doing, he could not say, but it would be easy to enough to find out.

It was a simple matter to reach out to them. It was something they did all the time, speaking to one another through thought. Only if a spellcaster had reason to shield himself did it prove difficult and for Darkhorse even that was often not a barrier.

Cabe . . .

He felt the first flicker of awareness.

A mind touched his. . . but it was not Cabe's. It was— It was his *own?*

Darkhorse broke the link he had been trying to forge with Cabe. What had just happened? It had been like touching his own reflection, viewing his own thoughts. He had never experienced such a backlash before, not in all the centuries he had journeyed across this world.

He reached out again, seeking to re-create the effect. There were many defensive spells surrounding both Penacles and the palace and although most of these had been attuned so as not to affect the Gryphon's allies, perhaps a newly set defense had accidentally caused the peculiar reaction.

What the shadow steed got instead was Cabe Bedlam. The sorcerer's mood was anxious. *Darkhorse! What happened to you? I felt your presence and then you broke off abruptly! Are you all right?*

Jam fine, Cabe. Something . . . it was nothing, simply a curiosity. I will tell you about it some other time. Perhaps you or your grandfather may have come across its like in your research.

Where's Aurim? Is he back in the palace?

Carefully, the ebony stallion explained the situation, playing up Aurim's interest in Jenna and how he thought it would benefit the lad. Cabe countered that it had been Aurim's attempt to impress Vergoth's daughters that had created the initial chaos.

Jenna seems different, Cabe. Besides, Aurim seems to understand that he needs to be careful. I think that he might need to see the outside more, meet those who have no affiliation with either the Manor or the palaces of Penacles or Talak. He has seen little.

196

Besides, he should be safe in Gullivan's.

There was a pause. *Maybe. I'll see what Gwen thinks. You're in the palace now, aren't you?*

I was going to join you. The Gryphon had said earlier he had need of me.

The need is greater now. We're with him at this moment in his quarters. I should have told you to come directly here rather than waste time talking to you like this. Cabe seemed to grow tenser by the moment. *Aurim should be all right. It's probably better that he's enjoying himself for a while. We may be here for quite some time. You'd better join us now.*

What is it? What do you mean?

Again Cabe paused, this time for much longer. *Just come.*

Thought was action. Darkhorse transported himself to the Gryphon's personal quarters. The room was wide, bright, and somewhat reminiscent of the forest: the work of the queen, no doubt. The king was of a more militaristic bent, although he, too, was a lover of beauty. Several shelves lined one wall, shelves filled with books and scrolls. An elaborate writing desk stood nearby. Several paintings and statuettes depicting animals and scenes from nature decorated the rest of the chamber save for one wall where an elaborate tapestry hung. Illustrated on it was a very detailed image of Penacles, an image so intricate that one could have located every individual building. If one stared long enough, it was possible to see the image shift on occasion. Whatever happened to the structure of Penacles was reflected in the tapestry, although that was not its primary function. The tapestry was the only way to reach the magical Libraries of Penacles.

The queen was not there, but the Gryphon and the Bedlams were. There were two other figures near the closed doors, figures that were not in any way human. They were tall, broad, and unless they moved, one would have thought them simply iron statues. They were more than that, however. Both were golems, constructs created by the Gryphon through great effort. When the royal family slept, the golems watched over them. They also made certain that no one attempted to use the tapestry without permission. Two identical creatures waited on the outside of the chamber.

"Darkhorse." The monarch of Penacles nodded to him. In his hand he held a peculiar, avian-shaped artifact. From the manner in which he held it, it was obvious that it was of some great importance. "A timely entrance."

"I am ever timely, Your Majesty! Cabe made his summons sound urgent. What is it? Has it something to do with that constructed bird you hold?"

"This . . . construct . . . arrived only moments after I left you. One of my guards found it and the moment he touched it, he felt compelled to bring it to me." The lionbird turned over the object. Viewed up close, it proved to be an even cruder representation of a bird than Darkhorse had first thought. "As far as I've been able to discern, it *flew* here but lost control when it passed through the first defensive spells. The compulsion spell activated when the bird was touched."

"A clever mage."

"And there aren't too many of those," Gwen remarked. "Even if there hadn't been a message inside, it would've been pretty obvious from what region it originated."

The eternal's ears pricked up. "Zuu?"

"Zuu," repeated the Gryphon. "The message was sent to me, but it was also addressed to Cabe."

The sorcerer held up a small piece of parchment. "In fact, it's written almost as a personal note to me, although I don't know who it could be from."

"And what is it about?" Darkhorse feared that he already knew.

"According to this, Zuu marched—or rather rode—against one of its small neighbors to the north. The message doesn't say when, but I gather in the last day or

197

two. More important, his forces include his Magical Order."

"He has begun his mad campaign, then?"

"More a testing of his strength, I suspect," the Gryphon interjected. "To see how his forces will do in battle. He will win, of course. The strongest foe he could possibly face is the Baron of Adderly, whose domain lies just north of Zuu's lands."

The shadow steed shook his head. "I have never failed to see the allure of conquering others! It has always looked far too complicated to maintain control afterward!"

"That it is," agreed the monarch of Penacles. "But that won't stop some from continuing to try. Once Lanith tastes a little victory, there'll be no stopping him short of full-scale war." The Gryphon looked up at the huge black stallion. "I have a favor to ask of you . . ."

King Lanith, clad in the traditional leather pants and jerkin of the brave Zuu warrior, pushed his short helm up by the nose guard and watched as his messenger returned at full gallop from the local baron's castle. He had sent what he considered a fair offer with the man. If the defenders surrendered, they would be relieved of all weapons and a small garrison would take over under an officer Lanith trusted. The baron's family would be transported back to Zuu where they would be hostages.

He could see that the offer had been spurned.

In his head, he heard the merry voice. *The brave baron insults you! He has the audacity to reject your kind offer. I suppose you'll just have to slaughter everyone inside.*

"Be silent, puppet!" Lanith muttered, ignoring glances from one of his officers. "When I want your advice, I'll ask for it!" Still, he had a point. Who was this country baron to think that he could resist an army of horsemen that blanketed the landscape for as far as the eye could see?

The messenger reined his mount to a halt and leaped from its back. Kneeling before his king, he said, "The man refuses to listen. He says that our riders will run their mounts into the ground and our archers will waste all of their arrows, but that we will never breach his defenses. He says that he will outlast us until finally exhaustion, frustration, and hunger send us riding back to our stinking stable of a kingdom."

Although the words were spoken plainly, they created a stirring among Lanith's officers. The horsemen of Zuu were respected warriors throughout the Dragonrealm. They had fought for a variety of causes since their nomadic ancestors had first chosen to settle in Zuu. The king's own brother had led a band that had fought hard to push back the Dragon Emperor's forces at Penacles. Blane had given his life and Lanith always pointed at the late prince as the example by which his soldiers, male and female, should live. There were a few who would have liked to point out that Blane had never believed in conquest, but they had wisely kept silent. However, no warrior of Zuu, whatever his or her feelings concerning the grand crusade, was willing to accept such insults from a country aristocrat.

"He's brought his destruction on himself."

"Do I send in the first wave, then?" asked his second, a graying warrior named Belfour. Like many of the officers but *unlike* the king, he wore the more protective padded metal vest and arm protectors common these days. In fact, with the exception of Lanith's special guard, the horse people were all better protected than their monarch. Bravery was one thing, but living to fight another day was preferable.

Of course, no one realized that the king was watched over by a hidden defender who would make certain that no weapon touched him. All they would see was that their ruler, self-declared conqueror of the Dragonrealm, was impervious to harm.

The image of a grand charge by his ready hordes enticed Lanith, but his unseen ally suddenly interjected. *The walls are strong. There are hidden pitfalls awaiting any of your eager riders who come in from the western side. What the human in the structure claims is also true. He could outlast you.*

"Then what—?" At the last moment, the king recalled that only he could hear the other. *Then what do you suggest? Why don't you just go in and deal with them?*

Oh, I'm not that powerful, great king, no indeed! Besides, if you wish to achieve your other desire, I must keep my presence as secret as can be. . . and where would the fun be without an epic battle? Did you know that there is a fault in the earth beneath the structure? A slight but significant fault?

I don't want to bring down the entire place! I want it fairly intact, you foolish imp!

A giggle briefly echoed through his head. *It will only cause a little damage. . . just enough to give you the time and entrance you need if your warriors are swift enough after the sorcerers do their work.*

The voice faded away, but Lanith needed no further explanation. "Ponteroy!"

A tall, overdressed man, narrow of face with a long mustache and thin, oily hair, rode up beside the king. He looked uncomfortable, probably because his clothing, while very elaborate, was more suitable to the cooler kingdom of Gordag-Ai than down here in the warmer southwest. Ponteroy performed a partial bow, then fixed beady eyes on his monarch. "Yes, my liege?"

"Prepare the Order. I've work for them. This is what they'll do." He signaled Ponteroy to lean closer, then whispered his orders. The officers tried to listen while pretending not to, but Lanith spoke too quietly. When he was finished, he waved the newcomer away. "You have your orders. Leave us . . . and do not fail, Ponteroy. I don't like failure."

"Yes, great one. As you command, great one." The newcomer nervously removed what at first appeared to be a small riding crop from his belt. The upper tip of the short staff was a crystal carved into the head of a horse, a head that glowed slightly the moment Ponteroy touched it. The mage saluted Lanith with the staff, then with some awkwardness turned his mount and rode off.

"Why isn't Saress here?" growled one of the younger officers, a female. "I don't like that slippery little serpent!"

Lanith silenced her with a glance. "Saress has other matters to attend to. Ponteroy has been paid his gold; that's all that matters to him and that's all that should matter to you. He knows what'll happen if he fails me." The king looked over his officers. "I trust all of you know as well."

More than one warrior paled. Lanith ignored them, staring at the stronghold of his foe. So far, his legions had barely suffered a scratch; he had conquered a pair of villages and a good-sized town, but nothing significant. The baron here was, in fact, the first true resistance that he had encountered. He could have simply allowed his officers to conduct a siege of the place, eventually overwhelming the defenders at the loss of many lives, but Lanith was impatient to complete this final testing of his might. This place was merely in his path. It was a bump in the road to conquest that he had to smooth before he could prepare for the real campaign against the true enemy. Gordag-Ai.

Gordag-Ai. Their lands were rich; they would easily feed his armies. Once he had his hold there solidified, he could turn on Talak. From there, he could ride into the Tyber Mountains and seize the still inexperienced emperor of the drake race.

One of his former officers had insisted that such a plan of attack could only lead to destruction and chaos, and that Talak would not stand for Gordag-Ai being assaulted because Talak's queen was the daughter of the rulers of Gordag-Ai. Talak, in turn, had treaties with Penacles.

But I have allies, too. In return for his aid, the drake confederation's leader, Sssaleese, would lead his forces in concert with the hordes of Zuu. Already Sssaleese had strengthened his hold on the lands west and north of Esedi, where Gordag-Ai lay. Talak could not stand against both and while the emperor nervously debated sending drakes against drakes, Lanith and his ally would crush the mountain kingdom ruled by half-faced Melicard.

Suddenly the thought of what he plotted began to overwhelm even the horse king. Gordag-Ai. Talak. Penacles. The drake emperor. So many powers and all of them against him. What could he possibly be thinking?

Victory is nearly yours, whispered his impish ally, scattering his anxious thoughts to the wind. *The first true step toward conquering the Dragonrealm takes place now. This is the test that shall reveal to your warriors their destiny!* The giggle that followed was loud enough to make Lanith wince in pain. *Your great sorcerers are ready to begin! All they need is your word!*

The last faded away just as Belfour informed him, "Your Majesty, there's a signal from Ponteroy. I think he's awaiting your command."

Lanith's fears vanished. There would be epic battles, tales to be told for generations to come, but his descendants, the future emperors of the Dragonrealm, would tell them. He would build an empire vaster than any the human race had dreamed of. There was no reason why the continent even had to be called by the worthless title of Dragonrealm once he conquered it. He could even name it after himself—

"Your Majesty—"

Stirring, the monarch of Zuu, future master of all that existed, nodded. It was the only acknowledgment Belfour needed to signal to the waiting spellcasters.

Lovely, oh, lovely, I cannot wait! came the voice in his head again.

At first, all that Lanith noticed was the restiveness of his many legions. His officers had primed them for war for months; now they wanted battle. Well, he would give them battle, glorious, victorious battle . . . but only a small taste of it today. As his invisible ally had more than once pointed out, it helped morale to know that you went into battle with victory a certainty. Once this day was over, they would be snapping at the bit to begin the actual move toward Gordag-Ai.

The horses suddenly shifted, growing uneasy. Several snorted and tried to back up. Some of the officers and soldiers had trouble keeping their mounts under control.

Lanith felt the earth below him tremble slightly.

Several heads appeared on the battlements of the castle. Someone raised a bow and shot at the surrounding force, but the single shaft fell short.

The tremor grew stronger. There were distant shouts of consternation from the stone fortress.

"Earthquake!" a young officer gasped. Others also looked shocked.

"Belfour, if anyone panics, I want them executed on the spot. Is that understood?"

"Y-yes, Your Majes-Majesty!" The senior officer's stuttering was not due to fear on his part, but rather the ever-increasing strength of the tremor.

"Ready our warriors."

"As y-you command."

A block fell from the battlements. Another followed. From within the castle came a cry, then another. Lanith smiled. Inside, panic had to be spreading like wildfire.

A crack opened in the ground just before the front gate of the castle, then another opened up toward the eastern side.

Moments later, a fault developed in the gateway. The high wooden gate, raised early on to prevent access to the attackers, came loose on one side, swinging open with a clatter that even the quake could not mask. Part of the gateway came crashing down.

"'That'll be enough," Lanith remarked.

Belfour raised a hand. Almost instantly, the quake began to die down.

"Signal the advance."

Horns blared. Officers shouted commands. Inside the castle, people were still crying out. Only one or two figures still remained on the battlements and they appeared dazed.

They dared defy you, great king! They mocked you and cursed you! They should be punished! They should be . . . examples . . .

King Lanith of Zuu nodded. The imp was correct. The imp was always correct. This country aristocrat and his little army deserved to pay for their insult to him. "Belfour!"

"Yes, my liege?"

"Tell the officers that all inhabitants of the castle are to be executed."

The senior officer's expression tightened. "Are you—?"

You must not grow soft now! They must be made examples to those who would defy you in the future. A little fear goes a long way, doesn't it, O great one? More lives may be saved by the loss of these insignificant few.

"Yes, I can see that," the monarch of Zuu whispered. To his second, he roared, "You've been given an order by your king, Belfour. Are you questioning it?"

The warrior swallowed, then looked down. "No, my liege."

"Then go!"

The landscape between the king's position and the baron's stronghold had already become a living wave of roaring, eager riders, a mounted army that was awe-inspiring even to him. He thought about riding with them, but this battle was hardly worth his while. Let his men see that he had faith in them. He had already ridden untouched into the last town, killing more than half a dozen of the laughable defenders the elders had mustered from the inhabitants. Any weapon that had sought to mark him had been turned at the last moment. The imp had kept his promise then, just as he always did.

A pair of archers fired from the battlements, but they were the only visible defenders now. The first of Lanith's warriors reached the broken gate and rode their beasts inside, their swords raised high. Even though the first ones would probably die, there was no way that the defenders would be able to plug the gaps now. It was only a matter of time.

As he watched his forces swarm around and over the battered castle, his one true ally's voice worked to relieve him of any uncertainties concerning his chilling commands to his second. *So much death, but it will all be worth it, O great one! You will unify the land, bring it to a glory that others have only dreamed of! Generations will sing the praise of Lanith the Conqueror, Lanith the Horse King!*

Horses. That reminded him again of the one promise that so far his unseen companion had failed to keep. Where was the mount he desired that would befit his glorious status? Where was Darkhorse?

Patience, Emperor Lanith! The shadowy presence giggled. *Already that is under way! Soon, very soon, you will have your wondrous, monstrous steed . . . and I will have my vengeance . . .*

THE HORSE KING
Chapter Four

Jenna was already waiting for him. Aurim fought hard to control his eagerness, the dazzling smile that spread across her face as he entered not at all aiding his struggle. After checking with his sister Valea to make certain that all was well at the Manor, his parents had decided to stay longer as guests of the Gryphon. He had been given the choice of returning or staying, which, in the young spellcaster's eyes, had been no choice whatsoever. So long as Jenna was in Penacles, he wanted to be there, too.

He felt a bit guilty. His parents had stayed because of urgent news from the western reaches: the possibility of a war of some sort. Aurim had had trouble paying attention, more interested in when he would finally be able to see the merchant's daughter. She was the first woman that the mage felt he understood. There were few women his age at the Manor and most of those treated him with the same respect they did his parents. It made it difficult to truly know them. When he visited the royal families of Talak and Penacles, the situation was even worse. True, there were more choices, but they were generally the pampered, overly delicate daughters of men like Baron Vergoth. The baron's daughters had actually been some of the more tolerable females he had met.

Jenna was different. She spoke her mind, but respected his as well. She admitted to her shortcomings, but seemed to be able to turn those shortcomings into something useful. Everything she said or did seemed to reflect his own desires, his own dreams. Around her, he felt more confident, more independent from his famous parents. Independence was important to him.

"Aurim!" The beautiful young woman rose as he neared what had become their favored table. She was clad in a forest- green riding outfit with gold trim, a fairly conservative outfit for someone from Gordag-Ai. Her hair was done up behind her and on her head she wore a peaked hat with feathers on one side of it.

He sat down. "I'm sorry I'm late, Jenna. My parents—"

"Should give you more freedom, Aurim." She frowned. "You are a great mage in your own right. You're more than old enough to be on your own. They should have to understand that."

"It's not that simple. They often leave me in charge of the Manor and its grounds. That's a big responsibility. I have to watch over what amounts to a village."

The frown vanished. "Your home sounds fascinating. I'd like to see it someday. I can't imagine drakes and humans living together in such cooperation. I know they live together in Irillian By the Sea, but humans have always taken a secondary standing there. Where you live, they work as friends!"

"It started when my parents were asked to raise Kyl, the Dragon Emperor, and it just grew into so much more. Many of the drakes decided to stay after Kyl departed."

Her hand slid forward, just barely touching his. "Do you think that we could go there? Just for a few minutes, I mean. You can do that, can't you? Transport us there? I know you could."

When she spoke to him in the tone she was presently using, Aurim was nearly willing to believe that he could do *anything*. He almost agreed to bring her to the Manor there and then, but just as the words reached his tongue, Aurim recalled that no one was allowed entrance into the magical domain of the Bedlams unless his parents knew first. They had good reason for setting such a rule. More than once, foes had sought entrance using false identities. Spies for a few of the Dragon Kings still sought to gain the secrets of the Manor for their respective masters.

"I'm sorry, Jenna. I've promised. Maybe if I introduce you to my parents and they got to know you—"

The hand quickly withdrew. "No, that's all right. Another time, perhaps. I understand if it's too much to ask."

Aurim knew that his face had turned scarlet. He had let her down. "I'm sorry."

"Please don't be." Her eyes appeared to sparkle. "I've an even better idea. Maybe you can help me. Would you teach me how to better control my abilities?"

Her request both flattered and worried him. Aurim wanted to help her, but then she might find out just how uncertain his own control was. Still, if he only had to make suggestions and didn't have to risk doing anything significant himself, then . . . "I guess that I could—"

"Oh, thank you!" Jenna leaned forward and kissed him lightly on the cheek. "Let's go to my room! We'll be able to work better there."

"Your room?" Aurim, raised to observe proprieties, shook his head. "That wouldn't be right, Jenna. I don't want you to get in trouble—"

"Oh, don't be silly, Aurim. I trust you . . . and you trust me, don't you?" She gave him a smile that would brook no dissension. "Besides, Gullivan speaks very highly of your family. I'm sure that he would see nothing improper about the two of us going to my room to talk, do you?"

Whatever misgivings he might have had, they were no defense against her beauty. Aurim finally nodded.

"Let's go now." Jenna practically had to lead him from the table. It was not until they reached the stairs that Aurim recovered enough to pretend that he was no longer concerned about what anyone might say. He did glance at Gullivan, but the innkeeper was busy with a customer.

Gullivan had a dozen rooms above the inn, most of them small but serviceable. There were two larger rooms, though, and one of these was where Jenna stayed. The furnishings were clean and well kept and the place in general was above the standards of all but the best inns. All in all, Gullivan provided something of a bargain, which was perhaps another reason why his business did so well.

Although there was some illumination from without, Jenna lit two oil lamps. Aurim now saw that other than one chair by a small table, there was nowhere to sit but the floor or the bed.

"We'll probably have more room if we just use the floor. Is that all right with you, Aurim?"

"Of course." Inwardly, he breathed a sigh of relief.

"Good." The merchant's daughter sat down on a wide animal skin that served as the only rug in the room. Aurim sat across from her, folding his legs as he generally did before beginning concentration exercises.

"I said I could only do this." She stared at her hand. It briefly glowed, then returned to normal. "But I can also do this." Staring at her hand again, she started to draw in the air with her index finger. A streak of light formed wherever her finger had been. In seconds, she had drawn the crude outline of what was possibly a horse.

Aurim blinked. The horse lifted its head, put one leg forward . . . then faded away.

"I can draw things like that and make them move a little, but that's all."

That's all? That she was able to do as much as this indicated that Jenna had more power than he had assumed. She was, in fact, what his father would have called a prime candidate for the school of sorcery.

Now there was a notion that appealed to him. Aurim wondered if he could somehow convince the merchant's daughter to leave her father's business for a time and study at the school. Not only would it enable her to better learn about the limitations of her skills, but it would put her nearby whenever he was able to get to

Penacles. Although it was possible that he could transport himself to Gordag-Ai, his lack of knowledge of the kingdom coupled with his distrust of his ability to correctly perform such a long-range spell made it doubtful that he would ever see her again if she returned home.

It was too soon to approach such a subject. *After* they practiced a bit, perhaps.

"You're better than you think, Jenna. You could become an excellent sorcerer if you put your mind to it."

"You're just saying that." She smiled wistfully. "It would be interesting. The things you must be able to do. Can you show me something now? I know you don't like to show off, but it would really mean a lot to me."

What could he say? He wanted so much to impress her, but since the incident in the palace, what little confidence he had once had in himself was virtually nonexistent now. If he failed, Jenna might laugh at him and ask him to leave.

"My concentration's been a little off today, Jenna. Couldn't I try to help you learn a little more about your power? Maybe we can get your images to last longer."

"Please, Aurim? It would encourage me if I saw some of what you were capable of performing." She looked down. "Not that I could ever be as good as you, but I want to experience what it must be like to have such power under your control."

Under my control . . . if Jenna only knew. Still, looking at her, Aurim found he could not resist another attempt. He would keep it small and simple, completely avoiding animation whatsoever. Well . . . maybe not. There were some old concentration techniques that he had once been good at—had been good at until his debacle in the Gryphon's palace—and if he cast the spells exactly the way he had, it was possible he might keep on going for a few seconds. Just long enough to impress his companion before things fell apart again.

"All right. Watch closely. I'm only going to do this for a breath or two." As she nodded, the young mage held out his hands, palms upward, and summoned up power.

An indistinct haze formed above his palms. The haze quickly defined itself into several tiny forms. The longer Aurim stared at them, the more distinct each became until at last he had re-created what had once been one of his favorite practice spells.

Each harlequin was colored blue and red and stood about two inches tall. They floated counterclockwise in a circle, but that was not all. Each little figure also performed a somersault. Over and over they went, much to the delight of Aurim's audience.

Without warning, the circle collapsed and the harlequins plummeted to the floor, where they faded upon contact.

Aurim cursed without realizing it. He slammed a fist on the wooden surface, sending shockwaves of pain through his entire arm.

"Aurim! Are you all right?" Jenna reached forward and took his hand in hers, studying it closely for any cut or bruise.

He tried to pull back, but her grip was surprisingly strong. The merchant's daughter locked gazes with him. "You shouldn't do something like that. You startled me."

"I'm sorry. It's just that the circle should have stayed in motion until I dismissed it! I've gotten worse, not better!"

"You're having problems with your spellcasting?" A look of concern crossed her features. "But you're supposed to be even more powerful than your parents! You are, aren't you?"

"As my father keeps saying, I have the potential. It's there, but I just can't seem to concentrate properly. I thought I was getting better with my control just prior to Kyl's ascension to the throne of Dragon Emperor, but afterward it all began to fall apart again. I don't know why, but it did. Very little I do works right."

She leaned forward and took both hands. "You must have gone through so much during that time. I imagine there were also a lot of changes afterward, maybe more work, more stress. I can appreciate the pressure you've been under. It's not easy being a merchant's daughter, being taught the business because my father has no son to turn it over to when he gets too old. Your parents act as representatives to the Dragon Emperor's court, too, don't they?"

"Yes."

Jenna nodded. "And you are left with more responsibilities when they are away."

"So's Valea."

"But you're oldest. In general, you're the one left in charge, aren't you?"

It was true, and sometimes he felt that the pressure was overwhelming. Valea sometimes said that he tried too hard, that he could not make himself responsible for every single matter going on in the Manor. Most of the activities that took place in and around the Manor did not require his watchful eye.

"I think that you've tried to do too much at once, Aurim. That's all. You need to turn away from everything else and let sorcery be your entire focus . . . but in a more relaxed manner. You need to become your strength, your power."

He laughed. "I thought I was supposed to be the instructor."

"Even a teacher can learn," Jenna countered, smiling again. Before Aurim realized what she was doing, the beautiful young woman leaned forward and kissed him. It was a brief, light kiss, but it left him completely befuddled. "I've got an idea. First, I'll teach you how to relax properly, then you teach me how to better utilize my skills."

It certainly sounded enticing to him, admittedly for more reasons than one. "How do you plan to make me relax?"

"My father taught me a few techniques." Jenna slid back a foot or two. "Turn your back to me."

Aurim did. The next thing he knew, Jenna had slid forward again, nearly nestling herself in his back. His heart beat faster. If this was intended to relax him, it was having the opposite effect.

"Close your eyes. Good. Now breathe slowly and let me do the rest."

The mage obeyed, although it was difficult to breathe slowly with her so near. Suddenly he felt her hands slide past his shoulders. Aurim twitched without meaning to, but Jenna stilled him with a single word. She touched his temples with her fingertips.

A tingling sensation spread over him.

Darkhorse and Cabe materialized at the edge of the Dagora Forest just a few miles west of the barony of Adderly. The sun was fast setting, which was just what they wanted. At the Gryphon's request, the pair had come to investigate the truth behind the message, and Adderly was the appropriate place to begin. If the horse king was testing his might, Adderly was his nearest reasonable target.

"I still do not see why we do not just return to Zuu, Cabe! We've visited the kingdom in secret before!"

"Yes, and the last time we were nearly caught by Lanith's pet sorcerers. I think they've learned a little since then, Dark- horse, especially if their numbers include the missing students:"

Deep down, the eternal knew that his companion was correct, but he still doubted that their present course of action would tell them anything worthwhile. Find Lanith, Darkhorse surmised, and one found the center of activity. They would learn more that way. The king of Zuu might have his own spellcasters, but Darkhorse doubted that any of them had skills worth fearing. Those that Cabe and he had encountered on their previous excursions a few years back had been as organized and competent as panicked sheep.

The shadow steed peered at the landscape before them. Adderly's eastern border seemed tranquil. There was no evidence of any battle. However, the castle of the baron was a few miles to the west and very much out of sight. If any struggle had taken place, the signs would be evident there, not here in this emptiness.

"Thank goodness there's no one here," the sorcerer remarked.

"Why would they bother to come here? There is nothing here, Cabe."

"True, but if they intended on invading the Dagora Forest, this entire area would now be overrun by more cavalry than I doubt anyone outside of Zuu has ever seen."

"I have witnessed the massing of hordesss far more vassst than what this human conqueror can gather," responded a harsh voice from behind them. "But I, too, am pleasssed that no such force camps jussst beyond my domain"

That Cabe was at least as startled as he was no compensation to Darkhorse. He did not like being spied upon, especially when he should have been able to sense this particular newcomer.

Cabe Bedlam's tone grew icy. "Lord Green. We were trying our best not to disturb you."

"Disssturb me?" The tall, armored figure walked closer. The setting sun left much in shadow, but it was clear that the dragon-helmed knight was not human. With the exception of his eyes--bloodred this time, although not always—the warrior was emerald-green. His armor was scaled, save for the helm, the crest of which was the startlingly realistic head of the menacing dragon. The lower half of the helm was open, revealing a flat, lipless mouth and daggerlike teeth. The scaled skin perfectly matched the scales of the armor and with good reason, for they were one and the same, the tough hide of a draconian shapeshifter.

The master of the Dagora Forest, the Green Dragon, had been watching them all the time.

"We didn't intend on encroaching long in your domain," Cabe added, clearly uncomfortable around the drake lord.

Darkhorse did not care for the drakes himself, but the lord of the Dagora Forest had always been friendly toward humans. Something, though, had changed the once-deep friendship between the Green Dragon and Cabe Bedlam into a shade of its former self. They conversed when necessary and met together when circumstances required it, but where once the scaled warrior had been welcome in the Bedlams' domain, he now never visited.

"You are not encroaching, Cabe. I undersssstand the reassson why you are here. Asss the power of my people, mysssself included, has declined, thossse like Lanith of Zuu have taken full advantage of it. I have been watching, and my agents, both human and otherwissse, have also been well at work."

"And have they found anything?" Cabe asked, still maintaining his distant tone.

"Very little." The Green Dragon looked from one to the other. "I have lossst at least five spies, all loyal volunteers. They entered Zuu . . . and did not return. I am quite certain that they are all dead."

This intrigued Darkhorse. The drake lord before them was one of the great powers of the Dragonrealm. He had access to rare artifacts and knowledge. His predecessors for generations back had worked to gather these things, providing the present lord of Dagora with many options when it came to such business as investigating the activities of a human monarch who had once been his vassal. "Have you looked for them?"

"I . . . have. Of courssse, demon sssteed. I do not leave sssuch things unfinished."

RICHARD A. KNAAK

There is something he fears about me. While fear was an emotion
Darkhorse encountered often from those he confronted, the drake lord had never
reacted like this. It had something to do with whatever had shattered the drake's
friendship with the sorcerer.

"Did you find out anything?" the spellcaster pushed, clearly desiring an
end to the discussion.

The scaly warrior looked away, obviously disconcerted. This time, however,
Darkhorse surmised that it was because of the results of the drake's investigation.

"Nothing . . . no . . . almossst nothing, Cabe. Each one left no trace, but I did
sssense twice a great emptinesss just before the link to me faded. I can't explain it.
They were not agents without protection." The Green Dragon looked up, eyes
locking on the sorcerer's. "Lanith controls sssome power, sssome *force*, that
makesss his insssipid Magical Order redundant and yet I cannot fathom what it
could possibly be! Only that it may be more than any of usss can deal with alone!"

The more he spoke, the more the drake's natural sibilance took over. The upper
hierarchy of the drake race prided itself on speaking the common tongue perfectly, but
whenever too emotional, they slipped.

"An emptiness," Cabe mused. "That's all you can tell us?"

"If I had more to tell you, believe me, I would. When I sssensed you, I debated
whether to sssay anything until I knew more, but then I quickly realized that I
have no idea how I *can* learn any more. Not without entering Zuu myself . . . and
I do not think that would be a good idea."

"What about Adderly?" asked Darkhorse. "Has anything happened to this
barony?"

The pause was far too lengthy for either Darkhorse or the sorcerer. "Adderly is no
more. A laughable offense that Lanith callsss hisss first great victory. A tessst of hisss
might . . . asss if Adderly had any defense of significance. The curssed horse king did
not even attempt to take the castle without the aid of his misssbegotten
ssspellcastersss!" The Green Dragon clenched his fists. "They ssslaughtered the
inhabitants even after they had sssurrendered! Monsssterss! They call usss
abominations and thisss isss what they do?"

Such an emotional admission from a warrior whose race was known for its
savage ways surprised even Darkhorse. It also made the shadow steed more eager than
ever to return to Zuu. This Lanith had been allowed too much freedom; he had abused
every notion of humanity. Darkhorse understood many of the reasons that the
Gryphon and the Bedlams had given for no one having gone to war with Zuu, but
he was now aware that such reasons mattered little anymore. There was no doubt now
as to either Lanith's intentions or his methods for achieving them.

"I can't believe Blane's brother could be like that." Cabe grimaced. "I knew Blane
for only a short time, but he was a good man, a brave warrior. He cared about people.
Can Lanith be that different?"

"Lanith wasss alwaysss the ambitious one, Cabe. Alwaysss the more driven. Yet
thisss is far more than I expected from him. The Lanith I recall did once have
compassion . . . but not now."

"Talk! Talk! All we do is talk!" The eternal had had enough of talk. Everyone
talked about how terrible things were and what a threat the horse king was. Well, it was
time to take action, not continue treading softly. "We waste precious moments
here! Lanith has moved, tested his power! He will move on from here, moving
north, no doubt! If we do nothing, he will be at the walls of Gordag-Ai before very
long! He may be marching there even now!"

The Green Dragon shook his head. "No, eternal, he isss not. Lanith returned to
Zuu after this massacre and now awaitsss some newsss. I know not what, though.

Only that his missstress, the sssorceresss Saress, is to bring it."

"Saress?" Cabe Bedlam looked up. "Do you know anything about her? Even the Gryphon can't find out much."

"Rumorsss, Cabe. Nothing more. Saresss is nearly as great a mysssstery to me asss thisss power that Lanith wields."

"Could they be one and the same?"

"No. I can tell you that, at leassst."

"We waste time here!" Darkhorse kicked up earth with one of his hooves. "Cabe, we should go to Zuu ourselves!"

His companion looked down at him, then at the Dragon King. The latter made no sound, did not even move. "Not Zuu, Darkhorse, but I do want to see the baron's castle. There might be something we can learn there. Are Lanith's forces still there, Lord Green?"

"Only a small garrison. There are many patrols, however. The bulk of hisss forces are encamped nearer to Zuu. I believe he likely intendsss to attack Gordag-Ai, but on the chance that he will sssuddenly turn east, I have kept a careful eye."

"We'll look over Adderly first, then. Do you mind, Darkhorse?"

He still desired to journey directly to Zuu, but the eternal trusted Cabe's opinion. "Very well."

By this time, the sun was barely a glimmer on the horizon. The Green Dragon had become a shadow among shadows. He backed away in silence. Cabe seemed disinclined to bid him farewell. Darkhorse swore that someday he would find out what had come between them . . . and if the drake lord had betrayed his friend in some way, the ebony stallion would see to it that the master of the Dagora Forest paid for his folly.

"Have you been to Adderly before, Darkhorse?"

He twisted his head around to look at Cabe. "I have passed through it. There is not much to see there. I have only seen the castle from a distance."

"There are hillsss to the north and some wooded areasss to the west and east," called the retreating drake. "Neither afford much cover, but for the two of you, either should be sssufficient."

Cabe stiffened, then twisted around so that he could face the nearly invisible figure. "My thanks, Lord Green."

"Take care, my friendsss." The Dragon King vanished into the forest.

Darkhorse's comrade stared at the forest a moment more, then turned back to him. "Do you know those areas at all?"

"I recall them somewhat. His suggestions have merit. Cabe, what is the—"

"The darkness will help us. Let's go."

"As you desire, Cabe." Feeling subdued, Darkhorse reared, then started westward. His hooves made no sound as he raced, and in fact, he left no prints in the earth. Now was the time for speed, yes, but also for stealth. Even if he did not fear for himself, he always tried to watch over Cabe.

The castle of the baron of Adderly was at first a black hill jutting upward just a short distance from the true hills that the drake lord had mentioned. One or two tiny points of light flickered near the battlements, but as Darkhorse and Cabe moved nearer, other lights materialized around the castle grounds. It became obvious that besides the garrison, there was at least one band of cavalry, likely a returning patrol, camping nearby.

"The structure looks unsettled," Darkhorse commented after a brief study. "As if someone had tried to crack it in two."

"Lord Green did say Lanith utilized sorcery. The baron and his people probably expected a more conventional battle." Cabe inhaled sharply. "Lanith killed them all . . ."

The shadow steed was about to remark on the last when he felt the slightest tug of power. Some sort of spell was at work and it had a familiar feel to it, although he could not say exactly how. It did not strike him as a major undertaking, but he nonetheless grew curious to study it.

"Do you feel something, Darkhorse?" his companion suddenly asked. "A spell of some sort?"

So Cabe felt it also. "I do. Shall we investigate? I sense nothing extraordinary about it, but I find myself curious as to its origins! It seems to come from the wooded area just east of the horse people's encampment. We can be there and gone before any of them notice us."

Cabe looked up, Darkhorse following his gaze. Only one of the two moons was evident and cloud cover mostly obscured that one. The sorcerer acquiesced to his companion's suggestion. "I'm curious, too. We'll have to watch carefully, however. There may be some danger we can't sense from here."

"And what danger is there that the two of us cannot handle?" The eternal chuckled quietly. "Lanith may have his tame spellcasters, Cabe, but you and I . . . there is nothing we cannot overcome together!"

"I wish you'd quit saying that, Darkhorse," whispered Cabe with a rueful smile. "I'm not quite as invincible as you think I am . . . and come to think of it, neither are you."

Despite the other's words, Darkhorse still felt confident. This was so much like times past. He and Cabe against the villainy of such as the wolf raiders, the burrowing Quel, the treacherous Toma . . . it was in times of adventure that the eternal felt most alive. He could not tell this to his human friend, though. Even Cabe, who knew him best, would not have understood the sense of pleasure that always underlined the shadow steed's emotions during such dangerous missions. Darkhorse felt needed at times such as this.

They reached a position near enough to the enemy encampment that they could make out individual figures moving about. The horsemen of Zuu appeared restive; Lanith had succeeded in stirring his subjects to war. They would be ready to ride the moment he commanded them to do so. Darkhorse snorted. While he enjoyed adventure, he found no enjoyment in war. All it did was waste lives.

"Ahead, Darkhorse," Cabe muttered. "By that small open area behind those trees."

He was already aware of the location, having sensed even before Cabe the strong presence of the spell. Again, Dark- horse thought that there was a familiar signature to it. He had confronted the creator of the spell in the past . . . but where?

Then a feminine voice whispered, "Get *away!* Not here!"

Startled, Darkhorse turned toward the voice. As he did, one of his hind legs touched what felt like the branch of a tree, only there should have been no tree, not even a bush, at that location.

An intense pressure closed in on Darkhorse from all sides, squeezing him with such force that it grew more and more difficult to maintain his form. Darkhorse grunted, fighting as the incredible pressure threatened to squeeze him into a shapeless mass.

A cry alerted the shadow steed to his rider's plight. Cabe was caught in the same trap and he did not have the malleability of form to survive for very long. The eternal was not even certain that he could survive very long. This was like no spell trap he had ever encountered.

It was already futile to retain his equine shape. Darkhorse drew his legs inward and then collapsed his upper torso. His struggling companion fell with it. The shadow steed immediately enveloped the sorcerer, shaping himself into a soft, spherical cell that would, for the moment at least, provide Cabe with some protection from the spell.

His head was the last vestige of his equine shape that he discarded. The snout retracted quickly until only the pupilless eyes and a slash that had been his mouth remained. His new shape would afford him a little extra time, but unless he found some way to disrupt the trap, both he and Cabe were doomed.

There was *one* other thing he could do for the sorcerer, Darkhorse realized, but even a death as hideous as what the pair of them faced would have been preferable to the human. Cabe had witnessed Darkhorse absorbing his enemies and it was a sight that the spellcaster had clearly abhorred.

There must be something! I am Darkhorse! There is nothing from this realm that can hold me! Yet . . . that was not entirely true. There had been other traps, other spells, that had nearly done him in. Somehow he had always escaped. This time, though . . .

Despite his best efforts, the pressure continued to squeeze him into a smaller and smaller ball. Before long, he would be too small for Cabe to survive.

In the midst of it, Darkhorse sensed an emanation that made no sense. It was his own power, yet it worked against him. It was as if he had designed this trap himself. That was foolish, though, no doubt the product of his rattled senses.

The pressure increased. Unable to withstand the added pressure, the eternal shrank yet again. Now he sensed the sorcerer's new discomfort. Cabe had folded himself up as best he could, but that was no longer sufficient. Darkhorse felt Cabe make one aborted attempt to disrupt the trap, but it held firm.

And so I shall discover what death means to me! I shall see if I, too, am granted an afterlife! He doubted the latter. Having been created in the endlessness of the empty dimension called the Void, he was not at all like the creatures who were born in the world of the Dragonrealm. When he perished, Darkhorse suspected that he would simply cease to exist.

For being so foolish, for failing to save his dearest friend, he expected nothing better.

The pressure increased yet more . . . then *decreased* just as the eternal was about to collapse. Seizing advantage of the shift, Darkhorse expanded as quickly as he could, trying to wreak what havoc he could on the spell. It continued to weaken and as it did, he pressed harder.

As suddenly as it had been sprung, the spell trap dissipated.

Free at last, he remained still, not even attempting to reshape himself. The eternal shifted his gaze and caught a glimpse of long golden hair in the darkness. Again he sensed a familiar magical signature, but he was too weak to give chase. Besides, Darkhorse was suddenly very certain that it was through *her* doing that the deadly spell trap had abruptly faltered. Only from the outside could anyone have affected such a sinister snare.

But why had she saved them . . . or warned them in the first place?

Unfolding as an oyster might, Darkhorse inspected the still form of his companion. He knew that Cabe still lived, but what condition was the human in?

At first the sorcerer did not move, but when Darkhorse prodded Cabe's mind with a gentle magical probe, his companion immediately stirred.

"Dark—Darkhorse?" Cabe awkwardly rose to his knees. He blinked, then stared in visible amazement at the peculiar shape of the eternal. The latter made no attempt to resume his equine form. What mattered most was whether the human was injured or not.

"How do you feel, Cabe? Are you well?"

"Well pressed," muttered the sorcerer. He touched his side, immediately wincing. "I think a rib . . . may be cracked. I could fix . . . this. . . eventually. .

. but I'll need s-some time."

A horn blared. Darkhorse heard men calling out and horses moving. "Time is not something we have, it seems! A wonder they did not arrive sooner than this! We were held—"

"No more than . . . a few seconds, although I agree that it seemed like much . . . much longer." Cabe grimaced. "If they have any more spells at . . . their command I-like this, I don't think that I can fight them j-just now, Darkhorse."

"On that I must unhappily agree, Cabe." The eternal attempted a limb. It was of the proper length, but rough-hewn, as if some artist had just begun work on a sculpture. It was proof enough, however, that Darkhorse could resume a shape capable of carrying his companion to safety. He adjusted his form immediately, gingerly raising his injured friend up.

Cabe seized hold of his mane. Given time, the sorcerer would be able to heal himself, but with Lanith's men approaching, all the pair could do was retreat.

His first movements were ungainly. Darkhorse had to struggle to recall the proper coordination of his limbs. The more he moved, though, the smoother his movements became.

Unfortunately, the delay allowed the first of the riders to reach them. Two warriors, one bearing a torch and the other a bow, urged their mounts toward the duo. A third horseman followed, sword in hand.

Darkhorse felt Cabe draw upon power. Dirt swirled up into the air, blinding men and mounts. The horses struggled against their masters, not at all willing to ride into the magical storm.

"Ride . . . Darkhorse!" Cabe gasped, his voice sounding more and more ragged. The spellcaster slumped against the re-formed neck of his comrade. "Ride!"

The shadowy stallion would have preferred to fight these first attackers off, but while he probably would have survived, he was not so certain about Cabe. He turned in the direction of the Dagora Forest, knowing that the best way to lose them would be among the thick foliage. Still weak, it was impossible for Darkhorse to transport the two of them away, but he had no doubt that he could outpace the patrol's mounts. They were, after all, only mortal steeds . . .

That thought came back to haunt him a moment later as a long row of flickering torches and dark, rapidly moving figures to the south warned him that a large patrol sought to cut them off from the safety of the forest. The riders moved with such precision and planning that Darkhorse wondered whether they somehow could read his thoughts. He increased his pace as best he could, but between his need to keep an eye on the injured sorcerer and his own weariness, the eternal found that outracing the horsemen of Zuu was a greater challenge than expected.

A fiery arrow shot past his muzzle, striking the ground no more than a few feet from him. His fear for Cabe's safety increased a hundredfold. Darkhorse sent a mental probe to his comrade, but the thoughts he received were jumbled. The sorcerer was alive, but barely conscious. It was all the human could do to maintain hold. Darkhorse shaped himself so as to better keep Cabe from slipping, but could do nothing to protect the sorcerer should the archer fire any more of the deadly bolts.

The riders continued to close. Everything appeared to be working as if someone had planned to capture or kill the shadow steed and his friend. Had they really known that the duo was here or had they simply *expected* them?

From somewhere ahead came the touch of another mind. A female. *Just a few feet more. I can help you, then. You must turn a little to the right, though! Hurry!*

To the right would take him even nearer to the oncoming riders, many of whom were evidently expert bowmen even on horseback judging by the increasing number of bolts that assailed him. Darkhorse almost demurred, but at the last moment decided to take the risk. He only hoped that he was not being played for the fool. The stallion altered course, at the same time pushing forward with what strength he had left. The spell trap had taken too much out of him; he had not felt so weak in decades.

Directly ahead, the woman informed him. *Only a few yards more.*

Her last words confused him. He was still far from the forest and there appeared to be nothing in sight. Darkhorse could not even sense any *sorcery.*

That was what made the hole that swallowed them a moment later even more surprising.

Chapter Five

Darkhorse stood in the midst of a picturesque field of lush, high green grass that covered the sloping landscape to the horizon. Several trees of different species stood tall among the grass, islands in an emerald sea. Birds flew among the branches, singing and darting about without care. Overall, the pastoral scene was a sight that should have gladdened the heart of any who came to this place.

The shadow steed could only think of how much danger he and Cabe might be in from this supposedly tranquil land.

Where was the night? Where was the moon? According to the sun's position it was roughly an hour after dawn. The shadow steed did not like the abrupt changes. Only sorcery could have twisted his world so much, making night into day.

Yet even the shift from darkness to light did not bother him as much as the presence of the gently swaying grass. Each blade that touched his legs made him want to jump back.

"It won't harm you," said the familiar feminine voice. "It won't harm anyone but certain drakes. You can thank your sorcerer friend for that."

A human female now stood among the tall grass. Despite being clad in a simple brown and white peasant outfit, the newcomer was impressive. She filled the blouse and bodice in a manner that Darkhorse knew would have garnered the attention of any male other than a blind one. Her features were slightly elfin, but a bit more full, more human. She had hair almost as golden as that of Aurim, save that hers appeared natural whereas his had been altered by an early juvenile attempt at sorcery. There was no visible streak of silver in her tresses, but he could sense that she was most definitely a sorceress or witch.

Her eyes glittered, but when the shadow steed tried to identify the color, he found it impossible. Sometimes they appeared emerald, sometimes golden, and sometimes . . . sometimes they were as red and narrow as those of a drake warrior. Who was this woman?

"I'm sorry," she added, smiling mischievously. "The blink hole wasn't supposed to work like that. I thought for a while that I'd lost you, but then it finally opened on this side."

"Finally?" Darkhorse snorted. "If that was a blink hole, I do not think that I have ever seen another one that took hours to cross through!" He looked again at the sun. "Is it truly the next day?"

"Yes." The smile faded. "But we can talk about that after I've taken care of him. Let me get him off of you."

"I think not!" He backed a few steps away, glancing quickly around at the grass. It did nothing but sway gently in the light breeze.

"I know what you're thinking. These are no longer the Barren Lands, as you can see, demon steed." She smiled again. "Cabe Bedlam is responsible for that. It's known that he and the Brown Dragon, the savage drake lord who ruled here, rode into this desolate region and only one of them departed alive. Sometime shortly after that, the grass and trees sprouted from the parched soil and everything became as it had been before the Turning War caused the creation of the Barren Lands in the first place. Cabe Bedlam brought life back to this domain. He'd hardly be in danger from it."

"Perhaps, perhaps not, human! This may no longer be the Barren Lands, true, but this is hardly an idyllic field! Among the green hills and oh-so-lovely trees of this new wonderland lie the bones of most of the drakes of clan Brown! This grand pasture *strangled* them to death, little sorceress! Every one of them! It took from them to build this deadly paradise and I do not doubt that it hungers still! Where did you think that it got the sustenance to revive itself, hmmm?"

Now her eyes briefly flashed crimson again. "I understand what happened, perhaps even better than you. The spell worked against the drakes of clan Brown because it was their master who tried to sacrifice your friend. He wanted the same results, but by using the blood of the grandson of the Dragon Master who'd caused the creation of the Barren Lands in the first place. The land is at peace now, though." She reached out a hand. Several of the stalks twisted against the wind to gently caress her palm. "I know. I've lived here long enough."

"Then you are foolhardy." Nonetheless, Darkhorse knew that he really did not have any choice but to allow her to treat his companion. Hours might have passed for the rest of the realm, but for Cabe and him, it had only been moments. Cabe could not help himself and Darkhorse was too weak to do much more. He could neither transport them to Penacles nor safely attempt to heal his companion's injuries. The female had been helpful so far. Perhaps it was taking a risk, but the eternal had to trust in her.

He would be watching everything she did, however. If even her slightest action seemed questionable . . .

"Very *well*. Take care of him . . . but know that I will be watching!"

"I'm sure you will." She waited for Darkhorse to kneel, then, without the slightest sign of fear of him, she carefully pulled Cabe from his back.

The grass moved toward the sorcerer, but just as Darkhorse was about to act, he saw that the blades had massed under his companion and were aiding the female in lowering Cabe to the ground. Those blades that were no longer needed retreated while others slipped under to form what appeared to be a soft bed.

"It's fortunate that you shielded him when you did. He has at least two cracked ribs, but I don't think much more than that," she whispered. Her hands moved upward, the fingertips gently touching the spellcaster's chest. "But his body's strong. He's in very nice form."

The tone of her voice suggested that her comment was not entirely clinical, but Darkhorse let it pass. Now that he saw her with Cabe, he suddenly knew who she was—and that knowledge disturbed him. Their previous encounter remained in his mind for one very good reason. It had taken place in Zuu.

"Step away from him"—the name she had used previously sprang to mind—"Tori."

She obeyed, not quite so confident now that he knew her identity. "We never really met. You shouldn't know me."

213

"I know you from a glimpse and also from detecting your presence when first you tried to seduce Cabe Bedlam. You are from Zuu, witch! You are one of Lanith's dogs!"

The last seemed to stir resentment in her. "I'd never be one of Lanith's puppets! I leave that to Saress and that popinjay Ponteroy! I'd never have anything to do with any of them!"

They might have sunken deeper into the argument, but then Cabe stirred. It was only for a moment, but it was enough to turn Darkhorse's concern to the more immediate problem. "I am taking him back to Penacles! Move away!"

"I won't. Look at you, Darkhorse. You might be able to knock me aside, but you're still too weak to travel by any other means than running That spell trap was designed specifically for you. It *had* to be. I was trying to see what it and the others were for—"

"Others?" He had sensed nothing.

She gave him a knowing smile. "Others. The area around the castle is dotted with them, but I've seen riders and their mounts pass through the traps without disturbing them. Only when you came across a trap did it spring. It was meant for you, demon steed, even if it also caught your friend in the process." The sorceress returned her attention to Cabe. "Now let me take care of him before his injuries grow worse."

Darkhorse relented, but he watched closely as the female delved into her work. She appeared to be earnest in her efforts, her hands carefully running over the areas of the injury. He sensed subtle uses of power over the ribs as she worked to mend them. Secretly, Darkhorse was grateful that it was not his task; he had been concerned about his clumsiness. Human systems were so delicate, so fragile. He might have caused more harm than good.

Cabe's expression gradually relaxed and his skin, which had grown so pale, was now pinker. He breathed with less difficulty now. Darkhorse probed with his power and found no trace of the injuries.

"He needs to rest now." As she rose, the grass shifted to better comfort the unconscious figure. Other stalks caressed the enchantress's arms.

"Thank you . . . Tori." The eternal eyed the lively grass with lingering distrust. How could it know the difference between a human and a drake warrior? Why would it protect one and kill the other?

"I did it because I wanted to, so don't thank me. Besides, it's probably my fault you came here in the first place. You got my message, didn't you?"

"You sent the message to Penacles?"

"It was the only method by which I thought that I could eventually reach Cabe." She smiled wistfully at the slumbering mage. "A pity I didn't latch on to him before he met the Lady of the Amber."

Darkhorse eyed her. "You are not quite the same female that Cabe encountered in Zuu."

"Things have gotten worse in Zuu. I can't even stay there anymore. I like fun, not war." She pretended to pout.

The shadow steed judged that Tori, if that was truly her name, was a person of masks. She pretended to be frivolous when that served her, serious when the situation called for it. At other times, he suspected that she switched back and forth without warning, putting those around her constantly off-guard. That, combined with apparently substantial abilities, made her formidable.

"Why Cabe? Why him? What do you expect of him?"

She started to put a hand on the sorcerer's arm, but Darkhorse's sudden glare made her pull back. "Because I've never known someone with the power he has. He's amazing. I don't think that there's another spellcaster who can match him power for power . . . and yet he keeps it all under careful control." This time the blond woman defied Darkhorse, lightly caressing Cabe's arm. Her expression was not light, however. If anything, worry now dominated. "He's the only one I can think of who has the power to deal with the thing in Lanith's palace."

"Thing?"

"Yes, thing. I wasn't certain until . . . until recently, but there's a power, a force, in Lanith's palace. . . an intelligent force. . ."

A power, a force . . . It was almost the same description that the Dragon King had used. She might have been eavesdropping, although that was doubtful since among the drake lord, Cabe, and himself, Darkhorse did not think that even someone as clever as the woman who called herself Tori could have remained undetected. She had also added something to the description. *An intelligent force* . . .

Intelligent? What did that mean? He wished that Cabe would wake so that he could ask him his opinion. Cabe and his wife were so much better at puzzling out such things. So, for that matter, was the Gryphon. He needed to get Cabe to Penacles. By this time, Lady Bedlam and the king of Penacles had to be worrying about them. "Can Cabe be moved?"

"I'd wait a little longer, just to make certain that I haven't missed something. He also needs some rest. Give him a couple of hours at least, demon steed."

Hours? Darkhorse had to let the others know what was happening, but he dared not try to contact Penacles from so far away. If Lanith had some powerful unknown mage working for him—that was the only answer Darkhorse had so far come up with to explain the "intelligent force"—then such far-reaching communication could not be trusted to be private. Darkhorse saw no sense in alerting Lanith as to their present predicament.

"An unknown mage . . ." he muttered. Could it be that the warlock Shade was alive? Shade had been both bane and hero to the realm over his centuries-long life, depending on which of his incarnations had been active. Many had thought that they had killed the warlock, only to discover afterward that he had been immediately reborn. Shade was *permanently* dead, though. He had to be. It could not be him.

Could it?

"I have to go now," the female announced. "There're things I have to do."

"Such as?"

"I have to search for someone, someone important to Lanith who hasn't been around lately. That could mean trouble."

The shadow steed snorted. "Could you be a little more specific, Lady Tori?"

His use of the title amused her. "'Lady Tori.' I'd like that if Tori were my real name. Maybe I'll still use it sometime." She looked down at Cabe. "For him I'd have been Lady Tori for the rest of my life."

"You are evading my question, little one, and are also far too late. As has been pointed out, Cabe is married, happily, I will add, and has children, too."

"Yes, and one of them is now a man, isn't he?" Her eyes sparkled, reminding Darkhorse momentarily of a Vraad, one of the race of sorcerers who had been the precursors of the present human population. "I've heard he's handsome." She dimpled, a sight no doubt designed to melt the heart of a human male but which only served to intensify Darkhorse's distrust. "Is that true, do you know?"

"If things are progressing as I believe they are," the ebony stallion responded, "then you are probably too late to snare the younger master as well. He has recently met one that I think has caught his fancy." He pawed at the ground. "Now! Perhaps you might clarify what you said . . . and also, I think, you might tell me your true name—"

"He's recently met someone, you say?" The golden-haired woman's expression darkened. "Interesting . . ."

215

THE HORSE KING

"I said—" Darkhorse got no further. The enchantress had vanished as abruptly as she had first materialized. He barely felt her depart. There was no sense trying to track her. In some ways, the female was more skilled than many of the other spellcasters that he had encountered over the centuries. There was also a peculiarity to her magical trace that he could not recall having encountered in another being.

Cabe shifted. The shadow steed wanted to wake him, but he knew that there was merit in what the enchantress had said about letting his companion rest. When Cabe was awake and fit to travel, the pair would immediately return to Penacles . . . and then Darkhorse would discuss with his friend their mysterious benefactor.

Aurim knew that his mother was anxious about his father's return, but he had grown up watching one or both of his parents vanish somewhere on some important mission, each time returning, and so he was less concerned than she was. He did worry, but what was there that his father and Darkhorse could not together defeat? They were two of the greatest powers of the Dragonrealm.

What was more important to him was seeing Jenna. Aurim was glad that his parents had not asked him to go back to the Manor. He suspected that Darkhorse had told them of his growing interest in the merchant's daughter, which was good. At this point, if his mother had requested that he return to the Manor to help his sister, the younger Bedlam would have refused. He was old enough to do so, too. They no longer had any hold on him. Aurim was his own man.

Jenna waited for him, but not at Gullivan's. She had suggested a change of scenery, a place where the two of them could better be alone. The river Serkadian, just a mile west of Penacles, had what she said were some wonderful idyllic spots, perfect for people trying to clear their thoughts and relax. While Jenna had been speaking in terms of sorcery, which was the supposed reason for the meeting, Aurim was more interested in the romantic aspects. He already knew that he wanted the relationship to blossom into something permanent. It was already impossible to think of life without her.

As Aurim rode, he tried to think of the proper things to say to her. She was a merchant's daughter, someone who had no doubt grown up hearing clever, fancy words from everyone around her. He, on the other hand, while somewhat familiar with the courts of two major kingdoms, had never paid much attention to protocol and such. Aurim knew few clever words and even fewer fancy ones. Everything that had so far run through his mind had sounded clumsy, oafish. His parents were no help. They had been married so long that even the simplest words seemed to relay meaning between them.

"What can I say to her?" he muttered as he neared the river. Lush trees lined much of the edge. There was a settlement north of here, but far enough away that it was unlikely anyone would disturb them. Here there was nothing but wild fields dotted with yellow and blue flowers and the occasional song of a bird perched high in the trees. A perfect setting, but not if he could not say the proper words.

"What do you want to say?"

Aurim started, not having realized that someone else was nearby. Jenna rode up to him from behind a small copse of trees, smiling all the while. She was clad in a bright blue and red riding outfit, another typical statement of fashion from Gordag-Ai. Her beauty made it even more difficult for him to think. "Jenna! I . . . wasn't . . . you startled me!"

She giggled. "Silly, that's what I wanted to do! I saw you coming and couldn't resist. Now what were you talking about?"

"Nothing. Nothing." Aurim tried not to squirm in the saddle. "Did you find a good place to stop?"

"I did. Just over there by that open part of the riverbank. Have you ever been here before?"

"I've hardly ever been to the river at all. Mostly I've seen the city. We're hardly ever in Penacles for very long."

She did not reply to that. They rode to the location she had chosen and, after taking care of the mounts, sat down on the soft grass. Jenna smoothed her riding outfit, then looked at him expectantly. "Did you do as I suggested?"

Aurim nodded. "I didn't tell anyone what we were doing. I decided to keep my progress a surprise, just like you said."

"They'll be so thrilled when they see." The young woman took hold of his arm and squeezed gently. "Just think what they'll say when you show them how you can perform without losing control of your powers!"

"You've done well, too," he countered. "You've learned quickly for such a short time."

"I think we've got much in common, Aurim. We both just needed someone who understood our lack of confidence. We needed each other."

He was certain that his face was burning. Jenna had shifted nearer as she had spoken and now only inches separated their bodies. The young mage grew more and more nervous.

"I want you to show me how well you're doing."

"What?"

The merchant's daughter rose without warning. She smiled down at him, then pointed at the river. "I want you to try something for me. Will you?"

Aurim struggled to his feet. "Jenna, I—"

"Look at this!" She cupped her hands before him. A moment later, a ball of blue light formed just above the palms. Jenna stared at it. The ball rose a few inches, then sank to its previous position. It then began to spin around. After a few rotations, Aurim's companion blinked. The sphere faded.

Her success thrilled him. In only a short time she had increased her control over her abilities far more than either of them would have thought possible. "That's wonderful, Jenna!"

"And I owe it all to you!" She hugged him. "Now, let me see how good you've gotten!"

"I—" He did not want to disappoint her. "What do you want me to do?"

"I want you to stop it." She pointed at the huge, rushing river.

The spellcaster was not quite certain that he had heard correctly. "You want me to . . . stop . . . the river?"

"Of course." Jenna moved closer until their bodies touched. She looked up at him, expectant. "I know you can do it. I really do."

Aurim's angle gave him a view of more than her arresting face. Embarrassed, he took a step back. Jenna did not let him completely escape, however. The young woman took hold of him by both arms and would not release him.

What could he do? He could no more refuse her than stop eating. His head tingling, Aurim finally nodded. "All right. I'll give it a try . . . but I can't promise anything."

"I know you can do it!" She leaned up and kissed him. While he was still recovering, sienna added, "Remember, you're the son of Cabe Bedlam and the Lady of the Amber! You're more powerful than *either* of them!"

For the first time, he actually believed that. In fact, the more he thought about it, the more his confidence grew. He *could* stop the river. Well, he would not actually stop the entire river, but what he had in mind would prove effective enough.

"What would you think if I created a dry passage through the river?" Aurim saw that he had her interest. "The water would keep flowing . . . it would just. . . um . . .

217

miss the area where the passage would be."

"That would make all the time we've spent together worthwhile." She squeezed his arm, her eyes bright with anticipation. "Are you going to start now?"

In response, Aurim stepped away from her and faced the Serkadian. It seemed simple enough now. He looked beyond the normal world, reaching into one of the levels where the essence of sorcery was visible. The lines were everywhere. Aurim tapped into them, drawing up the power that was both in and around him. He stared at the onrushing water.

I will do it! If he had any lingering doubts, one last glance at her face was enough to douse them. Before his heightened will, even the powerful forces of the river had to obey. Slowly at first, then swifter, a strange depression formed. The depression spread from one side of the riverbank to the other for roughly four or five yards. The water level on both sides of the gap did not alter in the least.

The depression grew deeper and deeper. On each side a wall of swirling water stood firm. As far as the river was concerned, the gap did not exist. That was the way Aurim planned it; he did not want someone either upstream or down growing curious about sudden changes in the water level. Word would then get back to the king and his parents, none of whom would have approved of this spell even if they *had* been happy that he had finally conquered his uncertainties. He could always tell them later, sometime after he had already proven to them that he was now capable of completely utilizing his vast abilities.

His spell squeezed the last of the water away. The river continued to flow smoothly along, sorcery enabling the water to leap instantly from one side of the depression to the other. Anyone standing between the two magical walls would hardly even get damp. Even though he had been certain that this time he would succeed, Aurim was impressed. Now his parents would be proud of him.

"I was almost afraid to hope," Jenna whispered, "but you did it. You *are* powerful."

"I know it's not quite what you wanted, but—"

"Oh, no!" Her face was aglow. "This is far better than even I expected! You've done excellently, Aurim!"

She wrapped her arms around him and kissed him hard. Aurim felt a tingle run through his body. He almost lost track of the world around him.

Jenna stepped back, eyeing him. Her expression was not one the young mage expected. The merchant's daughter looked slightly confused.

"Is something wrong?" he managed to ask once his voice returned.

"You *are* stronger than I thought." Jenna glanced at the river. "You'd better change that back."

"All right." It was easier to disperse the spell. The process took only the blink of an eye.

"I've outdone myself," his companion whispered. "What do you mean?"

In response, the attractive young woman seized him again. The kiss that followed made the previous one seem short and indifferent. Again a tingle coursed through Aurim. However, unlike during the last kiss, it did not go away. Instead, it spread, growing stronger at the same time. The world receded. Aurim almost felt as if he were watching himself from outside his body.

Stepping back, Jenna nodded triumphantly. "That's better."

Aurim tried to say something, but found that he could not. It was not that he was still overwhelmed by her passionate kiss, simply that he could not *move*. He tried to raise an arm, but nothing happened. The only thing the sorcerer could do was breathe and blink and he suspected that he was doing so only by permission.

218

Jenna had to notice his predicament, but instead of helping, she seemed very proud of herself. She also looked a little different. Slightly older, more lush of form, and with a different cast to her features, a cast more akin to those of the southwestern continent, not the northerly climes from which she hailed.

"Raise your arm," she commanded.

To his surprise, he did. Aurim tried to lower it, but his limb resisted.

"Lower it now."

He obeyed. He had to. *What's happening, Jenna?* Aurim wanted to ask. *What did you do to me?*

Perhaps his companion saw the question in his eyes, for she then said, "You're completely mine now, Aurim. Isn't that what you wanted?" She laughed, a harsh, pitiless laugh. "Of course you did. You had no choice. You were stronger-willed than I would've imagined, but I like a challenge. The others were simple in comparison, even if none of them were quite as naive."

Others? She had done this to others? Something registered in his mind. Talk concerning students who had vanished from the school of sorcery his parents had developed in conjunction with the kings of both Penacles and Talak. At least two students, possibly three. Were they the ones that Jenna spoke of?

Jenna continued to change both in form and clothing. Her hair tumbled down to her waist and her features were transformed into something not quite human, as if somewhere in her lineage was included elfin blood. Her curves were more arresting, the kind that Aurim had only dreamed of ever seeing. She clearly knew that he could not help looking over her new shape, for she briefly posed, giving him ample view of her ample charms.

"He's talked about a new step in his plans, you know," Jenna whispered, pressing her body against his again. "Breeding the strongest of his Order to one another to give him a new generation of even more powerful sorcerers." The enchantress leaned forward and kissed him soundly. Had he been able to, Aurim would have pulled himself away in disgust. As stunning as this woman was, her manner, her attitude, revolted him. "I think I like his plan better now, dear, lovely Aurim. You look much more delicious than that perfumed jackal Ponteroy."

The clatter of hooves caught the attention of both although only Jenna, of course, could turn to see who was coming. Aurim's hopes rose. Perhaps the Gryphon had noticed him depart. Maybe his father had even returned.

"They're a little early. I was hoping we could have had a little fun before they arrived." Jenna patted his cheek. "I know you're disappointed, darling. If I'd had my way, we'd have had a bit more time to better get to know one another. Don't worry, though, there'll be plenty of time in Zuu."

Zuu! For the first time the depth of his dilemma struck him. Not only was he a prisoner, but they were going to take him to the land of the horsemen. There was no telling what they planned to do with him once they had him there, although Jenna's words hinted at least of one intention.

The clatter grew louder, then abruptly ceased. A faint wave of dust drifted past Aurim and his captor. The sorcerer wanted so badly to sneeze.

"You're early, Captain."

"Not by my reckoning, Saress. I'm right on time."

Saress. Aurim stared at the sinister temptress. Everything about the woman he had been infatuated with had been a lie even down to her name.

"Did you think I might get carried away? Was that it?" she teased. "Come, Captain, you know Lanith has both my love and loyalty, which is why you should be more careful what you say."

"It isn't that," the unseen officer suddenly protested, not nearly so arrogant now.

Saress obviously had much influence with his master. "I just know how you like to be thorough. Sometimes that demands too much of . . . your quarry."

Saress winked at the captive spellcaster. "I don't think that there's much beyond this one, although we'll have to experiment further another time. Is our route planned?"

"Yes, we can skirt just south of the Dagora Forest. It's the most direct route."

"South of the Dagora Forest. Are you suggesting we ride through the Barren Lands?" The enchantress did not seem at all pleased.

Aurim heard the horse move forward. Out of the corner of his eye, he caught partial sight of a brown stallion and its rider, a tall figure clad in a simple brown outfit with a riding cloak. Strands of blond hair dangled from the rider's hood, but his features were otherwise obscured. "It seems the best way. The place is no longer desolate. Why should we avoid such an unpopulated stretch when it gives us the straightest route home?"

"Why, indeed?" Saress was still not pleased. Suddenly her gaze shifted to Aurim. "Then again, why take so long to get back to Zuu? Why not make use of new options . . . or at least test them out?"

"What're you talking about, sorceress?"

"He's strong, Captain. He's everything we thought he was and more. He parted the river to impress me, the dear boy."

For a moment the soldier was silent. Then, "He did that?"

"And I, for one, think he's capable of so very much more." The enchantress stared Aurim in the eyes. "Aren't you, Aurim? All you needed was a boost of confidence and I gave that to you with a few subtle spells and more than a few loving looks." She laughed lightly. "Yes, I think you can do it."

Aurim knew what she wanted of him, and knew that now he could probably give it to her. He did have the concentration and confidence, both of which had been built up by a serpent in human form. Yet if he was so powerful, how could he have been so easily snared? Why could he not escape?

It's not always a matter of power, his father had once said. *It's also a matter of using your power in the most effective manner.*

Saress was not as strong as he; he knew that. However, she had a far better grasp of her abilities than he did and she had used them to her best advantage.

"Gather the men, Captain. Our dear new companion is going to take us back to Zuu in the best dramatic fashion. Lanith will love it!"

"You're not serious! I'm not going to—"

"I've had enough argument." Saress waved her hand in the direction of the soldier, who stiffened in the saddle. "You'll get your voice back after I've proved my point." To Aurim, she added, "You will listen to everything I say, won't you, darling?"

To his surprise, he answered her. "I will."

"That's a good boy. This is what I want of you. You'll take everyone here—the two of us, my friend the captain, and his three playmates *and* all the horses—all the way to the royal grounds of Zuu."

Again Aurim spoke against his will. "I've never been to Zuu. I don't know the kingdom."

She took him by the arm. "Don't you worry, Aurim. I will give you a destination."

Reaching up with her free hand, she touched his temple. Instantly, the image of an open courtyard materialized in his thoughts. A huge stable covered one side of the yard and the tall walls of what had to be the king's palace or castle made up much of the remaining view. In the walls were carved the images of men on horseback. A banner fluttering from the top of the stable bore the head of a charger.

"Is that good enough?" Saress asked him.

"Yes." It was. He wanted to deny it, but could not. "Then take us there now, my darling Aurim."

Unable to resist, Aurim concentrated. He was finally the sorcerer he had dreamed of becoming . . . and now his dream had become his nightmare.

Chapter Six

It was more than three hours before Cabe stirred, three hours in which Darkhorse could do nothing but think and glare at the magical grass.

"Darkhorse?" Cabe's voice was weak, but in this quiet place carried well.

"Cabe! By the Void! I had begun to fear that you would never wake!"

"Dark—where are we?"

"In what was once termed the Barren Lands!"

"The Barren Lands?" The mage stared, taking in the trees, the birds, and, most of all, the endless sea of grass. He nodded. "Yes, I can feel it. These were the Barren Lands once. I've been here a couple of times since it changed; I'd recognize the sensations I feel anywhere."

The shadow steed felt nothing, but did not question his companion. He was simply overjoyed that Cabe was awake and well. At least, he *hoped* Cabe was well. "Are you all right, then?"

The human touched his side. "I think so." He shut his eyes for several seconds, concentrating. "Yes. Yes, I am. Thank you."

"I . . . I did not mend you, Cabe."

"No? Then who did?"

"It was . . . a female. A sorceress. In Zuu you once knew her as Tori."

"Tori?" Cabe's expression went from complete befuddlement to dawning recognition. "Tori. *She* was here? She mended my injuries? I don't remember anything other than escaping that trap."

"And that was done with her aid, too, Cabe. She assaulted it from the outside. Then, after you caused the earth to rise up and hinder some of our pursuers—"

"I did that?" The sorcerer shook his head. "I don't even recall doing that. I think I may remember holding on to you for dear life."

"She called to us. Told us to ride in a certain direction. I did. A blink hole materialized directly before us, leaving me little chance to avoid it. When we finally exited, though, it was to arrive here . . . several hours later."

"Several . . ." Cabe looked up at the sun. "I didn't even pay attention to the fact that it's setting! Gwen! She'll be worried! Did you contact her?"

Darkhorse could scarcely look at his friend. "I feared to do so. There was good reason—"

"I think I understand. You can explain everything else later, then. We have to get back to Penacles." As Cabe started to rise, he seemed to lose his footing. The sorcerer immediately sat back down. "Maybe I'd better do this a little slower. Looks like I needed the rest after all. Thank you for watching over me, Darkhorse."

"I am sorry I could do no more. Tori said it was wise to let you rest and I agreed."

The spellcaster rose again, this time with more care. "We'll have to talk about her and everything else *after* we reassure Gwen and the others." He blinked. "I didn't even think to ask you how you were doing. That spell trap seemed designed for you."

221

"It was. As you said, though, that is something else we can speak of after we assuage the fears of your wife, Cabe. As for me . . ." The eternal rose up on his hind legs. The grass spread away from him as far as it could. Darkhorse laughed as he dropped down on all fours again. "I am Darkhorse! How could I be anything but perfect?"

Cabe did not question his answer although it was clear that he did not entirely believe him. Darkhorse was still a bit weak, but not nearly so much as before. He had recovered enough that racing across the Dragonrealm would be a fairly simple task. They could be in Penacles just before sunset. Still soon enough as far as he was concerned.

The sorcerer mounted, groaning slightly in the process. "Maybe it would be best if we just rode back, Darkhorse. I don't think that I could stomach another sudden shift in location just yet. Is that all right with you?"

"Did the female miss some injury? Are you ill?"

"No, nothing like that." Cabe positioned himself for the ride. "It seemed to me that it would just be a good idea."

"As you wish."

"It really is a beautiful, peaceful land now," commented the human. "I'm surprised it's still empty. I'd think anyone would love to settle in a place like this."

Darkhorse held off comment. The sooner he was away from this land, the better. The grass still seemed too interested in the pair, constantly touching both of them whenever possible.

The grass, though, was hardly a threat compared to what they had already faced . . . and *would* face soon enough again. Lanith was indeed a danger to the fragile peace of the Dragonrealm if he had such power to control. Even Darkhorse was willing to admit that anyone who could set such a snare was a foe with which to be reckoned.

An intelligent force . . .

There was indeed much that they had to discuss after their return to Penacles.

Lady Gwendolyn Bedlam stood at the entrance to the Gryphon's palace, either relieved to see them or ready to throw something, Darkhorse was not certain which. Only when the sorceress finally met them at the bottom of the palace steps did her mood become more evident.

"Cabe! You're all right! Why didn't you contact us?" Her expression darkened. "What have you been up to?"

The sorcerer slid off Darkhorse's back. The eternal tried to quietly step back, the better to escape the brunt of any explosion, verbal or magical. He had a healthy respect for Cabe's wife.

Cabe tried to calm her. "It took longer than we expected to investigate the barony. We had to be careful, too, what with the possibility that any of Lanith's mages might be in the vicinity. I'm sorry we had to keep you anxiously waiting, Gwen."

Her gaze darted from her husband to the shadow steed. "Is that all? Nothing terrible happened?" She folded her arms. "I don't think that I believe you."

"I assure you, Lady Bedlam—"

"Never mind, Darkhorse." Cabe sighed. "I can't lie to you, Gwen. I don't know why *I* tried to make it sound as if nothing had happened. We'd have to tell you everything soon enough, anyway. Something did happen. I don't even know all of it. There's much that Darkhorse still has to tell *me.*"

"Then the best thing for all of us," declared the voice of the king of Penacles, "is to retire to my chambers and discuss this in privacy."

The Gryphon stood several steps above them, having arrived so silently that even the eternal had not noticed him. He was perhaps one of the few creatures who could consistently surprise Darkhorse, although, to be fair, Darkhorse was one of the few

222

creatures capable of consistently making the monarch uneasy.

It did not take Cabe very long to relate his story. The others listened carefully, Gwen's expression turning darker as the tale of the spell trap unfolded. By the time the sorcerer was finished, her hands had folded into such tight fists that her knuckles were bone white.

"You nearly died, Cabe! If not for Darkhorse—"

"It wasn't Darkhorse, darling. Not exactly."

"If I may . . ." The Gryphon poured himself a goblet of wine. He had made certain that his guests had been given both food and drink, especially the still-weary sorcerer. The king raised the goblet and sipped, his features momentarily shifting to that of a handsome gray-haired man with patrician features. The Gryphon could completely shift form for long periods at a time, but preferred the one with which he was most familiar. "Let us simply hear Darkhorse. Then we can take it from there."

The Bedlams nodded. Darkhorse debated leaving out some aspects of the adventure, especially the part concerning their feminine rescuer, but knew that Cabe would never allow him to do so. That in mind, he threw himself into the telling, making certain that no part of it, however small, was left out. Darkhorse even related his own sensations during the struggle in the sinister trap and his mistrust of their rescuer afterward.

His mention of Tori brought forth a variety of reactions from the trio. The Gryphon looked merely curious. Gwendolyn Bedlam kept her expression neutral but her narrowing eyes were a clear indication of what she thought of the mysterious woman's interest in her husband. As for Cabe, he first looked uncomfortable, then thoughtful, especially when the eternal mentioned that their benefactor had used a false name.

"I wonder who she is?" he commented after Darkhorse had finished.

"I would very much like to find out." Lady Bedlam gazed at her husband, who wisely kept silent.

"The identity of this good-willed enchantress aside," interjected the Gryphon, "what she and the lord of the Dagora Forest have said worries me greatly. What sinister force is it that Lanith has at his beck and call? A mage of great power? Why is he or she not leading the horse king's Magical Order, then? That position, according to my reports, is still filled by a woman named Saress, who shares more than her sorcerous abilities with Lanith."

"I had a thought earlier, Lord Gryphon." Darkhorse shifted uncomfortably. "I thought that perhaps it might be Shade."

"Shade is dead, demon steed. You saw to that yourself. He is truly and honestly dead. Do you think that he could have kept himself hidden for so long? That was never Shade's way, good or evil."

Cabe agreed. "Besides, you searched nearly every inch of the Dragonrealm. Shade was a Vraad, a last lingerer from their time. He had the most distinctive magical trace of any creature in this world, including you. One of us in this room would have noticed his presence."

Darkhorse did not entirely agree, knowing better than anyone how powerful the warlock had been, but he acquiesced. "I do not really think it was Shade, but I felt the need to mention it. However, it could very well be a Dragon King! Zuu is not that far from the domain of the Crystal Dragon . . . and none of us know much of his doings."

"No." Cabe's response was quick. "No, it's not the Crystal Dragon . . . take my word for that."

"But Darkhorse does make a good point, Cabe Bedlam. What about the others? Storm and Black to be precise." The Gryphon stroked his savage beak. "Better yet, Sssaleese. Yes, his fledgling federation would benefit if attention was drawn from it for a time by everyone's interest in Lanith's crusade. A treaty between the pair would also aid him. Sssaleese needs materiel, food. The Dragon Kings haven't been very happy with his presence and I know at least one has pushed Emperor Kyl to take some action against him. Kyl's held off. Sssaleese is strong enough to create a situation. The refugees from the broken drake clans believe in him. He gave them something that the Silver Dragon promised but then failed to deliver. Kyl is surely keeping that in mind."

"Sssaleese may be involved with Lanith, but I somehow don't think he's this force." Cabe sighed. "The Green Dragon didn't speak of the force as if it were one of his own kind. He talked as if it were something he could not identify. I think if it were Sssaleese, the lord of Dagora would've discovered that. The drake lord was honestly uncertain."

"So what we are left with is what we had at the beginning. A mysterious, intelligent magical force that may or may not be related to Lanith's Order of sorcerers." The king rose and began pacing back and forth like an anxious cat. "There were things I came across in the empire of the Aramites. Age-old forces left by the founding race of our world. I know that some of them *could* reach this land if they desired, but I've never noticed any sign. Lanith might also have made some pact with the Seekers or the Quel, but I doubt either the avians or the underdwellers would work with any human long."

Gwendolyn Bedlam cleared her throat. "Perhaps you should consult the Libraries."

"At this point, Lady Bedlam, that might be more trouble than it's worth. I wouldn't even know what to look under . . . intelligent evil forces? Mysterious entities? Even if an answer was in there, it would be in some godforsaken riddle or poem that we'd have to piece together. I don't have the patience for the Libraries of Penacles right now. However, I do have access to some other volumes that the last Dragon King here gathered during his reign. There may be something in them."

"There might also be something among the books and scrolls at the Manor," suggested Cabe. "Something that perhaps will help us detect and define this force without it noticing."

"So it seems we now know our next step." The Gryphon eyed Darkhorse. "You have no idea where this enchantress vanished to, do you? She's given us some information; I do not see why she just doesn't join us."

Cabe's mate did not look at all pleased with the suggestion, but only Darkhorse noticed. The shadow steed explained how she had vanished without leaving any discernible trace.

"Her powers seem almost as mysterious as this force working for Lanith," the lionbird commented. "Someday we'll find out more about her, but that can wait."

The Bedlams rose together. "We should return to the Manor as soon as possible, then." Cabe looked for confirmation from his wife before continuing. "We'll keep in contact whether we discover anything or not."

"I have agents out in some of the surrounding regions . . . and some other resources that I've yet to tap. Between all of us, we should be able to uncover some answers, Cabe."

"I, too, will do my best to ferret out some answers." Other than hunting for the enchantress, however, Darkhorse did not know what he could do short of invading Zuu. He sincerely doubted that either Cabe or the Gryphon would appreciate an effort like that, though.

"Aurim!" Gwen's outburst caught them all by surprise. "I nearly forgot about

Aurim! We have to tell him what's happening so that he doesn't wonder what's happened to us!"

"Well, that's easily taken care of, darling. Where is he?"

"Not in the palace. I think. . . I think he's with the young woman named Jenna."

"She has been staying at Gullivan's, Cabe," the eternal added. "Shall I go retrieve him?"

"No, I'll simply link with him." The master sorcerer closed his eyes, but the look of confidence on his plain features gradually shifted to one of uncertainty and puzzlement. Finally breaking off his attempt, Cabe glanced at his wife. "That's odd. I don't sense him anywhere."

"That cannot be!" Aurim's mother shut her own eyes. After several long, silent seconds, she, too, gave up. "He should be in the city. He should be."

"He may be shielding himself from us, darling. After all, he probably wants privacy."

"Perhaps . . ."

Darkhorse stepped forward. "I will look for him, friends! It is likely, as you say, that he wanted privacy. Have no fear! I can cover Penacles much faster than either of you. You may return to the Manor if you so desire. When I have your son in hand, we shall return there."

"What do you think, Gwen?"

With some reluctance, she nodded. "Thank you, Dark- horse. I'm sure it's nothing, but with all that happened to Cabe and you, I cannot help but worry a little."

"Perfectly understandable!" Already the shadow steed wanted to be on his way. His preference was always action over discussion. Now, at least, he could do something important, however minuscule it was compared to the overall situation concerning Zuu. Darkhorse had no doubt that Aurim and Jenna were somewhere nearby, acting as all young human adults seemed to during the early stages of a relationship. That did not at all mean that he condoned the younger Bedlam's carelessness, however. Aurim's position and abilities demanded that he not hide his presence from his family even in a kingdom where they were very respected. There was always some risk.

"Please emphasize that we would appreciate it if he could come home immediately. We'll need everyone's help, including his and Valea's."

"I shall do so, Cabe. Have no fear!" He reared and, as they watched, vanished from the palace.

The ebony stallion rematerialized directly inside Gullivan's. He had thought of materializing outside, but that would have brought too much attention to him. Darkhorse hoped that none of the innkeeper's customers would take offense at his sudden arrival. Anyone who stayed at Gullivan's was warned about the possible sudden appearance of spellcasters associated with the Bedlams' school. Of course, nothing could prepare them for Darkhorse, but he hoped for the best.

The same serving girl who had been frightened so easily the first time took one look at him and screamed. Gullivan burst out of the kitchen, eyes wide. When he saw the cause of the scream, the human sighed.

"Oh, it's you, Darkhorse."

"My apologies, Gullivan!" The eternal glanced around. Two gaily-clad merchants from Gordag-Ai had been discussing business matters with the pair from Irillian and another pair likely from Penacles. The men from Gordag-Ai stared open-mouthed while the others simply stared. One of the men from Penacles was trying to hide a smirk. He had evidently seen Darkhorse in the past and now was enjoying the foreigners' shock.

The innkeeper hurried over to Darkhorse. "How may I help you? Are you looking for Master Aurim, by any chance?"

"That I am, Gullivan! Very astute of you! Is he here?"

"I don't believe so. The young woman isn't here. That much I know. She stepped out earlier and hasn't returned."

"No?" This made Darkhorse's task much more complex, but he was undaunted. "Do you have any idea where she went?"

"Not me, but I'll ask in back. Maybe one of the girls or someone else saw her after I did." Gullivan bowed briefly and quickly retreated into the back room. A moment later, he emerged again, scratching his chin.

"Any word?"

"My son says that when he stepped outside earlier, he saw the girl riding off from the stable. She looked like she was packed for a trip."

"A trip?" What sort of foolishness had the young pair gotten into? If Jenna had packed for a trip, then it was likely that Aurim and she were meeting outside the city, possibly for a more private encounter. While the eternal did not begrudge his young friend such privacy, Aurim should have informed someone if he was leaving the safety of the city walls.

"Did your son say which way she rode?"

"She went north, but she could've easily turned another direction later on. Is there something wrong, Darkhorse?"

"Not as far as I know. Just two young ones with their heads lost in the clouds, I suppose." The eternal paused. "Tell me, Gullivan, where outside the city walls would a pair of young friends go to meet? What I mean is—"

The veteran soldier smiled. "I know what you mean, friend. I've watched the lad and lass. If I wanted privacy and I was willing to ride a little, I'd probably head toward the Serkadian. There's some lovely spots out there if you're interested in setting the mood."

"The river?"

Gullivan's smile faded slightly. "The river. It's very scenic in places. If one wanted a place to meet a young lady, there's some nice places along the river's edge, especially where the flowers are in bloom. Ladies like that sort of thing."

"Do they? Then I think that I shall go there and look." He dipped his head toward the innkeeper. "My gratitude, Gullivan, and if Aurim should return, please tell him that matters require his presence back at the Manor. Make certain that he knows that it is urgent."

"I'll be glad to do so, Darkhorse. If I may . . . is there something wrong?"

Darkhorse backed away a few steps from the innkeeper. "It is nothing to concern yourself with, Gullivan. Now if you will excuse me. ."

He vanished from the inn while the proprietor was still nodding, rematerializing a moment later near the western gate of the city. Two sentries on duty inside the wall leaped to attack position before they realized just what faced them. A family passing through the gate froze in terror, the man and one of the three small children crying out. Behind them, another man on a horse struggled to regain control of his frightened steed.

With some effort, the guards restored order. The braver of the pair approached the eternal slowly, saluting. "My Lord Darkhorse! I—we didn't recognize you at first! Greetings! I am . . . uh . . . Haplin! May I ask for what reason you honor us?"

"Easy, Haplin! Forgive me for my sudden arrival! I am in search of someone! Are you familiar with Aurim Bedlam, son of the sorcerer Cabe Bedlam?"

"I've only seen him from a distance, my lord."

"Enough to recognize him if he passed through these gates?"

Haplin frowned, then glanced at the other sentry, who shrugged. "We've seen no one like that, Lord Darkhorse. Just the usual merchants, farmers, moving families, and riffraff."

The shadow steed caught the second man glancing at a young woman accompanying an elderly couple into the city. After pondering for a moment, Darkhorse decided to try a different query. "Have you perhaps seen a young merchant woman?" He described Jenna as best he could, attempting to emphasize those features that the guards might best recall. "It would have been earlier this day."

"I remember her," called the second sentry. "She headed straight west, which I thought kind of funny since when I asked where she was going she said 'home to Gordag-Ai.'

"Indeed?" That struck Darkhorse as strange as it had the guard. Perhaps Jenna intended on returning to her homeland after her meeting with Aurim, but the eternal could not see the young woman making the journey all by herself. He also did not think that after the attraction the pair had shown for one another that she would separate herself from the young sorcerer that easily.

Something did not sit right. Darkhorse's uneasiness grew.

"I thank you for your time, friends!" The ebony stallion reared, which immediately caused a path to clear for him. Haplin saluted, but Darkhorse was already past him. Now more than ever, he wanted to reach the river quickly.

There was still no trace of Aurim. The boy had shielded himself well. As for this Jenna, what little power he had sensed in her was not sufficient to track her down. That meant that Darkhorse would have to physically search the area until he located the prodigal pair. It was the only way he could be certain that he would find them.

The short distance to the riverbank was no difficult hurdle, but the winding, foliage-rich landscape threatened to be. Two young lovers would do their best to find a secluded location, of which there were far too many from the looks of things. The shadow steed paused, then turned south. As he traveled, Darkhorse studied the ground for recent tracks. He also continued to search on another plane, seeking any momentary lapse, any accidental sorcerous trace left behind by Aurim.

A short time later, he at last found some clues. The tracks could have belonged to anyone's mount, but he sensed also a slim hint of sorcery in the vicinity. Darkhorse followed the mild trace, noting that the tracks also led in that direction. Ahead of him was what looked to be a perfect location for his quarry, a quiet, private opening near the riverside. Colorful flowers even decorated the area.

He heard nothing but the birds and the rushing water, but that did not mean that the two were not nearby. It could be that they had even noticed his presence and were keeping silent. The shadow steed hoped that was the case although he doubted it.

A moment later his fears were confirmed. The area was empty. Still, Darkhorse was certain that they *had* been here. The longer he remained, the more he felt the past presence of Cabe's son. Aurim had performed sorcery of some sort, sorcery of a high degree. The trace grew stronger the nearer Darkhorse moved to the river.

What had the lad done? Had something happened to both of them because of some spell Aurim had been trying to cast?

Darkhorse shuddered, then rethought matters. The traces that remained of the younger Bedlam's attempt were too delicate to be the by-products of a magical disaster. Whatever spell Aurim had cast, he had completed without problem.

Which brought the eternal back to the question of where the two young humans were now.

He glanced down, seeking tracks that might indicate the pair had ridden off elsewhere. His eyes widened as he found the two sets of hooves met at least three more.

227

THE HORSE KING

What company joined them? Bandits? Even at his worst, Aurim would be able to handle three bandits! All he would have had to do was reestablish his link with his parents.

Oddly, when Darkhorse looked for the newcomers' path of departure, he found nothing. According to the prints, the strangers had ridden up to the horses of the young pair and then all of them, Aurim and Jenna included, had simply vanished. There were no tracks leading away.

Doubling back, the eternal checked once more. Tracks led to the spot, but no tracks led away. Studying the river, Dark- horse wondered if perhaps they had somehow managed to cross it. Perhaps that was what Aurim had done, created a path or bridge across the river.

Had a fisherman been walking near the riverbank he might have noticed a wondrous sight. Unhindered by normal limitations, the huge, ebony stallion trotted across the vast Serkadian, his hooves not even touching the swift water. However, there were no tracks on the other side. Darkhorse searched for quite some distance in either direction along the bank, but found nothing, not even a trace of sorcerous activity.

He returned to the original site, mind racing. The evidence did not bode well. Aurim was nowhere to be found. Jenna had told the sentry that she would be returning to Gordag-Ai even though it was clear that she had indeed met with the young sorcerer. At least three riders had joined them and then the entire party had simply disappeared.

Disappeared. Spellcaster's work. Yet, Aurim's trace was the only strong one . . . although there was a very faint hint of something else. It reminded him vaguely of . . . of the female sorcerer who had rescued Cabe and him from the spell trap.

Something has happened to Aurim! His parents must be told!

The moment Darkhorse contemplated telling them, however, he found himself unable to move. The Bedlams were back at the Manor in the midst of important research, trying to puzzle out this sinister force working for King Lanith. By the time he retrieved them, there was no telling how cold the trail might be. It behooved him to try to track down the missing sorcerer first.

If they had not forded the river or ridden from this location, then the only logical assumption could be that someone had transported them away. That would require power and the longer the distance the group had to be transported the more power the sorcerer would need to expend. Jenna had not struck him as having that much strength—although Darkhorse was beginning to suspect that she had more than his cursory inspection had revealed—which left Aurim himself the logical choice.

But why would the lad aid his own captors . . . if that is who they were? The evidence was circumstantial for the most part, but the shadow steed was fairly certain that he was correct in his assumption. Now he needed to do something about it.

If Aurim had cast such a great spell, then there had to be some trace of his path. Travel by sorcery seemed instantaneous to most people, but the truth was that the spell still occasionally left a slight trace. At the very least, if Darkhorse was able to detect such a trace he might be able to follow the party.

It was a long shot even for him. Only because of the intensity of the young spellcaster's power did the eternal think that he might have a chance.

Steeling himself, Darkhorse projected his mind in a dozen directions. No human mage could have imitated his efforts, for their minds were restricted to a few petty planes of existence while the shadow steed, being a creature of the endless, empty Void, was open to many, many levels. However, he rarely looked beyond the ones known to most spellcasters of this world; there was always the danger of permanently fragmenting his mind. He was willing to risk some of that danger now, however, if only

228

it would aid him in finding Cabe's son.

*I allowed this relationship to grow . . . I allowed this to happen . . . Jam at fault .
. .*

Again and again his probing failed. Somehow, Aurim Bedlam had gained such control over his abilities that he had used scarcely more than the slightest amount of power necessary to complete the transportation spell. There was no sign of a blink hole nor any evidence of any other method of magical travel. Nonetheless, Darkhorse did not give up. He could not. There had to be some sign, some bit of—

And there it was. The trace was so very minuscule, only detectable on the very edge of human magical senses. Neither the elder Bedlams nor the Gryphon would have likely noticed its presence. Darkhorse had already missed it twice. Only because of his stubbornness had he finally taken notice. It was too faint for him to decipher which direction the party had traveled, but not too faint for him to follow using a spell of his own.

Without hesitation, Darkhorse opened a blink hole. There were other, swifter modes of magical travel, but because he was not certain what lay at the other end, the eternal wanted to have that extra moment in which to prepare himself. He suspected he knew just where Aurim had been taken. Now he could verify it.

The hole floated before him, a wide oval rip in reality. Darkhorse took one last glance around him, then entered.

What existed within the blink hole was a question even the shadow steed could not completely answer. He stood upon a path floating through a vaguely seen dimension of mist. In some ways it reminded him of the Void, but where now the light mist floated around him, in his home there would have been nothing but a great, bright emptiness.

Darkhorse moved along the path, knowing that he had already crossed much of the distance between Penacles and his destination. He had created this blink hole carefully, forming it so that with his power he could manipulate its time span. He would reach the end when he chose and not a moment before.

The path before him grew more distinct, a sign that Dark- horse had nearly reached his goal. He slowed. The blink hole was not supposed to open until he reached the very end. The shadow steed tried to gather his thoughts. There might be a dozen different threats beyond the hole, but Darkhorse was prepared. For Aurim's sake, he had to be.

The shadow steed willed the gap to open.

Nothing happened.

Perplexed, Darkhorse tried again. The results were the same. The path ended, but no doorway formed.

He turned back. Something had blocked the way. He would have to return to Penacles and plan anew.

Only . . . now it was impossible to see the path back. All that lay behind Darkhorse was mist. Endless mist. The ebony stallion tried to trace his route, but without the path, he had nowhere to go.

He was trapped. Someone had set another snare, catching Darkhorse because of his own arrogance and overconfidence. This time, there was no one to save him.

Chapter Seven

THE HORSE KING

Zuu.

Aurim had often dreamed of visiting the land of the horse people, but not as a helpless prisoner of the king and his vile, treacherous witch. He had no one to blame but himself, though. His father would have seen through her disguise, of that the younger Bedlam was certain. Only someone as simple and naive as Aurim would have fallen prey to Saress's masquerade.

As if sensing his thoughts, the enchantress turned and smiled at him. The two of them had been waiting here for the past half hour. Saress seemed not to care; whatever the king wanted her to do, she did. If he wanted her to wait, she waited. If he wanted her to trick and capture potential sorcerers for him, the woman leaped to obey. Worse, if what Saress had said of King Lanith's future plans was true . . .

"Patience, darling. He'll be along soon. Just . . . enjoy the sights."

She meant herself, of course. Saress was clad in a thin, low-cut outfit made entirely of leather. It covered little more than necessary. Aurim knew that it was a variation on the traditional jerkin and pants of the horse king's guards, but Saress had turned it from a piece of history to something with a much darker purpose. It was supposed to be seductive, and under other circumstances, he knew that it probably would have captured his full attention, but after what the witch had done to him, Aurim could only look upon her with revulsion.

Despite the spell that held him in stasis, Aurim still had use of his eyes. Rather than glare at his captor, the sorcerer chose to again study the room. This was supposed to be the throne room of the kings of Zuu, but it more resembled the interior of some old keep built in the days when Lanith's ancestors finally decided to give up their nomadic lives. Likely it was a reminder of that time. More than one palace had been built on the site of previous royal buildings. Perhaps King Lanith's throne room was all that remained of the original house of the first chosen monarch of the new kingdom.

There had been alterations since then, of course. High up the walls, someone had added barred windows. Someone else had added a number of torch holders shaped as astonishingly lifelike armored hands. They appeared to line the walls on both sides from end to end, but unable to move his head, Aurim could not be certain.

The dais before them was of the same dark granite as the walls, which meant that it, too, had probably been part of the original structure. The throne, however, looked new. Carved from what Aurim recognized as rare elfwood, it stood taller than even one of the Dragon Kings. The legs had been shaped to resemble those of horses, even down to the hooves. The armrests were the sleek backs of racing chargers, whose ferocious heads seemed ready to snap at anyone who approached too closely.

Forming the upper back of the chair were twin steeds who reared toward one another, forehooves clashing. Underneath them, a pair of swords pointing earthward completed the back. The entire throne had been painted a dusky brown, the most popular shade of the famous horses of Zuu. Only the leather seat of the chair gave it any variation.

It was the ugliest piece of furniture that Aurim had ever seen.

A door behind the throne suddenly opened. Saress immediately went down on one knee and, to his dismay, so did Aurim. A full dozen warriors of the king's special guard marched out in perfect order, then split into two equal groups. The warriors, evenly divided between male and female, lined up across from one another, forming a corridor of muscle extending from the dais to the enchantress and her captive.

Only then did the horse king enter.

A chill wind seemed to precede him, as did a darkness that no one else in the chamber noticed save Aurim Bedlam. Despite the many lit torches, the illumination suddenly appeared muted. Aurim shivered, a spontaneous reaction that not only surprised him, but pleased him as well. The reaction had been independent of Saress's control. That meant that her hold on him was not perfect.

Lanith was the tallest of the horse people that Aurim had so far seen. He was older and graying, yes, but hardly soft and weak. The horse king's features reminded him of a mountain chiseled by time and weather. Not handsome, but impressive. Lanith was clad in garments akin to those of his guard, an outfit that hearkened back to generations of fierce nomadic warriors. He might have stepped through the centuries himself, so menacing did he appear. The shadow and the chill added to the effect, which made the sorcerer wonder if their presence was planned. Aurim tried to probe the darkness, but found his probe deflected by some magical force.

With no further ceremony, the horse king seated himself, the darkness settling several feet above him. He glanced first at the captured spellcaster, then at Saress. A thin smile spread across his features.

"My love!" the enchantress called much too loudly. "I have for you a very special prize!"

Perhaps it was only Aurim's imagination, but he thought the monarch of Zuu was slightly amused by Saress's obvious attempt to seduce him with her outfit. "I'd imagine he must be, considering that you were supposed to remain in Penacles for another week. How good is this one? Better than the last?"

She rose, each movement an invitation to her king. Aurim, who was forced to rise with her, was fairly certain that Lanith had accepted more than a few of her invitations in the past, enough so that now she was the puppet and he the master. "Better than any of them! Better than any you hoped to add to the ranks! I have *him.*"

"Him?" The horse king straightened, studying the golden-haired mage closely. "Rich clothing for a student. A head of hair that almost looks like . . ." The air of disinterest faded. Lanith grew eager. "He's Aurim Bedlam!"

"You see? I said that I could get him and I did, my love!"

"Yes, at last." King Lanith stared at Aurim, finally frowning. "But if he's so powerful, then how could you take him so easily?"

Saress leaned back, her body momentarily pressing against her victim as she touched Aurim's chin in mock tenderness. "A young man in love is apt to think of little else. It was easy to wrap him around my finger and lead him along. Power without thought is easy prey."

"So it is." Because Saress had her head turned toward Aurim, only the captive saw that Lanith's gaze briefly shifted toward his pet sorceress as he spoke. "But is he that powerful?"

Saress abandoned her captive, joining the king at his throne. She draped herself over his left shoulder, allowing his eyes to linger on her form before pointing at Aurim. "He can create passages through rivers, passages wide enough to cross an army! His might is such that he transported five of us, including our *mounts,* all the way from the Serkadian River to your royal courtyard!"

"Yes, I heard about that." King Lanith's eyes burned into Aurim's. "I could make much use of someone as strong as you, young sorcerer. Would you serve me willingly if I paid you well? You could have almost everything you wanted . . ." His hand rested on Saress's own.

Once more, Aurim Bedlam's mouth moved of its own accord. "I would try to escape the moment I could."

The tall warrior almost stood. His gaze turned darker. "Is that so? You arrogant, pampered little colt—"

"He must answer our questions, my king," the enchantress interjected. "My spell requires it of him."

"Has he no will of his own, then?"

"Only in the privacy of his mind. The rest belongs to you—to you, Lanith."

"To me." The horse king leaned toward Saress. "Make him perform . . . some trick."

"As you command." Saress smiled at Aurim. "Show him your little harlequins, darling."

Parlor tricks. He was being forced to perform parlor tricks for his captors. Rage overtook fear. Aurim did not want to perform for them like a trained animal. He was a free man and a sorcerer. His arms rose halfway, but the young spellcaster tried to keep them from rising farther. He would *not* perform.

His arms stayed where they were. Aurim could not lower them, but neither did they continue to move on their own. In one sense it was a stalemate; in another, it was a grand victory for him. Saress's spell did not have complete control over him after all.

Unfortunately, King Lanith also noticed his success. "The boy's not obeying. I thought he had to do every thing we said, Saress."

"He does!" Seeming more embarrassed than fearful, the sorceress abandoned her position and stalked toward Aurim. The look in her eyes was anything but seductive now. Her prisoner had succeeded in making her appear foolish before the man she obviously adored. "I gave you a command. Do the little trick with the harlequins!"

His arms rose an inch higher, then settled back to their previous positions. Aurim smiled triumphantly, then smiled more when he realized that he now had control of his mouth again.

Saress slapped his cheek before realizing that her captive was now partially mobile. The moment she understood her danger, the temptress immediately stepped back.

"What's wrong, Saress?"

"Nothing that I can't deal with, Lanith." Despite her tone of assurance, though, the expression on her face, an expression only Aurim could see at the moment, was anything but confident.

His hopes continued to rise. She still had enough control to prevent him from speaking or casting his own spells, but that control was rapidly fading. Soon he would be able to take matters into his own hands.

"Naughty boy! No man leaves Saress!" The woman thrust her left hand toward him.

Aurim felt a crackle of energy surge through him that briefly stole from him the movement and force of will that he had regained. The sorceress smiled at Aurim again, but with renewed effort, the golden-haired mage swept away her second spell and further weakened her first. Now he had enough control of his arms to slowly move them as he desired. Aurim still could not summon enough strength to cast a spell, especially one to transport him away from this evil place, but he only needed a few moments more.

Beyond Saress, King Lanith did a peculiar thing. He leaned farther to one side and raised his head as if listening to someone nearby . . . only there was nothing but the sinister darkness. Then the monarch of Zuu looked again at Aurim.

"Cease your efforts, Saress."

"Lanith—"

"You're dismissed. That goes for the rest of you as well. Leave now."

The guards looked as perplexed as the enchantress. Aurim, too. What made the man think that he could face a sorcerer of Aurim Bedlam's ability? It would only be a few moments before the spellcaster was free. Better that the horse king departs with his witch in tow than face his former captive's wrath.

Despite her obvious reluctance, Saress was the first to obey. The guards followed slowly, each of them glancing from the captured sorcerer to their lord. At the doorway, the enchantress paused while the warriors filed out. Only when she was the last left did Saress finally depart. Even then, her eyes lingered on King Lanith until she was out of sight.

Throughout it all, Aurim continued to struggle for freedom. His arms were his. Then his entire body began to respond, slowly, then faster. He was only seconds from complete control, seconds from escape.

All the while, the horse king merely sat on the throne and watched.

The last vestiges of Saress's spell shattered. Aurim briefly paused, wondering whether he ought to do something about the king of Zuu. The man had ordered his kidnapping. He was ready to begin a great war. Surely if Aurim had the opportunity to capture Lanith, then he had to try.

The sorcerer glared at the figure on the throne. "King Lanith, you should've run."

His adversary looked anything but fearful. The king slowly rose, arms crossed. Aurim could sense nothing, but Lanith's attitude put him on guard.

"I run from no one, especially a pampered little magician with high ideals and, until recently, no control over himself. You think that a few little victories win a war? You've no idea about the workings of strategy, the playing of the game, the writing of the epic—" Lanith broke off, suddenly blinking. "I want him under control now, imp. I've no more time to waste."

Aurim had no idea what Lanith meant by the last, save that it gave some indication that the pair of them was not as alone as he had thought. He looked around, assuring himself again that no one had remained behind, and finally came to the conclusion that perhaps Zuu's lord was insane.

It was definitely time to depart. Aurim assumed that if he could transport an entire party across most of the continent, he could still send himself back to Penacles. He summoned up the necessary strength—

—and felt his effort suppressed by another force.

He wanted to try again, but suddenly his body was once more a prison. Aurim could not move, could scarcely even breathe this time.

A giggle echoed through the chamber. Aurim found himself raising his arms in a dramatic gesture, then flapping them like a Seeker trying to take off. He knew that he was an absurd sight, but he could not help himself.

The darkness floating above Lanith drifted toward Aurim, slowly coalescing as it moved.

"Stop the games," the king commanded the air. "Keep him still."

"As you command, 0 great majesty . . ."

Despite its merry tone, Aurim found nothing amusing about the voice. It was the voice of a creature who had no concern for human life or death. There was something vaguely reminiscent about the voice, too, as if he had heard another akin to it before.

"You've got him secure? He can't use his sorcery against me?"

"Oh, no, no, Your Majesty! He is your puppet to command! You want him to dance"—Aurim performed a wild, clumsy series of steps—"and he dances! You want him to—"

"Enough of the theatrics, imp!" Lanith strode up to his prisoner. "Little brat . . ."

The spellcaster could do nothing as the warrior king thrust his face near. In truth, what concerned Aurim more than the man was the creature that served him. Only now did he sense something of its presence and that only because the shadow was now an indistinct yet swiftly solidifying blob. What was it?

"So, Aurim Bedlam. I made you an offer, but it's clear that you won't accept it. I can't trust you to join me. Should I have you then executed? You're a danger to me, boy. Maybe I should have your neck stretched . . . or better yet, toast you over an open fire so that I'm *certain* you're dead. I've heard a good sorcerer is hard to kill."

For the first time, the young mage was glad that the spell holding him did not allow him any movement. If it had, King Lanith would have certainly noticed his fear.

"It would be such a terrible waste, though, great majesty," suggested the voice. "He is, after all, an asset in more than one way! He would lead your Order in battle and also act as bait!"

Bait? What does he mean? They had to want his parents. That was it. His empty-headed romantic ideals not only threatened him, but his family, too. Lanith probably intended on making all of the Bedlams his unwilling servants.

Of course, Aurim's mother and father were hardly the simplistic fools that he was. Lanith might have some pet creature working for him, but it could hardly be as powerful as the elder Bedlams or, say, Darkhorse.

Darkhorse? Thinking of the shadow steed made him stare again at the mysterious form. Now it vaguely resembled a tiny, humanoid figure, a black, faceless thing.

"He escaped once, imp. His will's very strong. Admirable at other times, but not now. If his will's strong enough, he'll escape again. I can't take that chance."

"A sorcerer is a terrible thing to waste, *Emperor* Lanith, but rest assured, where there's a will, there's a way to *crush* it thoroughly!" The tiny figure giggled, "I can make your will his will, if you like."

This intrigued the king. "You can do that? You can make him do what I want?"

"It is *difficult* to do," replied the demon in a tone that made Aurim suspect that it was anything but difficult. Lanith appeared not to notice, however. "But I think that I can turn him to your grand cause, great majesty . . ."

The creature had completely formed now. He—for lack of a better pronoun—resembled a foot-tall, unfinished puppet. Aurim saw now that the king's imp had eyes and he was almost certain that he knew whose they resembled.

"Do it, then. With someone of his power to guide the others, my Order will be the greatest weapon of war ever."

The puppet floated toward Aurim, eyes fixed on the sorcerer even though his words were for the king. "And let us not forget: as bait, he will garner for you the other great prize you desire, my lord!"

The creature was barely more than arm's length from the captive—and now there was no denying exactly who he reminded Aurim of. It had to be impossible. There could not be two such astonishing beings, yet, the proof was before him. Coming for him. Burning into his soul with pupilless, icy blue orbs just like those of-

"Darkhorse," King Lanith whispered, responding to his companion's last words. "Darkhorse."

It was worse than being trapped in the Void, Darkhorse decided. Nothing but mist surrounded him He could barely see his own limbs, much less anything that *might* have lurked nearby. At least in the clear emptiness of the Void Darkhorse had always been able to see that nothing watched him, nothing stalked him from behind . . . and nothing tried to reabsorb him, in the horrific process eradicating the sense of self that he held so precious.

At least I am safe from that! Any fate, any death, was better than the slow draining loss of his identity. It was one reason he had been so pleased when the Vraad sorcerer Dru Zeree led him back to the Dragonrealm. In the Dragonrealm, Darkhorse could hide from the one thing he secretly feared.

Such thoughts did not, of course, aid him now. It was possible that he might never escape this place, but the eternal planned to exhaust all options before giving in to such a fate. He could not re-create a blink hole from within the very nether region into which a blink hole opened, but there had to be a way of forming another exit. Darkhorse had traced his way from the Void to the Dragonrealm; this should be no more difficult.

Darkhorse soon regretted his confident thoughts. A scan of the misty nothingness with his senses revealed no trail to the dimension of the Dragonrealm. The place was a veritable blank in terms of sorcery. For the first time, the shadow steed grew anxious. His anxiety was not entirely related to his own fate, either. At this very moment, Aurim Bedlam faced possible danger. Worse, his family was ignorant of his disappearance, thanks to the eternal's mistake.

"I will be free of this place!" Darkhorse snapped out loud, more to shatter the unremitting silence than because he believed what he said. Without some path to follow, the eternal was at a loss.

He tried to review what had happened. The dissipation of his blink hole had been no accident. Some spellcaster had taken advantage of his travel spell and disrupted it at the most opportune moment. A very, very difficult form of attack, which meant a sorcerer of tremendous ability. It also meant a sorcerer who had some inkling of his plans or at least had kept a distant but careful eye on him.

But who . . . and why? One of Lanith's puppet mages? The missing students had promise. Perhaps one of them. Doubtful, but Darkhorse had no other answer.

A slight tingling in his head scattered all other thoughts. His magical senses came alive as Darkhorse realized that a thin tendril of energy now reached out to him from the mists. It was so very faint that Darkhorse kept expecting to lose it. Immediately he began tracking the tendril's path. The nearer he got to the source, the better the chance that he would find a way to return to the Dragonrealm.

On and on through the mist the eternal floated. The tendril never grew stronger, but neither did it weaken. Still, the longer Darkhorse followed, the more frustrated he became. Was this another trick? Was he cursed to follow this trail forever? Surely at some point the tendril would cease to be . . . and that would leave him once more stranded in the middle of nowhere.

Before him, a gaping hole burst into being.

Darkhorse was sucked through the newborn blink hole before he could even react to its presence. His equine form stretched like so much molasses, twisting and turning until little remained that resembled any sort of animal, much less a horse. The eternal cursed the multiverse, sorcerers, and sorcery in general as he fought to keep himself from tearing into several pieces. He dared not let that happen. The cost not only to himself but the Dragonrealm in general would be too great if even one fragment of his being separated too long. He knew too well what could result from such a disaster. If the fragment survived and, worse, thrived, it might become the monster people had often thought him to be.

Then, even as he began to believe that he could hold himself together no longer, Darkhorse fell into the Dragonrealm.

Unable to control his flight, the shadow steed plummeted earthward . . . but it was not earth he struck, rather water. Much water.

The splash as Darkhorse struck drowned out all other sounds. The eternal registered only that whatever lake or river he had landed in was very deep, for despite the speed with which he had fallen, he still did not touch bottom. Gradually the eternal's wild flight slowed until at last he floated, quite dazed, several feet below the surface.

Darkhorse slowly recovered, noticing only belatedly that he was drifting along at a good rate of speed. A river, then. The shadow steed regained enough control of his body to halt his progress, then, still underwater, started the process of restructuring himself. The legs formed readily enough, but it took him several minutes to re-create his head and tail and a few minutes more to add fine detail.

Suddenly Darkhorse sensed the presence of a spellcaster, likely the same one whose probe had led him back to the Dragonrealm. The unknown mage searched the waters for him, probing closer and closer. Darkhorse decided to save the other the trouble of searching any longer. The spellcaster might be the reason that the eternal had managed to escape the nether realm, but he also might be the one who had trapped him there in the first place.

The shadow steed burst through to the surface, rising above the water. He saw now that he had indeed fallen into a river. A forest covered the landscape as far as he could see. Suspicions concerning his whereabouts grew solid.

His attention shifted to a figure among the trees: The spellcaster he had sensed. Not a man, but a woman. Not any woman, either, but she who had gone by the name Tori.

Darkhorse swooped down on her, moving so swiftly that the sorceress had little time to react. He came to a sudden halt directly in front of her, one foreleg raised up, and glared. The eternal still floated two or three feet above the woman, which meant that she had to crane her neck in order to look at him.

"I have had enough of your games, female!"

"What are you talking about? I saved you!"

"And how was it I became trapped in the first place?" From the way her expression altered, Darkhorse assumed that he was correct. The enchantress *had* been responsible. "I know not what your plan is, but you may consider it a lost cause!"

To her credit, she did not back away. "I don't know what you're talking about! I arrived at this spot, saw nothing, and was about to leave when I felt your presence. You were here but not here. I searched and found you. . . somewhere beyond. After that, I kept working until I was able to open one end of a blink hole for you! If not for me, you'd still be . . . wherever!"

"I do not believe you. I believe that you are in part responsible for the kidnapping of Aurim Bedlam!" The shadow steed descended to the ground. The woman did not behave as he would have expected. She should have attacked or, if *she* was sensible, retreated. Instead, the sorceress acted as if she were now the offended party. Despite her defiance, however, Darkhorse pressed on. "And after you kidnapped Aurim, you worked to assure I would not be able to rescue him!"

"Which is why I also helped you to escape, I suppose." The blond sorceress shook her head. "That makes no sense and you know it, demon steed."

"What makes no sense, unless you are lying, is your sudden appearance at so opportune a time! I follow the lad's trail, discover that he and his captors have seemingly vanished, and when I try to follow, I find my spell torn about and my path back no more! Then you appear and lead me out! Tell me that your timely rescue of me can possibly be due to chance, female!"

"My name, if you have to have one, is Yssa."

"A name as false, no doubt, as Tori!" The shadowy stallion took a step forward. Yssa, if that was truly her name, had the good sense to retreat an equal distance. "You are avoiding the subject!"

"Believe what you will." The enchantress steeled herself, even daring to stare him in the eye. "No, my finding you was no chance thing, demon steed. You mentioned Aurim Bedlam during our last visit together . . . and how he'd met someone. I came to . . . to see who it was."

"Did you? How very, very inquisitive considering you had never met either of them." Darkhorse snorted. "Or have you? Aurim, likely not, but perhaps you did know the young woman Jenna!" Her blank stare did not suit him. "A merchant's daughter, so she claimed." He described her in detail, but Yssa still gave no sign of recognition . . . or did she? Yssa's mouth tightened slightly as the shadow steed added every bit of information he could recall about Aurim's lady. She knew *something*. *"You* still claim no knowledge?"

"I know no one who looks like that."

Darkhorse kicked at the ground, creating a tiny yet deep crevice. Yssa jumped. The eternal stepped forward. Yssa again retreated, but this time a tree trunk blocked her path. She looked ready to do another vanishing act, but Darkhorse shook his head. "No escapes this time, human! You will find it impossible to depart, I promise."

"I've done nothing but help you, demon steed. You've no right—"

He reared, sorcerous energy radiating all around him. His eyes flared. "I am Darkhorse! I do what I choose to do for what cause I care to take up! Someone dear to me and dear to others I care for is missing! You know much, but you think you can keep it from me!" The branches of the trees nearest Darkhorse shook wildly. He thrust his head so close to Yssa's face that it filled her view. "I *will* have answers!"

"Saress!" the stunned and frightened enchantress blurted. "It was Saress! I'm sure of it! I know she's journeyed to Penacles in secret in the past and each time she's brought back a young spellcaster for Lanith. Someone . . . someone I knew within the palace walls told me that she brought at least two, both of them ensorcelled! If Lanith can't pay them enough to be his lackeys, he's more than willing to take them against their will, and the easiest way is through Saress!"

"So, you pretended not to know her when I described her as Jenna! I do not like being lied to, human!"

"I didn't lie to you . . . not exactly. That wasn't Saress. Not her normal appearance. She's good at casting illusion, though. If it wasn't her, then I can't imagine who it could've been!"

The tree limbs stilled. The shadow steed allowed the aura surrounding him to fade, but he did not back away. "You know this Saress very well, I believe! How?"

"I've encountered her before. She . . . she nearly made me one of King Lanith's forced volunteers. She also killed a friend of mine in the name of her master."

Her sincerity was questionable, but Darkhorse sensed some element of truth in her words. He took one step back, giving Yssa just enough space to let her relax a little. Darkhorse did not want her becoming too relaxed, however, not until he was certain that he had all the information he required. "How powerful is Saress?"

"Powerful?" Yssa seemed uncertain what the eternal meant by his question. "She's fairly powerful. Not like Cabe Bedlam. Better than the others in the Magical Order, but that's not saying much." A long hesitation followed. "She might be a little stronger than I am." Her expression hardened. *"Maybe."*

"Is she this intelligent force?"

"No." She said it with such confidence that Darkhorse could not doubt her answer. He had suspected that Saress was not the dark power behind the horse king.

Darkhorse came to the conclusion that Yssa was not an enemy in disguise but rather an unruly, self-reliant witch who preferred her own unorthodox methods to working with others. True, she had passed along information to Cabe and the Gryphon, but more because it suited her purpose. Dark- horse was amazed that she had remained hidden from both the Dragon Kings and human spellcasters for so long, but then, it was possible that she was even more skilled than the eternal believed. Certainly the peculiar pattern of energy within her, the magical signature, was unique. In some ways it was also harder to read than most. There was much about Yssa that remained an enigma, but Darkhorse would worry about that after he had rescued Aurim.

How he was to do that, Darkhorse still did not know. Best to talk it over with Cabe and Gwen, however unnerving the thought of telling them about their son's kidnapping. In desperate hope that he was wrong, the shadow steed asked, "You are certain that this Saress is responsible? You sensed her presence where the boy vanished?"

Her nostrils flared as if she had inhaled something repugnant. "I could mistake her for no one else. She was there. If your friend also was, then they were together. It couldn't be coincidence."

"No, I thought not." That was it, then. He had to break the terrible news to the young sorcerer's parents. Darkhorse looked around, trying to orient himself so that he could head the proper direction back to the Manor. "This is . . . the Dagora Forest, is it not?"

Yssa looked uncomfortable. "Yes."

"Why here? Why bring me to this place?"

"This is where I was when I sensed you. I didn't notice anything near Penacles."

"Indeed? How very peculiar." It was also very suspicious. What the woman had told him sounded like the work of a powerful spellcaster. There were very few of those. Of course, this *was* the Dagora Forest, but surely that did not mean . . . "Yssa, what brought you to this place? Why come here after Penacles?"

"Because she came to see me, demon sssteed," answered a figure suddenly standing among the trees.

"Lord Green . . ." The Dragon King bowed in acknowledgment of his identity. Darkhorse shifted to better face the drake. Again he found himself wondering about Cabe Bedlam's sudden withdrawal from friendship with the armored ruler and how that affected his own standing. None of the drakes had ever considered the eternal a comrade, but this one had at least acted respectful. Now, though, the Green Dragon's anxiety shone like a beacon. The drake lord was worried about something.

Darkhorse thought he knew what it was, and the knowledge made him furious. Small wonder that the Green Dragon might fear his wrath. "It was *you*, was it not? It was you who trapped me in the first place! It was you who prevented me from rescuing Aurim!"

"I'm sorry," Yssa called, but her words were not meant for Darkhorse. Instead, she bowed her head toward the Dragon King and repeated her apology. "I'm sorry. I didn't think."

The drake lord waved off her apology with one mailed hand. "You could not know. It doesss not matter, my dear."

"You know her?" It was a conspiracy, then. The woman had to have worked with the Dragon King to trap him. Darkhorse did not know why they had dared snare him, but he would have answers even if both of them had to pay. The ebony stallion reared up, energy crackling around him.

"Pleassse calm yourself, demon sssteed. No harm wasss meant to you. I only sssought to prevent you from becoming yet another of the horsssse king's slaves. I wasss nearly ready to release you myself. I only needed to compossse mysssself for what I knew would be a very . . . sssensitive . . . conversation with you."

Darkhorse was not at all certain he believed the drake, but he dropped to the ground. "Then say what you must say, Lord Green, for I have a friend in peril."

"I will, but not here." Before the eternal could question him, the Dragon King raised one hand. As he did, their surroundings shifted. Gone was the forest, to be replaced by a cavern chamber, a vast natural room that Darkhorse recognized as the court of the Green Dragon.

The drake lord no longer stood before him, but sat on a huge stone throne. An arch formed from vines rose above the throne. The same vines coursed along the walls of the chamber, adding a sense of life to what might otherwise have been an empty, soulless place. Despite a lack of natural light, the vines seemed as healthy and fresh as if they had been growing outdoors.

"We risk no one listening in while we are here," explained the Green Dragon. "Not even whatever force it is that ssserves Lanith. I have also disssmissed the guardsss. There will be no ssspies of any sort."

All that might have been true, but Darkhorse still wondered about the presence of one other in the chamber. Yssa now stood to one side of the throne, as if she had every right to be there.

"What of her? What is her part in all of this, Lord Green? Too many questions have been dangled before me. Too many questions and not nearly enough answers!"

"Yssa is here by my permission. It isss too long since we ssspoke and that is a shame that I mussst bear. I am glad that she hasss at last come back to me."

"I had to," she responded. "I had no choice."

"Yesss . . ." The Dragon King seemed somewhat bitter, but his bitterness appeared to be directed at himself. "Of course."

"Yssa." For the first time, the name made some sense to Darkhorse. Many drake names had similar sounds. There had been Ssarekai, so loyal to the Bedlams, his human lords, that he had sacrificed himself in an attempt to stop the renegade Toma. Now there also existed Sssaleese, leader of the fledgling drake confederation. Yssa was a perfectly normal name—especially for a drake. "So . . . you are not human after all, female."

She looked insulted. "But I *am*, Darkhorse! I am . . . at least in part."

"Yssa *isss* human, demon steed," insisted the drake lord somewhat uncomfortably. "Her mother wasss a very beauteousss woman"—the Green Dragon reached out a hand to the sorceress, who took it after some hesitation—"and I . . . and I am her *father."*

Chapter Eight

"You cannot mean what you say, Lord Green! Such a coming together is . . . has always been . . ."

"Unthinkable?" The drake lord removed his hand from that of Yssa and leaned forward, red eyes staring defiantly into the eternal's own. "Do you deny the possibility that at least once in the past the two races have come together? Do you think that *no one* ever thought of such a combination?"

Darkhorse snorted. "I am not so naive. There have always been those of both races who found themselves attracted by . . . shall we call it the exotic, my Lord Green? Yet, that does not guarantee that their union will be blessed. We are talking of drakes and humans, after all!"

"Two races not so dissimilar as you think, at least based upon my ssstudies. There are those who find the new emperor attractive, if you recall."

Darkhorse recalled all too well. Cabe's own daughter Valea had been attracted to the young drake, who, admittedly, looked nearly human. Many of the latest generation of drakes seemed more human than ever, which made the potential for human-drake relationships more and more likely. The eternal did not like the notion; the Dragon Kings and their people had always been adversaries, the masters who needed to be overthrown or, at the very least, taught humility. "I do not deny such things, Dragon King, but what you say—"

"Isss only the truth. Yssa is my own, the only legacy I have of her mother." The drake lord looked away, obviously reliving the past. "Humansss have ever had a more ressspectable place in my domain, demon steed. Not quite the level achieved by those in the Manor, but I and my predecessorsss have always known the value of their kind. Humansss have ssserved in positions of authority in my realm. Sssuch a one was Yssa's mother. Penelope wasss her name. She looked much like her daughter, I mussst say."

"You've no need to explain everything to him, Father," Yssa protested with a glare at the shadow steed.

"But I would like to tell sssomeone, if only becausssse I have kept your presssence hidden much too long. I have acted ashamed of you, my daughter, ashamed of one of my own." The Green Dragon leaned back. "Her mother wasss a woman of rank here, one who kept my research records in order and kept track of my ssstudies. She was a valuable sssubject." His tone grew darker. "My matesss do their duty, but we have long gone passst love. Now we work only for the sssake of raising a sssuccessor. Penelope, however, shared my passions, and having grown up among my kind, she sssaw not the monster outside, but the kindred sssoul inside."

Darkhorse did not want to believe the Dragon King. He did not want to think that such . . . hybrids . . . existed, but it explained Yssa's peculiar magical signature. He also saw no reason for either of them to make up what would have seemed to most a preposterous tale. It also perhaps explained a few encounters Darkhorse had had in centuries past with spellcasters whose abilities and style had matched nothing he had known. Perhaps hybrids were not so uncommon after all . . . just secretive.

Perhaps.

"It wasss only once, but that wasss enough. The unthinkable happened. Penelope wasss with child. No one dared sssay what everyone knew, not even when she gave birth." The Green Dragon looked at his daughter. "She wasss beautiful even then. Mossst human infants are so . . . so raw. Not her. I thought of her as her mother reborn . . . which proved prophetic asss her mother died but a day later."

Silence followed, a silence finally broken by Darkhorse. "I am sorry."

The figure on the throne straightened. "I do not ask for your sympathy, demon steed. I only tell you what happened. Yssa is my daughter and although we have been essstranged for quite sssome time, we are no longer."

"Then I am glad for you, Lord Green! However, we have diverged from the reason I have been brought here! Why did you do it? More important, how dare you entrap me, leave me to float in the world between worlds?"

His words seemed to strike the Dragon King hard. "I did what I did to protect you, Darkhorse, not becausssse I am your foe."

"Protect me?" Darkhorse laughed. "Protect me! From what could you protect me, Lord Green? I am Darkhorse!"

"Which doesss not make you invincible, demon sssteed," countered the master of the Dagora Forest. He pointed into the air. "Sssomething resssides in the domain of the horse people, sssome force whosssse powers and origins I have been unable to fathom. My daughter callsss it a creature, although I myssself have not even been able to verify that."

"It lives." The enchantress shuddered. "I felt it." Her eyes narrowed. "But now that I think of it, it reminds me of something else . . . I don't know what, but something else."

240

"That we can worry about later, daughter. Darkhorsssse, I know of Aurim Bedlam'sss abduction. I sssensed his presence in Zuu, and one of my few remaining spiesss verified it. However, shortly after his arrival, it wasss asss if the youth vanished. I sense that he isss in there sssomewhere, but it is asss if he is shielded from my sssight now."

"Which makes it all that much more important that I rescue him as soon as possible! If that is all you have to say to me, Lord Green, then I shall be off!" The shadow steed took a few steps back. He intended to create another blink hole from this very spot, one that would open up in the court of King Lanith if necessary.

"Wait!" The Dragon King's voice boomed throughout the chamber. He stood now, one open hand held high. "Hear me out, Darkhorse! Yesss, you mussst rescue Aurim, but to go charging into Zuu isss to court disssaster! There isss another way, a more sssubtle way! I can help you there!"

The shadow steed held off departing. Inwardly he knew that he was risking much. What he should have done was go straight to Cabe, but that seemed far too time-consuming at this point. The Green Dragon, however, was also a planner— and he knew Zuu better than either the Bedlams or the Gryphon did. If there was a way to work around King Lanith's defenses, then the Dragon King was the one who would know.

"Very well. I am still listening."

The reptilian monarch inhaled, his eyes growing a little less fiery. "The gatesss of Zuu are still open for busssiness despite the rumblingsss of conquesssst. Lanith still encourages business, although why ssso many fools would continue to go there, I cannot sssay. Merchantsss still bring their waresss to the city and othersss still come to purchassse the kingdom's fine sssteeds. That will sssoon change, but for now it worksss for us."

Darkhorse understood what he was suggesting. "I am to imitate a simple mount, thereby gaining access into the city. A reasonable suggestion, but surely Lanith's sorcerers will be watching for such a thing. If this woman who tricked Aurim was indeed the horse king's enchantress, then they will of course watch for me. I suspect that she is powerful enough to detect my presence. Better to leap in, rescue the lad, then depart."

"The matter of detection is not a problem, demon sssteed." The Dragon King extended his hand. He now held in it a medallion, the center of which was a green gemstone. "Thisss is a variation on the tokens all travelers who enter Zuu mussst bear. Unbeknownst to mossst, they are also desssigned to detect any newcomer with sorcerousss abilities. Thisss one, in turn, will act asss a damper, shielding your powers from the senses of Lanith's sorcerers . . . even Saress."

"I would look a little out of place wearing such a thing and I expect that I could not absorb it within me, could I?"

"Your rider will wear it. Asss long as the pair of you are within range of one another, you will be protected. Once inside, you can contact a representative of mine."

It seemed a reasonable if still somewhat risky option, but Darkhorse had some misgivings. "Who is it who will ride with me?"

Yssa stepped forward. "I will, Darkhorse."

"Daughter, that wasss not—"

"I know Zuu better than even your spies, Father. I lived among the people." She spread her arms. "Look at me. I might as well have been born among them."

"Your mother's parentsss were from the kingdom, true. However, I cannot risssk having you —"

She would not be put off. "Who else could defend themselves so effectively?" Yssa turned to Darkhorse. "You've no choice but me, demon steed. Will you accept that or do I have to argue with you, too? The longer we wait, the more danger to your friend."

He was probably as leery as the Dragon King was of involving the female, but she was correct. Yssa was the one best suited to journey with him, the only one he could trust to also defend herself. Her knowledge of Zuu would be invaluable, too. "I accept your company, wo--Yssa."

"I do not," insisted the Green Dragon. "Yssa, I forbid you to—"

She snatched the medallion from his hand, then vanished, only to rematerialize a moment later next to the shadow steed. The Dragon King hissed, starting toward her at the same time.

Yssa leaped aboard Darkhorse, a riskier act than she likely realized. Darkhorse immediately shaped himself to better accommodate her weight, then turned to block the drake lord.

"She will not go with you, eternal! I have only regained her! I will not lossse her again!"

"The choice is mine, Father. You know how much I enjoy adventure!"

"You will ssstay!" Now a transformation came over the Dragon King. His arms and legs twisted, his hands curling into claws. He swelled in size and as he grew, leathery wings burst from his back and a tail sprouted from below. The vestiges of humanity quickly slipped away. The dragon head crest slid downward, remolding into the true visage of the reptilian monarch.

Within seconds, a huge emerald dragon had taken the place of the scaled knight.

Darkhorse backed several steps, but he was not daunted by the leviathan. Powerful though the Dragon King might be, the eternal had faced such strength before. If need be, he would defend himself, although the shadow steed hoped it would not come to that. The drake's concern was for the welfare of his daughter.

"Good-bye, Father!" Yssa called. To Darkhorse, she whispered, "Be prepared to leave here when I say so."

The dragon unfurled wings that nearly spanned the entire width of the great cavern. "Think what you do, Yssssa! Thisss is no tryst! Thisss is no game!"

"For once I agree with you, Father." The enchantress pointed at the massive dragon.

Light flashed before the dragon's crimson orbs. He roared, startled.

"Time to go!" Yssa called merrily.

Darkhorse followed her lead. The cavern faded even while the dragon sought to regain his sight. A moment later a vast field of wild grass formed around them. Darkhorse silently cursed his haste. He had transported both of them to the former Barren Lands.

The grass seemed to take note of Yssa the moment the pair appeared, straining toward her like a pack of puppies yearning to be petted. The eternal shifted ground, trying to avoid the tendrils.

"He always had such a temper," his companion remarked. "I knew that he'd grown careless, otherwise he would've never been diverted by such a simple spell. He'll give in now that he knows there's no stopping me." She peered around. "I wouldn't have thought you'd take us here."

"It was the nearest location that did not take us toward Zuu or back toward Penacles! Had I had a moment more, I would have chosen a better location. Away!" The last was directed toward the increasingly inquisitive blades of grass.

"They don't mean any harm." Yssa lowered one hand enough so that the grass could touch it. "They'd only harm a drake of clan Brown and there aren't many of those left."

"Nonetheless, I still do not like their inquisitiveness! Make them cease so that I can think!"

She whispered something to the plants, which immediately stilled. Yssa then smiled at the shadow steed, an action that did nothing to ease his tension. He was beginning to regret agreeing to take her on as his companion. If not for the fact that she knew Zuu so much better than he did . . .

"I only need a few minutes to create an illusion around us. We'll be a rider and mount from the southern horse ranches. All I have to do is weather myself a bit and make you look more like one of the browns they raise down there."

"I can easily form the proper disguise if you will but show me an image."

She nodded. "Good. The less spellcasting around us, the less chance of someone detecting it. The medallion's good, but it's got limits."

He twisted his head around to look at her. "Why are you doing this, Yssa? This need not concern you."

"But it does." That was all she would say, but a trace of anger in her tone hinted at something more. Her mood abruptly changed again. "Well, shall we begin?"

Yssa insisted on a quick journey to the south so that the shadow steed could study the horses raised there. Darkhorse needed only a few moments to inspect the creatures in order to make the adjustments to his form. His companion was delighted with his shifting abilities.

"Why do you always choose a horse, though?" she finally asked. "Why not some other form like that of a man? You could probably imitate one easily."

"I prefer this form. It has grace, beauty."

"But you could transform into something else . . ."

"With more difficulty than you imagine." That was not entirely true, but he saw no need for her to know all his capabilities. "I have adapted myself to the basic form of a horse, and having utilized that shape for so very long, minor transformations such as this are simple. It would require much more effort to adapt to a completely new shape, such as that of a man or a drake."

"A pity. It could've been handy."

The enchantress had also changed, although her transformation was simply an illusion. In order to avoid enshrouding herself in too powerful a spell, Yssa had kept her alterations minor, changing only enough to keep her from resembling herself. She still looked like a native of Zuu, but one more muscular and plain of features. Her outfit was simple and functional, the type worn by those more accustomed to herding horses rather than city life. Her clothing was real, albeit adjusted to conform with her illusionary appearance.

It was but a short leap to the vicinity of the city. Yssa chose a location that would give them the privacy their sudden arrival required. After all, their disguises would not have mattered much if someone had noticed them materialize. Once it was clear that they had arrived undetected, the pair immediately traveled to the main road, there joining others with business in Zuu.

"Less business than usual," the enchantress whispered. The eternal could not reply, but he flicked his ears in a manner they had decided would indicate his agreement. The southern road to Zuu was indeed less congested than it should have been. Horse trading was still important to the kingdom, which meant that there should have been many travelers riding to and from the city. A few merchants rode south, no doubt to buy directly from the ranches, but their numbers were far less than what would have been expected at this time of year. Not all the horses bred in Zuu were used for Lanith's armies. There should have still been a thriving business . . . except that many of the kingdom's customers now faced the possibility that their former trading partner now eyed them as future vassals.

Not every inhabitant of Zuu had to be pleased by the king's decision to expand his domain. Many of the merchants had to be suffering greatly by now.

To their surprise, however, the gates were no more well protected than during Darkhorse's previous visit with Cabe. The shadow steed had expected more security, but while several of the king's guard did patrol the gate, they asked no more questions than previous. Darkhorse received one or two admiring remarks, but otherwise the soldiers did nothing to slow the pair.

Before they were allowed to enter, though, the,. captain of the guard, a graying, hook-nosed woman taller and broader than the Gryphon, handed a token to Yssa. "You know the rules, right? Keep it with you at all times. You might be checked for it at any time by a member of the guard. Understand?"

"I do." The enchantress took the token and dropped it in a pouch tied at her side.

Darkhorse hoped that the medallion given to them by the Green Dragon functioned well. Between Yssa and him, the pair surely radiated much power. Even sorcerers as simpleminded as the bunch that worked for the king of Zuu could detect them given half the chance. Sorcerous shields were of no help, either. According to Yssa, someone among the horse king's hired mages, probably Saress, had devised the tokens so that the very shields that would have normally hidden the presence of the spellcasters actually betrayed them. That meant that neither Yssa nor the eternal dared add their own shield spells to that of the medallion.

No one confronted them as they journeyed through the city, yet Darkhorse could not shake his uneasiness. Everything seemed perfectly normal, but each moment he expected a legion of ragtag sorcerers to materialize from the shadows. He also still worried about the mysterious force King Lanith seemed to command. Even here in the city the shadow steed could detect no trace of its presence and yet he was certain that it lurked somewhere nearby.

Zuu itself presented nothing but the picture of calm and cleanliness. People still went about their daily business, arguing over prices in the marketplace or meeting with companions at the many taverns and inns around the city. Guards rode through the streets, but their manner was casual. Merchants from a few other kingdoms inspected horses for sale, a sign that business had not slacked off as much as Darkhorse had first supposed. Some folk, it seemed, were always willing to deal.

Despite all the horses, the streets and buildings of Zuu were among the whitest and newest-looking that the shadow steed had seen in quite some time. He noted men and women at work picking up after the horses. Others were scrubbing down a stable, one of many such structures located all over the city. The people of Zuu seemed to think nothing of the manual labor, however disgusting it might have seemed to some. Everything Darkhorse had heard about the horse people was true; they were bloodthirsty in battle, yet they also maintained a great belief in keeping their homes in order. The stench of hundreds of animals should have overpowered Zuu long ago, but one could barely smell them.

Yssa tugged lightly on the reins. Darkhorse slowed, then allowed her to guide him toward a stable.

As she dismounted, the enchantress took the opportunity to whisper, "My father has a man here. If anyone can give us some information about the palace, it'll be him."

He wanted to ask how *a* man who worked at a public stable would know much about the king's palace, but the coming of a groom prevented him from doing so.

"Good day to you," said the young blond man. "Can I help?"

"Is Trenlen here?"

The groom glanced back. "Trenlen's inside, but he's busy. Perhaps I could help you?"

"I'd rather wait. Trenlen's an old friend of my father's. He'll want to see me. You could see to my horse, though." She handed the reins to the groom, tossing him a coin at the same time. "Give him a good stall and some water. I'll take care of everything else as soon as I'm done with Trenlen."

"It would be no difficulty to rub him down—"

She smiled at him. Despite the plain features created by the illusion, she still had an effect on the young man, who blushed.

"I prefer to do that myself. He's special."

"All right." The groom stroked Darkhorse on the muzzle. "Come on, boy."

It frustrated the eternal to separate from his companion. What good would it do for him to wait in the stable? However, he had no choice. He would have to be patient while Yssa spoke with this Trenlen. He considered altering his appearance. Reshaping himself into a more humanoid form would gain him better access to things . . . but he was loath to abandon a shape that had served him so well.

He would be patient for the time being, but if the enchantress took too long, he would have to take charge of matters, whatever the cost. Each passing moment meant increased danger to Aurim. If not for the fact that he knew that Lanith wanted the younger Bedlam for his Magical Order, the shadow steed would have fretted more. Lanith would not want to harm Aurim; the lad had too much to offer the horse king if only the latter could bend the spellcaster to his will.

Be strong, Aurim. Be very strong.

Darkhorse's last glimpse of Yssa was of the sorceress entering the building next to the stable. Then his view became one of stall after stall, most of them inhabited. As he neared the first, the mare within grew anxious. The groom shushed her, but then the horse in the stall next to hers also grew jumpy.

They sensed the eternal's difference. Outside, the animals would have paid him little heed, but when trapped in close quarters with him, many horses were wont to grow nervous. Darkhorse wondered whether he would be able to stay here after all.

The groom evidently had similar thoughts, for he encouraged the shadow steed to a quicker pace. Soon they were past the other mounts and into an unoccupied part of the stable. Even then the young man with Darkhorse did not pause. The eternal began to suspect that he was going to end up back outside, but at the very last stall the groom finally halted.

"Can't go any farther, boy. I don't know why you make 'em so nervous, but they just have to be satisfied with you being all the way over here." The lad took a moment to stroke the eternal's muzzle. "Maybe they're just jealous because you look so good. I wonder if your mistress is trying to sell you to the master. Hope so. I'd get to ride you, then."

As much as Darkhorse appreciated the groom's good taste, he silently urged the boy to depart. While there was little the shadow steed could do from inside the stable, he could do nothing at all so long as his undesired admirer remained nearby.

Fortunately, the groom settled for watering him and then disappearing. By that time, the other mounts had settled down, although many turned a wary eye in his direction. Darkhorse ignored them, instead trying to decide what he dared risk.

Yssa had explained the range of her father's medallion and Darkhorse estimated that he was just barely within that safety margin. It was fortunate that the stable was not any longer; the shadow steed might have then risked the Order's notice.

Darkhorse was still debating his options when he heard someone approaching. It was Yssa, accompanied by a second, hulking figure with the look of a soldier upon him. The eternal tensed, suspicious that perhaps the Dragon King's talisman had not worked so well after all.

"I was beginning to think that you weren't in here at all," the enchantress whispered, her tone amused. "What did you do, scare all the other horses?"

"This is your partner?" asked her companion. Like many folk of Zuu, he wore his blond hair in a long ponytail. His round features were half-hidden by the thick, somewhat darker beard. "I admit he's a fine steed, but, my lady, that's all he—"

"You can speak to him, Darkhorse. This is Trenlen. He is one of my father's men."

"If you say so, then I am willing to risk speaking." The shadow steed chuckled as Trenlen's expression altered from disbelief to shock. "Greetings, Master Trenlen. You have a fine stable."

"I. . . thank you."

Yssa waited for the man to recover his wits, but when Trenlen continued to simply stare at Darkhorse, she finally snapped her fingers before him. "Pay attention, Trenlen. We can't remain here long."

"My. . . my apologies, my lady." Despite his best efforts to remain attentive, the man's eyes continued to drift to the eternal.

Sighing, the enchantress turned to Darkhorse. "We had a discussion concerning the palace and I think I've found out something of use to us. Lanith's sorcerers make their headquarters in what was once a part of the royal stables, but has long since been renovated. The king likes them near, but not too near."

"So Aurim is there?" Out of the corner of his vision, Dark- horse noticed Trenlen's eyes bulge. It seemed that each time the eternal did not behave like a real horse, the man was dumbstruck.

"No. I knew about the headquarters of the Order already and I didn't expect that your friend would be in there. Aurim Bedlam is too great a prize. Besides, he isn't one of Lanith's paid dogs. He's an unwilling recruit."

"So far you have told me nothing, then."

She frowned. "Just wait. Trenlen, tell him what you heard."

The stable owner recovered enough to explain, "Two of my daughters are in the palace guard. Brave warriors, brave lasses. They're loyal to my liege Green just as I am." His eyes narrowed in concern. "It's by their own choice they took such a position. They knew that it would help us keep an eye on Lanith. I've always been proud of them."

"I understand," returned the eternal, trying to maintain his patience. "They are to be commended. Yet, what news do you have?"

"Two things. One that I have known for a long time. That the king talks to himself at times, ignoring all others. Shadows seem to follow him, too. Maybe the work of his mistress, Saress. The other news I learned only two hours before you arrived. Saress arrived earlier with a young and—from my daughter's slightly biased description—handsome man who seemed to walk around as if half-asleep. He did whatever the enchantress told him to do."

So there was verification at last. The horse king did have Aurim Bedlam. "And is there more?"

"My eldest daughter was on duty when they brought the lad in. The king questioned him a little. Offered him a place in the Order. The lad said he'd try to escape if he could. In fact, from what my daughter said, it looked like the boy was already fighting their control."

Aurim had been fighting back? Perhaps there was hope. Perhaps Aurim had even already escaped. Darkhorse pressed, "Then what happened, Master Trenlen?"

"I don't know. The king dismissed everyone, including Saress. The last my girl saw of your friend and King Lanith was His Majesty facing the lad as if he didn't have a care in the world."

"Very odd. Is Lanith also a spellcaster?"

Yssa snorted. "Him? There's been no trace of sorcery in Lanith's family for as far back as anyone can recall. Until his interest in gathering sorcerers, this was one of the parts of the continent where you were least likely to find a spellcaster of any competence. The past monarchs of Zuu relied on the people's prowess with arms and their riding skills."

The shadow steed dipped his head in agreement. The people of Zuu had always been proud of their heritage. It had been a surprise to many when Lanith had chosen to augment his armies with sorcery.

A pair of men entered the stables, the same young groom accompanying them. Trenlen immediately reached out and rubbed Darkhorse on the neck. "Are you sure you won't sell him for less than that? I'd like him, but I can't afford so high a price."

Taking up the conversation, Yssa shook her head. "Not for a coin less, Trenlen. Take it or leave it."

Darkhorse watched the newcomers talk with the lad, then retrieve a pair of dusky horses. A minute later all three had departed.

When they were alone again, Trenlen exhaled. "We can't talk for too much longer. There'll be more folks in and out of here. Always gets busier toward evening."

"I have still not heard much of great aid to us," insisted the shadowy stallion. He glanced beyond the stable owner to assure himself that no one, especially one of the grooms, might suddenly surprise them again. "Do you know where Aurim Bedlam is now or not?"

"If my daughter is correct, he is being kept in a chamber below the throne room. It's a place where the king goes when he desires to be alone. . . or, as some say, to talk to himself without staring eyes around."

Yssa removed a small piece of paper from a pouch. "Trenlen's given me this. A crude map showing where this chamber is located in regards to the palace grounds." She unfolded the map and showed it to the eternal. The detail was sparse, but sufficient to give him some idea of where they had to go. "Will this be enough, do you think, Darkhorse?"

He eyed the large man. "You are certain of the accuracy of this map?"

"On my life and that of my daughters."

"It will do, then, Yssa. We must not wait any longer. I fear for Aurim."

Trenlen eyed the pair. "What will you do? You can't just go charging into the palace!"

"Leave that to us, Trenlen," the sorceress replied. "But it would be good if perhaps you could watch the doorway for a few moments. Make sure that no one comes inside."

The man still looked uncertain, but at last he nodded. "Aye, I can do that. Good luck to you."

As Trenlen walked away, Yssa whispered to Darkhorse, "It's best that he doesn't know any more than he needs to. We've risked his position just by coming here."

"I agree." The eternal shifted position. "Mount. We will be in and out of the palace before Lanith knows what is happening."

"Are you certain you can do this?"

"I am Darkhorse! Of course I can!"

THE HORSE KING

She smiled. "I love your confidence."

From the entrance came the sounds of argument. The loudest voice belonged to Trenlen. Darkhorse glanced at his companion. Trenlen had gotten to the entrance just in time, but judging by the others' insisting tones, there was no telling how successful he would be in keeping the newcomers out. By rights, the man could not keep customers from their mounts. He risked his business by doing so, not to mention raising questions better left unanswered.

An idea occurred to Darkhorse, one that would solve a small problem nagging him. "Yssa. I need a little more time for this. You had better help Trenlen delay them. Give me but two minutes, then hurry back. They must not enter, or they might see something they should not. I am going to have to create a very particular type of blink hole."

She looked uncertain, but finally agreed. "I'll do what I can."

"Then hurry." The shadow steed nudged her forward. Yssa ran toward the entrance, not looking back. Darkhorse watched her for a second, then backed into the most shadowy corner of the stable.

The woman was capable and had already helped him much, but what Darkhorse intended he had to do alone. He could not risk another's life nor could he risk his own concentration. The shadow steed had enough to concern him without also worrying about Yssa's safety. He had resigned himself to her presence, but secretly had hoped for some excuse to leave her behind for her own good. Now he had the opportunity.

The moment she was out of sight, Darkhorse acted. He did have to make a blink hole to enter the palace, but not one as complex as he had indicated to Yssa. Still, one part of his explanation to her had been true; no one else could be allowed into the stable while he was creating it. Blink holes oft times opened up with a bright flash that no one could have missed.

Darkhorse pictured the layout of the palace, combining what he knew of its exterior with what Trenlen's map revealed. It gave him a more than adequate path to create. Even if Aurim proved not to be in the chamber, Darkhorse expected to be able to sense the lad once he was so near. Cabe would have called him overly optimistic, but the shadow steed did not see it that way.

The hole opened up instantly, a glaring circle of light in the darkness of the stable. Several horses stirred, some of them kicking at their stalls or trying to pull free. Then, with one glance toward the entrance of the stable, Darkhorse sloughed off his disguise and darted inside. As he entered the blink hole, he thought he heard someone call out, but by then it was too late to stop him.

Darkhorse wasted no time trying to reach his destination. He wished that he could have used a quicker teleportation spell, but the shadow steed wanted *some* advance warning should there prove to be a defensive spell between himself and his destination.

A moment later, that proved to be a fortuitous decision, for Darkhorse nearly collided with a peculiar field enshrouding the entire palace. It was a complex warning spell, one that would have alerted everyone in the building had the shadow steed simply tried to transport himself inside. The field was an admirable effort on someone's part, probably that of Saress. None of the other spellcasters was likely this competent.

Despite its complexity, however, Darkhorse was not deterred. He had faced far more cunning spells. The knowledge gathered over centuries easily enabled him to cross through without causing even the slightest ripple.

He materialized in the chamber without difficulty, only to find that it was empty. Yet, Darkhorse still sensed the lingering presence of the young sorcerer. Aurim had been here not long before. It was very possible that he had missed Cabe's son by as little as an hour. Darkhorse, his sight completely adjusted to the gloom, glanced at his surroundings. The room was sparsely decorated. There were a few old tapestries on the walls, tapestries that were tattered and moldy, as if the chamber had been forgotten for several years. A single chair stood in the very center of the room, the only piece of furniture in sight. Dust covered everything but the chair and a path from the only door.

A slight tingle coursed through him. Something, some trace, reminded him of the past. . . but of what part of his past Darkhorse could not say. He searched with his power, but whatever it was was overwhelmed by Aurim's recent presence.

If the lad was not here, then where? The shadow steed reached out beyond the confines of the chamber, seeking the young sorcerer in every direction. Lanith would want to keep his prize nearby.

His probes met with no success, although once he thought he sensed Aurim. The trace vanished before Darkhorse could get a fix on it, though. He was forced to extend his search. As yet he had not sensed Saress or any of the other spellcasters, but the farther afield he had to search, the greater the risk that one of them might notice *him.*

Aurim, where are you? Darkhorse started to fear that Lanith had killed the young sorcerer, perhaps because Aurim would not agree to be his vassal. It was the only explanation that he had for not being able to locate the golden-haired spellcaster.

Darkhorse?

The mental plea was so tentative that at first the eternal did not realize what it was. Darkhorse sought out the source, but once more he was unsuccessful.

Darkhorse? Is that you?

Aurim? It felt like his friend, but still the shadow steed could not locate him. *Where are you?*

In a dungeon! Aurim sounded frightened yet relieved. *They've got a spell on me that won't allow me to use my powers to escape! Darkhorse, they tried to take control of my mind!*

Recalling how distraught Aurim had been when he had discovered that Duke Toma had once played with his memories, the eternal understood just how upset his young companion had to be now. Very few things frightened Aurim Bedlam as did the idea of another manipulating his thoughts. *Have they hurt you?*

No, but they'll be back to try again soon! Darkhorse, you wouldn't believe the power that Lanith controls! It—

You can tell me later, Aurim! The important thing now is to help me locate you so that we can depart this terrible place! You must concentrate! Concentrate as hard as you can so that I can find your position!

I'll try! The sorcerer ended the conversation, but did not sever the weak link. Instead, Darkhorse felt an increased sense of Aurim's presence. The younger Bedlam was powerful and even despite the handicaps his captors' spells had put on him, his will was great. In fact, it was more focused than Darkhorse could ever recall. If one thing good had come out of the kidnapping, it was Aurim's increased control over his will.

Slowly the eternal homed in on Aurim's location. Deeper down, as he had expected, but far more to the north. That placed Aurim near the vicinity of the Magical Order's living quarters.

Darkhorse had already risked discovery the moment he had abandoned Yssa and the protection of her medallion. By entering the palace he further increased the threat, yet he had no choice. *I must act the moment I know exactly where they keep him! We must be gone within seconds!*

He sent a subtle probe in the general direction of Aurim, trying to detect the nearby presence of Saress or any of the others. Darkhorse sensed nothing, but briefly he experienced a peculiar echo effect, as if his probe had turned around and detected his own presence. The effect was momentary and he shrugged it off. What was important was to rescue Aurim.

Darkhorse? Are you still there?

I am, Aurim. Prepare yourself Are you chained?

Yes. They're iron chains. If I could use my powers, they wouldn't matter.

Any guards?

No. They didn't feel I needed one.

That was good. One less hurdle. Darkhorse readied himself. *Very well, Aurim. Here I come!*

The short distance was nothing in comparison to his earlier treks. Darkhorse vanished from the one chamber, almost instantly appearing at his destination. He felt a brief disorientation that caused his vision to blur, but the sensation passed.

"Darkhorse! Are you all right?"

"Aurim?" The shadow steed twisted around, finally locating the sorcerer. Aurim Bedlam was chained against the far wall of his cell. Torchlight shone weakly through the bars of the small window in the cell door, just enough illumination to reveal the haggard, pale features of the young spellcaster.

With a snort of disgust for his companion's captors, the eternal stepped closer and inspected the chains. They were, as Aurim had said, simple iron chains. Under normal conditions, the lad should have been able to remove them without any trouble, even considering his past lack of control.

A simple glance by Darkhorse caused both bracelets to quietly open. Aurim rubbed his wrists, smiling in gratitude.

"We must be away from here immediately, Aurim! Mount up and I will take us back to your parents"

The sorcerer quickly obeyed, saying nothing. Darkhorse concentrated. No blink hole, this time. He needed the swiftest if least secure teleportation spell he knew.

The cell faded away. The vague outline of what Darkhorse knew to be the gardens of the Manor formed around the pair. They were nearly home.

That was when something pulled them back. "Darkhorse!"

He could not reply to his friend, so caught up was he in trying to fight the forces acting against them. Whatever power Lanith had raised, it was stronger than he would have believed. It was also the most unusual force Darkhorse had ever fought, for it seemed to come from a number of sources even though it acted as if it came from only one.

Lanith's sorcerers working in concert? Darkhorse could not believe that the ragtag bunch could summon such strength even together. More important, he doubted that they could coordinate their efforts so effectively. This attack was being guided by a masterful force.

An intelligent force . . .

His struggles went for naught. Darkhorse and Aurim finally rematerialized, but their new location was neither the Manor nor the dungeon. The shadow steed and his companion now stood in the center of the very same dust-laden chamber that Darkhorse had first visited in his search.

This time, however, it was not uninhabited. A single torch posted in the wall by the door illuminated the room enough so that they could readily see King Lanith sitting in the lone chair. The horse king's eyes gleamed as he stared at the ebony stallion. It was a possessive stare, one that unsettled Dark- horse more than it should have.

"At last. . ." Lanith smiled wide. "Magnificent!" Darkhorse attempted another spell. The same force that had brought him here crushed his attempt.

The horse king stood. "You're even more amazing than I could've believed! Truly you're worthy of being my mount!"

"Worthy of *what?*" Despite their predicament, Darkhorse could only laugh. *"I? You think me your mount? You are more than mad, King Lanith!"*

The monarch of Zuu paid his retort no mind, instead looking up past the shadow steed. "Aurim."

A pair of hands, Aurim's hands, touched the eternal on the neck.

Darkhorse lost all control of his form. His legs stiffened as if frozen and he found he could not even move his neck. When he attempted to alter his shape, nothing happened.

"He is yours, Your Majesty." The voice was Aurim Bedlam's, but there was a coldness to it that the shadow steed had never heard before. Darkhorse felt him dismount as he added, "Just as planned."

"Very good. Very good."

Aurim! the shadow steed silently called. *Aurim!* His call went unheeded, though. Either the sorcerer did not sense it or he had no desire to respond.

The young man stepped before him, then performed a mock bow. "I'll leave you now, Darkhorse, so that an old friend can have a word with you."

Without waiting for permission from Lanith, Aurim Bedlam, smiling pleasantly, vanished.

"Well," the king of Zuu commented to the chamber walls. "You did it. You promised and you delivered."

A giggle echoed throughout the chamber, a giggle that grew stronger with each second. Shadows formed by the king, shadows that began to solidify into one form.

"I told you I would, great majesty, oh, yes, I did! Did you think I would fail you? Never, never . . ."

Had he been able to move at all, Darkhorse would have shivered. He knew the voice. Now the eternal even sensed the growing presence of its source, a thing that he had thought long, long trapped in a place from which it could not escape.

It cannot be . . . it cannot be him . . .

Yet as the shadows became a tiny, ebony puppet that floated at eye level, Darkhorse could no longer deny the truth. Unbidden came the name that he had tried to forever eradicate from his memory.

Ice-blue eyes stared at ice-blue eyes. "And so the story continues . . ." The ebony being giggled despite having no mouth. "And what a part I have set aside for you, my brother, *my self.*"

Yureel . . .

Chapter Nine

Yssa sensed the spell even as she tried her best to aid Trenlen in stalling the two ranchers seeking to retrieve their mounts. Darkhorse had opened the way to the palace, which meant that she had to find some method by which to send the men away so that she could quickly return to him. The longer the hole remained open, the more chance there was of stirring the interest of the Order despite the talisman.

It was Trenlen who finally solved the problem. He put a companionable arm around each of the pair, saying, "Really, friends, it won't take long. The man's horse is skittish. He bought the thing in Gordag-Ai and you know what kind of horses they breed there." This brought some grudging nods from the men, both of whom, from what the enchantress understood, were members of a family controlling one of the largest breeding ranches of Zuu. "Why don't you come inside and we'll have a drink on me. I'd say that by the time we finish, the man and his horse'll be out of our hair. Isn't that right, darling?"

Yssa took his cue. "That's right. You take care of them, my love. I'll see to everything here. Gentlemen . . ."

The two men with Trenlen allowed themselves to be led away, the offer of a drink no doubt the deciding factor. Yssa watched them for a moment, then hurried back inside.

She caught sight of the eternal just as he stepped through a blink hole. The enchantress called out, but Darkhorse did not look back. The moment he was completely through, the hole vanished.

Damn him! What does he think he doing? Yssa rushed to the empty stall seeking some trace of her companion, but the huge stallion had left no sign. She blew very well where he had gone and the knowledge made her shiver. Poor Miklo had entered the palace and he had never come out. The memory of the last seconds of their link still remained with her. A sense of falling and falling without end . . . then nothing.

Darkhorse was far more powerful than lost Miklo, but that did not mean the magical stallion was immune from danger. That had already been proven to her. More important, Darkhorse did not understand Zuu and its monarch the way Yssa, who had lived here for many years, did. Yssa was old enough to recall Prince Blane and the old king. Lanith was neither his brother nor his father. He had become a driven man, capable of anything if it furthered his goal, and now he appeared to have the power to back his obsessive nature.

I have to talk with Trenlen! He might have a suggestion! The enchantress rushed back to the entrance, wondering how she could interrupt him without raising the suspicions of the two men he had invited for a drink. With Darkhorse gone, Yssa supposed that she could tell them that their mounts were now accessible. If they were still in so great a hurry, perhaps they would forgo the rest of their drink . . .

Unfortunately, she had scarcely stepped outside when she sensed the nearby presence of at least two sorcerers. Not Saress, whom Yssa knew too well, but a pair of less competent ones. They had some power, though. The enchantress tensed. Ponteroy, perhaps. He was the only other senior member of the Magical Order that Yssa had any respect for. The man was an overdressed dandy, but he did have skill of a sort . . . and at this moment he was much too close for comfort.

Reaching into her pouch, Yssa checked for the medallion. Its presence did not do much to comfort her. She found it highly suspicious that the two sorcerers she sensed were closing on her general vicinity from opposite directions. Perhaps she had been wrong to think the medallion had been strong enough to shield both Darkhorse and herself.

Whatever the reason, she had to leave quickly. Yssa did not want to endanger Trenlen. Lanith dealt harshly with spies.

She contemplated transporting herself away, but decided that doing so would do more to reveal her presence. The medallion had its limits. Yssa looked around, studying the vicinity. Better to lose herself among the evening crowds. Her illusion still held, so even Ponteroy, who had seen her once in the past, would not recognize her.

A busy inn a short distance down the street seemed the perfect destination. Yssa walked casually toward it, trying not to look around any more than what would be normal. The two sorcerers were very nearby. Now she sensed that one was definitely Ponteroy, his presence ever tinged by a dark, almost oily aura. It was hard not to underestimate him because of his appearance.

The inn was as crowded as the enchantress had hoped it would be. The tone was slightly more subdued than she recalled from her years past here, but that was not surprising considering the current situation. Lanith might have his people stirred up for war, but that did not mean that they did not contemplate the possible results of that war on their own time. Yssa knew that the majority of Zuu's inhabitants preferred the peaceful life. They were always willing to defend themselves or a cause they believed in, but conquest was not a national goal. That was a part of their kingdom's nomadic past. Only Lanith dreamed of creating an empire, but then, Lanith was king and in Zuu that was enough for the people. He commanded and they obeyed.

Locating a seat deep in the common room, Yssa did her best to look like a weary traveler. A serving woman glanced her way but did not immediately come over, more concerned, it seemed, with the male customers. Yssa, who had plied such a trade for a time, grimaced briefly. Men and women in Zuu might be more or less equal, but personal prejudices were rampant. She would be lucky if any of the serving women came by soon.

Even among so many people, it was not difficult for her to sense the presence of the nearby sorcerers. They were not trying to shield themselves, which possibly meant that they were not actually after her. Yssa hoped that was the case, but their path continued to hint otherwise. Now they were both so near that she almost expected to see one of them walk through the inn door.

A huge woman carrying a tray stepped in front of her. "Do you want food or drink?"

Ignoring the serving woman's flippant tone, Yssa replied, "I want some ale." Her eyes darted back to the door. "Some bread, too."

"I'm not certain about the ale, darling, but they'll certainly serve you bread in the dungeons."

The enchantress stared into the eyes of the serving woman. "Hello, Yssa," smirked the tall, plain figure.

She felt an invisible web fall upon her, a web of sorcery Yssa immediately knew had been designed to sap her of her strength. It would have worked, too, but the ploy was so typical of her adversary that even without forethought Yssa was prepared for it. Before the web could completely settle, Yssa vanished.

She reappeared an eye blink later in an alley not very far from the inn. The maneuver had been a risky one and only Yssa's comprehensive knowledge of Zuu had prevented her from possibly materializing in a wall. Such swift transportation spells were ever risky, especially those cast in the midst of danger . . . and there was no danger greater to Yssa than Saress.

I overestimated myself. She had evaded Saress for so very long that she had not sufficiently taken into account the other's skills. Yssa had told Darkhorse that the other sorceress might be a little stronger than she, but what she had failed to add was that Saress was also more practiced. Saress was at least a hundred years old, and it was said that at one time she had even convinced Azran Bedlam to reveal some of his secrets to her.

The alley was empty and Yssa sensed no sorcerers nearby, but she knew better than to believe that she was safe. The pair she had noted had possibly been decoys designed to keep her from noticing a shielded and disguised Saress. Now all three of them would be shielded. Worse, one of them *had* to be Ponteroy, who also could be quite devious. Saress would not waste her time working with the less competent spellcasters. She had been hunting for Yssa for far too long now to take such chances.

Hoping that the medallion would shield her to some extent, the disguised sorceress leaped to a new location. This time when she appeared, vertigo nearly overtook her. Yssa leaned against the wall of an elaborate house belonging to one of King Lanith's own generals, a veteran named Belfour who had been an admirer of hers when she had worked as a serving woman. Yssa often thought that it would have been better if Belfour had become king, he being remotely related to Lanith.

According to her sources, Belfour was supposed to be out in the field drilling His Majesty's armies, which was the reason she had chosen his estate for a momentary respite. Yssa doubted that Saress would expect her to use the home of so august a person as General Belfour. More likely the other sorceress would still be searching the vicinity of the inns and the grand marketplace.

It would have made sense to depart Zuu entirely and return to the safety of her father's domain, but Yssa was not quite ready to abandon Darkhorse despite his having left her. Of course, by this time the shadowy stallion should have rescued Aurim Bedlam and departed the kingdom for Penacles, but Yssa suspected that such was not the case. First, she was fairly certain that Darkhorse would have come back for her. Second, the confrontation with Saress had been too well executed to have been spur of the moment. Someone had been watching out for them.

The enchantress recalled her own words to Darkhorse. An intelligent force. She still recalled the first time she had sensed it. Never in her life had she felt such a peculiar, unsettling presence . . . although now that Yssa had spent some time around Darkhorse, she realized that there was something about the stallion that reminded her of Lanith's creature.

That was impossible, though. Everyone knew that there was nothing in the Dragonrealm like Darkhorse.

"So what do I do now?" she muttered. For years, Yssa had depended only on herself. She had not had to worry about others. Now she feared for a companion not even human. "You! What are you doing here?"

Startled, Yssa whirled around. Two soldiers, obviously members of the general's household guard, approached her with swords drawn. Yssa cursed herself for a mindless idiot. Of course they would be on duty even if their master was away. Being confronted by Saress so soon after Darkhorse's disappearance had left her much too befuddled for her own good.

She was not too worried, however. Swords might be a threat to most, but not to a skilled spellcaster. As the pair closed in on her, Yssa stared at their weapons.

The blades twisted, quickly intertwining with one another. Both men stumbled to a halt, tugging on their weapons. The enchantress concentrated, abandoning her latest location for the only one left that she believed to be safe. It frustrated her to keep running, but that was all that was left to her for now.

General Belfour's estate faded, to be replaced a moment later by thick forest. Yssa was back in the land of Dagora, her father's domain. She breathed a sigh of relief.

The sigh became a startled gasp as a hand took hold of her by the shoulder. She tried to vanish again, but nothing happened. Yssa tried one more time with the same results.

Her captor spun her around.

It had been quite some time since she had seen him, but Yssa could never forget Cabe Bedlam.

"I come here searching for my son and Darkhorse and find you instead. What are you doing here?" His expression indicated that he was not at all pleased to see her again.

The sorceress sought to regain her composure. She gave him the same smile that had enchanted so many without magic, but this time the results were not what she hoped. Cabe Bedlam was not at all moved by her beauty and her manner.

Belatedly, Yssa recalled that she still wore the illusion. He did not even know who she was, much less what she looked like. Seeing no reason to continue her masquerade, the enchantress dropped the illusion.

"You!" Bedlam's expression tightened further, as if he had suddenly found himself touching something rather foul. "Tori, isn't it?"

Rather disappointed in his lackluster reaction to her identity, Yssa did not immediately reply. The sorceress had changed since the last time she had met him, although admittedly their prior confrontation had been a short one. Perhaps this was simply a side that she had not noticed. Yssa was not certain that she cared for it.

"Darkhorse went looking for my son, who was supposed to be somewhere in Penacles. Darkhorse never came back with him and when I searched for both, I found no trace of their presence. It took some doing, but I tracked my shadowy friend to this general region . . . only instead of him, I sensed you."

"You *couldn't.* The medallion—"

Cabe's gaze cut off her protest. "I've the experience and knowledge of two lifetimes, although I can't expect you to understand what I mean. Sometimes it helps. Now, I'll ask you this once. What's happened to them? Some notions have been running through my imagination, but I'm hoping that you'll tell me I'm wrong, Tori."

Under his intense scrutiny, any thought of seduction faded. Only one thing interested Cabe Bedlam now. Yssa saw no reason to hold back. The master sorcerer was probably the only one who could really help her. "Lanith has your son . . . and I think he might also have Darkhorse."

"Tell me."

She did, trying her best not to leave anything out that might be of importance. The enchantress spoke of Saress and her masquerade, of Darkhorse's discovery and his determination to rescue Aurim as soon as possible, and of her own role in the situation. She ended with the shadow steed's disappearance and her narrow escape from the other spellcasters.

Yssa kept back only the truth about her origins. Knowing how Cabe Bedlam felt about her father, it made more sense than ever to avoid revealing the secret she had kept hidden so long.

As Yssa explained, Cabe Bedlam's expression grew so grim that the enchantress feared that some of his frustration and anger would spill onto her. Yssa did not relish facing the might of the strongest sorcerer in the land. Fortunately, Cabe's gaze finally shifted from her to the west . . . where Zuu lay.

"Damn Lanith . . . what right does he have to my son? What right does he have to *conquest?* All I've ever wanted for the Dragonrealm is peace!"

Knowing he required no answer from her, Yssa took a step away from the robed sorcerer. Although Cabe Bedlam's voice was still quiet, she could sense the energy building around him, sorcerous energy that he would eventually have to unleash somehow. Yssa had a suspicion that it would not be long, either.

"You didn't see Aurim in Zuu, did you?"

"No. I only know what I told you. Trenlen's daughters saw him."

"Who's this Trenlen, anyway? Why did he help you?"

Answering those questions meant treading in dangerous territory, but Yssa did the best she could. "Someone I know from when I still lived there. He doesn't care for what the king is doing. Neither do his daughters."

Cabe clearly knew that she had not told him everything, but fortunately, he chose not to pursue the matter. "Do you remember where it was Aurim was supposed to be?"

"Yes." She described the location, but he seemed dissatisfied.

"Be silent for a moment. I'll try something." Cabe shut his eyes before the enchantress could reply. Energy continued to gather around him.

Yssa sensed a spell, probably a probe since she noted no changes around them. The sorcerer was seeking the mind of his son.

Moments later Cabe opened his eyes, frowning. "Hard to say, but I think I know where they are. Strange, though . . ."

"What?"

"Darkhorse . . . it was as if he were in two nearby but different locations." The master mage waved off his 'own comment. "Zuu reeks with sorcery. It's even worse than we thought. Once I rescue them, we'll have to talk to the Gryphon. Lanith's gone too far."

"What are you going to do?" Yssa had a notion, but prayed that she was wrong.

Looking at her as if she should have understood immediately, Cabe replied, "I'm going in there, of course."

This was too much for her. Darkhorse she could understand charging into the fray, but Cabe Bedlam was supposed to have more sense. Had he not faced down the Ice Dragon, the Quel, Shade the warlock, and countless other foes? Surviving such adversaries required not only great skill and power, but also intelligence.

Yet . . . it *was* his son that the horse king had kidnapped. Even though her father and she had been estranged for several years, she knew that she would have tried to rescue him if he had been in the same predicament as the younger Bedlam.

"You don't know Zuu the way I do, though," she told him, feeling a sense deja' vu. "You need me. I know the city."

Cabe eyed her with some skepticism, probably recalling their previous encounter. "This is something I'd best do alone. This time, I know what to expect."

Before she could say anything more, the sorcerer turned his gaze in the direction of Zuu. Yssa sensed power rising from within and around the master mage. Once again, Cabe Bedlam's incredible power astounded her. The enchantress briefly toyed with her old notion of seeking him as the perfect mate, but she doubted that even at her most seductive she would be able to turn his head. The sorcerer had that look that said he was very much married and enjoyed being so. Yssa had never seen the Lady Bedlam, but decided that the other sorceress had to be someone very special.

"I see the barriers," Cabe whispered. "Interesting. Grandfather would've liked their design."

Yssa had no idea what he meant by that, but the matter was moot. Cabe Bedlam blinked . . . and was gone.

"More stubborn than Darkhorse," she muttered. That was it, then. Cabe Bedlam had gone to retrieve his son and comrade from Zuu. If anyone could do it, he could. That left Yssa with the question of just what she should do next. Return to her father? Not yet. Perhaps she should journey back to the former Barren Lands. It was the one place Yssa was certain that Saress would not find her, not that the witch was probably looking for her anymore. Saress certainly had better things to do than go pursuing Yssa yet again. They had played this game often enough.

The grasslands, then. No matter how stirred up her emotions were, the enchanted field where she had brought Cabe and Darkhorse after their last encounter always soothed her. It still amused her how anxious the shadow steed had been to depart it. The grass would never have harmed him. It probably could not have done so even if it had tried.

Yssa felt for the medallion her father had given her. Considering how poorly it had worked so far, she was tempted to just leave it here, but her father would be upset with her if he found out. She decided that she would return it after she had spent some time recovering her calm.

Yes, a rest would do her nicely first . . .

What sounded like the crackle of thunder made her stiffen. A sudden, powerful gust of wind threatened to push her against the nearest tree. Yssa sensed sorcery, but from exactly what source or direction she could not say.

A man-sized projectile materialized out of the air, flying past at a remarkable rate of speed. Only as it dropped toward the earth did the sorceress see that it *was a* man. Cabe Bedlam, in fact.

Too startled to act, Yssa watched as the other spellcaster plummeted to what certainly had to be his death. He had materialized far too high up and flown at far too swift a speed to land safely. Belatedly she raised a hand, trying to concentrate enough to cast a spell.

At the very last moment, the sorcerer's progress slowed. A small blue aura formed around him. Cabe Bedlam struck the ground hard, but not nearly so hard as Yssa had feared. Probably he had been knocked unconscious.

She started toward him but then had to leap behind a tree as the air opened up again. This time, a half-dozen figures appeared. They stood together, surveying the area with varying looks of interest and trepidation.

In their lead was Ponteroy. In one hand he held a short staff topped by a crystal carved into the head of a horse. Yssa knew that the gaudily-clad sorcerer used the staff to better focus his own powers.

Of the other spellcasters, most, including the older woman, were vaguely familiar to her, but their identities were not so important as the fact that despite their obvious anxiousness, they began to search the area very methodically. This was not the collection of misfits that she recalled from several weeks back. They still had rough edges, but the Magical Order looked much more like a cohesive fighting unit than Miklo had indicated during their final meeting.

"Look over there," Ponteroy commanded a youth, the only one completely unknown to Yssa. She suspected that he was one of the students kidnapped from Penacles, but now he seemed an eager servant of Lanith.

They were searching for Cabe Bedlam, of course, but fortunately, Ponteroy had chosen to focus on the wrong area. That meant that she had a chance to get to the sorcerer first and spirit him away before the others noticed.

Crouching and hoping that the medallion would do her some good after all, Yssa moved slowly toward where Cabe lay unmoving. Fortunately for the master sorcerer, he had landed behind some trees. Yssa also noticed that she could barely detect the unconscious spellcaster, which meant that he had woven a fairly complex shield spell around himself. That would not hide him forever, though, which was why she had to reach him quickly.

The sorcerer's still unmoving form worried her immensely. The enchantress began to wonder whether he had been more severely injured than she had first thought, but since he lay on his stomach she could not see what his face might reveal. However, when Yssa tried to turn him over, an invisible barrier more than an inch thick prevented her. No matter how she tried to move him, the spell would not allow her to get any grip.

"Sometimes you can be too safe," she whispered to the unconscious figure. Yssa quickly glanced at the hunters, now distant, only partially visible forms. The longer they took, the better. She needed time to decide how to get around Cabe's protective spells.

Then a second crackle of thunder made her look around with renewed anxiety. She sensed that someone new and much more capable had joined the pursuing mages, someone with abilities far more impressive than those of either Saress or Ponteroy. An unfamiliar voice said something unintelligible, something that made Ponteroy reply angrily. The newcomer added one more comment, then an unnerving silence ensued.

257

Yssa redoubled her efforts to move Cabe. She tried to pick up his head, but only managed to cause him to shift a little. However, the movement evidently was enough to wake the sorcerer. Cabe Bedlam groaned, then slowly opened his eyes.

Yssa leaned close, whispering, "I can't touch you! Let me touch you so that we can get out of here before they find us!"

He closed his eyes, seeming to drift off again. However, the protective spells around him lessened, then vanished. Cabe opened his eyes again. "Do what . . . you can now. My concentration is still too . . . I can't focus enough . . . yet."

Yssa nodded, seizing hold of him.

A figure clad in brown sorcerer's robes suddenly materialized at her side. Yssa looked up into an ugly face whose most dominant feature was one of the longest, sharpest noses the enchantress had ever seen. The spellcaster was bald, not even having eyebrows. He reminded her of a vulture.

"Here he's lying," the vulture called out, "and he's got someone with—"

A heavy branch suddenly swung down and swatted the bald hunter in the face, cutting off his words. With a groan, he fell back, stunned.

Having momentarily disposed of one foe, Yssa found her mind now blank. She had to take Cabe away from here, but the question of where was too much for her muddled senses.

From all around her Yssa felt the use of sorcery. The other spellcasters were acting in *concert* now, creating some sort of prison . . . and yet she could still not focus her mind. Should she take Cabe to her father? That did not seem wise. Should she take him to the grasslands? He might react to them the same way Darkhorse had. Why of all times was it impossible for her to think?

As if sensing her dilemma, her companion whispered, "The Manor. Take us there. Let me show you."

With one hand, he touched her forehead. An image of a place formed, an image so lifelike, Yssa almost tried to reach out and touch it.

It was a house, an abode, but like none she had ever come across in her life. Massive stone walls merged with barriers formed from the very earth. Chiseled marble and cut wood had been used to build much of the structure, but the right side seemed to have been built into a huge and still living tree. Atop the roof and overlooking the front entrance was a metallic figure, a tall Seeker. The avian creature was so realistic he seemed ready to swoop down on unsuspecting newcomers.

The building was at least three stories tall and wider than some barons' castles that Yssa had seen. A small army could have dwelled within those walls.

"There. The Manor," the sorcerer concluded. "Now you know where to go."

She did and just in time, too, for several yards away, a second figure materialized. He was not one of the original hunters, but Yssa knew that he had to be one of their fellows. Although escape was what she should have been concentrating on, the enchantress could not help staring first. Before her stood a handsome, golden-haired man who resembled a hero from the epics spun in the taverns of Zuu. Her heart beat faster and Yssa had to remind herself that this man was an enemy.

"Who're you?" he demanded. The voice was the same one that she had heard giving commands to Ponteroy.

Yssa desperately thought about Cabe Bedlam's home, the mysterious and legendary Manor. She pictured it as he had shown it to her.

"Stop—" the other sorcerer began. A brief hesitant look crossed his features, then fury took over.

His darkening visage was the last thing the enchantress saw before the world around her faded.

For a moment she and Cabe hung suspended in the middle of nothing, then, thankfully, a new scene unfolded. Gone was the forest, although in the distance Yssa could still see tall trees. Instead, the pair of them had ended up in a huge, well- manicured garden that stretched long into the distance. Some of the bushes had been trimmed into the shapes of animals. A marble walkway led toward what looked like a hedge maze. Here and there, benches dotted the area.

Someone cleared their throat. Yssa looked over her shoulder and saw a tall, scarlet-tressed woman dressed in a beautiful forest-green gown. Behind her was the back of a huge edifice one side of which was part of an immense tree.

"I would venture to say," the woman remarked in a very cold voice, "that you must be the one he called Tori. Now would you like to explain to me what you're doing with my husband?"

Knowing more than most about the legendary Lady of the Amber, Yssa involuntarily cringed.

"It's all right, Gwen," muttered Cabe. He untangled himself from Yssa and tried to rise. Halfway up, the sorcerer seized his head in both hands. "Except for every bone and muscle aching and an incredible throbbing in my head, that is. If anything . . . if anything, Yssa probably saved me from capture."

"Yssa? I thought her name was Tori and what's this about capture? You went to find our son." Lady Bedlam's tone grew anxious. "What's happened to him, Cabe? Where is he?"

"He's a prisoner of Zuu. The young woman he met in Penacles was evidently a sorceress working for the horse king. Saress was her true name, I believe."

"A . . . prisoner." Cabe Bedlam's wife grew furious again, but at least this time her fury was not focused on Yssa. "How dare that barbaric horse trainer hold my son! We have to get him back immediately!"

"That may not be so simple--" Yssa began, clamping her mouth shut the moment the other sorceress looked at her. She had made a mistake reminding Gwendolyn Bedlam of her presence.

"What she means," Cabe quickly interjected, "is that Zuu is better protected than I could ever imagine. I can't even get inside the city walls. In fact, when I tried, I was thrown back so hard it stunned me for several minutes. If not for Yssa, Lanith's spellcasters would've captured me." He shook his head, then grimaced in evident pain. "They acted in unison, nearly perfect unison. I felt it even as they hammered me. I don't think I've ever heard of spellcasters working so well together, not even the Dragon Masters."

He suddenly turned his face away from his wife, but Yssa, who now had a clear look at it, saw the anxiety and pain. Her suspicions about what she had seen just before they had escaped were now verified by his obvious pain. He knew the golden-haired sorcerer who had nearly captured them.

If she could not see his expression, Gwendolyn Bedlam could certainly read his turbulent emotions in his actions. The enchantress put a comforting hand on her husband's arm. "Cabe, what is it?"

Swallowing, Cabe looked at her. "Gwen, one of the attackers was . . . it was Aurim!"

"That's impossible!" She jerked her hand away. "He wouldn't—"

"And I don't think he did." The robed figure stared at Yssa. "Did you sense it? Did you get a chance to probe him?"

It had not occurred to Yssa to do any such thing. All that had concerned her was to escape, taking her stunned companion with her. "I didn't . . . I don't understand . . ."

"No, you wouldn't. I probably sensed him just before you did, I suppose. I reacted without really thinking. I could feel the presence of my son, but when I tried to speak to him through his mind in order to avoid alerting the others, I ran across—" He stopped,

259

clearly unable to believe what he was saying. "There was another mind overlapping his own. I couldn't even reach Aurim's!"

"Possession?" Lady Bedlam snapped. "Not possession! Not after what Toma did to him!"

An intelligent force Yssa recalled Miklo's last moments again. "The thing in the palace! The thing that Lanith controls!"

Oddly, Cabe Bedlam shook his head. "I would've thought so, but it can't be. That can't be what I sensed . . . and yet, what I sensed could not be the truth, either." He looked at both of them. "What I sensed . . . was *Darkhorse.*"

"What?" both women cried. Yssa wondered if Cabe still suffered from a concussion. He had to be mistaken.

"It was Darkhorse," he insisted. "I know Darkhorse's magical trace. There's nothing like it in all the Dragonrealm. *He's* seized Aurim's mind . . . and now it seems he's forcing our son to serve the king of Zuu, even if it means fighting us!"

Chapter Ten

Yureel.

If there was a thing in all of creation that Darkhorse feared, it was Yureel. He had believed he had seen the last of the monster, but here Yureel was, once more turning living beings into puppets to be wasted in horrific tableaus of violence all for the sake of the mad creature's personal entertainment. That was all any other being was to Yureel, a thing to be utilized for his enjoyment, then discarded when of no further value.

The shadow steed still could not move. The spell that Aurim had cast was a thorough one thanks to the guidance of the macabre little figure. Aurim Bedlam had probably been the thrall of Yureel since soon after his capture, a thrall now eager to do whatever his master desired. Somewhere deep inside, the young sorcerer's mind might still be active, but it hardly mattered. Darkhorse had seen few who could escape the control of the shadow man.

He himself had been one of those few, but now Yureel had him again.

Through Aurim's sorcery they had moved him to a stone structure that had, until recently, served as part of the royal stable. That was all he had been told by the king of Zuu, who, whenever he visited, stared at the shadow steed with a greedy eye. Darkhorse had been here for two days now, unable to move or even use his power to send a mental summons to Cabe or the Gryphon. It was clear that Yureel had spent much time plotting Darkhorse's capture.

Why this, Yureel? Why not simply do what I know you desire? Why not finish me? The sinister little demon had some wicked torture in mind. That had to be it. Yureel wanted him to suffer great mental anguish, vengeance for the ebony puppet's long imprisonment in the empty realm known only as the Void.

Perhaps that was why Darkhorse was here. Perhaps Yureel planned on keeping him here for a few centuries . . . but, no, that was ridiculous. Besides, King Lanith seemed expectant about something. *If the madman thinks—*

A dread rolled over him. Darkhorse sensed another presence, one so much like himself that only he could have noticed the difference.

The insane giggle floated about the chamber. A tiny speck of darkness in one far corner suddenly expanded until it formed a nearly human figure only a foot tall. Once fully shaped, Yureel floated serenely toward his prisoner.

"I do hope you've been enjoying the accommodations, brother dear!" The miniature phantom drifted to eye level. "I wanted you to feel at home since you enjoy that absurd form so much!" Yureel cocked his head. "Oh, dear. I forgot that you're speechless for now, aren't you? That'll teach you to be impolite to our gracious host."

Briefly granted speech in the room where he had been captured, Darkhorse had used it to tell King Lanith what he thought of his part in this. The would-be conqueror had not been amused, although Yureel had been. Nonetheless, the shadow puppet had ordered Aurim to silence the prisoner and Cabe's son had obeyed without hesitation.

"We had quite an interesting time shortly after you were captured, Darkhorse. A little side note to my growing epic. It seems a loyal friend of yours wanted to visit. He tried to enter without great Lanith's permission." Yureel giggled. "I'm afraid that we had to destroy him. I hope Aurim won't miss his father *too* much!"

Cabe? Cabe had already tried to rescue him? What was Yureel trying to say . . . that Darkhorse's dearest companion had been killed in the process? *Impossible!* he wanted to roar. *You are as bald a liar as ever, Yureel!*

"You have a twinkle in your eye! Are you trying to tell me something?" He giggled again.

Darkhorse felt the tingle of sorcery. An instant later Aurim Bedlam joined the pair. He bowed to Yureel, completely ignoring his friend.

"I've done as you requested."

The tiny figure turned. "Really? So soon? I'm so proud of you! Show me, quickly!"

Aurim stretched forth his arms. Something made of leather and metal appeared on the floor before him. It took Darkhorse a few seconds to identify the creation as a bridle and bit.

"Is that all right?"

"Lovely, lovely, indeed! And the best of all?"

The sorcerer actually smiled. It was a smile that made the shadow steed want to cringe, so much did it seem more the expression that Yureel would have worn . had the latter actually had a mouth.

"Here." Aurim pointed next to the bridle. A glittering, golden saddle materialized. A strip of silver lined the edge of the saddle and the horn vaguely resembled an equine head. To Darkhorse the object was gaudy, which meant that it likely had been designed by his counterpart, not the sorcerer. "Is that the way you wanted it?"

Yureel clapped his tiny hands together. "Perfection! Simply perfection!" He turned to Darkhorse. "You should be extremely proud of him, brother! He's overcome all of his inadequacies quite quickly, hasn't he?"

"He can't talk," Aurim commented.

"Let him . . . for the moment."

"Release me, Yureel!" cried the ebony stallion the moment he realized that the spell of silence no longer held. "End this folly before it comes crashing down on you!"

"You do like to pontificate." His tone switched, shifting from taunting to bitter. "Perhaps I should throw you into the Void so that *you* can try listening to yourself as you float trapped without hope! Trapped!"

"You were responsible for your own imprisonment, Yureel! You tried to turn a land into chaos and disaster! You caused death and destruction on a grand scale and felt nothing for the mortal lives you wasted! The sorcerers who finally discovered you and found a way to bind you could have destroyed you instead!"

THE HORSE KING

The shadow puppet's icy eyes narrowed. "But they couldn't, Darkhorse! They couldn't! For a long, long time, I wished that they had . . . for having tasted so much life, realizing that there were so many epics to create, I wanted more!" He giggled again. "And now, I shall create my greatest!"

He is more insane than ever! "Again with the stories, Yureel? What is it with you and your pathetic yearning to create these so-called epics? Is it because you so little understand the lives of the creatures you torment that you think you can learn something by manipulating them in scene after scene of devastation?"

Without removing his gaze from that of Darkhorse, Yureel snapped, "Replace the spell!"

Darkhorse found himself silenced again. He had apparently touched upon a tender point. Yureel looked ready to say something else, but was interrupted by another newcomer.

It was Lanith. The horse king was alone, probably because he wanted no one else to see his phantom servant . . . if the shadow man could be called *anyone's* servant. From what Darkhorse knew of Yureel, it was the horse king who was the puppet.

"How much longer, imp? I've been more than patient! When will he be ready?"

"Your timing is impeccable, 0 great emperor!" Both Yureel and Aurim performed bows before the king of Zuu, although the former's was decidedly perfunctory. Lanith, however, did not seem to notice the lapse. "Only this moment has your young but so capable master sorcerer completed the tasks I set before him!"

Aurim indicated the bridle and saddle. The horse king, unable to sense the incredible amount of power imbued into the items, seemed somewhat disappointed.

"This will do it? I've a hundred saddles better-looking than this, all made carefully by the best craftsmen in the kingdom. This hardly looks like a suitable saddle for a king, much less an item that'll make *him* behave as he should."

"You don't like the design?" asked Yureel with what sounded like actual disappointment. The floating figure indicated Darkhorse. "Well, you'll like what it does, I promise you that! Aurim?"

Retrieving the saddle and bridle, the young sorcerer turned to Darkhorse and stared.

The shadow steed felt the bit in his mouth and the strap of the saddle around his torso. Try as he might, Darkhorse could not free himself of the magical items his ensorcelled friend had constructed. Aurim's spell still held sway.

"Now release him."

"Yes, Yureel."

Darkhorse felt a great weight lift off of him, but it was immediately replaced by another, more subtle spell that he quickly realized emanated from the bridle and saddle. He could move his head a little, but that was all. The shadow steed still had no control over his general form.

"He's ready, Your Majesty," the sorcerer announced.

Yureel laughed, then floated to the stallion's head. Dark- horse could just barely see him in his peripheral vision. "As promised, great majesty, the only mount *fit* to be yours! A steed perfect for the conqueror of the Dragonrealm, the future emperor of all!"

"Magnificent!" Lanith strode to Darkhorse, who wanted to rise up and kick the king away but could not. The tall human stroked his neck, whispering what the eternal considered inane comforting noises that might have worked on a true animal but only served to annoy him further.

Lanith mounted, the action marred only by a brief giggle from Yureel. The warrior king adjusted his seating slightly, then said, "I want to take him out and run him around the yard."

"You have only to guide him as you would any other horse," Aurim replied. "He'll show only as much spirit as you desire, Your Majesty. The saddle and bridle ensure that."

"Seems a bit of a pity. I normally like to break in my own mounts."

Flittering around so that Darkhorse could see him, Yureel chuckled. "You will still have that pleasure, my wondrous majesty! The longer you ride him, the more he will see that he now only lives to serve you! There is plenty of spirit there to be broken and with a little guidance from me, he will soon be yours in mind as well as body!"

More lies, Yureel! Darkhorse tried to shout. *I will not break! Never! And if I know you, you do not expect me to. You have something else in mind eventually, don't you?* This was merely the shadow puppet's way of weakening Darkhorse. The ebony stallion already knew what fate awaited him. Yureel would not be satisfied until there remained but one of them.

"Open the gates."

"As you've got things well in hand, my glorious monarch, I'll not bother you with my unworthy presence. In my place I shall leave our most loyal Aurim."

Darkhorse could clearly hear the sarcasm in every word, but King Lanith noticed nothing. For the first time, the eternal began to realize how great were the strings with which Yureel manipulated his human "master."

"You're dismissed, imp. Aurim! Open the way to the yard! I want to see what he can do."

"Yes, Your Majesty."

As the sorcerer obeyed, Darkhorse caught one last glimpse of Yureel. The shadow puppet stared back at him, icy eyes glimmering with glee, as he faded back into the shadows.

"Come on, you."

It took Darkhorse a moment to realize that Lanith meant him. At first he thought how absurd it was that the king of Zuu would assume that he would quietly obey his dictates. Then, when his body began to move of its own accord despite his best efforts otherwise, Darkhorse realized just how powerful the bridle and saddle were.

Aurim stood by the open entrance of the stable, beaming with pride as the king and Darkhorse moved by. The shadow steed found he could move his head, though not turn it around. His body seemed to have the normal limitations of a true equine. Darkhorse looked at his young friend, but the golden-haired spellcaster merely smiled smugly at him, then looked up at the king.

Lanith urged Darkhorse out into the yard, where he forced the shadow steed to trot. The saddle and bridle functioned as if linked to the monarch's mind; they made Darkhorse do whatever his rider desired. The eternal watched in frustration as his ensorcelled body performed like a trained animal for the horse king.

Feminine laughter accompanied by clapping caused Lanith to finally rein him to a halt. Standing near one wall of the yard was Saress. The enchantress was clad in a very low-cut leather riding outfit. "May I ride him when you're done, my darling?"

Lanith patted Darkhorse on the neck in an obviously possessive manner. "Not just yet, Saress. Perhaps after I've grown more accustomed to him myself." The king stroked the eternal's mane. "Perhaps."

The enchantress pouted theatrically, then pretended to notice Aurim. "There you are!" She crossed the yard slowly, each step designed to attract the attention of both men. "Did you make the saddle? I can sense the spells on it, but they're tied together so intricately I'm amazed that anyone could do it!"

The king had guided Darkhorse around just enough that the eternal could see both spellcasters. Aurim did not seem to take Saress's compliments in the manner that she no doubt hoped he would. In fact, the young sorcerer looked very uncomfortable. Small wonder as the woman practically wrapped herself around him the moment she was near enough.

If she sought to make Lanith jealous, it was a losing cause. Saress's devotion to her king was so clear that Lanith had to know that all he had to do was snap his fingers to summon her to his side. The enchantress might find other males of momentary fascination, but her soul belonged to her master. In some ways, it was ironic justice, considering what she had done to Aurim and others.

"I made them, yes," Aurim answered somewhat hesitantly. No mention was made of Yureel, which confirmed to Darkhorse that Lanith did not share all of his secrets with Saress. The shadow steed wondered what she thought of Aurim's sudden loyalty to the king or if she even thought of it at all. The enchantress was not a thrall like the younger Bedlam; she was a willing servant. Surely Saress noticed some trace of Yureel's foul presence.

"Come." Lanith, sounding bored with the shift in conversation, turned Darkhorse away from the pair. He made the shadow steed trot once around the yard, then forced him to pick up the pace. Darkhorse tried to reject each command, but the saddle and bridle continued to override his will. Yureel had planned his revenge very well.

Around and around the yard Darkhorse raced, Lanith putting him through a variety of maneuvers that would have pushed even the strongest of mounts to their limits. The eternal performed all of them with ease, which only served to encourage the horse king to try yet more difficult stunts.

He could neither see nor sense his counterpart, but the shadow steed knew that Yureel watched him from somewhere, no doubt giggling merrily all the while. A startling thought occurred to him. *Was this part of Yureel's plan all along? Did he somehow manipulate matters so that I would be the one to come rescue Aurim?*

The macabre little figure had probably not planned things quite so perfectly, but if he had been in the Dragonrealm even for a short period, then he would have had time to study his adversary. He would have known enough about Darkhorse and his relationship with the Bedlams to know that sooner or later the shadow steed would involve himself if one of his mortal friends was kidnapped. That would explain the number of spell traps that Yssa had located around the barony of Adderly. Yureel could not predict *exactly* where Darkhorse would show up, but he could make a fairly good guess . . . and had.

"He handles magnificently!" Lanith called to the others, reining Darkhorse up in front of them. "Never has any king had a finer mount!"

"You look perfect, darling!" The enchantress abandoned Aurim, who looked quite relieved, and put a caressing hand on the king's leg. "Like a warrior god!"

"I do look good, don't I?" Lanith reached down and cupped Saress's chin for a moment, then looked up again and said, "Aurim, you've served me well. He obeys my every command perfectly. Every movement is flawless. He'll serve me well in battle. He'll put the fear into my enemies . . ."

Put fear into his enemies . . . Darkhorse had tried to keep from thinking about what Lanith might desire from him. He had hoped that the horse king might simply keep him in Zuu, but it was clear now that Lanith wanted to take full advantage of the eternal's abilities. The shadow steed was to be the king's warhorse.

He wanted Darkhorse to attack the very people the eternal had always fought to protect. Yureel's vengeance was to be even more terrible than Darkhorse had supposed; the shadow man wanted his counterpart to watch as his own substantial powers were turned on his friends.

King Lanith dismounted with a flourish. His face was flushed from excitement. "Saress! Summon Belfour and the others for me! Why wait any longer? Everything I need is mine!"

"Surely you're not—"

"And why not? There's no power strong enough to stop me! I've got an armed force like none other in the realm. My Magical Order's proven itself against the greatest sorcerer of the realm, Cabe Bedlam himself! Better still, the legendary demon Darkhorse is mine to control, mine to ride! I can't lose now! I will triumph against all foes! I'll be Emperor Lanith, ruler of the Dragonrealm!"

Aurim smiled obediently and Saress, after some initial expressions of concern and confusion, laughed and clapped her hands. They were the perfect puppets, Darkhorse decided, for the puppet king.

He wished that he could speak. Surely Lanith did not think that even with magic and arms behind him he could conquer the entire continent. The Aramites had managed to do that on the other continent, but they had only done so with a power rumored to be greater than Yureel and Darkhorse combined. Even so, their empire had crumbled, unable to stave off numerous rebellions that had risen nearly simultaneously under the Gryphon's guidance.

The monarch of Zuu tossed the reins to Aurim. "See to him. Make sure that he's ready when I need him. I want to ride him slowly through Zuu at the head of my personal guard, to show the people that our destiny is assured." To Saress he added, "Tell Belfour and the others I'll meet them in the throne room. They're to be gathered there in half an hour, no more."

"Yes, darling."

Aurim pulled on the reins. "Come."

Unable to resist, Darkhorse was led back into the stable even as the king gave Saress some last commands. The eternal heard something concerning "that witch," which either referred to Gwendolyn Bedlam or, more likely, the still missing Yssa.

With a gesture, Aurim sealed the entrance behind them, then led Darkhorse back to his stabling. Only then did the human look Darkhorse in the eye. "You won't be able to move now, so don't strain yourself trying." Perhaps he saw something in the shadow steed's stare, for Aurim abruptly removed the spell of silence. "You want to say something?"

Darkhorse forced himself to remain calm. This might be his only opportunity to break the lad free of Yureel's insidious spell. "Aurim, you must listen to me. This is not you. You would never serve a monster such as Yureel or this pathetic, would-be conqueror. You would never attack your own family or use your abilities to rain down destruction on people simply trying to defend themselves."

"If the king commands me to use my powers to aid his efforts, I'm bound to obey."

"You are *not!* It is a spell that binds you, not loyalty. Think! This is Yureel's foul doing! He has seized your mind, twisted your very thoughts. This is not *you.*"

The sorcerer's face went blank, then slowly his expression twisted, as if he fought with some inner demon. "No. . I'm simply loyal to the king . . . but . . . Saress . . . she fooled me . . ."

Darkhorse's eyes flashed. "Fight it, Aurim! You are stronger! You are not Yureel's pawn!"

"*Darkhorse.*" The young human looked ready to scream. "I can't—"

"You must!"

"I can't . . . really believe you'd think my hold on him was that weak, brother!" Aurim flashed a smile and giggled, sounding much too much like someone other than himself.

The eternal tried to probe the chamber, but the spell that bound him did not allow him that much power. Still, there was no doubting that Yureel was present nearby. "So, only a game again, eh?"

"A game, a chapter in our epic, call it what you will." The golden-haired man froze, his expression growing slack. "Just as you once told me, I'll tell you now. There is no escape for you and your friend, Darkhorse, not now . . . not ever."

"Yureel—"

Aurim giggled once more, then blinked as if waking. He studied the captive for almost a minute. Darkhorse felt the spell of silence envelop him again. "You'd better behave now. I've got to go."

The human seemed to have no recollection of what had just occurred. Darkhorse did not try to stop him from leaving, not that there was much he could have done. He could only watch as Aurim abandoned him to the silence and darkness of the stable.

The shadows only served to remind him of Yureel, who had proven as masterful as he was cruel. Yureel thoroughly controlled his puppets, utilizing their abilities proficiently so as to preserve his own strength for w lt w truly needed. Now he had control of one of the potentially greatest sorcerers alive; there was no telling to what limits the sinister little demon planned to push the younger Bedlam.

He will surely use the lad against his parents just as he plans to use me against them. If Novel follows true to form, he will probably do his best to see that Aurim injures or perhaps even kills Cabe and Gwen . . .

The very thought would have made him shudder had he still had the ability to move that much. Yureel's mad epic promised blood, destruction, and betrayal. The shadow puppet obviously understood human emotions to such a point that he knew that Aurim's family would find it difficult to unleash their full might against their son. Hesitation would be their fatal flaw, the key to eliminating the only opposition possibly able to put an end to the mad crusade before it spread too far from the borders of Zuu.

He will do it. He will make Aurim attempt to slay his parents . . . and if I am any judge of ability, the lad has the power to succeed.

Aurim had no control over his body. The monstrous thing in his head danced him around like a marionette, making him do this and that for a man the creature obviously disdained. And Darkhorse probably thought Aurim had betrayed him. Thanks to the younger Bedlam's work, the shadow steed was now also a helpless captive. Even if Darkhorse did not believe his friend had turned on him, Aurim felt as if he had.

As he marched obediently through the palace halls toward the throne room, Aurim struggled to regroup his thoughts. He had never felt so frightened in his life, not even when Toma had seized hold of his thoughts for a time. The drake had merely blocked some of his memories; he had never actually possessed Aurim. That had been unsettling enough, but his predicament now was . . . hideous.

Everyone in the palace assumed that he was now the loyal servant of King Lanith. Inwardly, that could not have been further from the truth. The link that the demon Yureel maintained with Aurim made him do whatever the graying warrior demanded, but only because Yureel desired it as well. Lanith was almost as much a puppet as he was. However, the dark imp dared not completely seize control of his so-called ally because others would have eventually realized that the king of Zuu was not quite himself. Besides, Yureel did have limitations of his own.

That was the only thing that gave him some hope. His captor did not have complete access to his thoughts, not if Aurim exercised some of the concentration tricks his parents had taught him. To be truthful, Yureel probably did not even care that Aurim still sought out ways to free himself. If there was one trait that both Darkhorse and the imp shared, it was a sense of overconfidence. Yureel believed that he now owned the sorcerer body and soul. Aurim hoped to prove him wrong, although he did not know how. All he knew was that he dared not lose hope. He had to escape, if only because he knew some of what his captor had planned for him. Aurim was to lead the sorcerers of the Magical Order in battle. He was to create a link between them even stronger than the one that existed now. Through him, Yureel would combine the Order's abilities to unleash such powerful sorcery as had not been seen since at least the Turning War, when human and drake power had clashed time and time again.

There has to be a way to free myself! There has to be! Already he had been responsible for injuring his own father. Only a brief moment of brittle control had allowed him to soften the spell he and several of Lanith's pet sorcerers had hurtled at the elder Bedlam. Aurim's rising hopes of rescue, dashed once already by his part in the capture of Darkhorse, had sunk swiftly again the moment Yureel's link forced him to attack his father. The thought had so repelled him, however, that he had been able to slow his movement just a fraction enough to decrease the intensity of the assault. Even then he had feared that he had killed his parent.

It had been even more chilling to join in the hunt to track his father down, especially with the increasingly bitter Ponteroy around. The other sorcerer had been told only a short time before that he was now third in rank behind Saress and Aurim and that news still stuck hard in the northerner's throat. The king himself had suggested that if the elder Bedlam could be captured, he would be a valuable addition to the ranks once he was "convinced" of the righteousness of Lanith's cause. However, Aurim believed that given the opportunity and the necessary seclusion, Ponteroy would have very likely *killed* Cabe Bedlam for fear that here would be another who would become his superior in the Magical Order.

Fortunately, it had been one of the less proficient mages who had found the injured sorcerer. And what had happened next had both startled and gratified the helpless Aurim. He had both heard and sensed the attack on his fellow hunter and had immediately transported himself to the spot. Instead of finding his father alone, however, there had been a woman—one of the most beautiful women Aurim could frankly recall ever seeing—protecting his father. Her presence had so startled him that even had he been willingly working for the king of Zuu, he would have hesitated that important fraction of a second.

When she and his father had vanished a moment later, Aurim had wanted to breathe a sigh of relief. He was certain that the woman had taken his father to safety. That meant that word concerning his plight would eventually reach the Manor and Penacles. They would realize that he could not possibly be voluntarily working for Lanith. Someone would come for both him and Darkhorse.

Which meant that he would probably do his best to capture or even . . . kill . . . his rescuers, be they his parents, the Gryphon, or even his young sister.

I can't let that happen! I've got to free myself from that monster before they come! How he could do that, though, Aurim did not know. True, he had had some minor success, but hardly enough to indicate that Yureel's control was slipping. Yureel was certainly not Saress, whose abilities were far more limited. The shadow creature was as powerful as Dark-horse, maybe even more so.

He nearly collided with another figure coming from a side corridor. Aurim at first thought it was a guard, but then he noted the garish, aristocratic clothing.

Ponteroy. The renegade sorcerer from Gordag-Ai sneered at him. "And good day to you, Master Bedlam. Shouldn't you be in the throne room? I've heard that the king wants all important members of his staff there. Of course, that no longer includes me, but I know it does you."

"I'm on my way there now," Aurim heard himself say. It amazed him the way Yureel had made him two people in one. The puppet half of him acted and responded as if everything he did was normal. Only occasionally did the true Aurim show through, mostly when Saress got too close, but also on occasion when dealing with jealous Ponteroy.

He started past the other spellcaster, but Ponteroy thrust an arm in front of him. The horse-headed staff gleamed in the dimly lit corridor, a sign that Ponteroy was ready to utilize his power. "Consider yourself fortunate, boy. It was your fault that those two escaped, but for some reason His Majesty has chosen to be benevolent to you, his new champion. He won't be so kind next time you make such a mistake. I know, trust me. Don't become too comfortable in your position. That could be disastrous for you."

"Is something the matter, Ponteroy?" Saress walked lithely toward them from the direction of the throne room.

The bitter sorcerer immediately pulled his arm back. "No, nothing at all, Saress. I was merely discussing a few minor matters with our new comrade here."

"You've some things to attend to, Ponteroy. See to them."

Summarily dismissed, the sorcerer from Gordag-Ai managed one final glare at his replacement, then stalked away. Saress watched him depart, amused by his anger and frustration. "Poor little Ponteroy! This demotion was just such a blow to his oily little ego. I don't know why he's so distraught; he's still being paid his gold."

"I've got to go," the puppet part of Aurim stated. He tried to work his way past Saress, but the enchantress would not allow him.

"There's nothing to worry about. We still have time. I'm supposed to be there, too, silly." She folded her arm around his, leaning close. "We'll walk together."

She was using him again. It had not taken Aurim long to realize that while Saress might find him desirable, he was in the end only a tool in her constant quest to maintain the attention of her king and lover. The enchantress was obsessed, and Aurim finally believed he knew what she wanted. Lanith was not married and had no heir. Saress wanted to be his queen.

Aurim doubted that Lanith would ever go that far. It was one thing to make Saress his mistress, but making her queen was an entirely different matter. Few humans anywhere would be comfortable with a spellcaster on the throne. In Penacles, the Gryphon had replaced the tyrannical drake lord. In Talak, Queen Erini kept her use of her powers to such minimal tasks that many of her subjects had forgotten she wielded them in the first place. These were the exceptions, however, not the accepted. Saress would never be queen, no matter how great her attempts to stir her master's jealousy.

Perhaps deep down the sorceress knew, too, for her attempts to seduce Aurim grew stronger each time they were alone. She might be devoted to Lanith, but Saress did not seem to mind the thought of a temporary lover.

Aurim shuddered, his own reaction this time.

"Even here in the southwest the halls are chilly, aren't they? We'll just have to stay closer together, I suppose." She led him slowly along the corridor.

Fortunately, the journey was short. He and Saress entered just as King Lanith, standing over a table where a large map had been placed, finished giving orders to an older officer Aurim knew to be General Belfour, the monarch's chief commander. Belfour looked none too pleased by the instructions his liege had relayed to him, but he nodded.

The horse king looked up as the two entered. "Saress! Aurim! Where by Haron's Mare did you get to? I've got plenty of things in store for the Order and I don't intend on saying them twice!"

"I was only retrieving our wayward friend, Your Majesty. Poor Aurim seemed lost in the halls and I was afraid he might not make it here in time."

Lanith punted. "All right, then! The two of you had better listen close, because there's going to be a few changes in the intended plan."

"Your Majesty," Belfour interrupted. "I really think that we should reconsider these changes. The terrain alone makes victory uncertain. Our riders will have a hard going with it—"

Lanith's darkening countenance was enough to silence the general. "Your protest's noted, Belfour . . . now put an end to it. The decision's been made." The would-be conqueror turned an evil grin on the two spellcasters. "Besides, terrain won't be so terrible a problem with the Order now working so well together, will it, Aurim?"

It was a curious Saress who responded before Aurim would have been forced to. "Exactly what do you have in mind, Lanith? Are we ready to trample Gordag-Ai?"

It had to be that, Aurim realized. King Lanith's reaction after riding Darkhorse made more sense now. With Aurim and Darkhorse now his to command, Lanith probably felt his forces were ready to attack the northern kingdom. Yureel had turned Aurim into the perfect link for the Magical Order, a link that would enable them to focus their combined might. With Darkhorse also ready to fight for him, the king had no more reason to wait. Gordag-Ai had no defenses strong enough to deflect the magical and physical forces of Zuu.

"We ride, Saress, but not to Gordag-Ai. I've changed my mind. A more important foe must be dealt with first, a foe whose defeat will mean more to the people than even conquering the northerners would've." He slammed one fist on the map, all but obscuring the name of the massive green land underneath. "Here."

Saress leaned forward, trying to read the map, but Aurim did not need to see the name to recognize the horse king's intended target.

It was Dagora, the vast forest domain east and north of Zuu. Dagora, land of the Green Dragon.

Chapter Eleven

The eyes of the Green Dragon came in many forms, some natural, some not. Among the more prevalent servants who patrolled his land were the elves. They were no longer his subjects, but it behooved any elf who chose to live in the immense Dagora Forest to assist in its defense and so a pact still existed. The Dragon King aided the settlements and in return the elves aided him in watching for and ousting any unwelcome newcomers.

Of late, the patrols had come to watch the west with great interest. Everyone knew that the human king of Zuu would sooner or later lead his warriors northward to attack the other human kingdom of Gordag-Ai and there was always the chance that a few stragglers might intrude in the forest. Besides, the drake lord had requested any news of the horde's progress so that he could relay it to his sorcerer associates in Penacles. They were taking this new conqueror seriously, even if the elves on patrol were less inclined to worry. Humans and drakes were always warring.

Sean Blackwillow led a patrol of four elves presently watching the eastern edge of Adderly. The horsemen had for the most part abandoned their bloody conquest almost immediately after taking it, but some activity still took place there. Sean was of the opinion that he and his friends were wasting their efforts, but it was his turn to lead a patrol and he always obeyed the dictates of the elders.

269

THE HORSE KING

"We get to go home tomorrow, don't we?" whispered a thinner, younger elf. This was his first patrol and he was proving the most irritating of companions. In Sean's erstwhile opinion, the coming generation of elves seemed to have no patience. Of course, the elders spoke the same way of him, but they were slow, cranky grandfathers .
. .

"Yes, Dyyn," he finally replied. "Tomorrow."

The four of them hid among the trees just a few yards into the thicker part of the forest. From their vantage point, they could see the easternmost hills of Adderly and, because of their exceptional eyesight, even the vague outline of the castle. Things remained unchanged, just as they had for the past four days.

Only—Sean squinted—suddenly there seemed to be a fairly wide shadow spreading along the western horizon. He stiffened, then moved a few feet forward, trying to see better.

"What is it, Sean? Another sheep?"

"Not unless sheep are swift and carry riders . . ." The lead elf blinked, hoping that what he saw was a trick of the still dim western sky. Unfortunately, the massive shadow continued toward them, coalescing slowly into identifiable human forms on horses. There were hundreds and hundreds in sight with more following with each passing second.

"What are they doing here?" asked Dyyn. "I thought that they already stole everything of value in Adderly. Why bother coming back?"

"Be silent, Dyyn." Sean's stomach turned. This was not right. The horsemen of Zuu were supposed to head north toward Gordag-Ai, not east. Not toward Dagora.

Yet, here came the golden horde, their impressive mounts quickly racing toward the edge of the forest. At the rate they were coming, they would reach the trees in no more than a quarter hour.

"Bracha, get the mounts." An older, stockier elf hurried off. To the remaining pair, Sean commanded, "You two spread out a little—"

A huge tree only a few yards in front of them burst out of the ground and flew high into the sky. Awestruck, the elves watched it go higher and higher. Only when a second tore itself free and followed after the first did they finally awaken to their danger.

"Bracha!" Sean cried. "Where are those mounts?"

A third and fourth tree shot from the earth, these so near that the three elves were pelted by a shower of dirt and rock. Sean signaled retreat. If Bracha would not bring the mounts to them, then they would go to him.

"What's happening?" Dyyn cried.

No one answered him, the answer so obvious even the young elf would soon figure it out for himself. Sorcery. Powerful sorcery. Sean knew that the human king had spellcasters working for him, but all reports had indicated that most of them were little more than sleight-of-hand artists. This attack . . . this attack was by someone much more skilled.

A tremendous crash threw Sean off his feet. He yelped as something jabbed him in the cheek. Blood trickled down the side of his face.

"Sean!" Bracha's strong hands took hold of him, dragging the injured elf to his feet. "Are you hurt bad?"

"What . . . what . . . ?"

"A *tree* just fell from the sky! A tree! I think . . . I think Dyyn's dead."

The patrol leader looked around. It looked as if about a dozen trees had rained down on them. An entire area to one side had been cleared, the trees lying in a jumbled pile. Sean did not see Dyyn, but he recalled the younger elf moving into the zone of destruction.

He put a hand to his cheek, wincing in pain when he touched the bloody area.

RICHARD A. KNAAK

Something hard and sharp still protruded from the wound. Bracha carefully removed it for him. It was a splinter of wood nearly four inches long. Sean considered himself fortunate that he had been so lightly injured. He looked around for the fourth member of the party. "Where's Iryn?"

"Over there." Bracha pointed behind himself. Sean could just make out the other elf and the mounts. "When I saw you go down, I yelled for Iryn to take hold of the animals for me while I got you."

"Thank you." Aloud, lingering crash in the distance warned Sean that not all the other trees tossed high into the air had landed. They had to leave now. The Green Dragon likely knew that something was going on at the edge of his domain, but the patrol had to report specifics not only to him, but to their own people.

Bracha helped him back to the mounts. Sean ignored his wound as best he could. It was inconsequential compared to the threat from the west.

"Bracha. I want you and Iryn to hurry back to our people. I'll carry the news to the drake lord."

"All right, Sean, but I do not see—"

A searing gust of wind nearly bowled them over. The animals grew frantic, fighting their riders for control. Behind Sean, a brilliant burst of light suddenly illuminated the entire area. A heat wave of incredible magnitude swept over the elves. Without even seeing it, the elf knew what had happened.

"Ride!" Bracha cried out, his eyes round with fright as he stared at what was occurring behind Sean.

The mounts needed no urging. They moved off at as fast a gallop as they could. Being elfin-raised, the animals could maneuver around forest paths that other horses would have found most difficult, sometimes impossible. Unfortunately, Sean knew that the thing now pursuing them would not be slowed by treacherously winding paths or wide trees. It would eat through such obstacles as if they were nothing.

He looked behind them and saw the wall of fire. It rose taller than the trees and the slight green tinge he noted was all the verification Sean needed to know that the fiery wall was yet another product of sorcery.

They will burn down the entire forest if they keep that thing alive for very long! Are they mad? What will they gain by reducing this land to ash?

The questions quickly became moot, for the wall moved with such swiftness that the heat washing over him became unbearable. Now only one thing concerned the elf as he and his companions fled and that was whether or not *they* would be able to outrace the wall of death.

Sean had his doubts.

The western edge of the forest was a blazing inferno and there was nothing Darkhorse could do to stop it. The coordinated power of the Order was so tremendous that it was very possible they would burn down all of Dagora if someone did not stop them. Unfortunately, at this point the only one capable of putting a halt to the wholesale destruction was King Lanith and he did not seem inclined.

The captive eternal suspected Yureel's hand in the matter. It served no real purpose for Lanith to destroy what he sought to conquer. This horrific assault on the forest was more to the tastes of Darkhorse's counterpart.

General Belfour, riding next to the king, asked, "Your Majesty, shouldn't they put an end to that fire now? We can't send the men in until things cool down a little and that will take time."

"A bit longer, Belfour. I want the drake to know what we can do to him." The king smiled triumphantly. "Don't worry, General. I don't plan on burning down the entire Dagora Forest. Just enough."

Darkhorse seemed to be the only one who noticed a shadowy presence around

271

the king and himself, a presence he knew to be Yureel. Yureel had not spoken to him since Lanith and his warriors had departed Zuu, but had made no attempt to hide the fact that he was there and obviously in contact with the horse king.

Curse you, Yureel! Cease this terror! If you will have a war, then have a war, not this wholesale destruction!

Whether it was his demand or, more likely, pure coincidence, Lanith raised his hand but a minute later. A soldier raised a horn to his lips and blew a long, low signal.

In the distance the towering wall of fire ceased. For some distance all that could be seen were the charred remnants of once magnificent trees. Darkhorse estimated that in the space of less than an hour, the king's sorcerers had burned away several hundred acres of ancient forest.

"Give the second signal."

The soldier raised the horn to his lips again and blew out a short series of higher notes. Darkhorse felt the sorcerers at work again.

"The path is cooled," the horse king announced. "Our warriors may progress. Everyone should be ready for battle the moment we finish crossing the charred region."

Everyone, including the shadow steed, knew very well that resistance would begin the moment they entered the forest. The Green Dragon surely had been notified of their presence the moment the sorcerers had first struck. The warriors of Zuu would face hidden archers in the trees, covered pits, surprise attacks on stragglers, and, of course, sorcery both human and draconian. Somewhere in the forest they would find another army, its warriors bitter and furious, awaiting them.

I must escape! I cannot allow this to continue any longer! Once more, Darkhorse tried to overcome the slave spell of the bridle and saddle, but all he succeeded in doing was weakening himself. Aurim had followed Yureel's orders to the letter.

Lanith noticed his momentary loss of strength. "I'll brook no hesitation from you, demon steed. Move."

A sharp pain coursed through Darkhorse as Lanith pulled on the reins, a new addition to his torture that had no doubt been whispered in the king's ear by Yureel. The saddle and bridle seized complete control again, forcing him forward at a quickening pace.

Scents mingled as Darkhorse stepped into the burnt portion of the forest. Smoke still lingered in some places. The shadow steed marked most of the scents as originating from charred trees and foliage, but his sharp senses also detected some sickly odors that he hoped were not what he suspected.

The warriors of Zuu spread out as they moved. Lanith did not rely on cavalry alone; he had foot soldiers as well. Even in heavily wooded regions such as Dagora the warriors of Zuu were not slowed much. Darkhorse had the least difficulty, but he began to have a grudging respect for the abilities of his mortal counterparts. The horses of Zuu were indeed remarkable.

They left behind the burnt ruins of the forest's edge none too soon as far as the shadow steed was concerned. If the eternal could still trust his senses, at least one blackened form that he had passed had been some unfortunate being, likely one of the elves who inhabited the domain of the Green Dragon. Darkhorse hoped there would be no more, but sooner or later Lanith's warriors *would* encounter resistance and then the shadow steed would be forced to battle those who should have been his allies.

There must be some way to stop this!! I will not fight for your pleasure, Yureel! Yet, he still had no idea how to keep from doing so.

All around them, the air was suddenly filled with hissing. One of the lead riders grunted in surprise, then slipped from his horse, a long bolt through his throat. Three other warriors within Darkhorse's view joined the first.

The bolts were not elven. In fact, from the brief glimpse Darkhorse got of one, they more resembled massive thorns from some plant. Lanith and Yureel had just gotten their first taste of the magical defenses of the Dagora Forest.

"Shields!" roared Belfour.

Above Darkhorse, the king stiffened. The shadow steed felt the growing presence of his counterpart. It was as if Yureel and not Lanith now sat upon his back. "Command the men to hold back, General Belfour. The Order will deal with this prickly situation."

Only Darkhorse heard the brief giggle that escaped King Lanith.

Belfour signaled a halt to the advance. Silence fell over the forest. The general glanced at his liege, but Darkhorse could not see what expression now graced the features of the warlord.

Someone gasped. Ahead of them, a dusting of white fell upon the trees. Wherever the dust fell, limbs and leaves crystallized and began to shudder. The sunlight that managed to shine through created a glare that forced more than one warrior to squint. The storm was short but heavy, lasting all of perhaps five minutes but covering everything in sight ahead of them.

"Give the order to move on again, General."

The senior officer nodded. At first, movement was slow and hesitant, but when no new rain of death fell upon the foremost soldiers, the pace of the advance increased.

When they reached the whitened area, the advance faltered again, but this time it was because of fascination, not fear. The trees and plants in this region not only looked crystalline, they were. One rider broke off a gleaming branch and brandished it briefly before being reprimanded by an officer.

In the center of the crystalline region, they came upon several barrel-shaped plants with hundreds of long, pointed spikes growing out of the sides. Each plant, though, had areas upon it where it appeared the spikes had been removed. No one had to ask if these were the sources of the hail of bolts. Like the other plants, though, these were also dead.

At sight of this, the morale of the warriors grew yet stronger, so much so that Darkhorse actually began to have hope. Yureel was allowing his human puppets to become too overconfident in their safety. However, the spines had been only the first line of defense. More was surely to come.

Lanith reined him to a slower pace. Belfour and the king's other senior officers followed suit, but the rest of the invading horde pressed forward, soon leaving their leaders far in the rear.

"Is something amiss, Your Majesty?" Belfour himself seemed uneasy, as if he shared the shadow steed's opinion concerning the increasing danger.

"No. Nothing's wrong." Although he spoke in the voice of the horse king, it was Yureel who yet held the reins. "Nothing *at all.*"

What do you plan, Yureel? What is going on? Surely you of all here would best know what danger lies—

Darkhorse paused in mid-thought, unable to believe what Yureel might be considering. It was wasteful, horrible . . . and so like his counterpart. He wanted to warn General Belfour at least, the elder warrior seemed to be more a man of honor than his liege had probably ever been, but the slave spell prevented even that.

Again, a brief giggle escaped the king. This time, one of Lanith's officers glanced his way, but only for a second or two.

The possessed king did a peculiar thing next. He reached down and patted Darkhorse on the head. The ebony stallion tried to shy away from the touch.

Far ahead, the forest ground shook without warning.

THE HORSE KING

Despite his superior vision, Darkhorse caught only momentary glimpses of what was happening, but it was more than enough. As if churned up by a legion of huge, burrowing Quel, the earth first shook, then crumbled. Huge gaps opened up in the soil, gaps in which startled horses planted hooves or unsuspecting infantry their feet. Warriors and horses cried out as they stumbled and fell, only to find themselves being pulled beneath the moving earth.

The possessed king urged Darkhorse forward, reining him to a halt only when they were near enough to the terrible sight to see everything. Around Darkhorse and Lanith pandemonium threatened to destroy what remained of the invaders' organization, but the horse king seemed unbothered. Lanith—or rather, Yureel—was far more interested in the disaster ahead than in what was happening to the rest of the huge force. Yet, despite his interest in what was happening to the unfortunates caught in the trap, the possessed monarch made no move to save them, instead perhaps actually *enjoying* the tragic spectacle.

Men, women, and horses were sucked under. Some souls attempted to find safety in the trees, but when they sought to take hold of a branch or trunk, their hands slipped away and they fell back into the earthen maelstrom, vanishing moments later with shrieks of despair. Some of their comrades tried to rescue them by throwing in ropes. This actually saved two or three, but at least one rescuer tumbled in before anyone could seize her. She disappeared beneath the surface before she could finish screaming.

Although they were the servants of his captors, Darkhorse agonized over each death. None of them needed to have perished. This entire war was the notion of Lanith and Yureel, possibly even only Yureel, although Darkhorse doubted that the king was an innocent in this matter.

Someone sounded a retreat, not that it was really necessary to do so at this point. With the exceptions of those attempting to aid the last few victims of the Green Dragon's latest defense, most of the warriors had already retreated some distance back.

"Who gave that command?" shouted Lanith with a snarl.

Belfour rode up. "My liege, it was me. I apologize, but there was no other choice! If someone hadn't given some signal, some indication that command still functioned, instead of a retreat we might've had a complete rout!"

Lanith's body quivered with barely contained rage. Belfour had interrupted Yureel's pleasure. The general could not have possibly realized how tenuous his situation, his very life, had just become.

Surprisingly, the possessed king calmed. "Very good, Belfour. You're to be commended, yes, indeed." Yureel's presence retreated into the background. More and more, Lanith sounded and reacted like himself. "Get them reorganized and have them pull back a hundred paces . . . for now."

"What kind of war is this?" muttered Belfour, still unaware just how near to death he had likely come. "Where are the warriors? Where are those we can bury good steel in? We can't keep fighting sorcery!"

"Sorcery's the drake lord's first defense, General," Lanith replied. "It's also his main defense. Cut through what he's got set up and he'll have to rely on his own warriors. Fierce but few compared to my proud, vast legions."

"I hope we *can* cut through these devil defenses!"

"Have you so little faith yet in my Magical Order?" The king snapped his fingers. Yureel might have receded into the background, but his influence was still strong. Darkhorse sensed that Lanith still listened to him. The horse king probably did not even realize that he had been momentarily possessed.

"You summoned me, Your Majesty?"

Aurim's arrival was so abrupt that even Darkhorse was startled by it. Only Lanith reacted as if fully expecting the young sorcerer to appear.

"I did. You see what lies before us . . ."

"Yes, Your Majesty."

"Deal with it."

"We'll do our best." Aurim made to leave.

The king turned Darkhorse toward the sorcerer. "You'll do more than that. I gave a royal command. I expect nothing but success!"

"Your Majesty, at least two of our number are hard-pressed to continue. It would be best if we could have an hour of rest. There are limitations."

"You'll rest when I give you the command and no sooner!" The king urged the shadow steed forward, then drew his blade and touched the sharp tip against Aurim's chest. "Deal with the trap. Clear the way. I want results! Men've died and there're those who must pay! They must pay!"

This last the king cried out so that all within earshot could hear him. Many of the nearest warriors nodded or muttered their agreement with his sentiments. More than a few clutched their blades, even brandishing them in a sort of salute to their monarch's demand for retribution.

And what would they think, Darkhorse wondered, *if they had seen their glorious king not more than a minute before enjoying the tragic deaths of their comrades?*

As Lanith withdrew the blade, Aurim Bedlam nodded. The shadow steed noted that the young sorcerer's eyes had a hollow look, as if Aurim was exhausted. Not surprising, considering the fact that he not only contributed greatly to each spell, but acted as the focus for all the others.

"It shall be done." With those words, the sorcerer vanished.

The horse king turned to his officers, his voice still loud enough for all around to hear. Darkhorse sensed the work of Yureel; no human's voice could have carried so well. "Cowards that they are, I say that they will pay! Afraid to face us with steel and bow, that's what they are! Well, if that's what they want, we'll answer them in kind and in blood until they have no choice *but* to meet us with arms!" The warrior king straightened in the saddle and even Darkhorse, his head twisted around as much as the bridle would allow, could see how the human wielded his sword against the distant, unseen foe to the east. "And when that time comes, we shall show them the same mercy that they showed our friends and kin here! Ten lives for every one of ours lost!" The horse king's eyes shifted to his officers as he cried out again. "Ten lives for one!"

Taking the cue, Belfour raised his own blade. "Ten lives for one!"

"Ten lives for one!" called out the rest of the officers obediently, each raising a weapon.

The cry was picked up by other warriors, until it became a chant. Lanith swung his blade around once, then again pointed it toward the east.

Perfectly timed, a green cloud formed over the heaving land. Yureel had coordinated the sorcerers' efforts with the king's words. Not so difficult a task when both Aurim and Lanith were under his sinister guidance, but the results were nonetheless spectacular. The cloud drifted down upon the earth and as it did, the convulsions slowed until finally they ceased altogether. The ground quickly reshaped itself, becoming flat and hard, perfect for men and mounts to travel across.

The warriors of Zuu continued to chant. Lanith paused to whisper something to Belfour, who caught the attention of the horn bearers. As soon as the land before them appeared stable enough, the general nodded. The blare of horns echoed throughout the area, even cutting through the chant. Slowly but with building determination, the

275

horde moved forward again.

King Lanith sheathed his blade, then, after most of his forces had already passed by, he urged Darkhorse on. The shadow steed contemplated throwing his rider, but regrettably, all he could do *was* contemplate his revenge. He was still as helpless as Aurim.

To everyone's surprise, they encountered no more resistance that day, although the terrain did become more and more difficult to traverse. By the time the sun neared setting, the invaders were exhausted from having to pick their way through thick brush and rising and falling landscape. Lanith grew furious at the slowing pace, but did not order the sorcerers to clear the forest for him as they had done in the beginning. After Belfour's fourth request, the king finally granted him permission to give the command to make camp.

The invaders might have had some knowledge of the Dagora Forest, but they could not know it as well as Darkhorse, who had crossed it time and time again over the centuries. However, the immortal could not recall so troublesome a trek in this region. He was of the suspicion that perhaps the Green Dragon had decided to be more subtle, that instead of outright assaults, the drake lord now utilized delaying actions such as small but significant alterations in the land. Not only would it frustrate the invaders, possibly make them more prone to making mistakes, but it bought the master of Dagora time to prepare for the massive force that had suddenly decided to invade his land.

Thirty, possibly even twenty years ago, it would not have been so possible for Lanith, even with his sorcerers and Yureel, to conquer his former master. However, with the coming of Cabe Bedlam and the death of the Dragon Emperor, the centuries-long rule of the drakes had begun to collapse. Humans saw that their draconian masters were no longer invincible. More important, the Dragon Kings, ever untrusting of their own brethren, finally began to turn on each other. The clans of Iron and Bronze tried to seize power from their emperor, only to be crushed. Treachery abounded. Green allied himself with humans, which enabled his kingdom to survive relatively intact, but his control over many of his human vassals dwindled, especially over distant Zuu.

The Dragon King was hardly defenseless, however, as had proven so far. Darkhorse had no idea what the drake's next move would be, but he suspected that the night would not be a calm one.

Making camp in the thick forest was not the most pleasant activity for Lanith's warriors, but they tried to make do as best they could. Because of the thickness of the foliage, Belfour tripled the normal number of sentries. In addition, members of the Order were divided into groups of three, with each group using their combined abilities to monitor the region around the massive encampment.

Aurim was exempted from this. Lanith wanted his prize sorcerer to sleep through the night, although if any of the spellcasters on sentry duty sensed anything amiss, they were to alert the younger Bedlam immediately.

Darkhorse found himself handed off to an aide, who seemed at a loss what to do with the eternal. The man first tried to deal with the shadow steed just as he would have with any normal mount, but when he found that Darkhorse neither needed nor desired anything, the aide threw his arms up in frustration and simply left his charge tied up to a tree next to the tent that doubled both as the king's personal quarters and his strategic headquarters.

The shadow steed had hoped that his caretaker would make the mistake of removing the saddle and bridle, but evidently the human had been warned against doing so.

Unlike his imprisonment in the palace, Darkhorse discovered that he could move, although if he tried to do much more than turn his head or take a step forward or back, he froze up for more than a minute. The eternal still could not use his power, not even to probe for any possible sorcerous activity in the forest around him. He had no idea whether the Dragon King even knew that he and Aurim were part of this sinister force. Darkhorse did not worry about himself so much as what might happen to Cabe's son if the Green Dragon tried to eliminate Lanith's most powerful tool, the Order.

Although he was fairly near to the king's quarters, Darkhorse could not hear what was going on inside save that Lanith appeared to be berating one of his staff. Not surprising, especially if the one being berated was General Belfour. Belfour was still the most outspoken officer, although he had so far never actually defied his liege. If Darkhorse was any judge, the general would have opted for continued peace rather than this war King Lanith so desired.

Be careful, General, lest Zuu lose its only voice of reason.

The eternal's ears twitched as a crackling sound rose without warning from the encampment's edge. At first he thought it was a new attack, but nothing more happened. The crackling continued to rise in intensity, causing some consternation among the warriors, who had just started to settle down for the night. Just as it seemed panic might arise, though, someone made an announcement that caused calm to resume. Darkhorse could not hear what was said, but gathered from the renewed quiet that the spell causing the noise was the work of the Order.

Time passed slowly for the captive. Belfour and the other senior officers departed the king's tent, vanishing into the encampment. Lanith made no attempt to check on his reluctant mount, instead evidently retiring the moment his subordinates departed. Darkhorse marveled at the horse king's attitude; the human treated the eternal as he would have any mortal steed. Away from combat, it seemed not to impress him that Dark- horse was so much more. The eternal resembled a horse and so Lanith treated him like one. It was almost insulting.

Yureel, too, was oddly absent, something that bothered the stallion. Neither of the pair required sleep and only needed rest if worn from battle or extensive uses of power. That Yureel had not come to taunt him meant that the shadow puppet had other things to occupy his time. Darkhorse wondered what the sinister imp found so diverting.

Time passed. Since the aide had departed, no one else had come to check on him. How long he stood facing the tree around which his reins were tied, Darkhorse did not care to know. On occasion, the distant, faint sounds of a sentry moving about or some warrior grumbling in his sleep disturbed the silence, but in general the night was quiet save for the calls of a few nocturnal creatures. After several futile attempts *to* do something more about his captivity, Darkhorse finally gave up.

He had nearly drifted off into *a state similar* to dozing when he sensed an approaching figure. His first thought was that it might be Aurim, but as he carefully studied the newcomer, Darkhorse realized that it was a warrior and a woman at that.

She approached him tentatively, as if not quite certain what to make of his imposing figure. The woman was typical of an inhabitant of Zuu, blond, tall, and muscular. She was no one that Darkhorse could recall, but the traditional outfit she wore reminded him of the king's Guard.

With a quick glance around her, the female stepped close enough to whisper. "My name—I feel like a fool to be doing this—my name's Rebatha. I was told you might be a creature called—gods!—called Darkhorse. Is that true?"

Unable to do anything else, the shadow steed nodded.

Rebatha looked uncertain. "Did you nod your head in reply? Maybe . . . if you really can understand me . . . stamp the ground lightly three times with your left front hoof."

Darkhorse obeyed, moving slowly so as not to frighten away his anxious visitor. Rebatha was clearly not supposed to be here. He now had a notion as to just who she was.

She watched him perform exactly as she had asked, shaking her head afterward in disbelief. "I didn't believe my sister or my father, but it must be true. You are Darkhorse, I guess. My father's Trenlen. He told me that you disappeared after trying to rescue your friend the sorcerer. When I heard King Lanith had a new mount, a horse like none anyone had ever seen, I had to find out if it was you. This was my first chance, though."

While he appreciated her efforts, Darkhorse wished that he could tell Rebatha to hurry and remove the saddle and bridle. Unfortunately, the spell of silence prevented that and it appeared that the woman did not realize that it was the equipment that prevented the eternal from escaping.

"I'm going to untie the rope and lead you away. Is there anything you can do, then?"

The saddle! The bridle! Can you not see that they are the reason I can do nothing? He twisted his head, trying to indicate the items, but Rebatha still did not understand what he wanted. As the woman turned to undo the reins from the tree, Darkhorse gave up his attempt to communicate. If he could at least escape into the forest, then it might be possible to find someone who would remove the magical bonds from him.

"I don't know what else to do," she whispered, tossing the reins over his back. "I'd better leave before they notice me missing. Can you escape on your own?"

At last something to which he could reply. Darkhorse nodded vigorously. Rebatha blinked, then began to back away.

"Good luck . . . I guess. I'd better leave before anyone notices."

The warrior vanished back into the camp; her departure as silent as her arrival. Darkhorse watched her until he was certain that she was safely away, thinking all the while of the bravery of Trenlen and his daughters. They had already risked much for him, a creature who they did not even really know. It now behooved him to make those risks pay off.

He moved slowly from his position, both because he feared disturbing Lanith and because of the possible danger of snagging the loose reins on a limb. No sentries were in sight, but they had to be nearby. However, the sentries were not as great a concern to him as the sorcerers were. Depending on what spells they had cast, they might take notice of him disappearing into the forest. If so, he hoped that they would simply think him some warrior's mount that had accidentally wandered off and assume that his master would soon retrieve him. By the time they realized otherwise, Darkhorse hoped to be far away and free of his bonds.

It does not matter whether they notice me or not, though, does it? I have no real choice, do I? This is my only opportunity to escape! With careful steps, he wended his way to the nearest path wide enough to enable him to enter the forest, then plunged in. He felt nothing as he passed through the area of the spell, but that did not mean that he had left the camp unnoticed by the sorcerers. Darkhorse chose not to worry about them, his path to freedom more important. The saddle and bridle prevented him from squeezing through extremely narrow gaps, which meant he had to constantly shift direction every time he was confronted by a breach too small. This slowed his flight, but at the same time meant that any pursuit would in turn be slowed.

That his opportunity had come so quickly had been surprising at first, but in retrospect could have possibly been predicted. Lanith could not help thinking of him as a horse even though he should have known better. Yureel clearly had many other deeds of evil to attend to, so he also had left the seemingly helpless shadow steed alone, probably on the assumption that the king would pay more attention to the guarding of his new prize. Aurim, the only other one who might have been concerned with Darkhorse, was trying to recover from the heavy stress caused by his monumental part in the Order's tasks. As for Lanith's warriors, their only concern was the as of-yet unseen enemy.

The path continued to be treacherous and was made worse by the fact that the saddle and bridle forced Darkhorse to remain solid. That meant that each step, each movement, caused branches and foliage to rustle or crunch. To Darkhorse, each noise echoed through the forest with the reverberation of a thunderclap. How did mortal creatures survive such racket?

Adding to his misery were the reins, which had long slipped off his back and since then had been catching on every other tree limb or bush he passed. It was a wonder he was making any progress at all, but fortunately, pursuit had yet to materialize.

Perhaps no one will discover my absence until the morning. He hoped so, but dared not slow down. The farther, the better—

The reins grew taut again. Darkhorse pulled up short. He was beginning to despise the disorder of the forest. The shadow steed backed up, trying to see what limb had snared him this time.

Instead of a tree, however, he discovered the reins in the hands of a being startling even to him, a being more at home in the forest than an elf.

"Little horse, little horse, where is your rider?" The figure, no more than five feet tall, resembled a tree herself. With his superior vision, one of the few attributes left to him, Dark- horse noted the barklike skin and leafy hair. She was nearly the same shade as the tree next to her. Her features were somewhat human, somewhat elfin, and very youthful. Some males of either species would have probably found her very exotic, although based on what little knowledge he had of tree sprites, any relationship between her and a male of another race would have been short and deadly. Tree sprites were born from shoots broken off and nurtured by their mother sprite; males of any sort were considered little more than sport and, when the woodland creatures were done with them, excellent planting soil. Only their fear of the Green Dragon kept them from mischief, that and their rarity. Few shoots took root and fewer still survived to maturity.

Whether she now acted as a sentinel for the drake lord or simply dwelled nearby, Darkhorse saw in her the possibility of either freeing himself or, at the very least, being led to the Green Dragon. The tree sprite would have no need for him and certainly a being as magical as she could see that he was no normal steed.

Darkhorse tried to indicate his predicament, but she pulled hard on the reins. "Little horse, come with me."

With strength far greater than that of a dozen men twice her size, the sprite pulled Darkhorse toward her. To his surprise, the eternal discovered that he had to obey; the same spell that gave Lanith control over him now worked for her. So long as she held the reins, the sprite was in command. Aurim had been very thorough with his spell.

If she takes me to the drake none of this will matter. That must be where she goes. What else would she plan?

"Come, come!" The sprite led him along a path that looked impenetrable at first, but seemed to open up just before them as they proceeded. However, while it was somewhat difficult to see the night sky from within the forest, Darkhorse quickly realized that he and his companion were heading southeast, not northeast, which would have brought him toward the caverns of the Green Dragon.

What is she up to?

It did not take long to discover the answer to that. The sprite led him to a secluded location where what first appeared to be a young sapling about two feet tall grew. However, the sapling twisted toward the sprite as they neared. Darkhorse's companion had led him to her offspring.

"Little one, do you see what I brought you? You will grow big and strong with this."

The sprite was not a guardian posted by the Dragon King; she was a mother seeking sustenance for her child. He noted the remnants of a pair of small animals nearby and a much larger mound that indicated that something roughly the size of a man had been buried there quite some time before. The sprite intended to slaughter Darkhorse and add his body to the sapling's larder. With such sustenance to support it, the sapling would grow into a more mobile sprite in only a few weeks.

The immature creature continued to lean toward them, reminding Darkhorse of the grass in the Barren Lands. The grass might have been harmless, but this creature certainly was not. Nor was her progenitor.

"Good little horse . . ." The delicate-seeming hands of the sprite had altered into long, wicked claws. She meant to tear open his throat.

Darkhorse could not move, but he was hardly fearful. A captive of the bridle and saddle he might be, but the eternal was still no creature of flesh and blood.

The sprite raised one hand, then slashed at his neck . . . only to have her claws glance off. She hissed, trying again. This time, the forest creature nearly broke one of her claws. Her second failure left her livid. Her other hand became entangled in the reins, causing her to try to tear it off. When that failed, the sprite moved closer and inspected the bridle.

"Sorcery?" Her interest piqued, she ran her hands over the saddle. Her tone grew merry. "Little horse, you have a pretty, pretty saddle . . . a pretty saddle that makes you so tough-skinned, yes? Must not get it bloody. Must take it off."

Still convinced that she could slaughter Darkhorse for food, the sprite worked at the fastenings of the saddle. Darkhorse stood as still as possible, not wanting to disturb the sprite's precarious attention span. Once he was free, she would see what it meant to threaten lives.

"Here," she whispered. "Here." The sprite tugged at the fastenings. They did not seem to want to open at first, but gradually Darkhorse felt her loosen the buckle.

"Please don't do that."

No, it cannot happen now! Not when I am so close! Dark-horse glanced to his side, already knowing who it was who had discovered them. Aurim. The sorcerer looked and sounded almost sad as he studied the eternal.

"I'm almost sorry you didn't make it." The young sorcerer reached out, as if trying to seize the reins from where he stood despite the fact that they were well out of his reach. "But now I'm going to have to take you back, Darkhorse."

Chapter Twelve

With one last tug on the partially loosened saddle, the tree sprite looked around

Darkhorse at Aurim. The shadow steed stared bitterly at his friend, frustrated that he had come so close to freedom, only to have it torn away from him.

The sprite's demeanor shifted the moment she realized what stood before her. All savagery vanished. She was now a delicate, vulnerable creature . . . and very much female. It was this she emphasized most as she moved closer to the sorcerer. Her movements were more natural than those of Saress, but still of the same school of seduction.

"Pretty, *pretty* man. Is this your horse? He's very pretty, too. Do you think I am pretty?" She was nearly close enough to put her arms around him. Whether the nymph hoped to seduce Aurim first or simply crush him with her incredible strength was a question Darkhorse would never know the answer to, for Aurim suddenly raised his hands to eye level, then brought them down toward the tree sprite.

He barely touched her, but the sprite transformed. She hardly had time to gasp as her arms stiffened and lengthened and her legs melded into one. Her feet sank into the soil, growing roots as they did. The sprite's face all but vanished as her neck thickened and her hair became a leafy canopy.

A few seconds later, where once she had stood, there was now a miniature yet adult tree.

"I'm sorry," murmured Aurim. His interest in the sprite faded. "You should've known someone would notice you pass through the detection spell we placed around the encampment, Darkhorse. You only got this far because the sorcerers on duty didn't make anything of it at first, but out of fear of the king's wrath and probably Saress's as well, they finally woke me."

Darkhorse twisted around to better face his friend. Aurim's brief moment of regret for the eternal had clearly passed and once more Yureel's spell held sway. Fortunately, it appeared that Yureel himself was not present. That meant that the shadow steed had only Aurim's affected mind to deal with.

What could he do against the sorcerer, though? So long as the bridle and saddle were attached, Darkhorse was little more than an obedient animal.

"Why don't you come to me, Darkhorse?" Aurim asked hesitantly. "You know I don't want to hurt you, but I've got to if you don't come willingly."

He sounded too sincere to be simply mouthing the words of Yureel. Aurim's will was stronger than even the shadow steed would have believed. *Perhaps with a little more time, he can free himself!*

What might happen in the future did not matter now, though. Aurim might be fighting against the spell that controlled him, but for now he was still a thrall to Yureel. Darkhorse wanted to go to his young friend and help him, but he could not do that until he himself was free and that was hardly what Aurim had in mind at the moment.

He backed away. So long as the sorcerer did not touch the reins, Aurim could not command Darkhorse to do anything. The reins seemed to be the key to controlling the eternal's actions.

"Please don't do this, Darkhorse. He'll make me hurt you. I won't be able to stop myself. It's taken me this much just to keep from attacking already. I—I don't think I'm strong enough to free myself from his will."

But you can! the shadow steed tried to roar. However, no sound, not even a whinny, escaped him. The spell of silence still held. Darkhorse's frustration grew tenfold. He *had* to be able to talk, he had to be able to tell Aurim—

"You are not completely his!"

The words startled both of them. Darkhorse blinked, then laughed. Aurim took a step back, hands raised. He seemed caught between attacking and retreating.

Darkhorse reared, kicking out with his hooves. The shadow steed had no intention of striking Aurim, but he wanted to keep the sorcerer off-guard for the moment. His unexpected success against the spell of silence encouraged him, but he could still sense that complete freedom was not his. The sprite had loosened the saddle, but while Darkhorse could feel it shifting back and forth, it was still attached to him. So was the bridle. He had regained some of his abilities, but not nearly enough.

Aurim, however, did not yet realize Darkhorse's dilemma. The stallion had to use that to his advantage. "I do not want to hurt you, either, Aurim, so I tell you now to stay back! You are not responsible for yourself! It is Yureel and Lanith who are the true enemies! You know that! Fight their control!"

"I—" The human shook his head. "You have to—"

His demeanor shifted, going from confusion to mockery. Darkhorse vaguely sensed a new presence. It was not exactly here, but its attention was.

Yureel! The shadow puppet had evidently discovered Darkhorse's escape and had linked to the sorcerer in order to recapture the stallion. The transference of control was slower this time, however, possibly a sign that Aurim had indeed shaken off part of the spell. Unfortunately, Darkhorse knew that Cabe's son was not yet strong enough to do more than delay the inevitable.

"Darkhorse . . ." The true Aurim momentarily broke through. Tears coursed down his face. "I can't—"

He suddenly seized his head and screamed. Darkhorse fell back, not at all certain what to make of the human's mad struggle. He wanted to help Aurim, but did not know exactly how. A part of him suggested running since nothing would be gained by both of them being captured. Only by regaining his own complete freedom could the shadow steed hope to help his companion recover his own.

Yet he made no move to depart. Aurim's struggle was so desperate, Darkhorse feared that the lad might be injured or worse. That he could do nothing to help made the matter that much more terrible.

Aurim screamed again. Darkhorse took a tentative step toward him.

The sorcerer gasped, then collapsed.

"Aurim!" Heedless of the possibility of a trap, Darkhorse trotted over to the still figure and inspected him. Aurim Bedlam was definitely unconscious. His breathing was slightly ragged, but steady. Even in the shadows of the night, the ebony stallion could see how pale and drawn the human was.

When the sorcerer still did not move, Darkhorse gently nudged Aurim's side with his muzzle. The human might have been dead, so limp had he become. Only his regular breathing kept the eternal from fearing the worst. Still, Aurim could not be all that well, not after such a titanic struggle. Darkhorse was amazed at the young man's incredible will. To have battled Yureel to this point . . .

I have to do something! I cannot simply leave him here. Now there is the chance to completely rid him of Yureel's foul touch. One major problem faced the eternal, though. How was he to move Aurim anywhere? The saddle and bridle still kept him trapped in a solid equine form, useless for lifting objects as large as the sorcerer's body, much less tossing them up onto his back.

He had only one slim hope. If his power was great enough to remove the fairly simplistic spell of silence, then perhaps, just perhaps, Darkhorse had enough ability to levitate the sorcerer. It was worth a try; he had no other ideas.

Thanks to the saddle and bridle, the shadow steed could not even estimate how much of his power he now controlled. He could only concentrate and hope that he did not fail. Levitating a heavy, still body was in some ways a much more complicated task than removing a minor spell such as the one that had kept him silent. Removing the simple silence spell had required only momentary effort; levitation demanded constant concentration and a steady flow of energy throughout the entire process.

Darkhorse focused on Aurim and imagined him slowly rising into the air. At first he grew optimistic; Aurim's arm rose, followed gradually by the rest of his form. However, Darkhorse managed to raise the sorcerer only a few inches high before he lost control and Aurim dropped back to the earth.

I will not be denied! Darkhorse readied himself and tried again, throwing his will into the task as he had not done in centuries. He was hardly used to such a relatively minor feat being so straining. He was Darkhorse, after all. No spell so simple should have defied him so.

Perhaps fueled by his growing ire, his second effort met with better success. Aurim's body shot up more than six feet into the air and would have risen even farther if not for the eternal's quick thinking. He regained control of the floating form, then immediately summoned the sorcerer toward him, keeping his concentration steady.

Darkhorse's most unsettling moment came at the very end, just after he had grown confident enough to believe success a certainty. He lowered Aurim to his back, but just as he was about to release his hold on the unconscious human, the loose saddle shifted somewhat. Aurim nearly slipped head first from the shadow steed's back. It was only through quick concentration that Darkhorse saved his young friend.

More cautious, Darkhorse repositioned Aurim so that this time he would be secure. Even so, Darkhorse knew that he would not be able to move very swiftly through the forest. The saddle would continue to shift around as he moved, upsetting Aurim's balance again. Carrying the sorcerer across his back also meant that the shadow steed now needed an even wider path. In a forest as thick as Dagora, that was bound to cause trouble at more than one point during their flight.

By now, Yureel had to know that he had lost his hold on his puppet sorcerer. The other members of the Order would also realize that one of their own was missing. Some sort of pursuit could certainly not be far behind. Darkhorse had to move on.

He passed the tree that had once been a thinking being. There was nothing Darkhorse could do for the sprite, but he did vow that he would alert the Green Dragon to what had happened. Despite his distaste for the creatures, her fate was a matter for her master to decide. If the drake chose to free her, so be it.

Handicapped as he was, reaching the Dragon King was still his best option. The drake lord had eyes throughout the forest; someone or something would take note of the huge black stallion and his unconscious charge. Hopefully, this time it would be a creature actually serving the Dragon King.

As the shadow steed traversed the thick forest, he continued to keep a wary eye out for Saress or any of the other spellcasters. For some reason the enchantress had not been part of the invasion force. Darkhorse supposed that her present duties now included monitoring Zuu while the king was away, although certainly Lanith could contact her through one of the other members of the Order if necessary. Still, it would have been nice to know where the treacherous woman was.

The night quickly aged. The shadow steed paused momentarily to assess two possible paths ahead. More than two hours had now passed since Darkhorse had left the region of the sprite and still he had come across no one who could help him. At this rate, dawn would soon arrive. *Where are your spies, drake?* Surely some creature other than the sprite dwelled or hid in this part of the forest. So far, the only signs of life other than the trees themselves had been the occasional cry of a night bird and the constant rustle of leaves as the wind blew—

It suddenly dawned on Darkhorse that although the leaves rustled even now, this time there was no wind. Something else was causing the branches to shift, something very large.

What dropped from the high, night-shrouded treetops was no bird . . . or, rather, *was* a bird, but also much more. It stood approximately the height of a human, but other than also having the general shape of one, the creature was avian. In many ways, it resembled the Gryphon with its predatory beak and its intelligent, searching eyes. However, where the king of Penacles often showed compassion, an aura of arrogance surrounded the newcomer.

Wide wings now folded, the avian pointed a taloned hand at Darkhorse's cargo.

"Stand aside, Seeker, I have no time for you!" The eternal kept glancing about the area. Where one Seeker lurked, there was generally a full flock nearby. Prior to the Dragon Kings, the avians had ruled this land, but their own audacity coupled with their continual war with the earth-burrowing Quel had led to their downfall. Rookeries still existed, though, and many Seekers still believed that they were masters of the Dragonrealm.

The avian, a male judging by his height, opened his other hand, revealing a medallion. The Seekers were renowned for the magical medallions they had created and many humans, elves, and drakes had hunted ruined rookeries looking for such prizes. Darkhorse, who knew how devious the devices could be, took several steps back until he heard fluttering behind him.

A second Seeker just a little smaller than the first and therefore likely a female blocked his path of retreat. Darkhorse wondered if they were aware that his power was hindered by his trappings. Certainly they wondered why he took such a slow, methodical route to bring Aurim Bedlam home. The avians were very familiar with the Bedlams, especially Cabe and his mad father Azran. Darkhorse suspected that the Seekers respected Cabe for his past dealings with them, but that did not mean that such respect transmitted into concern and respect for either the master sorcerer's friend or his son.

Seeming somewhat irritated, the first Seeker squawked quietly, then held the medallion up. The shadow steed readied himself for whatever assault the birdman planned.

Images flooded his head, images Darkhorse immediately recognized as originating from the mind of the Seeker. The avians could communicate with those of other races by either using their talismans or, better yet, touching their clawed hands to the forehead of the one with whom they desired to converse. Communication always occurred in the form of a series of images, not all of them necessarily based in reality. This Seeker had chosen the medallion, likely well aware what it might mean to touch the legendary demon steed.

In his mind, Darkhorse saw the Green Dragon, now seated on his throne, making a demand of a pair of elder Seekers. The image was followed by one of the armies of Lanith poised at the edge of the Dagora Forest. That picture, in turn, was followed by the vision of a blazing forest. Next came a series of swift scenes, all of them of flocks of Seekers rising swiftly into the night sky.

"So your flocks serve the drake lord of this forest, do they?" An interesting alliance. Seekers despised drakes even more than they did humans.

The vision shifted without warning, showing avian against drake in combat. The alliance was only temporary, foes joining together to combat a common enemy. Lanith's horde lay destroyed, their pitiful weapons no match for the combined might of the Seekers and the Dragon King.

"And what about his sorcerers? Your victory will not be an easy one, bird!" Pride was still one of the Seekers' greatest weaknesses. Too often they dove into conflicts, assuming that they were destined to be the victors.

The winged figure ignored his question, instead indicating the prone form atop the back of the shadow steed. An image of Cabe Bedlam materialized in Darkhorse's thoughts. The avian had made the link between Darkhorse's unconscious charge and the master sorcerer. How he had made that link became a little clearer a breath later when a vision of Yssa formed. Evidently the Seekers held her in as much respect as they did Cabe. For some reason, the eternal was not at all surprised. The drake's half-human daughter seemed to have a way with some creatures.

Pulling the medallion to his chest, the birdman indicated that Darkhorse should follow him. While the eternal would not normally have trusted the creature enough to obey, he decided that it was best to risk it at this time. After all, the Seekers only had to seize the reins to put him under their complete control, something he did not want them to discover. If he cooperated, they would not be tempted to forcibly lead him along.

One benefit of the avians' unexpected appearance was that any pursuer would think twice before attacking while the Seekers were nearby. Even the Order would pause. Seeker magic was a force to be reckoned with.

While it was clear the pair with him would have preferred to return to the sky, they remained earthbound for the trek, flittering through the woods like graceful yet deadly dancers. However, Darkhorse did not doubt that at least half a dozen more just like them lurked above, flying from tree to tree and keeping a silent vigil on the surrounding area with both their eyes and their medallions.

The Seeker behind Darkhorse suddenly bumped into him. He glanced as best he could at the smaller of the bird people, discovering her all too interested in Aurim. While reading the shadowed, inhuman features was oft times difficult, the stallion thought he saw suspicion and uncertainty in her eyes. She started to reach for the sorcerer's dangling arm, but Darkhorse took a quick step forward. She glared at him but could not match his icy gaze for very long. The Seeker retreated a few steps and did not try to touch Aurim again.

As pleased as he was to be making apparent progress, Darkhorse again grew impatient with the length of the journey. Surely the Green Dragon had to know where he was by now. Why did the drake not simply use his vast power to transport the eternal and his companion to his caverns? Why trust to the untrusting Seekers?

The lead creature paused without warning. Darkhorse looked around, but saw nothing significant about the location. The Seeker, ignoring his impatience, went down on one knee, lowering his head at the same time.

With the other Seeker keeping watch, the first avian raised his hands upward. Darkhorse could not sense any use of sorcery, but he suspected that his guide was trying to summon someone very far away.

When enough time had passed and still nothing had happened, the shorter Seeker squawked angrily. The male looked up at her and squawked back, his annoyance seeming to be focused more on his companion than the one he was trying to summon. When it was clear that there would be no more interruptions from the impatient female, the taller Seeker renewed his summoning.

As if in response, a figure formed in the darkness just before the male.

At last! the shadow steed thought, his exasperation having grown nearly beyond his control. *I will have some very choice words for you, drake lord, for making me journey this long when the situation is so dire!*

However, the newcomer was not the Dragon King, but a shorter, more familiar person.

Yssa.

"I'm here, J'K'I'RU—" The enchantress paused when she saw the steed and his cargo. "Darkhorse! You escaped! Is that . . . is that Aurim?"

"It is, Yssa, and while I am indeed happy to see you, perhaps you can explain to me how you come to be associated with these . . ."

"That can wait." She folded her arms tight. "I don't think that I want to let Lady Bedlam wait any longer than I have to. Not after our first encounter. She doesn't even know why I left so suddenly." Yssa turned to the male Seeker, reaching out a hand at the same time. Surprisingly, the avian, now standing, took her hand and held it. He squawked something, to which Yssa replied with a nod. "Thank you again, J'K'i'RU. I know it wasn't easy to convince your flock to do this, even for me."

"Do you actually understand that noise? What is this Jkiroo you've said twice already?"

"J'K'i'RU. That's the shortened version of his name. Don't ask me to repeat the full version; I don't think my mouth and lungs could take it. Yes, of course I understand him, just as I understood the grass."

She said it in such a matter-of-fact tone. Darkhorse doubted that anyone save perhaps Azran Bedlam had ever been able to understand the natural language of the Seekers. Most had to rely on either the medallions or being touched by the avians. Truly there was more to Yssa than anyone realized.

However, she was correct about one thing. Now he, who had been so impatient to end his journey, was delaying it further. Aurim needed to be attended to and the sooner the better.

Behind him, the female said something. The male shook his head, but she insisted. Finally, he squawked at Yssa, who nodded her head. "I'll tell him that."

"Tell who what?"

"A message for Cabe Bedlam. A personal one. This flock holds him in especially high regard because of something concerning his father . . ." The enchantress sounded somewhat puzzled.

"He can explain in more detail, but I will tell you that it is because of Cabe that many Seekers were freed from their servitude to Azran, his father. Azran was nothing like his son."

"So I've heard." She approached the eternal. "The saddle. It feels . . . evil. The rest of the equipment does—"

"Lady Bedlam is no doubt very upset, Yssa. We should go to her as soon as possible." He dared not let her continue speaking about the saddle and bridle until they had been removed. If the Seekers did not realize just how handicapped he was at the moment, he had no intention of illuminating them in that regard. Darkhorse did not trust them enough to not think that they might turn on Yssa, even if she was respected by them.

"You're right, of course." The blond enchantress held both hands out, thumbs together and fingers fanned out. The Seekers returned the gesture, the male actually touching palms with Yssa. Darkhorse, studying the hands, wondered if the gesture was supposed to represent a flock coming together in harmony. When there was time, he intended on discussing much with the young woman.

The Seekers suddenly darted up into the air, vanishing into the darkened treetops. Yssa watched them disappear, then turned her attention back to the ebony stallion and his unconscious passenger. "You can't transport the pair of you back to the Manor, can you?"

"No, I cannot . . . can you?"

"I think I can do it, but we might have to appear just outside the magical barrier that surrounds their domain. I don't think Lady Bedlam trusts me quite enough yet to let me immediately enter. I only made it last time, I think, because I was with Cabe. She's very protective of him."

"Like me, Yssa, she is very protective of all of those close to her." The shadow steed studied the darkened forest. "I am very distrustful of the lack of attention Lanith has given our escape so far. You had best send us on our way before that changes."

"I agree." She closed her eyes, concentrating.

The blink hole illuminated the entire area. The moment Yssa indicated everything was ready, Darkhorse wasted no time in entering.

Nothing hindered them as they crossed from one end of the hole to the other. Yssa and Darkhorse stepped out of the other end, only to find that what she had feared was true. They had not materialized on the Manor grounds, but rather in the surrounding forest. Darkhorse recognized the region and knew that another two or three steps would take him up to the barrier that prevented those without permission from entering.

"There's something I should warn you about first, Darkhorse. I nearly forgot. The Bedlams think—"

"Darkhorse." The voice that interrupted was that of Gwendolyn Bedlam, but the tone was hardly one of relief or greeting. Instead, it almost sounded accusatory. "What have you done to my son?"

"My lady?" He turned, nearly jostling Aurim loose, and found the legendary sorceress standing behind Yssa. An aura surrounded Gwendolyn Bedlam, a crimson aura that mirrored the outrage in her expression.

"Careful, Gwen," called Cabe from yet another direction. He, too, faced his old friend as if confronting a possible foe, but his expression was more a combination of curiosity and sorrow. "Let's hear him out."

"Our son lies on his back like some gutted stag. I want to know if he's all right before anything else happens, Cabe."

"He is not all right, Lady Bedlam. He has been through far too much. The sooner you are able to care for him, the better his chances of full recovery are!" The shadow steed sidled close to them so that the Bedlams could retrieve their eldest offspring.

The emerald-clad enchantress seemed to relax a little. Darkhorse, neck twisted to the limits the bridle allowed him, saw that the aura had faded somewhat. She was still furious with him for some reason, but parental concern had taken the forefront.

Aurim's still form rose from his back, the young sorcerer's flight guided by his father. Cabe Bedlam brought his son up to eye level, then floated him toward his mother, who immediately began to inspect him.

"He seems all right on the surface, but something's been done to his mind." She glared at Darkhorse. "What did you do to his mind?"

"I did nothing!" the eternal instantly protested. He slowly began to understand what was happening. As impossible as it was to imagine, they believed that he was somehow responsible for Aurim's condition.

Stepping forward, Cabe interjected, "Darkhorse, I felt your presence when Aurim and the other sorcerers attacked me. I also sense your touch in his mind. Everything points to you being responsible for possessing and possibly injuring our son. Can you explain that?"

"I can, but it would be better if we did so in the safety of the Manor. You must understand—"

"You're forbidden entrance for now, Darkhorse. I'm sorry. Gwen and I can't take that chance."

"Cabe! You cannot possibly believe that I would ever harm either you or yours! I am your friend! I was your grandfather's friend! *I* have stood by your line more times than even I can count! I have fought beside you against drakes and more! How could you, how could even your lady, believe that I would harm your son?"

Even Gwen was moved by his words. "I don't want to believe that of you, either, Darkhorse, but something did happen to my son and your trace is on him."

"Not *my* trace, my lady, although I can clearly see why you would think so. No, to my shame, that which you sensed earlier, Cabe, was not me . . . and yet I must also say that it was. The villain you seek is an abomination, a travesty of everything that I have sought to be, whose foul name is *Yureel.*"

"Yureel?" The Bedlams and Yssa stared blankly at him. He had hoped that at least the young enchantress would make the link between Lanith's mysterious intelligent force and what he had just revealed, but such was not to be the case.

"Yureel," Darkhorse repeated. "A creature whose trace is so very much like mine because . . . because once, before there were two of us, there was only one. Him." He shook his head. "I will say no more out here. We risk his presence by doing so. Besides, Aurim needs aid."

Cabe walked over to him, reaching out to touch his muzzle. The eternal felt a sorcerous probe enter his mind. He did nothing to deflect it, knowing that the spellcaster sought the proof of his words.

Stepping away a minute later, the sorcerer said, "I believe him." When he saw that his wife was about to protest, Cabe Bedlam added, "And yes, I also believe it's him, Gwen. I thought of that, too." The human did not bother to explain to Darkhorse what he meant by the last, but he did apologize. "I'm sorry, my old friend, but we've been on edge for the past several days. We know all about the armies devastating the western edge of the Dagora Forest and we're painfully aware that our son seems to be a part of the horse king's Magical Order, the ones most responsible for what was happening."

"The Gryphon's been speaking to the Green Dragon, although if they've accomplished anything yet, we haven't heard," Gwen added. "We wanted to go and confront Aurim ourselves, but the Gryphon convinced us that it was more likely we would fall prey to the same power that had taken him. Worse, it was even more likely we'd have to fight our son."

"Well that risk is past now." Cabe raised an arm high. "And I think we can take this conversation into the Manor now . . . unless there's still some objection?" He looked at his wife.

Lady Bedlam's gaze did not fall on Darkhorse, but rather Yssa. "I suppose not."

"Good." Even as the sorcerer spoke, their surroundings transformed. Now they stood in a hall that on one side was made of marble and on the other was carved from living wood. Newcomers always stared at the point where stone and plant melded with no discernible seam. The marble became the wood or perhaps the wood became the marble.

Yssa looked around in awe even though Darkhorse was certain that she had been here at least once since they had separated. It took quite some time to become even somewhat used to the Manor. Although the marble was bright white, almost as if it had been quarried only yesterday, the sense of great age was so evident that even the most jaded person had to stop and stare.

"Aurim needs to be put to bed," Gwen declared. "I'll get Valea to help me with him as soon as I have him settled."

"Please," interrupted Yssa. "May I . . . may I help you, too? I might know a few . . . unusual . . . methods that might work to heal him."

From her expression, Lady Bedlam was anything but pleased by this offer of assistance, but after glancing at her son, she finally acquiesced. "Thank you. Any assistance would be appreciated."

The two sorceresses and their patient vanished, leaving Darkhorse to deal with Cabe. This was not going to be a conversation that the eternal looked forward to, but he had no choice. It was time that someone knew about Yureel.

"She seems harmless," Cabe Bedlam remarked. "And more able than I would've expected after our first encounter, but Tori—or rather Yssa—isn't telling us everything, Darkhorse. Do you know anything about where she comes from? She's scarcely older than Aurim by sorcerer standards. She was born a decade before the death of the

288

Dragon Emperor; that much I've figured out, but just where is still a question. Actually, I've several questions concerning her. How did she escape the drakes' notice? What's her heritage? Yssa looks like a native of Zuu, but for some reason I think that there's more to it than that . . ."

Although he could have answered most of the questions rather easily, Darkhorse chose to remain silent on the subject. Those answers were best left to the young enchantress and her father. Knowing the truth would not help the present crisis and, in fact, might only serve to complicate things further. "I cannot say, Cabe, but that is an issue to be dealt with later, would you not say? We must speak of Yureel and quickly."

The sorcerer's mood shifted. "Yes. Yureel. I've never heard such a name . . . and you said . . . I still can't believe I heard it . . . you said that he's just like you? How can that be possible, Darkhorse? I don't think I've ever come across any mention in any of the journals and spell books I've collected of another creature like you!"

"Yureel is far more than simply a 'creature like me,' Cabe. Yureel is more me than I am, I regret to say. Did you not listen closely to my words when we were outside? Yureel and I share an origin. It is because of *him* that I exist at all!"

His last words seemed to reverberate about the hall. Cabe Bedlam stared wide-eyed at his friend, perhaps, Darkhorse pondered, seeing the eternal truly for the first time. Darkhorse had struggled for so very long for so many centuries to prove, mostly to himself, that he was a unique being. Now, Yureel's return had reminded him of the truth; he was nothing but the foul monster's creation.

"I think . . . I need to sit down for this," the sorcerer finally blurted.

"Allow me—" Darkhorse paused, recalling that he still wore the bridle and saddle. The shadow steed had been so unnerved by the coming conversation that he had completely forgotten about his impediments. "Before we do anything, Cabe, may I ask you to please remove these wicked trappings from me? They hinder my powers."

"Oh, gods, I'm sorry! Let me take care of your concerns and mine at the same time." The human waved his hand.

Their surroundings shifted yet again, this time becoming one of the more private regions of the vast garden. Cabe now sat on a stone bench. High, trimmed bushes shielded them on all sides from the world. It was a perfect place for what would be an unsettling conversation.

Darkhorse barely noted the change in scenery, though, for Cabe had, true to his word, at the same time removed the bridle and saddle. The sensations caused by their vanishing made all else insignificant. To Darkhorse it was as if he had been born a second time. He felt energy flow through him like a river filling an empty basin. The eternal wanted to caper about, fly up into the heavens, or simply shout his joy, but he immediately reminded himself that his freedom was insignificant compared to what he had to tell his friend. "My thanks, Cabe! You have been there to help me as few others have through the centuries. I have ever been in your—"

"Darkhorse . . ."

Cabe knew he was stalling now. The eternal steadied himself. Only Yureel could turn Darkhorse from proud and confident to uncertain and anxious. "I will make this as short and concise as I can then, for even simply talking about it unnerves me greatly." He stared at his long-time friend. "You know about the Void, the empty place from which I was spawned."

"I remember that when I was there I not only wanted desperately to get back here, but I wondered how you could've existed there so long without going mad."

"An astute question and one that I have asked myself since I first arrived in the Dragonrealm. Perhaps because I knew little else when first I came into being, it was easier to suffer my fate . . . but I digress." The stallion shook his head, sending his mane flying. "Let me start again and, please, this time I must get through this."

"Go ahead."

Darkhorse drew upon his renewed strength. He would need much of it in order to finish his tale. "Now there are two of us. Yureel and myself. Once though, there was only one." Darkhorse briefly glanced away, not wanting to witness Cabe's reaction to what he was about to reveal. "It was not *me*. That one was Yureel . . . my creator . . ."

Chapter Thirteen

Yssa helped Gwendolyn Bedlam guide her son to his bed. The young man was still unconscious, not a good sign in Yssa's mind. She found herself more anxious about his health than she would have expected, considering that their only encounter had been a momentary one. The young enchantress decided that it was probably because her time at the Manor had allowed her to know his family just well enough to understand what he must be like. What she had heard of him sounded amazing and quite appealing.

Control yourself Yssa! she silently chided. *He'd have no more to do with you than his father did!* Besides, Lady Bedlam would probably turn her into something grotesque if she discovered the younger woman eyeing her son with anything other than a clinical attitude.

He *was* handsome, though . . .

"How is he?" asked a voice from the doorway. Yssa turned to see Valea Bedlam, her complexion pale, walk toward the bed. To look at the daughter was to see a memory of the mother as she had been at that age. Once they reached adulthood, most spellcasters, especially those with better-than-average ability, did not age much over the rest of the three hundred or so years of their life span unless they chose to do so. Even then, with effort they could reverse the process for a time. Only when they had reached the end of their third century did it become impossible for even the best sorcerers to hold back the ravages of time any longer. At that point, they began to age normally, turning old and gray over the next decade, two, if fortunate. Few were the cases of a spellcaster completing a fourth century.

As for those with only a trace of ability, age generally came to them as it did any other mortal. Power was indeed life.

It was not then surprising to find that time affected the Bedlams little. Mother and daughter looked more like twins born a few years apart. Lady Bedlam was slightly taller and Valea's eyes were more like those of her father, but other than that, the differences were negligible. Both had a fondness for the color green, although where the elder Bedlam wore an elegant gown befitting a master sorceress, the younger was clad in a trousered hunting outfit that still somehow managed to be quite feminine.

They had spoken with one another only briefly during Yssa's initial visit to the Manor, but in Valea Yssa believed she had found an ally, perhaps even a friend. "He's still unconscious," she said now. "We only just lowered him onto the bed."

"He seems all right physically," commented Lady Bedlam as she ran her hand over her son's forehead. Her brow furrowed. She repeated the gesture, moving slower this time. "Odd. I don't sense Darkhorse's influence . . . or rather the influence of that thing that seems like him. Now it seems like he's just sleeping."

Yssa joined her. "May I?"

When Lady Bedlam indicated she had no objections, Yssa reached forward, touching her fingertips to the center of the unconscious sorcerer's forehead. She probed deep, trying to make certain that Aurim Bedlam was indeed free of the spell that had bound him. Her initial search verified what Lady Bedlam had said, but Yssa probed deeper yet. They had to be certain that he was cleansed of any influence.

Layer after layer of his subconscious gave way to her. Although Yssa did not try to read his mind, she did pick up general emotions, enough to know she had been correct about the sort of man he was. Very admirable. Much like his father was said to be. The enchantress was tempted to linger, but knew better than to do so with Aurim's mother next to her. Besides, nothing she had noted contradicted Lady Bedlam's conclusion.

And yet . . .

Exactly what it was she sensed, Yssa could not say. When she searched for it again, the enchantress found nothing.

"Well?" asked Gwendolyn Bedlam, her tone one of growing impatience.

The interruption broke her concentration. Whatever she believed that she had sensed had to have been the product of her own overwrought mind. "I can't find anything. He just doesn't seem to want to wake up."

Cabe's wife nodded. "From what Darkhorse said, this was more traumatic than when Toma seized control of Aurim's mind. Lanith made my son do things that he would've never willingly agreed to do, things that must have *revolted* him." Her hands tightened into fists. "We stayed out of this for as long as we could, first because Zuu had once been a great ally to us and we didn't wish to make the political situation worse, then because Aurim was a prisoner. It's terrible . . . generally I'm the voice of peace, but this time Lanith's gone too far! He has to be *stopped,* Magical Order or *not.*"

"I'll help in any way I can, Lady Bedlam."

Gwen eyed Yssa, possibly trying to find a kind way to turn down her offer. However, before the master sorceress could reply, her daughter interjected, "Anything you can do would certainly be appreciated, Yssa. I know I speak for my entire family, including my brother. I know he'd welcome your presence."

The last made Lady Bedlam's eyes widen briefly, but gradually she nodded. "Yes, we can certainly use your aid, not to mention your knowledge. You know Zuu better than any of us. Were you born there?"

From the tone of her voice and the slight shift of her eyes, Gwendolyn Bedlam was clearly still suspicious about Yssa's origins. So far, none of the Bedlams had *demanded* the truth, but Cabe's wife was not going to be patient with her much longer. Yssa recalled that her father had once acted as secret patron of the sorceress, but that had been long, long ago, before Nathan Bedlam, the Turning War, and the lady's own imprisonment by Azran Bedlam. If anyone might recognize her for the half-breed she was, it would be the woman before her.

"No, my lady. My grandparents were from there and I lived there for some time after I grew up, but I was born and raised in a small village to the north."

"I see." That seemed to settle matters for now. Lady Bedlam leaned over her son. "I wish I knew why he slept like this." She pushed a lock of hair back from his face. "I don't dare take a chance, not after last time."

"Do you think there's a risk of that, Mother?"

Yssa could not follow the sudden shift in the conversation. She looked at Valea. "What risk? Of what?"

It was the elder woman who responded. "Aurim wasn't the only one Toma seized control of. I nearly killed my husband. It was a spell, actually, not really possession, but it might as well have been. We can't risk that Aurim might not still be under some subtle spell." Gwen spread her hands, then again gazed down at her son. A pink aura formed around him. "That should hold him."

"Is that necessary?" Yssa hated the thought of him being bound. It did not seem fair after all Aurim Bedlam had already been through.

"I think so, yes." Lady Bedlam stepped away from the bed. "Now I can concentrate on what ails him without fear that he might attack us while under some carefully hidden spell."

Her words made Yssa think again about the momentary sensation she had felt while probing the sorcerer's mind. Perhaps she should not have so readily dismissed it as nothing. "My lady, I might've made a mistake. You might want to probe his mind again. For a brief moment I thought I sensed something, but it wasn't there when I looked again. Maybe you'd have more luck."

Lady Bedlam extended her hands over her son again. She closed her eyes, but opened them only a breath or two later. "I still sense nothing. I went very deep, too, just in case you might be wondering, Yssa."

While it was a relief to know that her fears had been nothing but empty air, Yssa could not help but be affected by the rebuke she sensed in Gwendolyn Bedlam's words. She began to wonder if Aurim's mother would ever trust her. Perhaps she thought that the young enchantress sought to bedazzle the son since the father had turned down her offer.

It was a reasonable thing to assume. Yssa had always wanted to find someone capable of understanding her and coping with her past. It would have to be a spellcaster; she had learned long ago that most normal humans either feared or sought to make use of her abilities. The drakes were no better. Cabe Bedlam, whose reputation for understanding was legend, had been the perfect choice—so she had thought at the time. Had he left his wife for her, though, Yssa suspected he would have quickly lost favor in her eyes. That was not the kind of mate she desired. The sorceress wanted someone she could trust enough to love and someone she could also trust to love the mixed-blood offspring that would come.

She had reminded both Cabe Bedlam and Miklo of the power her children would wield thanks to both their parents, but had done so only in the hopes it would be an added enticement. Yssa knew now that with Miklo that had not really mattered; he would have accepted her even if she had had nothing to offer him, even children. That she had not loved him in return would not have mattered. Poor Miklo would have accepted her and that would have been enough.

With Aurim Bedlam, however, it was different. Something stirred in her when she looked at him, something that had blossomed quickly since their first brief encounter. It was true that Aurim's power did impress Yssa, but her emotions went much deeper than that. Having touched his mind, she had discovered that the man behind that power was also worth knowing. The blond woman only hoped that she would have the opportunity.

"What do we do now?" Valea asked, gazing down at her brother.

"It looks to me like this will require some private study of my own, dear. Why don't you take Yssa and show her around a little more, darling? If I need either of you, I'll let you know."

Yssa found herself greatly disappointed by Lady Bedlam's dismissal. She said nothing, though, knowing it would only upset the woman. Lady Bedlam did not need more aggravation; her son's recovery was of the utmost importance and if anyone could bring him out of his slumber, it was probably her.

"Yssa?" Valea gently touched her arm. Lady Bedlam had already forgotten them, her attention completely fixed on the still figure. "Let me show you the main library. You didn't get a chance to see that before, did you?"

She actually had gotten a glimpse of it, but Yssa understood that the younger woman was trying her best to keep the peace. Or perhaps Valea feared that Yssa would say something regrettable in response to the rebuke. Yssa gave her a comforting smile. "No, I haven't really seen it. Is it far?"

"Not too far . . ." With one last worried glance at her mother and brother, Valea Bedlam led Yssa from the room. They did not talk at first, Yssa's companion seeming more concerned with getting as far away from her brother's chambers as quickly as they could. Only when they reached a staircase at the end of the hall did she start to calm down. "There's so much to see in the Manor. Every now and them I find some little thing I don't recall ever seeing and I've lived here all my life!"

"I know your mother is worried, Valea. I didn't take any offense from her attitude. She's also got a right to be a little leery of me. I did try once to seduce your father. To be honest, I'm rather surprised that you aren't my enemy."

"If you had tried to seduce my father *again*," Valea replied, her voice suddenly so very like Lady Bedlam's, "my mother would have been the least of your worries." Intense levels of power abruptly radiated from the young woman. Yssa now saw that the incredible abilities Aurim had inherited had also been passed on to the Bedlams' daughter. Whether she was as powerful as her brother, Yssa could not tell, but Valea Bedlam was clearly not someone with whom to trifle.

"I understand perfectly."

The summoned power immediately dwindled away. Yssa's companion smiled apologetically. "Good. I like you. I think my brother would like you, too."

Yssa felt her face redden: a rare occurrence. Valea's simple statement had embarrassed her as little else had during her colorful life. "Well, if he's as nice to others as you are, I'm sure that I'll like him."

"Good!"

Trying not to smile at Valea's enthusiastic response, Yssa focused on the path ahead. The staircase wound several times as it descended but the bottom was visible from where she stood. The Manor was a wonder in design. The enchantress pondered its creators, who, according to what Valea had told her the last time they had met, still remained a mystery to the Bedlams even after all these years. They had suspicions, but nothing verifiable.

"Is something wrong, Yssa?"

Realizing she had been standing and staring, Yssa shook her head and started down. However, a few steps later she happened to glance at the bottom and what the enchantress saw then made her stop. There was a figure at the bottom of the stairs, a figure that should not have been there.

It was Darkhorse, but not Darkhorse as she knew him. The huge ebony stallion looked distorted, as if he had forgotten how to form his equine shape. His legs were twisted, the body looked bloated, and the head was only in part formed. Worse, other appendages of varying design sprouted from his body.

"Rheena!" her companion gasped.

The shadow steed did not move. Yssa slowly descended, her eyes fixed on the bizarre tableau. What had happened to Darkhorse? Why was he frozen in place like some statue?

"Yssa, wait!" Valea darted down the steps to her side. "I think that it's just—"

"Look!" Before the blond enchantress's eyes, Darkhorse faded away. It was as if someone had erased the stallion. "We've got to find out what—"

Valea seized her hand. Aurim's sister was a surprisingly strong woman for her size. "Wait! Listen to me. It startled me, too, at first, but only because I've never seen that one!

Don't worry, Yssa, I know what it was now."

"What are you talking about? That was Darkhorse! He's in danger!" How could Valea be so calm?

Looking Yssa straight in the eye, the other woman quietly said, "It was a ghost. One of the Manor's ghosts. They're images from the past, usually, images that for some reason remain behind. Some of them move, some of them even talk."

"I've never heard of that!" Tales about ghosts and the like abounded throughout the realm, but Yssa had never confronted any such spirit herself. She knew something of the Manor thanks to her father, but he had failed to mention this interesting tidbit of information.

"It doesn't happen very often. Generally it's either Father or Aurim who sees them. I don't know why. I've seen my own share, though. You should witness the wedding scene; it's beautiful if a little sad when you think about the fact that the bride and groom are long dead."

"So the image we saw . . . that happened in the past?"

Here Valea hesitated. "I don't remember ever hearing about this one, but there's one way to be certain. We can ask Father. After all, he's with Darkhorse now."

That was exactly what Yssa wanted to do. The ghost had been too real, too immediate an image. The memory of its appearance still made her shiver a little.

"They're out in the garden maze," the younger sorceress announced, evidently having searched for them with her mind. "They seem to be all right. I didn't probe hard enough to disturb them. Darkhorse is telling him about something."

Yssa had forgotten that. Something about a creature like him. That in itself sounded fascinating, although also frightening if there was any truth to it. She hoped to ask the shadow steed some questions herself when she had the opportunity.

"I don't think I want to disturb them just yet, Yssa. There's another way to check, though. My father keeps a journal of sightings in his private library. He won't mind if I look there. He asked us all to record sightings whenever possible. It's a hobby of his, I suppose."

Yssa still wanted to interrupt Cabe and Darkhorse, but she was a guest, a somewhat undesired guest at that, and so it behooved her to follow the suggestions of her host. Fortunately, Cabe Bedlam's private library was nearby. The room was small but neat and consisted mainly of a desk and some shelves filled with journals, scrolls, and the like.

Valea reached unerringly for one of the journals. She opened the volume, then placed it on the desktop so that both of them could read its contents at the same time. To her surprise, Yssa saw that over the years, Cabe Bedlam and his family had listed hundreds of sightings. Fortunately, Valea evidently knew most of the listings by heart, for she ran through the list so fast that the other sorceress barely had time to read some of the entries. Those that she did read surprised her. Besides the wedding, which she spotted just before Valea turned the page, there were sightings of Seekers, sword fights, even a Quel. Oddly, many of the visions were mundane ones. Yssa even noted more than one listing concerning a woman cooking in the kitchen. There seemed to be neither rhyme nor reason to which images appeared.

Two toward the end of the listing interested her. One, recorded by Aurim, noted that Cabe Bedlam himself had materialized as an image. The other, recorded in turn by Cabe, concerned the drake Toma, with whom Yssa had long been familiar thanks to her father. Although he was now dead, simply seeing the renegade's name made her uneasy. To think that Toma had come so close to seizing control of both the Manor and the young successor to the Dragon Emperor's throne . . .

The listing was a particularly long one, but before Yssa could read more than a line, Valea interrupted her by pushing aside the journal. "Nothing! I didn't see one mention of Darkhorse in here. Now I'll have to interrupt them." The young woman sighed. "But first I guess that I'd better record this one, otherwise Father will probably scold me later on. He takes this so seriously."

While Valea wrote, Yssa took the opportunity to read the rest of the entry concerning Toma. The sighting had taken place not long before Emperor Kyl's ascension and had evidently been a shocking sight to the one confronted by it, namely Cabe Bedlam. He had noted that there had been several unusual factors concerning the vision, including the fact that it had been of a very recent event. The vast majority of the other sightings had been of things and events from the far past. More important, Cabe had noted that the image had probably been some sort of *warning*, the Manor's way of trying to alert its inhabitants to the drake's intrusion. Toma had actually entered the Manor, having stolen the identity of a trusted human scholar named Benjin Traske.

The entry was interesting, but Yssa could make no link between it and the image of Darkhorse they had witnessed. She leaned back, pondering the matter while her companion finished the new entry.

"Do you want to add anything, Yssa?"

Relegating the other entry to the back of her mind, the enchantress read what Valea had written. "No, I don't think I could add anything. You were very thorough."

"I have to be. Father generally questions us about the sightings later on. The more I write down, the less I have to try to recall later on. It's self-preservation."

"Then he'll want to know about this as soon as possible." Yssa straightened: "Is it far to where he's located? Your lands are vaster than some baronies. The garden seems to go on forever."

Valea giggled. "I know, believe me. It won't take us long to walk there, though. There's no reason to use a spell for something as minor as this probably is. My parents don't like us to waste our strength popping from place to place." She turned toward the doorway and her amusement vanished. "That's odd. I don't remember the door being closed."

Neither did Yssa. "One of us probably did it when we came in and we just forgot."

"You're probably right." Valea tried to open the door, but it remained shut. She tugged again with no better success. "I don't understand. It's not locked."

"Let me try." Yssa tugged, but also failed. Lacking the patience of her companion, she did not try a second time, but rather concentrated her power on the defiant door.

It still would not budge.

Valea looked at her. "Something's terribly wrong. You just tried to open the door with sorcery, didn't you?"

"I did. It should've opened easily."

"Maybe if we both try."

The pair stared. The door glowed bright green and quivered, but it remained sealed.

"Take my hand," Yssa commanded. They had one option of escape left, but she suspected that they had to act fast or not at all. "Don't lose your hold, whatever you do."

Once Valea obeyed, Yssa completely focused her attention on her spell. She had always been good at travel spells, be they blink holes or otherwise. What she planned should be simple.

At first, it seemed it would be. A circle of light formed before them. Yssa's hopes rose. The blink hole was forming perfectly . . .

Before the enchantress could open it, the hole suddenly dissipated. A slight backlash of power sent Yssa to the desk, where Valea barely kept her from falling onto it. Both women stared at the sealed entrance.

"That should've worked!" Yssa nearly hissed, but managed at the last moment to smother the sound. Hissing was a habit she had acquired as a child, but one she purposely worked to suppress for fear that others might discover her origin.

"Maybe I can contact my father . . ." Valea stared toward the ceiling.

A giggle echoed through the room, a malevolent, taunting giggle that did not sound human.

No! Yssa whirled around, but could neither see nor sense the source of the foul laughter. Valea shook her head as if trying to clear it. She had failed to reach her father, of that the half-breed enchantress had no doubt.

"What was that, Yssa? Where did it come from?"

Zuu. Zuu is where it's come from . . . A sense of dread rose within her. A short time past, the Manor had warned the Bed- lams about the drake renegade in their midst. She wondered now if perhaps it had been trying to warn them again. Darkhorse had said that the thing that served Lanith was like him, so much so that even Cabe could not tell the magical signatures apart. The mad image of Darkhorse, his form twisted into something perverse, might have been the Manor's unique way of trying to tell someone that the evil had gained access to what should have been the safest domain in all the Dragonrealm.

Worse, if what she believed was true, it was now moving against them . . .

Cabe Bedlam was his dearest friend and yet telling him of Yureel was a task Darkhorse found daunting. He forced himself to proceed, though, knowing that it was necessary. If anyone might be able to help him, it would be Cabe.

"I neither know when nor where Yureel first came into being or whether, like the Void, he was simply there when the multiverse blossomed. If age matters at all in that empty realm, Yureel is far, far more ancient than I. He existed there, floating about and, on occasion, inspecting the few bits of matter that slipped into the Void, but never finding their place of origin. I do not even know if at that time he cared where such bits came from. It is my suspicion that for as long as Yureel has existed, he has mostly concerned himself with his own amusement. Other matters, other creatures, existed only to entertain him."

"You say he was first," Cabe interrupted. "If so . . . how did you come to be?"

The stallion shuddered. "The notion was evidently one long in the forming. Its origin, I believe, was due to an encounter like none he had ever experienced before. Yureel himself told me of the encounter time and time again. He seemed to take particular pleasure in repeating it to me whenever I did not care to join in his foul games, which was often." Darkhorse faltered, recalling the ruthlessness of those games. It was fortunate that Yureel's opportunities for such sport had been rare. "A being of intelligence—Yureel described it only by saying that it talked and had six limbs—had the misfortune to be cast into the Void. Yureel, who had no name at the time and did not even understand the meaning of 'self,' found the hapless one. He was fascinated. Never had he come across such a thing. Yureel decided that he needed to completely understand what this new and unusual toy was like."

"What . . . what did he do?"

Darkhorse gouged the earth with one hoof. "He did as he had always done with the objects he found. He *absorbed* him, Cabe. Swallowed him as a pit of tar would a helpless riding drake. You have seen me open myself when touched by a foe and you have seen that foe vanish within as if falling forever. It is not a fate any would desire, but some might find it more suitable than what Yureel did to this one. He took in the lost one, took in his essence, his very being . . . and made it his own. Where there had been two, there was now only one, but one who now held much of the knowledge, the experience, and the power of the one taken."

The sorcerer shifted uneasily. "Darkhorse, are you saying that you can do this? You can . . . swallow . . . someone and make what they knew, what they *were*, yours?"

For quite some time, the eternal could not look at his friend, much less respond to the question. Finally, with a slow, regretful dip of his head, Darkhorse answered, "Yes . . . I can, Cabe. If I were wont to, I could seize a full-grown human, take him inside, and make mine all that he is." His icy eyes widened. "But I would *never* do such a thing! Never, Cabe!"

"I know you wouldn't, Darkhorse. I know."

What he could never tell the sorcerer was that he *had* done so, far in the past. In the Void, he had not understood what he was doing, only that this was what Yureel always did. In the Dragonrealm . . . there had been a couple of times when the only way to save others had been to take lives in such a manner. The ones he had taken had deserved no mercy, but he could not help feeling sorry for them nevertheless.

The story. He had to keep his mind on the story. "Now Yureel saw things as he had never seen them before. He knew that there were other places beyond his reach, places full of things, full of life. It frustrated him that he could not find these places, although I know he did try. The frustration grew worse the longer he dwelled upon it. When next he confronted a hapless visitor to the Void, he seized that one faster than the first, thinking it would help alleviate his frustration. It did not. It only added new dimensions to it. Now Yureel realized that the places he could not reach had to number into infinity. So many creatures, so many *playthings*, kept from him . . ."

The shadow steed paused, momentarily distracted. For a moment Darkhorse thought he sensed someone using sorcery to contact him, but when he tried to verify it, the eternal felt nothing.

"You don't have to go on if you don't want to," Cabe commented, taking his latest pause for reluctance.

"I need to." It had only been his distraught mind. That was it. Nothing more. "This has to be told." He shook his head, trying again to clear his thoughts. "As I have indicated, to Yureel, the unfortunates were nothing but entertainment. Those that he did not take immediately he generally killed soon afterward for one reason or another. However, it was not until he happened upon a pair of identical beings, creatures who spoke and acted together at all times, that a fantastic notion occurred to him. In his mind, they were the same being but in different shells. They had one another to ever work with . . ." The shadow steed thought over the last statement and corrected himself. "They were never *alone* . . ."

Yureel had taken them as he had taken the others, but this time he studied them closely first. If they could have each other, then why could *he* not have another "self" with whom to play, with whom to share his pastimes . . .

Never had Yureel found any being akin to himself, so he decided that he would create one. The concept of creating something was one he had learned from some of his toys, but until that moment it had made no sense. He pondered it long, testing out one process after another. Nothing seemed to work.

"Then he hit upon the answer, Cabe. If he could absorb other things, make them part of him, why could he not reverse the process and separate a piece of his being, give it strength, and make it grow into another version of himself? There had been incidents when he had misjudged some of the playthings he had found and they had injured him, separating one bit of his essence from the whole. Being a creature much like . . . shall we say a cloud or puddle, for lack of a better earthly description . . . he was generally unhurt by these attacks and always afterward reabsorbed the fragments. It had never occurred to him to do anything otherwise."

THE HORSE KING

"Didn't he ever miss a . . . a piece . . . before?"

Darkhorse understood. "Small fragments, yes, Cabe, but the small ones did not last. That, in fact, was something Yureel discovered for himself during his initial experiments. His first attempt was a tiny blob that he could manipulate but that had no intelligence of its own. He tried yet a larger one, but ended with the same results. It came to the point where Yureel understood that he would have to divide more or less into two *equal* parts to achieve his goal. Unfortunately, he had also learned that the constant attempts to divide *had* weakened him already. He needed to absorb more substance to make further attempts but in the Void there was little to find. His patience, though, had reached its limits and so Yureel dared to try one more time even despite his weakness."

Like a mass of wet clay pulled apart by an artisan, Yureel had stretched in two opposing directions. At first the creature had felt no change, but the more tenuous the physical connection between the two parts became, the more separate the controlling forces of each half also grew. The process also began to speed up, perhaps because the second portion now had some desire for existence of its own.

When had Darkhorse first experienced consciousness? Even the shadow steed could not really say. He thought he recalled some part of the separation, but if so, the memory was a faint one. More distinct were the first memories after the process had finally come to an end, when both shapeless forms had floated weak and unmoving in the vast emptiness. That weakness had threatened both and at one point the new "self" had been forced to retreat from the other, for in hunger the elder had tried to reabsorb his offspring. That was a memory that always haunted Darkhorse. Yureel had thought nothing of the separate personality he had created; he had been just as willing to reabsorb his new counterpart as he had his many ill-fated playthings. Yureel was a name that would come later. At this point, the two identified themselves by such concepts as "self" and "other self." In appearance, they were identical, but even from the start, subtle differences in personality became evident.

"It was when I first encountered a creature other than either myself or Yureel that I learned just how different we were, Cabe. The one who I found was nearly dead, but he struggled to live. I was curious, for I did not retain much memory of Yureel's encounters. The newcomer seemed weak, so I, who had regained strength by then, gave him enough to heal him. I wanted to know what he was and why he looked different. Naturally, my newfound toy was frightened, but he overcame that."

"How were you able to talk to him?"

The stallion considered this long before answering. "I cannot say for certain, Cabe. In the Void, it seemed much easier to touch the minds of others, especially those unshielded. I have not always found it so in the Dragonrealm. Regardless, we eventually did communicate and I found him so fascinating that I just wanted to listen and learn."

Something in his tone evidently made the sorcerer extremely uneasy. "What happened to him, Darkhorse? I can tell that something did." The human's eyes narrowed. "Yureel . he didn't really—"

"Yes, my friend, he did." Darkhorse kicked at the earth again. "He found me, not so difficult a task then, and was delighted with the new toy. Yureel seized him, wanting to play, and when I protested. . he grew angry and *absorbed* him."

"God!"

"I did not at first understand how terrible that was, but I did not think his actions right. You must understand; Yureel was not kind with his captives before he absorbed them . . . not kind at all. That was what drove me away more than anything."

Darkhorse paused to think, not wanting to say anything more that might hint at how *he* had been little better than Yureel. Best to move on to the end. The final fear that had sent him fleeing from his counterpart. "I will not bore you with the tale any longer. I will only say that there came a time when because of his cruel actions to the creatures he found, I did not want to remain near Yureel any longer. I started to drift farther and farther from him, but he caught up to me and demanded to know why I had left him behind. I told him that I wanted to be by myself, that I did not like his games." The shadow steed shuddered. "He said that I did not have to leave. He would simply reabsorb me and create a new playmate, a better one. Before I realized what was happening, Yureel was trying to envelop me!"

The sorcerer shifted uneasily on the bench. His face had grown pale with each successive revelation. "You don't have to go on, Darkhorse! Not if you—"

"I felt my mind, my *self,* dissipating!" the eternal cried, almost talking to himself now. "He tried to do with me what he had done with the others! I am sorry to say that at the time the realization of what they had suffered did not strike me; I only knew my own personal terror, that I was about to cease to be!" Darkhorse stomped the ground in an attempt to relieve himself of the remembered fear. "Yureel did not expect me to be able to resist. *Nothing* had ever been able to resist him! I left him stunned, no doubt also shocked, and fled through the Void until long past the time when I could sense his presence, much less see him in that empty place! I do not know how long I journeyed, for you yourself know how meaningless time can be in the Void, but ever I kept careful watch in case he had tracked me down. I feared him then, Cabe, just as I admit to fearing him now! After the Dragonrealm was revealed to me by a lost sorcerer, I believed that at last I was free of Yureel, but that assumption proved false. He had never ceased following me, so I later discovered. Once before he found his way into this world and only through luck did others succeed in banishing him, again, supposedly *forever.*" The stallion shook his head. "But forever is a long time. He has finally returned . . . and although I fear for the Dragonrealm, I fear more for myself."

Cabe Bedlam rose from the bench. "Why didn't you ever tell me this before?"

"The spell the other sorcerers used to bind Yureel in the Void seemed perfect. I thought him gone forever, unable to harm even those unfortunates who drifted into his realm. I thought myself rid of him."

"How long ago did this happen?"

Darkhorse hung his head low. "Your grandfather's grandfather had not yet been born. I know that because I knew the man. Zerik Bedlam, by the way. Among the spellcasters who forced Yureel back to the empty realm was the woman who would be his mother. I only remember her as Lamaria of the Hidden Grove."

"Someday, you and I will have a long talk about just exactly how many of my ancestors you've met." The human reached out, putting a calming hand on the shadow steed's muzzle.

Although Darkhorse was no true equine, he appreciated his friend's gesture. Telling the story had filled him with shame, not only for his own weaknesses, but the excesses of his brother, his other self. Yureel was a monster in every sense of the word, the demon that mortals had always mistaken for. Some of the sinister legends that had made the ebony stallion so feared had their roots in the battles against Yureel.

"He must be destroyed, Cabe. Somehow, we must destroy Yureel. He will not listen to reason, and no earthly prison is secure enough. There can be no safety from him. Somewhere in the past, he developed a fondness for epics. I think more than one mortal tried to placate him with such stories. Yureel now sees worlds such as the Dragonrealm as the setting for his own tales, and those tales always revolve around destruction on a massive scale. I believe that it was he who saw the taste for conquest in

Lanith's mind and then seduced the horse king with grand promises of an empire spanning the continent."

"But I can't imagine how Lanith thinks he'll win even with Yureel and the Order. All he'll do is maybe succeed in destroying the last vestiges of peace. The entire Dragonrealm could erupt as some kingdoms fight him while others try to take advantage of the chaos!" Cabe mentioned no names, but they both knew that two Dragon Kings, Storm and Black, were among those who would take such an advantage.

"Yureel does not care if Lanith is victorious! He wants only for the armies of Zuu to create such havoc that it takes years for peace to prevail! Yureel is anarchy, Cabe! That is all he strives for!"

The sorcerer looked shaken. "I can't believe that he's so terrible a monster. The way you talk about him . . . is he that much more powerful than you? I'd think the two of you would be equals, yet . . . you really fear him . . ."

"I do. Cabe, I have never been Yureel's equal. To be his equal, I would have to do as he does. That would give me but two choices. I could *absorb* power wholesale as he has always done . . . and spellcasters, of course, provide the greatest source of power . . ." Darkhorse gave thanks that Aurim had escaped the fate of so many others in the past. From Cabe's shifting expression, it was clear the elder Bedlam's thoughts ran a similar course.

"And . . . the other method?" the human finally managed.

"Yureel is a parasite in every sense of the *word,* Cabe! What he does not swallow whole, he often slowly sucks dry. I cannot be certain, but I suspect that he has been drawing strength from the sorcerers of Lanith's Magical Order . . . and was doing so from your son as well."

"He wouldn't!"

Darkhorse shook his head. "There is nothing Yureel would not do, friend! Nothing! If we do *not* destroy him, my foul twin will certainly destroy us . . . but only after we are nothing but empty *husks.* We must—"

His warning was interrupted by the sudden materialization of Lady Bedlam. The scarlet-tressed sorceress's expression was dark. The shadow steed found himself somewhat relieved to see her; her intrusion put a welcome end to his painful conversation. Rather would he deal with trying to free Aurim of the spell that bound him than speak more about the past he shared with Yureel.

"Darling, have you seen Valea and that woman?"

"I've not seen *Yssa* since the two of you took Aurim to his room. I expected Valea to join you there."

Gwendolyn Bedlam looked uncomfortable. "I found I didn't need help from either of them and so I asked Valea if she wouldn't mind showing that woman more of the Manor. Now I'm beginning to regret that decision."

The sorcerer shared a worried glance with Darkhorse. "Why?"

"Because I can't sense them anywhere. I wanted to ask Valea to look up something for me in the main library, but I couldn't locate her. I tried a stronger, more direct probe, but for all practical purposes, both she and that wood witch are missing."

"Valea wouldn't leave the Manor without telling us, dear, and you've got nothing to fear from Yssa. She's not a threat."

"Isn't she?" Lady Bedlam's eyes burned into those of the shadow steed. "What do you say, Darkhorse? Considering what she is, or at least is in *part,* wouldn't you say she might be a threat? I was a fool to let my daughter be alone with that creature . . . that abomination!"

She knows! It should not have surprised Darkhorse that Lady Bedlam had discerned Yssa's heritage. At one point in her young life, the Green Dragon had been

Gwendolyn Bedlam's patron, a tutor of sorts. She had lived among drakes and possibly had even come across half-breeds such as Yssa. Still, Darkhorse guessed that Gwen only knew that Yssa was part drake. "She is no threat, Gwendolyn Bedlam. I will swear on that. Yssa, whatever her heritage, has worked only to aid us against the horse king!"

"What are the two of you talking about?" Cabe demanded.

Neither answered him, Lady Bedlam staring long and hard into the eternal's inhuman visage. At last, the sorceress tore her gaze away, instead focusing on the Manor. "Cabe, can you detect our daughter anywhere? Either her or . . . or Yssa?"

The sorcerer shut his eyes, but opened them a second later. His expression now matched that of his wife. "I can't find either of them . . . but . . . but I'm sensing Darkhorse."

"He's here with us! Of course you'll—"

"Not here, but in the Manor!"

Now she looked confused. "You must be mistaken, Cabe. How could he be in there, too?"

"Because it is *not* me, Lady Bedlam! Not me!" A horrible realization crossed Darkhorse's mind. The eternal immediately sent a probe of his own toward the ancient edifice.

The search was no search at all. The building, nay, the entire domain of the Bedlams reeked with the magical trace that only to Darkhorse differed at all from his own. How, though, could the unthinkable have happened? The barrier should have noticed, should have prevented access—

No! Cabe had the right of it more than he realized! The barrier could not tell the difference! When Cabe allowed me access, Yureel, shielded by either his own sorcery or more likely that of Aurim, entered at the same time!

Yureel had succeeded in invading the protected domain of the Manor . . . and it was Darkhorse who had unwittingly provided him the *key*.

Chapter Fourteen

Yureel had invaded the Manor while their attention had been focused elsewhere. Darkhorse's counterpart had planned well. Too well. Where, though, was the monster now? He would not have fled already.

"Aurim!" Darkhorse looked at his friends. "We must see to Aurim!"

Lady Bedlam took control, gathering the trio together and immediately sending them to the young sorcerer's chamber. However, they discovered only an empty bed. Cabe did a quick check of the area, but could not locate either his son or the two other women.

"What a fool I was!" the eternal roared. "Each way I turn, Yureel has already planned ahead! He no doubt saw a rich opportunity when Aurim confronted me and made it *appear* the boy had broken free of his hold just so I would help him gain access to the Manor! I never would have believed that Yureel would risk himself so! Your home is the one place of which he should have been wary."

"Never mind that," Cabe interrupted. "What we need to do now is find the children and Yssa." He blinked. "I think . . . I think that I sense the women downstairs . . . in my library."

Lady Bedlam looked confused. "But we both tried to locate them earlier! How could you be able to do it now?"

"There presence is faint, but I'm certain it's them, not a false trail."

That was enough. In the blink of an eye, they were downstairs. Instead of Cabe's library, though, they stood in the hall just beyond it. The door before them was shut and Darkhorse and the others knew immediately that it had not been shut by a human hand. The moment Gwendolyn Bedlam tried to touch it, the door glowed a bright green around the edges.

Darkhorse stepped up to the bespelled entrance. "Leave this to me! Yureel might have incorporated a few more surprises!"

He reared up and kicked, but the door was not his target. Instead, the shadow steed first struck the left side of the doorway, then the right. Each strike was accompanied by a flash of crimson and after the second assault, little remained of the green band. Darkhorse moved closer and nudged the door with his muzzle.

It swung open to reveal two anxious women, their backs pressed to the side wall and their gaze riveted to the eternal's huge form.

Valea was the first to move. She ran to her parents, hugging them both.

Yssa paused at the doorway. "Thank you, Darkhorse."

"Yes, thank you," added Valea, coming over to hug him around the neck. "I didn't mean to pass you by."

"That is all right."

"We were sealed in," Yssa began. "We saw . . . we saw a distorted vision of Darkhorse . . ." She described what had happened.

"Yureel, yes . . ." Darkhorse snorted. "He is still near, too, I am certain of it!"

Cabe Bedlam's fists clenched. "He has Aurim. He has to have him. Valea, Gwen. Give me your hands."

Separating from the others, the Bedlams joined hands. Gwen and her daughter shut their eyes while Cabe stared toward the ceiling. Energy circulated between the three of them, so much that even the eternal was greatly impressed.

"He's at the western edge of the barrier," the sorcerer announced. "I see only Aurim, but I feel something else nearby. Aurim is trying to open the barrier . . ." Cabe pulled his hands away from his family, breaking the link. "I've strengthened the barrier. They can't possibly exit now."

"Do not be so certain of that—" Darkhorse began, but Cabe paid him no mind. The sorcerer vanished, leaving the rest of the party stunned by his sudden action.

"Damn him!" Lady Bedlam gathered her power. "Always willing to sacrifice himself! Stay here, Valea!"

She, too, disappeared. Darkhorse did not wait to see what the two younger women would do. He followed Gwen's lead. They would need his aid against Yureel.

A disturbing sight greeted him. The elder spellcasters faced their son, whose expression was answer enough as to the depths of Yureel's control. Aurim looked ready to attack his parents. Worse, it looked like he might even be willing to *kill* them.

Aurim looked his way. "Darkhorse! You'd better stay back! I don't want to hurt you, but I will if I have to!"

He still sounded so much like the true Aurim that it was even difficult for the shadowy stallion to believe otherwise. Only the fact that he could detect Yureel's foul presence in the area kept Darkhorse from wondering.

Trotting forward despite the warning, Darkhorse looked not at the young sorcerer but the slight shadow he could barely detect above the human. "Ever playing with puppets, Yureel! Are you so fearful, so untrusting of your power that you cannot face your foes directly? Are you so great a coward, brother?"

Cabe Bedlam stepped toward the shadow steed. "Darkhorse! What're you doing?"

He knew that the human feared for his ensorcelled son, but Darkhorse believed that what he was doing was their only hope. If he could goad Yureel into forming, then they had a better chance of defeating their foe.

The now-familiar giggle floated toward them. Over Aurim, darkness coalesced into the tiny ebony form that had taunted Darkhorse in Zuu. Ice-blue eyes identical to his own stared down in mockery at the eternal and his allies. Darkhorse heard more than one gasp from the spellcasters. It was one thing to be told that there was indeed another creature like Darkhorse, but another to actually be confronted by him.

"The tale spins itself rather well," remarked the foot-high puppet, "and the actors play their roles to the hilt! Oh, I am indeed appreciative of your efforts, my brother, my self! You have added elements without which surely my epic would have seemed hollow!" Yureel giggled again.

"Epics, stories, tales . . ." Darkhorse chuckled, mocking Yureel's mockery. "Never a truly original thought in your mind, though! You cannot even fight your own battles; you must use deceit! Well here is your opportunity to create an epic of your own, *brother.*" The stallion reared. "You and I have something to finish! Come to me! Let us at last end what should have ended long ago in the Void!"

The shadow puppet started to float forward, but halted before moving more than a couple feet from Aurim. "It was a brilliant notion to make you the mortal's steed, Darkhorse! He already desired you for that purpose! The thought of such humiliation and regret was delicious! A mortal would have commanded you and under his control, you would have destroyed these insignificant specks you claim to care for and wreaked havoc upon your beloved world!"

"Yet another of your plots that shall never come to fruition, Yureel! Yet another failure!"

"A failure? Oh, no! Hardly a failure! Short but so very enjoyable! Besides, I have many, many other chapters to add to my epic! If not as Lanith's ignoble steed, then I shall find another place for you, my brother, my self!" He giggled again. "Your friends, however, will have to live with minor roles . . . while they live. Are they the patient kind, Darkhorse?"

"What does he mean?" whispered Valea.

Yureel bowed. "We must depart."

"You shall not!" Darkhorse unleashed his power, aiming not at the torso of the small, shadowy figure, but rather between the pupilless eyes. Unfortunately, a gleaming, transparent shield rose up between the eternal's attack and his adversary. The spell dissipated as it struck.

Aurim smiled. Had Yureel formed himself a mouth, the smile he would have worn would have been identical. The younger Bedlam was proving all too well just how proficient he now was in the use of his abilities.

"It might have been extremely interesting to see what he could do against all of you," Yureel commented blithely, "but I have far, far more interesting games to play and, thanks to you, Darkhorse, the one point of concern has now been dealt with!"

They waited for Yureel to say more, but the puppet suddenly vanished . . . no, vanished was not quite right, because Darkhorse, at least, could still slightly sense his presence. Yureel was a master at hiding himself.

Aurim turned from them, moving as if he no longer even knew that they were there. There was no time for the others to react. The golden-haired sorcerer crossed through the invisible barrier surrounding the Manor grounds.

303

"That's impossible!" Cabe cried, looking at his wife. "Even Aurim shouldn't have been able to cross without my permission!"

Darkhorse was not so concerned about what Aurim should or should not have been able to do as he was about what Yureel had done at the same time. The shadow puppet had drifted through the shield in perfect unison with the human. Worse, Darkhorse sensed a subtle shift in the barrier spell. A sudden thought filled him with dread.

"Cabe! You must cancel the spell that protects your domain! Do it immediately!"

It was a sign of the master sorcerer's faith in his friend that Cabe Bedlam obeyed immediately. Darkhorse, however, did not wait to see the results of his companion's work, but rather leaped toward the barrier. It was a risky chance he took, considering the many things Yureel might have done to the protective spell, but the shadow steed knew that he had the most hope of catching the escaping pair.

The speed at which he reached the barrier was enough that if he was wrong, the backlash would possibly do him great damage. Darkhorse did not care. He was his friends' only hope to rescue the lad.

To his surprise, whatever Yureel had done did *not* affect the shadow steed. Darkhorse flew through the spell, only slightly slowed by it. He landed on the grass beyond and looked around. Aurim could no longer be seen, but his magical trace was still evident. The shadow puppet had not bothered to hide the trail, which was disturbing. However, Darkhorse had no intention of stopping the chase simply because of the possibility of a trap. He dared not.

"Darkhorse! Wait!"

Yssa had materialized before him. The eternal came within a hair's breadth of overrunning the enchantress, but turned at the last moment. Despite the danger of losing track of Aurim, Darkhorse paused to glare at the woman. "Do you realize just how close you came to possible disaster, mortal? Do you realize that a collision between us would have been more than simply two bodies striking one another? I am *exactly* like Yureel! A simple touch could have meant your death if I had been caught off-guard!"

"It was the only way to get you to stop!" she countered. "I couldn't let you go running off and getting recaptured, especially with the others being prisoners!"

"The others—?" Darkhorse blinked. "You stand before me as free as a bird!" He twisted his head around in the direction of the Manor. "I would assume that the others were—"

His voice died abruptly. A massive silver dome covered the Manor grounds for as far as he could see. Judging by the way it extended beyond the trees, it covered not only the Manor and the garden area, but also the homes of the many humans and drakes who lived under the protection of the Bedlams. Yureel had turned the barrier spell into a glittering, reflective prison. Darkhorse could not see Cabe and his family even though they surely had to be where he had just left them.

"I followed after you," the enchantress explained. "I didn't even think about what you'd said to Cabe Bedlam about trying to cancel the barrier spell until I reached it." She shivered. "It felt like forcing my way through hardening clay even *with* the aid of my powers. There was even a moment when I thought that I might become trapped halfway through."

"What about the others?"

"I don't know. I just know that when I turned around, no one had followed and *this* was in place. I think it's the barrier spell . . . but different."

"It is!" Despite the need to track Aurim, Darkhorse trotted back to the opaque shield. Even up close, he could not sense the spellcasters within. A mental probe proved futile; the barrier was impervious to his sorcery. Out of mounting frustration, the shadow steed rose up and struck it with his hooves. Bright sparks flew, but otherwise the silver shell was unaffected.

Yssa put a hand on the shield. "I can't sense anything. It deflects every attempt I make to contact them."

"Aurim had a hand in the making of this, albeit an unwilling one. The lad is possibly the most powerful spellcaster I have come across since. . since perhaps even the warlock Shade! When he and Yureel departed, I feared that this might be what my foul brother intended."

"**Is** there nothing we can do for them?" The enchantress was pale, in part because she was still recovering from her effort, but also because she, like the eternal, knew what it meant if the Bedlams remained imprisoned. Cabe and his family represented the greatest threat to Yureel's plots. Even against Aurim, the Order, and Lanith's legions, the Bedlams were powerful enough to counter the shadow puppet's dreams of mayhem. Yureel had his limits; he could not control all of his foes. Probably he had not dared an attempt on their lives for fear that it would be enough to destroy his hold over Aurim. At least, Darkhorse hoped that was the reason. Whatever the reason, sealing the others inside this prison had been Yureel's best opportunity to be rid of them without endangering himself.

Once more I have been too slow to realize! Once more he has made me a fool! To Yssa, he said, "There is nothing I can do. Aurim is the one best suited to return the spell to its original form."

"But he's—" Yssa hesitated, frowning. "I'm . . . I think I'm hearing something . . . it's *Cabe Bedlam."*

"I hear nothing!"

She quickly quieted him. "I hear him, but he's very faint! I think—" Her voice suddenly shifted, growing deeper, masculine. It was, in fact, Cabe Bedlam's voice. "*. . . do anything now. Tell Darkhorse that he needs to alert the Gryphon! He's our best hope now. We're all right here and the air seems unimpeded. I'm pretty certain that given time and the resources of the Manor library, we'll be able to escape. If the Gryphon can organize some alliance between drakes and humans in the east, they can keep Lanith and Yureel from pushing forward!"* Yssa paused, then in Cabe's voice, added, *"Don't go after them, Darkhorse! Please! Contact the Gryphon . . . Kyl . . . and the Green Dragon! Don't go charging off!"*

"Cabe! Can *you* hear me? I—"

The enchantress let out a gasp. "He broke the connection! Thank Rheena! I don't think I could've kept that up much longer!"

Darkhorse was hardly so relieved. He turned to the opaque wall. "Cabe!"

"He can't hear you. It took a lot to get through. I don't think it would've even worked . . . except that I'm more receptive than many spellcasters."

"So it would appear!" The ebony stallion kicked at the earth. "There is still hope of catching up to Aurim before Yureel can get him back to Lanith's armies. The spellwork will have weakened him enough to force him to travel by short leaps, not one long, direct jump! I cannot pass that chance up! The boy is our best bet to quickly freeing his family, not to mention severely weakening the horse king's Magical Order!"

"But what your friend said is true; we really need to speak to the Gryphon! I've heard much about him, Darkhorse. That's why I sent the messages to him, so that both he and Cabe Bedlam would be informed about what was going on. If anyone can help us, it's the Gryphon." Yssa bit her lip. "Cabe Bedlam mentioned my father. I should've returned to him by now. Maybe I can convince *him* to talk to the king of Penacles."

THE HORSE KING

As much as it pained him, Darkhorse finally gave in to Cabe's suggestions. Chasing after Aurim and Yureel *was* indeed folly, no matter how much the shadow steed wanted to rescue the young sorcerer. Darkhorse still felt guilty about Aurim's kidnapping; he should have kept a more careful eye on the lad.

The Gryphon. He was the best chance. With the magical libraries his to use, the lord of Penacles might be able to solve the problem of the altered barrier spell in short order. Cabe might have confidence in his eventual success, but Darkhorse had his doubts that such success would come soon enough. Yureel would have Lanith moving swiftly now that the Bed- lams were not a concern, and it would take some doing to get Black and Storm to agree to aid their rival Dragon King. Blue might be willing, but his might was concentrated on the eastern coast of the continent, which meant that by the time his forces reached Dagora, the armies of Zuu might have already overrun it.

"Very well!" The eternal tried to sound as confident as possible. He was all too aware of his missteps. "A suggestion, though. I would rather you speak with the Gryphon while I confront your sire. You have much knowledge concerning Zuu and its situation that would be valuable to him. You would also be more likely to convince him of working not only with your sire, but also the other drakes."

His companion did not sound at all convinced. "And what will you talk about with my father?"

"Matters which are too lengthy to discuss now. Cabe has done right to set our course." Darkhorse subtly summoned power. He had to do this carefully and quickly before Yssa could react. "If there is anyone who can help me deal with Yureel, it is one who has made a study of the techniques of sorcery utilized by past races. I have some questions to which he might have answers."

It was clear that she still was not convinced about his choices. "I think it would be better—"

Now. The eternal's eyes narrowed ever so slightly.

The protesting enchantress vanished in mid-sentence.

The Gryphon would understand her sudden appearance. It was not the first time guests had literally dropped in at the palace. Besides, Darkhorse had also taken the precaution of sending a magical missive to the inhuman king.

Now that Yssa was on her way, Darkhorse turned toward the west. Although he had spoken with the Green Dragon but recently, the shadow steed was not at all certain what greeting he would receive. Helping the drake lord's daughter trick her father was reason enough for the Green Dragon to shun him. With the war raging to the west, it was possible that would not even be able to get within more than a few miles of the drake's sanctum.

But I will because I have to! Readying himself, the eternal concentrated on the region of the Dagora Forest where he knew one of the entrances to the Green Dragon's caverns was hidden.

To his amazement, Darkhorse was not hindered by any defensive spell. With the forces of Zuu already so near, he would have expected the drake to have installed stronger measures to protect his domain. Was the situation already that desperate? Did Yureel and his puppet king already have the master of the Dagora Forest trapped against a wall?

Carefully, he trotted in the direction of the entrance. Hidden by both camouflage and sorcery, it was impossible for any except the most accomplished spellcasters to locate. Darkhorse, though, had made use of it once or twice in the past. He and the Dragon King might not get along that well, but circumstances occasionally demanded they meet. It would have been simpler to materialize in the caverns, but that method was surely now not open to him.

When Darkhorse did locate the entrance, he was somewhat disturbed. It was still hidden by camouflage, but there was no trace of any spell protecting it. Darkhorse paused before entering. The drake lord had never been a careless sort. This should not have happened.

Even knowing that something was definitely wrong, he finally entered. The cavern entrance was large enough to admit him; not surprising since it had originally been created with dragons in mind. Darkhorse picked up his pace as he descended, his eyes adjusting to the increasing darkness at the same time. Some natural illumination kept the tunnel from growing completely dark, but any human would have been hard-pressed to see more than a few yards at a time. The eternal could see ten times that distance.

No one barred his path, demanding the reason for his coming. Nor did Darkhorse sense any more spells, although in the past the caverns had been riddled with defensive measures. Now he was glad that he had chosen to come here himself instead of allowing Yssa to do as she had planned.

At last he entered the first chamber of the cavern. It was huge, wide, and entirely devoid of any trace of the drake or his clan. Darkhorse turned in a circle, trying to find some sign of life, some clue as to where everyone had gone.

Where are you, drake? Where are your people? The stallion moved in silence as he tried to sense the presence of anyone other than himself. The first chamber appeared to have been systematically emptied of all contents. He had the growing suspicion that it would not be the only chamber he would find so.

The next chamber he reached was as devoid of evidence as the first had been. A pair of vine plants grew together like a wreath over the entrance to the next major chamber, the only things that the Dragon King had been unable to move.

At last he found the throne room. The dais and the chair remained, but their trappings had been stripped away. sent a probe toward the chair and sensed a slight trace of energy, but nothing significant enough to investigate further.

He had seen more than enough to convince him that the caverns of the Green Dragon were utterly empty. The entire clan plus those members of other races who served the drake had abandoned the ancient lair.

Why? Why abandon this place? Things could not have grown so dire in so short a time! What has happened here?

No longer worried about disturbing someone, the shadow steed transported himself to some of the deeper chambers. He soon verified that the birthing areas, the clan sleeping chambers, and even the private chambers of the Green Dragon himself had been emptied. That the last rooms had been stripped clean particularly surprised him considering the vastness of the drake's collection of sorcerous antiquities.

The Green Dragon would not abandon his homeland. He would never do that. What does he plan? The abandoned caverns revealed no answers, however, and before long, finally decided that he had had enough of the place. With one last, brief inspection of the drake lord's chambers, the shadow steed summoned power for a return to the surface.

Instead, he found himself in another of the countless chambers that made up the huge underground labyrinth. Darkhorse glanced around, not recognizing the place. It was not among those he had inspected earlier.

"Now what?" he muttered. His concentration had not been at its best. Yureel could twist his thoughts around so easily it was a wonder that Darkhorse had not ended up transporting himself to the icy Northern Wastes.

Once more the eternal summoned his strength, this time his mind focused on his destination.

The new chamber in which he found himself was virtually identical to the previous. Judging by the odor, riding drakes had clearly made much use of this location. However, the habits of the animalistic lesser drakes did not concern him nearly as much as the fact that twice now he had failed to reach his intended destination. Darkhorse searched the caverns as best he could with probes, seeking some trace of a spell, something that would explain how he could twice err so terribly.

Still nothing. This made no sense, no sense at all. He had to be missing something.

A third attempt landed him in a sulfur-ridden, steamy cave where the temperature was enough to make most non-drakes collapse from heat exhaustion. Another birthing chamber. Other than a few pieces of shell, there was no sign that drakes had ever been here. Someone had very carefully removed every unhatched egg.

Each time he tried to transport himself to the surface, he landed in yet a different part of the cavern complex. Sorcery was at work, that was obvious, but it was of a sort so subtle that even Darkhorse could not readily detect it. *Trust the lord of the Dagora Forest to devise something so devious!*

In order to test the limits of the trap, Darkhorse trotted to the exit of the birthing chamber. Traveling by spellwork had failed; perhaps a physical trek was called for. He stepped into the tunnel beyond, fully expecting to be shifted to another location, but to his surprise, nothing impeded his progress. Perplexed but pleased, the shadow steed trotted swiftly in the direction that he assumed led to the surface.

Darkhorse moved from passage to passage without any delay. He was glad that nothing more had happened, but not at all lulled by the fact. Escape could not be this simple, not if the Green Dragon had gone through all this trouble. Each corner he turned, he expected some new trick to be sprung.

It was not until he passed yet another birthing chamber that he began to see the cunning with which the drake lord had set his snare. There should have been no birthing chamber this close to the surface. They were generally buried deep in the cavern complex where they might best make use of the world's inner heat. By this time, Darkhorse should have been near the entrance through which he had entered, a region far too cool for the sensitive dragon eggs.

Thinking of eggs made him think of Yssa, whose birth would certainly have been unique among the drakes. From what the Dragon King and his daughter had told Darkhorse, Yssa had been born like a human even though part draconian. He wondered what the event had been like.

He dropped the interesting but useless line of thought and pondered again his quandary. Spells sent him from chamber to chamber at random, while journeying physically meant an endless trek through the same tunnels over and over in some insidious loop. Either one by itself would have been insidious enough a trick on invaders, but both guaranteed that even Lanith's mages would have been left baffled and frustrated . . . at least for a time.

A wonderful ploy, Dragon King, but I wish you had considered the possible arrival of one of your allies! Had this intricate spellwork already been prepared when last he had been here? If so, it would have behooved the drake lord to warn him.

"Very well, then! If I cannot escape like that, perhaps a little random destruction will do the trick!" He did not like the thought of damaging the caverns of the Green Dragon, but the latter had left him no choice. Darkhorse summoned up as much strength as he could muster. No half measures now, not when so much depended on his escape.

Energy flared from him, crackling blue bolts that darted in every direction. Darkhorse left no part of his immediate surroundings untouched. If there was a point of weakness, he would find it.

The cavern passage was afire, the blue, flickering light blinding. Even Darkhorse had to readjust his vision. He did not lessen his assault, though. There was a way out of this trap, just as there had been a way out of so many others in the past.

Of course, he *had* required the aid of others to escape some of those traps . . .

A sense of displacement made him falter. His surroundings took on a surreal look, the walls shifting and the floor rising and curling. The disorientation grew worse, so much so that Darkhorse had difficulty even retaining his footing. His concentration faltered and with it his attack. The lightning storm dwindled, then faded away completely.

Nothing . . . the shadow steed tried to clear his thoughts in order to begin a second attempt, but the great weight of his failure made it nearly impossible to think of anything constructive.

"You have no idea how clossse you came to destroying my carefully desssigned trap. I am impressed, demon sssteed."

Still disoriented, Darkhorse sought out the source of the voice. As he did, his surroundings shifted again. Instead of the passage, he now stood in the throne room, but a throne room not stripped of its trappings. More important, the great chair itself was no longer empty.

"My apologiesss for not rescuing you sssooner, demon steed," the Green Dragon remarked offhandedly. Despite the drake lord's seeming indifference, though, Darkhorse sensed a strong level of tension beneath. The effects of the war, no doubt. "My attention wasss focused elsewhere."

A pair of draconian guards flanked the throne and another pair watched from the entrance. All of them were very much on edge. While the eternal did not fear them, he knew that now was not the time to antagonize the warriors. He would have to control his temper, however much he might want to berate the Dragon King for leaving him trapped so long.

"A very cunning spell, Your Majesty! A new piece of work, is it not?"

"Very new. You never actually left thisss chamber; you only thought you did. A hundred sssoldiers could fill the throne room and all of them would fall victim to the same delusion that you did. They would then be sssimple prey for my sssservants, who are protected by talismans also of my creation. Extremely effective, albeit draining to create, I mussst admit. Circumstancesss demanded it, though. The . . . intrusion from the wessst hasss become more of an annoyance than previously expected. Measures were taken should the unthinkable happen."

That was not comforting news. Dragon Kings were not prone to pessimism when it came to battle. Generally they went down fighting, still certain that they could snatch victory from defeat. "That terrible?"

"They have begun burning my foressst again!" The Green Dragon nearly rose, but remembered himself at the last moment. "I have sssquelched a dozen fire wallsss of ever-increasing magnitude and I fear that sssoon I will reach my limits. In the meantime, their warriorsss, whether on foot or mount, advance through what should be an impenetrable shield of thick foliage. You were in that trap longer than you think, Darkhorssse. Sssunrise isss upon us. Within the next few hours, they will meet my firssst line of warriorsss, elves and drakes who shall be outnumbered twenty to one. Each warrior facesss the enemy knowing that all he isss meant to do isss hold them off while I further regroup my other forces and once more futilely requessst aid from my counterparts." The drake unleashed a sharp hiss of contempt. "Counterpartsss . . . only the emperor himself has clearly promised me any aid, but his meager forces will not be here in time to keep the wessstern half of my beloved forest from being rooted up or charred by thossse barbarians! Brother Blue hasss stated in principle that he will help, but much of his power is maritime, which does me little good."

The drake did not mention either Storm or Black, but was fully aware how little

THE HORSE KING

help either of them would be. In their minds, it would be better to weaken Green *and* the invaders. Only then might those two move. "What of the confederation formed by Sssaleese? Is there no aid there?"

"Sssaleese's confederation ssseems to be more interested in the lands just wessst of Gordag-Ai, landsss once belonging to Bronze. If I were a paranoid being, demon sssteed, I would almossst wonder if thisss fledgling confederation hasss joined the invaders."

As if we do not have enough to concern us . . . Darkhorse remained silent on the subject. Sssaleese was a problem for another day. "If I may, Your Majesty, I know that events are at present demanding your attention, but I must tell you of terrible news."

A look of resignation on his face, the drake indicated that he should proceed. The shadow steed did, throwing himself into the events that had taken place since last the pair had met. He glossed over his enslavement in Zuu, especially the enchanted saddle and bridle, then focused on the details of Yureel's invasion of the Bedlams' domain. The Dragon King's expression became more and more unreadable as the eternal progressed, even when Darkhorse revealed what he knew of Yureel. The shadow steed saw no reason to keep hidden the truth about his adversary from the Green Dragon, who had ever been an ally of his friends. However, he was admittedly startled by the lack of emotion; it was almost as if the drake was not so surprised by Yureel's origins.

"A dreadful tale, demon sssteed, and very informative. You were right to sssend my daughter to speak to the lionbird. I would prefer her far from here at the moment and she can certainly deal with the lord of Penacles." The Dragon King steepled his fingers, red eyes narrowing in thought. "You give me sssome possible options, now that I know that the real threat lies not ssso much with the horse king and his insipid Magical Order, but with sssome creature from beyond the Dragonrealm! Yesss, I may have wayss of dealing with this monstrosity . . ."

"Oh?" This interested Darkhorse greatly. "And what manner of artifact or spell would that be?"

The Dragon King grew evasive. "Possibilitiesss, nothing more. There may not even be time to investigate them—"

The drake lord suddenly threw back his head and hissed. The guards nearest him dropped their weapons and went to his side, but he waved them off. Darkhorse's host was clearly in pain, but was not about to give in to it.

"Your Majesty," the shadow steed called. "What is it?"

"Can you not feel it, demon sssssteed? They've moved fassster than I thought they would! They're tearing my foressst apart again! My firssst warriorsss already prepare to meet them, but it will not be enough! They are hurting her, ssscarring her . . . my foressst!"

One of the guards tried again to help. "My lord! You mussst ressst! You have not ssslept sssince—"

"Away!" The lord of the Dagora Forest rose, his gaze burning. "Darkhorsse! Attend me!"

Before the eternal could reply, the Dragon King transported them to his personal chambers. They now stood in one of the rooms that the drake utilized for his researches. Shelves and shelves surrounded them. The Green Dragon's collection of sorcerous artifacts was unparalleled in the realm as far as Darkhorse knew. It seemed that each time the shadow steed saw it, the collection had changed greatly, as if his host continued to add so many finds that he constantly had to move the older ones elsewhere.

The Dragon King marched directly to a triangular, crystal array fixed on a stand set in the center of the chamber. The tiny emerald crystals, all identical, glittered even in the semidarkness of the chamber. He waved a hand over the center. "Show me!"

The array pulsated twice, then an image formed about a foot above it. Darkhorse was impressed by the clarity of the vision; this latest device of the Green Dragon's, whether new or some recent artifact uncovered, far outdid the previous viewing devices the eternal had seen his host utilize.

Regrettably, the scene it revealed was one that made the shadow steed's fascination with the construct irrelevant. Once more magical flames overran the mighty trees but this time the flames were a brilliant golden hue. They danced around the wooded region as if almost alive. In fact—Darkhorse peered closely—some of the smaller blazes *did* move as if they knew what they were about.

Even from here, he could sense Aurim's part in the spell. Yureel had set his prize puppet to work the moment they had returned to Lanith's encampment.

"They know my warriorsss await them! That ssserpent Lanith boasts of hisss hordes, but can only fight them with sorcery! He callsss himssself a warrior king? He isss a ssspoiled child with assspirations of greatness!"

As he spoke, however, the flames flickered out of existence, one merry blaze doing so just as it leaped for yet another defenseless tree. The Dragon King let out a weary gasp, as if the forest's reprieve physically affected him as well. He was not relieved, though.

"They come," he announced to the eternal. "Now that the morale of my warriorsss hasss been tested by their sssorcery, he sends hisss armiesss . . ."

The vision shifted, filling with row after row of armored, yellow-haired riders, each well armed. True to their tradition, the Zuu horde consisted of both men and women and many of the more capable ones that Darkhorse noted were of the latter sex. The look in the eyes of each told Darkhorse how terrible the odds were that the invaders might be turned early. The horse king, or possibly his hidden ally, had stirred them up, made them see themselves as their nomadic ancestors, whose fury even the Dragon Kings had long respected.

"They are about to meet." Without warning, the Green Dragon waved his hand over the array, eradicating the image just as the forces of Zuu reached the untouched forest.

"Why did you do that? Do you not want to see?"

"I know what will happen, jussst asss my commanders there do, too. Nevertheless, they will fight asss well as they can. The horse king will find out what it isss truly like to fight dragonsss. I have also already ssset other ssspells in motion." The drake lord hung his head, looking exhausted. "There isss nothing more I can do and yet I ssstill feel as if I have done nothing adequate. Thanksss to this creature you mentioned, this Yureel, and his puppet sssorcerers, I am at a great disadvantage." He looked up again, eyes brighter, a thoughtful expression crossing the flat, reptilian visage half-hidden under the helm. "Perhapsss, though, perhaps, now that I have your information, I have another option. Yes, a way of dealing Lanith a crippling blow by removing the threat of this creature and dessstroying hisss cursed Magical Order all in one blow . . ."

The last words startled Darkhorse. Any aid against Yureel was welcome, but not if it meant endangering Cabe's son at the same time. He took a step toward his host, assuring that he now had the Dragon King's attention. "You cannot touch the Order until I free Aurim!"

"I will do what I musssst do, demon steed, to preserve my kingdom and my own! Lanith musssst be stopped, and the besssst way to slow him isss to deal with the true power behind him. I regret any danger that might confront Cabe and Gwendolyn's ssson, but I am facing dessssperate times here!" The drake took up

311

a defiant stance before him. "If Aurim Bedlam must die to sssave so many more, then ssso be it. I will regret hisss death, but I will not regret causssing it, not when the other choice isss worse . . ."

The Dragon King turned away, his interest now focused on a shelf containing part of his collection. Darkhorse stared at the drake's back, but was so stunned by his host's decision that he could not yet bring himself to reply to the other's cold words. The Green Dragon intended to protect his kingdom at the cost of those dearest to the eternal and Darkhorse could think of no good reason why he should prevent that from happening. The Dragon King was correct; to leave Yureel and the Order untouched was to condemn many others to their deaths. Darkhorse's monstrous twin would not cease his horrendous crusade until someone forced him to cease.

To save a continent, Cabe's son might have to die . . .

Chapter Fifteen

"What're you do—?" was all that Yssa managed to blurt before her surroundings became the interior of the palace of Penacles. She clamped her mouth shut instantly, not wanting to accidentally bring every guard in the building to her.

Too late. Darkhorse had dropped her in the midst of the throne room itself and although the Gryphon was not there, sentries stood watch over the room. Four of them charged toward her, their swords ready. Yssa prepared herself, knowing that she might have to injure them.

"Stop!"

The single word acted like a thunderbolt, causing the guards to freeze where they were and the enchantress to leap in surprise. Only a few steps behind her stood the lionbird himself. Clad in the robes of state and standing much, much taller than she, the Gryphon was a sight that Yssa, who had lived among drakes, still found daunting. He was a creature of magical origin, it was said, the only one of his kind. Standing so near to him and sensing his great power, she could believe the tales.

"You are Yssa. I received notice of your coming just before you arrived." To the soldiers, he said, "This woman's no threat. Your speed is commended, but you may all return to your positions now. As for you, young woman, you will come with me."

While the guards returned to their posts, the Gryphon led Yssa out of the throne room and down the hall. After a short walk they came to a chamber that appeared to her to have been unused for quite some time. The lionbird ushered her inside.

"This palace is far too large for my needs, even with a family. However, this was the domain of the Dragon King Purple before me and he and his predecessors for some reason chose to build this structure over the site of their former caverns. They also had a preference for large chambers, of course. You've no idea how deep down this edifice goes and so much of it is wasted space." The Gryphon chuckled. "A strange lot, the drake clan Purple."

The chamber was nearly empty, which made it look even more immense. There were chairs and tables to one side, as if on a rare occasion the room was used for gatherings, but the last such gathering had evidently taken place some time past.

"I was here already, looking out the window, when I heard Darkhorse's summons. I come here to think sometimes, especially during a rising crisis such as that which plagues my neighbor to the west. No one will disturb us here and I'll be better able to concentrate." He grunted, a somewhat feline sound. "Toos used this for various occasions, especially when he was regent during my absence. At one time, it was where he entertained his military officers—" The Gryphon cut off. "Forgive me. My mind wanders sometimes. Old wars, old friends . . . the past."

From her father and the Bedlams Yssa knew that the Gryphon was more than two hundred years old, possibly even older. It was not just because he was a spellcaster, but because of his peculiar origins. The Green Dragon had not known the truth about those origins, though, and the Bedlams had not enlightened her either. She wanted to ask him about himself, but decided it was best to wait until a better time. Darkhorse had, after all, sent her with a task in mind.

"Did he tell you why I came, Your Majesty?" The Gryphon had such a regal aura around him that she wanted to curtsy.

"Only that it was urgent . . . which was why you were able to arrive in the palace in the first place. Did you think it was this simple to enter my home?"

She had not thought about that. A good thing that her host respected the word of Darkhorse. The king of Penacles had a reputation for taking the warrior's outlook on things and that probably included unexpected visitors trying to magically pop in. "It is urgent, Your Majesty! Very, very urgent! The Bedlams and their people are prisoners!"

"Explain slowly and precisely," he commanded in a tone that indicated he would brook no other manner of explanation.

She did, careful not to diverge at all lest the Gryphon's gaze turn baleful. His beak was far too sharp and his hands far too strong for her not to think of his predatory nature. The monarch was neither cruel nor capricious, but Yssa could not help being a bit fearful.

By the time the Gryphon had heard all, the mixture of fur and feather lining his neck stood fully ruffled. "Bad news. Worse than I feared. So this thing is not only like Darkhorse, but has visited the Dragonrealm before? That would explain some of the tales I've heard from time past."

"If he was here before, then someone succeeded in exiling him," the enchantress reminded her host. "He wouldn't have left on his own."

"No, he wouldn't have." The Gryphon stroked the underside of his beak with the back of his hand. "Hmm . . . it appears that I must consult the libraries anew. Days wasted on research that now holds no significance . . ."

"But what about the Bedlams? Can you help them?"

He looked at her as if she had just asked him if he slept on a perch in a cage. Yssa, entirely unnerved by his fierce gaze, nearly fell back over a chair. "Of course I'll do what I can, human! Do you think I'd leave my friends trapped like that? The Bedlams are one of the few chances we've got of stopping this carnage before it spreads too far! Think, woman!"

At first Yssa resented his attitude toward her, but as she studied his movements, she saw that the Gryphon was extremely upset. The spellcasters were obviously very dear friends of the monarch. *Good! He'll do what he can for them, then!* She had been afraid that he might relegate the family's predicament to a lesser priority.

"I'll go now. I think I know what to ask for, but it may still take days to decipher the blasted answer." He ignored her look of puzzlement, adding, "My mate'll see to it that your needs are met while you wait for me to return—"

The anxiety-ridden enchantress could not believe what she had just heard. *"Wait?* Are you suggesting I simply wait? Do nothing? I can help you search for an answer!"

The lionbird shook his head vehemently. "It would take me many hours just to explain how the Libraries of Penacles work. Even I don't fully understand them, human, and I've had years and years to study them. Even the Dragon Kings who ruled this city never completely uncovered the secrets of the books . . . a fortunate thing that. If this is to be done as swiftly as possible, it must be done by me alone, I'm afraid."

"But—" Yssa gave up. If she was any judge of character, the king of Penacles was not the type to change his mind. It did not sound like the first time he had made this decision. "All right. I won't argue with you about the books. I want the Bedlams freed as soon as possible. My—the Green Dragon desperately needs help and they seem to be the only ones willing to give it."

"I won't go into that with you, spellcaster, because while I know that it's not *completely* true, it mostly is. Some help has been sent and more is on its way. I know it's insufficient, but that's all that can be done at this point." The Gryphon led her back toward the hall. "Troia will see to your needs. After your adventures, you have to be exhausted."

She was, but Yssa hardly thought it was the time to relax. She wanted to help, if not with the Gryphon's work then with something else. Letting others take chances was not the enchantress's way. Her father called her reckless, but Yssa simply thought of herself as determined and capable.

What was there left for her to do, though? Darkhorse had already visited with her father and since she knew how much he respected the shadow steed's might, it was likely that the two were already working on some sort of plan of action.

All this planning and running around and yet there still seems to be nothing for me to do! People keep sending me away from where I'm really needed! If she could not help the Gryphon or the Bedlams, then she would return to where she would be of some use. She would return to her father. He would certainly be in need of her aid.

"Thank you, Your Majesty, but I've got somewhere else I have to be." Before the Gryphon could contradict her, Yssa summoned power and vanished from the palace.

She rematerialized by the side of the Serkadian River, far from her intended destination. The events at the Manor had sapped her strength more than Yssa had imagined. Despite the very early morning sun, the enchantress felt as if it were still the dead of night. She had rested at the home of the Bedlams, but that had not been enough.

Pausing only long enough to catch her breath, Yssa attempted another leap. She was certain that the Gryphon would be behind her at any moment. At the very least, he would not be pleased with her destination. The Dagora Forest was no place for anyone now.

No one except her.

Her second leap took her to a place where she could glimpse the ruins of the kingdom of Mito Pica. Ravaged more than two decades ago by the forces of the previous Dragon Emperor, it was a ghost that refused to be forgotten. Yssa had leaped to its vicinity only because she knew that the Gryphon would not think to immediately look here. His hesitation was all she needed. One more leap and she would be too far away for him to follow after. The king had far more pressing matters than hunting a recalcitrant young woman down simply so that he could turn her over to the safekeeping of his queen.

Her next jump took her near the Manor. As she rested briefly against a tree, the enchantress saw that Yureel's spell still held. The opaque shell still loomed over the Manor grounds. Yssa thought about trying to contact Cabe Bedlam, but realized there was nothing she could do except tell him that she had informed the Gryphon of their plight. The stress of making contact, however, would force her to rest even longer before attempting yet another leap toward her father's domain and she desperately wanted to reach the caverns as soon as possible. More and more Yssa began fearing for her sire. With Yureel to guide him, Lanith had to be making terrible inroads through the forest. Her father needed her help.

After several minutes, the enchantress decided that she was ready for the next jump. Fully rested, Yssa would have been able to make the remainder of the journey on this attempt, but she knew that it would now take her at least one more afterward. At least after this one, she would be well into the familiar forest.

Once again, Yssa summoned power. It was still somewhat of a strain, but not enough to make her think of pausing. Yssa materialized exactly where she intended, a small clearing many miles southeast of her father's caverns. It had been a favorite spot of hers when she had been growing up and one she had now and then returned to even when at odds with him.

Standing in the very center of the clearing, a weary Yssa spread her arms and looked up into the sky. It was very tempting to remain here for a time, absorbing the tranquility of the place, but she could not. She could only relax long enough to build up her strength. The power might be drawn mostly from the world around her, but her own will and power were required as well. Yssa did not have the capacity that Aurim Bedlam did. He had leaped from one end of the continent to the other . . . such ability was *astonishing.*

Just a few minutes . . . that's all . . . just a few minutes . . . "Well, it took some time, but I knew eventually you'd return to your special place, darling."

Yssa whirled, unable to believe she had heard the voice. She had been careless, not thinking that another knew this place.

Exhaustion overwhelmed her. Yssa tried to remain on her feet, but the grass looked so inviting and her head felt so heavy. A part of the enchantress's mind screamed at her to defy the exhaustion, see it for the spell it was, but the rest of her was all too eager to rest. She fell to her knees.

Saress's voice floated above her. "That's right, Yssa, dear. Just relax. About time you got here; I'm supposed to be watching Lanith's kingdom for him, not .hunting you down, but he seemed suddenly interested in you. Something to do with the shadow horse, I think."

Fight . . . it . . . Yssa slumped to the ground, barely able to concentrate, much less fight the spell. Had she not been so weary from jumping from location to location, Yssa was certain that she would have sensed the other woman's presence here, no matter how well shielded Saress might have been.

That did not matter now, though. Nothing mattered. Nothing but . . . sleep.

"Rest easy, Yssa. The long chase is finally over, but there's more to come for you. *Much* more."

"I cannot permit you to harm him, Your Majesty! There has to be another way!"

"If one would presssent itself, demon sssteed, then I would welcome it! Failing that, however, I mussst turn to the few options I have. There isss more at stake here. My so-called brethren have left me to my own devices. My young emperor will sssupply me with sssome aid, but it will be too little too late, as is whatever Blue *might* provide me! Now you've alssso come to tell me that the Bedlamsss are prisssoners, which leavesss me no other road upon which to travel—"

"Then help me free the Bedlams! You have all of this accumulated knowledge and power—"

"None of which I can ssspecifically make use of for your dilemma. I do not have the time to research the ssspell that Aurim and the shadow creature used to imprison them. Ssspeak to the Gryphon, if you will. I've heard preciousss little from him, demon sssteed, ssso I daresay he might have the time I do not!" The Green Dragon turned from him. "We have nothing further to discuss."

Darkhorse grew furious. "I will not be so easily dismissed, Your Majesty!"

"I think you will have to be. I have my kingdom to sssave and thisss will require doing sssomething I'd rather you did not sssee."

Darkhorse moved toward him, but before he could reach the Dragon King, the shadow steed suddenly found himself outside the caverns. Angry at the drake's disregard, Darkhorse started for the entrance, then recalled the trap. He did not want to get caught in the drake's web again.

I have to do something, though! The eternal regretted his coming here; the Dragon King's decision had only made the situation more volatile. By revealing the truth about Yureel to the drake, Darkhorse had actually endangered the younger Bedlam's life further. Aurim was possessed. He was not responsible for what he was doing and yet it appeared he would have to pay regardless.

The eternal was still contemplating his next move when he thought he sensed Yssa. It hardly seemed likely considering that she had to be in Penacles, but Darkhorse had already learned the hard way that it was best not to ignore such things. He turned around, trying to locate her. Perhaps Yssa had decided to return to her father the moment she had finished relaying the Bedlams' fates to the Gryphon.

He did not sense the young enchantress, but he did sense something else, something not at all welcome in the forest. They were fairly well veiled from sorcerer's sight, but Darkhorse still succeeded in sensing brief flashes of their presence. Soldiers . . . and not those loyal to the Green Dragon.

Focusing on their locations, Darkhorse transported himself. It was too coincidental that he would sense both Yssa and the enemy in the same area.

He arrived at the edge of a small clearing and had no trouble spotting those he sought. There were three of them, three tall, blond, armored warriors. One had her sword out and her attention on the forest around them while the two males prepared to lift up a still form on the grass. Even with the warriors' bodies blocking much of his view, he could tell that the form was Yssa's.

"What have we here? Trespassing?"

The warriors turned together, the two males pulling free their weapons. They were well trained and would have been a formidable sight to anyone other than him. One of the males joined the female in an advance toward the shadow steed. The third remained with their prey.

"I give you one warning, mortals! I am Darkhorse! Your blades will not do me any harm. You only condemn yourselves if you choose to attack rather than surrender."

They paid him no mind. Either they were fiercely loyal to the will of Lanith or they were also puppets of Yureel. Whichever was the case, they left Darkhorse no option but to battle them. He could neither allow them to kidnap the woman nor remain unhindered in the Green Dragon's domain. If they had made it this far, it was possible that there were others.

Without warning, the two warriors advancing vanished from both his sight and his magical senses.

"Now this is an interesting trick!" Darkhorse held his ground. "My compliments to the creator of your protective spells! Nonetheless, my demand still stands. Surrender or suffer the consequences!"

He heard the swish of the blade just before it struck him. Despite his bravado, the eternal could not help tensing when the invisible weapon cut into him. Fortunately, while the warriors' defensive spell was an effective ploy, their swords were still very mundane. The blade passed through his chest and out again with barely a ripple to mark its passing.

Laughing, Darkhorse took one long step toward the invisible pair. The shadow steed was not certain of their exact locations, but he was fairly certain that both of them jumped back when he moved forward. The third warrior remained visible, his expression anything but happy. He did not flee, however.

Darkhorse took another step forward. This resulted in another attack from one of the invisible warriors. The sword thrust was aimed for the eternal's throat. Darkhorse felt the blade penetrate, then sink deep. However, this time he did not allow the warrior to free his or her weapon. Instead, the shadow steed pulled the weapon in, trying to move quickly enough that its wielder would have no opportunity to let go. The ploy failed, though, his attacker too frightened to try to hold on. It was probably the only thing that saved the warrior from a terrible fate.

However, the second of the invisible warriors chose that moment to try to leap on the shadow steed. Darkhorse felt the weight of the man—at least he thought it was the man—as the latter landed on his back. Darkhorse snorted. Without the bridle and saddle, he now had full control of his form.

He never saw the hapless warrior, only heard his scream as his seating grew nonexistent and he fell *into* the shadow steed. The scream continued on for several seconds, sounding fainter and fainter, as if the man continued to fall. The one visible soldier paled and started to back away from Yssa. The other, once more visible, quickly joined her companion.

Laughing, Darkhorse trotted toward them. The two moved a few paces behind the still woman, then held their ground. He hardly cared what they did now, his first concern being for the enchantress. If they had severely injured her, then they would have good reason to fear him.

Still she did not move. Darkhorse sought out her mind, but met resistance. He tried to check her condition, but ran against the same wall. Someone had bespelled her; that was the only answer.

The warriors watched but did not interfere as he moved close enough to touch her. With one last condescending glance at the pair, Darkhorse used a hoof to gently nudge Yssa's side.

Yssa shattered, the fragments flying into the shadow steed's face. Each fragment exploded as it struck him, not only disorienting the eternal, but momentarily blinding him. It did no good to back away from the shower; the pieces of the false image followed Darkhorse wherever he went.

"Quickly now!" called a voice he recognized as that of Saress. "Take her before he can recover! The Lords of the Dead take him! He wasn't supposed to be here!"

"Yet here I am, Saress!" Darkhorse roared, shaking his head back and forth in a futile attempt to disperse the determined pieces. "And in another moment you will learn to regret that circumstance has led me here!"

"In another moment, demon, we'll be far from here!"

Even as she finished, Darkhorse sensed her cast a spell. He tried one of his own and managed to slow if not stop the distracting shower. The fragments continued to pelt the eternal, but now at least he could see some of what was happening around him.

What Darkhorse saw was Saress, clad in her twisted version of the traditional garb of a warrior of Zuu, opening a blink hole wide enough for her two remaining underlings and their prize, the true Yssa. The sinister enchantress noticed him focus on her and nearly lost control of her spell. She recalled herself at the last moment and smiled at her adversary.

"Good-bye, demon!" She waited until the others had gone through, then, with a last wave, stepped inside.

A second later another hole opened up only a few feet from where the first had been. From it emerged the warriors, their captive, and Saress, still smiling. Her smile vanished when she saw where the hole had brought her.

"What in the—"

"Welcome back, Saress!" Darkhorse chuckled, dispersing the last of the fragments. "Did you think I would let yet another escape me so? I am not disoriented now, female! Release your captive and I may allow you to live."

Her expression turned to one of dismay. Darkhorse did not add that he had been fortunate to turn her spell around. Had he been forced to try a second time, it would have been just as likely that he would have failed. Luck was at last on his side.

"You think I am to be caught unaware this time, witch? Release Yssa and surrender!"

Saress made the warriors stand aside. Her eyes narrowed as she walked slowly but defiantly toward the eternal. "You think you've won, do you? You think I'm defenssseless, do you?"

The enchantress opened her mouth . . . and *roared.* Suddenly she began to grow, swelling larger than a bull, then larger still. Her skin changed, becoming dusky brown, and her limbs twisted. Wings burst from her back, wings that soon spread the length of the clearing and beyond. The hulking form nearly filled the clearing.

There were few of the drake clan Brown still remaining and at first Darkhorse thought that he was seeing one of them. It slowly registered, however, that had she been a female drake, he would have recognized her as such even in human form. No, Saress was much more. Small wonder that at one time she had reminded him of Yssa. Saress, too, was a half-breed, albeit of a different clan.

The revelation was so unexpected that he was not quite certain what to make of it. Saress used his surprise to her advantage, seizing Yssa from her stunned companions, who fled immediately after. This was not a secret the enchantress would have shared with many, especially her beloved monarch. Lanith tolerated her sorcery because it served his purposes well, but from what Darkhorse knew of him, the king would probably have been less than delighted to discover that he had been bedding a being half draconian. Like most of the horse people, he believed in the purity of the human race. To him, drakes, although they had once been masters of Zuu, were little more than animals.

Wings flapping, the dragon rose into the air. Near the earth, Darkhorse was swifter and stronger, but in the air dragons still held sway. Darkhorse could follow, but so high in the sky catching a dragon was difficult, if not impossible. Despite that, the shadow steed immediately leaped after her, the abandoned warriors no longer a concern. Without Saress, they would soon fall into the hands of the Green Dragon's servants. The only thing that concerned him was rescuing Saress's captive.

Darkhorse raced higher and higher, his hooves already touching the treetops. Unfortunately, Saress was already a distant form ahead of him. Whether her transformation had been planned or an act of desperation, she stood a good chance of escaping him. Even for a dragon, the half-breed sorceress was swift.

He found himself wondering how well the two women knew one another. Perhaps their similar backgrounds had drawn them to one another at one time. While rarely on excellent terms with their counterparts, the Dragon Kings did meet with one another. Perhaps that was when the two half-breeds had first met. Judging by her strength, Saress was very likely one of the Brown Dragon's offspring or at least the offspring of one of the royal line.

This may be why Yssa spent so much time in the Barren Lands! To Saress, the re-formed domain would be death. The grass would take her.

Saress continued to climb higher and higher, which made Darkhorse's journey more difficult. He had limits as to how high he could fly and those limits were far less than that of a dragon. If she rose much higher, he might lose sight of her.

The speed with which she fled westward continued to impress him. Darkhorse soared over acre after acre of forest and yet gained little ground on his adversary. Saress was a huge but slim beast, perfectly designed to sweep across the heavens. Seldom had he seen a swifter drake.

Then . . . the landscape ahead altered in an alarming manner. Gone in many areas was the proud forest. Broken and burnt, the trees lay scattered in all directions. Smoke still drifted upward. Darkhorse could vaguely make out many tiny forms moving eastward, obviously the horsemen of Zuu and their counterparts on foot. There seemed to be a large area where the movement paused, which the shadow steed suspected had to be where the Green Dragon's warriors had finally met the invaders. The battle line resembled a madly twisted serpent, one that was unfortunately being forced east in most places.

Sorcery was also in use below, although Darkhorse could not say in what manner. Judging by how strong the trace was even at this height, some tremendous spells had been cast in the past few hours. Lanith, or perhaps Yureel, was pushing the Magical Order to its utmost. At this rate, it was very likely some of the weaker sorcerers might perish from exhaustion before the forest realm was taken, but if that meant a swift victory over the Green Dragon, the risk was no doubt worth it to the horse king and his secret ally.

So much devastation, so much chaos just for your personal entertainment, Yureel! Darkhorse turned his eyes from the earth, realizing that the distraction had enabled Saress to increase the distance between them. She seemed to be heading beyond the battlefield, most likely to Zuu. If she thought returning to Lanith's kingdom would save her from him, then she was sorely remiss.

A hole in the sky opened up ahead of the fleeing dragon.

Darkhorse cursed, picking up his pace as best he could. He had not thought that Saress would have had enough strength left to perform this feat of sorcery. If he pushed hard, though, the eternal was certain that he could reach her before she made it through.

A second hole opened directly before him. Darkhorse could neither turn nor stop in time to avoid it.

The other end opened up in a room, although what the eternal saw of it was only a flash of stone and what was possibly fire. He flew across the chamber, no more able to halt himself than he had over the Serkadian, and struck a wall reinforced by strong sorcery. Unable to shatter it or pass through, Darkhorse ricocheted off and rebounded across the chamber, crashing against the opposite side, which proved also to be reinforced. Each collision was also accompanied by a sharp jolt through his body, yet one more treat no doubt prepared for him by Yureel. Again and again, he careened against the walls, too stunned already to halt his mad flight.

By the time Darkhorse struck the floor several seconds later, he barely had the strength to even suffer the agony caused by the final jolt.

Unconsciousness prevailed. Darkhorse vaguely noted a passage of time, but how much was beyond his limited senses. He tried to gather his wits, yet every time something pushed him back toward the darkness.

What stirred him at last was a sound so terrible, the shadow steed wanted to return to his oblivion. It was a giggle. Yureel's giggle.

"A little late and a little sloppy, but all things have worked out for the best, don't you think, my dear boy?"

"Yes, Yureel," responded Aurim from nearby.

Darkhorse slowly recovered. His gaze, when he could at last focus, fixed on the source of the giggle. The shadow steed's malicious counterpart floated about four feet above the floor. Darkhorse tried to leap at him, but something held him fast.

He could neither reshape himself nor cast a successful spell. Once again he sensed Aurim Bedlam's work in this.

"I hope you'll forgive the long wait, my brother, my self! It was hard to draw myself away from the delicious tableau I've been so busily concocting. I think dear Lanith can make do for now, though, even without his prize sorcerer or his oh-so-majestic steed. The drake's warriors are admirable fighters, but their defeat is inevitable, isn't it, my brother, my self? Their first lines have already been routed."

The shadow steed was startled. *Routed? How long was I unconscious?*

Yureel must have noticed something, for he added, "Didn't you know? Of course not! How could you, having been trapped here for more than half a day!"

Half a day? It seemed impossible, another of the shadow puppet's grand lies, but. . . Darkhorse believed him this time. Half a day . . . How much destruction and death had occurred? What had happened with the Bedlams? He doubted that they had escaped yet. Yureel would not have been nearly so gleeful if they had.

The tiny figure clapped his hands. "Aaah, there is so much I could tell you about present and future events, Darkhorse, but it would be rather pointless now, wouldn't it? Poor, poor Lanith will be so disappointed, but I think the crushing of his former liege will assuage him! Besides, you made for a most unruly steed, you know!" Yureel giggled. "And a very sloppy one at the moment. You really should learn to hold up better."

Darkhorse glanced quickly around the chamber. The three of them were the only ones in the place.

"This is a private discussion." Yureel's tone was no longer merry and the change chilled Darkhorse. "My grand majesty has his little war to keep him occupied. As for the female creature who has accompanied you of late, she is for the moment enjoying a reunion with the king's Saress. They are two very intriguing beings I have yet to incorporate properly into my wonderful epic, but be sure that I will soon! They both seem fond of the lad here; I think there might be something in that. Poor Saress, though, will be so disappointed when she finds that she can't keep this Yssa. They've played quite the game of cat and mouse for years, I understand."

"Saress does not know of you, does she, Yureel?"

"She will in good time. That time is not yet now. She was useful, however, although I'm sure that she's still wondering what became of you. It was very fortuitous that she chose this time to bring you to me." By his tone, it had been more than fortuitous. The malevolent figurine drifted even nearer. "You've no idea how I missed you, my brother, my self. It was as if a piece of me had gone away . . . but that is the case, isn't it? Well, I've decided that the time's come for us to be together. No more games, no more epics, just the two of us together."

The two of us together. He could not mean what Darkhorse thought he meant. It had to be the shadow steed's overwrought imagination.

Yureel shifted closer until he was only a foot from his captive. "I should correct myself, of course. The two of us together . . . making only one."

It was true, then. He meant to reabsorb Darkhorse. Yureel intended to swallow him, make everything that the ebony stallion had been his own—and Darkhorse could think of no way to stop him. The old fear reared its horrific head, making it nearly impossible for the shadow steed to think, yet he had to or he would perish. If Yureel absorbed him, there would be nothing left.

"I so look forward to this, Darkhorse! You've lived an epic yourself, a story I could only dream of during my so lonely, so lengthy internment—"

"A sentence of your own making, Yureel! A kind punishment, considering your atrocities!"

"Kind? Kind?" For the first time, the shadow puppet nearly lost

complete control. "Better would it have been if they had destroyed me! Do you understand at all my isolation, my loss? I'd intended to let you learn about helplessness a little at the erstwhile hands of Lanith, but the mortal was clumsy. Well, my brother, my self, a lesson lost is one best not remembered at all. I will just have to satisfy myself with living off of your memories." He glanced back at Aurim. "I shall begin. Be ready."

Aurim nodded, his expression blank. "Yes, Yureel."

"You're a grand, good boy." Yureel faced his prisoner again, but now his form shifted, seeming to melt. At the same time he expanded, growing more and more to encompass an area as great as that which Darkhorse filled. With each passing second, the differences between the pair lessened until even Darkhorse would have been hard-pressed to find them.

"Perhaps I'll create another self at some point when I become bored. Perhaps that one will be more *manageable* than you were, Darkhorse."

The shadow steed struggled, but Aurim held him fast. There was no sign of recognition in his steady gaze. Darkhorse could expect no help from that quarter.

The black, floating mass that was Yureel reached out—and touched Darkhorse.

The eternal felt as if needles had pierced every part of him. Darkhorse roared as Yureel began to flow over him, then quivered as his foul twin intruded into his mind. Darkhorse tried to pull away, but could not. Slowly but surely, the monster began to absorb his essence.

No! I am Darkhorse! I am my own creature! I am distinct from Yureel!

We are one that has been separated far too long, brother, returned the intruder. *The separation is now at an end. Struggle if you will, but it will not even delay what is inevitable . . .*

He was right. Darkhorse could see that. Despite his defiance, despite his strong will, he was nothing to Yureel so long as Aurim held him in place.

"Aurim! Hear me! Break his hold! Your will is powerful! He cannot hold you and still do this!"

Aurim did not respond, though, save to stare down at the shadow steed.

Nothing! I am undone!

No, brother, you've been undone all this time! Now at last, the mistake will be corrected . . .

Darkhorse felt his mind drift. Yureel was tearing him apart . . .

We are one. What you are will be mine and with it I will turn the Dragonrealm onto its head and remake this land, this world, into my own dream! What a glorious epic I will create!

I—was all that the shadow steed could think in response. Already he barely remembered himself. His sense of being was slipping away, becoming nothing more than a fragment of his twin's powerful self.

He had lost to Yureel . . . for the final time.

Chapter Sixteen

Aurim did not recall much about his time in the Manor. He remembered a struggle for control in the deep recesses of the Dagora Forest, then, for a long time, nothing. When at last he woke it was to find himself in the midst of an intricate bit of spellwork guided by the monstrous puppet master. Disoriented, he had been

321

unable to prevent the completion of the spell that Yureel had used to trap his family.

Yureel had controlled him completely throughout the process. The creature had first marched him around the Manor's grounds like a toy soldier, then, while Aurim desperately tried to communicate with his parents, the demon had completed the spell turning the protective barrier into a prison wall. Only Darkhorse and the woman who had earlier rescued his father had escaped, although how *she* had managed to get through, he could not say. Darkhorse had been meant to follow in order that Yureel could trap him again. It had made the demon furious when, after escaping the inescapable trap, the woman had distracted his intended prey.

Still enraged, Yureel had returned him to Lanith, who had promptly called for a renewal to the torching of the forest. To Aurim, who knew the ways of the shadow puppet well by this time, it was harder and harder to tell when Lanith was himself or when he acted as spokesman for Yureel. Yureel whispered in the mind of the horse king, suggesting things and sometimes even giving outright commands through the monarch. Only General Belfour ever questioned the commands, but he usually quieted after one glance from Lanith.

Aurim hated linking to the other sorcerers, especially when it came time to launch another terrifying assault in the name of the king of Zuu. The bond the Magical Order forged was much, much deeper than those he had created with his own family. Each and every one of the other spellcasters' personalities became known to him and with only two or three exceptions, they were not people Aurim would have wanted to meet. Hysith was harmless and two of the others, students kidnapped from Penacles, were victims like the young Bedlam. Another student from Penacles, Willar Avon, had willingly joined in return for the gold Lanith had offered. As for the rest of the Order, they were mostly ruffians who had had the dubious fortune of being born with a better than average tendency for sorcery.

The worst, other than Saress, was Ponteroy. Each time they linked, Aurim sensed the other sorcerer try, ever so subtly, to undermine the connection his successor had created between the band. Ponteroy wanted him to fail just enough that Lanith would rename the northerner second in command. From little snippets of thought Aurim had gained through the connection, he knew that Ponteroy dreamed of seizing control of Zuu, but only if he could get Saress on his side. It was a dream that the gold-haired spellcaster knew would always remain a dream. Saress was Lanith's slave.

Each time before they bonded, the Magical Order formed a geometric pattern with Aurim the center. There were seven of them this time, the others having been forced by exhaustion to abandon the spellwork. The loss was fairly negligible; those with Aurim were the strongest of the group. Losing someone such as Hysith was not a major blow to the Order.

Burn the forest! Force them to fight in a more open area like true warriors! Teach the lizards and elves what humans can do! Lanith's words did not take into account that among the defenders were many humans as well. He did not care; the horse king spoke for the benefit of his warriors, who hung on every damnable sentence.

The drakes had finally tried sending some of their number in the form of dragons, but they had learned all too quickly the folly of doing that. It seemed that for months one of the details of the Order had been to cast spells on the arrows of the horse king's archers. The first dragons who had flown near enough had perished in a hail of remarkably accurate and deep-penetrating bolts, backed up by sudden lightning storms summoned up with ease by the sorcerers. It had not helped that many drakes had become so accustomed to humanoid form that they were actually clumsier in the ones in which they had been born.

Aurim watched the results of the spellwork. The fires raged strong, destroying all in their paths. Those who simply sought to defend their homes were perishing out there and it was *his* fault. They were dying in most part because of Aurim Bedlam's much vaunted power. All these years he had failed to reach his potential and now, when that potential had at last become realization, his abilities were the plaything of a demon.

Lanith commands that the fires be doused, Aurim Bedlam. It seems he wants to let his little soldiers play now.

The command passed along by Yureel came as both a relief and a new cause of grief. Aurim needed rest, having maintained the fires since being forced to imprison all those in the Manor. Yureel might control his body and be able to make him cast spells for hours at a time, but the weariness was ever Aurim 's.

He canceled the fires, but some of the spells he and the others had cast continued to play havoc with the forest and the Green Dragon's defenses. Allowed to sit, Aurim watched with sinking hope as Lanith's forces moved ever forward through the ravaged land. Nothing the drake lord had thrown against them so far had done more than momentarily delay the horde. Lanith had lost some warriors, but not nearly enough to stem the tide.

Father, what do I do? His parents could not help him now. Anything that happened would have to be of his own doing . . . and Aurim could think of nothing he could do. His great attempt to override Yureel's control had not only failed, but had led to greater disaster. *But I can't give up! I can't!*

He was still trying to find some answer when the demon seized control of his body again. *Come, Aurim, my friend! I've immediate need for you! An opportunity lost has suddenly arisen again!*

The invisible strings once again in place, Aurim rose to his feet against his will and turned to Ponteroy, who was watching the advance with far more satisfaction than he had. "Gather the others," Yureel commanded through him. "There is something that needs to be done."

"The king said we could rest for now," countered Ponteroy, likely more than uncomfortable in his extravagant clothing. "I, for one, follow *his* commands, not yours, boy."

Aurim's hand shot out, seizing the elegant sorcerer's arm near the shoulder. Ponteroy glared, then his face paled in pain as the hand gripping him squeezed tighter and tighter. Aurim felt Yureel pour a touch of sorcery into the grip, preventing Ponteroy from striking back.

"His Majesty'll appreciate what we're about to do, Ponteroy," Yureel added through his unwilling puppet. "Now do what I told you and make it quick!"

The hand released the other sorcerer, who nodded and hurried over to the others. Aurim heard Yureel giggle in his head.

Ponteroy soon returned to him. He was still pale, but bitterness had overcome much of his fear. "They're ready . . . well, five of them and myself. Is that enough?"

"That's enough. Oh, yes, that's enough," Yureel said, forgetting to sound like Aurim. They joined the weary but obviously cowed sorcerers, who had already formed their part of the pattern. Ponteroy took up his position. Aurim stood in the center of the group.

He comes! He comes!

Aurim's head jerked skyward. At first the ensorcelled spell- caster saw nothing, then a shocking sight materialized among the scattered clouds. A dragon. A sleek, swift one racing through the heavens. There was something familiar about it, though, and also something not quite right. It was as if there were two forms up there where only one was and neither of them radiated what passed for the magical signature of a true dragon. In fact, they reminded him more of—

There! There!

THE HORSE KING

His gaze shifted to a tiny speck some distance behind the disconcerting dragon. It was as black as night and even from here he could sense who it was. *Darkhorse!*

Oh, yes, my wondrous sorcerer, it's my brother, my self! Here I thought he'd gone and found some sense, but he's come back to me after all! Now we can proceed as I intended so long ago! Grand, glorious Lanith the Conqueror will just have to make do without his perfect steed. I've other, more important plans for Darkhorse . . .

Unable to stop himself, Aurim formed the bond between himself and the others. Once more their wills became subordinate to his, which actually meant to Yureel's. Their power joined with his own. Aurim Bedlam felt such strength that he was certain that he could do anything . . . except escape his own tormentor.

Now, the demon began, *you will do the following . . .*

The spell trap was very simple, but very well timed. Aurim stared at the swift figure, trying somehow to contact Dark- horse or give him some other warning, but Yureel's control was insurmountable.

When the shadow steed vanished through the hole that the sorcerer had created for the demon, tears of frustration slid down Aurim's face. Darkhorse was as good as trapped. The young spellcaster had been integral in creating the holding cell where the shadow steed now resided and he knew how strong it was. Darkhorse would not soon free himself.

That was it, then. Darkhorse had been captured. There only remained the Gryphon. Yureel had managed to eliminate the other major threats to his insane campaign. Aurim had little faith in the drakes organizing themselves before the forces of Zuu laid waste most of the western half of the continent. Kyl sought for a more unified race, but even those of his kind who believed in the cause could not help bickering with one another.

The new spell left him even more exhausted. In control of his own body, Aurim Bedlam would have collapsed, but Yureel kept him standing long after the others had settled down. Three sorcerers were always on duty, working in conjunction to monitor the spells already unleashed and watching for any new magical attack by the Dragon King. The demon secretly monitored each group through carefully crafted links to one selected member of the trio. Yureel's commands came as whispers in their heads, whispers they did not realize were not thoughts of their own. Aurim had once wondered why. Yureel simply did not possess all of them, but eventually realized that even his captor must have limits. Besides, it was clear to him that even the ensorcelled members were not possessed to the degree that he was. Like Lanith, they did not realize they were being influenced. Aurim Bedlam was Yureel's prize and received special attention.

A battle horn sounded, a sign that the horse king's men were beginning a new attack on the Green Dragon's domain. The battle had shifted to the mundane, with humans, drakes, elves, and others cutting one another down for what they believed. Not for the first time, Aurim wanted to throw up. He had never found war very glamorous and what little he had witnessed here from his exalted position had made it look no better.

Now you may get some rest, Aurim, my friend. There are some things to which I must attend before I visit my dear other self.

The young sorcerer barely had time to close his eyes before he blacked out. Yet again he had been reminded of how much Yureel controlled his existence. Aurim floated through a dreamless sleep, vaguely aware of things around him but not quite certain what they were. Only once did anything disturb his slumber, the voice of a young woman who called his name. He was certain that he knew her, but once the voice ceased, Aurim drifted off again, forgetting her.

Wake, Aurim Bedlam!

He nearly jumped to his feet in his attempt to obey. Blinking, Aurim looked around, only to find that he was no longer on the field of battle, but in the room set aside for him back in Zuu. The disorientation was enough to make his head spin and only by clutching it did the sorcerer prevent himself from passing out. Then he slowly realized that *he* had seized hold of his head, not Yureel. Gazing at his hands, Aurim wiggled his fingers. The minor movements thrilled him, so long had it been since this much control had been his. He took a few tentative steps from his bed—and suddenly his body began moving in a different direction.

"Well, that was a little bit of fun," Yureel commented with a giggle, suddenly floating in one corner of the room. His ice- blue eyes sparkled merrily. "The time has come."

With no more explanation than that, the sinister shadow puppet whisked him to another chamber, one Aurim recognized as the cell Yureel had forced him to create. On one side of the cell lay Darkhorse, terribly misshapen. Gone were all traces of the equine form of which his friend was so fond. Darkhorse was now a shapeless, still blob that spread across a good quarter of the chamber. A pair of icy blue orbs, identical to Yureel's save that they seemed dull and lifeless, floated in the center of the unsightly mass. Once or twice in the past, Aurim had seen Darkhorse in such a shape and he had been unnerved each time. Now, though, he only felt sympathy for him.

"He really must learn to pull himself together," Yureel said, giggling again.

The laughter seemed to cause the prisoner to stir. The eyes grew more alive.

Their captor noticed this and his next words were louder, more concise, just for Darkhorse's sake. "A little late and a little sloppy, but all things have worked out for the best, don't you think, my dear boy?"

"Yes, Yureel." Although the voice was Aurim's, the response was Yureel's. Once more, all the young sorcerer could do was watch as his every action was dictated by the foul creature.

"I hope you'll forgive the long wait, my brother, my self! It was hard to draw myself away from the delicious tableau I've been so busily concocting. I think dear Lanith can make do for now, though, even without his prize sorcerer or his oh so majestic steed. The drake's warriors are admirable fighters, but their defeat is inevitable, isn't it, my brother, my self? Their first lines have already been routed."

Aurim desperately wanted to hear more, but then another voice in his head caught his attention, the same female voice he had heard earlier during his enforced slumber.

Aurim Bedlam . . . can you hear me?. . . By Rheena, Mistress of the Forest, please say you do!

Someone was in his head, someone who had managed to do what Yureel had told him time and time again was impossible. *Who are you?*

Yssa . . . my name is Yssa . . . thank the Mistress that I finally got through to you! I've . . . trying to reach you ever since . . . sensed your presence! You are . . . you are Aurim Bedlam?

He acknowledged his identity to her, although it should not have been necessary considering their link. Obviously she was nearly as anxious as he was. *You . . . you're the woman who saved my father . . .*

Yes . . . my name is Yssa, but that's not important! I've tried to break through the barrier in your mind since . . . first brought here . . . listen to me . . . she thinks that I'm still under her spell. I've got to make this quick. Can you . . . anything . . . ?

He asked her to repeat her question. Their link seemed to be a tenuous one, which weakened every time Yureel made his body move or speak. The monstrous creature was saying something to Darkhorse, but Aurim paid his words no mind, wanting only to continue his conversation with Yssa. If she could break through, perhaps she could help him to escape Yureel's power.

THE HORSE KING

Can you do anything at all on your own, Aurim?

He told her the sad truth in as few words as he could, finishing with *I only managed to fight him in the forest. His will is overwhelming!*

But you've got such power, such will of your own! I felt it! I've heard about it!

Something in the way she spoke to him briefly encouraged Aurim. How could Yssa believe in him if there was not truth to what she said? In all fairness, a part of the young sorcerer knew that it was also the enchantress's beauty that played games with his hopes. Nonetheless, his hopes rose. *Maybe I could do something . . .*

As if stirred by her continuing presence, Aurim's mind began to race. His father had often told him how it had been during the worst crises that his own mind had worked best. Now the same happened to the younger Bedlam. One thing in particular interested him. How had Yssa managed to breach the sorcerous walls with which their captor had enveloped his mind when no one else had? What made her different?

Whatever the reason, it was possible she offered him options that he had not had before. *Yssa! Can you help me—*

Her answer was immediate and without hope. *No . . . I can't do anything except talk . . . you. Saress doesn't know how skilled I am at . . .*

Her last words faded as Aurim found his attention forced back to Darkhorse's predicament. Yureel had him doing something. He was casting a spell to strengthen the one holding the weakened shadow steed to one place. At the same time, Yureel began to distort and expand, coming more and more to resemble the shapeless mass that was his captive brother. The floating blob immediately moved toward Darkhorse, his intention quite clear. Yureel had spoken many times about what he intended to do with his counterpart once he tired of humiliating him. Now, it was very clear that the horrific shadow man had decided the ordeal of humiliation had come to an end.

Yureel will devour him . . . Aurim knew that what he thought was not quite an accurate description, but it was close enough. Yureel would absorb Darkhorse; there would be nothing left and the monster would be far, far stronger than he had been before. The sorcerer had witnessed the amazing extent of the shadow steed's power in times past; what would Yureel be able to do with so much more strength at his beck and call?

Worse . . . what about *Darkhorse?* Such a fate went beyond horror as Aurim knew it.

What is it? What . . . happening, Aurim?

He had forgotten about Yssa. *Yureel! He plans to make Darkhorse part of him!*

The enchantress's dismay more than matched his own, but she was less inclined to simply wait for the inevitable. *You've got to save . . . Aurim! You're his only hope! You . . . the power! Use it before . . . too late!*

I can't defeat Yureel on my own. Can't you help me?

Her presence faded more. *No . . . nothing I can do. I'd hoped if I could break through . . . you . . .*

Darkhorse roared in pain and agony, a sound that nearly deafened Aurim. Already Yureel floated partially atop his captive. The process of assimilation, as the monster had sometimes called it, would soon be complete.

Aurim! I had a chance to . . . you at the Manor! Your father said that you . . . power . . .

Yssa's words no longer made much sense. She had obviously used most of her remaining strength to contact him and all she had accomplished was to discover how helpless *he* was.

To his surprise, Darkhorse suddenly called out, "Aurim! Hear me! Break his hold! Your will is powerful! He cannot hold you and still do this!"

I can't! he tried to reply. But Yureel allowed him only to watch and keep

326

Darkhorse still.

Aurim . . . Yssa insisted, her presence momentarily stronger. With a little more concentration, he even managed to summon a vision of her. The enchantress was chained to a wall, her bonds radiating an emerald aura. Even at this dire moment, she looked beautiful.

Aurim, if there is any hope, you've got to push your will to its fullest now!

He had been saying he *couldn't* for so long, it was hard for Aurim to think otherwise, but if he did not try once again, Darkhorse would be no more.

What can I do? Fighting Yureel would be a fruitless task. There remained only one possible plan. It would enable him to avoid battling the demon directly. He had to try to send the shadow steed far, far away where Darkhorse would have the time he needed to recuperate.

Away . . . Aurim concentrated his efforts through the very spell the puppet master had forced him to maintain all this time, the one that kept Darkhorse still while Yureel devoured him. This was his link to his friend, an opening that might be turned to his favor *if* he had the will and power to do it.

Away . . . He did not know where to send Darkhorse. As far away as possible, he supposed. As far away as Aurim's will would permit.

Away . . .

Darkhorse roared—

"What is this, what is this, what is this?" Yureel cried, still formless but quivering in astonishment and swiftly rising fury. "Where is he? Where is he?"

Aurim! I felt . . . such power . . . what did you do?

He ignored Yssa's frantic question, his efforts concentrated on doing what he could to free himself. It would not take the demon long to realize just who had been responsible for snatching his prey from his grasp. Aurim did not want to be here when that happened.

Too late. *"You! It had to be you!"* The massive blob turned on him. "It can't be but it has to be! What did you do, human, what did you do?"

"I sent him far away," Aurim responded against his will. He had forgotten that Yureel could simply demand answers from him. "I sent him far away."

"Where?"

"I don't know." It was true. Aurim had not consciously chosen a destination.

The blob shifted nearer, Yureel's disturbing gaze never leaving him. "You don't know *where*, my little sorcerer? You don't know where you put him?"

"I only wanted to send Darkhorse away so that you couldn't hurt him." The captive spellcaster tried to keep himself from saying anything more, but his will was not strong enough. "I don't know where."

"I heard you!" Still shapeless, the demon expanded farther, filling more than half the chamber. He floated closer, a hungry look in the inhuman eyes.

He's going to take me now! He's going to take me! "Aurim, darling, I thought I felt—"

Saress had materialized, seduction clearly evident in her eyes. However, one look at the monstrous form hovering before them and the enchantress shrieked. Aurim could not really blame her; he wanted to scream, too. Yureel was only inches from him . . .

The demon suddenly withdrew, his form contracting and reshaping. Saress stopped shrieking and started to cast a spell, a dangerous thing for all of them considering not only how panicked she was but also how tight their quarters were.

"Grand and glorious Lanith," Yureel suddenly called. "I've need of you, O conqueror of the realm . . ."

"—Lipazar's Blade! You—" The horse king stiffened, then quickly studied those around him, finishing with the demon. Yureel had returned to his previous form and now he darted behind the monarch, as if frightened of what the sorceress could do to him. Aurim wanted to scowl; the monster was hardly in danger from Saress.

"What goes on here? Why've you brought me back here, imp? Have you found my steed?"

"Not yet, your glorious majesty! A problem arose with this sorcerer; he's proven willful when he shouldn't be! I was trying to remind him of his duty when the beautiful Saress materialized and mistook my deed for one that threatened both of their lives . . ." Yureel sounded timid.

Lanith turned to Saress. "Calm yourself. Yureel's no threat to you; he serves me . . . don't you, imp?"

"Yes, yes, I do, Lanith the Great!"

The enchantress quieted, but she was by no means convinced of the demon's complacency. Aurim prayed that she would remain suspicious; it would only serve his own chances if Saress continued to keep a wary eye on Yureel. She had seen him at his most terrible. Unless he wiped the memory from her mind, Saress would *have* to think the demon more dangerous than he now pretended to be.

"What is he, Lanith?" the sorceress demanded, thrusting a finger at Yureel.

"A servant, Saress. One who's worked hard to aid me in my conquest of the Dragonrealm."

The woman's brow arched. "Has he? I thought it was my Magical Order—and dear Aurim here—who had done so much!"

"Yes, yes, indeed," the demon cried. "They've performed marvelously, beauteous Saress! I . . . I've only done what little I could on the side."

"Why haven't I known about him, Lanith?"

"It wasn't wise to let too many know about Yureel, Saress. You can see for yourself what sort of reaction he receives. He serves me best by being unnoticed until too late." The horse king turned slightly toward the tiny demon and smiled at him. Yureel pretended to be honored.

Clearly the enchantress saw that Yureel had Lanith's ear. It did not sit well with her, but Aurim noticed that she was intelligent enough to cover her distaste before Lanith glanced her way again. The woman did not like being second to anyone or anything when it came to her beloved ruler. "You must forgive me . . . Yureel . . . but I sensed a great spell cast here, one that Aurim cast. I came to see what he might be doing down here when he should've been on the battlefield serving my dear king."

At last she had garnered Lanith's curiosity. "What spell is that, imp? Why would you drag Aurim here to cast a spell when he's needed on the field for the same reason?"

"I intended on using the aid of your precious sorcerer for a spell that would give us knowledge of the Dragon King's present position, but I discovered some . . . reluctance . . . on the lad's part, Your Majesty. As I first indicated, he seems to be having second thoughts." Yureel peered at Aurim, pupilless eyes growing colder. "Dangerous second thoughts."

"Oh?" The king also stared at Aurim. "I thought that was beyond him, imp. You said so yourself."

"I appear to have been remiss, glorious majesty! My apologies! I shall, of course, deal with the problem. Oh, I must assume that since your Saress is here, King Lanith, that she's accomplished the task you asked of her."

The horse king blinked. "Task? What task would—"

"The renegade enchantress, grand king! The woman who has danced around your city evading your Magical Order for the past several years! If Saress is here, then certainly she must've captured the woman!"

"Yes . . . I'd forgotten about that. Where is she, Saress?"

"I . . . have her in one of the dungeons, darling, but she's hardly worth the trouble to deal with now—"

The tiny figure floated away from the supposed protection of the horse king and took up a position that allowed him to gaze at both spellcasters without much effort. "I must humbly disagree, my lovely lady. More than ever she's of importance." Yureel studied Aurim closely. "Most important, indeed."

"She's nothing but a hedge witch!" Saress snapped.

"Oh, she's more than that, much, much more! Just ask her father, Lady Saress. You may have heard of him, I think."

As Aurim watched, the enchantress's visage paled. Yureel had struck a nerve. Saress actually looked frightened again. "I don't know anything about her father!"

"A great lapse in knowledge considering how long you've known *her*. One would almost think the two of you had grown up together, so familiar do you act with her."

"She's *nothing* to me."

"Enough of this babble," the horse king commanded, his expression one of increasing impatience. "I have a land and a Dragon King to conquer and this is delaying things! Bring me this woman now, Saress!"

She curtsied, managing still to display her obvious charms to the king as she bent forward. "I am ever at your command, dear Lanith."

Yureel giggled. Rising, Saress stifled what was likely a grimace. She took a deep breath, then slowly looked up at the ceiling. Power began to gather around her.

"The day is quickly waning," the shadow puppet remarked offhandedly.

The narrowing of her eyes was the only visible sign Aurim noted that indicated her bitterness with Yureel. "Come here, Yssa!"

No sooner had she finished the command when they were joined by the other enchantress. Aurim Bedlam found himself thankful that Yureel had not bothered to control his sight, for there was no one else in the chamber he would have rather stared at now than Yssa. She was even more beautiful than he recalled. Unfortunately, the blond enchantress was just as much a prisoner as he. A faint orange glow around her throat was the only evidence of the magical bonds that kept Yssa from using her own abilities, but its presence was sufficient to tell Aurim Bedlam that she would not easily escape.

King Lanith approached her, the gleam in his eye not one that Aurim cared for much. "This is her, eh?"

Evidently Saress was not pleased by her beloved monarch's interest in her rival. "She's nothing, Lanith. Not even worth trying to add to the Order. Leave her to me. I'll—"

"Be silent." The horse king's gaze drifted down, then up again. He cupped Yssa's chin, studying her face for much too long as far as Aurim was concerned. "Good form. Very healthy. Excellent breeding, I'd say."

With his back to her, Lanith could not see Saress's smoldering look.

Aurim tried to contact Yssa, but it was as if her mind had been shut away from his. He finally gave up, realizing that he could tell her nothing of value. They were both helpless.

Or were they? After his success in freeing Darkhorse, who was to say that Yureel's hold was that complete? Perhaps it had been his own distrust of himself that had made him such a pliable puppet. *I've got to try again.*

You will do nothing! commanded an enraged Yureel in his head. The confident, beguiling attitude the demon displayed for Lanith and the others was actually a mask; his fury had not abated. *Your chance is past! If you try again, my fine little human spellcaster, I shall do to your female as I intended to do to my dear twin!*

329

THE HORSE KING

Yureel did not wait to hear if he understood. The demon vanished from the sorcerer's mind, confident, no doubt, that he had made his point. Regrettably, he had. Aurim immediately ceased his attempt. He could not risk Yssa.

"She's a fine addition, I'll admit, imp, but what best use is she? Will she join the Order?

"Her?" Saress snapped. "Never!"

"In this I must agree with your fine lady, my majestic king! No, she is no use to the Order."

Lanith seemed puzzled. "But surely you can—"

"There is a position of greater value for her to fill, oh, yes, indeed," Yureel responded quickly. "She will buy you a victory over your former liege, the dragon man!"

"Now why would she matter to him? Is she one of that green lizard's servants? I didn't know he kept human mages."

The tiny puppet master giggled. "Oh, more than a servant, much more, much more . . . wouldn't you say, Lady Saress?"

Again the king's mistress grew extremely uncomfortable. She evidently knew what Yureel hinted at and it unsettled her greatly. "He values her, yes."

"So highly that he would risk surrender just for her?" the king asked, extremely skeptical.

Yureel gave a comic shrug as he drifted back to his supposed lord. "Surrender . . . possibly. Hesitate too long . . . definitely."

Growling, the horse king reached for the small, hovering figure, but Yureel was too swift. He easily dodged aside, then took up a position nearer poor Yssa. "No more games, imp!" cried the graying conqueror. "Tell me why the damned drake would bother with a human. He's fond of them, but not that fond!"

"Aah, but with this sumptuous lass, he is!" Yureel floated next to Yssa's face. Aurim could see her trying to keep an eye on the foul monster. The tiny figure indicated her visage. "She is rather attractive, wouldn't you say, my grand emperor-to-be?"

"There's no denying that."

"Exotic, yes?"

Lanith studied her for far longer than necessary. Only when Saress cleared her throat did he finally pause. "She looks like one of my people. . but there's definitely something else. Her blood's not pure. She's a mix."

"A mix . . ." Yet another infuriating giggle. "Oh, mixed well, indeed, wouldn't you say, Lady Saress." Using one tiny arm, he dragged Yssa even closer to Lanith. "A strong mix, your glorious majesty . . . strong, because she carries a most royal and . . . *draconian* . . . bloodline."

Saress gasped, then forcibly pushed all emotion from her countenance. Lanith eyed her, then studied the tiny demon as if the latter had completely lost his senses. "What are you saying? You sound as if you're trying to tell me that this other woman is a . . . is part. . ."

"Part *drake*, yes."

"Impossible!" The horse king seized Yssa by the shoulders arid looked her over again. Had the bound enchantress been able to use her abilities, the monarch of Zuu would have been no more than a blot on the wall now. "And yet . . . maybe not . there's something about her. . . I've seen draconian females in human form . . ."

"She's far, far more than those little creatures, great and glorious Lanith! More so because she is also the child of the Dragon King himself."

Lanith was clearly skeptical. "How did you discover this fantastic secret?"

"Spies, searching, guesswork . . . a combination of events." The creature glanced surreptitiously at Saress.

Aurim caught the look, then the brief, frightened expression that again crossed the visage of Lanith's mistress. For the first time, Aurim noted some similarities in the women's features.

If what Yureel said was true, could that also mean that Saress was . . . that she was . . just like Yssa?

No wonder you shake every time Yureel mentions Yssa's heritage— Aurim paused in mid-thought, the demon's revelation finally sinking in. Yssa was not quite human. Not *human.* It did not startle him as much as he might have expected, but then, he *had* grown up with drakes. He saw them as few others did, as a race as beautiful and terrible as any other. They were people like himself and many of them, when compared to some humans such as Lanith or even his own grandfather, Azran, were better. The Dragon Emperor's own sister, Ursa, was his sister Valea's close friend.

"Part drake . . . part *animal* . . ." Lanith released her, disgust growing. "Well, she may be of use, then, if the Dragon King will acknowledge her."

"He will, my lord, oh, he will."

"He'll not surrender his kingdom for her, though." The would-be conqueror walked around Yssa, studying her again, but his mind was clearly focused on other matters than her appearance. "No, but as you've indicated, he'll probably hesitate if he does care for her. He'll be afraid she'll be injured—"

"Or tortured," added Yureel with a giggle.

—and that will cost him. It could cut the war down by half. Then we could turn toward Gordag-Ai as originally planned. They'll fall in half the time it'll take to conquer Dagora, especially if that drake Sssaleese can keep his pledge . . ."

Aurim did not follow the last but what he did follow made him even more anxious. He knew the Dragon King Green well enough to realize that what Yureel said was true. For someone he really cared for, especially one of his own, the drake lord *would* hesitate and that hesitation, manipulated by the horse king and the demon, might very well prove the fatal stroke.

"Magnificent!" Lanith suddenly cried. He laughed and, without warning, reached out to pet Yureel. The tiny figure remained still, although Aurim caught a hint of contempt in the inhuman eyes. "Magnificent! Once my former liege the drake has fallen, all his wondrous magical treasures will find better use in my hands! His fall will also reduce the power of his brethren, who'll realize too late that they should've aided him, the stupid lizards!"

"With Dagora yours, my great and splendid king, there will be no way they can even hope to stop you . . ."

Aurim doubted that. He still believed that Lanith could not succeed in the end; the continent would never be his. It was true, though, that if Dagora fell to him, any chance of putting an early end to the horse king's campaign would fade.

And we can't have that, now can we, little Aurim? My epic is far from complete! Yureel's chilling voice echoing in his head was enough to make the sorcerer cringe.

I think you've had enough fun for now. Recall that her life is in your hands! She is a valuable tool against the drake, but I will sacrifice her if I have to, Aurim Bedlam! And in case you've forgotten—The spellcaster's left hand suddenly thrust itself upward, stopping only an inch or two before his face. The fingers formed a tight fist. —*I'm still very much in control!*

"Imp! I want to return to the field! Belfour'll have the troops over the northern ridge by now, what with the Order's help. That means that we're getting damnably close to the center of the drake's domain and he'll defend it harder than any other place we've taken yet. Now's the time to remind him of his darling daughter!"

Contact between Aurim and Yureel ceased, but the hand remained where it was. A reminder. "Most definitely, Emperor Lanith, most definitely! I'll have Aurim whisk us there in but a breath! If anyone asks, you can say that he transported you here because of a matter of urgency. It would not be the first time you've made such use of your little sorcerers."

"I don't need to explain my comings and goings to anyone, imp . . . but it would be best to return before Belfour and the others get too nervous. Saress, you know the half-breed best; I want you with her for now in case she manages some trick." Without waiting for a reply, the horse king turned again to Yureel. "My mount is still missing, imp. What've you done about finding him again? I've had to commandeer one of my aide's mounts for now."

The demon did not even hesitate. "Worry not about him for the time being, my lord. Your great victory is near at hand. I'll keep an eye out for your steed, I promise you. I want to find him *nearly* as much as you do."

"All right. Then let's get back to the field. Now."

"As you command." And to Aurim, "Send them."

He could do nothing but obey Yureel. If there had been any hope before, certainly there was none now, not for him, Yssa, his family, or certainly the Green Dragon. Yureel had all of them dancing, even those who did not realize it. Only Darkhorse was free of his sinister twin's machinations.

The only question was . . . could Darkhorse return from wherever Aurim had sent him?

Chapter Seventeen

What happened to me? was Darkhorse's first question. He tried to focus, but the sudden shift in location had left him disoriented. It had certainly not been his own doing; between Yureel and Aurim, Darkhorse had been securely and efficiently imprisoned—

Aurim? It seemed the only conceivable answer. Somehow the captive sorcerer had managed to overcome Yureel's control, if momentarily, and been able to send Darkhorse away. That had to be the answer; nothing else made more sense. Perhaps with Yureel so occupied with absorbing his twin, the foul little monster had allowed his mastery of the human to slip just that precious little.

Where had Aurim sent him, though? For the first time since arriving, Darkhorse focused on his surroundings. Aurim Bedlam was a clever person. It had to be somewhere where the sorcerer trusted him to be safe.

Then again . . .

Where by the emptiness of the Void am I? It was like no place the shadow steed had ever visited either in the Dragonrealm or beyond. He *was* beyond the world of the Dragonrealm; that was immediately obvious.

Everything around him seemed unclear, as if his sight were failing him. That was not the case, though. Even up close, the peculiar plants—if they were plants—remained slightly unfocused. He shifted toward one and prodded it with a primitive appendage. The plant, a bluish, a cucumber-shaped thing with hairlike leaves, immediately quivered. A moment later a piercing bell sound shook Darkhorse so much that he immediately retreated from the alien object.

The cucumber plant's reaction set off another similar plant nearby. That, in turn, caused yet a third, then a fourth, to also peal like bells. The uproar shook Darkhorse to his very being, but there seemed to be nowhere to turn. Each direction he looked, similar plants blocked his path . . . and more and more of them were reacting to the first one.

The clamor grew maddening. Darkhorse could not have held together a form even if he had had the strength, so jarring was the noise. He finally gathered himself together as best he could, peered up at what he supposed passed for the sky but looked more like congealed fog, and flung himself upward.

The atmosphere was almost as thick as it looked, but slowly Darkhorse made headway. Somewhere above him was the way out of this peculiar realm. All he needed was a little time to locate it.

Something brown, round, and twice his size darted past him in the thick mist. Although it did not return, Darkhorse decided to push harder, not wanting to encounter any more of the strange world's inhabitants. Past experience had taught him never to assume that any creature was harmless.

The noise below grew faint, but before the eternal could relax, a second brown thing darted by. This time Darkhorse caught sight of a wicked appendage resembling a cross between a claw and a tongue. The glimpse encouraged him to yet greater effort. He did not like the notion of seeing whether or not he was immune to the dangers of this world. His friends needed him.

With what power he had at his command, Darkhorse probed the very fabric of the bizarre world, seeking any trace of a way out. Every place he had visited had some weak point that could be used to journey elsewhere. There might be an infinity of alternate realms, but they were all linked in some way. Once he escaped this one, he could begin a thorough search for the way home.

The fact that the shadow steed had never visited this world before reminded him of just how powerful Aurim was. As Cabe had always insisted, it was only the boy's will that held him back. With only minor control over his power, he had performed a feat the likes of which few master sorcerers were capable. Of course, the younger Bedlam's desperate gamble had provided Darkhorse with a new quandary. This world was unfamiliar to Darkhorse, which meant that the next one might be, too. Exactly how far from the Dragonrealm had the sorcerer thrown him? The shadow steed did not claim to know all of the infinite variety of realms, that being impossible, but he did know quite a few. This one was not remotely similar to any he had visited.

He abandoned his musings as two discoveries vied for his attention. The first concerned his path out of this realm, a tiny thread in the fabric of his present location that hinted of an escape route. Only a search would reveal the truth.

The second discovery concerned the fact that one of the winged brown things had decided *Darkhorse* was worth investigating.

He sensed it just below him, its pace far slower than that of the first one. It flew in an oval pattern that drew tighter with each circuit. Darkhorse estimated that it would likely attack after three more revolutions, which meant perhaps two, maybe three minutes at most. That gave him very little time to investigate the path ahead. If it was a false trail, he might uselessly push himself against it and waste his preciously small reserves of strength just before the thing decided to attack.

Darkhorse did not even contemplate trying to absorb the creature. Not only did the notion revolt him, but somehow he suspected that doing so would be more to his detriment. This realm was unsettling. If necessary, he might take the beast, but only as a last resort. What it might want to do with him, he did not even want to know.

Seeing beyond the thread proved more difficult a task than he anticipated. Like the sky itself, the edge of this realm felt thick and uncooperative. Darkhorse increased the intensity of his probe; the thing below him had already completed one and a half revolutions and gave signs of preparing to rise. Dark- horse did not doubt it intended to attack.

The barrier gave. Beyond the edge he sensed the hints of other worlds, other dimensions. The eternal had no time to consider which path might be best; the beast below had abruptly turned from its pattern and now rose toward him at a speed Darkhorse would not have thought possible in the thick atmosphere. He caught sight of a pair of the wicked appendages focused at him. What had looked at first like a tongue now extended ahead of the beast at a rate even swifter than the creature's own speed.

Unwilling to meet it with his weakened skills, Darkhorse followed the thread out of the misty realm.

The world of the brown thing flickered, then transformed into a sun-burnt, arid plain where everything held a reddish tinge. A massive crimson sun filled more than a third of the sky. There was no sign of life, past or present, and very few landmarks save the occasional worn mound of rock.

The shadow steed paused to recover. Fortunately, the path behind him had closed the moment he had passed through. Darkhorse could sense no trace of his pursuer.

An inhospitable world, he noted as he gathered his strength for the next part of the journey. So many dimensions he visited were like that. A few of them even made the Void seem interesting. This one threatened to be an addition to that list.

After what might have been hours . . . the massive orb did not seem to move so it was difficult to say . . . Darkhorse finally began his search for a new route. Unfortunately, although he soon found many threads worth following, none of the paths seemed familiar to him. The shadow steed at last chose one that resembled a world he had crossed long ago. While it was not the one he knew, sometimes similar realms were closely linked to one another. Sometimes.

Darkhorse still bore no resemblance to the animal from which he had taken his name. He had decided to conserve his energy until he managed to return to the Dragonrealm. There, the eternal knew places where he could take the time to recuperate. Out here, where he was not even familiar with the landscape, Darkhorse did not want to trust that he could stay in one location long enough without risking himself to something like the brown, clawed creature.

Hoping for the best, the shadow steed opened the path to the next dimension and flew through. He landed this time in a world much like that of the Dragonrealm save that all the colors seemed to be wrong. The sky was light green, the clouds were pink, and the landscape itself, a wild, grassy field, was colored what could best be called golden blue. In the distance, Darkhorse could hear what sounded like birds, but he saw no trace of them, not even a tree where they might have perched.

Seems calm enough. The eternal was not lulled, though. The former lands of the Dragon King Brown were proof enough of how lethal calm could be. Nonetheless, Darkhorse needed rest.

The oddly colored field went on forever. In fact, the more Darkhorse stared, the more he was convinced that he was seeing much, much farther than should have been possible. Perhaps this was a larger world than the one he was used to. He was tempted to explore it a little, but each minute he delayed his return meant further possible danger to his friends.

He suddenly realized that he was being watched.

Unhindered yet by a set form, Darkhorse shifted his eyes to the back so that he could see his watchers. A flurry of yellow burst from the grass behind him, scattering in many directions. The creatures that had been watching him looked for all the world like huge toads with legs and wings. Some flew off, others ran away on their four gangly legs. However, one of the creatures still remained, its eyes more intent than those of its fellows.

This is not a beast. The eyes were too intelligent, too knowing.

Stretching its wings, the toadbird *transformed.*

Darkhorse caught only a glimpse of a humanoid shape wrapped in a black, obscuring cloak before the figure faded away. The shadow steed floated over to where it had stood, but there was nothing, not even a magical trace.

He noticed that the field had become deathly silent.

I had better leave. Darkhorse performed a hurried search of those paths he could sense easiest and found a single route that seemed vaguely familiar. The way was a difficult one, but not impossible. It was also the only choice he had. He gathered his strength, then opened the way.

A hooded figure, either the same one or another just like it, materialized in front of him. The general shape was humanoid, but the thing inside the black cloak was definitely not human. A pair of narrow, amber eyes stared back over what seemed a short but toothy maw. One hand was visible, a hand with only three blunt digits.

"I am departing your world, friend! There is no need to be alarmed."

The hooded figure did not respond, but suddenly a second identical creature materialized next to it.

"I mean no harm. I am simply a lost traveler. But a moment more and you shall never see me again."

A third formed on the other side of the first one. Another materialized to the shadow steed's right. In rapid succession, several more appeared, each of them twins of the first. Dark-horse realized that they were forming a circle around him.

The eternal decided to simply depart. However, when he tried to do so, a strong force pulled him back to the ground. He tried once more with no better result.

By this time, the hooded beings completely surrounded him. The first one raised its hidden hand into view, revealing a crystalline sphere. The creature spoke, but the clacking noise it made did not translate. The eternal shook his head. Whether or not the hooded creature comprehended his response, it chose to say nothing more. The crystal, though, remained in view.

"I am no threat to you! Neither have I any worth to you. Release me and you shall be bothered by my presence no more!"

The circle grew tighter as each figure took a single step toward him. The pull on him grew stronger. *If they move much closer, the force will be too great to counter . . .*

He studied his undesired companions. Raw force would not by itself free him. He needed to put them off-guard, disrupt their concentration. What could he do that would—

The answer came to him. On the surface it seemed absurd, but with creatures such as these, it had the potential. it was also a simple answer and simple answers, he had discovered, were most often the best.

Darkhorse *laughed.*

The sound shattered the silence in a way his protests had not. Startled, the hooded figures stepped back, clearly less certain of their superiority. They had probably never heard such a loud, raucous noise before.

Taking advantage of their confusion, Darkhorse again tried to depart the foreign realm. Once more he failed, but this time the force combating him proved weaker. The shadow steed scarcely paused before renewing his efforts. His would-be captors had begun to recover from their startlement. Brandishing the sphere high, the leader waved the rest forward. They were slow to obey, but obey they did. Even as Darkhorse pushed to free himself, he felt the pressure increase dramatically.

I will not be denied this time! The eternal flung himself toward the leader of the creatures, who stumbled back so quickly that it lost its footing and fell into the deep grass. The crystalline sphere went flying from its hand.

While the others moved to aid their fallen comrade, one sought after the lost artifact. At the same time, Darkhorse turned back to the path he had opened and leaped toward it.

The same force tried to seize him again, but it was not as strong as the previous attacks. Unfortunately, it did cause him to lose control of the opening and, worse, broke his link to the path itself. The eternal battled free of the spell and desperately tried to reestablish the link in time, but his concentration had been shattered and the best Darkhorse could do was seize for what he hoped was the path he had chosen.

The realm of the hooded creatures and the flying toadbirds faded behind him, but Darkhorse did not have time to revel in his triumph. His haphazard departure left him spinning out of control and unable to leave his quickly chosen route. He had only a short glimpse of a watery world before he passed through to yet another realm without slowing in the least. Darkhorse managed to regain some control of his flight, but the second world vanished before he could even identify it.

He nearly left the third one behind as well. Only with a supreme effort did the eternal keep himself from being flung yet farther along. Finally breaking away, Darkhorse fluttered down to what proved to be gray mountaintops. Snow capped the peaks, but the cold was not a factor. Darkhorse chose the nearest and landed on a ledge.

It was a testament to his weariness that only after a long rest did Darkhorse note his surroundings. At first he could scarcely believe his luck. The eternal rose and surveyed the landscape for some miles around, but he hardly needed visual verification. This world had a familiar scent to it, a very familiar one. Not only had Darkhorse been to this place in the past, but he now knew what path he had to take to find his way back to the Dragonrealm. It was a lengthy trek, but at least a familiar one. If he set a good, steady pace, he would be able to recoup some of his strength by the time he returned home.

Home. Yes, the Dragonrealm was his home, more so than the Void had ever been. He could not allow Yureel to lay waste to his home, not even if it meant that Darkhorse had to sacrifice both of them to save it.

The sooner I depart, the better. There is no telling how much time has passed. The danger of moving from dimension to dimension was that time might pass more quickly in one world than another. It might be that only an hour had passed in the Dragonrealm . or it might be that *years* had.

Darkhorse rose slowly, shifting shape as he did. He would return to the Dragonrealm in the form in which he was known. In a sense, Darkhorse knew that it was his way of showing himself that Yureel had not crushed his will. The shadow steed was far from beaten; his twin would discover that soon enough.

But do I have the strength to defeat him? The shadow steed had to hope that he would have the strength by the time he confronted his monstrous counterpart. Yureel was his concern and no other's.

Fully restored to his favored form, Darkhorse took one last look at the landscape around him. The cloud-enshrouded mountain peaks could not be called the most attractive sight that he had ever seen, but Darkhorse savored the image nonetheless. It was very possible that this would be the last peaceful sight he would see.

No time for hesitation! Tearing himself away from the view, Darkhorse located his path to home. Yureel awaited him, probably eager to renew contact. Darkhorse did not want to disappoint his brother.

After all, they were family.

Realm after realm, dimension after dimension, the shadow steed passed on, never slowing. Worlds flickered by at an incredible rate. Darkhorse could not remember the way being this long. How many more worlds could there be? How much time had passed in the Dragonrealm in the meantime? The Dagora Forest could be a wasteland, its master slain, perhaps, by Aurim Bedlam himself.

Do not think of that! The lad was strong; in the end, he would resist Yureel. He had to. It was unthinkable that Aurim could become, even unwillingly, a greater terror than his grandfather had ever been.

Yet, Darkhorse knew all too well how strong Yureel's will was.

He passed through another realm with scarcely a glimpse at it, but as the eternal departed, he at last sensed that his final destination was at hand. The world Darkhorse entered next was one very near to the Dragonrealm. Darkhorse had not come this way in some time, but if he was correct, the shadow steed suspected that only one more realm separated him from—

As he crossed into the next realm, a wall of water put a shuddering halt to his journey. The darkness of the depths welcomed him. It was not always possible to predict exactly where a path between dimensions opened and this one had evidently opened in the midst of a body of water. In fact, as Darkhorse finally slowed his descent, he realized that he had fallen into a sea . . . and a very deep, cold one at that.

Recovering his equilibrium, the eternal darted upward toward the distant surface. Gradually the darkness gave way to the first glimmers of light. Fish swam above him, dispersing wildly as he rose among them. A long, narrow shark nearly as large as Darkhorse studied the ebony form for a moment before evidently deciding that the newcomer was too much to take on.

Darkhorse broke through to the surface and although he did not need to breathe, he inhaled and exhaled deeply once in order to relieve himself of some of the anxiety that had built up within. Then, rising upward until his hooves barely touched the surface, Darkhorse looked around. However, other than water there was nothing in sight.

He was in the middle of nowhere with no immediate sense of direction to guide him, but there was at least one thing that Darkhorse knew. He *had* returned to the Dragonrealm. Despite his certainty that he had had at least one more realm to cross, Darkhorse had instead plunged his way into the dimension of his adopted home. That he had miscalculated meant nothing to him in the face of such a revelation. Darkhorse was home and that was that.

Which way *was* home, though? The cloud cover, which hinted at a quickly approaching storm, made it impossible to judge direction by the heavens and the weary traveler's incredible trek had left his mind more addled than he had realized. He *should* have been able to sense in which direction to travel.

A few minutes of rest. That is all it will take. A few minutes of rest and I shall be able to orient myself.

However, even as he thought that, Darkhorse noticed that the sea had already begun to rise and fall with increasing intensity. Darkhorse dodged one wave that threatened to wash over him. The wind picked up. He did not move, though, his attention fixed only on the task at hand.

A column of water burst up behind him. Darkhorse turned, intent on avoiding it, but halted when he saw that the column was only a thin, quickly vanishing skin over something far more imposing. The thing within the column continued to rise higher and higher until it *loomed* over the weary eternal.

The maw of the creature was large enough to swallow five Darkhorses whole. The eyes were green and glittered of their own accord. From the lower jaw, fleshy strips that gave the appearance of a beard fluttered in the wind. Its skin was a brilliant ocean blue and the scales that covered it were streamlined for swift speeds through the water, an element probably more natural to it than the land upon which it had been born.

"You are Darkhorsssse," the sea dragon, a male, burbled, spraying the eternal as he spoke. "We were all told to watch for you, yet I never dreamed that you would come to be in my region. I thought it could not posssibly be true, but I invessstigated regardless. You are Darkhorsssse."

A wave roared over the behemoth, but the dragon scarcely noticed it, his concentration completely on Darkhorse. The sea now had a somewhat ghostly look to it, a sure sign that Darkhorse was losing the battle of wills. He concentrated what strength he had left to shifting the eventual destination of the spell to elsewhere. It had to be somewhere the shadow steed could recuperate. Darkhorse could barely hold his own now—and this to a *drake*.

Where? Where would I be safe? It was impossible to think. He could only hope that his own instincts would preserve him.

With one last effort, he finished altering the dragon's spell. Then, before the beast had the opportunity to realize what had happened, Darkhorse dropped his own defenses and allowed himself to be taken.

The shift struck him hard. Darkhorse fought unconsciousness throughout, but the struggle grew more difficult with each passing moment. He did not even know that he had landed elsewhere until it occurred to him that earth and not water lay beneath him. Through fading senses, the eternal realized that he lay sprawled in a field—but not just any field. If he was correct, he had transported himself to, of all places, Yssa's favored domain.

As if to verify his fears, several stalks of grass bent down and touched him lightly on the head. More of them followed suit even as Darkhorse faded into unconsciousness.

He had journeyed back from far beyond the Dragonrealm, struggled against creatures on a foreign world, battled the will of a huge drake even though greatly exhausted already . . . only to fall helpless into the Barren Lands.

Now he was *its* prisoner.

Chapter Eighteen

Darkhorse woke to birds singing, the wind gently blowing, and the spreading realization that he felt stronger than he had in many days. He also remembered *where* he was, a bit of knowledge that destroyed any pleasure at finding himself fully recovered from his long ordeal.

Leaping to his feet, the shadow steed glared at the grass around him . . . only to find that for several yards in each direction it lay limp and, curiously, quite dead. He nosed at some of it, but the blades remained unmoving. Darkhorse probed the area around him and found not one living blade. He estimated that he stood in the center of a circle of devastation whose diameter had to be at least thirty yards, yet outside of the circle the grassland remained as pristine as ever.

What happened here? Darkhorse recalled little of his hurried departure from the sea and nothing that would have caused the destruction around him. If it had been his doing, he regretted it. While the enchanted land made him nervous, Darkhorse did not indiscriminately destroy. The grass had harmed neither him nor his companions. He held no malice against it.

Trotting to the edge of the circle, the eternal eyed the healthy blades. They did not try to reach for him as they had in the past. Curious at this shift in behavior, Darkhorse put one hoof onto the untouched portion of the field.

Blades of grass darted toward his leg. He started to remove it, but the plants were swifter, wrapping quickly around the limb. The wary traveler hesitated, not wanting to further raise the ire of the field. It might be demanding some sort of reparation for the loss of so many. He waited, seeing what the blades would do next.

A tingle ran through him. Darkhorse felt a fresh surge of strength. He felt almost willing to take on Yureel and the entire armed force of Zuu by himself. The sensation spread. He *was* Darkhorse, after all. What creature in all the Dragonrealm was more powerful, more—

"Insane!" The ebony stallion tugged the leg away, retreating several steps at the same time. The grass around his leg fluttered to the ground, now as lifeless as that under his hooves.

But I did nothing . . . nothing. . . The tingle had died down, but the sense of growing strength did not. He felt nearly invincible. Darkhorse fought down his urge to race off and do battle with Yureel and tried to understand what had happened to make him feel so confident. The sense of growing strength had begun the moment the blades had coiled around his leg, almost as if he had been feeding off their energy.

Feeding off of their energy? But he had done no such thing! It went against his respect for life. Battle was one thing, but he was no murderous creature like his twin. He would never have done something so uncaring, so heartless. The plants had done nothing to harm him. Yet, if Darkhorse had not stolen the life force from the blades of grass, then . . . then that meant that the grass had *willingly* sacrificed itself for his recovery.

"Impossible . . ." Was it though? How else to explain his rapid recovery? He had witnessed for himself how the grass had reached out and taken hold of him. He had even sensed the power flowing from them. The plants *had* given their lives.

It must be for Yssa. The land here is fond of her It must know that I . . . that I am her friend. The notion might have seemed outrageous to most, but Darkhorse had long ago come across evidence that the Dragonrealm itself also contained a consciousness of sorts, rumored by scholars to be the last spiritual traces of those who had founded the world. Whether that was the case, he had witnessed enough startling revelations during his lengthy life span to know that his present theory was a possibility.

It might even know that she is in danger. Cautiously, the shadow steed trotted to the edge of the circle again. He felt somewhat foolish for what he was about to attempt, but Dark-horse saw no other way. There was no one creature with which he could specifically speak.

"Hear me, grassland! I know not what force lies behind you, but whether it be the spell that restored a dying land to your present glory or whether another force entirely is to be credited, I thank you for your great sacrifice! No more must be given, though! I am well and ready, thanks to you!"

No breeze blew across the field, but the blades fluttered regardless. Darkhorse blinked, almost willing to swear that the rustling sounded like the name *Yssa.* That was nonsense, though . . . was it not?

Regardless, he could remain here no longer. Yssa, Aurim, and so many others depended on him and even if he failed in the end, Darkhorse at least had to try.

"I will do what I can for your friend and mine," he added, not wanting to chance offending the grassy region if it *had* spoken to him. "I must go now. Thank you."

The blades rustled again, but this time he made out no reply. Dipping his head once in gratitude, the shadow steed backed to the very center of the circle, then focused. There was only one person who might be able to help him. The Gryphon. He hoped nothing had happened to the king of Penacles during his absence. Yureel had to know that the Gryphon was a threat, which meant that like the Bedlams, the lionbird might be in danger, if not already a victim.

I can but hope. With one last glance at the rustling blades, Darkhorse concentrated on the throne room in the palace of Penacles. The Gryphon would help him.

A moment later, though, he found himself not inside the palace, but rather outside the gates of the city proper. The shadow steed probed and found that the defenses around Penacles had been greatly strengthened, enough so that Dark horse doubted he could have penetrated them even at his best. The eternal sought to contact the Gryphon. Surely the king would grant him entrance once he knew who it was.

He received no response. With so many cunning spells in place, it was possible that the Gryphon was simply hidden from his probes, but Darkhorse suspected that the truth was that the inhuman ruler had departed his kingdom. It had not been uncommon in the past for the Gryphon to take personal risk in order to aid either his friends or his very kingdom, and bearing that in mind, Darkhorse could think of only one place where he might readily find the king.

A quick thought was all that was needed to send him on his way. He materialized exactly where he desired, which regrettably answered one question immediately. The opaque shell still covered the domain of the Bedlams. Darkhorse feared the worst. Whether he had been gone from the Dragonrealm for weeks, months, or even only a few hours, there was no saying what might have happened to the Bedlams and their people since his departure. Air flowed through the shell, but what if Yureel had set some other deadly trap into motion? Darkhorse tried to contact Cabe, but the wall would not allow him access of any sort.

Someone stood to the right of him.

"So, you aren't dead, Darkhorse."

Clad in plain robes that likely hid a breastplate beneath, the Gryphon nodded to him. The king of Penacles looked very weary, not a good sign at all. The Gryphon was a skilled spellcaster, one of the best and certainly one of the most knowledgeable. If he looked so defeated, circumstances had to be extremely dire. "How fare you, Your Majesty?"

He gestured at the shield. "It speaks for itself, doesn't it? I'd rather go into battle against an army of Aramites than play with this infernal trap! I've no more tricks to pull, no more forces to throw into the situation. I've been defeated at every turn . . ." The Gryphon blinked. "No, not completely. I have established contact within. They're still all right, although growing restless. Cabe thinks he knows something about how his son manipulated the field, but he still isn't certain that he can alter it without Aurim's assistance. I never dreamed that the boy was so *powerful.*"

"So the only way to free them is to bring Aurim back."

"No, eventually Cabe will find a solution. I may still have some luck, too. The trouble is we don't have the time. In the past week, the Green Dragon's all but buckled under to the damned horse king—"

"The past week?" Darkhorse thought back over his long journey. "How long since last you heard of me, Lord Gryphon?"

"It must be nearly two weeks. That's why I began to believe you dead. I didn't think you'd let things in the west go unchecked for so long, not to mention abandoning your friends. You've never been a coward, Darkhorse."

Nearly two weeks. Not as lengthy an exile as it might have been but far too long for the good of the land. Considering what he had last learned while Yureel's captive, he was amazed that things were not worse. "What was that you said about the lord of the Dagora Forest? The drake is not fighting back?"

"Delaying tactics and very weak ones. His forces nibble at the enemy but do not clamp down. As for sorcery, it's as if he's suddenly bereft of the art. I thought it might be because of Aurim Bedlam, that he might not wish to harm the boy, but I don't think the drake's that compassionate."

The Green Dragon might not be that compassionate when it came to Cabe and Gwen's children, but there was another whose presence might make him hesitate. Saress had captured Yssa and there was no reason to believe that the latter had escaped. The drake cared deeply for his half-breed daughter. It would not surprise Darkhorse that the reason for the Green Dragon's predicament was Yureel's use of the young enchantress as a bargaining chip. The cursed creature knew that he could best prolong and increase the devastation he desired by having Lanith defeat the drake. That would bring the other Dragon Kings in at last, but at the same time the resources of Dagora, including the drake lord's sorcerous collection, would be in Yureel's hands.

More important, a victory by Lanith over a Dragon King would garner him support from others who despised the drake race or saw the opportunity for advancement. A victory over Dagora meant the possibility of bringing the entire continent to war. Everything that Cabe had worked for would collapse. Kyl could not possibly keep his people from resuming their own war against humans. His race was as passionate about their beliefs and desires as Cabe's race was. In the end, there could be only one victor in such a cataclysm.

Yureel.

"Is there no hope for Dagora, then?" The eternal could not believe things had deteriorated so much.

"I was able to send some support . . . not much because my spies report that my good neighbor the Black Dragon has managed to organize his human fanatics and his clans under his heir. They're prepared to move at any moment and it'll be toward Penacles if they think I've weakened myself enough. Kyl sent some aid, too, but without the Green Dragon to coordinate their efforts, they can't do very much. More than half the forest has now been overrun by Zuu. I'd have never thought it possible, but it's happened . . . with the aid of sorcery, of course."

It always came down to that. Regardless of the strength of his fighting force, Lanith's true might lay in the vast reservoir of sorcery available to him through Yureel, Aurim, and the Order.

There is no other choice, then. Everything . . . the freedom of the Bedlams, the defeat of the horse king, the salvaging of Dagora, and the rescue of Aurim . . . it all demands I confront Yureel and end this. The Barren Lands had granted him as much strength as he dared command. It behooved him to see that he did not waste the gift.

Perceptive as always, the Gryphon noticed his shifting mood. "What is it, Darkhorse?"

"What will you do now, Your Majesty?"

"Return to Penacles for the time. Besides Dagora, I've got to keep an eye on Lochivar, Irillian, and Wenslis. Gordag-Ai, too, if the rumors I hear about the drake confederation are true."

It was as Darkhorse had guessed. The Gryphon had already overextended himself.

THE HORSE KING

Not only did he have to deal with the various kingdoms most affected by the war, but he also had to work to free his allies.

I can look to him for no aid. It would not be fair. "Darkhorse—"

The huge stallion stepped back. "My best wishes for your success in all matters, Your Majesty. My best wishes and dearest hopes."

"Darkhorse, what are you planning? I know you, eternal! Don't do anything—"

He did not wait to hear the rest of the Gryphon's warning, mostly because Darkhorse feared that he might end up agreeing with him. For everyone's sake, he had to see this through.

However, the sight that greeted him when he materialized a moment later in Dagora nearly sent him fleeing back to the king of Penacles. Oh, the forest here still stood, but the trees were gray and leafless, clearly dead of some blight. Worse, the area was littered with dead. The Dragon King's warriors had finally confronted Lanith's horde. Most of the bloody, mangled remains were those of the defenders, but there were many blond corpses, not to mention those of dozens of horses. The half-skeletal remains of a good-sized dragon lay among several crushed trunks, testament to the futility of such might against the horse king's linked sorcerers. Dragons made easy targets.

The battlefield was days old and the only life remaining consisted of rats, carrion crows, and other scavengers. Dark- horse kicked away one overly eager rat scurrying near his hooves. He loathed them not because of what they were but because of what they represented.

This is not far from the caverns of the Green Dragon. I wonder if this time the place will be abandoned in fact, not fantasy.

He abandoned the horror of the field, choosing a destination near the eastern caverns. The western entrances had to be held by the enemy. Zuu had conquered *more* than half the forest, that was clear now.

The forest here seemed undisturbed, but it was deathly silent, a sure sign that the war raged not far away. The Gryphon had indicated that the Green Dragon had not surrendered despite the threat against his daughter, but his hesitancy had cost the drake too much already. Even if he decided to throw everything wholeheartedly into the next battle, it was possible that he would lose badly.

Darkhorse tried to contact the Dragon King, but received no response. He was disappointed but not surprised. Still, the shadow steed hoped that the drake lord would soon notice him. The longer Darkhorse had to wander the forest, the more likely that Yureel would sense him.

Blast you, Dragon King! We must speak! What could he say, though, that he had not said earlier? In the Green Dragon's eyes, Darkhorse likely appeared to be an unnecessary interruption.

A blink hole suddenly opened in front of him.

Stumbling back, the shadow steed awaited whatever threat lurked at the other end of the hole. However, instead of some new danger concocted by Yureel, a lone drake warrior stepped out. The newcomer held both hands open so that Darkhorse could see that he was unarmed.

"Pleassse, demon sssteed! You mussst come thisss way! Quickly! Hisss Majesssty begsss you not to hesssitate!" The warrior's crimson eyes nearly pleaded with the eternal to hurry.

So the Green Dragon would see him after all. Darkhorse trotted toward the hole. From the tone of the anxious drake, the war had the clan against the wall.

The armored figure suddenly drew a blade and hissed, but he was not looking at Darkhorse. Something darted past the shadow steed, burying itself in the throat of the hapless drake. Even as his companion collapsed, already dead, Darkhorse saw more

342

than half a dozen warriors on horseback come charging toward him. Darkhorse paused before the entrance, greatly tempted to repay them for the drake's death. Then he realized that he had detected no trace of the riders, which meant that there was at least one sorcerer nearby.

That proved to be more than correct. A trio of robed figures, one of them bearing the unmistakable stench of Yureel, materialized a short distance away. The lead sorcerer, a figure Darkhorse recognized as once having been a student in Penacles, pointed at the ebony stallion.

Darkhorse leaped through the hole, hoping that the Dragon King would be quick in sealing it behind him.

The other end of the blink hole opened into the inner sanctum of the drake lord. Darkhorse whirled around as soon as he was through, prepared now to block the way if the sorcerers' spell followed. Fortunately, the blink hole had already vanished.

"You have a habit of demanding . . . my attention . . . at the worssst of times, demon sssteed."

The Dragon King slumped on a chair near the viewing artifact, his eyes fixed on the scene floating above it but his mind clearly many other places. His words were distant.

"My apologies! I have been away for quite some time and this was the first opportunity I had to contact you."

"Away?" The Green Dragon finally stared at him. "Until you materialized in the foresssst, I had become certain that you had perished at the . . . handsss, isss it?. . . of your brother." He rose slowly from the chair. "He hasss my daughter, demon. He hasss my daughter, and like my foresssst she isss hisss to do with asss he pleasesss!"

Darkhorse trotted up to the drake, forcing the tall figure to stare up at him. "I know that all too well! I was there when she was taken. Strange, though, I never took you or your brethren to be so fearful for the safety of your females. They were there for breeding purposes only."

The reptilian lord looked ready to strike him, but apparently thought about the consequences. Instead, he turned away and walked slowly toward one of the shelves housing his collection of artifacts. Darkhorse noted that many of the shelves were now empty.

"You do not know usss as well asss you think. In the passst I've been forced to deal with rebellious children, but that doesss not mean that I did not mourn them in quiet." He hissed. "I will admit that Yssa isss a ssspecial cassse. I cannot explain why."

Having known her for a time, Darkhorse thought he already understood. Yssa brought a sense of life to her surroundings that not all the foliage decorating the caverns could have matched. She was one of the most determined mortals he had met.

"It may—"

"I've changed my mind," the drake commented, reaching for a small box high on one shelf. "Your coming here might be the key to sssalvaging my kingdom and my daughter."

His tone did nothing to encourage the eternal. The Dragon King sounded as if he were willing to do anything. He had already threatened Aurim's life. "I will not help you kill Cabe's son, drake!"

"That isss an option I find beyond me. To attack the lad isss to attack the entire Order. The oddsss against sssuccessfully completing that operation are great. No, I propossse insstead a multipronged asssault that will have asss its culmination the exile of thisss monstrosity Yureel and the ressscue of my daughter."

He was mad. Darkhorse was certain of it. "You say that attacking Aurim is a futile gesture but trying to save your daughter while at the same time exiling Yureel is *not?*"

"Not with thisss!" The Green Dragon turned and held forth the artifact. It was a box, aged beyond belief, but still sturdy. There was a pattern on the lid, but time had worn away so much of it that only a wing was still identifiable. "Not with this . . ."

"Get that *away* from me!" Darkhorse reared, nearly causing the drake to back into the shelves. Fear swept over the eternal. He knew what the box was. He had seen its like before. Once, he had even been a prisoner of one.

Being trapped within the box had been worse than being lost in the Void. At least in the latter one could move. In the box, there was nothing put pain.

"Yesss, it isss of Vraad make," the Dragon King remarked, referring to the ancient race of sorcerers who were the ancestors of the humans.

"I *know* it is of Vraad make! I know what the cursed box is! By the Void, how many of the monstrous things did they create? Must they all survive the centuries?"

It had been the Vraad Dru Zeree who had led him to the Dragonrealm, but it had been another Vraad, the militaristic clan leader Barakas Tezerenee, who had taught him fear as only his twin had before. Lord Tezerenee had used one of the boxes to break him. The box was a prison, one in which Dark- horse had been trapped, helpless. He had been forced to obey the edicts of the ruthless Vraad leader until rescued. The memory was countless centuries old but as fresh in his mind as ever.

"Destroy it! Destroy it!" The eternal backed farther away, nearly upsetting some of the shelves behind him.

Cradling the box in his hands, the Dragon King stared defiantly at him. "I will not! Thisss isss the only one I have left! Thisss is the only thing I have left that I believe will deal with the creature . . . and you will help me, demon sssteed!"

Darkhorse fought his fears down. "Help you with what?"

"To *trap* him with thisss, of courssse! I'd wondered if you, with your knowledge of Vraad waysss, would recognize it. You do, sso you alsso know how it worksss . . . and it ssstill doesss. With it, we shall capture the monster, ressscue my daughter . . . and perhapsss Aurim Bedlam as well."

"Exactly what do you have in mind?" Darkhorse was certain that the strain had unbalanced the drake, but his plan did have a remote possibility of success, which was more than the stallion could say for his own idea.

Seeing that he had his companion's undivided attention at last, the Green Dragon smiled. The image made Darkhorse wonder just what Yssa's mother could have seen in him. He was exotic, yes, but he was a *drake*. Darkhorse doubted he would ever understand love.

"There isss little time remaining." The reptilian monarch visibly forced himself to calm down. "I must now defend not only the west but the south asss . . . as well. The land lost to the horse king and his familiar resembles a jawbone now with the sharpest fangs just to the south of my cavernsss. Men, drakes, elves, even Ssseekers have perished by the scores, and but for the sorcery Lanith has at hisss beck and call, I could end this insufferable war in a few hours. As brave and ready as they are, the warriors of Zuu are alssso pragmatic. They'd know better than to continue if the Order wasss eliminated."

Darkhorse was not so certain about that, but he did not comment. "You said we would also try to *rescue* Aurim, not kill him."

"Yes, yesss. Hear me, then. It isss you who bear much of the responsibility for success. You will locate my daughter, who isss, I believe, far behind the lines accompanied by Lanith's witch. You must take her from the witch—"

The eternal let loose with a short, bitter laugh. "Yureel is certain to notice me!"

"So much the better. His attention will be divided. When he comes to deal with you, I will come and deal with him."

He was proposing to leap behind the lines of the enemy and face Yureel head on. The Green Dragon appeared to have a great death wish. Even if he succeeded in trapping Dark-horse's twin, the Order would make short work of him. Either Aurim or one of the other sorcerers under Yureel's spell would then release the insidious monster.

At that point, they would all turn on Darkhorse.

When he informed the Dragon King of this, the helmed drake disagreed. "The Order will not be a problem. In fact, they will be the caussse of even greater distraction for the demon."

"How so?"

The smile that now spread across the Green Dragon's half-hidden features was as grim as any Darkhorse had seen in years. "The Order—including Aurim, I hope— will be hard-pressed to aid Lanith'sss horde, much less their true master. I intend to throw everything I have at Lanith's army. *Everything.* Once the box and its contentsss are sssent far, far away, the hold the demon had on the young Bedlam will surely fade. That, then, will weaken the Order to the point where they will fall from exhaustion quite quickly. Their ssstrength without Cabe'sss son is not so great a danger."

The shadow steed nearly turned him down there and then. It was a risky plan at best. Even supposing the impossible happened and they were able to exile Yureel again, how long could the drake's defenses hold out? Lanith still had Ponteroy and the other sorcerers, and their combined powers were not so weak as the Green Dragon might think.

"I will do thisss with or without you, Darkhorsssse. You'll have to admit the oddsss are better with both of usss working together. What other hope isss there?"

"The Gryphon—"

"Hasss too many concerns of hisss own! It isss either this or defeat."

It went against his better judgment to agree, but Darkhorse had found enough fault in his own judgment recently to make him uncertain. The Green Dragon had fought in wars past; he was certainly a better strategist than the eternal could claim. Besides, what other plan did they have?

"Very well. I agree."

The drake hissed in obvious relief. "Good. I had little hope for sssuccess on my own, being unable to both rescue Yssa and confront the demon. I have officers who can deal with the battle itself, but no one I could trust to aid me on this mission."

Unspoken was the fact that although the Dragon King had a male heir to his throne, he dared not risk him even for Yssa. Drakes with the markings designating them future Dragon Kings were rare and so each of the monarchs kept careful watch over their successors. The Green Dragon's heir would be helping to coordinate defensive efforts from somewhere deep within the cavern system, well away from the battle. It was a curious arrangement at times, especially considering that many Dragon Kings came into power by eliminating their progenitors.

"When do we begin this?"

Again the drake smiled grimly. "Asss they say, 'there'sss no time like the presssent,' is there?"

Death. More death. More and more death and not a thing that Aurim could do to stave off the flow. If anything, he was responsible for the rising casualties. The spells that the Order focused through him laid waste to acres of forest and hundreds of defenders. Lanith's warriors suffered losses as they pushed for the Dragon King's stronghold, but that made the matter worse, not better. The defenders had done their utmost to rout the invaders, but against sorcery that left the Green Dragon's own spells wanting, they were helpless.

Another day and we'll be pounding at the lizard's door. His head'll decorate a lance soon after -

Aurim mentally cringed at the thought. Of late, he had found himself thinking such things. Yureel's control had crept deeper into his mind, threatening to soon turn the sorcerer into a loyal, very willing servant to the monster's evil.

General Belfour rode up to him. "Any spellwork?"

"Only the protective shield," Aurim's mouth responded.

"I don't like it. Why the sudden lull? The drake's troops withdrew, too. If it wasn't for the fact that our own need the rest, we'd be after them all the way to the Dragon King's lair. This doesn't bode well."

Thankful for any respite, Aurim Bedlam hardly wanted to question the retreat, but that part of him controlled by Yureel had to ask, "Does the king want us to stir them up? We could create another fire wall."

"The king's in conference," the veteran snapped. To the sorcerer, by now familiar with the older warrior's personality, that meant that Belfour had noticed his monarch talking to himself. None of Lanith's warriors were privy to his relationship with the demon, so to them the horse king had to seem mad. Still, no one dared talk of removing him from the throne. Not only were the warriors of Zuu trapped by their own sense of tradition, but Lanith had proven he wielded great power. "We'll probably have an answer before long."

Aurim snapped to attention, his eyes suddenly darting skyward. The reaction was a combination of both parts of him in response to the sudden sensing of a familiar presence. A study of the clouds revealed nothing, though.

"What is it, spellcaster?"

He struggled with himself, trying not to reveal what he had sensed. Belfour noticed his hesitation and urged his animal nearer. The general looked ready to slap Aurim on the cheek.

Fortunately, or rather unfortunately in Aurim's eyes, the sorcerer lost his struggle to keep his secret. "Darkhorse. He's near . . . or getting near."

"Darkhorse? That beast is back?" Envy and distrust vied within Belfour. He had not made it a secret that he would have dearly loved a steed such as his king had briefly owned. "I'd better alert His Majesty to—"

The earth rumbled nearby, the sudden quake sending the three spellcasters presently on monitoring duty to their knees. Belfour's horse reared in surprise, forcing the general to concentrate his full effort on retaining control. Aurim maintained his footing, but before he could gather his wits, a heavy wind threatened to push him back into the general's anxious mount.

Ahead, a horn abruptly blared, immediately followed by several more.

"They're attacking!" Ponteroy called needlessly from nearby. The other sorcerer had been drinking some of the sickly sweet wine he transported daily from Gordag-Ai. Now he stood, a purple stain spreading across the chest of his otherwise immaculate jacket, and hurriedly began organizing the rest of the Order.

The rumble increased in intensity, spreading both to the north and the south. The magical wind matched it, blowing so hard that some of the weaker sorcerers had to be aided by their fellows. Slowly, they formed a ragged pattern, an empty spot in the middle left for Aurim.

In the midst of it all, he sensed the swiftly approaching presence of Darkhorse. The stallion was heading to the south, beyond the rear of Zuu's lines. Aurim was happy that Dark- horse had survived his haphazard exile, but bitter that now he would have to try to capture the shadow steed again.

Yssa. It was the only answer. Darkhorse had to be heading toward Yssa.

"Don't just stand there, brat!" Ponteroy snarled. "If we don't do something, the drake's attack will force our warriors back and his sorcery will scatter *us* all over the landscape, too!"

Yureel's conditioning seized hold. Unless contacted directly by the demon, Aurim had to obey the monster's primary dictate. He was to work to counter the enemy's spells, then lead the Magical Order in attempting to destroy the source of the spellwork.

Despite the dread that rose within him every time he joined with the others to spread havoc and death among the horse king's foes, the young spellcaster now felt a shred of hope. Occupied as he was with defending the legions of Zuu, he could not immediately turn and attack his old friend. Yureel would have to face Darkhorse alone, at least for the time being.

Unfortunately, Aurim also knew that the demon had already planned for his twin's inevitable return . . . and this time the puppet master would brook no escapes.

Chapter Nineteen

There! She is there!

Darkhorse focused, opening a path to where Yssa was held prisoner. Despite the Dragon King's plan, he wanted to move in quick and be gone with the enchantress before Yureel even made his appearance. The stallion doubted he would succeed in doing so, but he had to try. He would be better able to concentrate on his foul twin if he did not also have to worry about his friend.

When he materialized a breath later, it was to the consternation of half a dozen guards and the sorceress Saress. The guards, much more used to the sudden shifts of battle, recovered before Saress. Three of them split away and tried to come around to the eternal's back. The others moved forward, spears in the hands of two, the third—a scarred woman—carrying a crimson rope. Darkhorse sensed sorcery present in all the weapons. As he had feared, Yureel had expected him to return.

"Away with all of you!" the shadow steed roared, trying to frighten them off. Beyond the three in front, Saress guarded the entrance to a tent wherein Darkhorse could sense her captive. Darkhorse contemplated leaping over the heads of the trio and charging Lanith's witch, but he suspected that Yureel had kept that notion in mind as well.

The three who had moved around him also carried spears, weapons that they seemed quite willing to use despite the reputation the shadow steed had for dealing with his adversaries. Darkhorse twisted around as no mortal horse could have and reared at the nearest guard. The man stood his ground and jabbed with the spear, managing to prick the shadow steed's right foreleg. A shock briefly jolted Darkhorse, who immediately retreated a step.

He heard the swish of the rope, caught a brief glance of it as it circled his head, then felt the noose settle around his neck. Darkhorse started to retract his head, but the moment the noose tightened, he lost control of his shapeshifting abilities.

"I've got him!" cried the woman.

So she did, but roping Darkhorse and keeping him under control were two different things. He sensed the same spell that Aurim had cast on the saddle and bridle, but thanks to the sacrifice of the enchanted grass, the eternal now had the strength to defy it. He reared, something the guard had not expected him to be able to do, and pulled his would-be captor forward. The moment she was near enough, Darkhorse kicked her soundly, sending the stunned warrior flying back into one of her companions.

Seeing his two companions collapse was enough to make the remaining sentry before Darkhorse lose much of his confidence in his sorcerous weapon. He started to back toward the tent.

"Get back up there, you fool!" shouted Saress, but she made no move to back the guard up.

The other warriors were not so reluctant. Another shock coursed through Darkhorse as the trio attacked. Deciding to risk further pain, the shadow steed kicked with his rear legs. Another shock briefly assailed him, but the agony was worth it in the end, for Darkhorse managed to stun one guard and knock loose the weapon from another. The third met the shadow steed's gaze and, after staring into the inhuman orbs for but a moment, dropped his weapon and fled.

Darkhorse had no more time to waste on them. The shadow steed reared, then planted both front hooves hard in the soil. The earth cracked, the tremor nearly upsetting the balance of the warriors around him. At the same time, Darkhorse created around himself a bright green aura that crackled like lightning. "Flee before I devour you, you insignificant little worms!"

Dropping their weapons, the remaining guards fled, leaving only Saress.

Shrugging off the noose, Darkhorse confronted the sorceress. "Step aside, witch, and I may forget that you exist."

She hissed defiantly, but when the eternal took another step toward her, the sorceress quickly vanished. Darkhorse hesitated, then trotted into the tent.

Yssa stood there, arms and legs stretched outward. Thin, silky strands circled her wrists and ankles, keeping her from moving, but otherwise she looked untouched. Even Yureel knew the value of a healthy captive, it seemed. Darkhorse probed the strands, which ended in midair, and found his twin's taint on them. Disgusted, he quickly disposed of the magical bonds.

"Come with me, quickly, Yssa! Before Yureel arrives!"

She tried to say something as she approached, but no sound escaped her. The eternal detected a spell similar to the one Aurim had used to keep him silent. Annoyed that he had not noticed it earlier, the shadow steed removed it, too.

"Darkhorse! You shouldn't have come here! He's expecting you to—"

The horribly familiar giggle floated through the tent, seeming to surround the pair. Darkhorse's eyes narrowed. Even now he could not sense Yureel. The malevolent puppet had worked hard to shield himself.

"Too late! Too late, my dear sweet sorceress!" Yureel coalesced in a far corner of the tent. The miniature figure drifted toward them. "I knew that you would eventually return to me no matter where the boy sent you! Ever the hero, my brother, my self? I'd think you'd learn a new game by this time!"

"And so I have!" Using his jaws, Darkhorse seized an unsuspecting Yssa by the arm, pulling her completely off the ground. Before Yureel could react, he had carried the enchantress out of the tent.

A tall, fearsome figure blocked their path from there. "Father!" Yssa gasped.

The drake thrust out one gauntleted hand at them. "Down, demon sssteed! Now!"

Darkhorse did not have to ask why. He could sense Yureel just behind him. Still gripping the Dragon King's daughter by the arm, he fell to the ground.

"No need to grovel, Darkhorse, it won't do you any—well, the lizard king! This is a surprise! My brother must've mentioned me to you, I see! Come to visit your offspring or come to surrender to the inevitable?"

"I've come to sssend you back where you belong, abomination!" The reptilian monarch flipped open the box.

Yureel giggled at the effrontery, no doubt thinking the Dragon King completely mad. The giggle died abruptly, though, as the floating demon's feet began stretching toward the open compartment. Snarling, the malevolent marionette tried to pull away, but his bottom half surged toward the box. Yureel began to look like an uncooked gingerbread man being stretched in two by some insane baker.

"Stop it! I command you to stop it!"

"Command all you like!" hissed the Green Dragon. "Welcome to your new home!"

With each passing moment, Darkhorse expected his twin to pull free, yet the pull of the artifact would not be denied.

"Release me! Release me or I will destroy you!" Yureel twisted and turned, ice-blue eyes wide with growing comprehension of what fate awaited him if he did not free himself quickly. Unlike Darkhorse, Yureel had never faced the boxes before.

"In, demon!" The Dragon gasped; Yureel was clearly stronger than he had expected.

There was nothing Darkhorse could do to help. If he interfered, he might find himself caught in the very same trap along with his twin. Worse, he might even accidentally free Yureel instead of assuring his imprisonment.

"You . . . will. . . stop!" Rocks burst from the ground and pelted the Green Dragon, but the attack was weak. Yureel dared not focus too much of his power on the drake; he needed everything to combat the tenacious pull of the Vraad box.

It was now only a matter of seconds.

The struggling figure stretched thinner and thinner as more of him seeped into the box. Yureel grew so sheer that it was possible to see through him. He grasped at the sky, as if trying to gain some handhold on the distant clouds.

Then, with one long howl of anger, the last of the shadow puppet vanished into the artifact.

The drake immediately shut the lid.

"Do you really have him, Father?"

"If you could feel how the box shakesss in my hand you wouldn't asssk such a question, my daughter."

Darkhorse glanced quickly around. Saress had to have warned King Lanith by now, and while by himself the lord of Zuu was little threat, he still had the power to command the sorcerers. Until the Dragon King disposed of the cursed box and its doubly cursed contents, Aurim remained a slave to Yureel. Their victory could still turn into disaster if Cabe's son gathered the Order and confronted them. "Dispose of the box, now, Dragon King! We do not have much time remaining to us."

"I . . . am. . . trying!" The Green Dragon clutched the artifact with both hands, as if trying to squeeze it out of existence. "It is . . . resisting my attempts to cast it out of our world."

Even without the use of a probe, Darkhorse could sense the tremendous force with which Yureel sought to free himself of the Vraad device. For the first time, the eternal wondered if the ancient box would hold out against the might of his vile counterpart. Perhaps time had taken a toll on the Vraad artifact after all.

"Darkhorsssse, I think it may require both of usss—"

Whatever else the Dragon King said, the eternal did not hear. Sorcery was at play around them, familiar sorcery.

"I think you've got something that belongs to me, lizard."

THE HORSE KING

The horse king suddenly confronted them, but he was hardly alone. Not only did a now-smiling Saress lean on his shoulder, but Aurim, the oily Ponteroy, and two other sorcerers flanked the pair. The younger Bedlam still stared at Darkhorse as if recognizing him only as an enemy of his master.

"Keep back, vasssal, unless you'd care to lossse your precious ally!"

Lanith's expression shifted to mild confusion. "I'm talking about your dear, sweet daughter, lizard. She's my special guest and I'm here to see that she'll stay that way. Come here, woman."

Before the Dragon King could retort, Aurim Bedlam interjected, "He has Yureel in that box, Your Majesty. That's what he meant."

"Does he? That box?" Fascination and indignation clashed as the horse king squinted at the artifact. "Now that's clever." He extended a hand. "Give it to me and I'll at least let your half-breed child live, lizard. Oh . . . and your death'll be relatively quick and painless, I suppose."

"Are you not leaving your warriors and your remaining spellcasters to face a storm of death, Your Majesty?" Darkhorse asked, trying to shake King Lanith's confidence a little. "They might be wondering where you are even now."

"My people are dedicated to me. They're warriors of Zuu, horse. The finest in the land and willing to prove it to any who disbelieve. If it costs some of them their lives, so be it. In the end, Dagora will be mine. After that, Gordag-Ai, then probably Talak."

"You fool!" The drake lord hissed, struggling more and more with the box. "Even with your spellcastersss you will eventually losssse! Can't you ssssee that the demon isss playing you like a puppet?"

It was the wrong thing to say. The horse king pointed at the box. "Take it from him, Aurim. Feel free to hurt him while you do it."

But at that moment the Vraad artifact suddenly blazed with light. The Green Dragon snapped one gauntleted hand away, the palm already a fiery red. However, he refused to release the box, though his other hand must be suffering terrible pain.

Yssa started toward her father, but Darkhorse used his power to drag her back, knowing it was already too late to help the Dragon King. There was nothing either of them could do.

The box exploded.

The explosion hurtled the Green Dragon back toward the tent, whether dead or not, Darkhorse had no time to discover. A pitch-black cloud rose above the cracked remnants of the foul device, a cloud with icy blue eyes. It surveyed those assembled, at last fixing its murderous glare on the scorched form of the drake.

"I'll burn him, I'll tear his limbs off one at a time, I'll spread his body across every land in the continent!" Yureel reshaped himself, but now he was larger, less cohesive. "I'll kill him, then kill him again!"

Focused as he was on Yureel's horrific return, Darkhorse forgot about Yssa until it was too late. The blond enchantress suddenly darted away from her companion, trying to reach her father.

"Yes, yes, yes!" Yureel ranted, eyes glittering in swelling anticipation. "You'll do even better, dear one! I hope your father survives long enough to hear your cries!"

"You'll do nothing!" roared Darkhorse, but as he moved to intercept his twin's spells, he found something holding him back.

"You won't do anything, Darkhorse," Aurim stared blankly at him.

"Very good," commended the horse king. "Hold him there." Lanith took a step toward his shadowy ally. "Don't harm her, imp! She's got too much potential. We can use her to strengthen the Order, make her help conquer her father's own land! Just do with her as you did with Bedlam here."

350

"Her mind's all wrong, you fool!" Yureel seemed to no longer care about pretending he was servant to Lanith. "Just like that witch of yours!"

Lanith clearly did not understand, but Darkhorse thought *he* did. Yureel could not control either half-breed the way he could humans. Something in the half-breeds' minds must differ from the minds of true humans. He wished he had the time to discover just what. Any advantage was welcome.

A brief, low moan escaped the Green Dragon. Yureel turned toward him again, his interest in his former captor renewed.

"Leave him be, damn you!" The Dragon King's daughter seemed not to care that Yureel had the power to tear her limb from limb.

A brave and impetuous young woman . . . and one about to die horribly because of those traits. Darkhorse struggled to help her, but Aurim held him at bay. The shadow steed stared at his young friend. Aurim stared back, expression still indifferent.

Gathering his will, Darkhorse tried to contact the mind held prisoner within the sorcerer's body. He knew that some part of Aurim had to be there; it had revealed itself in time to save him before. Perhaps there was a chance Darkhorse could stir the true Aurim to action.

In his mind, he called the human's name over and over. The sorcerer's expression tightened, as if he was not at all at peace with himself. Darkhorse took the change as a sign and pushed harder to reach his friend. *Aurim Bedlam! This is not you! You have the power to shift the balance here! You must!*

As the ebony stallion fought to reach the sorcerer's mind, Yureel looked down upon the drake's defiant offspring. "Yes, you're absolutely right! I should leave him alone . . . at least for now! I *should* play with you first! I'll make your death an epic in itself!"

Standing her ground, Yssa cast a spell. A cloud formed around reel, but the shadowy figure shrugged it off with scarcely any effort. He moved nearer, reshaping and solidifying into a massive, dark figure very reminiscent in outline of an armored warrior, a drake to be precise. Even the eyes seemed half-hidden now by a pitch-black helm. The dark knight stood at least a full foot taller than Darkhorse.

"Kapio's Charger!" gasped the horse king. Darkhorse suspected he had never seen his ally in anything but the most minute of forms. "Imp—"

"Why don't you change, too, little witch?" Yureel taunted the defiant woman. *"She* can do it"—Saress blanched and quickly retreated a few steps behind Lanith—"you can certainly do it, too."

Yssa's response came in the form of another spell, this one a score of bright flashes that burst into and out of existence accompanied by a loud explosion. Briefly startled, the shadow knight backed up a step . . . and walked into a cage formed from the earth. As the entrance of the cage sealed itself, the enchantress fell to one knee, gasping.

"The box could not hold me," Yureel casually remarked, putting one massive hand against the front of his cage, "and it was your only hope, dragonspawn." The cage shattered, pelting all of them with bits of earth. He stalked toward Yssa, each step leaving small craters. "Now, how shall we begin with you?"

As he reached for her, his hand swelled, growing all out of proportion to the rest of his form. Yssa tried to vanish, but Darkhorse sensed Yureel counter her attempt. She was still trying to transport herself away when the fearsome knight lifted her up by the waist.

"Perhaps I'll squeeze you apart first, then absorb the leftovers . . . "

Try as he might, Darkhorse could do nothing to free her. Aurim kept his powers in check. He stared again at the young sorcerer. *Aurim! Do not let this happen!*

THE HORSE KING

Yureel tightened his grip. The enchantress first gasped, then moaned as the shadowy knight started to squeeze the life out of her.

A silver scythe formed between Yureel and Yssa and without pause *sliced* clean the hand that held her.

Hand and enchantress dropped the short distance to the ground. The severed appendage immediately released her and scurried back to its master, who absorbed it and formed a new hand to take the original's place.

Aurim stepped in front of the king, eyeing the monstrous shadow with new and growing defiance. "I've . . . killed for you. I've ravaged . . . a land . . . for you. I've seen more . . . death . . . than is right for. . . any one person. . . to want or have to witness!"

"Return to your place!" commanded Lanith, reaching for him.

The younger Bedlam glared at the horse king, who suddenly thought better of touching a powerful spellcaster in anger. "I am."

"You little whining traitor!" Ponteroy raised his staff, but Aurim blinked and the staff suddenly burst into flames. Gasping, the other sorcerer dropped his fiery weapon and kicked it away. A slight wave of Aurim's hand sent the burning staff flying in the direction of Lanith's advancing warriors. A breath later, they heard it explode.

"Go home, Ponteroy," Aurim added. "I know your former liege in Gordag-Ai will be pleased to see you. You've told me that often enough."

"No—" was all the arrogant spellcaster managed to spout before vanishing. If Aurim *had* sent him back to Gordag-Ai, it was doubtful he would be returning soon, if at all. The kingdom's spies likely knew every traitorous action the overdressed sorcerer had been involved with since his arrival in Zuu and without his staff, Ponteroy was not as much a threat.

The two remaining sorcerers retreated to Saress, who still watched Lanith nervously. Her own fear that he would realize what she was kept her paralyzed.

Not so Yureel. "Naughty boy! Behave yourself or I'll just have to strike you from my epic!"

Aurim's expression instantly slackened. He started back to the other spellcasters.

"Fight it, lad!" Darkhorse roared. Belatedly he realized that Aurim had dropped the spell holding him prisoner, probably at the same time the sorcerer had turned on his foul master. Now nothing prevented him from using his power. The ebony stallion immediately focused on Yureel, trying to strike between the eyes. If he could distract his murderous brother—

Yureel easily deflected his spell, but as Darkhorse had hoped, the attack gave Aurim the reprieve he needed to recover control of himself. The young sorcerer gritted his teeth and stared at his former master. Aurim was frightened, but doing his best to face the source of his fears.

Two of the spears dropped by the sentries rose into the air and darted past Aurim. Behind him, the king of Zuu, sword drawn, tried to protect himself from the unexpected attack. Lanith had clearly intended on stabbing the spellcaster from behind, realizing, perhaps, that without Yureel, his own dreams of victory would remain just that. If it meant sacrificing even so valuable a pawn as Aurim had been, so be it.

The treacherous monarch managed to deflect the first missile with his sword, but the second came too fast. Lanith tried but failed to raise his weapon in time. The head of the spear buried itself in his shoulder. Grunting, the horse king dropped his weapon and stumbled back.

Hissing, Saress went to his side. She pulled the weapon free, passed her hand over the wound, then signaled the other spellcasters to come to her aid. "I've stopped the bleeding, but more needs doing! Get him away from here and see that he's healed completely or you'll face me later! Go now!"

The two immediately took hold of the king and carried him away. Saress stood and glared at the source of his agony, the Dragon King's daughter. Yssa, though, had already forgotten the murderous king, her concern once again for her injured father. She did not even notice the other woman start toward her.

Knowing that the drake lord's daughter was too distracted to be of good use, anyway, Darkhorse called out, "Take him away from here, Yssa! Somewhere safe! Do it now!"

Looking relieved yet guilty, Yssa carefully scooped up her father. The drake's hand was a burnt ruin, probably unsalvageable even through high sorcery. The Dragon King breathed in short gasps. Yssa hurriedly opened a path of escape, clearly aware of how weak the drake had already become.

With an inhuman roar, Saress flung herself after her disappearing rival. Occupied with Yureel, Darkhorse could do nothing to stop the furious sorceress. Saress vanished only seconds after Yssa and her father did.

Yureel continued to prove more resilient than the stallion had hoped. The dread knight had so far fought Darkhorse and his companion to a standstill, something that should not have been possible. True, Yureel had always maintained greater reserves of strength due to his horrific habit of eventually devouring any source of power he came across, but Darkhorse was at his peak and Aurim was possibly the greatest spell-caster in generations. Even Yureel with his parasitic link to the other spellcasters of the Order should not have been able to stand against the pair, unless. . . Aurim was unconsciously holding back because his confidence had begun to erode again.

"We have him, lad! Keep at him!" He hoped he sounded encouraging. Aurim needed to believe in himself.

The human did not respond and his face was horribly pale. He still worked alongside the shadow steed, but it was clear that he recalled too much of his enslavement. Fear made him hesitant, something that threatened to be fatal for both of them.

Aurim! He cannot harm you anymore! You have proven your will superior to his! Darkhorse repeated himself, uncertain as to whether the boy paid any attention to his plea.

He made me . . . I couldn't do a thing, Darkhorse . . . he made me kill for him! I thought I was strong enough, but now I don't know . . .

But you saved Yssa and the drake! You broke free, Aurim! You broke free!

At first Darkhorse believed that his words had had no impact on Cabe's son, but then he sensed a new onrush of power behind the spell that Aurim cast next. Yureel certainly felt something, too, for although the spellwork itself was invisible, the shadow knight's reaction was anything but. Yureel's form glowed crimson and he stumbled back, crushing the tent.

"You are ours, Yureel!" Darkhorse meant his cry not only for his twin but for Aurim, too. The young mage needed more encouragement if the pair of them had any hope of victory. Aurim had finally freed himself of Yureel's control and now had the insidious demon at the disadvantage, but events had a habit of changing quickly in such dire situations. "Your epic will have to remain incomplete!"

The monstrous creature regained his footing. "I'm very disappointed in both of you, brother! You've misbehaved! I will just have to absorb you . . . but not before I teach you your place."

"Your power is not enough to withstand both of us, Yureel. That should be obvious even to you!"

He expected Yureel to retort again, but instead the shadow knight did something

353

that caught both Darkhorse and Aurim completely off-guard. He flung himself into the air and flew off toward the east, his speed so great that he was little more than a speck by the time either of his adversaries realized what had happened.

"Darkhorse—"

"Aurim! Mount quickly!" Darkhorse waited only long enough for the sorcerer to obey, then leaped into the air after their foe. Yureel had already flown halfway to the battlefield, a destination dangerous even for so deadly a creature. What he planned, Darkhorse could only guess.

Still behind the Zuu lines, Yureel began to descend. The shadow steed could not readily detect who or what Yureel flew toward, but he thought he sensed sorcery there. A sudden suspicion started to gnaw at him.

"Hold tight, Aurim! We must reach him before it is too late!"

The sorcerer had already wrapped his arms around his friend's throat, but he tightened his grip. Sorcery was in play all over the battlefield despite the fact that both armed forces had come together, and it was likely difficult for the spellcasters to separate friend from foe. Even one stray spell might be enough to slow Darkhorse and possibly brutally injure the human astride him.

Yureel disappeared from sight, but Darkhorse still sensed his presence below. He now also sensed the presence of several sorcerers: the remnants of the Magical Order. Without Aurim, Saress, and Ponteroy, the Order was severely weakened, but the potential for danger still existed. If anyone knew best how to exploit that potential, it was Yureel.

"Be ready, Aurim. I fear the worst."

They were suddenly buffeted by earsplitting shrieks from every direction. Aurim screamed, and it was all the eternal could do to keep from following suit. The shadow steed spiraled toward the ground, just barely able to maintain control. In the distance, he caught sight of at least half a dozen figures positioned in a recognizable geometric pattern.

In the center stood the huge, shadowy figure of Yureel. Darkhorse touched the earth still facing the group. A quick probe verified his fear; Yureel had taken Aurim's place as the Order's focus. Worse, he had thrown off the mask of independence under which they had operated. Now he controlled each and every one of them.

"Darkhorse! He's made them like me!"

"I know that, Aurim! We cannot allow that to dissuade us, though."

"You don't understand, Darkhorse." The sorcerer gripped his companion's mane tight. "In a link of that complexity, they become so much more than a group of low-level mages."

Darkhorse understood that also, but before he could say so, Yureel and the Order struck again. Tremendous pressure threatened to flatten the eternal to the ground. Next to him, Aurim fell first to his knees, then on his face.

"We—must—work together! Give me your mind!" The moment he said the words, the eternal realized his grave mistake. Animal fear overwhelmed his friend, fear based deeply in the human's recent captivity. Aurim saw Darkhorse as too much like his twin.

The pressure continued to build, but now the ground changed, liquefying. Sorcerer and shadow steed quickly sank. It was all either of them could do just to keep their heads above the surface.

"Aurim! I am not Yureel! I will not seize control of your mind and body! We will work *together*. It is the one weapon we have that he can never understand well enough to use himself. We must link and become one together, not one held by the will of the other!"

The spellcaster shook his head. "I can't! Not again!"

"If you do not, then we have no hope. I must intertwine our powers so well that whatever Yureel attempts, he will be unable to separate them. Divided we are two against many. Together . . . we have the power to see to it that he will never cause such devastation and terror again."

Aurim nodded. His mind opened up to Darkhorse and although the eternal still sensed some lingering fear, he also noted building resolve. This time, Aurim Bedlam would not falter.

It was nearly too late. Darkhorse bound his power with that of the sorcerer just as Aurim's mouth sank below the surface. The human's eyes widened, but he did not give in to panic.

It is done! We are one in our strength now. The binding briefly gave Darkhorse a sense of double thought, but he immediately sorted out his own mind from that of his young companion. With the stallion to guide them along, the pair lifted themselves from the earth.

Yureel forced his thralls to attack again, but this time the pair shrugged off the spell. With Aurim once more atop him, Darkhorse closed in on his counterpart. Neither he nor his companion attacked in turn; the spells they cast simply acted to deflect those of the Order toward the forces of Zuu. Each time Yureel attacked, he dealt damage to his own cause.

At last, only a few yards separated Darkhorse and his brother. Yureel looked slightly smaller and less fierce; controlling so many during so relentless a struggle had taken a toll even on him. The spellcasters looked even more bedraggled, but they had no choice.

"You are wasting your weapons, Yureel," taunted the shadow steed. "You can never make use of their full power while their spirits are trapped. Your very desire to control means that full control can *never* be yours."

"Still you preach, my brother, my self. Still you preach and no one listens!"

"Look around you! The power you threw against us has instead fallen upon the warriors of your supposed ally! Do you call that control? In the past few minutes, you have probably done more damage to the legions of Zuu than the Dragon King's own forces have."

Yureel hesitated, icy orbs shifting momentarily in the direction of the two battling armies. Like Darkhorse, he could sense that the horse king's warriors no longer had the advantage; the deadly spells the shadow steed and Aurim had redirected had struck Lanith's army at its most vulnerable points. The power that the dark knight had thrown at his foes had caused such damage that in some places the defenders were now pushing westward.

"My epic . . ." Yureel glared at the duo. "All my lovely work . . ."

"Worry not about your epic so much as yourself, Yureel. The box might not have been able to hold you, but there are other cages. The Void awaits your return."

"I will not go back there! I will not! I will not! Never again!" Arms burst from the shadowy giant's body, enough arms with which to seize the defenseless sorcerers around him. The arms retracted the moment each had hold of its prey. Darkhorse tried to sever the limbs as Aurim had earlier, but Yureel was too swift. The unmoving mages disappeared into the recesses of the knight's monstrous torso without so much as the slightest scream.

"God!" Aurim nearly slipped from his back. Darkhorse could not help shivering. He never ceased to be amazed at Yureel's complete lack of respect for life. The sorcerers had meant no more to him than a blade of grass or a fly.

Yureel no longer seemed weary, pushed to the edge of defeat. He looked stronger now, stronger and larger. The ebony knight had threatened to absorb his twin and make all that Darkhorse had been a part of him. He had done exactly that with the mages.

Their lives and especially their *power* were his.

By themselves, they had not been spellcasters of great ability. As part of the Order, their combined might had made them strong, but not impossibly so. As a part of Yureel, though, a part of his very essence . . . Darkhorse feared that once more his brother had snatched victory from him.

Only the two original arms remained, and now the shadow knight held a pitch-black mace. Yureel, already more than twice the height of his brother, raised the sorcerous weapon high. He moved as if fully revitalized.

"I've enjoyed our game so very much, my brother!" the murky titan bellowed. "But now the game ends, Darkhorse . . ."

Chapter Twenty

Yssa propped her father against the tree. Her guilt at leaving Darkhorse and Aurim behind had been countered by the Dragon King's serious condition. She hoped that she had the time and power left to stabilize him before it was too late.

Darkhorse Aurim . . . forgive me for not being there to help you.

She already knew that healing the drake's hand was beyond the scope of her capabilities. Had it occurred because of a normal fire, she might have been able to repair it. Unfortunately, the potent energy wielded by Yureel had caused the damage and true to the monster's parasitic nature, it continued to ravage the limb even now. As much as she hated to think it, the enchantress knew that a good part of the arm would have to be removed in order to save her father. Taking a deep breath, Yssa knelt on the grass and prepared herself for the inevitable.

A shadow fell across her.

"You hurt my Lanith, you little hedge witch!" A strong blow against Yssa's cheek sent the blond woman falling against her patient. Through teary eyes she looked up at her attacker.

"I think I'll give him your head asss a presssent," Saress hissed, expression anything but human. "After I'm through with it . . ."

General Belfour noticed the two sorcerers first, then the weary form between them. His brow, already furrowed in worry from the way the battle had suddenly turned, formed deeper valleys when he recognized the somewhat bedraggled figure. The general turned the reins of battle over to his second in command, then urged his mount toward the newcomers.

"Your Majesty!" Lanith's eyes flashed open at the sound of his voice, searching the area around him as if expecting something. Belfour, who had seen that look before, nearly clamped his mouth shut, but his curiosity got the better of him. "Your Majesty, what happened to you?"

The monarch looked down at the wound near his shoulder. Belfour had never seen a wound so—blue—but when he started to repeat his question, King Lanith cut him off with a wave of his hand.

"Your Highness," one of the sorcerers began, trying desperately to keep the wound covered at the same time. "We've only just begun. Neither of us is as powerful as Saress—"

"Saress . . ." Lanith looked up at his general. His tone seemed almost clinical. "She's a half-breed, drake abomination, Belfour. Kill her when she returns."

While removing the influence of the enchantress from his king had always been high on the veteran warrior's list of goals, the revelation of her origins nearly left him speechless. "A . . . *drake*, my lord?"

Lanith ignored him, eyes on Belfour's mount. "Give me your horse, General." He reached out to touch the bow and quiver hanging on the saddle. "Leave everything."

"My horse?" Meridian had been the warrior's favored battle mount for years, trained to obey a variety of signals and defend his master at all costs. There were times when he was fonder of the animal than he was some of his family.

"Your *horse*, General."

"Majesty, your wounds—" the same spellcaster began, cutting off Belfour before he could lodge a protest.

With speed that belied his injuries, Lanith drew a knife from his belt and thrust the blade into the sorcerer's stomach. Gasping, the man collapsed as his life quickly fled. The lord of Zuu pulled the blade free, wiping it off on the dead man's robes, then glanced at the remaining spellcaster. The other mage blanched, then scurried off in full panic.

"Worthless trash. When this is over, I'll rebuild the Order anew." The king stared at Belfour, who immediately dismounted and handed the reins to him. Lanith climbed up and, without another word, rode off.

The general watched Lanith vanish into the distance, then belatedly noticed that something was happening far ahead of the king. It seemed to be some sort of panic, as if they did not have enough trouble with the chaos spreading from the middle of their lines. The entire tenor of the war had shifted, just as General Belfour had feared from the start. Deep inside, he had known that this entire campaign had been madness, but as an officer of Zuu, he had been bound by his post to obey his monarch.

What would happen now, when it could no longer be denied that the king had not only led them to ruin but was insane as well?

Frowning at his own thoughts on the subject, the aging warrior quickly began searching for a new mount.

The mace struck the ground, causing tremors and opening a crevice wide enough to swallow a man. Sorcerous energy from the monstrous weapon scattered over the area, most of it in the direction of Darkhorse and his companion.

Yureel obviously did not care that they had moved closer to the battle. If some of Lanith's warriors were too slow-witted to get out of his way, he simply crushed them. All the gargantuan shadow desired was the destruction of his foes. He gave them no time to think, striking again and again without pause. The pair could do nothing but back away and defend.

This is madness! Darkhorse knew that at the rate they were retreating, he and Aurim would very soon be in the midst of the Zuu army. Already Yureel had scattered several riders, killing two in the process, and while that benefited the Green Dragon's defenders, it did nothing for the shadow steed. It was not that the link between Darkhorse and his human friend had grown any weaker, just that Yureel's vicious, rapid attacks kept the eternal and his companion at constant bay. Worse, the memories of his imprisonment in Zuu and the fate he had nearly suffered there had begun to return each time Yureel neared him. Yureel had almost swallowed him and still would again if given the opportunity. The deaths of the sorcerers had reminded him too much of the probability of that. Try as he might, the shadowy stallion could not forget.

"Darkhorse! We have to take the offensive!"

He heard Aurim and agreed with him, but the mace, as much a part of Yureel as the hand that wielded it, crashed into the ground only a few yards away. Darkhorse felt a slight pull from it, as if it sought to draw him into it. He knew then that if Yureel struck him even lightly, he would be absorbed.

THE HORSE KING

The shadow knight giggled again, icy blue eyes bright beneath the helm. "You were always the lesser of the two of us, my brother, my self! Let me end your miserable existence so that you can live on in my own glory! I'll even preserve a little place in my story for you, Aurim Bedlam, perhaps a little tale of a boy who sought but never found his full potential . . ."

The mace came down again. Darkhorse moved almost too late. Yureel missed him by less than a yard, but energy released by the strike threw stallion and rider several feet into the air. Aurim slipped from the shadow steed's back, falling some distance away.

"I'm tempted to take you first as you've slipped from me far too many times, brother, but I think I'll start with your little mage friend first as an appetizer and savor you as the main dish! Since you two are linked, I know you'll fully enjoy his agony."

Yureel kept the mace pointed toward Darkhorse as he reached for Aurim. Darkhorse eyed the ebony weapon, then Cabe's son.

Rearing, he charged the huge figure. Yureel reacted, but too slowly. Darkhorse ducked below the mace, not that he would have cared at this moment if it had hit him. All he intended to do was grant the sorcerer time to escape. Even with the power bequeathed to him from the Barren Lands, Darkhorse knew that Yureel had the advantage. The shadow steed's own deeply rooted fear, a fear as great as that which Aurim had suffered earlier, worked against him. He did not want to be engulfed by Yureel.

The shadow knight fell back as they collided, but recovered quickly. Seizing Darkhorse by the throat, he shook the shadow steed hard. "So eager to rejoin me as all that? Very well, I'll be happy to grant your desire."

Darkhorse! The link! Our power together, remember?

Aurim's words made perfect sense, mirroring as they did his own earlier ones, but for some reason he could not take them to heart. This was *Yureel.* Darkhorse of all creatures knew his twin best. Yureel had been first. Yureel had always been stronger.

You said that together we could beat him, Aurim reminded him, sounding more like Cabe Bedlam. *Together. One. A u r i m —*

Let me take over. I'll do it. You said I could.

He felt Aurim take control of the link between them. The shadow steed wanted to warn him about the dangers, but to his surprise, the human manipulated it as if he had done so all his life.

With a shriek, Yureel dropped him. Darkhorse fell to his knees, then stared up at his twin. The shadow knight held his head in his hands and howled. His form became less defined and he seemed to shrivel a bit.

Aurim Bedlam, eyes closed and back straight, pointed one hand at their adversary. His control of their combined might was flawless; Darkhorse could not have done better. Yureel had only himself to blame; in the process of utilizing the lad as a pawn, he had shown Aurim what he could do. The boy remembered everything, it seemed.

We're still not one, Darkhorse. You've got to join me completely in order to let this work

The student had to remind the teacher of his own lesson. Another time Darkhorse would have laughed. Now he could only hope that he would be able to give Aurim what the sorcerer needed.

He opened himself up, giving all that he could to the effort. As if struck, Yureel fell to one knee. He was only vaguely humanoid now and much smaller than he had been a moment before. The shadow man finally tore his hands away from his head and tried to reach for his attackers. However, he moved as if the very air around him had solidified. Yureel managed one step closer, but the effort caused him to shrink more.

Through their connection, Darkhorse knew what Aurim planned. It was justice of a sort, the same kind of trap Yureel himself had had the sorcerers set in Adderly. The pressure on each side of Yureel increased tenfold, pushing him into a smaller and smaller place. Like Yssa, Aurim had built a cage; but unlike the enchantress, he had the power and skill to make it inescapable.

It was in your mind, Darkhorse. I hope it was all right to use it.

Darkhorse said nothing, allowing Aurim to control the situation. All that mattered was finishing with Yureel, and the spellcaster seemed to know exactly what had to be done.

Yureel abruptly shrank to a foot tall, trying, perhaps to escape the trap through some sort of trickery. Aurim matched him immediately, though, giving the monster no extra room in which to move. He did not want Yureel coming back to plague them again.

"Don't send me back!" the tiny figure suddenly cried, the icy eyes wide and pleading. All trace of the fearsome monster had vanished. Yureel sounded like a frightened child. "Destroy me, but don't send me back!"

For the first time, Darkhorse sensed Aurim falter. If they exiled him, they could never be certain that Yureel might not return. On the other hand, the shadow steed knew that Aurim had been sickened by all those his sorcery had injured or killed in the name of the king of Zuu, even if he had not truly been responsible. Even destroying Yureel might prove too much for the lad's mental state.

"Darkhorse, what should I do? *I* don't think I can kill him!"

The shadow steed himself did not know how to answer. To be rid forever of the fear of Yureel had always been his dream, but to dispose of him in a manner so . . . so . . . much like what his twin himself might have chosen . . . did not sit well with Darkhorse either.

"I know a place," he finally said "a place far, far away from which I doubt even Yureel can escape . . . especially if we work together to fashion this cage into one stronger than the last."

Aurim stared at the imprisoned figure. "I wanted to . . . after all he's made me do . . . after all those whose deaths he caused. . . I wanted to make him suffer for all of them . . . but I can't."

Recalling his own fears of eternal imprisonment in the box, Darkhorse replied, "He will suffer, Aurim. Sending him to exile in his cage will be a far more effective punishment."

"You can't, you can't, you *can't!*" Yureel roared. "Don't send me away! I was so *lonely!* I couldn't bear it again, Darkhorse!"

"You will have to bear it, Yureel! For all that you are responsible for, you will just have to bear it. After all, you really have no choice, do you?"

The tiny figure's eyes dulled. All the fight appeared to have drained out of Yureel now that he was a helpless prisoner. "No choice. Yes, my dear brother, my self. I've no choice . . ."

Ice-blue eyes met ice-blue eyes.

Yureel began to swell.

"Aurim!" Darkhorse flung himself between the sorcerer and the cage.

The cage held the forces unleashed by the shadow puppet for only a breath, maybe two. Not even the combined might of Aurim Bedlam and Darkhorse could contain it any longer. The burst of energy rose ten, twenty, even thirty feet into the sky and even farther along the ground. Raw power raged over the shadow steed, who now completely covered his human friend.

Darkhorse was on fire, but he did what he could to protect Aurim, if not himself.

THE HORSE KING

The agony became so great that the eternal screamed loud and long. Still the murderous wave washed over him, threatening more and more to tear him apart.

At last, the level of pain decreased. Darkhorse shivered, astonished—no, unable to *believe*—*that* he still lived. He remained where he was until the last vestiges of the terrible assault had faded, then, with each movement still agony, the shadow steed slipped off of Aurim.

Despite the protection Darkhorse had given to his companion, he saw that the spellcaster, too, had suffered. Deathly white, Aurim could not even rise at first. Only after several anxious minutes did he manage to sit up.

"What . . . what happened?" Color began to seep back into the human's face.

Still in the process of refining his form, Darkhorse indicated the ravaged area where the cage had stood. A gaping, blackened hole marked it. The words came harder than Dark- horse would have imagined. It was not as if any thing related to the notion of love had ever existed between the ebony stallion and his darker half. "Yureel could not stand the thought of returning to exile."

The battered Triage paled again. "Do you mean that he *destroyed* himself?"

"It was that or face a fate he feared more." Darkhorse snorted. "I had not thought he feared exile so *much,* even knowing how terrifying it was to him. I did not know he would choose this last path until I saw the death in his eyes."

Aurim buried his head in his hands. "I killed him. In the end, I killed him after all."

"No! Yureel's end was his own doing and one that should not be wept over! Too many died for his madness for you to even consider taking some blame! You tried to be humane; Yureel did not even know the word *existed.*" Darkhorse glanced again at the devastated area. "Do not pity him, Aurim. If there was ever one creature not deserving of pity, it was Yureel."

The sorcerer looked at him, finally shaking his head. "I think that no matter what he was and what he did, I'm going to pity him a little, Darkhorse. I didn't know he hated imprisonment so much he would do this."

Too weary to argue, the eternal simply shook his head. He would never completely understand humans.

A hissing sound made the shadow steed stiffen.

Aurim cried out. A long shaft was buried in his thigh. Darkhorse looked for the source, wondering who had recklessly chosen to remain behind when all the other warriors had fled from the vicinity of the deadly duel. He saw in the distance the lone figure of King Lanith, mounted, preparing another arrow. Even without attempting a probe the shadow steed knew that the arrows were all enchanted. They were the same bolts used to penetrate the hides of dragons and magical shields. The sorcerer was fortunate that it had not completely pierced his leg.

"I'm all . . . right . . . Darkhorse," Aurim Bedlam called through clenched teeth. "I can deal with the arrow. I can."

Gratified by the news, the shadow steed refocused on the would-be assassin. Fury at the human's continued audacity fueled Darkhorse to renewed effort. Lanith might have been a pawn in many ways to Yureel, but he was hardly without guilt in matters. Yureel would not have chosen him otherwise. The blame for much of the destruction and death that had occurred and *would* have occurred lay at the feet of the horse king.

Darkhorse reared, daring Lanith to try for him. He doubted that the enchanted arrow would harm him, but even if it did, it would not be sufficient to keep him from stripping the human from his mount.

The horse king aimed, his target Darkhorse's head. Another breath or two and the shadow steed would find out exactly how deadly the arrow could be.

Lanith jerked straight in the saddle. His arrow shot harmless into the air, landing far to the warrior's right. The king dropped the bow and gripped his mount's mane. He weaved back and forth, glaring at the shadow steed, who was mere moments from reaching him.

King Lanith, ruler of Zuu, the horse king, tumbled to the ground, an arrow in his back.

Slowing to a trot, Darkhorse approached the sprawled figure. As he did, he noted a second rider approaching from behind the horse king; General Belfour. A sword hung from the man's side and he wore a bow looped around his shoulder, but the veteran warrior's hands were empty.

"That will be close enough, General," the shadow steed called when Belfour had come within a few yards of his king. "I intend no trouble, Darkhorse." Belfour showed him open palms. "I only came in search of my liege." The warrior peered down at the limp form. Blood pooled beneath the king's body; Lanith was clearly dead. "A perfect strike. I warned him that he shouldn't count on that magic shield around him. Sooner or later, it would fail him. The Dragon King has many fine archers and we're certainly near enough to the lines to be in danger." He shook his head. "I *did* warn him."

"Against normal weapons his shield might have held, General, but both wounds he received were from ensorcelled shafts." The eternal probed the arrow. Not only had it been enchanted, but he was fairly certain that the Magical Order had done the enchanting.

General Belfour leaned forward, one hand resting on the quiver. Surreptitiously studying the shafts within the quiver, Darkhorse knew that he did not have to look far to find the horse king's assassin.

"If you've no qualms, demon steed, I'd like to take my lord and my horse, which he borrowed, and depart."

He eyed the officer. "What will happen now, General Belfour? What about his war, his dreams of conquest?"

The human straightened, his face a perfect mask. No one who met him later would realize that he had murdered his own monarch. "This war was wrong, and *I* am certain that the king had just come to believe that. All that would've been accomplished in the end was tearing apart the Dragonrealm, something we don't need. We had no right to start this in the first place. As senior officer, it's my duty to withdraw our forces from Dagora and return to Zuu. A royal funeral must be prepared. Then, since the king had no direct heir and his brothers are all long dead, one of his nearest kin must be chosen to take his place."

"You are his cousin, are you not, General?"

Belfour actually looked surprised. "Yes . . . I am . . . and I suppose if they ask, I'd take the throne, if only to prevent anarchy."

"I believe you would make a good monarch, General. You look to be a man who believes in peace, not conquest, a man who would realize how rich his kingdom is already. Rich enough, in fact, to aid those whose lives have been ruined by this futile war."

"Yes . . . yes, I'll do what I can."

The shadow steed nodded. "See that you do." He paused, then added, "His brother Blane was a good man."

Belfour dismounted. "Aye. He would've been a good king."

One last thought occurred to Darkhorse before he could take his leave. "What of Saress and the Order?"

"My king's last command was to kill the witch if I saw her again. Something about her disgusted him. It's a command I'll fulfill if the opportunity comes. Sorceress or not, I'll see it done." Belfour removed the shaft from Lanith, studied it, then tossed it aside. He wrestled the king's corpse onto the back of the horse he himself had just ridden, then reclaimed his own. "As for the Magical Order, Zuu prospered for centuries without mages and the like, and what's worked so well for so long is just fine with me."

"That will be good news to many." Darkhorse turned. "Fare you well, General Belfour, and good luck with your future."

"A moment," the warrior said. "Two things I'd tell you still. The first is to watch out for the drake Sssaleese in the north. The king might not have liked his kind, but he was more than willing to deal with them in order to advance things. Watch the north."

It only verified facts that Darkhorse already knew, but he nodded his thanks, nonetheless. "Sssaleese will be watched. The second part?"

Looking somewhat uncomfortable, the general finished, "If you should ever come to Zuu again, you will be welcome. I promise that. It is owed to you and yours."

Darkhorse turned and departed without a word in response. It would be a long time before he would consider returning to the kingdom of the horse people. First he would wait and see how the new monarch fared.

Aurim waited where Darkhorse had left him. The sorcerer had removed the arrow from his thigh and not only stopped the bleeding, but healed the wound, too. The shadow steed was impressed. Even for Cabe, wounds of a sorcerous nature took more time. Some wounds, like the one that had taken the Gryphon's fingers, could never be completely healed.

"I heard your conversation with the general through our link, Darkhorse." Aurim was pale but otherwise in reasonable condition, all things considered. "I heard everything."

"We can sever the link now, Aurim. " Darkhorse chose not to speak further about Belfour and his friend did not press.

"No, if you don't mind, we still have a few more things to do." The young human stood, looking stronger by the moment. "And they can't wait any longer."

Darkhorse nodded. Linked to Aurim, he knew exactly where his friend wanted to go.

The Manor.

"Mount, then. There is nothing more to keep us here any longer." The eternal could not help glancing at the scorched area that marked the last of Yureel. "Nothing at all."

Chapter Twenty-One

When at last the Bedlams had been freed and Darkhorse had been able to verify that General Belfour had kept true to his word by withdrawing the forces of Zuu from Dagora, the shadow steed made a visit to the forest kingdom. No word had come as to the Dragon King's condition. There were even rumors that he was dead, rumors that some of his fellow monarchs seemed eager to believe.

Darkhorse might not have worried save that he had not heard from Yssa since she had fled from the battle with her injured father. That Saress had been not far behind made the matter more vexsome.

The eternal materialized before one of the entrances to the drake's caverns and waited. He knew that they were aware of his presence from the beginning, so it came as no surprise when a dark-skinned human appeared from behind a tree. The middle-aged human, clad in evergreen robes that marked him as one of the reptilian monarch's senior aides, bowed before Darkhorse.

"Is there something I can do for you, demon steed?"

"I would speak to your king."

The news did not please the aide. "His Majesty is very occupied at the moment—"

"It's all right, Gyman," interjected a female voice.

Yssa stood near the cavern, her clothing and demeanor a tremendous contrast to the vital enchantress Darkhorse had come to know. While the brown and tan gown still hinted of Zuu, it covered her far more than the dresses she had worn in the past. More important, her features were devoid of all traces of pleasure at seeing her friend again.

"Yssa! You do live, then!"

His remark brought a faint smile to her face. "That should be obvious."

"And your father?"

The smile vanished. "Come see for yourself."

Darkhorse found himself standing in the chambers of the Dragon King, the enchantress beside him. On a bed formed entirely by plants of a thousand varieties, the master of the Dagora Forest lay sleeping. His chest rose slowly, with intermittent hesitations, and occasionally he twitched as if in pain.

His left forearm was gone, the stump bound with white cloths.

"He'll recover in a few weeks, but until then, I don't dare leave him." She looked over her shoulder where two sentries, one human, one not, watched. "My bro—his *son* and heir almost ordered him put to death, a drake tendency I've never cared for. I convinced him in the end that our father would still be able to rule well. He believed me."

"And is that so?"

"Yes."

The shadow steed turned away from the unconscious Dragon King. "What happened to Saress, Yssa?"

She looked down. "She followed us. I brought Father to the first place I could think of where I might be able to help him. I hadn't even begun before she appeared and struck me. I thought we were both dead."

"But you are not. How did you defeat her?"

"I didn't. You see, I took my father to the Barren Lands." Yssa looked again at the drake. "She knocked me to the ground and reached for Father. That was when the grass took her."

The grass? It took Darkhorse a moment. The grass had taken Saress— "Her father *was* of the drake clan Brown."

"Yes. You know how Cabe's spell worked. The grass knew her bloodline despite her human appearance. There was nothing I could do." She shivered. "It was over in little more than a minute."

That would save the new king of Zuu the duty of fulfilling his predecessor's last command. Darkhorse was not entirely dismayed at the fate of the sorceress.

"I really need to see to him, Darkhorse," Yssa added, indicating her parent.

He was being asked to leave already. The shadow steed saw no reason not to oblige her. When the Green Dragon was better, Darkhorse would visit Yssa again. "Very well. I am glad that you are well, Yssa."

"Wait. . ." She reached up and briefly hugged him around the neck. In a quieter yet still tense voice, she said, "I know most of what's happened. I know you and Aurim dealt with Yureel and that the two of you also freed everyone trapped at the Manor, but I just wanted to find out if everyone is . . . feeling well."

Knowing exactly who in particular she meant, he responded, "Everyone is well. Cabe provided food and there was water and air aplenty. As for Aurim . . ." He noted the way her interest grew at mention of the lad's name. "He will never forget what Yureel put him through, but he is doing fine. His skills and confidence have grown tremendously. You should visit sometime. I think he would enjoy that."

"I doubt his mother would, though." She smiled as she said it, a sign to Darkhorse that the enchantress *would* be visiting soon.

"I will go now, Yssa, but I hope to see you before long."

"You will. All of you. You've my gratitude for many things, Darkhorse."

With a dip of his head, the ebony stallion returned to the surface. He started to open the path to the Manor, but at the last moment chose to turn west.

A brief run brought him to the site of the battlefield. Most of the dead had been removed, but the devastation remained. No spell would restore the Dagora Forest this time. The burnt and shattered trees would have to be cleared, then new ones would be planted. Darkhorse knew the Green Dragon well enough to understand that despite the immensity of the project, the drake would see that it was done. The shadow steed wished him the very best of luck. He would try to assist. After all, it had been his brother who had caused all of this.

His brother . . . Their origins might have been linked, but from then on he and Yureel had been two entirely different creatures. There had been no love, no kinship, no sense of family. In the end, they had only existed as enemies.

"Family . . ." he whispered. In the physical sense, the eternal had no family, especially now that Yureel had destroyed himself. Still . . . he thought about the times he had shared with first Cabe, then Cabe's children. There had also been Queen Erini of Talak and her daughter. He had even shared good times with Melicard, Erini's dour husband, and the Gryphon. Even now, the Bedlams awaited his return to the Manor. Lady Bedlam had decided that a holiday festival was in order to revive everyone's spirits. She had made a special point of reminding Darkhorse to be there. Coming from Cabe's wife, that meant much.

Family . . . The shadow steed turned from the ruined forest. Come the morrow, he would do what he could to assist the inhabitants of Dagora in resurrecting the western half of their realm, but today . . . today . . .

Today he needed to be with family.

DRAGON MASTER

Obsession wears many faces . . .

I

The bronze mask wore a smile. The entire false face, in fact, had been shaped to be jovial, with small crinkle lines at the end of the open mouth and between the arched brows. Even the eye holes had been carved to indicate merriment.

Merriment . . . or mockery.

The hood of a vast, green cloak hung just over the top edge of the mask, obscuring the rest of the wearer's head. That same cloak draped over wizard's robes dark brown as the figure sat upon the cracked, crumbling stone throne.

Within the mask, eyes so gray as to be almost colorless watched intently. A true mouth with just a hint of white beard surrounding it set with teeth clenched. Hands scarred and gnarled gripped the ends of the ruined arm rests.

The decrepit throne sat upon a broken dais in a huge, devastated cavern. On each side, massive, winding columns carved from the stone dwarfed the figure. Towering statues lay shattered on the floor, their identities eradicated by some explosive force. Parts of the ceiling had clearly caved in, broken stalagmites and stalactites now intermingled together in toothy displays.

"Now," he rasped.

A tremendous roar erupted from a high, dark passage far ahead.

Through the passage burst a huge dragon, his greenish, scaly skin tinted with what could only be described as a bronze accent. He reared up, his head nearly touching the ceiling, and roared again his displeasure at his recent captivity.

Narrow, reptilian orbs of crimson marked the puny figure on the throne.

"At lassst! Now isss my vengeance! I will burn your flesh from your bonessss!" the leviathan rumbled. He inhaled, preparing a monstrous blast of flame.

The masked wizard raised his left hand and whispered, "Genin. Hala."

From two smaller passages below him emerged a young man and woman, both clad in hooded, light green robes. Their expressions were in general blank, but their eyes focused on the beast with hatred mirroring the one who had summoned them.

The dragon paused briefly when he noticed them, then clearly dismissed the pair from his thoughts. Only his captor was of importance. As one, Genin and Hala raised their left arms, pointing at the great beast.

Lightning without any source suddenly struck the dragon from every angle. He roared in agony and astonishment, so harsh, so deadly were the attacks. Scorch marks dotted his body, the scales burnt completely through.

"Houndsss! Jackalsss!" Twisting, the winged behemoth raked at the two, but came up short when an invisible barrier suddenly blocked his way.

From the young woman, Hala, came a momentary gasp. Then, her face resuming its almost inhuman calm, she fixed her gaze again on their adversary.

"Too slow . . . " muttered the seated figure. "You are all linked. Use that. Finish now."

The young spellcasters nodded simultaneously.

The invisible force that had blocked the dragon's claws now buffeted him back. At the same time, every sharp rock formation near the iron-tinted leviathan shook loose.

Now pinned against one wall, the dragon tried desperately to flame his keepers.

But before he could, scores of stalactites and stalagmites flew at him, pincushioning the bronze giant before he could exhale. He roared in agony. Great rivers of blood shot forth, splattering everything save the three tiny figures. The dragon's roar transformed into a pathetic whimper.

The beast stilled.

Genin lowered his arm.

Hala lowered hers.

The gargantuan corpse tumbled to the cavern floor, its collapse creating a tremor that shook the entire chamber for several seconds. Genin and Hala turned their unblinking eyes to the one who commanded them.

"Better . . . " he remarked, nodding his head slightly. "Much better . . . "

"Thank you, Master Tragaro," the pair piped in unison.

Without another word, they filed out the way they had come. Tragaro leaned back and stared avidly at the dragon, savoring the death.

"Soon . . . very soon . . . we shall rise again . . . "

II

From atop his horse, the wizard Cabe Bedlam eyed the hilly landscape ahead, noting the lights flickering in the distance.

"Gordag-Ai," he whispered. "Perhaps the answer lies there. I suppose it's worth checking out."

His mount, a huge, shadowy black stallion, twisted his head around at an impossible angle to look at the gray-robed figure. Startling eyes of ice-blue—eyes with no pupils—narrowed in amusement.

"After a week of running around every hill and mountain, questioning every peasant and dwarf, we're *finally* going to enter the city?" the steed asked. "Truly this is a glorious day!"

"Hush, Darkhorse! Even out in this wilderness someone might hear you!"

The black stallion snorted. "What would I fear from man or drake?"

"Too many things," his human companion returned, taking a quick look around. "Your reputation precedes you by several centuries, you know. We don't need that now."

Cabe Bedlam wore plain, cloth robes, the type a pilgrim might don. The hood covered most of his dark hair and, more importantly, almost all of the wide, silver streak marking him as wielder of magic, a wizard or a warlock. His face bordered on the unprepossessing, which aided in his present masquerade. No one would ever take the slightly upturned nose, broad mouth, and farmer's jaw for the features of one of the most powerful mages in all the Dragonrealm. In truth, Cabe came from a lineage that had produced many of the most famous and infamous spellcasters, including both his grandfather Nathan and his treacherous father, Azran.

Hidden from Azran, who had betrayed his fellow wizards, the Dragon Masters, in their war to rid the lands of the monstrous Dragon Kings, Cabe had been secreted magically for almost two centuries before his elven guardian had dared try to raise him among mortals. That mistake had started a chain of events that had seen the elf's death, Azran's destruction of the Red Dragon clan, and much, much more. From it, though, Cabe had emerged as a powerful force for humanity—and a leader despite his own protests.

And in the process, he had gained a wife—the fiery, magical Lady of the Amber—a family, an estate . . . and the true friendship of the legendary eternal, the enigmatic creature called Darkhorse.

Darkhorse himself came from an empty realm beyond reality, the endless Void. The shape he wore was one of his own fancy, taken when he had entered the land centuries before. If necessary, the eternal could manipulate his shape with the fluidity of water, becoming anything he desired. However, his fondness for his present form kept him from rarely doing so and the name he had gained because of his chosen appearance made his inclination to become something else even less.

He had befriended others of Cabe's line, but Darkhorse seemed to have a special kinship with his current rider, willing to sacrifice himself if necessary to save the wizard or his family. When Cabe had informed the shadowy creature of his intended quest, Darkhorse had quickly volunteered.

In truth, the dark-haired spellcaster was grateful. When news had come to him of the disappearances, he had naturally been concerned; young men and women vanishing so near the enclaves of the Drake Confederation boded ill. However, when Cabe had heard that these were men and women who had shown some potential with magic—that had stirred worries much, much greater.

When one Dragon King—Brown—had died trying to slay Cabe himself, his human vassal, the lord of Zuu, had begun his own campaign for power. Lanith had gathered by guile and force a small but deadly group of half-trained mages, pawns not only of him, but his own true master, Darkhorse's twin, Yureel. Before Lanith's plan had been foiled and the Horse King and Yureel slain, many had died.

Even before then, Cabe and his wife had begun to gather young humans with the gift into schools where they could be cautiously trained. The Dragon Kings had, over the centuries, attempted to control or eradicate any such humans, but always a few had survived and flourished. Now, with no such threat, more and more were appearing.

And now some of them were *disappearing*.

Gordag-Ai had produced its share of mages, including the present queen of Talak, Erini. They had been free of the yoke of a Dragon King longer than most realms. Because of Erini, restrictions against magic had loosened and now that her nephew, Edrik, sat on the throne, he even employed a few for the good of the kingdom.

But Cabe had come to wonder whether Edrik might now be desiring to be the next Lanith . . . and that was why he had hesitated to enter the city.

Darkhorse turned his head forward again. "I shall endeavor to keep my identity secret, friend Cabe."

Cabe patted him on the neck. "I don't want to lose you."

The ebony stallion snorted, but clearly appreciated his rider's comment. The pair moved on, heading toward the great wooden gates leading into Gordag-Ai.

Guards with high, forked helms, bronze-colored breast plates, and wide-hipped military pants watched warily as he and others entered. The banners of the kingdom, a fierce red ram on a field of black and white stripes, fluttered overhead.

In contrast to the broad, almost cumbersome garments of the locals, the buildings were short, narrow, and packed together. Although not nearly so expansive as Talak or Penacles, Cabe still saw no reason for Gordag-Ai to be so cramped. However, as he studied the people, he noticed that they seemed more inclined than in most places to bump against one another, almost as if on purpose.

Something Queen Erini had once said of her homeland came to him. "We are a close-knit people, we of Gordag-Ai. Surrounded by drakes so long, we came to cherish the presence of one another . . . "

Whatever the truth behind her beliefs, certainly the Gordagians, as they were called, spent much time finding excuses to talk. Several tried to strike up a conversation with each newcomer who entered. A number of onlookers peeked from the open windows and for the first time the wizard realized that, despite their narrowness, Gordagian buildings had more openings than normal—and thus more places to lean out and see or speak with a passerby.

At a clean if old establishment called the Mountain Herder, Cabe dismounted. After going through the pretense of tying Darkhorse to a post, the supposed pilgrim stepped inside.

His smiling host, a young, fair-haired man, came up to him. "Welcome, traveler! I am Brode! Please! Have a seat! Some ale?"

Taken slightly aback by the robust manner of the innkeeper's greeting, Cabe hesitated before agreeing. "An ale would do wonders for my parched throat, good man. Do I also smell stew?"

"Oh, aye! My wife, she's finishing it up now! Just be a few minutes!"

With the utmost earnestness, Brode guided his newest customer to a seat. As the wizard sat, he glanced around at the others. Brode had five patrons, all but one clad in local clothes. The fifth wore plain trader's garb with small badges sewn in at the shoulders that indicated he originated from Talak, far to the east. All seemed perfectly at ease with the innkeeper's overenthusiastic nature.

After Brode had brought him his drink and meal, Cabe leaned back. Outwardly, it appeared he relaxed, his eyes half-shut while he occasionally took a sip or a bite, but in truth, the wizard now reached out with his senses, trying to detect any disturbance along the invisible, intangible lines of force that crisscrossed everything and everybody. Even the slightest hint of magic would register.

But after a good hour, he detected nothing. His food gone and his ale nearly down to nothing, Cabe focused his will in the direction of the king's palace. He had seen it from afar as he had entered, a towering, slim structure that gave its monarch a view of everything for miles around. Cabe wondered about the safety of such a needle in the wind-thrashed regions of the northwest, but the tower seemed to take each blast in stride.

The one question remained was how often the king made his way up to the top, certainly a feat requiring exceptional health and patience.

From the palace, he at last noted a slight hint of magical action. The spell, however, was of such minute proportion as to be almost nonexistent. Cabe would have used more magic simply to douse the oil lamps that illuminated the room. Ignoring the faint signal, Cabe turned his focus elsewhere—

Without warning, a force of such magnitude that it made his head feel as if it had been kicked by Darkhorse's hooves overwhelmed him.

Groaning, Cabe nearly fell forward onto the table. Everything swam. The other patrons glanced his way, although none rose to help.

Brode, just coming from the back, noticed the wizard's agony. Cabe managed to pull together as the innkeeper approached.

"Are you not well?" the young man asked anxiously.

"Too long on the road, that's all." The wizard paid for the meal and drink. "I'm all right. I'll be going."

"We also have some fine rooms—"

"Perhaps later, I—" Cabe paused as he sensed the aura of magic approaching.

Through the doors entered three helmed men, soldiers of Gordag-Ai. On the breastplate of the leader, a stout but ready veteran with a thick beard, hung an amulet . . . the source of the aura.

The commander looked directly at the wizard, pointing.

Brode immediately backed away from his guest. The other patrons removed themselves from the premises.

The trio loomed over Cabe, who tried to analyze the spell work of the amulet. Protective, yes, but not dangerous. Certainly not the cause of his earlier distress.

"You are the mage," rumbled the leader.

The fact that he stated Cabe's calling as fact, not question, meant that no pretense would convince the soldiers otherwise. The wizard nodded.

"I am he. Is there a reason for disrupting my repass?"

"It is requested you come with us, mage. An invitation by his majesty, no less."

Edrik? Cabe had not planned to speak with the young king, but the fact that Edrik knew of his arrival intrigued him. "And will I be wearing those upon my arrival in the royal court?" he asked, indicating the iron cuffs worn at the side of each guard. "As a safety measure?"

The bearded veteran kept his craggy face expressionless. "His majesty requests your willing presence."

Which meant no cuffs. Did Edrik know exactly what mage he had invited?

Sensing the tension building within the soldiers despite their polite attitudes, Cabe nodded, then cautiously rose. Brode had vanished into the back room.

The officer led, with Cabe flanked by the two other guards. As they stepped outside, Cabe noticed that, for the first time, the area had emptied out. Word traveled fast.

Darkhorse gave an equine snort as they appeared. The wizard blinked, signaling his companion to maintain his pose as a simple animal.

A fourth guard sat mounted, the reins of his comrades' steeds in his hand. The bearded soldier indicated that Cabe should retrieve his own horse.

Patting Darkhorse's flank, the hooded mage mounted. Surrounded by what could pass for either an honor guard or determined captors, he rode off toward the towering palace.

III

"I've my suspicions, yes, I do, that you're a very, very special wizard."

The king of Gordag-Ai was young, barely eighteen, and the wide, jeweled throne of cherry wood made him look even younger. He wore the noble, crested crown of his line slightly askew over his thin, blond hair. Edrik had soft features—not fat, for he was as thin as a rail -- and dark, blue eyes. His nose was arched and his mouth was full. Even without being monarch he would have attracted women, especially those with the innate desire to mother him.

Next to him stood the bearded officer and from Cabe's study of the man here was a soldier who would give his life for the slight ruler.

"What say you, General Majjin?"

Majjin eyed their guest up-and-down impassively. "I'd place a wager you're right, majesty."

The imperial chamber of the Gordagian monarch was a simple affair compared to the plush courts of some kings. Good, sturdy oak walls trimmed in gold surrounded the occupants. Carvings of mountain animals decorated those walls. A gold chandelier with over fifty candles illuminated the room and a purple carpet crossed from the entrance to the dais on which the throne sat. Above the seated figure and his general hung the ram banner of Gordag-Ai.

Cabe decided to end the guessing. "You are correct, King Edrik. I am Cabe Bedlam, a friend of your aunt."

The young monarch smashed his fist against the throne's arm rest. His eyes widened and he grinned, making him look even younger. "I knew it! When they detected you, they said you were a powerful mage! Very powerful! I was certain it was you, especially after someone reported you riding on a huge black stallion!" Edrik suddenly looked around. "Majjin! Where's the stallion?"

For once, the officer looked a bit disconcerted. "Majesty, I could hardly bring an animal into the royal court! It is in the stables where it belongs—"

"Majjin, you fool! Don't you know what that 'animal' is?"

"I prefer to be considered a *who*, not a *what*," boomed a voice from everywhere. "and I have graced the courts of a hundred and more regal kingdoms by invitation!"

The Gordagians whirled this way and that, searching for the source. Majjin had his sword out and stood protectively over the seated king. Edrik, on the other hand, had an expression even more awed than that which had greeted the announcement of Cabe's identity.

Looking to the shadows in the corner to the left of the throne, the wizard spotted the two telltale blue orbs. Cabe smiled, which caused Darkhorse to chuckle.

Edrik and Majjin turned toward the shadows. Majjin extended his blade, as if a simple steel weapon could do anything against the eternal.

"Careful, general," Cabe warned. "It doesn't pay to antagonize him."

There was truth to what he said. Darkhorse was a loyal comrade, an avenger of wrongs, and he understood humans enough to know simple concern and fright, but if Majjin persisted, the magical stallion might choose to see him as a danger . . . and *absorb* him.

Absorb was perhaps the wrong term, but Cabe had never come up with any better description. He had witnessed drake warriors and taloned beasts fall *into* Darkhorse, fall and keep falling as if into a bottomless abyss, finally vanishing. Only one being had ever emerged from that abyss and that had been the warlock Shade, a figure as potent in his own right as the eternal.

"It's him!" shouted Edrik, now very much the youth. He would have risen and gone to the shadows if not for Majjin's blocking arm.

The huge, ebony steed emerged from the black corner, forming out of the very darkness. He loomed over the two Gordagians.

"Your majesty!" roared Darkhorse, dipping his head. "I knew your great-grandfather, Edrianos V! A cheerful, cheerful man!"

Grinning from ear to ear, Edrik returned, "That wasn't my great-grandfather . . . that was my grandfather's great-grandfather!"

"Was he? Aah, how time flies, as they say! My error!"

With a graceful, silent leap, the eternal flew up into the air, then landed with a twirl next to Cabe.

"You were supposed to remain inconspicuous," the wizard remarked dryly.

"Have I not?" his companion asked in utter innocence.

The king squirmed free of Majjin. "But why come incognito, master wizard? Gordag-Ai's no enemy of yours! You corresponded with my father and grandfather both!"

Cabe bowed his head. "And may once again I give my sincerest sympathies for your father."

"My thanks, master wizard," Edrik returned with equal solemnity. "The sickness took him swiftly."

Edrik's father, Ermanus X, had been king for only a few scant years when struck down, leaving the young prince, already without a mother since birth, to fend for himself. His aunt, the only sibling of Ermanus, had passed on what knowledge she could, but Erini lived far away in Talak. Edrik had been forced to grow up quickly.

"You have not answered the king's question," reminded General Majjin sternly.

"Majjin! Behave! He's Cabe Bedlam, the master wizard! He doesn't have to—"

"But I do," interrupted the spellcaster. "The general is correct. I was remiss in not simply going to you, but—"

Now it was the bearded commander's turn to interject. "But you were concerned about the wizards his majesty has been gathering . . . and whether my liege seeks to use them aggressively."

Cabe's brow furrowed imperceptibly. The general was a shrewd man.

"The lessons of the Horse King are not lost on Gordag-Ai, Master Bedlam. Nor is lost the fact that some of his wizards came from our realm. Be assured, though, that his majesty gathers his for the peace and security of the realm, not dreams of conquest."

"The Drake Confederation is not stable," Edrik added.

The dragon clans that had gathered in the northwest represented the survivors of more than half a dozen distinct lines, all with histories of turmoil and competition between them. That they had held together for more than a decade had more to do with their distrust of the rising human kingdoms than any true alliance. If Sssaleese, the unmarked drake who had gathered them, lost control, the repercussions would avalanche over Gordag-Ai.

"Be assured, King Edrik, that Gordag-Ai will not be alone if the Confederation collapses. In addition to myself, both the kingdoms of Talak and Penacles watch the situation." Marriage, of course, bound Talak to Gordag-Ai. Penacles, on the other hand, was ruled by the half-human Gryphon, sworn foe of the Dragon Kings in general.

"I know that," responded Edrik, returning to his throne. "And you should know that you're our guest while you're here, Master Bedlam."

"I thank you, but my work is best done if I continue to move about."

Majjin grunted. "You're looking for these lost kids. The ones with magic."

"I am."

"You think the drakes took them?"

Cabe spread his hands. "It seems a distinct possibility . . . but I hope not."

" 'Distinct possibility'? Hell, man! What else could it be?"

"That remains to be seen. Your own wizards have detected nothing?"

Majjin gave him a sour look. Edrik frowned.

"Our wizards are hardly of your caliber," the king returned. "Den's the best. He's the one who created the spell that let us know you were near." The young ruler looked to a guard. "Summon him."

A few minutes later, a young, slightly-bearded man not much older than the king appeared. Clad in a plain, white robe, Den was tall, thin, and very studious. He peered at Cabe through two thick lenses attached by a metal clip to his nose.

"You sent for me, your majesty?"

"Den, this is Cabe Bedlam, the master wizard."

Den nearly lost his lenses. "M-Master Bedlam!" He went down on one knee. "An h-honor, sir!"

"And beside him is the legendary Darkhorse."

The thin spellcaster gaped, having somehow not noticed the towering stallion before.

"I'll take that as a greeting!" chuckled the eternal.

Cabe bid the young man to rise. Den had thinning brown hair, but the silver streak was still quite evident. "So you cast the spell that detected me? I'm impressed."

"To be frank, it was to detect any magic. If I may say so, you and your—your companion—radiate power greater than anything I've ever experienced!"

But Darkhorse and I both shielded ourselves from the presence of other spellcasters, Cabe thought. *This Den has much, much potential if his spell noted us despite that.* Out loud, he replied, "But a fascinating feat, regardless."

Den beamed.

"We summoned you for a question," Edrik interrupted. "You know the rumors we've all heard. Have you detected any other magic or spells that you haven't told me about? Even the slightest hint?"

"No, your majesty—but, in truth, I've been more focused on the west. You know why. Master Bedlam was just a fortunate mistake on my part!"

Cabe shook his head. Don't underestimate yourself."

Den adjusted his lenses. "Thank you, Master Bedlam, but I don't."

"This region is not the only one from which potential spellcasters have vanished," Majjin pointed out.

"No, but it's where the most have." Cabe glanced at the general. "I take it you've been making your own inquiries for some time."

"And will continue to do so. Gordagian citizens have been kidnapped. It is an affront to his majesty."

This received a nod from the king. "Whatever help we may offer you, master wizard, it's yours."

"Actually, Den would be of use . . . if he doesn't mind."

The novice mage nearly lost his lenses again. "It would be an honor—but how may I serve you?"

Den's awe reminded Cabe how he himself had felt the first time he had realized he wielded great power. "Your spell is better than you think. I'd like to see if we might be able to refine it."

Before Majjin could protest, Edrik cut him off with a wave of his hand, replying, "Certainly, Master Bedlam! The skills of all my spellcasters are yours to command in this effort."

"Thank you, but for now, I only need Den."

Den looked embarrassed. "Actually, I did have some help in the matter. You'll want her, too."

" 'Her'?"

At that moment, another robed figure entered apprehensively. "My lord, forgive my impertinence for disturbing—"

"And here she is now," burst Edrik, barely able to restrain himself from rising to greet the newcomer. Cabe noted a rueful smile momentarily grace Majjin's bearded face. Both the general and the master wizard recognized the king's infatuation with the newcomer.

She wore robes akin to Den's but while slim filled them much more attractively than he did. Her hair was long, straight, and brown—quite unremarkable—but it framed an ivory face such as cameo makers adored. She had deep brown, steady eyes that looked older than her by far. Cabe guessed the woman to be only a year or two older than Edrik.

"We were just speaking of you," the king went on, trying to recover his decorum. "Den rightly reminded us that you are just as responsible for the magic detection spell I wanted cast around the kingdom as he is. You came up with the variation that allowed us to extend it even further."

The woman blushed hard at his praise, making Cabe think that she shared his infatuation. Out of the corner of his eye, he noted Majjin having to restrain his expression. The general did not like his lord to be entertaining any thoughts of romance with a spellcaster.

"You honor my efforts too much . . . "

"Hardly," remarked Den. "I couldn't have done it without you."

Edrik clapped his hands together. "Then it's settled. Master Bedlam, you have the full compliance of two of my best—"

She gasped, looking full at Cabe, then Darkhorse, finally registering why a traveler's mount would be allowed before the king. "Bedlam! You're Cabe Bedlam!"

"Now whose reputation precedes him?" jested the eternal.

"They are yours to use, Master Bedlam. Den, you already know, but allow me to introduce to you—"

The young woman stepped up to Cabe, staring deep into his eyes. Once again he had the sense of more years than her young form indicated. "Hala, Master Bedlam . . . you may call me Hala."

IV

Bedlam . . .

How long since he had heard that name? Two centuries at least.

Tragaro clenched the armrests.

"Bedlam . . . " he whispered. "Nathan . . . "

Below him, where in the distance the huge corpse of the dragon slowly rotted, more than a dozen young figures in hooded robes stood positioned. The pattern they created multiplied their meager power, channeled it however Tragaro desired. When he had wanted the dragon dead, the others had channeled their magic through Genin and Hala, his prize pupils. Now, they did so for their master, enabling Tragaro to watch through the eyes of Hala, study both the one who bore Nathan's name and the dark beast that ever followed a Bedlam.

Tragaro matched the bronze smile of his mask. The Twins would be coming into perfect alignment very soon. How appropriate that a Bedlam should make himself available.

"Yalak, Tyr, Basil . . . you and the rest shall be avenged. The blood of the drakes will be spilled! The Dragon Masters will be reborn!"

He reached out at the image in his mind, the Bedlam, and tried to wrap his gnarled fingers around the throat. Although Tragaro failed, of course, he still derived some pleasure from the thought.

Making Hala's eyes shift, Tragaro peered at Darkhorse, ever a Bedlam's hound. The black beast would have to be removed first. The masked wizard laughed. "Easily done . . . easily done . . . "

Cabe felt some guilt at not having mentioned one fact to the king—the fact that he had a particular reason for wanting to reshape Den's spell. The memory of the terrible mental blow he had suffered in the inn remained with him. Someone had twisted the lines of force so essential to magic with such disregard that it had nearly killed Cabe simply by his noting it.

There were many advantages to being so sensitive to magic, but not if it meant suffering again such an attack. Cabe had no desire to repeat the incident. He hoped Den's spell, properly altered, would make that possible.

It turned out that the tip of the towering palace belonged not to Edrik, as Cabe had always assumed, but to the Gordagian wizards. Being wizards, they had decided to make the trek much easier for themselves and had installed a permanent travel spell—called by some as a blink hole. One end of the hole remained fixed at the ground floor of the palace, the other opened into the mages' wing high above. One merely walked in one end and appeared out the other.

It did not surprise Cabe that the Gordagians knew such advanced spell work. At the behest of Edrik's father, some of the older ones had studied for a time at the school in Penacles that the Gryphon had set up. Both the lord of Penacles and the Bedlams had done what they could to see to it that a new generation of properly-trained spellcasters would become a reality.

After several introductions to awestruck young mages, Cabe left a cheerful Darkhorse with the rest while he joined Den and Hala in private in the tip of the high tower, where the spell they had created constantly scanned the kingdom.

Cabe studied the arrangement. In the center of the ten-by-ten room stood a pedestal on which four delicate crystals—red, blue, yellow, and white—had been set. Each represented a direction on the compass. Dangling over the center was a nut-sized lodestone. With his heightened senses, Cabe noted the intertwining and binding of the magical forces from one stone to the next, then how they were tied into the natural lines of power crisscrossing everything.

"This is indeed astounding. Excellent work."

Den adjusted his lenses modestly while Hala simply blushed.

"Show me this here," he went on, pointing to questionable details within the matrix the pair had created. Cabe already had a good notion as to how he could do what he planned, but he wanted to be certain.

The two explained their creation, verifying his beliefs. It would be a simple task to amplify and adjust their detection spell.

The task took less than an hour, thanks to his companions' aid. Hala was especially helpful, seeming to read his mind much of the time.

Cabe pushed back the sleeves of his robe as he studied their work. Now the spell's range extended far in every direction, even allowing for the detection of magic residue, the sorcerous imprint left by a spell already cast.

"Generally one of us is always here," remarked Den. "But I was called down so quickly I forgot to ask someone to replace me."

"So where do you usually sit? With your eyes on the lodestone?"

"Yes, Master Bedlam."

They stepped back respectfully as he sat and stared. For a minute, Cabe merely eyed the lodestone . . . then his surroundings faded. Suddenly, the wizard could see in all directions, see all parts of the lands encompassing Gordag-Ai and beyond. He could see every line, from the strongest to the most minute.

Over and over Cabe scanned the realm and beyond, finding nothing of note. He sensed the other wizards in the tower, sensed the innate magic that was Darkhorse, even sensed his own inherent power—but no trace of that which had struck him down.

And then . . .

To the north—No!—the southwest—No!—the north again!

Two sources?

Frowning, Cabe concentrated. The north became the apparent direction, but then so did the southwest again. Try as he might, it proved impossible to pinpoint anything more about either location. They were incredibly well-shielded. Only his manipulation of the Gordagian spell had made any notice of them possible.

Two sources. Two points of investigation.

Two possible threats?

He pulled himself free. "I've located something. I don't know what, but there are two places." Cabe pinpointed the directions. "Each seems as likely as the other."

"Which one do we investigate first?" asked Den.

"We investigate nothing. You've done your part. Darkhorse and I will take care of the rest."

"But if you both go after one, the other might vanish," Hala pointed out. "And if you separate, there will only be one of you near each."

Cabe had considered that himself, but had come up with no good answer. He did not want to risk the young wizards nor any of Majjin's soldiers. They would be more a danger to themselves than assistance to him. Yet, he did not like the idea of splitting away from Darkhorse.

"Master Bedlam," she continued hesitantly. "I know that you want to do this as quietly as possible and that you don't want to risk others . . . but perhaps there is a way to do this. It—it's not exactly what you hoped for, but it might work."

"Speak."

She looked at him with those eyes. "I know you don't want us going with you to either place, but—but what if we came along part of the way, guided you to a point, then waited for you. That way, if something seemed amiss, we could more quickly contact help. Den could go with Darkhorse and wait at Primar's Point. I could travel with you as far as the Myridian Pass. We could stay linked better that way."

He frowned. Some part of him intended to reject the overly-simple plan, but another part grasped at it. At the very least, it would give him something to counter Edrik's and Majjin's objections when they found out he had gone ahead without their consultation.

"Very well. We'll do it."

Hala's beaming smile made him smile back despite his misgivings.

Darkhorse, too, had not been overly impressed with the youthful human's suggestion, but he bowed to Cabe's wisdom. If his friend thought the notion satisfactory, than so be it. Still, leaving Cabe did not suit the eternal and he insisted that Hala alert the other wizards of Gordag-Ai at the slightest hint of trouble. They, in turn, would contact him.

Now he raced north, toward Primar's Point. High hills dotted the landscape and huge rock formations loomed in the distance. The discerning eyes of the stallion noted ancient dwarven markings, signifying an old trade route now long grown over.

"We should be there soon, should we not?" he rumbled to Den.

The human clung tight to his mane, his faced planted in Darkhorse's neck. The suggestion that he ride the eternal had at first excited the novice wizard, but the actual experience was proving too much as Darkhorse nearly soared over the earth.

"S-soon! Yes!" gasped Den, clutching his lenses so as not to lose them. "Not much farther!"

Despite the waning day, both Cabe and Darkhorse had agreed that urgency insisted they investigate the two locations immediately. Both man and eternal had the ability to traverse the great distance quickly when necessary. Cabe had created a Blink Hole with the assistance of Hala while the shadow steed had simply started running . . . the swiftest method of all.

A sharp-edged geological formation materialized far ahead. Primar's Point. The knife-blade shape was unmistakable. Several red curving strata in the formation gave it a bloody look.

The woods thickened. Burdened with a rider, Darkhorse was forced to pick his way along. The descending sun left in its wake deep shadows everywhere.

"You know where best to await me?"

His voice muffled by the stallion's mane, Den replied, "Around the eastern side of the Point! There's a clear rise where—where I can sit and c-concentrate!"

"Excellent! We shall make for that and—"

He got no further, for suddenly the path turned . . . literally before his *eyes*.

"What's this?"

Den dared look up. "W-what's wrong?"

"I am not certain! Hold tight!"

Darkhorse attempted to pull away from the path, but an incredible force tugged him back along it. His body suddenly rippled and from the gasp that escaped the human, something of a similarly unsettling nature had happened to him.

"D-Darkhorse! I can't—"

"You *will* hold tight!" To guarantee that, the eternal shifted his form, allowing Den's legs to sink into the stallion's sides. Black flaps then wrapped over the legs, effectively sealing Den to his mount.

"I am going to try to pull free again! Be ready!"

Without waiting for Den to reply, the shadow steed threw his power against that which held them—and this time he felt the spell give.

Stallion and rider turned off the path, heading up a gray hill.

"What happened back there? What was that spell?"

"I am not sure! I think—" but Darkhorse got no further, for suddenly he saw that he now ran *downhill*.

His attacker had planned for his escape.

Curiously, there was something remotely familiar about the spell work. Darkhorse had come across its like before, but not as the victim. Who had it been . . . ?

He had no more time to think about it, for now he once again ran the path. If the insidious incantation acted as Darkhorse suspected, he would be running along the same short distance until the caster decided to halt the attack.

That, of course, assumed that it was *supposed* to end. The intention might be for Darkhorse to continue running forever and ever . . .

Atop him, Den suddenly realized in what they were trapped. "A time loop! I've read of them, but the knowledge and skill needed . . . "

He did not go on nor did Darkhorse need him to do so. Such a spell required much ability. Their adversary had to be as nearly skilled as Cabe, but very few mages still lived who could claim such a degree of talent.

Still lived?

Memories dredged up. Incomplete ones, but enough to remind Darkhorse that the last caster of such a spell was now long, long dead. He had been an ally, not a foe . . .

But who?

"D-Darkhorse? I think—I think I've got an idea!!"

At this point, the eternal was willing to listen to anything. "Tell me! Quickly!"

"It—it's a time *forward* loop! A normal wizard couldn't break it in either direction, but you might if you reverse, with every iota of your power pushing that way—"

"I will have no greater effect! The spell will just adjust with me!"

Den fiddled with his lenses. "But if I use my magic to stretch it forward at the same time, it might be too much strain!"

Darkhorse had already thought about the fact that few spellcasters could match Cabe's abilities, much less his own. It was highly likely that whoever had set the trap would be near the limits of their power. This was a trap requiring constant reinforcing until the victim gave in, at which point it could be bound to the one trapped, sealing him from reality for as long as desired. The strain had to be incredible.

"Very well! We can but try!"

He sensed Den focusing. Despite the loop, there were still lines of force everywhere, one thing the unknown casters could not prevent. It was the key fault in the spell.

"Now!" the wizard shouted. "Now, Darkhorse!"

The eternal's legs twisted, now facing backwards. Without a pause, Darkhorse raced that direction, sensing his route through magic.

He felt Den pushing with his own power toward the other end of the loop. As far as the spell was concerned, it was as if they tried to run in two directions at once.

Their surroundings rippled . . . then a brief sensation of displacement nearly caused Darkhorse to stumble. He compensated, tasting freedom—

Something plucked Den from his back despite the shadow steed's precautions. The wizard screamed.

Darkhorse's tail became his head as he reversed himself entirely. He quickly searched around for the human.

A tree shaped like a monstrous hand had the wizard in its grasp.

Snorting at the petty attempt, the ebony stallion charged toward his trapped companion.

But instead of being grateful, Den, his lenses gone, shook his head and shouted, "No, Darkhorse! No!"

Too late did the eternal see the slight rippling on the trail ahead.

He raced into the second time loop—

V

"I dislike leaving you here alone in the pass, Hala."

"I grew up here, Master Bedlam," she replied, turning her much older eyes to his. "I'll be safe."

That they discomforted him had nothing to do with attraction. Hala was pretty enough, but Cabe very much loved his wife, the sorceress Gwen. Rather, when he looked deep into them, he felt as if Hala had lived much harder than her few years warranted.

Although thanks to the slow aging of wizards he barely looked older than her, he pointed a fatherly finger and insisted, "What goes for me goes for you. At the slightest hint of trouble, give me warning. That goes for alerting your comrades in Gordag-Ai, too."

"I'll do what's right," she murmured, lowering her gaze.

The blink hole had opened almost exactly on target, in great part due to Hala's added concentration. Linked to both him and the spell, she had helped guide them here.

The Myridian Pass was a beautiful gap between two mountains where the colored strata of thousands of years of cutting by the nearby river stood revealed for the few admiring travelers to wander through. The rock alone made for a wonderful spectacle, but the onrushing water, with its swift rapids and lush green banks, added even more dimension. In addition to the plant life, great herons nested across from where the wizards stood, barking to one another or flying over the river in search of food. Their

377

presence seemed to belie the notion that something sinister might be going on not that far away.

Gazing at the descending sun, Cabe estimated no more than half an hour before the high walls of the pass caused everything to be plunged into darkness. The Twins would then be ascendant, with Styx, the pale one, slightly more dominant. Tomorrow, the two moons would be in perfect alignment with one another, a time of high sorcery.

Cabe shuddered. It had been at such a time that as a youth he had nearly been sacrificed by the Dragon King Brown. Brown had hoped to rejuvenate his realm. Two hundred years before, during the Turning War, the Dragon Masters, with Nathan Bedlam at the lead, had literally twisted the landscape upon itself. They had crushed the power of Brown, nearly decimated his clans, and left in their wake the most desolate of places—the Barren Lands.

It had been Brown who had perished that night, inadvertently felled by Cabe's burgeoning magic. Now, for the first time since then, the Twins were preparing to align . . . and Cabe could see no good coming from it.

But he had another, more immediate matter on his mind. A short teleportation spell would send him near to his destination. The sooner he investigated the site, the sooner he could be away from here.

Reaching out with his mind, he touched Hala's ever so carefully. *Do you sense me?*

I do.

He did not probe her thoughts deeper, desiring only to maintain the link. Hala was a very capable young woman. She would be prepared to act should the need arise.

Materializing a moment later as close to the estimated location as he dared, the wizard gazed around. Little seemed different from where he had just left Hala. The river continued along its course and more herons nested in the distance. A few squawked at him as they soared overhead. The area looked beguilingly peaceful, if much more shadowed.

He sensed a faint magical signature from the nearest mountain and headed that direction. It was very likely he would find nothing. What would the missing youths be doing out here?

The pale moon appeared over the peak. Once more memories flashed, this time memories of a brave band of mages seeking to free their kind from drake rule.

Cabe stumbled to a halt. Faces he did not know—and yet did—passed before his eyes. Among them he saw one very much like his own, so much so that he knew it could only be his grandfather's.

Then . . . Nathan Bedlam's face turned about, became a mask that became Cabe's visage . . . .

And suddenly he stood with the others, a group of four, this time, four if one did not count the hissing bronze dragon upon which one of the wizards rode.

"I cannot foresee the best outcome of this," Yalak commented, his tall, lanky body topped by an oversized head covered in gray and silver hair. He lowered what he called the Egg, a rounded, glass artifact he most favored when trying to view that which might be. "I have looked in every direction of the future, but nothing takes dominance. We win or we lose."

"Well, that was pretty useless," grumbled Basil. Clad in armor and cloak, he looked more like a warrior than a wizard and, in truth, his spells were all more akin to the ways of the former. He preferred direct battle, not subterfuge.

"We'll have to go ahead, regardless of the outcome, then," Cabe's own mouth said. The voice was deeper than Cabe's, however, deeper yet much more weary. One robed arm pointed up at the brown-robed figure atop the dragon. "What say you, Tragaro?"

RICHARD A. KNAAK

"You know my opinion, Nathan," Tragaro retorted. *His trim, black beard and penetrating, pale eyes gave him an ominous appearance. He turned his gaze to the beast upon which he rode, patting its head as if the drake was preferable company. From his tone, clearly he and the others had been at odds for some time on the subject they discussed.*

Nathan/Cabe sighed. *"Each of us has an equal voice in all matters. That was agreed on long ago."*

"And yet it is ever the Bedlams who lead the way. First you, Nathan, and now you foist your sons upon us as our leaders! Dayn, perhaps, but Azran is unstable, as bad a seed as any Dragon King!"

Basil snorted. *"Says the man who mesmerizes drakes to fight their own!"*

The dragon appeared to take offense at this remark. The leviathan hissed sharply at Basil.

"Be still, Sssorak!"

The dragon lowered his head, chastened. *"Yesss, Massster Tragaro."*

"My sons are my sons," Nathan/Cabe responded, biting back anger. *"And they are loyal to our cause . . ."*

Loyal to our cause . . .

Loyal to our—

With a grunt of pain, Cabe nearly keeled over. He clutched the nearest formation, trying to steady himself. Even the surge of power that had struck him during his visit to the inn had not dealt so harsh a blow.

Yet, the pain passed very quickly. The pain, yes, but not the recollection of what he had experienced.

In his first years as a wizard, he had lived through similar episodes. Memories from his grandfather, inherited by Cabe when Nathan himself, seeking to save his dying grandson, imbued a part of his own spirit, his very soul, into the infant. For a time, that had meant that, in a sense, they had been two in one.

In the end, that which was Nathan had sacrificed itself in combat with the fatalistic Ice Dragon. Relived memories such as this had ended at that time.

So why, Cabe now asked himself, am I experiencing them again?

Head still clearing, he glanced up at the rocks.

A young man with flowing brown hair half-hidden under the hood of his light green robe stared down blankly at the wizard.

Cabe took a cautious step back—and noticed a dark-skinned woman little older than the man perched upon another rock. She wore robes identical to her companion.

Without turning, he sensed at least four more figures standing in various locations above and around him.

Cabe had found the missing youths . . . and they had found him.

Cautiously raising his hand, he called out, "Hello!"

They remained silent, their eyes never leaving him, never even blinking once.

Then, the first figure suddenly raised both arms toward the wizard, cupping the hands together as if catching something precious within.

The hair on the back of Cabe's neck rose as he felt an incredible onrush of power. The hands opened.

A fierce ball of glittering emerald energy burst toward the master wizard, growing rapidly as it approached. Cabe stood his ground, only raising one hand in defense.

Barely an inch from his open palm, the monstrous sphere exploded, dissipating rapidly in a blinding display of green sparks.

One did not survive long as a spellcaster in the Dragonrealm without keeping some defensive spells handy.

He did not bother to talk to them again. Their eyes, their mechanical movements said it all. They were under some sort of control, either a spell or mesmerism or—

Mesmerism. There had been something about mesmerism in the flashback Cabe had suffered . . . .

He had no time to worry about that. Someone had control over several very capable novices and had melded them into one linked unit. They had underestimated Cabe's abilities, however. He sensed he could defeat them yet, but he had to give warning to Hala so that she, in turn, could let Darkhorse know. With Darkhorse to aid him, rounding up these poor puppets would be child's play.

The same young male began focusing power. Cabe realized that he intended an attack identical to the first. Apparently the puppets had limited skills.

As he prepared to deflect the second assault, Cabe opened his mind to the Gordagian. *Hala! I've found—"*

Searing pain erupted in his head and raced quickly through his entire system. Dropping to his knees, he screamed. Only barely did Cabe recognize that the horrendous assault on his mind and body came, not from those around him, but through the young woman to whom he had linked his thoughts.

But by then it was too late.

The stench of decay filled his nostrils, stirring Cabe from the comforting darkness. He tried to stretch aching muscles, but found neither his arms nor his legs would move. His limbs were pulled tight, so much so that he wondered whether they would soon tear free of his helpless torso.

"You are awake, Bedlam . . . do not play that you are not."

With tremendous effort, Cabe forced open his eyes.

He floated, untethered, high above the ruined floor of an immense cavern. Nothing physical bound his arms and legs; he simply floated helpless and immobile.

Torchlight enabled him to barely make out at the edge of his vision the source of the stench. A huge dragon, several days dead, lay sprawled to one side. Its armored exterior had been pierce several times over by scores of sharp stalactites and stalagmites.

"They are most promising students, my children are."

Without warning, Cabe plummeted earthward. Only at the last did he suddenly swerve upright, coming to float just a few feet directly before a figure seated on what the wizard recognized as the ruined throne of a Dragon King.

"Soon, with my expert guidance, they will become masters. *Dragon Masters.*"

The many implications of the audacious declaration sent chills through Cabe. His captor spoke as if he knew the Dragon Masters well, spoke, in fact, as if he had been *one* of them.

But of the Dragon Masters, only Cabe's wife had survived, and she had only done so because of being trapped for two hundred years in a magical block of amber cast by Azran. The rest had all perished during or just after the Turning War.

The smiling mask of bronze did nothing to assuage Cabe. Nor did the grin behind the smile, for it held a cunning madness the likes of which he had not seen since confronting his father.

"Who are you?" he finally blurted.

His question caused a narrowing of the pale eyes within, eyes that should have been familiar. "Nathan was a much quicker sort, whatever his failings. The memory I supplied you should've been sufficient to introduce me, to remind you . . . "

Nathan . . . the Dragon Masters . . . the memory had been an implanted one, not part of his grandfather's legacy.

The other Dragon Masters. There had been several, but Cabe had met two as undead—Basil and the scholarly Tyr—and knew of Yalak. Of the handful in the vision, only one matched at all what glimpses Cabe could get of the face behind the mocking mask.

"Tragaro?"

Now the eyes gleamed. They were demanding eyes, ever snaring Cabe's view. He wanted to look around him, concentrate on escape . . . but Tragaro's eyes would not let him.

"The grandson will redeem the sins of the father and grandfather. How appropriate. I thought to simply slay you first, to pay for their betrayals, but this is so much more justice! The Dragon Masters will achieve their goal at last! The drake menace will be cleansed from the land, only their stinking carcasses," the other wizard gestured at the huge corpse. "left as monuments to their foul reign."

"But the Dragon Masters are dead!" argued Cabe.

"No more . . . I have rebuilt them." With a wave of his hand, he raised Cabe up so that the prisoner could see the gathering figures. In addition to the ones who had confronted Cabe, several others now stood awaiting Tragaro's word. Cabe counted more than a dozen.

At their head stood Hala and the young man who had confronted him in the pass.

"I have trained them. They'll be more unified than the first Dragon Masters were. They will obey my commands utterly! This time, there will be no treachery . . . "

Cabe was very certain that they would obey. Gazing at each face, even Hala's, he saw the same blank expression. Puppets, indeed. Obedient to every whim of the figure on the throne.

Tragaro brought his captive back to him. Behind the mask, the eyes glared. "The betrayal of the Bedlams left me injured and my mind ruined. For generations, I did not even know myself! Then, gradually, it all came back. The ambitions, the hopes, the deceits, the failures. I finally knew what I needed to do, but it took time, planning . . . and now all comes together at last!"

"There's no need for this! The power of the drakes is failing, Tragaro! At least half of the Dragon Kings are dead, some of the others in precarious positions. Most of the human lands are independent! It is only a matter of time before—"

The masked mage clutched tight the arms of the throne. He leaned forward and hissed, "Time isss up! The drakes will be crushed utterly and the land put to order! There will not be one stinking reptile left!" Tragaro relaxed, smiling. "And you will make the dream a reality quicker than I had even hoped."

All the while they had spoken, Cabe had been carefully probing with his senses the spells holding him in place. He had a suspicion as to how to unbind himself, but he needed just a few moments more.

"You'll receive no help from me and there are others who will keep you from this genocide. Drakes and humans are beginning to learn to live together! At the Manor alone—"

"I am aware of your disgusting experiment, the housing of drakes and people in one settlement, working together like brothers and sisters!" He slammed his fist on the stone. "Never!"

"Tragaro—"

"And as for other opposition, Bedlam . . . they will either see the light of day, as you will . . . or they will be obstacles quickly removed." The hooded figure held out his hand. In the palm, a tiny red sphere materialized. "As the demon steed has been."

Cabe glanced into the sphere—and saw Darkhorse racing along a stretch of trail. The scene went on for three, four seconds . . . then repeated itself. After the fourth viewing, he realized what the mad mage was trying to show him.

Darkhorse was imprisoned in a time loop.

381

Dismissing the sphere, Tragaro clapped his hands. "It is time for the newest to be added our ranks! Bring him forth!"

Two more robed figures stepped from a passage nearby, dragging between them someone familiar to Cabe.

"Den!"

The Gordagian glanced up, squinting. His lenses were nowhere to be seen. "Master Bedlam?"

"There is only one master here," their captor interjected. "Come to me."

Den was pulled bodily before Tragaro, then made to look into the Dragon Master's eyes.

"You become a part of a legacy few are worthy of being," Tragaro informed Den. "You will shape the future, recreate the world . . . "

His eyes never blinked. The two figures holding Den made certain that the latter could not turn away nor even shut his own eyes. He had to look into Tragaro's.

"My mind is your mind, my thoughts your thoughts. As I command, so shall you act . . . "

Den briefly struggled, then suddenly relaxed. He stared at the Dragon Master, now also never blinking.

Tragaro leaned back again. "Join the others."

No longer held, Den stiffly backed away alongside his former guards. In silence he moved next to Hala, then awaited Tragaro's next command.

But the masked wizard looked instead to Cabe.

"Now . . . you shall join us, Bedlam."

VII

Darkhorse ran. Darkhorse ran again. And again. And again.

And in contrast to most trapped in such a spell, a niggling little part of his mind remained aware of the infernal repetition. That part grew more and more adamant in its refusal to remain imprisoned so.

But while there had been Den to aid him in escaping the first trap, now the shadow steed had only himself. What the human had suggested had worked perfectly because there were two of them, one to focus all his energies one direction, the other to do so on the opposite. To escape this loop, the Darkhorse had to rely only on himself.

As he again raced along the short stretch, Darkhorse sought some weakness in the loop. He already knew what he would find, though. Each repetition—and there had been hundreds of them by this point—had revealed only that the spell had been sealed completely, clearly the work of a master mage.

Yet—to his astonishment, when Darkhorse dared check once more, it was to indeed sense a weakness. A minute one, yes, a weakness most victims would have been unable to take advantage of, but for the eternal it offered hope. The only hope he had.

As the loop repeated once more, he probed at the weakness, tried to further stress it. Each time the trap began its vicious cycle, Darkhorse pushed more, stretching the weak point to its utmost.

The path shimmered . . . then stabilized again.

Others might have been completely discouraged, but Darkhorse saw the brief shimmering as proof he was near to success. He focused his power upon the stress point again and again. The danger constantly existed that if he wore himself out too

382

much, he might lose what hold he had and become completely immersed in the trap. If that happened, he would never escape . . . and would not even realized any more that he had wanted to do so.

Yet again he struck at the weakened area.

The path shimmered . . . then twisted in a madcap arc that defied the laws of nature. The sudden shift threw the eternal into a swirling, chaotic landscape in which earth became sky, then earth, then sky, and so on.

"I will not be imprisoned!" he roared.

Of all things Darkhorse feared, imprisonment was perhaps the most monstrous. There had been incidents during his long visit to the Dragonrealm when he had been captured and held by the whims of others, forced to exist in tiny, black spaces without any certainty of ever tasting freedom again. Born in the endless, open Void, such prisons were worse than death to him.

Urged on by such notions, Darkhorse pushed harder, striking at the weak point even as he vainly sought to reach a stable footing.

And suddenly . . . the entire world collapsed in on him.

The fear that he had made his situation more terrible faded almost immediately as the eternal's surroundings normalized. In a most uncharacteristic fashion for him, the ebony stallion clumsily steered off the path and crashed into a copse of trees. Any other creature would have shattered their bones against the trunks, but instead Darkhorse merely melted through them.

He came to a rest several yards up an incline, thoughts still in a tangle. Shaking his head, Darkhorse cleared his mind. The first thing he noticed was that the sun was now early in the sky, meaning that at least one night had passed. Hoping that it had been no longer than that, the stallion immediately began searching the area, his fear for the humans, especially Cabe, mounting.

Of Den he noted no physical sign, but when Darkhorse searched with other senses, he noticed a faint magical signature which vaguely resembled the young Gordagian's. Uncertain whether or not he merely headed toward another trap, the shadow steed raced after the dissipating trace.

Yet, he had barely covered more than a few miles when he came across a sight entirely unexpected.

A column of Gordagian troops on horseback, General Majjin at their head, moved methodically toward the north.

Racing ahead, Darkhorse came around toward the front of the column, nearly materializing before Majjin himself.

The general's horse reared in surprise. Majjin cursed at both the animal and Darkhorse, the latter receiving some exceptionally virulent expletives.

"By Vramon! Do that again and—demon or no demon!—I'll run you through!"

Ignoring the futile threat, Darkhorse demanded, "General! What are these soldiers doing here?"

"Think I don't keep track of the our wizards' activities? I smelled something amiss and convinced the king to let me take a more tried-and-true method of hunting down these missing people! After questioning his pet wizards, I calculated that the north was the more likely target and it looks like I was correct! This is a Gordagian problem and it'll be solved by Gordagians, demon, whether you and Master Bedlam like it or not!"

The eternal snorted. "This is high sorcery, general! I was myself attacked and your mage Den is missing! For that matter, I have not been able to contact either my friend or the young woman Hala!"

"Then it's even better that we've come!"

"Better? Have you heard nothing I have said? Mortal, there is magic afoot here of the likes even I would not have expected! Your toy warriors will be nothing to it! You must turn around and—"

"Turn around?" The bearded officer looked aghast. "Gordagians do not turn and flee like rabbits!"

With that, he urged his reluctant mount forward, guiding his troops around the blue-robed figure.

Darkhorse snorted, but from much past experience knew when it was fruitless to talk to some humans. He himself had a legendary propensity for rushing headlong into danger, but even he recognized the risk inherent here. Someone who wielded magic with as much skill as their unknown adversaries did would hardly be daunted by the column. All Majjin would do was get himself and his men slain.

Turning about, the shadow steed raced past the soldiers, vanishing far ahead. Whatever the threat, he had to meet it first. Not just for the sake of the Gordagians, but for the missing wizards . . . especially Cabe.

He only hoped he was not already too late.

Cabe had never been so clear on the focus of his existence. He had never understood his duty so plainly.

The drakes, and those who would prevent their demise, were to be destroyed. That was it. At Master Tragaro's command, he would summon the full might he possessed and squash any enemy.

Cabe stared at the empty air, knowing his cause was just. He had to make up for the treachery and mistakes of his family. He had to make amends for Nathan, who had led his compatriots into disaster, killing most in the process. Cabe also had to rectify the evil perpetrated by Azran, who had slain Yalak and others, then abandoned the rest at the most crucial of points during the war.

Because of the Bedlams, Tragaro's fellow wizards had perished. Such crimes demanded justice, and by serving Tragaro utterly, Cabe would see that justice was done.

"M-Master Bedlam?"

The tentative voice registered as more of an annoying buzz at first. Cabe chose to ignore it, wanting his mind clear for Tragaro's magical summons.

"Master Bedlam! Please! It's me! Den!"

The ensorcelled wizard's brow furrowed as he tried to push the voice away. However, something deep within him stirred, something that urged him to listen.

"You must hear me! Quick! I don't know how long before he realizes that I'm not under his control!"

Cabe blinked, the first time he had done so since staring into the pale eyes.

"Master Bedlam! Speak to me! His mesmerism didn't hold for me, I think, because of my poor eyes! I lost my lenses! I'm not powerful like you, just lucky! You have to have the strength! You must be able to break free of his enchantment!"

The urge to reply grew more powerful. Question arose, uncertainties as to why he so wished to follow blindly the dictates of Tragaro.

"Master—" Den suddenly cut off with a strangled cry.

"I sensed an emptiness where there should be obedience. I sensed a will where there should only be my desire."

The gurgling grew more frantic.

Cabe felt a sudden urge to look, but his eyes would not obey. The Dragon Master had not given him a command, after all.

"Occasionally, there are those who lapse or cannot be trained," the harsh voice went on. "They are a distraction to the rest. Therefore, they are removed."

Den cried out. A strange, crackling sound hurt Cabe's ears. His nostrils vaguely detected a burning odor.

After a short silence, Master Tragaro's masked face filled his view. The eyes snared Cabe's own.

"All is as it should be. Clear your mind of any other concerns. Your only need is to obey my commands . . . "

The questions all but ceased. Only a slight uncertainty refused to die, but it was so tiny that, at the moment, even Cabe did not notice it.

Tragaro suddenly pulled away, his gaze looking to the side. "What's that?" he said to the emptiness. "Show me!"

After a long pause, he looked again at his latest addition to the ranks. Cabe awaited his word.

The Dragon Master gave it. "The abysmal fools! They would save the lives of drakes by their actions! Therefore, they ally themselves with the reptiles! It is by their own choice they must suffer!" To Cabe, he added, "And it is time to begin paying for the sins of the Bedlams! The Twins are ascendant! Your power will be at its peak! Follow me!"

Without hesitation, Cabe obeyed.

VIII

Unlike the Gordagians, Darkhorse chose to move with more stealth. He had learned his lesson and knew his foes to be crafty. If they had captured or slain Cabe, they were among the darkest and deadliest he had ever known.

A creature formed of a magic, he could meld into the land. More important, he now focused all his power on evading detection, creating a shield he hoped that would make him a blank to anyone watching.

That he also sensed nothing of Cabe disturbed Darkhorse. That a mage as capable as his friend could be so easily overwhelmed did not bode well. They had confronted a variety of evils in their time together and while both had nearly perished more than once, matters had always come to a good end.

Now, Darkhorse was not so certain.

Beyond the pass, the eternal slowed. He could sense traces of magic here and there, peculiar traces that were different from one another yet also the same. Curious, he probed them deeper, with the same results. They were and were not the same signature.

Then Darkhorse sensed a much more welcome trace, that of Cabe. It was faint, almost completely faded, but identifiable.

And it drifted amidst all the rest.

He was surrounded, Darkhorse decided. Still, from what he could judge of the other traces, they lacked the intensity he would have expected of powerful spellcasters. True, together they represented a respectable level of ability and strength, but certainly not sufficient against the Cabe Bedlam.

So what had happened?

Scarcely had he delved more, though, when he sensed the casting of a major spell. Not near him, but rather further south, likely within the pass—

The pass through which General Majjin and his troops now journeyed.

Darkhorse nearly teleported himself there immediately, so anxious was he to warn the humans. Then it occurred to him that to do so would be to announce himself to whoever had cast the spell. For the sake of everyone, the shadow steed had to keep his own escape as secret as he could.

He raced back, utilizing swiftness no ordinary equine could match. The trees were blurs, the land a vague flash of images. Darkhorse ran as he had never run before.

And as he ran, a feeling of dread spread over him . . .

Tragaro's new Dragon Masters materialized throughout the two sides of the Myridian Pass, unblinking eyes fixed on the approaching column below. Although scattered for some distance, they might as well have been standing shoulder-to-shoulder, so well-linked were they to one another.

At the forefront, Tragaro had placed his most favored 'pupils'—Hala, the young man Genin, and the one who would be the experienced hand who wielded their combined might . . . Cabe Bedlam.

As for their master, the elder wizard remained within the ruined chamber, eyes within the mask alight with anticipation. The dragon had been a tremendous test, yes, but this would be the first in the field. This would prove to him their readiness. The ease and swiftness with which they destroyed the column would tell Tragaro whether they were ready to strike at the crumbling confederation of drake clans to the west.

He had little doubt of the outcome. Without the Bedlam, it would have proven more troublesome, but with him there was no question.

The niggling sensation rose anew in Cabe's head as the Gordagian column neared. Cabe was certain of his task, for it had been given to him by Master Tragaro, but a tiny part of him protested. That protest grew, especially when he felt the others begin to meld their minds together in preparation for giving their united power to him.

They interfere with the planned destruction of the drakes, came Tragaro's thoughts. *They must therefore share the drakes' fate.*

He understood that to be fact. It made perfect sense. The protesting dwindled again.

At the head of the column, Cabe made out a face vaguely familiar to him. A bearded officer. The man looked this way and that, clearly wary of his surroundings, but willing to push on despite that wariness.

It would be a fatal mistake.

Raising his arms, Cabe prepared his spell. At the same time, he felt the others begin to feed him their might.

Near his feet, loose pebbles began to quiver. The quivering spread, touching other loose rocks and stones farther and farther away—and in the direction of the encroaching soldiers.

Hala and Genin stepped beside him, linking to Cabe and further increasing the intensity of the spell he cast. Now the ground shook with more vigor, enough so that those below at last became aware of something amiss.

But as Hala's mind touched Cabe's, something else happened. An image briefly filled his thoughts, an image of a young, studious wizard—lenses perched on his nose—trying to awaken him from some nightmare.

"Den?" he murmured.

The vision faded, but in its wake it left more uncertainty. Cabe hesitated, the spell faltering.

Tragaro's imposing presence touched him instantly.

Bedlam! They approach! Let the mountains fall upon them!

Cabe fell back into the rhythm of the spell. The ground shook with more vehemence. Loose boulders and rubble tumbled toward the Gordagians.

The bearded commander looked up, made out the several figures high above. He shouted something to his men and several tried to ride toward the towering ridges, but the tremors drove them back.

This is not right! This is murder! a voice in his head cried.

He belatedly realized it was his own.

And at last Cabe Bedlam truly stirred from Tragaro's spell.

Swinging his hands palm back to each side, he struck both Hala and Genin in the chest with simple but effective bolts of raw force.

With cries of startlement, the two flew back several yards, landing hard. Hala lay prone, but Genin attempted to rise.

Cabe sent another bolt his direction.

They were not dead, not even badly injured. Tragaro had made puppets of them and Cabe had no desire to slay innocents if he could prevent it.

Of course, that did not mean that the innocents might not try to slay him.

Tragaro did not wait to respond to Cabe's betrayal. Suddenly the rest of his 'flock' refocused their combined energies, turning them instead on the more dangerous enemy in their midst.

The ground beneath the wizard's feet transformed, becoming a giant hand that sought to crush him in its grasp.

Before the fingers could close, though, a swift black form flew past, snagging Cabe and dragging him off.

With a toss of his head, Darkhorse set his human friend atop his back, then turned to avoid a horrendous shower of icicles that nearly perforated both of them.

"Darkhorse!" Cabe gasped as he clutched the shadow steed's mane. "He said you were trapped!"

"There is not the trap that can hold me—not without a little help from friends, of course!" The stallion sobered. "Young Den somehow worked to reach out to me from afar, paving the way for my freedom!"

"Den . . . Darkhorse . . . Den is dead! He tried to free me, but Tragaro murdered him!"

Cabe had rarely known the eternal to miss a step, but Darkhorse did so now. "*Tragaro?* Impossible! Tragaro is dead!"

"He seemed very much alive, although with that mask I can't say what condition his face was left in!"

"Ma sk?"

"A bronze one with an evil mirth to it. You can see his pale eyes and mouth through it."

Darkhorse paused atop a ridge, gaze not on Cabe but the robed figures turning to face them again. "The eyes sound like Tragaro's, but I am certain he perished! I am certain I saw his corpse!"

Their debate ended abruptly as the ridge upon which they were perched suddenly gave way, the hard rock turned to soft, useless sand. Darkhorse leapt away. Cabe noticed and appreciated that the ebony stallion consistently steered Tragaro's novice Dragon Masters away from General Majjin's troops.

"This must end!" Darkhorse roared. "Yet I don't wish to harm these if I can! They are pawns of another!"

"I agree, but if we need to hurt them to keep this from going further, we'll have to! We can't risk more lives, not the Gordagians nor even the drakes!"

The ice-blue eyes of the stallion studied the robed youths. "Are they truly any danger to us when we are together, Cabe?"

"By themselves, no, but Tragaro is linked to them and he amplifies any threat a hundredfold!"

"I feared you would say that. We may have to slay some of them yet."

Den's screams flashed through the wizard's head once more. Cabe could not allow any more to suffer or die. "No . . . not if I can help it. I think we need to split up again."

"Not a wise move."

"Listen to me! I need you to keep them at bay, prevent them from either leaving or casting any spells at Majjin and his men!"

The shadow steed's head twisted around to stare into Cabe's eyes. "And what is it you intend to do in the meantime?"

Cabe's set his mouth tight. "I'm going to face our masked friend."

"Folly! We should face him together!"

"He'll either summon the others back or use the moment to destroy the Gordagians! Either way, innocents will perish!"

"And if you go alone, you might!"

But the wizard's mind was made up. "Keep things going here and he'll either be forced to split his efforts or concentrate solely on me. If he does the latter, then you'll have a chance to rescue those he's ensorcelled."

"Cabe—"

"No more arguing." Cabe focused on what he recalled of Tragaro's domain. The clearer the image, the more certain he was of materializing in the right location. "I've got to go now!"

"Beware! Your grandfather Nathan considered Tragaro a most accomplished Dragon Master!"

As he vanished, Cabe managed to call back, "Then, I'll just have to be better . . . "

IX

Once again, a Bedlam had betrayed him. Once again, the cleansing of the land had been thwarted—at least for a time. The dream of a realm free of dragons was his only purpose, the only reason he had persevered so long.

Tragaro rose from the ruined throne, gnarled hands cupped together in anticipation. This Bedlam assumed himself as clever as Nathan or Azran.

He was about to discover that Tragaro was cleverer by far than all three.

Cabe choked back a gasp, but not because of the stench. He had been prepared for the odious smell of the decaying dragon, but what he had not been prepared for was the blackened, crisp skeleton almost at his feet.

The final, charred remains of Den.

Disgust and regret gave way to anger. Den had done nothing more than try to save Cabe and Darkhorse. Tragaro had burned him alive simply for that.

"Such emotion. Its like brought the Dragon Masters down and left the lands in the claws of the drakes for another two centuries."

"I knew you were about," Cabe said without turning. "I assumed you wanted to announce yourself dramatically. It seems your way."

He sensed the spell as Tragaro cast it and quickly turned to counter. The shining silver shield came up just as the rocky projectiles struck. The stalactites and stalagmites shattered, showering both mages with rock.

Tragaro immediately gestured. The projectiles' remnants reformed around Cabe in an attempt to entomb him.

388

Without even a movement, the younger wizard dispersed the fragments again.

"I also assumed you'd try something like that," Cabe remarked, nodding his head toward the massive corpse. "since it worked so well before."

"I merely test your skills, Bedlam. You answer some questions." The smile within the smile stretched menacingly. "Now I begin in earnest."

The stone floor beneath Cabe's feet suddenly cracked open. A hot gust of wind rising up barely warned him in time of what was to follow.

As Cabe threw himself to the side, a burst of molten lava shot up, striking the high ceiling.

The surface on which Cabe had landed suddenly liquefied. His right foot sank in to the shin. He tried to push himself up, only to have his hand sink as well. When he tried to pull either free, it was to find both mired completely.

"I am a Dragon Master . . . " Tragaro quietly uttered as he approached the floundering form. ". . . and you . . . you are not even worthy of the name Bedlam."

Cabe sank beneath the liquid stone.

"Not even worthy at—"

Tragaro raised his arm over his masked face as the black tar suddenly flew up and over him. The Dragon Master vanished under the torrent.

Face grim, Cabe rose from the hole created by his surprise assault and searched for his adversary. Yet, as the liquid stone splattered to the floor and resolidified, it left no trace whatsoever of the other spellcaster. As quick as Cabe had countered Tragaro's vile work, so, too, had the dark wizard reacted in defending himself.

A bony, blackened hand clutched Cabe's throat from behind. Twisting, he stared into the sightless sockets of Den's skeletal visage.

The knowledge of just who he faced nearly did Cabe in . . . no doubt exactly as Tragaro intended. The regrets, the hindsight, they stifled Cabe's reaction, made it hard for him to consider any escape.

His air cut off, his heart pounding madly, Cabe struck wildly at Den's skeletal form. Yet, the ghoulish corpse did not explode as it should have. Instead, the force of Cabe's spell scattered in every direction, even at its own caster.

That which had been the novice wizard pulled Cabe high, dangling the struggling mage like a trapped animal.

Cabe shut his eyes.

Den shuddered and released his victim as a lance that gleamed as bright as the sun pierced his burnt torso where the heart had once beat. The corpse staggered back.

Utilizing what magic he could, the wizard landed somewhat unsteadily on his feet. Rubbing his throat, he watched as the Sunlance suddenly flared. From his grandfather, Cabe had inherited the ability to call upon the Light Of Kylus—the last the elven name for the sun—and create a gleaming shaft that always struck its mark. The first time he had used the ability had been by pure accident, when the Dragon King Brown had attempted to kill him.

But where Brown had simply fallen dead, the animated corpse now glowed as brightly as the lance. The light grew brighter, blinding. Cabe could no longer even see the dead Gordagian's form.

Then, with one last sudden flare, the Sunlance vanished again . . . and with it went the last traces of Den.

"A Sunlancer . . . " Tragaro's voice declared . . . for once a hint of respect in it. "The Bedlam isss a Sunlancer."

Still gasping for breath, Cabe turned to meet the Dragon Master. He took little pleasure in the fact that Tragaro also breathed heavily. At least the elder mage could stand without the fear of teetering. "A Sunlancer, yes. It's a family tradition. One I'll share with you firsthand unless you give in now."

Tragaro laughed harshly. "You are in no condition to summon a second such marvel, Bedlam. Your last trick is played, whereas I have still one more at hand . . . "

His strength nearly depleted, Cabe nonetheless tried to ready himself. The longer he delayed, the more likely that Darkhorse would have the other situation resolved. Bereft of his mesmerized slaves, Tragaro would be a danger more possibly contained.

If Cabe survived, that is.

The masked figure simply stood there, both mouths grinning. Cabe tried his best to detect some twinge of spellcasting, some hint that his foe was preparing his next magical attack. Tragaro was too far away for any physical assault, even with a dagger, and against such mundane assaults, the younger mage kept himself well-protected, anyway.

Then, Tragaro opened his mouth.

Out came a thick stream of pure flame.

Darkhorse expected Tragaro's ensorcelled pupils to continue their assault against him, but, to his dismay, they turned from the shadow steed and instead renewed their efforts against General Majjin.

Rather than have the good sense to retreat, the Gordagian commander ordered his men off their horses. The soldiers spread out through the pass, trying to get near the mages. Several had bows out, the intention obvious. Majjin planned to save the kidnapped spellcasters even if he had to kill them to do it.

Yet, it was Majjin's men who suffered loss. The first archers to get close enough to have a chance suddenly found the earth opening under them. Two men screamed as they plummeted into the sudden chasm. Another scrambled to safety, only to have an unnatural wind thrust him back over the gap. He plunged, his cry cut off as the chasm shut tight again.

Majjin, however, was not one to be daunted even in the face of deadly odds. He continued to spread out his forces, perhaps trying to draw the mages into too many fronts and thereby splinter their efforts.

But the robed figures seemed not at all put off by the general's tactics. The tremors increased and rock slides began everywhere. Herons cried out and abandoned their nests.

As if taking its cue from the birds, the river suddenly left its banks, rushing over several Gordagians who had headed toward it. Five vanished, while several more floundered about, their armor weighing them down dangerously.

Darkhorse trod across the raging water. With his mouth he snatched one struggling soldier, then formed appendages on each side to seize others. Seeing no more, he reluctantly departed the river with the four he had saved and brought his precious cargo to the frustrated commander.

"Are you daft, human? Your warriors die left and right and you simply send them in for more! Be gone from here! We will deal with this madness!"

But Majjin ignored him, instead continuing to shout orders. He still planned to get archers near enough to strike.

Darkhorse swore, something he had learned well from humans. So long as the Gordagians refused to retreat, he could not attend to the wizards properly without more lives lost.

The rock slides grew more tumultuous, forcing him once again to race hard if he hoped to save those caught beneath them.

It was all up to Cabe, then. Darkhorse could only hope that his friend could deal quickly with Tragaro . . . assuming that the latter had not already slain him.

The impossibility of what the Dragon Master had done nearly enabled his surprise to put a quick and fiery end to Cabe. There had been no casting of a spell, no use of a magical talisman.

Tragaro had simply opened his mouth and breathed fire.

All of this Cabe registered in less than a second. Experience, not skill, saved him now, for he had survived by expecting the unexpected time and time again. The flames caught his robes, even singed his right hand, but he rolled away, dousing the fire while at the same time moving out of the dark wizard's view.

Another burst of flame shot out, scorching the ruined column Cabe planted himself behind. The other wizard flattened to the ground, barely avoiding annihilation. Given a few more moments, he hoped to have the strength to fight Tragaro . . . but it seemed doubtful that Tragaro would give him those few moments.

Nothing remained in Cabe that could, for now, counter the incredible flame the older spellcaster breathed. It was in itself magical, yet not created by magic. It burned hotter than any fire Cabe had created, possibly burned hotter than even a Sunlance.

Then, of all things, an old expression came to him, an expression more apt now than anytime in the mage's life.

Fight fire with fire.

It was certainly worth a try . . . and would use up what reserves Cabe had managed to scrounge.

He would place himself squarely in Tragaro's sight, certain and terrible death his fate if he failed. Aware, though, of what little other choice was left to him, Cabe leapt up and waited for the inevitable.

Tragaro breathed on him.

The spell Cabe cast was a simple one, so simple that he feared the Dragon Master would know it for what it was and react in time.

But Tragaro did not, so confident was he of victory. The flames came within a foot of Cabe. The younger wizard could feel the incredible heat. Sweat poured down over his face.

And, as he had hoped, his spell sent that same fearsome fire back into the bronze visage of Tragaro.

Perhaps Tragaro was resilient to the flames, but the metal certainly was not. The bronze glowed bright, burned hot—and Tragaro shrieked. He clutched at the mask—yet seemed incredibly resistant to removing it. Instead, he let the sizzling metal sear his flesh.

Humanity bested Cabe's desire to stand back and avoid further threat. He leapt toward the still-shrieking figure, casting a quick spell that he hoped would keep his own fingers from burning to the bone.

Through the mask, Tragaro's eyes blazed with pain, but when he saw Cabe trying to remove the cause of it, he stumbled back.

That the elder mage had the strength and endurance he had stunned Cabe. Anyone else would have been writhing on the ground, their flesh roasted.

Yet Tragaro still suffered terribly and despite his reluctance to part with the mask, Cabe refused to back down. He darted forward, snaring the bronze piece and using all his might to rip it away.

Along with it came the Dragon Master's *own* face.

In horror, Cabe stared as Tragaro's eyes and mouth stretched in a comically macabre fashion, as if his flesh had become tree sap. Tragaro howled even more and snatched desperately at the mask, but did so too late.

And with the false face finally gone, the other wizard's countenance transformed.

All trace of beard, of any hair, vanished . . . and with them went Tragaro's nose as well. Only a slit remained. The Dragon Master's mouth became little more than a long slit, one that spread far wider than on any normal person. His skin darkened, transforming to the color of moss but touched by a hint of the same bronze cast of the mask.

Even Tragaro's hands transformed, curling inward and growing longer, taloned. Scales developed that swiftly covered the skin.

The eyes remained pale, penetrating, but they had also changed, turning into slits more akin to a lizard or some other reptile.

Darkhorse had believed Tragaro dead with the rest of the original Dragon Masters and it appeared he had been correct. What stood before Cabe now certainly could not be the venerable wizard.

But it *could* be a drake.

A drake called . . . *Sssorak?*

"My masssk!" he hissed. Without the false face, every vestige of humanity was giving way quickly. "I will have my masssk!"

Despite the heat it retained, Cabe did not release his hold. The mask radiated magic of its own, one with a signature not unlike that he had sensed around the false Tragaro.

He had even trained a drake to fight its own . . .

"You don't need this," the wizard insisted, trying to put a peaceful end to the struggle. "You're not Tragaro. You're a drake. You've no reason to want to destroy your own kind."

Sssorak hissed. He looked larger, more bestial, and the robes he had worn as Tragaro now fit very tight. "They mussst be desssstroyed! Their monsssstrous reign must end!"

The drake looked ready to exhale again. Cabe had never come across a drake who could exhale flame or poison mist while in a humanoid form, but Tragaro's beast did not even resemble a normal drake. He looked trapped between human and dragon. There were rare cases of magical crossbreeding, of beings whose lineage could be traced to both races, but such was not the circumstance with Sssorak. He was fully drake . . . but either he or Tragaro had created of him something else as well.

Before Sssorak could inhale again, Cabe held the already half-melted face up. The drake instantly clamped his mouth shut, but he continued to expand in size. From his back, lumps pushed through, lumps recognizable as vestigial wings. Behind Sssorak, a small, narrow tail slapped the stone.

Still holding the artifact, Cabe approached the panting beast. "You must listen to me . . . Sssorak. You're not Tragaro. You're as much a puppet of his legacy as your new Dragon Masters are of you. You're a drake!" He studied the coloring closely. The bronze tint of Sssorak's otherwise green scale was not some residue left by the melting mask. "And right now you work to help destroy what's left of your own clan as well . . ."

The inhuman eyes stared uncomprehendingly. "Give me my masssk, Bedlam . . ."

With a roar, Sssorak, his body still transforming, leapt at the spellcaster.

X

The change came suddenly, so suddenly that Darkhorse first suspected it a trap.

The tremors ceased without warning, quickly followed by the collapsing of one of the robed figures. The others held their ground, but they moved slowly, almost haphazardly. To the eternal, they looked like nothing less than marionettes whose strings had broken or become entangled.

Yet while Darkhorse took relief from this turn of events, General Majjin saw it only as an opening. He quickly ordered his archers forward again. One managed to get just within range before the shadow steed noticed him.

As the soldier took aim, Darkhorse cried, "No!"

But the archer got the shot off regardless of the warning. Darkhorse was too far away and any spell he contemplated took too long to cast.

The shaft hit its target in the chest. The target, a young, brown-haired woman with sleepy eyes, gasped and crumpled.

"No more!" roared the eternal, filling the view of the nearest archers. Confronted by the sight of a pitch-black stallion ten times the normal size, the hardened fighters broke.

Darkhorse charged toward the general, shrinking back to his preferred dimensions as he neared Majjin. Even then, he made for such an imposing sight that it was all the bearded officer could do to keep his war steed from bolting.

"General! You will cease! Can you not see that they are no longer a threat? Look at them! Now they are the helpless victims you sought to save! Do you still intended to slay them?"

"It could be a trick," muttered Majjin. "They're wizards! They can't be trusted—"

"No? Not even as much as a soldier sent to rescue them who instead decides to execute them without first checking?"

Majjin's countenance reddened from anger, but he finally nodded. Signaling to another officer, he commanded all archers to hold fire.

"Thank you, general." Darkhorse eyed the man close. "Give me a moment and I will attest to their condition."

Without waiting, he whirled about and, to the astonishment of the soldiers, raced up the steep mountainside, heading from one ridge to another.

As he suspected, the threat was most definitely at an end. Several of the young wizards, including the two Cabe had attacked, lay unconscious. The others sat or stood in a daze, most holding their heads or staring blankly.

Just as he had done with the soldiers in the river, Darkhorse seized several of the stunned novices and brought them back down to Majjin. Once those had been delivered, he raced back for more. The speed with which he moved left his charges breathless, but Darkhorse could not think of that. No matter how fast he raced, precious seconds continued to pass.

Precious seconds in which Cabe might still die.

Sssorak's claws nearly rent Cabe. The wizard rolled back, the drake's hot breath almost as deadly as the flames themselves. Sssorak now stood twice as tall as the human and his wings had grown some, but he still looked trapped between forms. He lacked the false armor appearance of a humanoid drake warrior, but the open visage was not that of a man, nor was the body that of a true dragon. It was as if Sssorak did not know what he should be now that he was bereft of Tragaro's mask.

Although they fought, Cabe still pitied the drake. He well understood the enmity between humans and drakes, the results of centuries of domination by the latter, but Tragaro had done something unforgivable to Sssorak. He had twisted the mesmerized drake so much, Sssorak was willing to slaughter both races in pursuit of his dead master's dream.

And it seemed nothing could convince the drake otherwise.

"This is not the face you should wear," Cabe insisted. "You are a drake . . . a

393

dragon, Sssorak! Tragaro's usurped your identity! Everything you've done in his name goes against your very nature!"

"You will not ssspeak of the massster ssso!" Again, Sssorak sought to exhale flame, but again he feared to destroy what remained of the mask. "He taught me the truth, made certain I could carry on without him! The massster taught me everything I mussst do!"

That made Cabe's decision for him. He had failed to reach the drake with talk. Perhaps Sssorak needed more.

"Tragaro is not your master . . . not any more."

With that, the wizard set the mask aflame again.

The spell was a short but intense one, giving Sssorak no time to counter it. Already softened and distorted by the drake's own fire, the false face had little resistance.

Cabe let the molten mass drop at his feet. "There is only you now, Sssorak. Only you."

"Noooo!" The drake dropped to the ground, crawling over to and scratching at the melted remains. His breathing turned ragged as he sought vainly to save what little still resembled the original artifact. "Tragaro . . . Tragaro . . . "

Stepping back from the pitiful sight, Cabe contemplated his next move. The fight appeared to be out of Sssorak, but the question remained as to what to do with the drake. Return him to his own kind, whom Tragaro had trained him to despise? Bring him to the Manor, the Bedlams' home, and try to fit him into the human/drake settlement within it?

As he pondered the possibilities, he sensed the arrival of another.

"Cabe! I came as soon as possible! Are you all right? Is the danger past?"

He smiled wearily at Darkhorse, grateful for the eternal's presence. "I'm all right. It's—"

"You murdered him!"

The startled wizard turned to find Sssorak standing over the puddle of bronze. Atop his not-quite-human, not-quite-draconic visage he had slapped the bent eye holes and partial mouth—all that remained of the mask. His flesh sizzled where the hot metal touched and a few streaks of burning bronze dripped down his face, but the wild-eyed drake did not seem to notice.

"You murdered the massster!"

Sssorak inhaled, his chest swelling grotesquely.

Both Cabe and Darkhorse reacted instinctively, striking—as they had done so often in the past—in tandem. A bolt of wicked blue lightning from the wizard struck Sssorak full in the mouth, shutting it in mid-exhalation. A tentacle from Darkhorse tightened around the chest.

Trapped, the flames reversed, seeking an outlet but finding none.

Sssorak swelled up like a water sack.

Darkhorse enveloped Cabe, creating for him a safe, secure cocoon.

The drake *exploded.*

Within the safety of the cocoon, Cabe grimaced, furious with his own weakness. He sensed every agony suffered by the shadowy stallion as the furious forces of the dying drake washed over the chamber.

Yet, as quickly as it had begun, it ended. Darkhorse peeled away slowly, reforming, rather unsteadily, his favored shape.

The torches had been destroyed, but bits of dragon flame illuminated the chamber, revealing the carnage. Of the ancient throne and the columns, only shattered bits remained. The rotting corpse of the other dragon had been nearly reduced to blackened bone. The stench of burnt and decaying flesh forced Cabe to cover his nose with a cloth.

Of Sssorak, there was no trace. Only a few fragments of bronze left any indication of his past presence and only one of those was still recognizable as part of the mask.

The twisted bit of smile gleamed dully in the light of the dying flames.

"And so it ends," declared Darkhorse, snorting. "So much for new Dragon Masters! Imagine! A drake, of all things! He must have have been mad! I knew it was not Tragaro! I knew he was dead all along!"

"Yes, Darkhorse, you were right."

They had returned to Gordag-Ai, returned to the court of King Edrik. The young monarch had taken the ensorcelled students into his house and promised that they would be cared for until they could be sent to their respective homelands. Any who wished to study with his own wizards could, of course, remain. The king was happy to provide them with whatever they needed.

Edrik was young, but not stupid.

However, one of Sssorak's puppets had already chosen to leave. Hala had not even come back with the group, instead riding south, toward Zuu. She had other family there, she had said, who would welcome her.

Cabe had noted Majjin speaking with her earlier. Whether or not the general had actually encouraged her departure, he did not seem disappointed with the choice. It meant a likely end to the king's infatuation with her and nothing would please Majjin more. The situation bothered Cabe and he made a note to check on Hala as soon as possible. She had been no more guilty than the rest and did not deserve such treatment, but as he could prove nothing, Cabe had to let it stand as it was for the time being.

He and Darkhorse now left laden with gifts from the king for the entire Bedlam clan. The eternal was in fine spirits; not a creature of material things, Edrik's gratitude had been his present and Darkhorse savored it. More than anything, he enjoyed the friendship of others, possibly because there was no other being like him in all the land.

"At least this was a situation nipped well in the bud! Who knows what would have happened if he had been able to make true use of the Twin's ascension! True, there were some deaths—and I mourn Den's most of all—but if things had continued on, the entire western half of the continent might have been thrown into chaos and war within only a few days! We were fortunate!"

"Yes, fortunate."

The shadow steed mistook his mood. "We could not save everyone, Cabe! Den, the soldiers, and those other young spellcasters who perished in the name of this false Tragaro have all been avenged, at least! All the wrongs have been righted!"

The wizard nodded and from there on pretended his mood was lighter, but for the rest of the journey, he thought of the one victim who could never be avenged.

Sssorak. The drake had lived for over two hundred years as the twisted, hate-blinded pawn of a man obsessed beyond reason—a dead man. Tragaro had nearly created a worse threat than the drakes he had so hated and in the process he had tortured his servant well beyond the point of madness, a crime Cabe could not forgive, whatever Sssorak's race.

No, Sssorak could never be avenged . . . but perhaps now, so the wizard hoped, he could be at peace at last.

DRAGON MASTER

RICHARD A. KNAAK

A WOLF IN THE FOLD

Suffer not the children . . .

I

The cavern glittered, its walls encrusted with a multitude of crystals of varying proportion. The flames from the two torches set in niches on opposites ends of the chamber were all that were needed to create the dazzling light that filled his surroundings.

He fidgeted, but not because the constantly-shifting illumination bothered his wide, feline eyes. No, the young, brown-furred figure fidgeted for a far better reason—to try to escape the black ropes which bound him from head to foot.

Although only a small child, the captive tried his best to hide his deep fear. His father and his mother were the bravest people he knew and he tried to emulate them, but it was so, so difficult. They knew everything, could defeat any enemy.

But they were back home and he . . . he had no idea where he was, save that it was a place worthy of any nightmare.

As if to accentuate that thought, a fearsome figure suddenly filled his gaze. Immediately he ceased his fidgeting.

The monster stared down at his him with narrow, red orbs. It had a long, slim snout that ended in a tiny but toothy mouth. The snout constantly shifted up and down, as if the behemoth sought to absorb every scent.

A scaled arm as thick as the child's torso reached forward to test the bonds with heavy claws designed for digging through mountains of rock and earth. The monster shook him as it tested the ropes.

"The ropes will hold," said a toneless, seemingly disinterested voice.

The beast turned to its right, giving the captive a glimpse of the layered armor that covered its backside. Embedded between the various plates were yet more crystals, their purpose unknown. They gave the monster a yet more surreal appearance.

It unleashed a shrill, hooting sound in response to the distant speaker. The beast's peculiar voice echoed through the massive cavern.

"He is unlikely to free himself," answered the voice to what apparently had been a question from the creature. "He lacks yet his father's frustrating tenacity to survive, not to mention his mother's grace."

The creature the child had seen twice before, but the speaker was a new thing. His eyes could not help but be drawn to the voice—human if not containing a touch of humanity.

The gargantuan watch dog shuffled aside as the other drew near. To the captive's momentary relief, the newcomer was indeed human, although of an unnerving appearance.

Beneath a shocking head of utter white hair—hair that clearly had not turned so pale due to age—could be found a plain visage utterly devoid of identifying feature or emotion. In truth, the human's countenance might have seemed a dead one if not for the scathing hatred boiling over in the eyes.

Under a tattered but serviceable traveling cloak could be seen clear evidence of armor and arms. As the figure approached, the tell-tale squeak of metal followed,

397

A WOLF IN THE FOLD

reminding Darot of his father's soldiers.

From within the cloak, an arm shelled in midnight black stretched forth. Unlike the monstrous giant, though, the human reached for the straps binding his prisoner's mouth tight.

The cloak slipped back as the arm moved, revealing the other limb.

Darot's feline eyes widened further. What he could see of that arm revealed a twisted, withered appendage, one long dead. Armor hid most of the effect, but near the shoulder and the hand, the horror lay unveiled. The arm looked as if something had burned it away, leaving but a mockery behind.

The cloaked human noticed his eyes. The good hand swiftly retreated—the better to push aside the garment and give the child a good look at the travesty.

"A pretty sight," Darot's captor remarked with the same unsettling lack of interest. He might as well have been commenting on some insect he had found wandering near his foot.

His scaled companion hooted loudly.

The icy-haired man did not look at the beast. "The Quel, he thinks it's dangerous to keep you breathing. He's for skinning you and wearing your fur for a trophy."

If he hoped to put more fear in the heart of the child, he readily succeeded. Despite wanting so desperately to be like his father, Darot sniffed and tears dripped down his cheeks.

His plight did nothing to touch the cold heart of the soldier. "I, on the other hand, want to keep you alive long enough for you to see your damned parents flayed and made into a new cloak for me."

The constantly-shifting glitter only added to the human's horrific aspect as he leaned closer. Even the animalistic Quel was preferable to the evil that young Darot could sense in the man.

"By now, the note is delivered, the stage is set. Your father will come running, knowing it to be a trap . . . but still he will come running." He straightened, absently touching the twisted limb with the good. "And I will pay him back a hundredfold for this and other indignities."

From the same shadowed entrance through which the human had emerged came a second towering Quel. This one hooted in a slightly deeper tone, clearly relating something of importance.

The cloaked figure nodded, then said to the beast, "The tunnel's ready, then?"

The second Quel responded with a different, higher note.

"Then have the others to keep an eye on the master of Legar. He likely will not stir himself from his seclusion . . . but we must be certain of no interference."

With a final note, the armored behemoth departed. Darot's captor allowed himself the first sign of emotion, a thin, almost nonexistent smile.

"Everything falls into place . . . " The smile faded, almost as if it had never been. "But I must be careful. He is a tricky one. He may suspect that what is on the surface is not the only act. He may yet realize the full extent of my vengeance . . . "

The first Quel uttered a sound. The human glanced at him, nodding. "Yes, I'll be along in a moment. I've just one more thing to say to the boy."

With his good hand, he reached within his cloak, going behind him. From there he removed a weapon that Darot had not noticed despite its size.

The mace had a crystalline head shaped like a jagged diamond, a head that, as its wielder brought it forward, began to glow as crimson as the Quel's orbs. The handle had been crafted from what seemed platinum.

"To replace the one lost," he explained cryptically. "Mark it well, child. You see it? You understand it can hurt just with a touch? Nod, if you do."

Darot quickly did.

Lowering the arcane weapon, the pale figure thrust his face within inches of his captive's. Up close, the darkness in the eyes grew staggering. Darot wanted to look away, but knew that if he did, the man would hurt him.

"Try nothing foolish. I won't hesitate to punish you." The human's eyes narrowed dangerously. "Your father would vouch for that. He knows of what I'm capable." A hint of a frown graced his pale features. "Perhaps he's even mentioned me. Orril D'Marr? You might want to remember that name, child . . . after all . . . I killed your brother."

II

The missive had but two parts to it, both simple but dire in their implications. The first was one word, a location.

Legar.

The second, perhaps more ominous than the remote peninsula, was a symbol, a black, stylized beast's head.

"Looks like a hound," General Marner finally decided. The burly, mustached soldier had officially served as chief officer of the kingdom of Penacles for the past three years, a position in which he still did not feel comfortable despite having more or less filled it for several more years. To him, to many in the fabled City of Knowledge, his role should have belonged to the lanky, red-haired Toos. Toos had been the long-time companion of the king, taking on the role of regent on what he had considered a temporary basis when his lord had sailed overseas to discover his lost origins. During that time, Marner had taken over his commander's position. When the king had returned, Toos had gladly stepped down and so had Marner.

But shortly thereafter, Toos had died, the victim of an assassination attempt on another. The king had naturally chosen the one with the most experience to replace his old friend and Marner had tried to live up to the reputation of his predecessor.

At the moment, he was dearly wishing that Toos still lived.

Someone had kidnapped the prince from under his prodigious nose.

"The sign is that of a wolf," his monarch responded in a tone which Marner had not heard since the loss of General Toos. Claws swiftly darted forward, shredding the parchment adhered to the door of Darot's chamber by the curved dagger. "To be more specific . . . the wolf god of the Aramites."

"The Ravager? Wolf raiders? In Penacles?"

The king cocked his head toward Marner in a manner akin to a bird of prey eyeing its next meal. The movement was not accidental; the lord of Penacles, after all, resembled much a hawk in appearance.

He was not human, at least, not for the most part. To those who saw him, the king was a cross between man, bird, and lion. He had the visage of the bird, but a regal mane both of feathers and a hair. His arms, when visible, were covered in a downy fur somewhat golden brown in color, although of late a hint of gray had finally touched it. His hands were almost human, but ended in slightly curved fingers from which claws stretched and retracted at his will.

The loose garments he wore—red robe, golden jerkin and pants—gave the pretense of a form wholly manlike. In truth, although the torso was mostly so, save for the fur and the nubs of what would have been wings, the legs were bent backward at the knees. In addition, the specially-made leather boots hid the fact that his feet were both birdlike and feline in design—long, slender, and clawed.

Human, avian, leonine . . . small wonder, when he had washed up near dead and totally devoid of memory on the eastern shores of the vast land called the Dragonrealm that he had taken as his name the most descriptive term for what he was.

The Gryphon.

As the tattered remnants of the note dropped to the carpeted floor, he looked down on his commander. "The room has been searched?"

"From top to bottom. No sign of forcible entry, my lord." Marner glared at two cloth-covered forms. The guards who had been assigned to the prince. "The poor lads were stabbed with their own blades."

"Their attacker was known to them, then." They both knew what that meant, but the Gryphon stated it nonetheless. "One of the curs is in our midst."

"Aye, my lord." Marner removed his hawkcrest helmet and went down on one knee. "I am guilty for my failure in protecting your son. My position . . . my life . . . is forfeit to you, your majesty."

The lionbird waved away his words. "I am growing old when I cannot sniff out a wolf raider. You want to redeem yourself in your own eyes, find the traitor in our midst. I rely on you while I am away."

"Away?" purred a feminine voice from down the corridor. "Away where?"

The Gryphon bit back a curse. He had hoped to be gone before she heard the news. "You shouldn't be up. The healers said—"

"I bore one son on the battlefield, the other during the storm that tore the roof from the eastern half of the palace. I suffered a miscarriage the next time after, but I swear that this child will be born!"

She moved with a natural grace only slightly hindered by her bulging belly. The silken emerald robe played off her tawny, feline fur. A matching pendant on a silver chain rested on her chest. She walked barefooted—as was her way—on slim, tapered feet ending in short, curved claws. Similarly, her hands, lightly furred, ended in longer, sharper ones that, like her mate's, retracted.

Under short brown locks two mildly-pointed ears rose erect. The feline visage was both human enough and exotic enough to have made her one of the most alluring women in the fabled kingdom.

Veiled, catlike eyes narrowed further as she approached the Gryphon. "The staff's been trying to keep me in seclusion. I finally had to threaten my nurse with the promise of a quick trim of her fine long hair . . . " Her claws stretched forth in emphasis. "What's going on, Gryph? Where is our son?"

"Troia—"

"I fought an empire at your side! Don't play games!"

He sighed, never able to hold out against her. "Troia . . . Darot is missing. He's been kidnapped . . . " As he spoke, the Gryphon's form shifted. Gone was the creature of legend, in its place a handsome, regal figure with flowing hair, cleft chin, and an aquiline nose. Around his mate, the king tended toward such a form. "The mark of the letter is that of the wolf raiders . . . "

Few times had he seen the cat woman lose her composure. When she had been forced to slay her treacherous mentor, Lord Petrac, she had broken up after the act. The second, more tragic time, had been when Troia had discovered the murder of her first born.

Then, as now, the act had been that of the Aramites, the dread wolf raiders.

"How? How?" She burst past them, racing into Darot's chambers. The Gryphon and Marner quickly followed after. Troia threw aside the hand-crafted bed sheets, shoved aside the elfwood frame. She flung open and charged into the vast closet.

"Troia!" roared the king.

"He only recently received his life name, too!" Among Troia's people, infants were given a name at birth, then a new one when they had survived at least four years. She had chosen the name 'Darot', after a hero of her race. Darot had gone around proudly for months after being receiving his new name, pretending he was the legendary figure and doing mock battle with amused soldiers.

"Your majesty!" echoed the general.

"Nothing's been touched! The room is as calm as if he still sleeps!" She pointed at the nearby wall, where Darot's favored bow and practice sword hung. To the right, an ebony statue of a shadowy stallion stood, a gift from the king and queen of Talak, who knew that Darot found the subject fascinating. The statue represented the ethereal creature called Darkhorse, an immortal who was ally and friend of sorts to the youth's parents. "Perhaps he's simply wandered off on one of his explorations!" Troia desperately suggested. "Like the time he managed to enter the Libraries!"

The Libraries of Penacleshad existed before the City of Knowledge had risen up around it. There were many legends concerning the Libraries' origins, including the notion that the complex had been built by the ancestors of the modern humans, the Vraad sorcerers. The Libraries were magical and could only be entered through the vast tapestry hanging in the king's personal chambers and guarded by golems. The tapestry, a masterpiece of magic itself, revealed Penacles as it was up to the moment. Whatever alterations took place, the tapestry added them instantaneously.

The Gryphon shook his head. "No, Troia, he can't get in again without my permission. He only passed the guardians the first time because he used his blood link to me. They now have different orders." He considered. "Besides, the Librarian will not let him wander about there any more."

The sole figure—perhaps *figures*, as the Gryphon had never been certain if each to whom he spoke was the same—was that of a bald, gnomish little man in voluminous robes who hid behind a sarcastic and condescending personality the knowledge of the workings of the Libraries. Each time someone entered, they were met by what seemed the same creature, this no matter what corridor it was.

On his one visit, Darot had slipped past the usually adept gnome and had run through the edifice, pulling out book after book to see what was in each. Unfortunately, unless one had a specific question and knew which book held the key, all the pages were *blank*.

Not realizing this unique fact, Darot had gone along looking for one that had something inside . . . in the process leaving a lengthy trail of scattered tomes behind him.

The queen suddenly grabbed for the headboard of her son's bed, slipping onto the latter and gasping for breath. Despite the ease of the previous two births, Troia had been suffering during this last pregnancy, so much so that the Gryphon had ordered her to bed rest.

"It's to be a son . . . " he heard her whisper. "Another son . . . but not to replace the *previous*! Not like last time!"

The Gryphon came to her side, helped her sit. General Marner vanished from the room, returning with a mug of water.

As he leaned toward his mate, the Gryphon's countenance changed again, reverting to the fearsome avian who has been the death of many Aramites before, including those who had slain his eldest, Demion. In a voice tinged with hatred for the ones who would perform such horrendous acts, he whispered to her and himself, "No . . . . not like last time . . . . "

401

A WOLF IN THE FOLD

III

To reach the southwestern peninsula from Penacles by normal means took weeks and the Gryphon suspected that the kidnappers had not simply ridden off and hoped to be there before him. They were already at their destination, of that he was certain. The wolf raiders were warriors, true, but they, too, relied on magic at times. To travel such a long distance, they would need a simple but massive spell, one that could be utilized to enable a large force to ride through at once.

A blink hole.

Cold Styx hovered in the night sky as he raced along astride his favored beige steed, following a trail visible only to the object in his hand. The traces of magic would have been impossible to note even for many versed in the arts, but the Gryphon had picked up many tricks and secrets during his long, adventurous life. One of those now helped him see the faint trail of energy left by the artifact that the Aramites would have needed to create the hole.

He had ridden around the area of the city all evening, knowing that somewhere out here the villains had accepted their precious cargo from the traitor and had then departed. The spells protecting Penacles from Dragon Kings also worked against blink holes created by kidnappers. They would have been forced to enter physically through the city gates, which should have drawn some suspicion. Therefore, it was more likely that they had waited outside for their cohort to perform the actual deed, then bring Darot to them.

More than those who now held his young son prisoner, the Gryphon wanted the fiend who had betrayed an oath to accomplish the perfidious act. He hoped Marner would find the perpetrator by the time he returned—*assuming* he returned.

"No . . ." the Gryphon muttered. "*We* will return."

Even in a land filled with shapeshifting dragon lords, demonic steeds, and more, the Gryphon could not and would not ride out undisguised, even at night. Two hundred-plus years of seeking freedom for those oppressed by the Dragon Kings had made him nearly as legendary as the Bedlam family, the most renown line of wizards and sorcerers. In his role as monarch, he had ruled over more than five generations of humanity, which surely marked his appearance in the eyes of his subjects. Maintaining the transformation that he used when around Troia was more of a strain than even she knew, but for love of her he suffered through it. Away from the palace, though, the Gryphon instead relied on illusion. However, even such a spell demanded a constant stress on his magical abilities, meaning that he would have to rely most on his strength and battle skills should some new situation arise. But such a reliance bothered the Gryphon not in the least, for he was more a warrior than wizard, anyway, and it was those skills he would need most when confronting the wolf raiders.

On a wooded hillside barely a mile from the walls of the city, he abruptly reined his mount to a halt. The night wind ruffled his feathered mane. The Gryphon cocked his head, eyeing the path before him.

He extended his hand, letting sit on his open palm the object that had led him to this point.

In the dim moonlight, the crimson gem suddenly flared bright.

Ahead of the king, the empty air rippled as if due to the advent of a ghost.

The unsettling effect vanished almost the moment it appeared, but the Gryphon had seen enough. The image had been faint, but still a telltale sign that a blink hole had recently opened here. The portal had been removed, but the residual traces left were just enough for him to use.

Placing the crystal in the pouch at his side, the Gryphon used what limited magic remained to him to bind the residue to his power. He urged it to resume its past casting, become once more what its creator had desired.

And suddenly a gap opened up, a shimmering tear in the fabric of reality. It widened, not only large enough for horse and rider, but for a small force of soldiers.

"One or a hundred," the Gryphon murmured. "I'll take you all down if so much as a scratch mars my son . . . "

With that, he urged his steed into the portal.

General Marner drew a line through the second name on his list of suspects. He had nine in all, those whose alibis had not been available at the time of the initial investigation. The second and eighth now had cleared themselves of possible wrongdoing.

He lifted up the parchment, eyeing the rest. One or more of them had aided in the kidnapping.

"Well?" asked a voice from the door. "Did you find the vermin?"

Quickly rising, the general rasped, "Your majesty! The king specifically ordered you back to bed—"

"My son is missing." Troia said it in such a way that Marner could think of no further reprimand. Had he been in her situation, would he have simply let everyone else take charge?

"I want to help you," the cat woman muttered. "I need to help you."

He frowned. "My lady, your infant—"

"Is due in another month. Don't worry yourself, Marner. I don't plan armed combat. I just want to offer . . . my senses."

"I'm afraid I don't—"

She maneuvered herself to a chair in his spartan quarters. Marner, still feeling like an interloper, had only a few personal items in the chambers that had served the indomitable Toos for generations. In the back of his mind, Marner kept expecting the fiery-haired, foxlike mercenary to return to his post even despite the small matter of his death.

The queen's deep eyes drew the officer to her. Like many of the soldiers directly serving the palace, Marner was infatuated by his mistress. It was a respectful infatuation, of course, everyone knowing their proper place. The pendant she wore had actually been presented by Marner and some of the soldiers under him on her last birth anniversary. To a man, each would have given their life for the queen.

Correction. There was one who likely would have preferred to give the life of the queen for his own.

"I grew up fighting the Aramites, Marner. For all the history my husband shares with them, mine was, in many ways, a more intense, more personal struggle."

"Your majesty, I still don't know—"

She raised a hand to silence him. "My people are hunters, creatures of the forest. We live by scent as much as anything else."

The general blinked. "Are you trying to tell me—"

The veiled eyes drew him nearer. Marner stirred in discomfort, improper emotions stirring. "Yes. I know the stench of wolf raider. It's very unique. I've been distracted, but that's changed. Send each of them before me, general." Troia smiled grimly, revealing an entrancing set of teeth—pointed teeth. "I'll do whatever I have to to sniff our traitor out."

The blink hole had deposited the Gryphon in the midst of a grass-filled landscape. In the dark of night, he could not at first get his bearings, but after a short ride, it became obvious just where the kidnappers had exited.

He could not see the city itself, but the gradually ripening equine smell wafting from the south was enough to identify the region as near the kingdom of Zuu, famous for its horses. His illusory visage twisted into an expression of frustration; Penacles and Zuu, while not enemies, were also not on friendly terms. The latter was one of the few kingdoms employing wizards of its own and while none approached even the Gryphon's level of mastery, any notice of his presence by one could cause a costly delay.

The kidnappers would have faced the same risk, which made him wonder why they had chosen to open the portal so far from their obvious destination. One explanation could have been a lack of magic upon which to call; the Aramites likely had no true sorcerers among them. Most of the *keepers*, as they were called, had perished during the war when suddenly cut off from the seductive power of their god.

But one *had* survived, albeit touched by madness. He it had been who had first led the wolf raiders to Legar, to what they had hoped a new base and a new source of magic. That keeper had died, as had most of the Aramites, when the Crystal Dragon, lord of Legar, had unleashed a spell that had shaken the earth, bringing it down on both the invaders and the subterranean Quel infesting the region.

Legar had been quiet since then, even its enigmatic master silent. The Gryphon's spies and secretive spells had revealed nothing. It had been as if the land had become a complete wasteland, devoid of life.

The perfect domain for a wolf raider.

He rode for as long as he could during the night, finally forced to stop for the sake of his horse. Secreting himself in a small valley, the Gryphon rested as best he could. Each time he shut his eyes, the images of his sons filled his thoughts. Darot was almost the exact image of his elder brother, which only served to remind the Gryphon of how much the first loss had touched him.

It had taken years, but he had gained his vengeance. The Aramite officer who had been responsible had died in the destruction of Legar. That had not erased the pain, but it had given some sense of justice. Few times had the Gryphon lost control of himself, but few adversaries had touched him the way Orril D'Marr had.

His eyes shot open. "Orril D'Marr . . . "

No . . . that path led to insanity. The cold, calculating young wolf raider lay crushed under tons of rock and earth. He could have no more survived than the scores of other Aramites who had fallen prey to the Dragon King's desperate act.

It had to be someone else . . .

With dawn, he raced off to the southwest, aware that his destination lay not all that far ahead. The Gryphon began steeling himself for the journey into the uninviting realm. The Legar Peninsula had always been an inhospitable land. The heat rose to unspeakable levels and the ever-present sunlight combined with the natural crystal deposits to make travel during daylight all but blinding. Wildlife consisted of the typical desert dwellers. The dragon clan itself had always been small and, like their lord, seldom seen. They likely would be no trouble, if they still even existed.

The Quel were another story. They lived deep beneath the earth there, burrowing through rock and creating vast, underground chambers. Until the wolf raiders, all but a handful had been caught in a perpetual sleep, the product of a spell gone awry centuries before. The Aramites had awakened the rest by chance and only the destruction of Legar had prevented further catastrophe. Still, the odds were better that some of the huge, armored diggers had survived. The Gryphon knew that he would have to keep an eye on the ground, watch for any sudden shifting that could not be explained by one of the realm's incessant tremors.

Late in the afternoon, his surroundings changed, becoming more and more akin to what he expected of Legar. His only moment of danger during the trek so far had been a small patrol to the south. The huge, blonde riders in leather jerkin and pants had clearly been from Zuu and, as was the kingdom's way, some of the warriors had been women. Zuu made very little distinction between the sexes when it came to work and war.

Fortunately for him, the patrol had turned back to the east without noticing the stranger in their land. That had not been due to lack of effort, but rather the Gryphon's own superior experience. More than two centuries as a mercenary and warrior had, at least, benefited him in some way.

At last, he reached Legar.

The high, rocky hills glittered even from more than a mile away. The clouds that had earlier threatened some rain stopped almost exactly at the recognized border, giving way to a relentless sun. A dry, harsh wind blew from the peninsula, offering the newcomer a taste of what to expect.

Without hesitation, the Gryphon entered.

At first, the trek seemed a simple one. While uneven and rocky, the path was not the worst, especially for a horse as well-versed as his. That enabled the Gryphon to focus his attention on the seeking signs of the kidnappers. Near Zuu, the effort had not been so difficult; a party of riders left much of a trail in grasslands and fields. However, here in this dry, hard region, the clues required a more cautious, expert eye.

Several times he reined the horse to a halt so that he could investigate marks. By now the Gryphon knew that there had been five riders, one of them likely his son. The party had stayed close together and had ridden as if the demon Yureel had been at their backs. They feared something . . . but not pursuit.

Their leader?

Still mulling over that question, the Gryphon directed his mount through a narrow, winding pass. The hills rose high and foreboding around him, then finally opened up just as the sun set.

And beyond them at last he witnessed the ravages of the Crystal Dragon's attack.

It looked as if the entire world before him had been literally raised up in the air, turned upside down, then dropped. No inch had been left untouched. Legar for as far as the eye could see was a realm torn asunder.

The horse snorted uneasily, stamping its front hoof at the same time. The Gryphon also hesitated, recalling the actual devastation. In many ways, what had happened here reminded him of the events during the desperate war against the Dragon Kings by the wizard Nathan Bedlam and his allies that had culminated in calling the struggle the Turning War. Then, the area of destruction had been elsewhere and the results had finally made the bickering drakes ally themselves long enough to deal with the upstart humans.

Rocks as huge as some of the hills through which he had ridden lay as if tossed about by some giant child. Sudden gaps plummeted deep into the earth, the pebbles that the Gryphon threw into one never making a sound to indicate that they had reached the bottom. Even after years, many areas had not yet settled, the groan of shifting earth assailing him as he traveled cautiously along.

His quarry aided his journey now. By careful study, the Gryphon located their path, the safest through Legar. Even still, he knew that the land could be treacherous and so he finally walked the horse, hoping eventually that he would find smoother ground ahead.

The Gryphon did not realize just how dangerous the peninsula still was until a short time later, when he discovered the bodies.

Initially, he had mistaken the glitter for just more crystal. Only as he drew near did he recognize the glint as from metal.

The Aramite and his horse had died together, crushed into one almost pastelike substance by the rock fall. The familiar black armor that had put fear into a continent for centuries had served as much of a buffer against the tons of stone as silk. Blood stained much of the area, the sun already drying it to a faint crimson chalk.

For several terrifying moments, the Gryphon searched around, trying to discover whether or not Darot had suffered a like fate. Eventually, it became clear that only the one horse and rider had perished. Scratch marks revealed that the others had continued on. Like him, they were now on foot.

The descending sun brought some relief in terms of temperature, but mounting frustration in terms of the pursuing father. The Gryphon dared not travel at night; one false step could quickly end his life. He did not fear for himself, but what the wolf raiders would do to his son if he did not make it to Darot. There would be no use for a young child, then.

Just before the last rays of sun vanished, the Gryphon came across what appeared the most stable patch of ground so far. More or less flat, it was flanked to the north by several jagged plates of baked earth rising yards into the sky and on the south by a gaping ravine.

Alone and feeling as dry as his surroundings, the Gryphon removed the illusion, returning to his true form. In preparation to entering Legar, he had filled several sacks brought with him with water. Already a third of those sacks had been emptied. The Gryphon took one, then held it so that his horse could drink. The animal eagerly swallowed the contents, licking at the empty bag until its master finally pulled it away.

Satisfied that the horse had been watered, he led it to where a few gaunt, skeletal shrubs somehow had managed to grow. The fare was not the best, but it would keep the steed alive.

Seeing to his own needs, the Gryphon drank some more water, then dug into the shrinking bag of rations. Some dried, salted meat served him for now. He had long learned to survive on little during his campaigns and had eaten as healthy as possible before setting out.

A slight tremor shook his immediate surroundings. Pausing in his meal, the former mercenary waited it out. The tremor ceased almost immediately. The Gryphon waited a few moments, then resumed eating.

Styx drifted high in the sky. Of his bloody sister, there was no sign. The pale moon enabled the Gryphon to see for some distance, not that there was much at which to look.

A second tremor started, this one nearer and more severe. Dropping the meat, he leapt up and prepared to move to safety.

His mount neighed. The Gryphon started toward the animal, intent on calming it.

The earth beneath the horse gave way.

The animal shrieked as it dropped from sight. The Gryphon made a desperate grab for the reins, but they slithered out of his reach, vanishing into the dark gap.

Before he could collect himself, the ground near his feet burst open and a huge rock thrust skyward.

No . . . not a rock. Even in the dim light of night, the Gryphon recognized the monstrous outline.

A Quel.

The Gryphon tried to cast a spell, but felt a force disperse the magic. He cursed silently, recalling that the crystal-embedded ridges of a Quel's shell gave it much protection from all but the most powerful attacks.

The giant underdweller emitted a deep hoot, then pulled a blunt spear from the earth and jabbed at his prey. However, by then the Gryphon had rolled away, coming to a crouch at the edge of the hole down which his unfortunate mount had fallen.

The end of the spear sank into the hard earth just inches from him. He immediately grabbed at the weapon, pulling it free despite the Quel's tremendous brute strength.

Again the Gryphon felt the ground quiver. This time, however, he was not fooled. Using the spear as a pole, he leapt away just as a second hulking form burst up from below.

The first Quel slashed at the Gryphon with claws nearly a foot long. Had they actually cut, they would have spilled the latter's insides all over the unforgiving landscape. Instead, as the Quel lashed out at empty air, his more agile opponent used the spear as a pole again—throwing himself up and over the armored behemoth.

The Quel turned, trying to snare him. The Gryphon flipped the spear around, bringing the point up.

He embedded the point in the creature's throat, the softest part of the Quel's shelled hide.

As the one dropped, two more erupted from the soil. Still moving, the Gryphon retreated up a massive rock in the hopes of better gauging the enemy's numbers.

But the rock shifted, tipping over and throwing him at an awkward angle. With a grunt, the Gryphon struck the ground shoulder first.

As pain coursed through him, one of his attackers seized the Gryphon by the mane. The Gryphon squawked as the huge creature twisted his head back.

Claws out, he slashed at the Quel's long, almost tubular mouth. Blood splattered the Gryphon's avian visage, but he failed to disrupt the shadowy behemoth's grip.

The other Quel closed in on him. Muscles straining, the Gryphon flipped, turning upside down in his captor's claws and wrapping his legs around the stocky head. The injured Quel hooted, adjusting his grip so that he could deal with the unexpected assault.

It was exactly what the Gryphon desired. He pulled his head free, leaving bits of his mane behind in the process, then dropped without warning. A normal man would have fallen on his back, possibly cracking it, but the Gryphon twisted again, managing to land on his feet and duck under the Quel's groping arms.

A spear point came within inches. The Gryphon rolled past it, darting with inhuman agility between two of his assailants.

He leapt up onto a more stable position, then crouched. The Quel turned as one, at least four broad, armored figures seeking his death.

Though they were native to Legar, this attack could be no coincidence. Whoever led the kidnappers had alerted the underdwellers to his eventual incursion. They had calculated that he would have to choose this particular area for his rest stop and had dug a tunnel to it.

The Gryphon eyed the dark path, seeking a way past the four. He spied another rock just behind the furious Quel. It would require a prodigious leap even for him, but it would put the Gryphon far enough ahead of his foes to keep them from ever catching up.

Two of the Quel abruptly bent down, thrusting their snouts into the earth and digging furiously. As they disappeared below, he noted them coming his direction. They hoped to undermine this rock as some had the last one.

Without hesitation, the Gryphon jumped.

But just as his feet left the rock, one of the remaining Quel did a peculiar thing. He bent low and turned his back to the Gryphon. The Quel curled, creating of himself a massive ball.

And suddenly a glittering blaze of light completely blinded the Gryphon.

His concentration lost, he tumbled earthward short of his target. He nearly broke his beak and his arm as he fell face first. Head pounding, the Gryphon struggled to regain his equilibrium.

A heavy fist pounded him into the ground, followed by another and another . . .

He managed to turn and swipe at the nearest. Claws rent flesh and fluids soaked his hand. A fierce gurgle gave indication of the harsh wound that he had dealt one of the Quel—

But then the pounding increased and under the relentless onslaught the Gryphon finally faltered. He tried to roll himself into a ball, but even that brought no protection.

A glaring, red orb broke through the swirling lights still assailing his eyes. It filled the Gryphon's gaze.

A force a thousand times harder than the blows he had suffered struck him . . . and the Gryphon knew no more.

V

Three more had been eliminated from his list, but the four remaining General Marner could not exonerate. They were all known to him, but he could not let that be a factor.

One worked in the royal kitchens, another served in the house staff, and two were members of the palace guard. The latter pair had even contributed to the necklace that their queen wore.

Marner had suggested that since Troia desired to be present, they should hold these final talks in the throne room. She had declined, stating that the general's office would be sufficient. Yet, while the queen found no fault in the bare walls and simple oak furniture, the general felt as if he lived in squalor. He quickly ordered the guard stationed inside the door to start the interviews, hoping that doing so would take his mind off his shame.

Syl Cordwain entered first, left leg dragging slightly. He acted as tutor for the young prince. The slight, balding man at first appeared incapable of any treachery, but Marner and the queen knew that his background included several years as a spy for the king. Syl had infiltrated nearly every major kingdom and Dragonrealm during his career and his knowledge of the known lands had made him the perfect teacher for one who would some day have to rule a place prized by every enemy.

"My queen," Syl whispered, kneeling.

"Good Syl," Troia returned, absently touching the gem.

"We've some questions," the general informed the tutor.

"So I would imagine."

For the next hour, Troia and Marner delved into every aspect of Syl's life, trying to draw clues as to his innocence. Their subject answered well, but ever it was on their minds that he had spent many a year in a career where twisting the truth meant life or death. It had only been the maiming of his leg that had forced Syl to shift to a new branch of service to his monarch.

"Tell me about your leg," the queen asked at one point. Marner glanced her direction, noticing that her nose twitched. When she had said that she could sniff out a wolf raider, she had in some ways meant it literally.

Syl went into his tale and when he had finished, the queen rose and touched him gently on the shoulder. "You've paid much following the dictates of my husband."

"My father served him before. I consider it an honor." His pinched face darkened. "Would that I had been near when the fiends took the prince."

He said it with such conviction that Marner desired to believe him, but again Syl's background worked against him.

Alone with the general, Troia remarked, "I sense no taint on him and he's nearly given his life more than once for the kingdom . . . yet . . . "

"Let us see the others."

In next came Henrik Bronzesmith and Juren of Taflur, two men Marner had, until this incident, considered among his best. The familiar scent of garlic pervaded Juren, who had a fondness for Penaclesean blood sausage. Henrik, broader of shoulder and a foot taller than his clean-shaven friend, tried to smooth his thick brown beard.

Both men went down on one knee as a guard shut the door. Despite being clad in the familiar silver and blue armor most recently chosen for the palace guard, they carried no weapons. General Marner had wanted no potential threat near the pregnant queen.

"Henrik," he began, not bothering to read through the notes he had earlier written. "Three years good service. Juren . . . nearly the same." Part of the case against the pair had to do with their recent addition to the ranks. They were less known to the general's staff despite their clean records and sterling behavior. Still, that alone could not condemn them.

"Taflur," Troia murmured. "Where is that?"

"N-north of Penacles, my lady," Juren sputtered. "Toward the Dagora Forest. A s-small village, if you please."

Both men had served in the kingdom's army prior to joining the palace guard. Their commanders had recommended them highly. Yet, Syl Cordwain was an example of how cleverly someone could infiltrate another realm and be thought of as a loyal member . . . he had spent some three and a half years in the service of the human administrator who ran the affairs of Irillian By the Sea for the Blue Dragon.

"You were not born in Taflur," Marner reminded the young soldier.

"No, sir. My family were refugees from Mito Pica. I was born just after they escaped its razing."

The general grunted his sympathies. Mito Pica, once a proud, shining example of human civilization, had been destroyed by the forces of the present Dragon Emperor's sire. They had been searching for Cabe Bedlam, grandson of the notorious Nathan Bedlam. The grandfather had been responsible for gathering mages to fight the Dragon Kings some two centuries prior and while the spellcasters had failed, their legacy remained burned in the drakes' memories. Yet, in trying to destroy Cabe, they had set in motion a sequence of events that now left half the continent free of their domination.

But for many of those in Mito Pica, that freedom had come at the cost of their lives. The ruins still lay untouched, the tales of bloodshed so terrible that few journeyed there.

Gazing through draped eyes, Troia looked at the larger of the two. "Master Henrik. You were born in Penacles?"

"Aye, my queen."

"You have family here still?" Her nose twitched once, twice.

"None, my queen. I was a lone child and my parents died from disease when I was young."

"No distant relations?"

He shrugged. "None to my knowledge."

Seeing her interest in Henrik, Marner recalled what he could of the man. Again, a sterling record, but . . .

"Henrik . . . you went away as a youth, seeking your fortune. That's what you told me once."

The bearded soldier's brow furrowed, but he answered, "Aye. Fool boy wanted to see what he could make of himself."

"Where did you go?"

"Zuu. Talak. Grandion. Wenslis. Morgare—"

The queen straightened. Only Marner noted the slight tensing of her form as she did so. "I don't recognize the last one."

"Obscure little region southeast of here, my lady," the commander informed Troia. "Near the realm of the Black Dragon."

"Oh?" Troia's claws extended ever so slightly. Her nose twitched more actively. "Really? Henrik . . . did you ever enter the mist lands—"

She got no further. Without warning, Henrik leapt from his position, coming at the queen with such ferocity that even she was caught unaware. From out of his sleeve slid a razor-thin blade of ebony barely larger than his palm.

General Marner stood, stunned by the action. Battle-trained reflexes finally took over and he threw himself in front of Troia.

But he needn't have bothered. A pair of hands caught Henrik's wrist, twisting it violently. The blade flew harmlessly away. The traitorous guard snarled and threw a heavy fist at his own attacker.

Juren ducked his blow, but lost his grip on Henrik's wrist. The larger guard used the moment to shove his comrade away and start for the door.

"Stop him!" roared Marner.

The guards near the exit moved to block Henrik's path. At the same time, Juren reached down and seized the fallen blade.

With a roar, Henrik rammed his way into the other soldiers. The three collided against the door, cracking it. One guard fell. The other struggled with the much larger Henrik.

Juren threw the blade.

Troia rose. "No! We want him alive!"

The blade caught its target in the back of the neck, leaving a long, bloody gash. It then slipped onto Henrik's armored shoulder, finally dropping to the floor.

The wound, while serious, startled the assassin more than it injured him. That, however, proved to be enough. Marner and the second guard joined the first, finally overpowering Henrik.

Arms secured, the prisoner was turned to face his would-be victim and his former commanding officer.

"My life, my soul, belongs to the Ravager," he uttered.

"What's that?" snarled Marner.

Standing, the cat woman eyed Henrik with loathing. "An old Aramite oath. They all swear it in the name of the creature they think a god."

Henrik spat her direction, his shot falling just short. General Marner rewarded his behavior with a slap across the prisoner's rough face.

Henrik shook his head as if dizzied by the blow, then smiled savagely at his captors.

"So now we have our wolf in the fold." The commander studied Henrik's wound. "Deep, but not too deep. You'll stay alive long enough to be questioned."

The Aramite continued to grin.

Turning to his queen, Marner bent his head. "Your majesty, this is my failure. I should've delved deeper into his past, discovered whether he was the true Henrik."

"The raiders are very devious, general. They pattern themselves after their so-called deity."

"Our Lord Ravager will smite you down!" Henrik rasped. "Your blasphemy will be punished!"

Daring a step closer, Troia replied, "How strong is your god? He seems to have left you bereft of an empire, Aramite."

The prisoner growled and shook his head. Sweat covered his brow and his skin went pale.

"I think you're undermining his faith a bit, my lady," remarked General Marner. "He's not looking all that confident now."

Despite having already been spat at, Troia moved yet closer. Her large eyes narrowed abruptly and her nose twitched as she sniffed at Henrik. "He's not looking well at all," she announced suddenly. "General, I think I detect—"

Henrik suddenly roared in obvious agony. His eyes widened and flecks of foam spilled from his mouth.

"A healer!" shouted Marner. "Get a—"

But it was already too late. With one tremendous convulsion, the wolf raider folded over. He shivered once, twice . . . and then fell limp in the guards' hands.

Quickly looking around, Troia cried, "Juren! Leave that be!"

The other soldier, just about to pick up the assassin's blade, hesitated. "Your majesty?"

"The blade! It carries the Bite of the Ravager! It's poisoned!"

Juren withdrew, staring with dismay at the hand which had wielded the weapon earlier.

Moving lithely for one very pregnant, the queen stepped over to him. She took the hand and inspected palm and back very carefully.

"No cuts," she informed them. "No scratches." Her gaze went to Juren's. "You are safe."

"Likely all that garlic he eats would've killed the poison, anyway," the general commented. Still, he was relieved that Henrik had not managed to take another victim with him. He patted Juren on the back. "You did your job well, lad."

"Thank you, sir . . . but . . . never I thought it'd be Henrik . . . "

"None of us, lad . . . " To the queen, Marner said, "I'll see that the palace guard's tightened up from here on, your majesty. There'll be no more of these curs among us!"

Touching the gem in her pendant, Troia nodded. Her mind was clearly on the assassin. "I was still probing. There was a chance he could have passed questioning. He had no reason to commit himself so quickly."

"Likely he thought he'd never get a better chance to do you in, my lady. Fanatics, that's how you and the king've described them before."

"Yes. Willing to do anything for a would-be god who would just as well eat them. Thank goodness, at least the Ravager can do no more harm."

"Why's that, your majesty?" Juren piped up.

"Because, thanks to my husband and other powers, the Aramites' lord is sealed in a hidden place, never to be released. Only the king and those who imprisoned the Ravager there know its location."

General Marner glared at Henrik's prone form. "Well, there's one less who'll try to avenge that beast. That'll be a lesson to the rest, mark me."

Troia nodded, but her eyes disagreed with the commander's evaluation. "Let us hope so. Let us hope so."

VI

Voices. They were the first thing to penetrate the darkness that had swallowed the Gryphon. Most of them were incomprehensible but recognizable, the savage hoots of the hulking Quel.

The lone human voice barely rose above a whisper, but its toneless quality immediately set his nerves on edge. He knew that voice, a voice of the dead.

"I could care less whether he slew two or two dozen of you," the speaker remarked. "You know the key is for him to live, for now. That's why I punished the one in charge of the attack. He let fury override reason. There will be vengeance, but calculated, timed."

As the Gryphon stirred to waking, the injuries caused by the Quel also awoke, nearly making him cry out. Only decades of life as a hardened mercenary enabled the Gryphon to keep still, pretend that he lay unconscious.

"He will reveal what I desire and lead you to what you desire. That was our agreement," continued the voice. A Quel hooted, then the voice added, "Yes, he should be."

The sound of footsteps echoed, growing nearer. The Gryphon did not move, did not alter his breathing. He had often fooled his adversaries into thinking he was unconscious. Perhaps again—

"Enough games," murmured the uncaring voice.

Something touched the Gryphon on the shoulder. A horrific shock tore through him, one that made the injuries insignificant by comparison. This time, the king of Penacles could not keep from shouting. His roar of pain repeated endlessly in the glittering cavern.

And through tear-drenched eyes both avian and leonine, he beheld the bland face of a corpse.

Injury had weathered the shaven countenance more than the past few years had warranted, but there was no denying the emotionless expression, the burning eyes.

There was no denying that Orril D'Marr hovered over him.

In the one hand revealed by the figure's dark cloak, Orril D'Marr wielded a frightening recreation of his favored weapon. The magical mace had been designed for both battle and torture and the Aramite had used it for the latter reason quite often. In a true moment of irony, he had been grabbing for a handhold during the final moments of Legar's destruction and had instead gripped the head, at last suffering a taste of what his victims had endured.

But the mace had been destroyed, lost in the devastation. In fact, when last he had seen the Aramite officer, D'Marr, too, had been tumbling into the great crevice formed by the collapse of tons of earth upon the Quel's stronghold. The wolf raider should have been mangled to a pulp, his body crushed under the earth and rock.

"My Lord Ravager watches over me," D'Marr remarked, as if reading his prisoner's thoughts. "I suffered some injury, but nothing that could not be healed . . . " Just for a moment, a flicker of bitterness touched the mask that was his face. " . . . nothing, save what you did to me."

Handing the mace to, of all creatures, a Quel, he threw back the thick cloak he wore, revealing the twisted, maimed remnant of his other arm. The flesh was even more

412

pale that that of the face. The hand, if it could still be called such, resembled a scaly set of skeletal talons.

"When the Quel found me, miraculously whole despite all, they chose, for reasons of their own, to allow me to live. For their needs, they required my health and so they used their magic . . . at the same time enhancing me where necessary." He paused, as if expecting his captive audience to ask just how. When the Gryphon remained stonily silent, D'Marr shrugged and went on. "But they could do nothing for this." With effort, he raised the arm slightly at the shoulder. "The full force of my power mace went through it, burning away most of the muscle, the nerve. The rest atrophied from inability to use it." Utter hatred radiated in the eyes, a monstrous contrast to the rest of the frozen visage. "A few seconds longer gripping the head and I would've died."

From behind him came a second, larger Quel. This one had a slight crest atop his elongated head and as he neared, the Gryphon noted how the creature holding D'Marr's weapon moved respectfully aside.

The Quel leader hooted, the same call that the Gryphon had first heard upon awaking.

"You're absolutely right," Orril D'Marr replied to the beast, his gaze never leaving the Gryphon. "He is probably wondering."

A cry burst from somewhere behind the king. The Gryphon immediately tried to turn, only then registering that his arms and legs were bound by thick, iron manacles. The manacles were attached to short chains nailed into the rock upon which he lay. Try as he might, he could not pull them free.

"You did come for your son, didn't you?" mocked the wolf raider. "Your second son, that is?"

Another of the armored Quel carried a struggling bundle before the prisoner. Darot saw his father and both relief and fear filled his eyes. He had clearly been crying for some time, but the Gryphon could hardly fault the child for that.

"You'll note that he's quite well and almost untouched. You may wonder why that is."

The Gryphon eyed his nemesis, but said nothing.

"The Quel and I . . . we came to an understanding. Thanks to you and that wizard, Bedlam, you accomplished what their mortal foes, the Seekers, never could." The Seekers were an avian race that had supplanted the underdwellers as rulers of the land before the coming of the Dragon Kings. The two races had battled long and hard against one another. "You destroyed their world."

The Crystal Dragon had actually done that, but the Gryphon, Cabe Bedlam, and the enigmatic Darkhorse had contributed to the chaos, if not by choice. Of course, neither the Aramites nor the Quel would see it that way.

"My armored friends, they would finally rid themselves of the Dragon King, but with their numbers reduced and their home in . . . shall we say 'disarray'? . . . they lack the strength."

"And they think to gain it from you?" the captive finally said. Despite the situation, he eyed the wolf raider with disdain. "A squalid pack of mongrels with barely a place to call their den? What strength could you add that could deal with a Dragon King, especially the Lord of Legar?"

Orril D'Marr almost reached for his mace, but then evidently thought better of it. To the Gryphon, he quietly replied, "The strength of a god."

The fur and feathers on the back of the Gryphon's neck stiffened. It had been more than vengeance that had sent the Aramite after him.

"You were there." D'Marr snapped his fingers and the Quel brought Darot closer. "You were there when our Lord Ravager was tricked into imprisonment. You know where he is kept . . . "

"And where he'll stay for eternity."

Darot suddenly cried out through his gag. The Gryphon's eyes burned red as he watched the creature holding his son rake huge claws ever so lightly over the youth's cheek. A hint of blood trickled down.

The Gryphon tried to draw upon his magic, but immediately sensed a dulling of his powers. At the same time, he noticed many of the gems filling the cavern flicker as if alive.

"No wizardry here, misfit. Not unless it falls into Quel wizardry."

"My son has no part in this. Release him."

The frost-haired figure glanced at the child. "I can do that, misfit. I can let this son live, where the other didn't."

Memories of the limp body of Demion filled the Gryphon's thoughts. Darot's brother had been older, old enough to see battle. His parents had kept him secreted as well as they could, but the Aramites had come across him.

And without compunction, Orril D'Marr had killed him.

He would do the same to Darot. The Gryphon could not imagine losing a second child, not even with a third on the way. "I won't fight you, wolf, You and your grotesque friends can do with me as you please. The boy deserves better."

"You know what we want. Give us that and I promise your get will be sent to his mother."

Something about the way D'Marr said it, as devoid of emotion as it was, set the Gryphon even more on edge. "What do you mean by that?"

The Aramite looked at his Quel comrades. "They are creature directly to the point. They would torture your child or you right now, using straightforward methods." D'Marr gave him an empty smile. "I, being civilized, prefer a more mentally-debilitating method first."

"That burrower touches my son again and they'll find nothing left of him but a scraped-out shell . . . " He eyed the creature hold Darot, letting the Quel read his meaning.

The huge beast drew ever so slightly into his shell.

"Look at him . . . " Orril D'Marr commented to the Quel leader. "Even now he can make one of your minions cringe. You see why we do it my way?"

The Quel nodded, responding with a slight, drawn-out hoot.

"Oh, yes, it will work. He just has to decide how much he values his family and who, if necessary, he wishes to lose less."

Darot whimpered.

"Speak plainly . . . if you can, cur!" snapped the Gryphon.

This time, D'Marr did reach for the mace. The head flared as he brought it toward the Gryphon. The latter did not flinch, knowing that that was exactly what the Aramite desired.

Finally retracting the sinister weapon, D'Marr whispered, "Speak plainly? Very well, I'll speak very plainly." He pointed the mace to the left, where the grim figure of another wolf raider materialized from the darkness. Dust still covered the ebony armor. Here was one of those who had transported Darot.

In the Aramite's hands sat a peculiar-looking and ominous crystal arrangement about the size of a small cat. Ten, small blue stones hovered magically above a crimson one that fit snugly in an oval, bronze tray set in the human's palms. As the Gryphon studied the blue gems, he noticed that they slowly shifted position, creating a descending spiral.

"Set it directly between the two of them."

Another soldier, also covered in dust, brought forth a wooden stand, which he placed several yards before the Gryphon. At the same time, the Quel holding Darot positioned the child on a rock across from his father. With impressive efficiency, the armored beast used its huge clawed digits to bind the Gryphon's son to the rock.

Meanwhile, the first wolf raider put the arrangement on the stand. The Quel that had been identified as the leader of the underdwellers stepped up and adjusted the crystals, not only turning them so that the Gryphon could see them better, but setting the blue ones into a pattern that moved more rapidly than the previous.

The massive creature hooted at Orril D'Marr.

"Yes, that should do." The frost-haired villain turned again to his adversary. "Here it is, misfit, in plain words. At a pace of roughly two hours each, one of those blue stones will cease to glow. It'll drop. You have until only the last one remains to tell us where the caverns are and prove that you don't lie. If there's any doubt, or you think that you can hold off from answering . . . " He looked over his shoulder at Darot.

The Gryphon could guess the rest. At the end of that time, if he did not give them the truth, they would harm his son. His gaze fixed on Darot and he wondered if the boy understood that threat.

"Aah . . . you make the logical, if incomplete, conclusion." Stepping between the king and Darot, Orril D'Marr held up another crystal, this one emerald in color. "But there remains one more element, a further enticement. You are a warrior born. The life of your son might be something you'd be willing to sacrifice. Therefore, I've added a further incentive."

The emerald flared. As it did, a foot-tall image materialized.

An image of Troia.

The barest ghost of a smile traced D'Marr's lipless mouth.

"Before the last stone drops, when your son is already dead by your choice, you have one last opportunity to give us the information. If not . . . with the final gem's fall, your mate . . . and your coming child . . . will also die."

VII

General Marner entered the royal chambers, going down on one knee before the queen. "Forgive this intrusion, your majesty."

Troia sat in a simple chair, a goblet in one hand. Next to her, a small, elegant marble table held a pitcher of spring water. Behind her, almost shadowed, two slim female forms stood watch. They were clad as ladies-in-waiting, but their expressions were hardly those of soft aristocrats. Toos had chosen both women with care. The younger, blond one could match the best dagger tossers at fifty paces. The older, more attractive brunette knew how to handle a sword better than many of his men.

Even still, both were not nearly as deadly as their mistress.

"Your visit is hardly that, general. You've some news for me?"

"Aye. We made a thorough search of Henrik's chambers. At first we found nothing out of the ordinary."

The queen fingered her pendant. "You said 'at first' . . . " Marner reached into a pouch on his belt, cautiously removing the contents. A black cloth surrounded them. He peeled it open, then showed the items to the queen. "In a space carved out of the wall and hidden with a false front, we found these." As she leaned close to inspect them, he warned, "No nearer, majesty! The vial contains the same poison as tipped the blade."

A WOLF IN THE FOLD

The black, opaque bottle was tiny, barely half the length of her thumb. That spoke much for the potency of the foul liquid within.

Tearing her gaze from the vial, Troia hissed.

The ring was as black as the bottle and instead of a stone, a metal image decorated it. Both could clearly see the savage, lupine head.

"The final damning evidence," she muttered. "No clue as to his efforts?"

"None, but I hardly expected any. He would've destroyed such things. The only reason he kept the vial was due to necessity and, as for the ring . . . I chalk that down to obsession with his god."

Troia nodded. "I'm rather glad that you found the rest of the poison. I've been wondering where it might be."

"As to that, young Juren leant his aid there. He's tried to recall any peculiar behavior Henrik ever showed. This came from one memory." Marner grunted. "Lad feels worse than the rest of us. He considered Henrik a friend."

"How is he faring?"

"I've done my best to show him he's done well, but he still thinks he nearly got you killed through his ignorance."

Troia's feline eyes became mere slits. "I'll talk to him. Let him know how grateful I and my mate are."

Her last words suddenly darkened the mood further. Troia gazed toward a window, staring, not by coincidence, to the southwest.

"Gryph must be in Legar by now," the queen said. "I should be with him. Darot needs me."

"With all due respect, the king was correct. As capable as your majesty is, you are nearly ready to bear your child . . . perhaps the heir to the throne."

She gave him a sharp look. Her claws extended fully and Marner momentarily expected to earn new scars on his face.

Then, Troia retracted her claws and nodded. "You're right, but I'll be damned if I like it."

"He'll bring Darot back. He will."

"I have to believe that, general . . . just as I have to believe he'll be coming back himself."

Marner departed the presence of the queen feeling less satisfaction than he had hoped from the encounter. They had their assassin, their traitor in their midst, and now all they needed to do was pray that the king would find the other villains and rescue the prince. It had to work out that way. The Gryphon had ruled Penacles all Marner's life . . . even the life of Marner's father and grandfather. The king had battled demons, Dragon Kings, and sorcerers. Surely the outcome of this sordid episode would be no different.

And yet . . . how many of those past adversaries had actually infiltrated the kingdom? The general had studied the records of his predecessor enough to know that very few had managed such a feat and none had managed anything as outrageous as this.

Which gave him the uneasy feeling that his end of the matter had not yet been settled.

But what had he missed? Nothing, so far as he could see. Henrik had been the man inside, the one who had tricked the guards, murdered them, then stolen the young prince away. From there, it had been in the hands of those waiting beyond the walls.

All of this had been validated by Henrik's last, foolish act. There could be no doubt as to his guilt.

Then why did ghosts of doubt still haunt Marner?

He went about his duties constantly at war with himself over the situation. Toos

416

would have no doubt tied up the matter simply and cleanly. Yet, on the surface, things concerning the present situation seemed just as simple and clean to the general. Had his predecessor lived with such ridiculous doubts after each case? The indomitable Toos?

"Of course not," Marner chided himself.

As night drew near and the palace settled down, he removed his helm and went to his quarters. The commanding general of Penacles's armed forces had a varied and unusual list of duties far different at times from that of most of his counterparts. He acted as major domo for the king, saw to the personal running of the palace guard, and still had to deal with the military might protecting the kingdom. If Marner had any grudge against the late Toos, it was that his predecessor had set such high standards that *no one* could possibly match him.

Yet, the general tried.

As he entered his room, he uncoupled his sword sheath and set the weapon aside. Seating himself at the table and planting his booted feet atop it, he drank some ale. When forced to attend formal functions, Marner drank the elegant wines, but for his own personal consumption he enjoyed the heavy ale popular among the troops. The thick brew provided nourishment and increased the stamina. A good soldier just had to know his limits.

Still the question of Henrik plagued him, tempting Marner to drink more than was his wont. He finally shoved the flagon away and brooded. Perhaps if he once more inspected the traitor's trail he would finally be able to rest.

He almost left his sword, but force of habit made him latch it on again before stepping out. Only a few torches lit the hallways at night. Accustomed to the shadows, the veteran officer strode determinedly down the corridors, nodding to the occasional sentry.

After some time, he came to section where the palace guard itself was quartered. The sprawling complex that was the palace enabled the king to keep a good-sized contingent of ready soldiers nearby. Built to accommodate the Dragon King who had once ruled here, most of the rooms were immense. This enabled each member of the palace guard to even have their own individual spaces, divided from those of their comrades by tall partitions.

The sentries at the entrance snapped to attention, but Marner quickly put a finger to his lips. He had no desire to awaken his men. With stealth commendable for a human—no one could match the king or queen—he headed toward the late Henrik's cot.

Marner seized a candle from the short table next to the cot, then lit it with the tinder left behind by the late resident. At his order, nothing had been disturbed since last he had inspected the place. Putting the candle aside, the general quietly turned over the blankets and inspected the rails. As before, he found nothing. Marner searched under the table, studied every personal item . . . and yet again he found nothing.

Some minutes later, the bulky fighter straightened. He stared down in disgust at the objects before him. With one last grunt, Marner doused the candle with his fingertips and started out.

Force of habit made him check on the slumbering figures as he walked past. Each of them he considered good men, which had been in part why Henrik's betrayal had struck him so hard. Like their commander, the sleeping men would have given their lives for their king and queen. The Gryphon and his mate did not rule by power alone; they also ruled by common sense and compassion. Marner could think of no better master and mistress to have.

Some of the beds lay empty, those men on duty. The general absently acknowledged each, knowing those on night activity often had the riskiest tasks. The kidnapping of the prince proved that.

417

Still frustrated, Marner headed for the exit. He thanked the heavens that none of the slumbering soldiers had noticed his search. They might have thought that their commander had lost his wits—

Hand on the door, Marner suddenly looked back into the darkened chamber.

With the same stealth that had enabled him to already once cross a room full of crack troops without waking any, the general hurried along. His narrowed gaze rapidly shifted from left to right and back again, studying each individual section.

And then he came across the one he sought.

The bed should have been occupied. He had been here long enough for the soldier who used it to return from any necessities. The palace guard lived by strict rules. No one went wandering aimlessly about the building.

So where had Juren gone?

VIII

Orril D'Marr had not tried any physical torture on either father or son. He had even fed Darot and allowed the child to deal with nature, then had bound the boy again. The Gryphon had been provided with some water, but no one had even suggested that he be released for even a moment. Still, overall the Gryphon had been treated far worse by captors over the decades, including other Aramites.

He knew it was not because of any civil streak. Orril D'Marr was simply letting him see that the wolf raider controlled entirely the situation. The lives of both were his. That, in turn, made it clear that the lives of Troia and the unborn infant were just as much D'Marr's to save or execute.

It was typical of the wolf raider. Orril D'Marr did everything with a mask of indifference draped across his face. Only the results revealed his true, monstrous self.

A slight clatter set every nerve in the Gryphon afire. Two stones remaining. When the next dropped, they would come for Darot.

He eyed the two Aramites left guarding him. One had always been watching him, which had made any plans of escape futile. Of late, however, the two men had become bored. Now they spent more time playing some secretive game of wager than paying attention to their captive. The glances toward the Gryphon had grown less frequent.

The noise made both men look up. One smiled maliciously at him, then both resumed their game.

He had to act now. Surely this time they would forget him long enough . . .

The Gryphon began contorting his legs.

When they had brought him here, his captors had chained his wrists and ankles. They had left his boots on, securing the bonds tight enough to make it impossible for a normal man to slip free his feet. The Gryphon had to assume that the Quel had been the ones to do that, for surely if the Aramites had done it, they would have realized the error in doing so.

His muscles ached and his bones felt ready to crack, but still he silently twisted his legs, trying to slip his feet free. The long, avian-leonine appendages were narrower than human feet. The special boots kept them set so that he lost no mobility even though he nearly stood on his toes. When transforming to a more human shape, the Gryphon even often left his lower limbs unchanged, since those were not visible. Only around his family did he generally make a full transformation and usually when the occasion allowed him to make use of other, more mundane footwear.

418

Now that habit offered him his only hope.

The braces squeezed tight against his flesh as he pulled upward. The task was made all the more difficult by his having to keep the chains from rattling.

Darot watched his father, but whether or not he understood what was happening, the Gryphon could not say. To his credit, the child remained silent, drawing no attention to them.

Suddenly, one foot slipped free. The chain rattled slightly as the boot shifted, but the Gryphon managed to keep it from doing enough to attract the guards' attention. His foot remained inside, his toes bent to keep the boot from falling free.

A moment later, the second slipped free. Again the metal links rattled.

One of the Aramites looked up. He tapped his comrade on the shoulder and pointed at the Gryphon.

The two black-armored figures approached, the first drawing his blade. Neither appeared overly-concerned, but both were veteran fighters.

"My son could use water. So could I."

"He'll live without it, if he lives at all," smirked the first. "And we've orders to give you nothing more unless you tell us what we want."

"I'll be happy to tell you mongrels where to go . . . "

"Beast!" The second moved to slap the Gryphon hard with his gauntleted hand. "You'll learn your place!"

The hand flew toward the captive's face.

The Gryphon pulled both feet free, using the rock and the chains on his wrists to swiftly fold his body upward. As he moved, the claws of each toe extended to their full length.

Razor-sharp nails tore out the throats of both men.

Neither had even a chance to gasp out a warning cry. They froze for a moment, then one slumped toward the Gryphon while the other fell back.

With one foot he caught the second, pulling him forward. Both corpses fell on the Gryphon. He heard a muffled gasp from Darot, but after that his son quieted.

Slowly the Gryphon let the body on his right slip to the ground. The second he held near. With his free foot, he reached toward the guard's belt.

The keys jangled as he removed them. The body shifted, almost causing the Gryphon to lose the precious items. He quickly compensated, managing to keep the keys snagged on one one claw.

Lowering the second raider, the Gryphon twisted his legs upward, nearly folding himself in half. His back strained and the keys slipped to one side. With a silent curse, he brought them around so that the other foot could seize the one he needed.

Each second he feared either one of the Aramites or a Quel would come in to check on the guards, but the shadowed entrances remained empty. Before him, the cursed clock that D'Marr had wrought with Quel magic continued to shift, the next stone already dimming. The minutes raced by as the Gryphon struggled to get the key into the lock and turn it enough to open the cuff.

The harshness of the click so startled him that he lost his grip on all the keys. They dropped to the hard cavern ground, their crash echoing even more than the opening of the cuff had.

Darot shifted nervously, but the Gryphon stilled him with a shake of his head. Turning his wrist, the king freed his hand, then tugged on the other.

In the tunnels leading to the cavern there came the sounds of hooting.

Grabbing at the keys with his foot, the Gryphon brought them up to his hand. He thrust the principal one in the lock and quickly turned it.

Darot made a soft sound through his gag.

The Gryphon looked toward the tunnels.

A WOLF IN THE FOLD

A hulking Quel wielding a spear emerged from the darkness, its gem-encrusted, segmented shell glittering in the light of the cavern's own crystals. The narrow red eyes took in the two bodies and the struggling captive . . . then the creature let out a loud cry of warning and charged.

Despite the key, the manacle would not yet open. The Gryphon tugged hard at it as his attacker approached, but still it did not give.

The Quel thrust. The point of the lance came at the Gryphon's chest.

He twisted around, using the remaining chain to enable him to swing out of the weapon's range. The point smashed against the rock, breaking off.

Ignoring the metal cutting into his wrist, the Gryphon propelled himself around the rock, swinging quickly toward his attacker's blind side.

The Quel started to turn, but in comparison to the Gryphon, he moved as if in slow motion. The prisoner wrapped his legs around the broad neck and squeezed.

Its breath cut off, the snouted beast instinctively pulled away.

The half-open manacle could not hold up to the strain. It snapped in two.

Pulling himself up, the Gryphon sank his hands into one of the ridges that divided each segment of the shell. He buried his claws in the tender flesh within.

Shrieking, the Quel abruptly fell back.

Before his adversary's massive weight could crush him against the floor, the Gryphon squirmed free. The Quel's desperate attempt proved a costly one for the underdweller, for, having failed to grind his foe into the ground, he now had to push himself up.

The Gryphon did not allow him that chance. Seizing the broken lance shaft, he jammed it into the open area under the snout.

With a last hissing squeal, the creature stilled.

But other cries already filled the tunnels, some of them human. The Gryphon hurried to his son, slicing Darot's bonds with one action.

"Come!" He led the child into the corridor that offered the least echoes of threat. Whether it also offered entrance to the surface, the Gryphon could not say, but he thought he sensed a slight hint of air current indicating so.

The clink of armor warned him of their approach before the wolf raiders could strike. Shoving Darot against the far wall, the Gryphon ducked under a sword blade. He slammed his fist against the armored chest and although the action pained him greatly, he had the satisfaction of watching the Aramite stumble back.

Claws out, the Gryphon slashed at the sword arm. One nail dug deep in the wrist where the armor by necessity ended. The wolf raider cursed, dropping his weapon and falling back as he he tried to bind the deadly cut.

As the second marauder drove forward, the king seized the fallen blade. The two battled for several precious seconds. At last, the Gryphon came under the other's guard, then caught him along the nose.

With a cry, the Aramite dropped to the ground, face crimson. Without compunction, the Gryphon ran him through, then turned to confront the first. However, the other Aramite had already fled, a trail of blood indicating that he would not likely live long despite his retreat.

His son in tow, the Gryphon continued on. A short distance later, he paused at a crossroads in the tunnels. By now, Darot had removed his gag, but he remained silent, trusting in his father.

Sniffing the air, the Gryphon chose the passage on the right. After only a few steps, he grew certain of his choice. Pausing to make an inspection of the walls, the Gryphon finally looked down at his son.

"Listen, Darot. You'll do exactly as I say?"

"Yes, father," the child whispered.

"Can you crawl up to that gap there? That one there. See it?"

Darot finally nodded. His eyes were as good as his father's when it came to the dark, but he lacked the latter's experience in ferreting out hiding places.

"Can you climb up there?"

At three years of age, Darot had been found climbing up the high walls of the palace. Rather than be frightened, as the servitors had been, his parents had watched him with pride—and then gone up to retrieve him. Some day, he would surpass both in his skills, but only if he survived now.

"Yes, father," the youth declared.

"Do so. I'll go to the entrance, lead those there deep in the tunnels. Wait until we're all past, then climb down and leave. Head toward the east . . . you recall which direction is east?"

"Yes, father." Most human children would have been unable to do what the Gryphon hoped of his son, but like any predatory creature, the offspring of the king and his mate matured at a quicker rate. Theoretically, Darot could reach home.

Realistically, it was the only hope the Gryphon had.

"I have to go find the human with the snowy hair. You understand that?" His son nodded, shivering at the same time. The Gryphon could hardly blame him. There were few humans who had filled him with the dread that Orril D'Marr did now. The Gryphon had no illusions that he would readily defeat the maimed Aramite. "He wants to hurt your mother. I have to stop him."

"I know, father."

Ducking down, the king gave Darot a quick, strong hug. He then guided the child up as Darot climbed toward the hiding place.

Pressed against the back, the boy was nearly invisible even to his father. The Gryphon nodded grim satisfaction, then headed toward the exit to freedom.

Just within sight of the night-enshrouded surface, the Quel came for him.

He immediately turned and fled back into the cavern complex, leading them away from his son just as he had planned. The three massive creatures crowded the corridor, their gem-encrusted shells radiating a dim light as they pursued him.

As the Gryphon spun around a corner, he nearly collided with another of the beasts. Fortunately, the Quel was as startled as him. The Gryphon used the Aramite blade to sever the head while the Quel still gaped.

Those pursuing unleashed harsh hoots of warning, which were immediately picked up by others deeper in the complex. A human voice—Orril D'Marr's—loudly but emotionlessly commanded them to close in on their prey from the very walls. The Gryphon was well aware that D'Marr expected him to hear that command and react accordingly, but he hoped that instead he would do what neither the underdwellers or D'Marr had in mind.

It was the only way he could hope to save Troia and the infant.

IX

General Marner could have summoned the entire guard, but instead he chose to seek Juren himself. It could be that he was wrong—he prayed he was wrong—but, if not, a troop of soldiers tramping around the building would only alert the other soldier to his suspicions.

Marner ran over the details again. On the surface, nothing proved that Juren was anything other than what he claimed. Still, he had been the one to react swiftest and his first action had been to toss the dagger at Henrik. What had seemed a survivable wound had become a death sentence thanks to the poison.

But that did not mean that Juren had known his strike would slay his comrade. Neither did the fact that he had been trying to pick up the dagger afterward indicate anything other than a soldier doing his duty. There was no reason for General Marner to be wary of the missing man.

And yet . . .

Without at first realizing it, he headed in the direction of the royal chambers. If his concerns had any merit, it behooved him to check on the security of the pregnant queen. She was well protected, but the kidnapping of the prince proved that even the best protections did not always work.

That thought came back to haunt him but a moment later when he noticed the slumped forms near the gilded doors.

Sword ready, he moved with stealth to the dead men's sides. Like the other guards, they had been killed with their own blades. One wore an expression of outright astonishment, as if he could not believe the identity of his killer.

Small wonder when it had been one of his own comrades.

Marner noticed then that one door was ajar. Cautiously, he nudged it open with the tip of his blade.

A single lamp remained lit within. It offered just enough illumination to reveal two more corpses . . . the female companions of the queen.

As he neared them, the general noticed a significant difference in their deaths. Blood splattered everything. The women's throats had been ripped apart. It looked more the work of an animal than a human being.

But then, in his opinion, wolf raiders were less than either.

At first he saw no sign of the queen, but then a faint blood trail from one of the women led him back to the doorway. Stepping over the dead guards, Marner searched for more telltale spots.

They led him toward the rear of the palace, toward where one of the huge balconies open during grand balls overlooked the ceremonial gardens. Below the balcony in question, Marner recalled, a huge fountain with a pointed spire had recently been constructed, a gift from the mountain kingdom of Talak.

Marner hurried his pace.

As he neared his destination, he suddenly noticed that all the torches ahead had been doused. Swearing silently, the commander planted himself against one wall and felt his way to down the vast corridor. His vision adjusted some as he went, enabling him to make out shapes.

And as the balcony came into view, he made out one shape in particular. Pregnant or not, there was no mistaking the queen. She stood as if frozen, her gaze turned toward the outside.

Marner started forward—and pulled back a second later when he noticed the other figure nearby.

His suspicions that it was Juren were verified when the figure raised a tiny, glowing emerald up, staring at it as if awaiting something from it. Juren wore an expression far different from his humble, youthful one. Marner recognized the fanaticism, the utter obsession Juren had to his cause.

The general could only assume that dark cause now demanded the queen's death.

Moving slowly toward the traitor, Marner held the sword high. One quick stroke would remove both the crystal and Juren's hand.

But as he readied the strike, the younger soldier suddenly slipped aside. He clenched his fingers over the crystal, dousing the dim light. At the same time, he drew with his other hand his sword.

"General Marner . . . I was coming to see you later, sir."

"For what reason? To add me to your list of victims?"

Although he could barely make out Juren's shape, much less his countenance, the commander knew that the latter wore a callous smile. "Yes, sir. Exactly that."

The general lunged, almost catching Juren in the throat. The traitor brought his own weapon up, deflecting Marner's blade. They traded blows for a moment, with Juren quickly forced back onto the balcony. Marner's hopes rose as the wolf raider barely kept his guard against the elder fighter.

Too late did the commander realize that Juren played him.

As they neared the still figure of the queen, Juren suddenly leapt toward her. He did not seize her or run her through as Marner feared, but rather simply pointed the tip of his blade at her swollen stomach.

"Drop your weapon, general. Do it now. The dagger on your belt, too."

Marner hesitated, then tossed the sword to the floor. He did the same with the smaller blade. That still left him with another that Juren could not know about, one that could be used the first moment that the traitor's concentration lapsed in the least.

But Juren was no fool himself. "What to do with you, eh, general? Each moment I keep you alive, you endanger our plan . . . "

"What? To kill the king's family?"

Juren snorted. "No . . . to free our god!"

Recalling what he had heard concerning the Aramite deity, Marner retorted, "Pretty petty god, if he needs the likes of you to help him escape."

"He was weakened! Our faith lacked and it cost him! But we grow strong again!"

How had the likes of this one slipped through, Marner wondered. Every word was seeped in zealous loyalty to the beast called the Ravager.

"So what you want is the information that the king has. That's why you kidnapped his son."

"We know the misfit well," Juren answered, referring, so the general gathered, to the Gryphon. "Only his family could break him. It nearly did when he lost his firstborn . . . "

The general shifted ever so slightly, noting with relief that Juren did not see him move. He needed to stall the villain a little more. If Marner could unhook the other dagger—

"How did you manage to drag the boy out of here? I could understand you being able to kill the guards, but there was no sign of a struggle—"

"The sons of the wolf inherit his cunning," Juren replied, as if quoting something. He continued, "Who best to quietly rouse a youngster from his bed and guide him to our waiting arms? Who better to slay guards without they're having any prior warning?"

Marner could not conceal his sudden intake of breath. He gazed at the shadowy form of the queen. "The pendant . . . "

"Aye. A thoughtful gift from her loyal servants . . . suggested by Henrik and *me*, if you recall."

He did . . . now. "You slew Henrik!"

"He gave his life for his god. It was all planned ahead." Juren held open his palm, in the glow of the crystal revealing his manic expression. "This, the one she wears, and another held by my Pack Leader are all part of the same. Through this, I link to the last, communicate with Lord D'Marr. He gives the order . . . I send the queen leaping off the rail."

It made no sense to keep her alive . . . unless . . . . "You're keeping her alive in case the king's willing to sacrifice his second son."

"He may be capable of that . . . but will also he suffer the loss of his cat and the last of their get?" Juren shook his head. "Even the vaunted Gryphon has his limits, general."

Too true. Darot would be the example that would prove to the king that he had no choice. If he did not give them what they wanted, they would then have Troia kill herself . . . and slay the third son in the process.

"Twisted minds," he murmured. Marner turned his arm slightly, feeling the hidden blade position itself. He expected no aid from the palace guard; Juren had chosen the most secluded spot for his deviltry.

The wolf raider edged closer to the queen. He held up the stone so that Marner could see her blank expression. The general could also make out the drying blood on her clawed hands.

Juren had used Queen Troia as the means of murdering her own bodyguards.

" 'Tis nearly time, general. I thank you for giving me something to distract me, but now the game's ended. She's got just a few minutes left to her . . . more than enough for one last hunt."

He held the crystal toward General Marner. To the latter's horror, the cat woman turned and stared at her subject.

"Which will it be, general? Can you kill your queen . . . or will you let her slay you?"

With that, Troia raised her hands. The bloody claws extended to their fullest . . . and the queen leapt at Marner.

X

Orril D'Marr stood in the glittering chamber, gaze fixed upon the macabre timepiece the Quel had made at his request. In his palm rested the final triplet. Only one blue stone now hovered, a stone whose slow descent he watched avidly.

That still did not prevent him from noticing when he was no longer alone.

"I thought you'd come sooner," he remarked without turning.

The Gryphon crept out of one of the dark tunnels. He had spent the past hour evading the pursuing Quel and Aramites. Several of each lay dead and the rest followed false trails. The Gryphon had utilized valuable time just so that he and his nemesis could be left uninterrupted.

"Slay me and she dies," D'Marr commented, turning slowly toward him. His ruined arm he left hidden under his cloak. "My agent will know the mission is lost and will therefore take action."

"You plan to kill her, anyway." The Gryphon strode toward the wolf raider, gaze shifting constantly as he sought traps. Orril D'Marr was too calm, even for him. "That leaves me with little inclination to save your own miserable existence, cur."

"But one word from me and she will be spared. She . . . and your unborn."

"One word that you'd never give, D'Marr."

The wolf raider bowed slightly, keeping the crystal visible. "You do know me . . . ."

A sense of dread filled the Gryphon.

He leapt up just as the floor exploded.

The Quel leader burst through, savage claws nearly ripping off the Gryphon's leg. The Gryphon landed just as the huge creature fully emerged.

424

Orril D'Marr actually laughed. "I imagine you think you were responsible for the rest running off on fools' chases! We knew you wouldn't show yourself unless we made it clear that I was alone."

But suddenly the Gryphon bounded toward the Quel, taking him by surprise. Out came the blade the king had seized from the dead Aramite.

The leader of the underdwellers tensed, awaiting the inevitable assault. D'Marr watched in amusement as the Gryphon sought to take on an opponent far larger and better prepared than him.

As he dropped upon the Quel, the Gryphon suddenly twisted. His feet came first, striking his gigantic adversary hard. The Quel shook but held his ground.

Using the beast as a launching board, the Gryphon flung himself on top of the Aramite.

Startled, Orril D'Marr thrust the crystal into his belt and reached with his good hand for his mace. He succeeded only in loosening it before the two of them collided.

Releasing his grip on the blade, the Gryphon seized the mace. He struck the wolf raider hard in the jaw, then rolled away.

The Aramite lay still, stunned by the attack. The monstrous Quel hooted as he charged.

Praying that D'Marr's new mace acted like the old, the Gryphon twisted part of the handle, then thrust.

As the glittering head sank into the armored hide of the Quel, a flash of crimson lightning coursed over the huge form. The Quel shrieked, but could not pull away.

The Gryphon had only hoped to stun the leader, but what happened next astonished him. The back of the Quel began exploding, one burst after another resounding harshly in the chamber.

It was the way of the Quel to plant crystals of various significance and power in the folds and creases between their armored plates as they matured. With age, the folds tightened, keeping the crystals forever held in place. The Quel used them not only to somehow ward away much of Legar's oppressive heat, but also to absorb and adapt the natural magic of the world and use it.

And now, years of potent power stored by their leader had been unleashed.

Fire raked the Quel as he struggled to free himself. The Gryphon pulled back, but the fury continued unabated. Still shrieking, the Quel leader stumbled into one wall of the chamber—and set that too into magical combustion.

An arm suddenly snaked around the Gryphon's throat, cutting off his air. Orril D'Marr's maddeningly calm voice whispered, "You've chosen death for her . . . and your offspring."

For a human with one arm, D'Marr was surprisingly strong. The Gryphon had no doubt that the Aramite had been strengthening his remaining limb since first the Quel had discovered him, but it was more than that. Now he understood what his foe had meant about being 'enhanced'.

Instead of struggling against the impossible, the Gryphon propelled both of them backward. He heard a startled gasp from D'Marr just before the latter collided with the nearest wall.

The wolf raider let loose with a grunt of pain. His arm shifted, allowing the Gryphon all he needed to free himself.

The chamber still sparkled with unleashed energy, but the Quel leader, although burnt badly in several places, now appeared to have recovered. Meanwhile, from the tunnels emerged several Aramites and other Quel, all intent on seizing the Gryphon.

He twisted around, pulling D'Marr in front. Thrusting the head of the mace just under the wolf raider's chin, the Gryphon shouted, "Get back! No one comes closer or I use this on him!"

The Aramites immediately obeyed, but the Quel were less inclined. They moved cautiously, seeking to avoid the harsh injuries that their leader had suffered.

"Your allies seem not to care a whit about you, D'Marr. Remind them of your importance."

He expected his foe to reject his suggestion, but D'Marr called out, "Do as he says. Stay back."

The underdwellers looked to their ruler. Leaning against one of his followers, the stricken Quel eyed the two with blazing orbs. A sound more like the hiss of a snake than a hoot finally erupted from his blackened snout.

The others surged forward.

Orril D'Marr's men looked to him.

"Stop them, of course, you fools!" he snapped, revealing more emotion than the Gryphon had ever noted before.

The wolf raiders threw themselves on the larger, brawnier Quel. The Gryphon expected the humans to be slaughtered, but D'Marr had evidently planned for such a contingency, for his fighters maneuvered with purpose about the slower beasts, aiming for those specific spots where the armored hides gave way to soft flesh.

This by no means meant that the Quel were instead cut down. As one fell to the twin blades of two Aramites, another Quel seized the first of the pair, raised him up over his head, and threw him across the chamber.

Mayhem filled the cavern. With no knowledge of numbers, the Gryphon could not estimate who had the upper hand, but that hardly mattered. All he cared about was escape. Troia and the baby might be dead, but Darot still needed his father.

"Come!" he snapped in D'Marr's ear.

As he steered his prisoner toward the exit leading to the surface, the Gryphon noticed the one-armed wolf raider try to toss something aside.

The emerald. The king almost ignored it, certain that he could do nothing to save his mate and unborn child, but then wondered why D'Marr should go through the trouble of trying to surreptitiously dispose of the supposedly-useless crystal.

On a hunch, he shoved the Aramite forward, then used the moment to sweep up the crystal. D'Marr tried to run, but the Gryphon seized him again, using the mace to keep him under control.

As they ran through the passage, he evaluated everything he knew about D'Marr's twisted mind. If the raider still needed the crystal to slay Troia, he would have kept it secreted on him. If he no longer needed it—meaning that Troia was already dead—the Aramite would have simply let it fall, not tossed it aside so carefully.

But if Troia still lived . . .

Behind them, a human scream echoed. The clash of arms resounded like thunder. A frantic hoot cut off suddenly. Despite the danger still nearby, the Gryphon abruptly halted, tossing his captive against one side of the tunnel and putting the mace as close to Orril D'Marr's bland countenance.

"The crystal. How does it work?" When D'Marr said nothing, he touched the wolf raider ever so slightly with the mace. The Aramite flinched, his eyes if not his expression revealing the pain he had just suffered. "Tell me now."

D'Marr remained silent.

The Gryphon had neither the time nor the stomach for torture. The sounds of fighting grew closer, possibly meaning that the wolf raiders had begun a retreat out of the chamber toward the surface.

Searching his memory for all he knew of crystal magic, the Gryphon came to a dire decision. He might be condemning Troia to the death she had so far avoided, but he had no other choice.

Dropping the stone, the Gryphon turned the mace so that the hilt hovered above

426

the former.

With all his might, he smashed the crystal. A brief flare of power brightened the tunnel, revealing only Orril D'Marr's guarded countenance.

Pressing his beak close to the Aramite's face, the Gryphon snarled, "If she's dead, I'll rip your flesh from your skull with one snap!"

Shoving the wolf raider forward, he went in search of the exit and Darot.

XI

"Rip his throat out," Juren commanded, sneering. "Rip it out!"

But as she leapt, the queen suddenly twisted in mid-air. Even her pregnant state did nothing to lessen her agility as she came around and turned the claws that had been about to slash Marner across the face and throat against the traitorous guard instead.

Troia ripped open the right side of Juren's cheek. He cried out, stumbling back and dropping his sword. His hand immediately went for a dagger in his belt.

Troia landed in a half-crouched position, for the first time showing some awkwardness. She pressed one hand against her stomach, clearly fighting to keep her baby safe.

Juren drew the dagger.

General Marner threw his first.

The blade sank into the Aramite's throat. With a gurgle of astonishment, Juren dropped both the knife and the crystal, then staggered back.

And over the rail.

Marner heard the inevitable crash, but paid it no mind. He knelt anxiously beside his queen.

"General . . ." she gasped. "I think I'm about to give birth."

He studied what remained of the pendant, curious as to its demise. The emerald gem had cracked, as if some great force had struck it. Marner had no doubt that only that had prevented the queen from attacking him instead of Juren. The king had promised to explain it to him, but with so much else going on . . .

"She fares well," a familiar voice suddenly announced.

"Praise be," returned the general, looking up.

It had been rough going for the queen, the birth of her third son more strenuous thanks to events. She had managed the actual act quickly enough, but then had fallen ill. Over the next week, she had eaten little. Her condition had been no better when the king and prince had arrived. The Gryphon had immediately ordered everyone away from her, then had ministered to his mate himself.

Two days later, the queen had begun to show recuperation. Now she not only fed herself, but her newborn as well.

"And the child, your majesty?"

"Trajan has good lungs."

The baby's lusty voice now filled this section of the palace. To Marner, he seemed to be declaring his place in the royal family, a place nearly stolen from him by Juren.

Thinking of Juren made him think of another, more foul personage. "I've done as you commanded, my liege. His cell is solid rock not only in terms of the walls and ceiling, but also the earth. It's been doubly-reinforced there, in fact. Nothing could

427

possibly dig through."

The Gryphon nodded darkly. "Let us hope so." The avian countenance brightened again. "You have my gratitude, general. You risked your life for Troia."

" 'Tis my duty, your majesty. I could do no less than my predecessor would have."

"Marner . . . Toos was a friend, a comrade, from well before my reign. He wielded a magic of sorts, too. I do not expect you to be him. You have your own skills and I wouldn't have chosen you to replace him if I hadn't agreed with his judgment. You are deserving of the position."

Touched, Marner knelt. "I thank you my lord."

The lionbird shook off the matter. "Now we must return to the matter of D'Marr."

"He will be executed, of course."

"Not until he's told us all we can drain from him. This new resurgence of Aramite activity bodes ill. I expect that there are others with plots akin to his. They want their god back, Marner, and I intend to thwart them in that effort."

"You can rely on me," the general offered. "Come the morning, I shall begin in earnest on the wolf raider."

"Let's hope we have that long."

"Your majesty?"

The Gryphon blinked, then shook his head. "Just anxiety. I know where you've buried him. D'Marr won't be going anywhere."

A child's laugh caught their attention. The Gryphon's form immediately shifted, becoming that of the noble, silver-haired man. He smiled warmly at the sound. "Darot plays with his brother. It's good to hear them both! Come, Marner! Let me show off my son . . . both my sons!"

His hands were bound so that he could do no harm to himself. He could not eat without aid. They kept him chained against the wall, with no light by which he could study his surroundings.

Even in the deep cell under the palace in which they had put him, Orril D'Marr could hear the faint sounds of the infant son of his enemy. In the dark, his face could not be seen, but for one of the rare times in his life, the Aramite wore a frown. That frown, along with eyes also hidden by the blackness, barely hinted at the intense venom he felt for those above.

They planned to come for him in the next day or two, using what methods at hand to pry knowledge from him. They would seek to find out more about what others like him intended, what others were doing to restore the glory of the empire and find their stolen god.

They would learn nothing from him. Nothing. He was loyal to the Ravager. He would not betray his god.

A sound, a so slight sound, reached his ears. He had heard it more than once since his recent incarceration.

The sound of claws digging at rock.

They had followed. Whether or not as allies, the Quel had followed him. He had learned that the creatures were very vengeful and they likely blamed him as much as the Gryphon for the debacle. Their leader certainly had no love for the Aramite, not after the injuries suffered because of D'Marr's weapon.

Orril D'Marr welcomed them either way. They would keep him from the Gryphon's interrogators and there stood a chance that, given the opportunity, he could convince them of his continued value alive.

If not . . .

Expression once more emotionless, the wolf raider set his head on the stones near where he heard the scratching. He shut his eyes and listened.

And waited . . .

A WOLF IN THE FOLD

A GAME OF GHOSTS

The past will always catch up . . .

I

She watched the three drake warriors rummage through the remains of what had been some twenty-plus years ago a merchant's grand home. The ruined estate—now enveloped by forest—lay on the outskirts of an even more vast ruin, that of the kingdom of Mito Pica. Outwardly, There was not much left of the once-stately house, mostly a scorched foundation and a crumbling, crushed roof. The rooms, the riches, the inhabitants, they were buried deep under that refuse, untouched even after so long.

There were few foolish enough to intrude into this accursed land and drakes were not among those Marilee Cord would have expected. Even more curious, they did not even seem all that interested in the burnt, overgrown rubble. It was as if they were just biding their time.

Marilee started to retreat to the others, only to hesitate when one of the drakes' savage mounts let out a low hiss. The reptilian beasts peered behind them as the three armored figures held their long, sharp swords ready.

But the interruption proved to only be the arrival of a fourth warrior. While the helms of the first three drakes were dramatic enough with their savage, dragon head crests—crests that were, in fact, representative of their true natures—that of the fourth was startling in its intricacy. The blood of a Dragon King flowed through this one, even if by being here the egg from which he had hatched had clearly not borne the royal markings needed to become an heir.

A humorless smile played across her pale face. The hint of blue gray in their mail armor identified them for Marilee. She had something in common with this foursome, at least in respect to their all being refugees of a sort. What survivors of long-ravaged Clan Iron were doing so far west from either their former domain or the drake confederacy of which they were supposed to be part was a question that intrigued her, but not enough to risk herself.

As the last hint of sunlight faded, Marilee, her dagger ever held ready, backed away. She and the others would decide what to do about these intruders. True, their color might not be gold, as the slaughterers' of Mito Pica's innocents had been, but they were drakes. If there were only four, then the vote would very likely be for blood, no matter what the cost. It had been a long time since the band had shed drake blood.

It was far overdue.

A sharp crack to her right made her freeze. The branch she had been pushing aside broke off, creating more racket.

Hisses arose from the drakes. Marilee remained still, hoping that they would lose interest.

Instead, she heard the slight rustle of movement toward her location. Another brief hiss warned her that at least one of the warriors was already too near.

Marilee broke into a run.

Sharp hisses rose. The foliage behind her shook violently. Marilee wanted to

431

stand her ground, but she could not face four drakes by herself.

Something huge crashed through the forest to her left. The panting hiss of a riding drake warned her that one of her pursuers—likely the leader—was mounted. The monstrous beast tore apart the young, bent trees between the reptilian warrior and his prey.

The others were on the far side of the ruined city and thus no help to her. Marilee believed that she could outrun the drakes on foot, but not the mounted one. The forest was not thick enough to slow his beast appreciably.

Marilee stumbled over an upturned root. She fell against the thick tree trunk and though the moment cost her only a second or two, it was long enough to enable her foremost foe to reach her.

The riding drake snapped at her, but missed. Its rider hissed and slashed at Marilee with a blade longer than her arm. The deadly edge scraped along the trunk where but the moment before the brown-haired woman had stood. Bits of bark flew at the diving Marilee.

"Human ssscum!" the rider rasped. "You'll not be warning him!"

She paid his words no mind, more interested in survival. Her dagger was woefully inadequate against either his sword or his mount.

He swung again, but a thick branch Marilee could not recall seeing blocked his attack. The blade sank deep, but not deep enough to cut through the wood.

The drake's mount lunged toward her, only to snag one forepaw on another upturned tree root. Marilee thanked her good luck, but doubted it would last unless she ran as hard as she could.

To her relief, the path ahead opened up just enough for her to push on. Behind her, Marilee heard the drake hiss in frustration as he chopped at the branch. His monstrous mount let out a roar that echoed his master's fury.

Then, the rider let out an odd gasp that caused Marilee to dare look back. Her eyes widened to saucers as she witnessed the armored figure hefted up like a tiny infant by a branch curled around his throat. The snarling drake struggled as he rose out of sight.

Bereft of its master's control, the hulking mount snapped futilely at more and more roots and branches that gathered around it. Already, two legs were entangled.

And somewhere farther back, one of the other drake warriors suddenly shrieked.

Shaking, Marilee spun away from the riding drake and resumed running. The path ahead continued to offer her just enough of a gap to allow Marilee to keep her pace up. Behind her, shouts arose among the drakes and one of the mounts hissed sharply. Fortunately for Marilee, the sounds grew fainter, as if the gap between her and her foes was growing. Yet, still she ran.

Only when the lithe woman finally ran out of breath, only when her heart threatened to explode, did she finally come to a halt. By this time, it was very dark. Marilee planted herself against a tree trunk and while she fought for air, she listened for pursuit.

All was silence. Stepping out, Marilee squinted, but saw nothing but black forest.

Common sense said to keep fleeing, but instead Marilee—as she too often had in her life—found herself choosing to dive back into potential danger. She headed to where the drakes had last been. The more the chilling silence dominated the region before her, the quicker her pace became. She had to see what had happened—

And then, just as abruptly, Marilee came to a horrified halt.

The tableau before her so shook the woman to her soul that she dropped her dagger without noticing. She stared at the grotesquely twisted corpse and how it remained posed as it did.

A GAME OF GHOSTS

Marilee's mouth gaped, but no cry escaped.

She whirled around and ran even as she had not when pursued by the drakes. Marilee ran and when she could run no more, she stumbled on a step at a time. Behind her, there was only silence . . . but that was enough in itself to keep her going.

II

A chill ran through the wizard Cabe Bedlam as he materialized. It was not that the wind was particularly cold or strong, but rather the spellcaster's instinctive reaction to these surroundings. Even though he had been raised here, Mito Pica held nothing but guilt for him. After all, the city had been razed, many of its people slain, all because of *him*.

If not for his blue wizard's robes and the great, tell-tale streak of silver in his otherwise black hair, most who had met him would not have immediately taken the youthful figure for arguably the most powerful mage in all the land. With his strong jaw and crooked nose, he looked more like a farmer, something which had caused more than one rival to underestimate him. Cabe could have altered his features, but was quite satisfied with them. They reminded him of who he truly was, not who almost everyone believed him.

Cabe fought back a sneeze. Even after more than two decades, he could still smell scorched land, the burning bodies. Each and every one of those who had perished remained a black spot on his soul, for the servants of the Dragon Emperor had been seeking him when they had torn asunder the city that had unknowingly given the grandson of the legendary Nathan Bedlam succor. Nathan Bedlam had led the Dragon Masters—a group of mages dedicated to freeing humanity from the harsh rule of the drakes—into what had come to be known as the Turning War. The mages had lost as much from treachery in their own ranks as they had the power of the Dragon Kings, but at least they had dealt the drakes a terrible blow.

Nathan himself had perished in part due to seeking to save his dying grandchild, then only an infant. He had also put Cabe in the hands of his most trusted friend, the half-elf Hadeen. Hadeen had been the only parent Cabe had ever known, a good thing since the wizard's father had been the mad sorcerer, Azran.

Hadeen . . . the tall, slim half-elf had looked no older than Cabe did now, but had actually been more than two hundred years old. Indeed, Cabe's own youth had lasted almost as long, Hadeen keeping him magically hidden for two centuries in the ill-fated belief that doing so would gradually make the Dragon Kings forget that a grandson might exist.

Cabe peered at the forest, noting the new growth and that which had survived the razing. So much life in a place of so much death. A shame the main city itself is still a blackened skeleton..

It was still two hours before sunset, more than enough time for what he planned here. Cabe had no desire to remain in Mito Pica come the night. Even more than most, the spellcaster saw Mito Pica as place of tortured spirits, ghosts. Ghosts that condemned him each and every moment of his life.

Cabe slowly strode through the woods toward his intended destination. Even Gwen, his wife and a powerful enchantress, did not suspect the depths of his guilt. Cabe Bedlam heard the cries of the dead day and night . . . and that was what had

433

brought him back here this day, the very anniversary of Mito Pica's destruction.

He peered up at some of the taller trees, recognizing a few giants. Cabe never liked to materialize at his final location; it was as much out of respect as it was guilt.

The forest remained quiet save for the occasional call of a crow. There always seemed to be crows here, Cabe noted dourly, as if they were hoping for some great bounty such as upon which their ancestors had feasted. The wizard was tempted to cast some sudden noise in order to scare them away, but held back out of respect for the long-dead.

He passed a few bits of rubble—the foundation of some farmer's home—and paused for a moment to see if he could recall who had lived there. That Cabe could not remember either a name or even a face troubled him. Time was gradually blurring his memory and of all those who had survived—not a great number and mostly children—it was he who should have done his utmost to remember all he could.

Please forgive me, he asked the fading memories. *I've tried to make amends* . . .

A young woman giggled.

Cabe spun. He saw no one, but there was no doubt in his mind that he had not imagined the sound. Wary, the spellcaster stepped forward—and then stumbled to a halt as a glowing figure suddenly formed among the trees ahead.

A woman with long, flowing black hair leaned down as if seeking to pick up something. The hair obscured her face. She moved with gentleness, as if the burden she sought was precious. Her gown was elegant, but of a style he could not place.

The wizard started toward her, only to be distracted by the clatter of metal against metal coming from his right. Cabe had been involved in too many wars over the years to not recognize the distinctive shifting of armor.

To the naked eye, the wizard acted instantly. To Cabe's eye, he reached out to the crisscrossing lines of energy invisibly covering the world and used some of that energy to cast his spell. The area he pointed at exploded in light, not only giving Cabe a view of whatever threat might be there, but also hopefully stunning that threat.

But what the wizard saw instead staggered him for its horror.

Arms outstretched, the drake warrior first appeared to float above him. That illusion quickly gave way to another, that the drake had been bound to the branches of the nearest tree.

But what the gaping mouth, the ghastly rips in the limbs and torso, the drying blood and the milky, staring eyes actually revealed was that the branches of the tree coursed through the drake's body. Two branches thrust out from the mouth, others from the wrists and ankles. A huge limb impaled the warrior through the chest, but Cabe doubted that it had been what killed the drake. Indeed, from the contorted expression, the victim had suffered horribly before finally being granted death.

Leaving some illumination, the wizard approached. As stunning as the sight was, Cabe remained attentive enough to note the drake's coloring. He had not seen a warrior of Clan Iron for decades, though he knew that that the survivors were part of a confederacy in the northwest. This drake had no business being here.

Yet what other force had also not only thought as Cabe, but acted on that belief?

Even so close, Cabe could not sense the spellwork used to slay the intruder. Not for a moment did the wizard assume that this force would be benevolent toward him; experience had taught him just the opposite.

The drake had been dead at least a day. Blackbirds had already picked at the corpse, though they appeared to find the scaled form not much to their liking. Cabe studied the drake for a moment more, then finally decided to move on. Curious as he was about the warrior's demise, it behooved the wizard to stay as far away as possible from the situation.

But barely had Cabe taken more than a dozen steps when he came upon the next and much larger victim. The riding drake's macabre pose made that of its presumed master seem gentle by comparison. The savage mount had obviously struggled longer and more desperately than the warrior, but the results had been the same. A large branch thrust out of its huge maw and another through its barrel chest. Each of its limbs were stretched wide, smaller but no less sturdy branches sprouting near the paws. Despite its immense girth, the riding drake hovered several feet off the ground. Dried blood stained the earth beneath.

Cabe swore. As he maneuvered the light for a better view, he was rewarded with another dark form hanging from a tree farther on.

The second rider had suffered no less than the first and not far from him hung his own mount. Cabe shuddered. He did not know if there were more victims, but what he had seen thus far was enough to warn him that he had better move on by more efficient methods.

With little effort, the wizard vanished from the grotesque displays, appearing a breath later at a more familiar, if also personally saddening, tableau. Barely visible within a great sprouting of vegetation was what had been a small, unremarkable cabin. While it seemed no different than a number of other tiny ruins surrounding the devastated city, this one in particular touched Cabe.

After all, it had been the only home had had known for far longer than he had even realized.

Cabe turned his attention to a towering tree only a few short yards from the cabin. Stepping closer, he bent down on one knee, then shut his eyes in contemplation—

Something very hard struck him on the back of the head. As Cabe toppled forward, his last fading thought did not concern the failure of the protective spell he generally kept around him, but rather that perhaps Mito Pica had finally chosen to claim the one responsible for its destruction.

Marilee and the four other ragged figures eyed the unconscious spellcaster with some surprise. She looked at the short, onyx staff she had used to hit the wizard and finally grinned. "It worked!"

The nearest trees suddenly shivered, as if some strong wind blew through them. That there was not the hint of a breeze was not lost on the five.

"Bertran! Silas! Grab the wizard! Quickly!" As an afterthought, she handed the staff to Silas. "Take this and use it as I did if he stirs at all! Now hurry!"

The two larger men did not need further encouragement. They dragged the limp form between them as Marilee and the other pair guarded the rear. What exactly they guarded against, they could not say for certain.

When Bertran, Silas, and their burden were far enough away, Marilee jerked her head back. Obeying her signal, her remaining companions gratefully raced after the others.

Marilee waited a breath more, then turned to follow.

A woman's shriek filled her ears. It was followed by sobbing.

Reacting instinctively, Marilee looked back.

A dark-haired woman in an elegant and archaic gown the color of honey lay sobbing. Even though Marilee knew that there should be no such person in the forest, no such living person, she could not help hesitating.

The gowned figure looked up. Despite the gloom, she was perfectly visible to Marilee and so it was that Cabe's captor could see every detail of the other woman's face.

Marilee gasped. Shocked at the sight, she stumbled back . . . and collided with something hard and metallic. Realizing what it was, Marilee turned to defend herself.

The mailed fist struck her hard in the jaw, knocking her as senseless as Cabe

435

Bedlam.

III

Every nerve in the wizard's body burned. The desire to return to the numbness of unconsciousness proved great, but Cabe's instinct for survival insisted he accept the pain and try to awaken.

He heard murmuring, but it seemed some distance from him. Steeling himself to the continued agony, Cabe managed to open his eyes just enough to see something of his surroundings.

In the faint illumination of a day the wizard at first mistakenly took for dusk but realized was much earlier, a drake warrior grinned evilly at him.

It took a moment for the mage to realize that things were not as they first appeared. The drake was not grinning at him; rather, the half-seen face was twisted into an expression of agony well-matched to his own.

Other details became more apparent, such as the fact that both Cabe and the drake lay on their sides facing one another. Both were bound tight by rope, surely a jest if someone expected such simple material to hold either prisoner for long. However, the drake continued to lay still and when Cabe sought to magically shake shed his own bonds, the agony coursing through his body trebled.

A low, ragged hiss that Cabe recognized through the haze of pain as the drake's laugh revealed that the wizard's fellow prisoner was not unconscious after all. Gritting his teeth, Cabe met the drake's fiery gaze.

"The great—the great wizard Bedlam ssstill dies even dessspite our failure . . . "

"It's a little too soon to assume my death," Cabe murmured back. "Others have learned that to their dismay."

The drake was undaunted. His faltering breath was not due to the ropes but rather his injuries, the extent of which were more severe than Cabe earlier estimated. The other prisoner was dying.

"The foolsss do not undersssstand the—the weapon. Unless—unlessss they do asss the Aramite showed usss—you will sssuffer constantly until the pain finally ssslays you . . . "

Aramite. Wolf raiders. Cabe knew the ebony-armored humans well, the fragmented factions of a once-mighty empire that had spanned an entire continent. Now, they controlled only small portions of that land and had turned to piracy to support what remained of their power. The wolf raiders had their own unique style of sorcery that now centered around blood, but Cabe suspected that the weapon that had been used on him was older, dating back to when the Aramites had been ruled by a creature they believed was a god.

Who the Aramite was who had delivered to the drakes this weapon was a moot point; the wizard, his family, and especially the king of Penacles—the literally-titled being called the Gryphon—would no doubt be on the wolf raiders' assassination list. It was the Gryphon who was in great part responsible for the fall of the Aramite empire.

But what these survivors of Clan Iron desired with Cabe's death was a question with many possible answers, none of the good for the Dragonrealm as a whole. The drake confederacy had a treaty of noninterference with most of the human realms. Their nominal leader, Sssaleese, was a drake who constantly had to look over his shoulder at rivals who considered their higher-caste births as reasons they should rule.

436

The last Cabe had heard, Sssaleese still held sway, but perhaps this party of killers represented a new force rising in the confederacy.

The mage noted that when he thought of these subjects, his mind was not impaired. The weapon's spellwork evidently responded to his magical abilities, perhaps feeding on them and turning them back on Cabe. That might explain the powerful force he had felt before blacking out.

The pain continued unabated throughout his conclusions and though over the years Cabe had become skilled at dividing his thoughts from any physical distress, he finally had to give in to that pain. Exhaling sharply, he shut his eyes and fought to keep from blacking out. Tears coursed unchecked down his cheeks. In the background, he heard the drake's hacking laugh.

Another voice suddenly intruded, a harsh male—and human—voice. There was a growl and then a heavy thump. The drake's laugh twisted into a grunt as full of pain as that Cabe felt.

Someone grabbed the wizard by the shoulders and pulled him to a sitting position. The action allowed the wizard to focus on something other than his distressed state.

But when he opened his eyes again, it was to stare into a pair of crystalline ones. Cabe exhaled in dismay—and the eyes vanished, replaced by the gruff countenance of a bearded man.

"What'd you do with her, mage?" the figure demanded. He set a well-worn knife at Cabe's throat. "What demon's trick've you used on Marilee?"

"Easy, Bertran!" called another from somewhere behind the towering man. "We don't want him dead, not if he can still return her to us!"

This in no way assuaged Bertran. "He'll give her back to us if he wants his death to be quicker and cleaner than what he left our people to!"

"I've done nothing—" A hard slap from the back of the hand wielding the knife cut Cabe off.

The drake dared laugh again, this time not just at the wizard, but their captors. Bertran whirled on the injured warrior. "You're only alive for one reason, so remember that!"

"Then—then you are in trouble—for I—I will not be your guessst much longer . . ." And as the drake declared that, blood accenting his words dribbled from his lipless mouth. He no longer laughed, but merely coughed harder and harder in search of air.

"Stop that, you damned lizard! Stop it or I'll—"

But the drake let out one last great hiss—that again ended in a hacking cough—and slumped. The narrow eyes lost their fire, the grew milky.

Bertran spat at the corpse. "Marilee never should've bothered to have us save him! See what's all happened now?"

Saved him? Focusing his thoughts, Cabe asked, "What did you save him from?"

The big man sneered. "You came from the direction he did. You saw what happened to his comrades and their beasts, didn't you?" When Cabe had nodded, Bertran pointed at the drake. "The other pair, they were skewered nicely. This one had managed to steer clear for awhile, but the forest finally got him! The branches were crushing his bones . . ."

"Was a noisy sight, wasn't it, Bertran?" someone jested.

"Aye . . . Marilee, being Marilee, she had some pity and thought maybe we could also learn something about why they were here. We were about to cut him free, but the branches just let him go for us."

Cabe straightened. "The branches—the branches let him go?"

"Guess the ghosts favored us that moment, we being their kin." Bertran sheathed the knife, then reached for something strapped to his back. "Gave us the drake and he gave us enough to know how to use this on you."

The Aramite device was a short, ebony staff topped by a fist-sized crystal in whose center shifted what to the wizard thought looked suspiciously like fresh blood. Cabe could not see any method by which to control the staff's power, but assumed it had to be simple if someone unversed in magic could manipulate the weapon even to some degree.

"Now, I've answered your questions, mage, so we're going to get back to what's important . . . " Bertran's scowl grew. "Marilee. Don't think because I talked calmer I'm any less ready to gut you! You've got one chance and that's to give her back to us and now!"

"I didn't—do anything—but I can help if you release me—"

Bertran raised the staff to strike Cabe, but two of his companions seized him before he could.

"Leave 'im be, Bertran!" begged one.

"He's the only one who can bring her back!" added the second.

Cabe had had enough. He had seen what some force in the forest had done to the drakes. A human woman was not likely to last much longer against it. "Would you just—just tell me what happened after I was knocked senseless . . . "

His emphasis on the last word did not go unnoticed. The second man whispered something in Bertran's ear.

"She sent us ahead . . . " Bertran finally told the wizard. He went on, giving what sparse details existed. Cabe continued to fight his pain, forcing it into one part of his mind as he surveyed his captors better. A very ragtag bunch, most of them young, but a few older than Cabe visibly appeared. The older ones wore clothes that still marked them as once of Mito Pica. The garments themselves were not that worn, but it looked as if their wearers had gone to the trouble of retaining the padded shoulders, arched collars, and other aspects of style popular at the time of the city's demise.

How many loved ones did they lose? How many? The mage tried not to think about those deaths, more deaths that he blamed on himself. With that guilt came a new rush of agony. Cab groaned and bent forward. The voices faded away. He knew only the pain . . .

Do you play chess? asked a voice that suddenly came not from without but within. It jerked Cabe back to his surroundings. He knew and despised that voice.

It was Azran's.

Where did you find this set? asked another speaker whose identity equally shocked Cabe. He could never forget the voice of the man who had been his real father.

"Hadeen?" the mage murmured.

Silence reigned around him. Blinking his gaze clear, Cabe saw why. Everyone, even Bertran, was staring to the wizard's left.

There, two vaguely-seen figures—their translucent forms glowing—sat in the middle of darkened forest leaning over a chessboard not only of unusual size and make, but with pieces that, in contrast to the murky players, even from a distance gave indication to tremendous craftsmanship. Indeed, the fine details of the pieces seemed to magnify before the mage's eyes and, in doing so, revealed to him that he had seen this set before.

He looked in shock from the set to the pair. For a moment, the player on the left defined enough to reveal a handsome, youthful man with features just sharp enough to hint that he was not entirely human. Clad in forest green and earth brown jerkin, shirt, and pants, the leather-booted figure looked more like a hunter than one who had been very much in touch with the spiritual aspects of elven life. Hadeen had made many sacrifices to raise the grandson of his best friend.

438

Then, a harsh, clinking sound drew Cabe's attention back to the board. A single piece lay tipped over, Azran Bedlam's undefined hand next to it. Cabe could not help but look at where his birth father's face should be and even though it bore less detail than the ever-blurred visage of the accursed sorcerer Shade, the wizard could not help feel as if Azran stared at him. Shivering, his pain momentarily forgotten, Cabe chose to eye the board rather than Azran.

Only then did he notice that there was something else wrong with the fallen piece. It had been shaped to resemble a huge wolf in mid-leap, but now the wolf's head was nothing but a piece of shredded metal, revealing a hollow interior.

The players and the game vanished without warning. Several of Cabe's captors turned to one another in consternation.

"We should leave this place, Bertran!" someone insisted. "They're growing stronger!"

"They won't harm us! We're blood!"

"How do you know? Maybe the wizard didn't have nothin' to do with Marilee! He was knocked out!"

Cabe forced aside both their troubled mutterings and the resurgence of his own pain as he finally recalled just why this particular board seemed so familiar. It was now the property of the master of Penacles, the City of Knowledge . . . and to Cabe's memory, the set was whole, its individual pieces unmarred. Yet, according to these phantasms one had been ruined, as if some force within had exploded free.

And although his current plight should have demanded his complete attention, Cabe Bedlam had the distinct feeling that understanding just what the shattered piece represented might mean more to his survival than anything else.

IV

The throbbing pain overwhelming the right side of her face finally stirred Marilee to consciousness. She groaned, which in turn caused a hissing intake of breath from somewhere to her left.

The hulking form of a drake warrior filled her horrified view. Marilee tried to move, only then noticing that her arms and legs were bound. She recognized her pursuer, although he was in a much more ragged state than previous. His armored body was covered in scars, revealing that the scales were indeed part of his flesh, not metal as they appeared. One particularly nasty scar ran across the drake's throat.

"You humansss . . . ssso weak! I thought I'd ssslain you with that light ssslap!"

"Why didn't you?" she couldn't help ask despite the obvious risk in doing so.

"Becaussse—" The drake pulled himself together and spoke with more precision. "Because you will bring me two things. The staff . . . and the wizard. That should not be such a terrible thing; your hatred for the wizard is almost as great as mine."

She managed a sneer. "I despise drakes even more than him! He might've been the reason my family and others perished, but your kind wielded the blades!"

"Those were warriors of Clan Gold, against which our lord revolted unsuccessfully." He waved off any further explanation. "Your cooperation isss not necessary, only that I have you. Your friendsss, they will come for you and they will bring Cabe Bedlam to me!"

As the drake made this last declaration, a sinister creaking sound arose from every direction. Marilee anxiously looked around, but saw nothing at first.

Then, she realized that the trees surrounding them leaned much closer than before. The long, twisting branches looked especially eager to reach the drake, but something held them back.

Her captor laughed. He opened his left hand to reveal a small cube that faintly radiated a dark green light. "Another toy from the wolvesss," the drake explained unhelpfully. "Meant to be usssed in conjunction with the staff you found on Sssorus. It protects againsssst magic and the sssupernatural . . . quite effectively, too, ssso I discovered."

As he said the last, the drake indicated his throat. Marilee pretended to care, her mind racing on how to save herself from this danger. Bertran would no doubt be planning something, but he also had the wizard with which to contend. They only knew the basics of the device they had found on the injured drake and it was possible that even now Cabe Bedlam might no longer be a prisoner.

That possibility actually heartened her briefly, something Marilee immediately experienced mixed feeling over. She and her band had heard of rumors of the wizard's yearly pilgrimage to the ruined city, a time when the ghostly memories of Mito Pica seemed to stir to greater life than ever. There had been arguments as to his reasons for returning annually, but most believed he felt guilt over his part in the bloody event. That Cabe Bedlam might suffer anguish had not in the least redeemed him in the eyes of those who had lost family and lives, but now Marilee desperately wished that the mage would appear and take on both the drake and the sinister force surrounding the pair.

"I sssaw you take Sssorus, but . . . wasss detained," her captor went on, leaning closer as he talked. His breath—a carnivore's sickly-sweet breath—assailed her. "He wasss badly injured, yesss?"

"Probably dead by now," Marilee dared admit, waiting for the drake to strike her for saying so.

He merely shrugged. "A warrior fallen. All that mattersss in the end isss the wizard's death. You should want that, too."

She saw a chance. "I'll be glad to help—"

The drake chuckled. It was not a pretty sound. "Oh, you will, human. Now that you are conscious, you will . . . "

He reached for Marilee.

The latest wave of agony subsided enough to enable Cabe to focus on what his captors were doing. He estimated that he had been overwhelmed by the staff's foul power for at least a quarter hour. It had struck him only moments after the apparitions had vanished. The mage cursed the Aramite device not only for the pain it inflicted, but more so now because it had prevented him from trying to decipher what he had witnessed.

There were ghosts in the Dragonrealm. Some were actual spirits, some were memories burnt into reality itself. Cabe was very familiar with both, but especially the latter, for he and his family inhabited an ancient sanctum—part tree, part stone—simply known through the ages as the Manor. It had housed many inhabitants over the countless centuries, most of their lives a mystery even to the wizard. The apparitions that Cabe had seen now looked akin to the Manor's memories, but the fact that they had focused on an element of his past was disquieting.

Bertran interrupted his struggling thoughts. "You look pretty sane again."

Cabe ignored the inaccuracy of the man's statement. Bertran needed him to help with the missing Marilee and that meant hope of ending this waves of pain.

When the mage said nothing, Bertran held up the Aramite device. "Maybe you understand this enough. Tell me how to make its power weaker and I'll use it to help you."

There was a very good chance that Cabe's captor wanted just the opposite information. Knowing how to lessen the agony also likely meant understanding how to make it worse. Still, Cabe decided that he had to take the chance. Through the Gryphon, the wizard had learned much about both the older magic wielded by the Aramite sorcerers called keepers and the newer, possibly more vile arts they utilized now.

"Hold it—hold it close." When after a brief uncertainty Bertran obeyed, Cabe studied the head and handle of the staff, deciphering the Wolf Raider script and runes.

"Well?"

"Grip the very bottom of the base. It should—" Another wave of agony threatened the mage. "It should turn halfway to the left!"

Bertran did as bade. "It did. Now what?"

"Runes—runes on one side. Five in a row." Cabe gasped. "Are there?"

"Five. I see 'em."

The wizard inhaled. "First and fifth. Touch them together. That should do it. Tap my head . . . lightly."

The strain grew overwhelming. Cabe's head spun.

Without warning, his agony diminished. It did not fade completely, but became far more tolerable.

"Did that do it?" growled Marilee's man. "Say something, spellcaster."

"Maybe you should hit him again," someone suggested.

"No!" The wizard drew back as best he could just in case his warning had come too late. He was not certain that another touch might not reverse matters again. Cabe could not say why its foul handiwork had not entirely ceased, but at least it appeared to be at a manageable level. "No . . . the staff's magic has lessened. Eventually, it should fade away . . . I hope."

To not only prove his first point but discourage any thought that they might keep him under their control, he made his bonds turn to dust. One of the other men immediately threw a knife at Cabe, but he had been expecting just such a reaction. The blade froze in the air a few inches from his throat, then changed into a dozen blue and green glowing moths that scattered into the dark sky.

"I trust that'll be a sufficient display to deter any other notions of attacking me," the wizard quietly remarked.

Most of the others nodded quickly, but Bertran looked furious. He swung the staff at Cabe, at the same time snarling.

Cabe softened the ground enough to make the large man's boots sink up to the ankles, then solidified it. Bertran struggled in vain to reach him. In growing desperation, Bertran finally threw the Aramite device at his adversary. Fortunately, used so, the insidious creation was no danger. Cabe took pleasure in forcing the staff to turn head down and bury itself deep in the soil at his feet.

He did not destroy it, aware that it might be needed in some manner. Cabe had no idea what had happened to Marilee and was not positive that she was even alive, but if she was, he might need the Aramite creation to rescue her.

Bertran continued to rail at Cabe, but the rest were clearly subdued. The wizard stepped within the imprisoned man's reach. Bertran swung at Cabe, only to have his fist stop in mid-air. Cabe sighed, admiring the other's determination, but wishing that he would learn quicker.

"I will still help you find her," he told Bertran. "And the sooner you calm down, the sooner we can begin."

Reason finally returned to the man's gaze, but he could still not simply accept the reversal of their positions. "All right. Just don't try anything . . . "

"I won't," Cabe responded, holding back a brief moment of amusement. Then, the seriousness of the situation returned to his attention. "I need you to lead me back to where you took me. That's all. When we're close, you can return to the rest here."

Bertran shook his head violently. The tawny-haired man gritted his teeth. "I'm going with. We find her together."

There remained just enough of the staff's influence to still give the wizard a headache even more aggravating than Bertran was proving to be. Bertran would be little more than a hindrance and possibly great trouble for Cabe if some force attacked the man during their quest, but the mage finally nodded. It was more and more clear that Bertran was deeply in love with Marilee and would sacrifice himself for her safety if necessary. That redeeming trait alone was enough for Cabe to take the risk.

He would not leave the man unarmed, though. With a gesture, Cabe sent the staff flying back to Bertran's grasp. As the latter stared in confusion at this offering of trust, Cabe turned in what he assumed was the general direction they had to head.

A moment later, Bertran trotted a step ahead of him. With an anxious glance at the wizard, he murmured, "We turn right at that crooked tree . . . "

Cabe nodded, his mind already on beyond the crooked tree to where others trees, far more murderous ones, might already have Marilee.

V

There were voices around them, the voices of the long dead. While they frightened Marilee, she was still more familiar with them than her captor. The drake— the mighty warrior—was growing more agitated as the muttering increased.

"What are they babbling about?" he demanded not for the first time.

Her mouth bound, Marilee could hardly answer him. It gave her a slight bit of satisfaction to know that the drake was so disturbed, but it would hardly save her.

She hung from one of the nearby trees, her legs tied together and her arms wrapped as much as possible behind her and around the trunk. In tying her up, the drake had nearly ripped her arms off. The strain was still making her tear up.

When he had first begun his work, Marilee had hoped that the neighboring trees would somehow use the opportunity to seize the drake, but now that he appeared to know how better to wield the other artifact, the trees appeared unable to even reach within several yards of him. In fact, any tree as close as a dozen yards simply grew limp.

What exactly the drake had in mind, Marilee did not know. She only hoped that Bertran had enough sense to turn to the wizard for help. They could always deal with Cabe Bedlam afterward.

Marilee felt conflicted by her sudden hopes that the wizard would come to her aid. In some ways, she resented the mage for that even though he had done nothing. Marilee had grown up hearing the stories of the older survivors and learned to hate the wizard based on those stories. She did not like anything that contradicted that to which she was accustomed to believe was true.

But if Cabe Bedlam did come rushing to her rescue, she would be very, very grateful.

A savage crackling drowned out all other noise. Marilee recognized the sound of a terrible fire . . . but there was no sign, not even a hint of smoke.

The drake whirled around, clearly seeking the source. He swore when it became apparent to him that this was merely another ghostly memory of the city's fall.

"Thisss isss a place of madnesss I will be happy to be rid of." He kept the device gripped tight. Even with little more than one hand, the imposing warrior had been able to easily handle Marilee by first tying her securely while she lay pinned face down by his knee, then tossing the rope he had evidently salvaged from his dead mount over the branches and hoisting her up. There had been two incidents when his hold on the device had been precarious, but to Marilee's disappointment, the drake had managed retain his grip.

Beyond the range of the protective effects, the trees stretched as best they could toward the intruders. Marilee did not trust that those branches would leave her be, which left her praying that the drake would not station himself too far from her.

Her captor intended a straightforward trap for the wizard, its effectiveness in its simplicity. She was the bait. Even more than Marilee, the drake hoped—nay, was certain—that Cabe Bedlam would come. Then, that same device that kept the ghostly forces at bay would supposedly do the same against the legendary mage's power.

And then the drake would use the very long, very sharp sword he kept at his side.

The whispers grew in intensity again. Marilee thought she made out a few random words, but before she could make sense of them, the area grew bright with flame.

The drake cursed and instinctively drew his weapon. Only as that happened did both he and Marilee see that although the fire burned strong, the trees remained untouched.

The city is reliving its final throes, she realized, feeling Mito Pica's suffering. Marilee had witnessed several supernatural visions during her pilgrimages to her former home, but there was something different happening. It was as if Mito Pica's dead were stirring as they never had before.

With another frustrated hiss, the drake sheathed his sword. "Thisss city should ssstay dead insssstead of crying ssso much."

Marilee felt her blood boil at the callous remark. Her parents, her brother and sister, and so many others had been slaughtered out of hand. She fought against her bonds in a futile attempt to reach the warrior.

Her attempts only earned his mockery. "Ssstruggle hard! Let the wizard sssee and hear that you live . . . that he can ssstill sssave you!"

Marilee's gag cut off her epithet.

The eerie fire ceased as abruptly as it began. The trees to the south ceased thrashing.

Another low chuckle echoed in her ears. "And even your pathetic ghostsss play to my advantage! They announce hisss arrival asss good asss a loud war horn!"

He slipped between the trees, vanishing from her sight. Marilee twisted as best she could in order to see the wizard's arrival. She had to give warning.

The other trees stilled. A silence more unnerving than the all the visions Marilee had thus far experienced tonight covered the area.

And then, ever so slowly, a dark-haired human figure approached from the darkness. Marilee made out enough of the face to recognize Cabe Bedlam. The wizard was not as tall as she recalled and he moved with a hint of hesitation. Even the great mage seemed small compared to the cursed souls haunting the forest.

Marilee shook her head, but he did not notice the warning. Her muffled cry also failed to gain any reaction.

Cabe Bedlam remained a half-shadowed figure as he neared, but Marilee could still not believe how youthful the man looked. She had only glanced at the mage previously before her own capture. This latest irony did not escape her; Cabe Bedlam not only lived while hundreds of others had perished, but he also had the benefit of enjoying the bloom of life longer than most humans.

Her bitterness quickly faded as the wizard drew closer yet. He looked around as if searching for something even though Marilee was quite visible. The man was walking into an obvious trap. She wondered if he was that confident in his power and, if so, would that prove to be a fatal mistake?

Painfully aware of the range of the drake's possession, Marilee noted when Cabe Bedlam paused just a few yards beyond. She tried to give some sort of warning not to advance, but he continued to utterly ignore her. Marilee tipped her head in the direction that her captor had hidden, only to have the wizard turn away from her to look at something else.

The drake attacked . . . leaping out from a location behind Cabe Bedlam. He easily wielded the sharp blade with one hand while keeping the other a tight fist.

With one mighty stroke, the drake cut a deadly arc across Cabe Bedlam's throat. The sword slashed through without pause. Marilee tried to scream.

Cabe Bedlam dissipated.

"What by the Dragon of the Depthsss?" rasped the drake as he recovered his balance.

A sound like a crack of thunder made both look in the direction from which the apparition had come. In the gloom, they saw a huge tree with long, draping branches toppling toward them.

Marilee struggled to escape, but the drake simply stood his ground. He stared at the oncoming tree with clear disdain.

She realized that he thought it another apparition, like the flames.

But as the falling tree neared, the drake obviously realized his error. He tried to fling himself away, but did not succeed. As the tree crashed, the massive crown engulfed Marilee's captor.

At the same time, the limbs of the tree where she was bound twitched despite there being no wind. Marilee stilled, hoping that she was not about to join the drake's fate.

The limbs paused. When after several seconds they did not move, Marilee dared take a breath and try to make sense of the situation. Despite previous evidence and the drake's assurances, the ghostly presence in the forest had finally managed to overcome the device. True, the tree had fallen from beyond the thing's protective range, circumventing its power, but the illusion of Cabe Bedlam could have had only one source.

Yet, the illusion confused her in another manner. She had never heard tales of the ghosts doing such things. This bespoke of a conscious, active mind. Marilee considered the fact that it might actually have been the wizard's work after all, but when first one minute, then another, and then another passed without Cabe Bedlam's grand entrance, she dismissed that notion.

There was no movement from the crown. Marilee hoped that the drake was dead, but knew how hardy the race was. She struggled against her bonds again and finally felt some slight loosening.

A woman screamed.

Marilee jerked her head toward the sound. Once more she beheld the woman in the gown. The other female knelt as if trying to pick up a small bundle.

There was no other sound, but suddenly the gowned woman whirled as if discovered. She put her hands up in protest and in doing so revealed her face to Marilee again.

As before her eyes glittered as if crystal.

There was a shout from the south. Marilee recognized Bertran's voice and forgot all about drakes and apparitions.

But her pleasure at his arrival dampened when she saw who was with him. Marilee's earlier hope that the wizard would come to her rescue faded, replaced by the hatred built up over the years.

Bertran rushed up to her, the big man dropping what she recognize as the staff used to subdue Cabe Bedlam and trying with his bare hands to tear her free.

"Step away from her," the wizard ordered.

Bertran obeyed. Cabe Bedlam stepped near Marilee.

The slight rustling of leaves made Marilee look beyond both men to sudden movement at the crown. She tried to give a warning, but the gag prevented her from making more than a moan.

"Something's dampening my power," the mage informed Bertran. "I think I can free her, but it'll take me a moment more."

The rustling increased, but neither of her would-be rescuers noticed. Cabe Bedlam shut his eyes in concentration.

Summoning all her strength, Marilee screamed as best as the gag allowed her.

But her cry was drowned out by the clash of arms and the cries of several beasts. Bertran and the wizard joined her in peering to the east . . . where suddenly a horde of earth-brown drakes as aglow as the gowned maiden rushed forward seeking battle.

VI

The scene upon which Cabe had arrived had proven to be a curious one. He and Bertran had heard the crashing tree and feared the worst for Marilee, only to find her bound but whole.

No ghost had seized the young woman, that was obvious. As to who her captor had been, Marilee would be able to answer that. Of course, seeing where the tree lay, Cabe had suspected the point was moot.

It should have been simple for him to release the woman, but Cabe's first spell faded even before it could come to fruition. He knew it was not the work of the staff and wondered if the supernatural presence in the forest had something to do with it.

Focusing his concentration, the wizard had attempted another spell on the captive . . . and that was when the drakes had come charging through the trees.

It took Cabe only a moment to realize that these were not living, breathing warriors, but apparitions. They glowed of their own accord and some literally charged through those trees. Yet, what more struck him was the coloring of these drakes. They were of an earthy shade, marking of them a clan not only far flung from this land, but one that had already been decimated two hundred years earlier during the ill-fated Turning War.

And certainly not a clan that had had anything to do with with razing of Mito Pica.

The ethereal warriors vanished. Cabe hesitated for a second, then returned his attention to Marilee. This time, the ropes fell away. Bertran caught the woman, then helped her get her footing. The big man was slow to release his hold and Marilee did not rush him.

Then, her eyes widened. Pushing past Bertran, she pointed at the fallen tree's massive crown. "He's still alive! He's still alive!"

Cabe glared at the crown. Nothing dampened his spell this time. The leaves burst from the branches and the branches twisted away, revealing what lay beneath.

Nothing.

Marilee looked around. "He's got to be near—"

The wizard cursed himself for underestimating their mysterious adversary. "He's not human, is he?"

"No! It was a drake—"

"The color of iron, I assume." After she nodded, Cabe shut his eyes and concentrated. He could not sense the drake's nearby presence, but suspected he knew the reason. "Did he carry some artifact, some talisman?"

Marilee nodded. Cabe did not bother to ask what it looked like. That it was of wolf raider make like the staff would make sense. The Aramite sorcerers needed gold to finance their efforts and more than a few of their macabre creations had made their way to the Dragonrealm.

He noticed that both of his companions were eyeing him with increasing suspicion. Cabe sighed, understanding that their long-bred hatred of him was on the rise again now that they were under the mistaken belief that the drake had fled. Retreat he had, but the warrior was still near. If the drake managed to survive the forest, he would seek once more to fulfill his mission . . . which Cabe knew was his death.

The forest . . . to the wizard, of more importance than either the would-be assassin or the vengeful survivors of Mito Pica was what was happening to the forest itself. *Why are there apparitions that have no relation to the city's destruction?*

Given the moment to think without incessant pain coursing through him or the need to rush to rescue someone, Cabe knew the answer. It was one that both made perfect sense and yet startled him as few things could.

He started in the direction from which the drake horde had charged, only to have the Aramite staff suddenly thrust before his face.

"Stop right there," Marilee growled, the weapon now in her possession. Behind her, Bertran looked torn. Cabe had saved the woman Bertran loved, but her bitterness toward the mage was evidently stronger than her gratitude.

"That's ill-advised," Cabe muttered.

"You saved my life, but that doesn't make up for the hundreds of others lost here, including my parents—"

Bertran put a hand on her shoulder. "Marilee. I've been thinking. I don't think we—"

She shrugged off the hand. A sheepish Bertran looked at Cabe.

The wizard frowned. Marilee let out a yelp and dropped the staff, which in her mind had grown as hot as a red poker. Cabe had actually not burned her, but simply let her feel the illusion of intense heat.

He gestured and the staff came to his hand. The woman gritted her teeth and grabbed for an empty area by her waist where presumably she usually kept a knife. Then, her expression turned to one of intense exhaustion.

"I've imagined . . . I've thought of taking you down most of my life," she murmured.

"Not that it'll matter to you, but every night I relive the destruction of Mito Pica. I lost someone very close to me here." As Cabe said this, he felt some more guilt. The statement was and was not true, if what he imagined was in part the reason for this evening's events.

Marilee eyed him. "Didn't know that."

Before the conversation could continue on into an area uncomfortable for Cabe, a woman's sobbing echoed through the forest. The wizard noticed that it startled Bertran and him more than it did Marilee. "You've heard that before?"

"I've seen her, too—there!" She pointed past his left shoulder.

Quickly looking, Cabe swore. The glowing, vaguely-defined shape of the gowned woman he had also seen earlier drifted among the trees. While the rich, black hair still obscured her features, her stance indicated some dire need.

But something else confused him. If what he believed was true, then he would have expected her to be heading the same direction that he had intended. Instead, she was moving toward the actual ruins of the city.

Despite that contradiction, Cabe chose to pursue the apparition. The vision headed toward what was left of the city wall. Beyond the wall, the silhouettes of several jagged shells that had once been towering buildings seemed to hungrily await Cabe's long-overdue return. Marilee's overriding hatred for him despite the rescue had stirred up his own guilt more than ever. Every fragment of Mito Pica still standing looked to him like the outline of a tombstone.

He expected her to walk through the wall, but instead she turned and began to hurry along its length. The mage picked up his own pace. His curiosity was only matched by his frustration. Despite his best efforts, he could never make out her face. Her hair continued to drape over whatever features should have been visible, as if the long tresses had a life and purpose of their own.

At what had once been one of the great gates but was now a mangle of rusted, scorched metal and shattered stone, the apparition entered Mito Pica. As Cabe attempted to follow, the branches of the few remaining trees ahead shifted in an attempt to block his path.

Behind him, Marilee swore. Cabe knew that she and Bertran had followed him, but since they no longer represented a threat to his safety, he had deemed that they were better off near him.

"We're safe for the moment," he whispered. "Stay close to me and nothing will happen."

"But you saw what the trees did to the drakes!" she whispered back.

"That's because they were drakes." Cabe frowned. He wanted to go after the spirit, but also wondered why the force he suspected behind all this would stop him. Was not the apparition part of his message, a message possibly for Cabe himself?

A woman's scream echoed from the ruins ahead.

Despite aware that the trees probably sought to keep him back for good reason, Cabe gestured. A wind thrust the branches aside, allowing the trio to continue through into the city.

There was no hint of animal life in the darkened ruins, not even the small vermin one would have expected. The areas above were devoid of birds, the ground of any small, scurrying forms. There should have been some inhabitants, but the wizard even noted an absence of insect sounds.

"We shouldn't be in this place," Bertran rasped. "We shouldn't disturb the dead . . ."

They appear very disturbed already, Cabe thought sourly. Or at least one in particular, if I'm correct.

Cabe was fairly certain as to the identity of the force ultimately responsible here and knew that he should have gone directly to the other's last resting place, but the female vision continued to demand the mage's attention. There had to be a particular reason for her materializing again and again.

There came renewed sobbing. Cabe pushed his way through two centuries of vegetation-overgrown rubble, moving deeper into the city. More than once, the mage thought that he would finally catch up, but the gowned woman always remained just far enough ahead.

And still he could not see her face.

Bertran swore as he stumbled over an unstable piece of stonework. Cabe looked back at the pair. "I shouldn't have let you follow me. I never thought to journey this far into the city. If you retrace our steps, you should be all right."

Marilee shook her head. "I need to find out about her, too. I saw her. I want to know who she was, why she's in more torment than the others. What is she and why we can see her . . . "

Now the wizard understood why she followed so docilely. Hinted at was that the woman was actually hoping to find other spirits that might be active. Cabe had suspected the reason, but now had his verification. "You want to find your parents."

For a brief moment, Marilee looked much younger, much less assured. Cabe saw the child left alone after the city's tragic fall.

"I know that sounds mad," she finally answered. "But I thought with everything so alive this time, maybe there was something going on. Maybe this ghost knew about others . . . " Her expression revealed how foolish that notion now seemed even to her.

"I'm sorry—" the wizard began.

Bertran interjected himself between them. "There she is! By the fallen inn!"

Even as they looked, the apparition moved on again. She continued to seem to have a reason in her journey. She headed toward the tilted remains of a roofless house, then suddenly veered toward the right down a narrow stone avenue.

Cabe's gaze narrowed. In the dim light of the moon, he could see the once fine iron fence, parts of which still stood tall. Beyond that fence, some distance away, a turreted estate house—one turret collapsed in—beckoned.

The wizard searched his memory for who this might belong to, but failed to find an answer. He watched as the ghost flitted through the wreckage and headed toward the crumbling edifice.

But as Cabe once more followed, Bertran growled under his breath. The mage turned to see the big man staring wide-eyed at their destination.

Bertran took hold of Marilee's arm. This time, he would not let her pull away. "Marilee. You ain't going in there . . . "

She was as confused as Cabe. "Why, Bertran?"

"That there's *Vale*."

VII

The name meant nothing to the wizard, but Marilee swallowed hard. "I never saw it. Only heard it. That's his place?"

"Aye, and if there's ghosts that mean us ill, the outcast will be one!"

"Who is the 'outcast'?" Cabe asked, simultaneously probing the estate grounds.

Bertran nervously shrugged. "My pa, he only just warned me never to go too near Vale. He said the outcast might steal me away!"

Marilee visibly shivered. Cabe, who thus far sensed nothing, wondered what connection this had to the phantasm. He also cursed himself for allowing this pair to follow him rather than do as he should have and first seen them safely to their companions.

Shrieks assailed them again. The ruins around the trio burst into flame . . . or rather, once more, the memory of flame. Shadows flitted here and there that the wizard decided represented the fleeing populace. His guilt mixed with his growing curiosity. Why were the dead of Mito Pica so violently awake? They had never been like this in previous visits.

"There's light in there!"

A GAME OF GHOSTS

Following Marilee's astounded gaze, Cabe saw that illumination did indeed fill the Vale house. He wondered at that name, nothing about the estate showing much that would match the descriptive title. While clearly there had once been many trees, that was as close to a vale as an estate within Mito Pica could manage. The landscape otherwise had no similarity, the only other features a set of crumbling statues the outlines of which made Cabe believe they had once represented various forest creatures.

Without warning, Marilee plunged ahead. Bertran grabbed at her, but too late. Cabe decided that a spell might not be the best thing for everyone in such a place—not unless absolutely necessary—and hurried after.

He managed to seize her arm. "Where do you think you're going?"

"I heard her! She called to me!" The woman looked past him to the house. "Momma!"

Cabe saw that he had let things go too far. "Bertran! Take her with you! I'll provide—"

But as he spoke, Bertran ran past him. "Pa!"

Marilee slipped free. Now entirely heedless of their own prior concerns, she and her companion hurried on toward the house.

Cabe started a spell intended to send the two far away, but hesitated. Instead, he grimly pursued them. Somehow, the mage was certain that this revolved around him. One way or another, this force wanted Cabe to come to it.

Alive or dead, I'll make you regret that if any harm comes to those two, he warned the mysterious power.

Make way for the Lady Asrilla! a ghostly voice abruptly cried in his head.

Simultaneously, an ethereal carriage drawn by six white and clearly transparent horses rushed along the crumbled street. The speeding wheels paid no mind to the stone and other rubble filling the street. The rounded carriage raced passed a gaping Cabe, who caught a glimpse of a crest the center of which was a wyvern wielding a lance. The crest meant nothing to the wizard, but the name, although one he had not heard in almost two decades, struck him to the core.

Lady Asrilla. Of Mito Pica.

His grandmother.

Cabe had never known her, for she had died giving birth to her second son, his father. With Mito Pica destroyed, he had never bothered to seek that part of his family. He had assumed that they had perished with the rest.

But whether they had or not, Cabe knew that his grandmother had died long before, which made this phantom coach a very, very strange specter.

He wanted desperately to follow this new trail, but Marilee and Bertran were almost at the house already and Cabe believed that if he let them go alone they were at far more risk. If he had to trade his life for theirs, then so be it.

But he would do so fighting all the way.

No longer willing to hold back, Cabe transported himself to the front entrance just before the pair reached it. Marilee and Bertran paused.

"Your loved ones are not within," he bluntly told them. "You are bespelled."

From Marilee, he saw some understanding. Bertran, however, started forward again.

She blocked his way. "Bertran!"

He gave her a befuddled look. "Pa?"

"Stay here," Cabe ordered. He drew an arc. A transparent golden shell formed around them.

That done, the wizard created another glowing sphere, then stepped through into what had once been a wide front hall. Cabe peered left and right, but only saw more

449

evidence of the great house's collapse. He moved deeper into the structure, finally entering areas where there still remained something of a ceiling.

A tattered tapestry fluttered on a far wall. Cabe would not have even noticed it save that in the light of the sphere he saw that just enough of the image remained to reveal a landscape.

A vale.

He made his way to the tapestry. For some reason, the landscape looked familiar even though the wizard was certain that he had never been to such a place.

The sobbing began anew.

Cabe wended his way out of the room, then hurried after the sound. At the far end of the hall, near where a huge double staircase had collapsed in on itself, the female figure slowly climbed into the air.

The wizard took another step . . . and the floor gave way.

It happened so quickly that he barely had time to shield his landing much less even stop his fall. Cabe hit hard, but not enough to do more than briefly knock the breath out of him. Even then, he was ready for the expected attack.

But nothing happened. Cabe summoned the sphere to him, possibly casting the first light on this chamber in decades.

The wall bore the sign of the vale, the image carved by some very skilled artisan. It stretched across the stone wall, but where it once would have been the focal point of the chamber, now what had burst through the wall itself more than stole that role away.

The roots were immense . . . and black even in the sphere's glow. Cabe could have sworn that they briefly shifted when first the illumination fell upon them. He waited, but when they did not move again, he turned to study the rest of his surroundings.

The dark-haired woman stood watching him.

He gasped, but not merely because she was there. As surprising as the roots had been, they were less shocking to him than the fact that the woman's feature were now visible to him. More to the point, that her eyes were visible to him.

Crystalline eyes that glittered even in the least light.

Cabe had seen eyes like those before. They were the eyes of a Vraad, the ancient race of sorcerers from whom all humans were descended. Very few knew of them or that the only known survivor—if he could be called such—was the cursed warlock called Shade.

But father, she began, talking to the air. *he still thinks me only his servant . . . a servant fond of him, but nothing more. I can prove his duplicity to Uncle and then he can convince the Dragon Hunter! Nathan will listen to Uncle!*

The wizard stood at a loss. First, here was a phantom bearing the mark of the Vraad, but speaking of another time . . . a time when Cabe's grandfather Nathan had lived.

Still speaking to some silent, unseen memory, she vehemently shook her head and added, *No! Whatever I felt for him doesn't matter! He'll bring everything down on us! The Kings already suspect you might not be as loyal as you seem. If they knew that you and Uncle did still speak—*

There came a shifting behind Cabe. He whirled—

This time, there was no question about the roots moving.

The sobbing renewed. Feeling as if he were in the middle of a tug of war, Cabe looked back at the spirit.

Now, she was swollen with child.

If it was possible, the dark-haired woman was even more pale than before. She lay on some cot or low bed that the mage could not see, one arm reaching out and the other holding her belly. In place of the golden dress, the ghost now wore a simple

450

ivory birthing gown, the color of which only served to make her look even closer to death's door.

Please . . . please keep him alive! I . . . I beg you . . . you have the power . . . the power, Nathan! Forget me . . . forget his father . . . forget that thing I still fight in my head . . . save my . . . save my son . . .

Cabe Bedlam forgot about ghosts, forgot about huge roots, forgot about all else. He knew exactly what was playing out here. This was a significant birth, one at the end of the ill-fated Turning War. In its way, it would decide the outcome for two more centuries of Dragon King rule . . . stunted rule, but still rule.

As with Mito Pica, the blame fell upon him. The impending birth hinted at before him was the wizard's own.

And this woman . . . this Vraad . . . was evidently his *mother*.

It was at that moment that he was struck hard from behind. As Cabe fell to the floor, he heard the unmistakable hiss of a drake.

Barely conscious, Cabe tried to push himself up . . . and as he did, he looked directly into the face of his mother.

The ghost smiled with sinister satisfaction, a smile most definitely aimed at Cabe.

I've waited so long . . . she murmured in his head. *And now I have you . . . my darling son . . .*

VIII

Bertran pounded against the shell. "It won't break! I can't break it! Blasted wizards!"

He received only silence from behind him. While he considered himself a fairly adaptable man, Bertran was always glad to have Marilee's quick wits at his side. She usually had a plan or could come up with one on the spot.

"What do you think we should do?" he finally asked. Forgotten was the enchantment that had made him think his long dead father had called to him. Once more, he only saw how manipulating a wizard could be.

Hearing nothing from her, he turned. "Marilee, are you—"

Bertran found himself alone.

Cabe never completely blacked out, but neither did he remain conscious enough for several precious seconds to know what was happening. All he could think was that the ghost of his mother was trying to kill him . . . or worse. Yet, he could not fathom why.

There also remained a niggling doubt. He missed some vital clue, some truth. There had to be more than what appeared on the surface. He had lived too long to not have learned to never take anything at face value, not even ghosts.

Slowly, he regained his senses . . . and only then discovered that he was bound tightly by the huge roots. Cabe immediately concentrated—

The roots tightened, cutting off his air and threatening to break his bones.

The moment he ceased his efforts, the roots loosened just enough to let him breathe. Cabe found no relief in the fact that he had not been slain outright; that meant that his captor had other intentions for him.

A low hiss from his far right suddenly warned him that he was not alone. The sphere he had cast remained floating a few feet above the center of the chamber, giving the wizard sufficient light. The vines granted him the luxury of shifting his head just enough to see the iron drake standing in the shadowed corner. The drake stood utterly still and if not for his low, steady breathing, might have seemed dead.

If not dead, he was certainly under control of the same force keeping Cabe a prisoner. The drake provided it with some actual hands. That he had gotten near enough to the spellcaster to hit him had to be due to the obviously weakening but still somewhat potent power of the Aramite device.

A clinking sound echoed through the chamber. A tiny object rolled into view below the sphere.

It was the shattered chess piece from the vision involving Azran and Hadeen.

So cold, so alone for so long . . . then given freedom only to feed some contemptible wizard's little plot! He thought he controlled me, but I was stronger . . .

The vision of Cabe's mother formed again. The crystalline eyes stared hungrily at the captive mage.

This isn't my mother, Cabe realized. It wore her form, but the eyes were not hers. They represented something else inhabiting her.

So clever, the little half-blood, the phantasm said without moving its lips. She drifted toward him. *Played right into his hands and his hands played into mine! He wanted all that power in a malleable vessel, one from which he would eventually draw everything to him . . . but I was stronger . . .*

She gestured and the chess piece rolled closer to Cabe. He could better see the top, where it was clear something within had escaped. What had Azran unleashed and why? Cabe still did not understand, save that it was Vraad in origin.

He remembered something his captor had said. His mother was a half-blood?

Hadeen! the wizard thought, imagining the half-elf who had raised him. *Did you know?*

The drake suddenly lurched forward. However, he did not walk toward either Cabe or the apparition, but rather the crest to mage's left. As the scaled warrior stepped up to the wall, the roots there pulled away. Cabe could not make out the exact details, but saw now that there was a face carved below the crest.

This was a crypt.

The drake pulled back a fist, then struck the wall. The crash of his fist against the stone resounded through the chamber. Cracks already created by the roots spread farther.

Without hesitation, the drake struck again. This time, not only did the stone crack, but so did some of the bones in the drake's hand.

Despite what should have been a horrific injury, the scaled warrior continued to pound at the wall. Cabe felt actual pity for the drake, who was killing himself for the apparition's desires.

The roots stretched out, carrying Cabe forward, then turning him toward the task at hand.

No sooner had that been done, then some of the stone fell in, revealing a darkened area behind the wall. The drake now tore at the hole, making it bigger. His breath grew ragged and blood dripped from his hands, but he had no choice but to continue.

And at last, what lay within was revealed.

The tomb was a simple one, with the house crest evident over the silver and stone casket, which itself stood upon a waist-high marble platform. Someone had placed a vase of white roses by one end of the coffin, which Cabe assumed was where the head was.

But the simple elegance of the tomb was ruined by the insidious roots, which sprouted from the casket itself. Cabe frowned, wondering about the contents.

A GAME OF GHOSTS

The ghostly female joined the drake as he entered the tomb. She turned to smile at Cabe, who was revolted by the fact that it wore his long-lost mother's form. *They thought they sealed me in, she mocked. but I would not be sealed in again! I fought. I raged . . . and was rewarded when all fell around me . . .*

At some unspoken command, the drake worked as best he could with his ruined hands to open the coffin. With a long moan, the top slid back.

Cabe was not certain what he had expected.. The true body of his mother, he supposed, either intact or decayed. Instead, a familiar golden substance covered the entire interior and whatever remains might have been placed first place.

Amber. The same substance in which Azran had sealed Lady Gwen for two centuries until Cabe had released her. Its preservative qualities, especially enhanced by magic, were renowned.

Azran had used it as a punishment, but aware of what held him prisoner, Cabe was certain that whoever had cast this had done so to contain something that needed to be contained.

My will was stronger than hers, stronger than his, stronger than all of theirs . . . she began anew. *Though he tore my essence free the moment he pulled me from Dru Zeree's foul prison, he failed to subdue my will! It grew within her, changed her . . .*

The drake warrior slammed his fist against the amber. There was more cracking of bone, but nothing more. The roots shoved Cabe closer to the tomb. Although she was in sight now, the ghost continued to speak in his mind.

But then the infant grew strong enough to pull me two ways, weaken me. She prevailed . . . for a time. The infant was born . . . tearing me apart!

Suddenly, she was in front of Cabe, the hungry crystalline eyes burning into his soul in search of something. The wizard shut his eyes, only to have some force open them wide.

Child of mine you are as much as hers . . . more! Dear, sweet Dru would not let me have his darling daughter, but I shall cherish you . . . for the few moments I need to take back what's mine!

As she spoke, another image briefly overlapped her. Cabe saw a strikingly beautiful yet ominous woman with short scarlet and ebony hair and tear-shaped eyes. He did not need to see that the eyes were crystalline to know that this was the ghost's true image.

No sooner had it materialized then the other image faded. The twisted vision of his mother—whose name he still did not know—smiled. Cabe shivered.

Now . . . be a good son and open the way . . .

The roots shoved him all the way to the casket. As he closed, the amber took on a slight illumination of its own.

And briefly, ever so briefly, Cabe saw the woman within.

It was the same woman whose form the dark spirit currently wore, but with a softness that the ghost did not have. Her eyes were closed and so Cabe could not see if they had turned crystalline, but one thing that did catch his attention in that moment was her expression. There was a sadness that touched him.

Her hair was also swept back from ears, revealing something else that he only noted after the image had faded back into the thick amber. She had slightly pointed ears. His mother did indeed have elven blood in her.

The roots tightened. The wizard gasped for breath.

Open the way, my darling . . .

It occurred to him that with all her power, the apparition seemed entirely helpless where the amber was concerned. Cabe eyed the the casket, seeking now the spell matrixes.

At first, he thought somehow that he had cast it himself. It was his signature . . .

453

but with a subtle difference.

Grandfather's, the mage finally understood. *Nathan cast this.*

Now he understood why she needed him. The complexity was one that rivaled even a Vraad's. There were elements to it that only Nathan could touch . . . or someone who was also Nathan.

The tragic path to Cabe Bedlam's birth was also one at least as complex as the spell he now inspected. He knew from Gwen that Nathan had sacrificed a part of himself to save his grandchild, who came to the world already dying. That part of Cabe's grandfather had only fully melded into him after the younger Bedlam had fought against the Ice Dragon. The wizard also knew that all humans had Vraad blood flowing through them, but had thought it diluted by the thousands of years since that race's fading.

But now Cabe understood that his father had attempted something even more vile than he could have imagined. In his lust for absolute power, Azran had taken this captive Vraad female's essence and instilled it in Cabe's pregnant mother. The mage already knew that his father had intended to sacrifice him and draw his already potent life force into his own body, but by adding including the Vraad into the development of the baby, Azran had created the potential for an even more powerful prize.

The roots began to tighten again. Cabe immediately worked on the spell, but part of his mind still dealt with the truth in the hopes that it might lead him to some escape. He carried within him strong Vraad essence, the powerful life force of the Bedlam line, and the fairly immediate presence of elven essence as well.

Cabe Bedlam had always wondered why he had grown so powerful even being the grandson of Nathan and the son of Azran. There had been more to it. Much, much more. *I am the amalgamation of several potent aspects of magic . . . a thing that could never happen by nature alone. I should not exist.*

But that was a moot point. Not only did he exist, but he had loved ones and people to protect. Aware that the Vraad spirit grew impatient, Cabe continued to play at obeying. He needed to buy time until he could find escape.

As he probed deeper into the spell, he once more caught a glimpse of his mother. She was dead, Cabe knew that, dead sacrificing herself for him. Only now did he also see the black flower resting over her stomach. It looked as if it had been plucked full from the ground, for the roots trailed off her body toward the back and vanished below her. Although he could not see where they went, the spellcaster knew too well. While she might not have been able to shatter the amber, the Vraad had managed to penetrate it to a degree so that she could seek some outside power to fully free her.

But evidently, the only power that could was the same power—so to speak—that had imprisoned her in the first place.

Once again, the roots threatened to crush him.

Come, my darling . . . mother would leave this place . . .

That she was mad, the wizard was certain. That she was a danger to the Dragonrealm, Cabe knew as absolute fact, especially if she not only took back what had been stolen from her, but also all else that was him. She would be one of the most powerful spellcasters to ever walk the world.

I should never have followed so gullibly! I should have listened to him, not chased phantoms! As he berated himself, Cabe finally discovered the key to dissolving the spellwork. He kept his thoughts as well-shielded as possible. The Vraad might be strong, but she could not read all his thoughts.

Again, the mage received a tantalizing glance of his mother. He wondered why that kept happening. The Vraad already wore her form; she did not need to tease him so.

Then, Cabe thought about the fact that his mother was a half-elf. He knew what

454

often happened to elves when they died. He had seen it happen to his adopted father.

The wizard placed his hand on the amber casing, hoping that he was not about to set the vengeful spectre free.

Another hand—a feminine one—touched the casing from the opposing side.

Without raising his own hand, Cabe looked in surprise at Marilee . . . or rather, something that wore Marilee's form.

IX

The eyes met his.

The dark roots suddenly released the wizard. They lunged for the Vraad, who stood stunned at this turn. Despite the fact that she was an apparition, the first root to reach her actually managed to wrap itself around her ankle.

A savage hiss echoed throughout the chamber as the drake grabbed his sword with his ruined hands and severed the end of the lunging root. The Vraad dissipated, leaving Cabe and Marilee with the ensorcelled drake.

The roots now darted for the scaled warrior, but even injured as he was, the drake wielded the blade expertly. Pieces of root lay scattered everywhere.

Cabe almost pulled his hand free, but then Marilee's hand slid over and pressed down on his. The wizard chose not to struggle, letting whatever used the woman to continue.

The roots began to curl into themselves. As Cabe watched, they quickly withered. At the same time, they also withdrew toward the coffin and the amber.

As if drunk, the drake now stumbled toward the mage and his companion. There was no doubt from the way he gripped the sword that he was after the pair. The Vraad still controlled him, even if that control had grown shakier. Well aware of the might of even a wounded drake, Cabe tried to cast a spell while still maintaining his link with the amber.

But again, 'Marilee' interfered. She squeezed the mage's hand, making him look back at her. The woman said nothing, but there was a look in her eyes that made Cabe halt his casting.

The roots receded faster and faster, finally vanishing into the casket.

The drake dropped to his knees, then collapsed in a heap.

At the same time, Marilee also slumped forward. Cabe caught her before her head would have hit the amber. He pulled her around the casket, then set her against the nearest wall. Satisfied as to her health, the wizard checked on the drake. While still badly injured, the would-be assassin breathed regularly.

Searching the drake, Cabe found the Aramite creation. There was little power left in it, but that did not matter to the mage. With much satisfaction, he crushed it.

Despite the apparent victory, Cabe sensed that the Vraad had not been entirely contained. There was something he felt that he had not done and that he should have done, but all that mattered at the moment was to get Marilee—and the now helpless drake, he supposed—to safety.

No longer caring about spells attracting ghosts, Cabe did not take long in sending both unconscious figures to the floor above. When that was done, he paused to gaze at the ruined tomb of his mother, whose name he still did not know.

But there was someone who could tell him. The same someone he should have listened to earlier. The spectral carriage had been the most blatant summons yet.

"Farewell," Cabe whispered to the amber. "I'm sorry."

He vanished from the chamber, materializing a breath later in the room above. With another brief thought, Cabe summoned a new sphere.

Unfortunately, in its illumination he now saw that there was no sign of either Marilee or the drake.

Concentrating, Cabe probed for either one. There was no sign of them, but he did detect Bertran's presence where he had left the big man. Sending the sphere a few yards in advance of him, the wizard headed to the entrance, hoping that Bertran could shed some light on the situation.

He spotted Marilee's companion as he neared the arched entryway. Bertran continued to pound his fists against the barrier, only halting when he, in turn, noted Cabe's return.

The wizard expected anger, but instead Bertran looked horrified. The man shouted something, yet no sound escaped him. That had not been part of Cabe's spell.

The stone entrance collapsed on the mage.

It was fortunate for Cabe that with the destruction of the device his defensive spells had been fully restored, but even still he risked being crushed to death. Warned by Bertran's expression, he managed to draw a shield above him just as the first heavy stones dropped. Even then, the force of the collapse pushed the wizard to his knees.

As Cabe struggled to free himself, a figure towered over him. He looked up into the savage, half-visible countenance of the helmed drake.

A drake with crystalline eyes.

"Were you thinking of leaving?" the Vraad asked through her puppet, the drake's croaking voice mixing with a sly, feminine one. "But you wouldn't let anything come to harm these poor innocents, would you?"

The Vraad-possessed drake gestured past Bertran to what had been a decorative statue that vaguely resembled a wolf. Although the head still remained, most of the features save one eye had been worn away by time.

But that was not so important as the fact that the statue peered with malevolent intention at Marilee, who was pinned beneath one half-shattered paw.

"I had a very nice pet similar to this one once," the spirit merrily continued. "Or rather, a series of them! Every Cabal was always so loyal, so obedient! They would snap off someone's head at my merest whim, just to please me . . . "

The statue's carved mouth ripped open, revealing sharp stone teeth. In a grating voice, it asked, "Feast, mistress?"

"Not yet, my dear . . . " The drake grinned at Cabe. "Not if my sweet son does as his mother asks!"

"You—are not—my mother."

The possessed warrior raised one hand. The stone wolf opened its jaws and set them around Marilee's throat. Cabe noticed that Marilee was not conscious. The spirit that had inhabited her for a time—his true mother, he still believed—had gone back to her rest once the amber had been resealed.

But why had not the same happened with the Vraad?

"I am your mother," the ghost insisted with indignation. "And I will teach you to say, if only before you die, 'Yes, Melenea, you are my dear mother!'"

As she spoke, Cabe at last noticed something different about the drake. Insinuated in his armor and spread among the scales was a number of tiny black roots. From what the wizard could see, they all originated somewhere on the warrior's back. Cabe had the notion that if the drake turned, there would be a black flower there.

Melenea had outwitted them, setting in place a link to the outside that even the sealing of the amber would not sever. She had no doubt done so the moment that she had ensnared the drake.

A GAME OF GHOSTS

The sinister spirit saw his interest. "Oh, yes! I've had so long to plan, so long to think of all contingencies! I have a thousand plans for a thousand situations, most of them well-crafted over the ages trapped in that chess piece by dear, accursed Dru!"

Twice she had mentioned that name, one vaguely known to Cabe through his contact with Shade. Another Vraad and, if the hints that Shade had made once were true, one whose bloodline consisted these days of the Bedlams.

He did not think Melenea knew this. She had made no such comment. She might know that the legacy of the Vraad race ran through him, but not that her tormentor was the progenitor of the wizard. For the first time since he had learned of the ancient sorcerers, Cabe wished at least that one had somehow survived. There was a shift in Melenea's tone that hinted that, despite her bravado, she feared this Dru Zeree.

Suddenly, a voice echoed through Cabe's mind, a voice that the apparition also clearly heard.

Now who said you were allowed out of the game, Melenea?

The voice was ghostly, yet dominating. It had all the arrogance, the power, of a Vraad . . . although Cabe recognized it as someone he had known well, someone who was certainly not Vraad.

And with that declaration came the giant shadow of a chess piece shaped like a lunging wolf, but lacking a head.

For just a moment, the ghost lost her confidence. The ensorcelled drake let out a frightened hiss and stumbled back.

Then, the brief look of uncertainty changed to one of fury. "Not a very nice trick—"

Melenea's own animated wolf howled as a ball of pure force sent it flying through the air and far beyond the estate. Cabe paid scant attention to the distant sound of stone shattering as he moved against his adversary. He reminded himself that this was the spirit of a Vraad, not a living one. The ghost had many limitations.

The drake was still one of them.

Melenea expected a magical assault; she did not expect a physical one. Cabe threw himself at the scaled warrior, hoping that he had guessed right.

The possessed drake tried to grab him, but while Melenea controlled the body, the hands still had broken bones. The drake's grasp was not perfect, enabling Cabe to maintain his hold on the wrists despite the warrior's greater strength.

"My foolish little child," Melenea hissed through her puppet. "Is that the bessst you can—"

Her derision ended in a shriek as another figure came up behind her and tore at the black flower Cabe had been certain had been there. Bertran—released by the wizard—pulled hard, his might managing to stretch the flower's roots tight and thus weakening the Vraad's hold.

Yet, while it weakened, it did not break. The wizard knew that he needed a force far more powerful than Marilee's companion, no matter how strong the man. Using the distraction, Cabe reached deep and found the drake's mind. He awoke the would-be assassin and let him feel the strangling roots, feel the insidious presence taking over his body. In addition and perhaps most important of all, the mage sent an image of what had happened to the drake's comrades in the forest, a dread reminder of what had happened the last time plants had entwined his kind. With it, the mage sent a suggested course of action.

The drake reacted just as Cabe hoped.

He transformed . . . but this time far more swiftly than those slain had likely attempted. It would put a tremendous strain on the drake . . . but the only other choice was continued enslavement.

Cabe flung himself back, at the same time casting both Bertran and the unconscious Marilee to safety. The wizard barely had time to do this before several tons of dragon began to grow before him.

The metamorphosis from armored knight to legendary behemoth was one that ever amazed Cabe. The iron drake swelled as if about to explode. His body arched and knees bent backward. His arms stretched forward and from his back burst two vestigial wings that immediately spread wider. The dragon's head crest slid down over the face, revealing itself the drake's true countenance.

The roots of the black flower strained, but this time they could not hold. One by one they snapped, until at last the baleful bloom hung loosely from one long tendril.

A golden aura created by the wizard swiftly surrounded the flower. The aura solidified, becoming amber.

Summoning the captured flower to him, Cabe probed it. He could sense a faint presence within. The struggle had greatly weakened the Vraad, just as he hoped.

Then, the wizard remembered the dragon that he had unleashed.

But his would-be assassin chose that moment to let out a ragged roar. The great beast twisted around, seeking something.

Seeking Cabe.

The dragon had a chance to take him. Cabe knew that. The dragon knew that. The huge head loomed over the spellcaster. The huge maw opened wide . . . but the dragon did not lunge.

And then . . . the blue-gray behemoth slumped backward. The gargantuan body fell toward the ruined house, crushing in what remained of the entrance and the front hall. The injuries and stress created by the Vraad's possession had proven too much even for the nameless giant, although Cabe had not intended that. The wizard had hoped to talk peace with the dragon.

He could have attacked, Cabe definitely knew. *He could have attacked.*

That the dragon had not could only mean one thing to Cabe. Drakes had a code of honor, though that code was not always as humans understood it. This one knew that the wizard had freed him from his captivity, given him a chance to strike back at the Vraad. In return, Cabe's nemesis had foregone his task, even though death was nearly upon him.

It meant that the mage would have a difficult time finding out who had paid the drake to hunt him down in the first place, but that was a trail for a different time. Cabe had things to settle here . . . first and foremost ensuring that the foul apparition never escaped again.

X

He materialized in the tomb, appearing right before the amber-encrusted sarcophagus. The moment he did, the amber there turned transparent, revealing his nameless mother. The wizard had a fair idea who she might be, even if he still did not know what to call her.

She was at rest, that much he somehow felt. Cabe believed that she had sensed when he had finally bested Melenea.

Thinking of the Vraad, Cabe brought forth the imprisoned flower. It looked like an exact duplicate of the one with his mother. Cabe wondered if he would ever find out the odd reason for that flower, which had given the malevolent spirit a foothold in the mortal world.

The Vraad waited for me all that time, the wizard thought. *She could never truly be free unless I enabled her.*

His grandfather had no doubt fashioned the spell to be one that only he could ever remove in order to ensure her permanent captivity. Yet, Cabe's birth had from the start left a way out. Already bound to his mother, Melenea had surely known of Nathan's sacrifice of part of his own essence into the infant. It was a rare mistake on the elder Bedlam's part.

Setting the smaller piece atop the enchanted coffin, Cabe delved with his mind into the core matrix of his grandfather's spell. There, he began dismantling the heart of all Nathan had done here.

As he expected, the Vraad made an attempt to escape through the partially-unraveled spell, but in many ways now torn between two places, her power was laughable. Cabe shunted aside her feeble effort, then made his changes.

The smaller piece of amber sank seamlessly into the larger, but ceased long before the two flowers—the grown from the first—could ever touch. Then, the wizard redid the overall matrix, adding his own unique touches. He also corrected for the unsettling and peculiar nature of Vraad magic, making certain that there would never be a repeat of the near escape.

And finally, when all that was done, Cabe stepped back from the tomb and with a gesture recreated the wall as it had been, minus the accursed roots. Not satisfied yet, he left the underground chamber, reappearing next to Marilee and Bertran. The two stood a safe distance from the estate, much of which was covered with dead dragon. He had already explained to them what he intended, but they still looked from him to the dragon and back again in complete disbelief.

"Can you really do that?" Marilee asked. "He's dead."

"A dragon is magic, even in ways many of them do not understand. That magic is still in him and it'll enable me to do just as I promised."

With that said, the wizard immediately concentrated on the huge corpse, seeking that inherent magic. He had never cast such a spell, but was confident that he could succeed.

Touching the lines of force that crisscrossed all things in the mortal world, Cabe directed them into the dragon. The dragon's magic intertwined with those forces, joining power to power.

The estate erupted in a staggering display of colors. They represented only the merest fraction of the forces Cabe now put into play. All that was the iron drake—a creature of death—now began to transform the very grounds.

The land shook. Marilee instinctively seized Bertran's arm, which the big man was clearly glad to give. Cabe gave both a reassuring look, but secretly set in motion a protective spell just in case.

The unleashed magic engulfed and absorbed the estate house, then spread forth. As it did, the outline of the landscape continued to shift and things began to sprout from the ground.

Trees. Dozens and dozens of trees. Their seeds had come from those scattered by the forest beyond. Left to themselves, they would have rotted away, but Cabe's spell had gathered them together, nurtured them, and accelerated their growth. Before two minutes had passed, where once the estate house had stood there was now a copse of trees, with more adding to the ranks like a growing legion of sentinels.

In their midst, one other feature added itself. A stream fed by water redirected by the spell flowed through the wooded area.

It was not exactly a vale, but it was as close as could be fashioned here.

Moreover, the virgin forest would continue to spread through the ruins of Mito Pica, taking the former city over as had not been possible before. Cabe did not know if Melenea's presence had kept Mito Pica so desolate, so full of misery, but she had certainly contributed to it. Now, her part, at least, was at an end.

As for the Vraad, her spirit was sealed far, far below the surface, with the forest roots creating a barrier not even one of the massive, burrowing Quel could have penetrated.

"It's—it's beautiful," Marilee finally whispered. Bertran merely nodded.

"This is the testament to our loved ones that Mito Pica should represent," the wizard replied. "It can never replace them, nor do I expect it to make you and the rest forgive me for what part I played—"

"We've been wrong about that. You weren't responsible. I can see that now and I'll make certain that the others learn of it."

Cabe shook his head sadly. "They'll just think you under a spell."

"Those who know me won't . . . and we'll convince the rest." In their conversations since the Vraad's defeat, she had said nothing about her possession by Cabe's mother and the wizard had not brought it up.

He doubted that it would be so simple for her to convince the others, but let her words pass. "You needn't walk to them. I can at least still send you off safely to your chosen destination."

The two quickly shook their heads. "We're good with walking," she continued. "Besides, it looks like it's going to be a beautiful day here . . . for once."

"As you like." Cabe stepped back. "In that case, I'll bid you farewell."

Marilee gave him a smile. "Thank you, Master Bedlam . . . for changing everything."

"No . . . thank you for forgiving me."

Before she or Bertran could say anything else, the wizard vanished. There was someone else he had to thank, someone he should have thanked long, long ago.

Cabe reappeared not that far from where the other drakes and their mounts had perished. He could not see the area where the remains had been, but believed that by now there was nothing left. For the one who had slain them, the drake bodies would have been a scar on an otherwise peaceful forest.

He returned to the tree before which he had knelt. Once again, the mage marveled at its height, which was greater than that of trees he knew to be much older. The good health and immense size of this giant should hardly have surprised him, for any tree touched by the spirit of an elf—or even a half-blood—generally prospered well.

Knowing no other way to begin, Cabe quietly said, "Hello, Hadeen."

The branches rustled despite no wind. The noise of their rustling seemed to create the spellcaster's name. Cabe . . .

Feeling suddenly like the youth who had found his world turned upside down by drakes hunting him for merely being the grandson of Nathan Bedlam, Cabe bowed his head. "You're the source of so many of the frightening visions people have seen here, aren't you? You did what you could to keep anyone from coming within her reach and becoming a puppet, a set of hands for her, as the drake did."

There was no answer, but Cabe felt certain he had things correct so far. After a moment's consideration, the spellcaster went on, "You also tried to warn me in particular and I ignored those warnings. I'm sorry." When there was still nothing from the tree, he bluntly asked, "You've been both trying to counter her and warn me each time I visited, haven't you?"

Now the branches rustled. *Yes . . .*

"She tricked you and grandfather somehow. She managed to find a way to at least partially reach freedom . . . but couldn't do anything more without me. It was because I had part of her and part of him. That made me unique, the only one with the power to undo grandfather's spell."

Yes . . .

"Azran released her. He found her a prisoner in that chess piece . . . that same set the Gryphon has now."

There was silence. Cabe frowned. The first part of his comment was definitely truth.

"The Gryphon's set is fake, a copy, isn't it?"

Yes . . .

Hadeen was not trying to be uncooperative. The half-elf had been part of the tree so long, even this much speech was an effort. Using the 'ghosts' was easier, but they were limited in what they could pass along.

"You said nothing the other times . . . or did I just not understand?"

Yes . . . tried so hard . . .

The effort put into the last was staggering. Cabe shivered, thinking how long he had ignored what Hadeen had wanted him so desperately to know.

"She was stronger this time, wasn't she? She only managed to finally pierce the amber recently." The mage considered. "Once you had passed on and Mito Pica fell. Then, she finally had no one to keep her under control."

This must be kept between us . . . another voice suddenly urged in Cabe's mind. The wizard spun around to see two glowing figures. One was Hadeen . . . and so was the other.

No. After a moment, Cabe saw that there were some slight difference. The second half-elf also wore more elegant clothing.

The Dragon Hunter did his part, the second continued. *He could not know that the seed had literally been planted. The demon spirit fooled us all there.*

We must remove her from the tomb—Hadeen began.

No! This is where she lies . . . with me and with no other! She is my only child, my heart! The stories about me will keep most away from our home. In the Vale, she will find the peace she needs . . .

And the peace ever eluding us, eh brother? Hadeen pointed out. *It is not our fault we were cast out. We did the right thing, even if those of our elven side did not understand.*

Most of what Hadeen said went all but unheard as his term for the other caught Cabe utterly by surprise despite the obvious resemblance between the two figures. *Brother?* If so, that meant that while he had not been Cabe's actual father . . . Hadeen had been his *granduncle.*

Ignoring the apparitions, the wizard turned back to the tree. "The master of the Vale was your brother? She was your niece?"

Even though there was no response this time, Cabe knew that he was correct. He now also understood that there had been many reasons why Hadeen had chosen to live on the outskirts of Mito Pica with Nathan's grandson. He had not only been seeking to protect the infant . . . but had been working hand in hand with Cabe's other grandfather to keep the Vraad spirit ensnared in the body of Hadeen's unfortunate niece.

The mage's mind spun. He knew that his wife, Gwen, who had lived in that time, did not know any of this. Nathan had lied even to her. She had only been told that Azran had taken a servant as the vessel for his child. Still, there had to have been some clues to the full truth. There was more involved here, but Cabe knew that it might take him a long time—perhaps a lifetime—to find out even a fraction of that.

Cabe sensed Hadeen's spirit already receding into the essence of the tree. With

461

the Vraad vanquished, there was little to hold Hadeen to the mortal world. Only protecting Cabe had enabled him to keep some sense of self since the city's fall and the death of his mortal shell.

This is only the beginning, the spellcaster decided. *Vanquishing Melenea was only one piece of a vaster puzzle . . . all about me.*

He knew of only one place to begin. Penacles. The City of Knowledge. The Gryphon was the only one other than Gwen who had lived in that time and he had not spent two hundred years frozen alive. If there was someone who knew what had happened, it was the Gryphon.

And if he knew, Cabe would also demand to know why the lord of Penacles had kept all of this from him.

He gazed at the expansive crown of the tree, seeing in it the face of the half-elf. With a nod, Cabe murmured, "Thank you for everything . . . "

There was no rustling. The wizard had half-heartedly hoped for some reply, but knew enough about elves to understand that Hadeen had given him more than should have been expected. The half-blood had loved his foster son—and grandnephew—that much.

Cabe focused on Penacles. He saw no reason to waste any time. He wanted answers, at least some answers—

The branches rustled. *Hadrea . . .*

The wizard stiffened. He waited, but there was nothing else.

Hadrea. His mother. Cabe had her name. He could picture her now, picture her when she had been alive and vibrant.

Ignoring the moistness growing in his eyes, the wizard began casting the spell that would take him to Penacles. As he finished it, he suddenly called out to the tree, "Thank you for everything . . . father . . . "

And as he vanished, he thought he heard the rustling branches form one last word.

Son . . .

RICHARD A. KNAAK

DRAGON MOUND

(Available in Hardcover & ebook)

Lightning crackled nearby, splitting a tree, which nearly fell across his path. Evan's steed did not hesitate, racing as swiftly as the wind toward his destination despite the fact that the bolt that had almost hit the pair had come not from above but from before them.

Evan drew the jeweled blade, certain that someone or something already expected him.

Perhaps a hundred yards or so from the dragon's mound, the baleful animal at last halted to a slow trot. The knight noted his mount's wariness as they approached the vicinity, almost as if the horse sensed something he could not.

"What is it?" Evan whispered.

The damnable steed's only reply came in a dismissive flick of the ears. Evan frowned, at last peering out into the wet, foggy gloom for answers.

Someone whispered.

He turned in the saddle, seeking the speaker, only to be snared by another voice coming from the opposite direction. Both spoke unintelligibly, but with tones of urgency.

A pale figure moved through the trees, seemingly unconcerned by either the downpour or the lightning. The knight leaned forward, squinting. It took Evan a moment to recognize the fur-clad form of an ax-man from Tepis—a warrior from the battle some two centuries before. The fur had been stained by something dark and the figure's head wobbled as if not entirely attached. No living being this, but rather some specter wandering the earth.

Despite his mount's disagreement, he forced the animal toward the murky figure. What part this apparition played Evan did not know. He grew tired of unanswered mystery after unanswered mystery—

The ashen steed drew up short as a veiled, feminine figure in armor burst forward from the brush, waving her sword. She made not a sound and when the horse rose up and kicked at the horned helm of the attacker, his hooves went through her. She continued on, one of Haggad's lithe and deadly Knights of the Veil, swinging at foes Evan could not see.

He shivered, the ghosts of memory a faint thing compared to this. The worn knight shifted his gaze and through rain-drenched eyes watched as his most ancient nightmares more and more took on form and fury. From the mists emerged a Wallmyrian archer, his gut spilled open by a sword, readying his bow for another volley. The empty stare of death greeted Evan when he sought the man's eyes.

Beyond the archer, a knight in old Rundin wear straggled along, one leg twisted, armor soaked in blood, and half his head and helm missing.

And in the background, the whispers and the thunder of the storm gave way to the mournful wail of battle horns.

A bolt of lightning from the vicinity of the mound struck the earth nearby, startling man and mount and briefly illuminating the area for a mile around. In that

463

instant of light, Evan Wytherling beheld a sight so blood-freezing that he nearly turned and fled, whatever the consequences to his tarnished honor and his cursed quest.

The dead had come in force to replay their roles in the great battle.

They formed from mist, from rain, from thin air. Elfin warriors with skin paler than even in life marched toward the mountains, some without limbs, some without heads, some crawling along with only one hand to push them forward. Trolls pincushioned with longbow shafts tottered toward them, grotesque faces made more so by death. A scorched and mangled skeleton swung at an almost perfectly preserved Rundin warrior.

From above came the roar of a dragon. Evan immediately looked up, but saw nothing but the overcast heaven. He returned his gaze to the ground just in time to notice one ghost in particular, a ghost who stared back . . . no mean feat as the wraith's massive head lay cradled in his arm.

"Come to play, boy?" sneered the bony, snow-eyed visage. In his other hand he waved a wicked, toothed sword stained with dried blood. "We've waited long for you . . ."

Evan fought to control his mounting distress as he greeted the foul apparition in turn. "Hello, General."

"Meek as a kitten! You've been away from good bloodshed far too long, boy! No more fire in your gut . . . just water!" The rail-thin specter tapped his steel-gray breastplate where a dozen or more heavy swords had been driven into his torso. "Look at me, boy! I don't even have a gut anymore and yet I'm still more alive than you!" The gaunt face cracked into a skeletal smile again. "Why don't you come down and play a little? I'll get the fire going in you again . . . before I split your gullet . . ."

Control yourself, Evan urged. The macabre figure before him could not hurt the knight; none of these apparitions could. They were phantasms called up by latent magic seeping from the cairn of Grimyr. At worst, they might steer him toward madness if Evan gave them substance with his fear. Even the monstrous figure before him, one of those best guaranteed to strike at his innermost being, did not really exist as a threat. The veteran knight had faced far more dangerous ghosts and knew the difference. "You are long dead, General Haggad. Go back to your rest."

"But I'm not done with this world yet, boy . . . and not with you, either. You owe for a lot of deaths." The wraith held his nearly hairless head up high, the better for Evan to see the soulless eyes, the outline of the bone beneath the very thin layer of dead flesh. "You owe Novaris, especially."

The silver knight's skin tingled. Evan pulled quickly on the reins, trying to urge his mount elsewhere. The horse obeyed without argument, perhaps sensing the same danger that his rider had.

A bolt struck the drenched earth a scant distance from them.

The force threw the stunned crusader from his horse. Evan heard the animal shriek, then he himself cried out as he bounced against rock and wood. His outfit did little to cushion the blow; he doubted that even his full armor would have aided. The stunned knight rolled forward, unable to stop and yet somehow still managing to hold on to his weapon.

Another bolt struck, ripping open the earth and unleashing a new element to the storm already raging, a torrential rain of dirt and stone. Clumps of dirt pelted Evan as he tried to stop himself. A crevice opened before him and the knight nearly tumbled into it, but at the last moment Evan managed to drive the tip of his sword into the remaining ground. He held on and wiped his eyes clear, finding himself staring into a black chasm that seemed to go on forever.

The rain continued to torment him, but no new bolt struck. Gasping, Evan pushed himself up to his knees, looking for Haggad. The ghost had vanished. All the ghosts had vanished, as had his horse. Laying his blade on his knees, the bedraggled warrior pulled off one muddied glove, put two fingers in his mouth, and let loose a high whistle. A moment later, he heard whinnying, but from impossibly far away.

Forcing himself to his feet, Evan again surveyed the region. The phantom warriors had indeed vanished, but somehow he knew that he had not seen the last of them.

A lupine howl cut through the storm, a howl answered immediately by one just like it, then another, then another, and another still. From all sides.

Evan immediately whistled again, but once more the reply came from too far away. The shadowy steed should have been able to reach his rider by now, and that they still remained separated by so much distance indicated that something interfered. Estimating the direction from which the horse's call had come, the mud-soaked knight trudged on, sword at the ready for whatever he would next face.

The howls grew nearer. Evan picked up his pace. He suspected the creatures would not be so easy to deal with this time, not with the numbers that he estimated hunted him and certainly not with so much power radiating from the vicinity of the mound. As with the wraiths, the wolves were clearly tied to Grimyr's tomb.

Thinking of that, Evan paused. Through the abilities Centuros had bequeathed upon him, he found he did sense some evidence of Novaris's magic, but it still seemed too faint, too old. The sorcerer-king must have set this trap long, long ago, which meant Evan had a good chance of outwitting it; the spell had to stay true to how it had been cast, unlike a thinking creature.

A more opportune decision Evan could not have made, for just then, a dark form with claws and teeth leapt upon him, humanlike eyes glaring into his own. Knight and beast rolled once, then Evan kicked at the lower torso of his attacker, freeing himself. He brought the blade up, cutting into the stomach region. As before, no blood, no organs, spilled forth, yet the creature howled as if dealt a deadly blow, then, with a sigh, evaporated.

By now they had to know that to face his sword directly meant their doom and yet still they most often tried to charge him. Did they not fear the weapon?

From both his left and right came a new pair seemingly forming out of thin air. Swinging the sword wide with both hands, Evan Wytherling severed the head of one monster, then cut across the chest of the second. The first fell, fading even as it hit the drenched and ruined ground, but the second staggered toward its intended prey as if driven by a force it could not fight. Evan felt little pride as he finished the wounded shadow beast, his adversary moving so clumsily that the knight simply thrust his jeweled blade through it to the hilt.

The hair on his neck rose as shadows in every direction separated from the surrounding trees and moved in on him. Evan glanced around, saw that he stood surrounded by more than a dozen of the murky demons. Vulnerable they might be, but sheer numbers would tell a sorrowful end to his tale after all, unless . . .

He had never cast the spell with so little preparation, but all his years of working the wizard's magic had to help him now. Muttering the words of power under his breath, Evan spun in a circle, dragging the tip of his sword over the earth. In the wake of the blade's path, a faint blue line of light grew into being.

Perhaps realizing what he intended, one of the beasts leapt toward the remaining open area. Evan muttered faster, completing the spell, then tugged the tip of the sword until it touched the beginning of the blue loop.

Airborne, the lupine monstrosity could not halt its attack. It fell across the glowing boundary that raggedly encircled the desperate knight. No cry. No gore. No ash. Its entire body simply evaporated inch by inch as the spell's victim crossed.

A second creature pulled back just before it would have committed itself. One of the half-seen monsters snarled, others following. They jostled as if trying to urge some of their members forward, but no one desired to achieve the fate of the first. As willing as they were to directly chance his sword, they clearly saw no value in throwing themselves uselessly at such a barrier.

Protected for the moment, Evan fell to one knee, gasping again for breath. Still the rain poured down, giving him little respite. Nonetheless, the knight took what rest he could get, ever, of course, keeping his eye on the beasts.

This had turned out to be a very personal trap, he realized, but one that should have been beyond Valentin's abilities. That Valentin could affect the town, Evan understood. The crimson warrior lay imprisoned directly underneath its center . . . and Evan now recalled at least in part the pattern Pretor's Hill itself created. The town's layout formed a sign of power, one that amplified a spell cast in its center. No coincidence, that. Novaris's hand surely had prompted the early settlers to assist in building the method of their own destruction.

Still, could the spell have been so well set that Valentin could reach out even here and cause such disaster for his adversary? The only other explanation seemed less likely. For all his attention to detail, even the sorcerer-king would have been hard-pressed to put together such an elaborate spell designed to last centuries and strike only when Evan appeared. Surely Novaris, if he lived, had not been so fearful of one determined yet weary warrior?

Questions and more questions, none of which he should have been presently wasting his time on. The creatures would not simply stand and watch; they were more than animal. Evan had a disturbing feeling that he knew more about them than he thought he did. He sensed a familiarity that went deep, went back to a time before he had been sent upon this endless quest.

At that moment, the faint voices began again . . . but this time there were words that Evan could make out.

whywhywhywhywhywhy . . .

lostlostlostlostlost . . .

betrayedbetrayedbetrayedbetrayed . . .

lostlostlostlostlost . . .

whywhywhywhywhywhy . . .

The sword slipped from Evan Wytherling's frozen hand. He knew not the names, but he knew the voices. They were voices from the war belonging to men he had once fought beside in that previous life. Evan clutched his ears, not wanting to hear those voices, be reminded that their owners had all perished in that battle, their lives, so many lives, wasted because of the ambitions of one sorcerer.

Nothing shielded his ears from the voices, though. They seeped through his clenched hands, ripped into the cloth of the hood of his cloak, repeating endlessly words of condemnation.

The lupine hunters crouched close, possibly waiting to see if through madness Evan himself might cross the barrier.

"This is not real," he muttered at last, almost throwing the words at the watching pack. "This is a spell of yours, Novaris, a spell to make your enemies do themselves in! I am stronger than it!"

Yet no sooner had he uttered his defiance when the next and even more foul step of his torture commenced, for the indistinct faces of the furred horrors surrounding him shifted, grew somewhat identifiable. They were not, however, the faces of beasts, but rather those of men, lost men, dead men. Slaughtered, left for the carrion crows. Each and every one of them.

Evan knew them all by face, if not by name.

And each mouthed the same words over and over . . .

why . . . lost . . .

betrayal . . .

He shut his eyes, trying to will the faces and words away. Memories welled up within, adding to his desperate situation. Faces Evan had not recalled in decades passed through his mind. Bloody skirmishes long fought replayed themselves. The whispered words continued on in the background, now accompanied by the low, consistent beat of war drums and the mournful wail of horns signaling the doomed into battle.

Despite his strong struggles, Evan Wytherling found himself slipping deeper into despair. He had never imagined reaching such a point and certainly not here. Emotions he had cast aside for so very long poured forth, the guilt of two hundred years at last seeking its due in full. The stricken knight grabbed for the hilt of the sword, uncertain at that moment whether he needed it to fend off foes or put an end to his own miserable condition.

From beyond the circle came a familiar cry, one that ripped through his despair, tore him from his descent into relentless guilt. Evan looked up in time to see a massive, pale phantom burst through the startled creatures, turning them once more into shadow beasts, not condemning ghosts. Great hooves struck out at the nearest, sparks of magic flying as the lupine horror fell back, stunned.

Reaching forward with the sword, Evan muttered a few words, eradicating the protective circle. The massive stallion charged up to him, turning so that the human could immediately leap onto the saddle. Evan did, then clutched at the reins. One of the beasts sought to pull him back down, but the knight's mount turned again, enabling Evan to strike. His attacker fell back, one arm severed.

The pack reformed, pressing them from two sides. Forced to higher ground, the pallid steed had to fight for footing. Evan noticed burns on the animal's sides, evidence that the steed's attempts to reach him had been fraught with danger. Disturbing enough how quickly this trap had worn the veteran warrior to the core; now Evan saw he could not even rely on the full strength of his companion.

The horse stumbled, something he rarely did. Evan nearly slipped off. He peered around them, trying to judge the landscape. They were within but a few yards of Grimyr's mound.

Another grim notion occurred to him, one that risked much but might save them. Limited though his own skills at magic might be, the tricks Centuros had taught him could still help Evan reverse his dire situation. Given a few moments' respite, he believed he could seize control of the magic spell and turn it. During that attempt he risked leaving himself open to attack, but that might be unavoidable.

Tugging hard on the reins, he steered his mount toward the dragon mound just as the shadows closed. Kicking at the nearest fiends, the animal reluctantly obeyed. Evan himself did not entirely like his choice of action but felt it best. They were already being herded farther and farther from safety.

In the rain the mound almost took on the shadowy shape of the great leviathan buried within. How Grimyr would have roared with anger if he had known that someday Evan would try to use what remained of the dragon's magic against the very power Grimyr had once served. As for Valentin, Evan realized that this might be his chance to put an end to the crimson knight's foul curse. Surely his suspicions had to be correct; Valentin had to be drawing power from this same source through his ancient link to Grimyr.

He sensed the presence of magic, a presence much stronger than during his previous visit. The moment they reached the edge of the mound, Evan leapt off, landing several feet up its side. The baleful steed snorted, then turned to a defensive position. The horse understood that he had to buy his rider precious time.

467

DRAGON MOUND

The soaked knight climbed farther up, trying to locate the highest point of the mound. He heard the nearby growls of the shadowy beasts and the defiant snort of his horse. Evan knew he did not have long; the stallion could not take them all on.

At last finding a satisfactory position atop the dragon's tomb, Evan prepared to drive his blade into the wet earth. He did not intend opening a passage to the rotting remains of the reptilian beast; instead the sword would act as a focus, as a way of drawing what magic there was to Evan's hand.

"Grasping at straws, boy?"

The suddenness of the voice nearly made the knight stumble backward off the mound. Regaining his footing, he glared at the apparition of General Haggad, who stood but a few feet to his left. The general's cadaverous head smiled from the crook of his arm. As usual, the bloodied, jagged blade remained a fixture in the ghost's other hand.

"You are becoming tiresome, General."

"And you are becoming desperate and pathetic, boy. Give in to your guilt. Give in to the past. This isn't the course you want to take."

Evan kept his expression masked, although inside his anxiety swelled. Haggad could be no less devious in death as in life. "You are nothing but the product of a madman's spell, General. You've failed to drive me mad, so you might as well go."

"I'd like to cut you wide open," the snow-eyed ghoul commented cheerfully, "to see how yellow your blood's become . . ."

The silver knight turned from him. "I have no more time for you, General."

"Then you'll have no more head, boy!"

Evan twisted around, but too late. Haggad's fiendish blade cut through the air in line with the paladin's throat. Sheer reflex caused Evan to reach up with one hand in a futile attempt to stop the jagged blade, but the general shifted, bringing his wicked weapon over.

The blade sliced completely through Evan's neck.

He gasped, waiting for the blood, waiting for oblivion. Yet, no blood seeped onto his hand, no darkness swallowed him. Slowly the truth dawned on Evan; the sword had not beheaded him. General Haggad's weapon had been as insubstantial as the specter himself.

The wraith laughed, a mocking, chilling sound. The body of the general shook so hard the head nearly toppled from the crook of the arm. "He said I'd be able to have some sport with you even though I couldn't touch you, boy! What a gullible little fool still after all these years!"

Though breathless, heart pounding, Evan composed himself again, realizing that Haggad's tactics had been designed to stall him, nothing more. Restoring the grimness to his features, the knight once more prepared himself for the spell. He lifted his sword. He could do this. He knew enough from Centuros to turn the evil on itself.

"I wouldn't do that if I were you, boy! He wouldn't like that!"

"Who?" Evan mocked, despite his efforts to remain indifferent. "Who? Valentin? Novaris?"

"Novaris? The Master's long gone from here, Wytherling, and Valentin, loyal that he is, is a mad dog, to be sure! No, I mean himself, boy! You know best not to disturb the dead . . ."

Evan reminded himself that he spoke only to a projection, that General Haggad stood there as only the simplest of ghosts. Some could do physical harm, but Haggad could only taunt, pretend. He had no real power over the knight save what Evan gave him . . . and Evan would give no more.

"Your games are over, General," Evan said as he focused on his sword. "Go back to being dead."

"You first, boy."

Just before Evan would have plunged his sword into the ground, the earth beneath his feet suddenly gave way, collapsing inward. Evan stumbled back, arms outstretched as he tried to regain his balance. His blade, which made contact with only air, was unnaturally propelled upward and over, landing far.

He rolled off the mound, collapsing facedown at its base. Groaning, Evan moved slowly, the air knocked from him.

Some distance away, his mount gave out a warning cry.

Darkness enveloped Evan, a darkness deeper than the night and even the storm warranted. With effort, Evan rolled onto his back, seeking his blade.

Laughter not that of the wraith assailed his ears, sent his head pounding. He knew that laugh, knew it erupted from no human source.

Something large and powerful struck him.

DRAGON MOUND

THE TURNING WAR: DRAGON MASTERS

(Legends of the Dragonrealm)

Nathan finally landed, every bone in his body shaking as he struck. Rock and earth continued to spill down around him, but his spell held strong.

Head pounding, Nathan managed to focus on his surroundings. As he did, it became readily apparent that what he lay in was no natural passage created by the flow of lava. What little the mage could see of the walls had the look of having been hewn by hand.

He tried to reach out with his mind to Yalak's. Not at all to Nathan's surprise, some invisible force cut off his attempt.

The rubble around him began to shift despite there being no tremor.

Leaping to his feet, Nathan illuminated the underground cave. A blinding blue brilliance spread everywhere . . . and in it stood revealed what he counted as at least a dozen ominous shelled shapes.

And two dozen glittering eyes fixed upon him.

Despite their girth, the shelled figures moved through the rubble with astounding fluidity. Nathan knew that they were not Quel, that race being confined to the Legar Peninsula a rarely seen. These creatures' shells were akin to those of turtles and even their heads --- or rather their sharp, sharp beaks --- had some general similarity, but there the resemblance ended. The faces were broader, squatter, and a malevolent intelligence filled the eyes. In their thick fists, they held short daggers with twin blades.

Jaruu . . . Nathan had never seen the beastmen before, but knew of them from tales of the Red Dragon's domain. The Jaruu were supposed to serve the Dragon King and so should not have been about to attack him . . . yet, these clearly were.

"I am here in the name of the emperor!" Nathan shouted. The Jaruu could understand Common speech, even if they did not speak it themselves. It was the language preferred by the Dragon Kings, after all.

Nevertheless, the Jaruu did not slow and their intent for Nathan was made more apparent by the low hisses more than one emitted.

The mage wished the creatures asleep, only to have the spell fade without even slowing the Jaruu. Frowning, Nathan took a measure of his foes. He waved his hand across, sending rock flying at his attackers. Three went down under the onslaught, but the rest ducked their heads deep into their shells, each utilizing a ridge atop to further shield themselves from his magical attack. At the same time, they continued to converge on him.

Nathan did not ask where his comrades were, assuming that they faced troubles of their own. Someone had arranged all this, leaking the information carefully. Nathan had to assume that it had been the Gryphon. No magic had been involved in digging out the ground underneath the illusion. Any use of such would have lingered long enough to warn Nathan and the others when they had arrived.

As this all ran through his head, Nathan continued to cast. Concerned that the Jaruu attacked under some misbelief that he threatened their master, Nathan was determined not to kill them. He only wished that he could be certain that he could stop the creatures from doing harm to him.

There was no use in attempting another spell directly focused on the Jaruu. Nathan was certain that it would fail just as the first had. The rocks had only worked because they had been the true target of his spell.

The blue glow began to fade. Darkness would not bother the Jaruu, who dwelled most of their time below ground to avoid the heat of the surface. Unfortunately, the light did not bother them either, or else they would have shown some hesitation after his illumination spell.

The foremost Jaruu reached him. It thrust the blade at his throat ---

The tip broke off, Nathan's magical shield holding. However, the Jaruu did not seem at all perturbed by the damage to the weapon. It immediately dropped the ruined dagger and sought to crush Nathan's throat in its huge hands.

"Awaayyy!" snarled a reptilian voice that echoed throughout the area. *"Awaayyy!"*

The thundering cry was followed by an angry roar.

The Jaruu froze. Nathan saw the conflict in their inhuman orbs. They wanted to continue their attack against the mage, but a primal fear now stirred within them.

Again came the roar, this time louder and obviously nearer.

One of the Jaruu broke, turning and rushing into the darkness beyond Nathan that took it farthest from the direction of the roar. That caused a flood of retreat by the other shelled creatures, quickly leaving the wizard alone save for those Jaruu he had managed to knock unconscious with the rocks.

No . . . Nathan realized very quickly that there was still someone else with him.

"Very clever . . . you picked the one thing the Jaruu feared. I wonder how long it will take them to comprehend that they ran from a spell of your making and not actually their master?"

Part of the darkness peeled away, but remained nearly as unfathomable. Nathan took one glance at the long, flowing black cloak and hood and especially at the murky face and immediately cast a new spell.

The six silver bolts should have pinned their target to the nearest wall, but instead simply melted as they neared the other figure.

"There is no reason for that," Shade murmured. "The Jaruu were not my doing. I only made use of the moment to speak with you."

"You're condemned by a dozen decrees from the emperor," Nathan retorted, a new attack already unleashed. He watched as the air solidified around the warlock ---

--- and then softened again.

"I've been condemned a thousand times more by countless others." Shade shook his head. "Some of them succeeded in having those decrees carried out. You yourself was the tool twice, if you recall."

Recalling not only those battles but aware of so many of the other stories told about the hooded figure, neither of Nathan's attacks had been meant to slay this current incarnation of the warlock; that possibly unattainable goal he would this time leave to Lord Purple and the emperor.

While his mind raced over what spell would work against a legend, Nathan also strengthened his own defenses. In addition, another concern constantly demanded his attention.

"Where are my friends?" Nathan demanded, purposely not mentioning that one of them was his son. That might put unexpected focus on Dayn. "Where?"

"Following a false trail. Have no fear for them. I won't hold you long."

"You won't hold me at ---"

A chill coursed through Nathan as yet more of the darkness separated itself from the walls. This time, it took on a shape not at all humanoid, but rather equine. The *shadow* of an equine.

"The lord of the Hell Plains is aware of us!" the booming voice declared to Shade. "This is best done and done now, my friend!"

"It will be, but I need Master Bedlam here to understand."

"I understand that you'll never take me," Nathan promised, well aware of his chances against not just *one* being of myth, but *two*. "Neither you nor this demon . . . "

"I am merely *Darkhorse*, nothing more," the towering creature retorted, sounding very offended. "not a demon . . . well, not in the absolute true sense of the word . . . I think."

While Shade emitted a brief chuckle at the stallion's almost childlike response, Nathan found nothing to laugh at. Every tale concerning either of the pair raced through his thoughts as he sought some weakness or at least an avenue of escape.

Another roar echoed across not only the cave, but the region above. There was no doubt of the reality of *this* one.

Glancing at Nathan again, Shade sighed. "Too late. This was not how it was supposed to---"

Tremendous claws ripped open the gap through which Nathan had fallen. Fire immediately swept into the cave, washing over everything and everyone . . . including Nathan.

Darkhorse dissipated much the way shadows did in the light of day or the brilliance of a fearsome inferno. Shade, on the other hand, *threw* himself at the other spellcaster, enveloping Nathan in his cloak.

As that happened, for the first time the elder Bedlam sensed the nearby presence of his son. Nathan tried to contact Dayn, but a different force prevented him this time. He knew that its odd magical signature could only belong to Shade.

The ground shook . . . then all was quiet.

The darkness receded. Shade pulled away from Nathan, who instantly leapt to his feet . . . and paused as his *new* surroundings became evident.

They were still in the Hell Plains, that much was evident not only from the stifling heat, but also from the jagged craters in the distance. Nathan recognized one particularly ugly and active crater and knew that Shade had teleported them miles away from their previous spot.

But what caught his attention more and at least for the time being prevented him from renewing the battle with Shade was the ruined structure before the pair. Little remained but the foundation and a few bits of wall, but Nathan could sense strong traces of ancient magic . . . and among them a trace that for some reason that appeared naggingly familiar to him.

"We hoped that we could bring this about gradually, but matters are racing faster and faster toward utter calamity," the hooded figure casually commented. "He will probably be angry at me for this, but I think it best it done here this way."

"What is this place, Shade? What madness do you have in mind ---"

A gloved hand rose. "Please, call me 'Vadym' . . . this time."

I will call you nothing instead, Nathan warily thought to himself . . . then wondered if the warlock could hear that thought. Shade gave no hint that he did, but the many legends bespoke of the accursed spellcaster having a thousand and one abilities no one else could claim.

"It seems safe enough for now," Shade continued, the murky countenance turning briefly to the ruins. "No sign of their presence, either."

THE TURNING WAR: DRAGON MASTERS

Nathan had no idea what the last meant, but it seemed to hint at someone other than those the wizard would have thought of. *Not the rebels? Not the drakes or their servants? Who, then?*

"The entrance is sealed by several wards. Allow me."

Before Nathan could protest, their surroundings changed yet again. Once more they stood in an underground chamber, their new destination --- illuminated by a small, emerald ball of light cast by Shade --- even more obviously hewn by intelligent means. Again, there arose not only disturbing, ancient traces of magic, but also that one hint of something so familiar.

"Where are we?" Nathan asked.

Shade cocked his head. "Where last the truth tried to reveal itself . . . and did not. Even the Gryphon does not know about this. Only Darkhorse and I --- who were here, then --- would recall it." The warlock grunted. "Not even the current lord of the Hell Plains knows, despite this being the work of his sire . . . "

Nothing of what his sinister companion said made any sense to Nathan. He also kept wondering at his own hesitation. This was *Shade*, declared threat by the Dragon Emperor. Nathan understood that he should have not ceased trying to subdue the warlock for an instant.

But the same misgivings constantly remaining with Nathan after recalling Yalak's lost cousin now stirred more than ever. Nathan's world was no longer as simple as he had once imagined it. Why it had suddenly become so complex, so full of unsettling questions, the mage could not say ---

The chamber shook, but the tremor was mild in comparison to the last one, as if the epicenter were much farther away.

"The lord of the Hell Plains is persistent," Nathan's faceless companion murmured. "Let us hope he keeps his focus on Darkhorse . . . "

"I still have no idea why you brought me here," Nathan snapped, finally having enough despite his misgivings. In the Red Dragon's fury, the drake lord might cause harm to some of the party, including Dayn. "but my s--- my friends need me. Consider that the only reason I don't try to take your head . . . "

The spell he launched with those words *should* have worked. Certainly, Shade did nothing to stop him. So near, Nathan would have sensed the warlock's unsettling magical trace the moment the hooded figure cast anything. Yet, it was something else that nullified the wizard's attempt to depart even before it was finished.

"You will fail each time, Nathan Bedlam. The stone's matrix survives well. The spell is ancient. Cast by one of my kind, although not for this purpose." The hood tilted slightly to the other side. "I never *have* found out just how or where the previous Red Dragon discovered it. I should do that ---"

Mind racing madly, Nathan backed away. He wore a small dagger at his waist, but doubted that it would be of any use. Shade likely had a dozen different protective spells around him that would ---

Nathan stumbled over something. To his dismay, he lost his balance. Worse, he could not even cast a minor spell to keep from falling back.

Much to Nathan's surprise, his drop abruptly slowed. As if held by giant invisible fingers, the mage gently dropped to the ground.

"You should really be more careful," Shade remarked.

With a glare, Nathan put a hand to the side in order to push himself to his feet --

Instead, he gripped a disturbingly long rock.

Shade chose that moment to better illuminate the chamber. The glow he created enabled Nathan to better see what it was he gripped.

It was what remained of a bone. That much, Nathan had already grimly

474

assumed. What he had not expected was the blackened condition of the piece, nor that the bone was so fragile that it crumbled in his grip. An incredible heat had scorched the bone . . . and presumably the flesh upon it.

And what Nathan had taken for another rock --- the one upon which he had slipped --- had been another fragment. Indeed, as Nathan's gaze took in a larger view, the mage saw the full skeletal array . . . and knew without a doubt that it was human.

He quickly looked back at Shade.

"I would have saved him, if I could, but the trap was a cunning one and caught even me by surprise."

The sadness that Nathan heard in the warlock's voice surprised the wizard, but it did not answer a most basic question. "What does this --- what does *he* --- have to do with me?"

"Everything."

With little choice and hoping that it would somehow lead to his freedom, Nathan concentrated on the mysterious remains. Crouching near the burnt bones --- and noting how the entire area surrounding them had been likewise put to the flames --- Nathan saw nothing he could tell about the victim save that, as the warlock had said, it had been a man, not a woman. No garments remained, those obviously burning to ash with the flesh. A few solidified globs of metal marked what might have been a buckle or buttons.

With Shade clearly offering only riddles, Nathan searched for some other clue. Only after staring for nearly a minute and seeing nothing new with only his eyes did he at last understand that it was with *other* senses with which he actually had to study the remains. This *had* been a fellow wizard, after all, even if one that had evidently been considered a traitor by at least one Dragon King.

He peered at the tableau before him as he did when casting a spell. Not only did Nathan see the lines of force coursing through everything, he saw the gathering of raw power here and there . . . a natural occurrence. It was not a spell that enabled him to do this; this was simply a natural ability of all those with power and thus not apparently affected by whatever dampened Nathan's ability to cast.

But all other thoughts vanished as Nathan's eyes once more swept over the bones and he saw what Shade had wanted him to see. This had been a wizard, yes. Although greatly fragmented, his magical trace still remained. That bespoke of a level of power comparable to Nathan's own, something not that common . . .

Yet, no sooner had the wizard delved a bit deeper than his heart skipped a beat. This was also source of the trace he had sensed both here and earlier. Despite the fragmentation, it was still much stronger than he had previously noted, enough that he finally recognized why it had seemed so familiar. Parts of the trace were akin to his own.

The scorched bones were those of a *Bedlam*.

THE JANUS MASK

(Available in Trade & ebook)

It was, G'Meni had to admit, a handsome enough face by present standards. The nose was perhaps just a tad too big as far as he was concerned and the mouth had a mocking cast to it that still unnerved him after more than a decade, but those very features were considered aristocratic by the standards of most, the type that leaders and lovers wore. Eyes of forest green and a head of stark black hair would have completed the picture of the man and soon they would again, now that the baron had chosen at last to make use of his greatest triumph.

He opened the top of the small glass case and removed the face from its container.

The mouth opened and closed once, a reflex that the squat, mustached alchemist was long used to seeing. All of the faces moved when one touched them. Sometimes the mouth worked or the nostrils flared. Once in a while, the eyelids opened, revealing the empty space behind them. G'Meni had made a long study of the properties of the dormant faces, determining what made one more mobile than another. He had come to the conclusion that it was the personality of the one from whom the face had been cast that dictated the random movements. The more vibrant the life, the more active the face.

Ten years had done nothing to render this particular face passive-but then, Viktor Falsche had never been what one would have called passive. Bloodthirsty and impetuous, yes, but never passive.

Still holding the face in his hands, G'Meni looked about the chamber, long oily mustache whirling wildly. "Where are they? They are late again! This will never do!"

His view took in walls overburdened by half-completed experiments, notebooks, jars of samples, and, on one side, the special ceiling-high case, normally locked, from which the container holding the lifelike mask had been drawn. it was a pleasant enough place, to his mind, but it revealed no answer to his question. Before he could repeat his query, however, there came the sound of marching, boot-clad feet. The pace with which the newcomers moved indicated that they knew very well that they were late.

G'Meni scratched the scarred wreckage that was all that remained of his nose, the end result of long ago leaning too close to one of his more explosive experiments, and chuckled at their evident fear. Their fear was a triumph, a major one, in his constant war of bickering with General Straas. To put fear into the minds of the general's men was to put a trace of fear into their commander's own mind, for were they not an extension of the bearded, arrogant soldier himself?

Yes, indeed, they were. Very *much* so.

There was a knock on the door. G'Meni rose to his full inch below five feet, used one hand to straighten his black robe, and tried to look as menacing as possible. "Enter and be damned quick about it, you slow-witted zombies!"

The door swung open and a soldier clad in the blue and gray half-armor of the Guard stepped inside. He saluted. His pale features were rough-hewn and, save for the sleepiness hinted in his eyes, the clean-shaven face was that of a butcher, a methodical killer. But for the lack of a beard, he perfectly resembled General Straas as the general had looked some fifteen years earlier.

A second soldier clad like the first entered. He, too, saluted. His features were identical to those of his companion. Only the color of their eyes differed, one man having blue and the other hazel.

"Well? Did you bring the one I asked for? He must be just right for Baron Mandrol, you know! This is a special occasion."

"Someone put him in the wrong cell," answered the first, in a tired drawl that was typical of his kind. "It took us several minutes to find out just which one, Master G'Meni."

The face in the alchemist's hands began to twitch. "Well, don't just dawdle, then, you idiots! Bring him in!"

The first man snapped his fingers. Two more guardsmen, copies of the rest, entered the laboratory with a third, much abused figure stumbling between them.

"Be careful with his arms, dolts! He won't be much good if you break them just yet! Save that for the masque!"

Looking rather chastened, the two soldiers loosened their hold a bit on the prisoner.

G'Meni eyed the four members of the baron's Guard. Perhaps it was time to ask the general for a new fitting. These men were becoming sloppy, not at all like the warrior whose visage they wore. It would require some work with the special acid he had prepared for such eventualities, but the wounds would be minor. He would broach the subject with the baron first. Straas was not going to be at all pleased to be forced to shave his beard after five years. He had grown it specifically to erase some of the unsettling resemblance between himself and his drone soldiers.

"But that can wait," the alchemist mumbled. With his chin, he indicated a long, angled platform fitted with manacles. "Put him on the table. Quickly, now! Your ineptitude means that I will be preparing him nearly up to the time of the masque!" He shook his head at the need for such rushing. G'Meni was a believer in quality workmanship where such a task was concerned. He wanted this to be the crowning masterpiece of his career, the focal point of the greatest of the baron's masques.

"And who better than you?" he whispered, gazing down at the flattened visage. The mouth worked again, followed almost immediately by a flaring of the nostrils. *Eager for life again, Viktor Falsche? Enjoy it while it lasts! If you only knew of the revenge I have taken . . .*

"He is ready, Master G'Meni."

"Then step back so that I can take a look at this one."

The prisoner, some peasant from the cells, was of the right height and build and his hair was only slightly lighter than desired. A little dye would take care of that. The eyes were green, but more emerald than forest. Still, they would do, too. The man looked and stank of several days in the company of the other refuse that populated the baron's dungeons, but a thorough cleaning would deal with that. The cleaning could take place *after* this part of the process.

G'Meni blinked, leaned a little closer, and studied the battered countenance of the peasant. "Give me a little more light."

One of the guards seized a lit oil lamp and brought it forward. In the increased illumination, the prisoner's features became clearer. The alchemist chuckled. He would have recognized those features anywhere. The long face, the broad, flat nose, the extended cheekbones . . .

One of your earlier trysts, my baron? He has to be one of yours with a face like that. An idea formed, one that the bent figure quickly quashed. He dared not risk such a feat; it could very well undo all that he had accomplished these past several years.

The guards would have noticed the resemblance to the baron, but they knew Mandrol's feeling toward his bastards. The children were a symbol of mortality to him, a symbol that he, too, must pass. The baron did not like being reminded of that, and so such children were to be removed when discovered. No one in Viathos Keep would think it amiss to make use of this one for the coming masque. In fact, the more G'Meni

478

thought about it, the more it would be the crowning touch to the event. Two birds with one stone, so to speak.

He realized that the peasant was staring back at him, cold fear evident in those green eyes. "What is your name, my boy?"

The "boy" was in his mid-twenties, a tad too young for G'Meni's preference in this, but old enough to make do. He hesitated, as was not surprising in the presence of the baron's most trusted adviser and the land of Medecia's second most feared name, then finally croaked, "Emil."

"Emil." Typically dull peasant name. "Well, dear Emil, you have been chosen for a great honor, you have. *You* are going to be a guest, a very *special* guest, at the baron's great ball tomorrow evening, isn't that wonderful?"

From the shudder that visibly coursed through the peasant's rank body, G'Meni gathered that Emil knew some of the tales that surrounded the monthly masques held in the grand ballroom of the castle everyone still insisted on calling Viathos *Keep*. It was to be expected. Had he not received such a reaction from the peasant, then the alchemist would have truly been surprised.

"Yes," he continued, holding up the unsettling visage in his hands for the chosen one to see. "You are going to attend the ball just like the nobles and courtiers. You will even have a special place of honor, one reserved for only the greatest of the baron's associates."

As if in response, the face twitched. The nose wrinkled and the mouth opened and closed. The chained prisoner could not help but be attracted by the movement. His eyes bulged as he watched the mask continue to make a pretense at life.

G'Meni allowed him to gape for several seconds. "It is fascinating, is it not? You have heard stories about this, haven't you?"

The peasant managed to nod, his eyes still fixed on the horrific thing his captor held so gently.

"I cannot take credit for the design, although I can take credit for the perfection. The baron himself is to be congratulated for this creation. It is, I can easily say, his crowning achievement." All knew of the baron's lifelong delving into sorcery and alchemy. "The synthesis of two astonishing schools! The power of magic and the knowledge of science combining to create *this*."

His audience did not seem as admiring of this marvel as G'Meni was. In fact, the peasant muttered something under his breath. At first the stooped figure could not make out what it was. He had the frightened Emil repeat the words, encouragement given in the form of a slap by one of the gauntleted hands of a guard.

"Death . . . mask. . . the death mask . . ."

The words were an offense to G'Meni. "Death mask, indeed! This is a symbol of the continuance of *life*, not death! This is, in its own way, an honor!" Balancing the face in one hand, G'Meni indicated the great case. "Each of those slots contains the perfect reproduction of the baron's most worthy adversaries through the years. Each of those faces was taken with great care and respect from their dead or dying forms in such a way that there remains a reflection, a hint of personality, of the original! Do you know the intricacy involved in such a feat? All of our work through the years!" The alchemist shook his head at the sheer ignorance of the masses. "It is ever the fate of the learned to be misunderstood and misjudged by those who do not know better."

His audience did not seem convinced. G'Meni looked up at the guards and saw little more comprehension despite the fact that they of all people should have understood the complexities of what he and his patron had accomplished. He wondered why he always tried to explain to such obviously unfit audiences as this bastard son of the baron. Better to get on with the process. Time was already slipping past.

Still, he could not help talking as he proceeded. It was the part of him, G'Meni always believed, that desired to educate and illuminate the ignorant despite their never seeming to *appreciate* his efforts that made him do it. That and his affection for the sound of his own voice.

"The highlight of the ball is a morality play of sorts, you must understand. A retelling of events in the great life of our baron. You have been given the honor of portraying a central figure in that play, one who certainly has earned a place of respect in my heart."

The prisoner shook his head, his eyes unable to turn long from the otherworldly object resting in G'Meni's palms.

"You do not feel up to the role, I am sure." The alchemist raised the wrinkled face to the horrified visage of his subject. "Rest assured, it will seem more like a dream. The mask will guide you. I believe you may even *sleep* through it. I've never been quite certain of the extent. Depends on the personality of the mask, you know."

"Mother of God . . ." the peasant was finally able to whisper. G'Meni already had the face mere inches from Emil's own.

"You will *be* Viktor Falsche, my loutish friend, and you will be as he was . . . until he died."

He pressed the underside of the mask against Emil's countenance.

There was a muffled scream that quickly faded. G'Meni paid little mind to the reaction save to note that it was part of the normal chain of events for the process. That pleased him; the mask had been waiting for so long that, reflex actions aside, he had still been a bit afraid that it had lost some of its potency. *Should have known . . . Viktor Falsche was always so lively.*

The false face stretched and remolded, shaping so as to conform to the contours of the host and yet still retain the features with which it had been instilled. The alchemist watched the process take place with pride in his heart. The masks were as much his children as they were the baron's.

At last, the rippling and twisting of the features quieted, leaving in their wake what seemed an entirely different man. G'Meni noted that even unconscious, the figure chained to the platform shifted to a more defiant, arrogant position, as if ready to fight even in the land of dreams.

"It has melded well," he informed the guards. "Inform the baron that all will proceed on schedule. He shall have his special anniversary masque tomorrow and there he shall reaffirm his position with a replaying of his greatest triumph . . .the humiliation and death of Viktor Falsche, rival and pretender."

"Yes, Master G'Meni." The identical soldiers departed, save for the first who had entered.

It took G'Meni a moment to notice the presence of the remaining guard, so absorbed was he in examining the fine, almost invisible line revealing where the mask ended. "What *is* it? I am extremely busy!"

The soldier indicated the prone form. "Is it safe to leave you alone with this one? I remember Falsche. I remember how---"

"You remember *nothing.* Your general recalls, and that memory is of years past. Forget it. If this were truly Falsche and not simply a shadow mask of him, I would perhaps worry, but there is no reason to fear. This puppet is mine to lead, mine to direct. He will play his role and then he will die. is that too much to understand?"

"No." Despite the response, there was still a hint of unease in the face. Even the eyes looked less sleepy.

G'Meni waved him away. "Your concern is noted. You may depart now."

The soldier saluted, then disappeared through the doorway.

480

RICHARD A. KNAAK

When he was finally alone, the squat alchemist delved once more into his Work. There was so much to do. The guards no doubt believed that once the face was in place, the rest was simple, but that was not how G'Meni saw it. He was a perfectionist, an artisan, when it came to the process, and that meant that he had to put the ensorcelled figure through a series of tests in order to ascertain just what level of possession had been attained. This Viktor Falsche had to be perfect, save for the flaw that would lead to his downfall tomorrow.

"You shall need a washing, too." He sniffed, looking over the figure. That would be the first test. A full head-to-toe cleansing would require extensive physical activity, which would inform G'Meni as to the strength of the link between the mask and the host. "Then, I have a *special* series of experiments designed just for you."

He paused then, noting something amiss just before the left ear. A crease. There should have been *no* creases, but there it was. "This will never do, you know! We cannot have you losing face before the climax!"

Chuckling at his own jest, the robed figure turned away to search for the adhesive he had created for just such emergencies. It was not as permanent as the liquid that was applied to the faces of Straas's drone soldiers, but it would hold for the length of the morrow's ball.

"No, indeed." He chuckled again, still very much amused at his humor. "We want you just perfect tomorrow when you face Baron Mandrol and the Lady Lilaith DuPrise."

As he finished speaking, a chill coursed through him, nearly causing him to drop the container he had just picked up. Not knowing why he did so, G'Meni whirled around and stared at the figure on the platform.

The prisoner had not moved. He still lay as the alchemist had seen him last, sleeping the slumber of the deeply entranced.

Master G'Meni's mouth curled slightly upward into a rueful smile. "Only you could do that to me after ten years of death, Falsche! Hmmph! I wonder how you will affect the Lady DuPrise."

He turned back to the table and the container and began measuring out a proper amount of the adhesive. Too much would be almost as detrimental as too little.

Behind him, the eyelids of the figure slowly opened, stared momentarily at the alchemist's hunched back, and then slowly closed again.

ABOUT THE AUTHOR

Richard A. Knaak is the New York Times and USA Today bestselling author of The Legend of Huma, WoW: Stormrage, and nearly fifty other novels and numerous short stories, including works in such series as Warcraft, Diablo, Dragonlance, Age of Conan, and his own Dragonrealm. He has scripted a number of Warcraft manga with Tokyopop, such as the top-selling Sunwell trilogy, and has also written background material for games. His works have been published worldwide in many languages.

His most recent releases include *Shade* --- a brand-new Dragonrealm novel featuring the tragic sorcerer --- *Wolfheart* --- the latest in the bestselling World of Warcraft series, and the third collection in his Legends of the Dragonrealm series. He is presently at work on several other projects, among them *Dawn of the Aspects* for World of Warcraft and a new Dragonrealm saga concerning The Turning War, which fans can find out more about on his website.

Currently splitting his time between Chicago and Arkansas, he can be reached through his website: http://www.richardaknaak.com. While he is unable to respond to every e-mail, he does read them. Join his mailing list for e-announcements of upcoming releases and appearances. He is also on Facebook and Twitter.

ABOUT THE ARTIST

Ciruelo Cabral was born in Buenos Aires, Argentina on July 20, 1963. His formal art training was limited to a few courses in drawing and advertising design, after which, at the age of eighteen, he immediately found work in an ad agency as an illustrator and at twenty one he became a freelance illustrator and started a career as a fantasy artist.

In 1987 Ciruelo traveled to Europe and settled in Sitges, Barcelona, Spain. He then embarked on a search for publishers for his "worlds of fantasy", eventually finding them in Spain, England, the United States and Germany, and through this means he reached a broad audience. Among his US clients is George Lucas, for whom he illustrated the book covers of the trilogy "Chronicles of the Shadow War".

He has also created a number of rock album covers, Steve Vai's The 7th Song and The Elusive Light and Sound being two of them. Other clients include Wizards of the Coast (Magic cards), TSR, Berkley, Tor, Warner, Ballantine, Heavy Metal magazine, Playboy magazine, etc. He also worked with Alejandro Jodorowsky on a comic story published in France in 2006.

In 1990 Ciruelo illustrated **The Book of the Dragon** to be published by the Spanish publisher Timun Mas. Foreign rights to this magnificent book were sold to Paper Tiger, London, in 1992, who had also published his first artbook: **Ciruelo**, in 1990. In 1997 the book **Luz, the Art of Ciruelo** came out. This third book features over 160 full color illustrations, a number of pencil sketches and ink drawings laid out in 128 pages. In 2000 his fourth art book **Magia, the Ciruelo Sketchbook** was published. In 2006 a special little book came out, **Travels Notebook**, with drawings and texts by Ciruelo. In 2008 his book **Fairies and Dragons** was published, containing many illustrations accompanied by a story written by himself. In 2010 **Dreams Notebook** followed the line of **Travels Notebook**. In 2012 his art book **Infinito Interior** was published featuring over 80 paintings.

He lives with his wife Daniela and their kids, Angelo and Lys in Sitges, a quaint and magical town near Barcelona, on the shores of the Mediterranean Sea.

Please check out his work at his website www.dac-editions.com

CPSIA information can be obtained at www.ICGtesting.com
Printed in the USA
BVOW05s1651210615

405457BV00015BA/278/P